"Penny."

The stiff and stilted tone of voice as well as his clipped manner let her know Jason was only speaking to be polite and wanted to get it over with as soon as possible.

Fine with me.

He kept those sexy, daring brown eyes on her, though. The straight and serious line of his mouth made her long for the days when those lips held smiles only for her.

Even though she secretly longed to see him smile just once, so she could see if the sight of those perfect teeth, those full lips and the dimple in his right cheek still had the ability to make her heart stop, she knew it was a lost cause.

And she didn't have time for things she couldn't change, wrongs she couldn't correct.

She only needed to bury her grandmother and get out of town so she could have the nice, private breakdown she'd been putting on hold since she got the news.

"Jason." He wasn't the only one who could give a one-word greeting. She would have been willing to forgo speaking at all. She could do very well without the just-under-the-surface bad feelings threatening to bubble over and explode.

Books by Gwyneth Bolton

Kimani Romance

Protect and Serve

GWYNETH BOLTON

became an avid romance fan after sneak-reading her mother's romance novels. In the nineties, she was introduced to African-American romance novels, and her life hasn't been the same since. She has a B.A. and an M.A. in creative writing and a Ph.D. in English. She teaches writing and women's studies at the college level. When she is not writing African-American romance novels, she is curled up with a cup of herbal tea, a warm quilt and a good book. She currently lives in Syracuse, New York, with her husband, Cedric. Readers can contact her via e-mail at gwynethbolton@prodigy.net or visit her Web site, http://www.gwynethbolton.com.

PROTECT *and* SERVE

Gwyneth Bolton

This novel is dedicated to my mother Donna Pough,
my husband Cedric Bolton and every reader who has
reached out and shown me love. I appreciate and
love you all more than words could ever express.

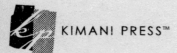 KIMANI PRESS™

ISBN-13: 978-0-373-86075-3
ISBN-10:   0-373-86075-7

PROTECT AND SERVE

Copyright © 2008 by Gwendolyn D. Pough

www.kimanipress.com

Printed in U.S.A.

Dear Reader,

Thanks for taking the time to read Jason and Penny's story. This novel started with two questions: If home is where the heart is, what happens when you broke that heart long ago? Can you ever *really* go home again? Penny and Jason have some history, and they have some issues to work through before they can really connect and make their way back to one another. But their story, like other lovers-reunited stories, gives us hope for people being able to work out their differences and find love again. I've always wanted to write novels set in the city where I grew up—Paterson, New Jersey. When I wrote my first novels, the characters wanted to be from everywhere but places I'd actually lived in before. Imagine my surprise when this smart and sassy sister popped into my head, started whispering her story to me, and I realized she was a girl from home! I'm so happy the characters in my HIGHTOWER HONORS series are proving to me that I can go home again and take all of you with me. Be sure to pick up my September 2008 release, *Make It Hot,* for the next installment in the HIGHTOWER HONORS series.

Gwyneth Bolton

Acknowledgment:

First I want to thank God for the many blessings in my life, especially the blessing to share my stories. I'd like to thank my family: my mother, Donna, my sisters, Jennifer, Cassandra, Michelle and Tashina, my nieces Ashlee and Zaria and my husband, Cedric. I want to send lots of love to my friends Angelique Justin, Jennifer Thorington-Springer, Cheryl Johnson, Kimberly Dillon-Shively and Yolanda Hood. And I want to send thanks and lots of love to my writer friends who read sections of *Protect and Serve* at various stages and offered comments and feedback. Thanks, A.C. Arthur, Jennifer Talty, Kari Townsend and Eleanor Shields.

Chapter 1

The worst part about funerals was, you had to make nice and be cordial to people you either despised or couldn't care less about. There was something about death that brought out all the clichés: *Life is short. You never know when you're going to go. Treat each day like it's your last.* As if coming face-to-face with mortality would make a person want to "get right" before they had to explain to Saint Peter why they didn't do better.

Penny Keys understood all of this in theory. But with Big Mama gone, she didn't care about the niceties and what she *should* be doing.

Sophie Hightower embraced Penny as if the woman had been Big Mama's closest friend, and ran off at the mouth about how good it was to see Penny again. And it was all Penny could do not to haul off cussing in the funeral home and shake up the staid and calm wake.

"Thanks, Sophie." Penny couldn't bring herself to fake pleasantries of any kind to this evil-mouthed, hateful old woman. She could barely manage a smile. Ever since getting the call from her mother, telling her Big Mama had passed away, Penny hadn't been fully thinking or feeling. She'd functioned. She'd organized, planned, taken care of everything. But feeling? That was gone.

Heartbroken, dejected, lost…

Those words didn't even begin to describe her mood. They certainly couldn't cover the large hole that seemed to stretch on and on in her spirit. She only remembered feeling this empty one other time in her life. She'd had no idea the hollowness in her heart left over from that loss had any room for expansion. Yet there it was, growing and threatening to take her over at any moment if she dared let go of her tenuous grip on control.

Penny gave the funeral home another once-over, but still couldn't find her mother, or anyone else who might save her from cursing Sophie out and making a mockery of Big Mama's wake. Anyone, that is, but the man who caught her gaze immediately. *Jason Hightower.*

She knew the very second Sophie Hightower caught the passing glances between her and Jason, because the old woman's fake smile dried up, and her well-wishing facial expression hardened ever so slightly. Sophie's lips twisted as if she'd bitten into something bitter, and her shoulders reared back, causing her overly large bosom to poke out even more than the pointy cones already did. The tall, rich-mocha-complexioned woman with the full figure would have been considered forbidding on a *good* day. Once she had her panties in a bunch over one of her precious nephews possibly falling victim to an unworthy 'hood girl like Penny, forget about it…. *Attitude overload.*

Penny straightened her back and swallowed. She felt her hands clenching together at her side. She resisted the urge to take a scrunchie out of her purse, put her long locks in a ponytail, dig out the Vaseline and take off her earrings in preparation.

I will not cause a scene. I will not—

"So, when are you going back to California, Penny? You know there's nothing for you here." Sophie's right eye slanted, and her lip tilted in a bit of a snarl.

Get thee behind me, Satan. I will not cuss this old woman out at Big Mama's wake. I just won't do it. I don't care what you have this old biddy say to me.

As if on cue, Jason, with his confident swagger and cocky demeanor, came walking over.

Was it just her, or did the people in the crowded room of the funeral home seem to part and make way for Jason as he zeroed in on her? Penny hadn't seen him in fifteen years and didn't want to face him now. It didn't appear she had much choice.

She tried to focus on anything else in the room besides him—the metal folding chairs in the corner, the stack of church fans piled on the wooden table along with a big white guest book and carefully folded programs. Even with those things to gaze at, her eyes still managed to find Jason's again.

Those dark brown pools full of accusation and allure would surely be the death of her—or, at the very least, the end of her sanity—if she continued to look into them.

"Hi, Aunt Sophie." Jason gave his aunt a big hug, all the while keeping his eyes fixed on Penny.

He had changed from the eighteen-year-old love of her life. His athletic build appeared stronger, more substantial, if that were possible. He was still tall. And his deep mahogany complexion was still flawless. For some reason, however, this grown-up Jason seemed larger than life. His presence filled the room, and left her feeling a barrage of things she didn't dare try and label. The dark, navy-blue designer suit he wore fit as if it were custom-made for him.

They must be paying police detectives well these days, Penny thought wryly, as she let her eyes roam Jason's appealing but also very off-limits body.

She was there to bury Big Mama, and that was it. As much as she despised the meddling Sophie Hightower, the woman was right. There wasn't anything here for Penny—anything or *anyone.*

"Penny." The stiff and stilted tone of voice as well as his clipped manner let her know Jason was only speaking to be polite and wanted to get it over with as soon as possible.

Fine with me.

He kept those sexy, daring brown eyes on her, though. The straight and serious line of his mouth made her long for the days when those lips held smiles only for her.

Even though she secretly longed to see him smile just once, so she could see if the sight of those perfect teeth, those full lips and the dimple in his right cheek still had the capability to make her heart stop, she knew it was a lost cause.

And she didn't have time for things she couldn't change, wrongs she couldn't correct.

She only needed to bury her grandmother and get out of town so she could have the nice private breakdown she'd been putting on hold since she got the news.

"Jason." He wasn't the only one who could give a one-word greeting. She would have been willing to forgo speaking at all. She could very well do without the just-under-the-surface bad feelings threatening to bubble up and explode.

"Sorry about Big Mama. She'll be missed. I used to stop by and check up on her a couple of times during the week. I never would have thought we'd lose her. Seemed like she would be here forever." His eyes softened a little, then hardened again just as quickly.

Big Mama never told me she was visiting with Jason twice a week.

But Big Mama wouldn't have. When Penny called, it was all about Penny. And Penny was sure that when Jason visited, Big Mama made those moments just for him. That was her way.

The huge lump that had taken up residence in her chest since she had gotten the news of Big Mama's passing began to throb. Big Mama was really gone, and there was nothing she could do about it. The thought of it made her want to curl up in a corner and just weep until she ran out of tears.

But there was too much to do now. She could cry when she went back to Los Angeles. Right now, she needed to get the wake and the awkward reunion with Jason and his evil aunt over and done with.

With no time to get choked up, Penny took a deep breath. Taking another, she relished the calm that overcame her body.

Sophie cleared her throat and stepped back. "Yes, she will be missed dearly. The Deaconess Board at Mount Zion won't be the same without her."

Giving Penny a quick and cutting glare, she added, "I'm going to leave you to greet the rest of your guests, dear. Come along, Jason. Penny can't be rude and spend all her time talking to us."

Subtlety had *never* been Sophie's strong point.

Jason nodded to his aunt and then returned his intense stare to Penny. "You can go ahead, Aunt Sophie. I'll catch up with you."

No, you go, too. Follow your dear, sweet aunt. I can't deal with you right now, Jason Hightower. Urgh…

Penny inhaled and exhaled.

Remember…calm, girly, calm.

She wondered what kind of visualization technique she could use to ease her nerves and get her through the wake and the proximity of the former love of her life. The image of Sophie Hightower's head being compressed in a metal vise held some appeal.

A bright, gleaming, false smile covered Sophie's face just before she cut her eyes at Penny. "Fine. I'm going to go and find my baby brother." She turned to her nephew. "Be sure not to tie up too much of Penny's time." She draped her scarf across her shoulder and haughtily took off across the room.

Penny watched Sophie waltz away, all the while mentally crushing the woman's head, until Jason's smooth baritone interrupted her concentration.

"It's good to see you back, in spite of the horrible circumstances, Penny. Too bad you couldn't have visited when Big Mama was alive."

How did his cocky, tell-everyone-what-they-need-to-be-doing personality not bother me all through high school? Oh, wait…it did—until he made me fall in love with him….

Penny swallowed. Being home again had dredged up enough of her feelings of guilt. She didn't need Jason to remind her of all the reasons she was a horrible person.

She knew she should have visited more. During the time she'd been away, she had spoken to Big Mama five, sometimes six times a week. Penny had flown her grandmother out to Los Angeles for visits at least once a year. Once she had finished school and could afford the costs, she'd never neglected the woman who had raised her.

Penny pursed her lips and narrowed her eyes. "Big Mama understood better than anyone my reasons for moving away and staying away. And most important, she knew I loved her."

"Are you sure about that? Because from what I could see, that woman missed you and mourned you the entire time. And for you to stay away that long shows what a cruel, heartless, selfish—" Jason took a deep breath, glared at her and cut himself off.

She knew he'd been about to say something that couldn't be taken back. It wouldn't have been the first time.

The two of you deserve each other—a backstabber and a slut. I can't believe I ever trusted either one of you. The harsh words he had spoken fifteen years ago echoed in her mind as she took in his mahogany face. The ruggedly handsome and manly face glaring at her right now had residual traces of the anger that had covered his more boyish face fifteen years ago.

She braced herself as best she could, given the fact that she had just lost the only person in the world who understood her and loved her unconditionally. And the only other person she had ever loved with her whole being was standing in front of her, blasting her in a creepily déjà vu manner.

She inhaled and exhaled several times. "You need to calm down, Jason. This is not the time or the place. If you cared about Big Mama as much as you claim you did, then you wouldn't disrespect her wake like this."

A hand rested on her shoulder and stopped her from saying more. Praying it wasn't her mother, Penny turned around.

Terrill had finally made it.

Penny let out a sigh of relief.

"Everything all right?" Terrill spoke the words to her, but his serious hazel eyes remained fixed on Jason.

Giving him a heartfelt hug and greeting, Penny felt herself shake just a little. She had no idea how much longer she was going to be able to hold up. But at least with Terrill—one of her oldest and dearest friends—there, she wouldn't have to go it alone.

"Everything is fine, Terrill. I'm glad you were able to make it."

She had just seen her friend before she left Los Angeles, so she knew Jason's presence was what made her extra happy to see Terrill. She leaned on Terrill's sturdy shoulder and clasped the arm of his suit jacket.

Terrill smiled at her and winked, his way of letting her know he was there for her no matter what.

Most of the people in the room were checking Terrill out. Success seemed to exude from him in ripples, and those who'd known him when he and his mother lived in a small one-bedroom attic apartment were either happy for him or jealous. The way eyes darted and conversations took place behind hands showed that Terrill had given many of the folks in the room something to talk about.

In fact, given the history the three of them shared, the room was probably abuzz with gossip.

She was very proud of Terrill, because she knew what it meant for both of them to make it from their inner-city neighborhood in Paterson, New Jersey, to their positions as movers and shakers in Los Angeles. Not many people from Warren Street who attended PS #10 and then Eastside High School ended up where they were. The two of them were kids from the 'hood who'd done well for themselves.

Shocked by how much she needed someone to lean on at this moment, she let out another sigh. Shooting a hesitant glance at Jason, she couldn't help but notice the intense anger in his glare.

Whoever said time healed all wounds told a big lie.

It seemed as if everyone in the funeral home had their eyes on the trio. Penny lifted her hand to her right eye and rubbed it across the tiny scar she had gotten when she was twelve. Although it was barely noticeable now, whenever Penny felt uncomfortable or put on the spot, her hand found and worried the small mark. She circled it with her pointer finger for a minute before she forced herself to put her hand down at her side.

So what if everyone in the funeral home was probably waiting to see if the three former best friends would cause a scene? She refused to turn into a ball of nerves for their entertainment.

As an image consultant, she knew the importance of appearances. The only thing a person really had any control over was the image he or she put forth. The perceptions of others might have been out of her hands, but that didn't mean she had to play to anyone's expectations.

"Hey, Jason. How's it going?" Terrill made an attempt to reach out to his old friend and got a harsh stare and a sneer for his trouble. His warm-honey complexion took on a tint of red when his former friend snubbed him. He slanted his hazel eyes and nodded.

"You're right, Penny. This isn't the time or the place." Jason gave her a once-over before walking away, and didn't even bother looking at Terrill. "It wouldn't even be worth it, anyway."

Her heart stilled, and a pain so sharp it could only be the reopening of an old, barely healed wound throbbed in her chest. Chancing a glance at Terrill, she couldn't help noticing that he had been seriously stung by Jason's words, as well. The two men hadn't been able to say a kind word to one another in fifteen years.

Terrill squeezed her shoulder, and she knew he was trying to let her know he didn't blame her for losing his best friend. His attempt at comfort made the pain even worse.

Looking at them now, no one would be able to tell people used to jokingly call them the Three Musketeers and tease them about being joined at the hip. They had been best friends since grade school, and the three-way friendship hadn't changed when Jason and Penny became high school sweethearts. They hadn't thought anything would be able to come between them. But they had been wrong.

Jason hated Penny and Terrill now, and it was all her fault. The realization that it was too late to correct the past caused a sharp pain in her chest.

Penny cringed.

If Jason Hightower could still hurt her with his words in the same way he had when she had left Paterson years ago, then she had no business being back here.

As soon as the funeral was over and done with, she was getting out of there as fast as her feet could carry her.

As Jason walked away, he mentally chided himself for losing control the way he had. There was something about seeing Penny again after so much time that brought back all his emotions about what had happened when they were seniors in high school and thought they had had their entire lives in front of them.

Seeing the man responsible for ruining all his dreams come up and comfort the woman he would *always* see as his did nothing to soothe Jason's raging emotions.

Neither of the two people who had betrayed him in the worst way possible had been home in years. Terrill had come back more often than Penny, who hadn't been home once since she left. He had run into Terrill off and on through the years, but could never bring himself to speak to the man.

Of the two of them, Jason didn't know whom he blamed more. Thinking of Terrill's betrayal made the blood run cold in his body. Numbness had come over him when he saw his former best friend, the man he had thought would one day stand with him at his wedding. Any emotion he felt seemed to be layered with ice, and he liked it that way. He didn't think he would ever thaw when it came to Terrill.

And Penny? Well, seeing her in person again for the first time in fifteen years caused his blood to boil and his body to run hot.

Anger. Hurt. Attraction...?

His conflicting feelings made for one jacked-up combination, as far as he was concerned.

How could he still be attracted to her?

Seeing the two of them together made him run hot and cold at the same time, and Jason wasn't comfortable with the impact their presence had on him.

It didn't help that Penny still looked gorgeous. The simple black dress she wore clung to her curves in ways that brought scandalous thoughts—certainly thoughts he shouldn't have been having at a wake—to his mind. The designer sandals with lots of straps and stiletto heels did things to her calves that caused his pulse to quicken.

But that was nothing compared to what it did to his heart to see that toasted-cinnamon face, those bold copper eyes and that beautiful sandy-brown hair, all in the form of a woman whom had grown up to be just as beautiful as he'd always known she would be. Her hair was styled in those thin sister-locks and hung loose around her face and down her back. The sisterlocks had soft blond and bronze highlights that shimmered and beckoned to him to reach out and caress them.

"I heard Terrill saw the light and got rid of that little slut soon after they left town." Aunt Sophie had snuck up behind him, and now she tilted her head toward the corner of the crowded funeral home where Terrill sat with Penny.

Jason didn't know how he felt about the fact that his aunt had probably seen him watching the two of them make their way to a set of folding chairs in the corner. He knew for sure he didn't like his supposedly saved and sanctified aunt calling Penny a slut, no matter how much the name seemed to fit.

He had even called her that himself, once upon a time.

Now, in spite of how she had hurt him, he regretted lashing out at her. Years and some distance had him rethinking everything that happened back then. Maybe it was his cop's instincts, or his cold-case training, but something about those past events still nagged at him.

"Is that any way for the president of the Deaconess Board to talk, Aunt Sophie? I swear, your mouth is worse than some of the criminals I arrest." Jason pinned a disapproving gaze on Sophie, in hopes it would halt her bad talk about Penny.

"I'm just calling it like I see it. I'm just letting you know your friend Terrill had the sense to let her go. You should, too. A girl like that is bad news. Just look at her mama." Aunt Sophie paused and hissed as she sucked her teeth in disgust.

"And Doreen, God bless the dead, as hard as she tried to make sure that Penny didn't end up like Carla, look at her. She threw away the best thing that ever happened to her and went off to California, dancing in music videos. It's a wonder Doreen didn't drop dead from the shock of it."

Sophie offered a dramatic pause and threw her head toward the heavens for effect. "Her daughter whoring her body

for crack cocaine, and her granddaughter whoring her body
for God knows what to the tune of that god-awful rap music.
Lord, have mercy!"

Jason counted to ten before saying a word to his aunt. The
woman meant well; he knew she did. She had been the one
who had comforted him when Penny had broken his heart.

He also knew as well as anyone that Penny had used
those few videos she'd modeled in to help pay for college.
She was a successful businesswoman now, who didn't
trade in on her looks—her still gut-wrenchingly beautiful
looks—to make a living.

He chanced another glance at Penny and found himself
lingering again over her soft, cinnamon-toned skin. She
had always been shapely, and what had been a knockout
body when she was a teenager had turned into a to-die-for
body in the woman. Her curves spoke to him from behind
her black wrap-style dress, and he silently reminded
himself that they were in a place for mourning, not sali-
vating. Captivated, he tried to get past the in-your-face realization that his copper-eyed girl had turned into a
gorgeous woman.

Just as he was about to open his mouth to let his aunt know
what he thought of her snide remarks, he stopped himself,
wondering why he felt so compelled to stand up for Penny.
She had no loyalty, and she certainly didn't deserve his.
Shaking his head, he walked away from his aunt.

Deciding he needed some air, he walked outside of Lee's
Funeral Home and took big gulps. Taking in the vibrant street
life happening all around him on Rosa Parks Boulevard, he had
to wonder why he'd bothered to show up at the wake at all.

Sure, he had loved and respected Doreen "Big Mama"
Keys as much as anyone. But he could have just attended the

funeral and paid his respects the next day—*from a distance.*
As it was, now he'd be seeing Penny two days in a row.

Glancing across the street, he noticed his brothers—
Lawrence, Joel and Patrick—exiting their vehicles. Lawrence
stopped to talk to four teenagers hanging on the corner, who
immediately hustled to hide their dice and cash. Jason kept
his eyes focused on them, in case they gave Lawrence any
trouble.

Lawrence, a well-known narcotics detective, actually
worked this part of town, so Jason doubted his brother would
have any trouble. Lawrence saw a lot more action as a narc
than Jason did as a forensics expert and cold-case detective.

The teenagers cleared the corner, and within seconds
Jason's three older brothers were standing in front of him.

All three shared the trademark Hightower rugged good
looks. They were tall, had skin in varying shades of mahogany, and their looks had been known to drive women wild.
Joel and Patrick were both firemen with the Paterson Fire Department. And he and Lawrence were both detectives with the
Paterson Police Department.

"Hey, 'lil bro." Joel reached out and gave Jason a quick
hug.

Lawrence and Patrick followed with the same greeting,
and then they all just stood there.

He could tell that they were trying to feel him out, that they
wanted to ask if he'd seen Penny yet.

"We came to pay our respects," Patrick offered, clearly
sick of the silence. His older brother normally had little use
for small talk or other common niceties. He was a shoot-
from-the-hip kind of guy whose brash manner normally
didn't go over well with the ladies.

"Yeah. That's good. You should," Jason responded.

"*She* here?" Never one to mince words, Joel seldom bit his tongue. However, he usually tempered his demeanor with wisecracks and his playboy charm. He was definitely the ladies' man of the family.

Jason caught Lawrence giving Joel a why-did-you-bring-that-up look.

"She's here," was all Jason could say in response.

"Well, it was a long time ago, Jason. You need to just let it go. You guys were young. You've moved on. She's moved on. It was the past. Don't be all sulky about it fifteen years later. And for Pete's sake, don't cause any drama at the wake." Joel was only a couple of years older than Jason. But Jason swore when it came to getting in his business and trying to boss him around, Joel had the older brothers beat.

"Joel is right, Jason. This isn't the time. And besides, women are scandalous, anyway. We all know this. Don't let her deceit get to you." Patrick, still bitter over his divorce and his cheating ex-wife, wouldn't give any woman the benefit of the doubt.

Catching his woman in bed with another man must have been hard on Patrick. Even five years later, he still hadn't really gotten past it.

Jason could sympathize with his older brother in more ways than he had ever let any of them know. He had never told his family the full story of his breakup with Penny.

He took a deep breath. After years of distance, he suspected that the things he'd been made to believe back then might be false. He was determined to find out, one way or another, *once and for all*.

"I agree. Shake it off, baby bro. Be the bigger person. Let it go." Lawrence slanted his left eye when he spoke, as if it would help make his point more clearly. Lawrence was suspicious of just about everyone, and it probably had a lot to do with the things he had seen working in the narcotics division of the police force. But he was a stand-up guy who always tried to do the right thing. The only problem was, he *always* encouraged others to do the same.

Since Jason didn't want to have this conversation with his brothers, especially not on the front steps of the funeral home, he just nodded.

His brothers accepted his nod as confirmation that he'd let it go. But Jason wasn't certain he really could. Watching as they entered the funeral home, Jason let the pep talk his brothers had given him stew for a moment. Yes, he could be the bigger person and not confront Penny, but he needed to know a few things. He still had some burning questions. Pieces of the puzzle didn't fit.

Since solving old crimes and mysteries had become his job, he looked forward to having the chance to apply his cold-case detective skills to this very personal area of his life.

He would have to work on his approach if he was going to solve this case. He hadn't meant to approach her with such an attitude. But there had been something about seeing her again. And when Terrill showed up…well, that had been the last straw.

"This is a tough time for Penny, you know. Big Mama was the only person who was always there for her, no matter what. She's taking it hard, so you really need to lay off about the past."

Terrill! Speak of the devil.

Jason turned to see his former best friend, and it was all he could do to contain himself. He had already made the mistake of showing them he still felt hurt by their betrayal, and he didn't want to let them see any more of his vulnerability.

"Shouldn't you be inside with her, then, if she's so torn up? Isn't that what lovers are supposed to do for one another? Comfort? Console? Why are you out here talking to me?"

"I'm out here because, despite what you think, I want what's best for everyone involved. She doesn't need the stress. It's bad enough she has to deal with Carla, and you know how that can be." Terrill ran his hand through his close-cropped, naturally curly hair and sighed. "You don't need to be all hung up on a past you barely understand. There's a lot you just don't know, Jason. If I could tell you without breaking confidences, I would."

Jason watched kids ride their bikes down the crowded street, took in all the hustle and bustle of the inner city on a spring evening. Paterson's streets came alive, pulsing with energy, once the days became warmer and longer. There might not be a lot of flowers in bloom or trees blossoming in the tenement jungle, but spring was definitely in the air. While feeling the pulse of his beloved city, Jason counted to ten.

It didn't work.

The fact was, Terrill was the same pretty boy who'd gone off to Los Angeles with *his* girl. He was the same former record company intern who had made it possible for Jason's girl to dance in rap videos, thereby torturing Jason for years, because he could still see her everywhere but she was no longer *his*.

If anyone in the world knew how much Jason had loved Penny, it was Terrill. For those reasons alone, Terrill's betrayal was unforgivable.

"Oh! Now, you have morals. Where were they fifteen years ago, when you stole my girl?"

Terrill threw his hands up and shook his head. "I give up, man. I tried, but you're stuck in the past. You need to let it go. And like I said, lay off with the guilt trips on Penny. She doesn't need that right now."

Watching Terrill walk away, Jason was almost tempted to chase him and finish the fight. It was a fight fifteen years in the making, and he was sure they would have it eventually.

Maybe the wake wasn't the time and place. But he *would* get answers—especially from the woman who'd broken his heart.

Penny let out the breath she hadn't been aware she was holding when she saw Jason leave the funeral home. And she smiled when she saw the other Hightower brothers coming in to pay their respects. Patrick, Lawrence and Joel had always been like unofficial big brothers to her. She missed the closeness she used to have with their family.

If only things could have been different….

"Penny, baby, it's so good to see you. You look good. I'm just so sad I'm seeing you under these circumstances. How're you holding up, baby?" Jason's mother, Celia Hightower, gave her a big hug, followed by her husband, James Hightower.

Seeing the other two adults who had provided her with a place of refuge when she was a kid, while her only other constant source of support lay in a coffin, made her chest swell up. But she refused to break down and start crying. If she started, she feared, she'd never stop.

She stood in front of Big Mama's casket, and the only thing she could think was how someone who was so much larger than life, someone who had *been* life to her, could possibly be gone.

The makeup the mortician had put on Big Mama seemed a few shades too dark for the light-complexioned woman

Penny had known. Penny touched the long, wavy hair that Big Mama and her own mother shared but had skipped a generation with her.

She remembered it had been Big Mama who taught her to be proud of her thick, sandy-brown hair when she wanted soft, jet-black hair like Big Mama and Carla's. When Carla complained that Penny's hair was just too much to handle, Big Mama had taught Penny how to love and tame her mane.

Penny let the good memories wash over her and fought back her tears as she touched Big Mama's cheek.

Mr. Hightower kept his strong arm around her. "She's in a better place now. She's with the Lord."

Why do people always say that? How do they really know? Penny wondered as she continued to caress Big Mama's cheek.

"She was so proud of you, Penny. She talked about you all the time. And she loved you, Penny. We're all proud of you, baby. And we miss you." Mrs. Hightower smiled brightly. The woman sported a full and shapely figure and a warm demeanor. She wore a beautiful black skirt suit and a delicate string of pearls with matching earrings.

Penny moved with the Hightowers away from the casket. She couldn't look anymore and she couldn't listen to them anymore. If she did, the lump in her chest that was threatening to explode any minute would be her undoing. And she couldn't lose it at the wake. She had to hold it together.

Mrs. Hightower's kind eyes made Penny remember all the times she had let her help out in the kitchen or had taken her shopping. Celia Hightower used to say she wanted to spend some girl time and get away from a house full of men and boys.

Even before Penny and Jason became a couple, Mrs. Hightower had taken Penny under her wing as the daughter she never had. Seeing her, and missing their bond, made Penny feel even worse—as if it were possible for her to feel any worse.

"Thanks, Mr. and Mrs. Hightower. I just wish I could've seen her before she died. She wasn't even sick. It—it just happened too fast. I never got the chance to—"

Her voice choked off, and Penny took a deep breath. She couldn't break now. There was just too much to do. She could have her breakdown when she returned to Los Angeles.

"She knew, baby. She knew you loved her." Mrs. Hightower patted her hand and smiled. "Now you be sure to stop by and catch up before you head back to the West Coast. Don't you leave here without coming to see me! I've missed you, sweetie."

Penny felt the weight of the guilt she'd been feeling since finding out Big Mama died grow and press her chest down. She had never wanted to lose contact with Mr. and Mrs. Hightower. She loved them. They were like the parents she'd never had, the parents she'd wished she had. Spending time in their home while growing up had made her feel normal and, most important, loved.

"She could come over for Sunday dinner," James Hightower offered. He stood over six feet tall and shared the same deep mahogany complexion as his four sons. He seemed to be the aged but still handsome template for those classic Hightower looks.

Penny took a deep breath. She remembered Sunday dinner at the Hightowers' after church. And she knew she couldn't sit through one of those family gatherings, no matter how much she secretly yearned to do so. No way could she do it.

"I'll try, Mrs. Hightower," Penny offered, hoping that would be enough. "But I better move along and see some of the other guests now."

"Go ahead, baby, and we'll see you on Sunday." Mrs.

Hightower patted her back with a smile and pushed her on her way.

It occurred to Penny to say that she hadn't said she'd definitely be there. But given the determination Mrs. Hightower always had, she knew better than to say never.

Carla slipped out the side door of the funeral parlor as soon as she saw him. He was probably the last person she wanted to see at her mother's wake. But there he was. If she could give him the slip, the way she had been doing since he got out of jail, that would be a good thing. If she could keep giving him the slip until she managed to talk her daughter into taking her back to Los Angeles with her, that would be even better.

Who would have thought both of those men would be out of jail at the same time? When your past came back to shoot you in the behind, it sure as hell came back blasting. For sure, this was more stress than her hanging-on-to-recovery-by-the-skin-of-her-teeth behind could handle.

She wouldn't have her mother to help her stay clean this time. It had been hard enough doing so with her mama alive and giving her positive encouragement.

How will I stay clean with Mama dead and those fools breathing down my neck?

There was no way. She would have to find a way to get Penny to let her move back to California with her.

Yeah. That would work.

She ducked into the corner store and realized she didn't have a whole lot of cash on her. Okay, she didn't have *any* cash on her. She'd run through the money Penny sent her every month a week ago. And with Mama's death and all, Carla didn't think it was a good time to beg Penny for some more ends. Plus, she had to save her favors for the big stuff, like getting the hell out of Dodge on a one-way ticket to Los Angeles.

Carla only had enough for a single cigarette. If the bodega followed the new laws, she wouldn't be able to get one, unless they had those individually wrapped cigarettes. Not every store carried them. Since she was trying to quit smoking, too, and had been doing well, that might have been a good thing. But she needed *something*. For sure, cigarettes were the lesser evil.

"Y'all sell loosies?" Carla patted her hair down and took a glance out of the window. Her heart stalled, and she ducked. The jerk must have followed her.

She saw him walking in front of the store. He looked like a dang-gone wild beast on the prowl.

Oh, shoot!

"We not supposed to split up the pack, *Mami*. It's against the law." The smooth Puerto Rican brother leaned against the counter and looked at her cringing on the floor. "Who you hiding from? Your boyfriend?"

He was handsome, if you liked those gooey-sticky caramel latte brothers with the deep, dark bedroom eyes. She liked her men taller, darker and a little more dangerous. Well, those tastes hadn't gotten her anywhere but crouched on the floor hiding. So maybe she should give *Papi* a try?

Carla didn't get up from her crouching position. "Did he pass by?"

"Yeah, *Mami*, he passed. You scared? You look like you scared." The store clerk had a humorous expression on his face, and his lips were tilted in a half smirk.

If she hadn't wanted him to sell her a loose cigarette so bad, she might have cussed him out and asked him what the hell he found so dang funny about her situation. But years of hustling had taught her a little something about the value of a good game face. Plus, he was cute, if you liked that type.

Carla stood and sucked her teeth in what she hoped came off in a joking manner and not the pure disgust she felt.

"How the kids say it these days? I ain't nevah scurred." She batted her eyes and then winked at him. "So what's up, *Papi?* You gonna sell me that loosy or what?"

"Well, normally, I wouldn't be breaking the rules. But you seem like a nice lady. So I'm gonna do you a favor. What you smoking, *Mami?*"

"Newports." She gave her lips a seductive lick for good measure. "Regular." She smoothed her wavy hair back. The stuff never held on to any hairstyles like she wanted it to. But most men seemed to like the long hair.

"I'm gonna give you this pack of Newports, *Mami.* You gonna give me your phone number?" He took a pack of cig-arettes down, slid them across the counter with a book of matches and winked at her.

Carla noticed the wedding ring on his finger as he made the slide.

Men ain't worth a damn!

She smiled slyly as she grabbed the cigarettes and slipped them in her purse. "You think your wife would like it if I gave you my number, *Papi?*"

He shrugged. "What my wife don't know won't hurt her."

Ain't that a blip?

She started walking out of the store. "Well, in that case, it's 777-9311." She busted out laughing.

"That's not your number, that's a song. Oh, why you playing me, *Mami?*"

Carla let the door close, all the while chuckling to herself.

Once outside, she tried to decide if she should go back to the wake and ride back to the house with her daughter in the family limousine provided by the funeral home, or head home on foot. If she didn't ride back with Brat, then the girl would be in the limo all by herself.

Like it or not, they were the only family either of them had left. And without her own mother there as the go-between, it was going to be hard getting her daughter to see that.

Carla reasoned that if he was really gone, then it would be safe to go back. And she sure didn't feel like walking home. She headed back to the funeral parlor, puffing on a cigarette and trying to think of a way around the latest crazy predicament in her life. But as she came up to the funeral home, a large hand snatched her into an alley.

Her pack of cigarettes fell into a puddle of water, and she reared up to curse whoever had grabbed her.

"What the hell!" She struggled and tried to pull away, only to get slammed against the brick building for her trouble. She looked up at the idiot who held her, intent on telling the fool she didn't have any money or anything worth stealing, but then she saw it was *him*.

Dang!

"You think you slick or something? You know I been looking for you. I put the word out, and you act like you couldn't even get at a brother. Since I had to hunt you down, I ought to bust you upside your damn head." The same mean, angry face she still saw in her nightmares glared down at her.

She had to strain her neck to really get a good look at the man who towered above her in a threatening manner.

"I didn't know you was looking for me. I hadn't heard anything. Shoot, I didn't even know you were out. How'd that happen?" She hoped her game face was still in place.

Because dealing with this animal without one would be foolish, to say the least.

His lips curled into a sneer. "It happened. That's all you need to know."

"Well, that's good." She smiled and tried the old batting of the eyes, knowing it was probably useless with this one. "I'm glad. But since you out and all, then you probably know my mother passed away. We burying her and all, so—"

"Yeah, my condolences. I just saw yo' mama the other day, when I stopped by there looking for you. I guess she ain't tell you I stopped by, huh? Nah, I guess she wouldn't have, since she seemed pretty heated that I even rang her doorbell. And I see yo' little daughter is home and all grown up." He licked his lips in a disgusting manner, and an evil leer crossed his face.

If he stopped by Mama's house, that might have been enough to make her have a stroke and die. Shoot! I'm so sorry, Mama.

Carla mentally kicked herself. Once again, her mistakes had made her mother suffer. She made a silent promise to her mother and herself. She would try and get it right this time. She was going to get herself and her child out of Paterson, and she was finally going to be a good mother. She had to…

"No, my mother didn't mention you had stopped by." She couldn't help but narrow her eyes, and she knew her voice had lost some of its fake pleasantness. She knew she needed to keep layering it on, if she wanted to escape the alley unscathed. But it was hard to do, when she thought about her mother lying in a casket inside.

"So, I see your boy beat that murder rap. You seen him yet?"

Answering his question would be too tricky. Even though they were no longer together, she knew this fool still had an irrational and psychotic jealous streak, especially when it came to her ex. She looked down at the pavement and thought for a minute.

"No."

The flat of his hand moved as soon as she uttered the word and knocked her upside the head so hard her head bounced against the brick wall.

"That's for lying. I know you saw him." He slapped her upside the head again. "And that's a warning. Stay away from him. Your baby's daddy is *still* off-limits to you. Just 'cause we ain't together no more don't mean any of *that* has changed."

Carla tried her best to keep her eyes focused on the ground, because if she looked at him, she would probably lose it. She didn't want to give him the benefit of her tears. And she wasn't sure looking in his smug, arrogant face wouldn't make her cuss him out.

Cussing him would no doubt have her explaining a bunch of bruises to Penny. And if she was going to get Penny to take her to Los Angeles, she needed to play it clean.

No stress. No drama. No idiots from her past set on ruining her, especially not *this* idiot.

He took her chin in his hand and lifted her face. Leaning in, he covered her mouth with his, and she let him kiss her.

"You still belong to me. And I'm only going to give you a little bit more time to come to that conclusion. So you go ahead and bury yo' mama and send yo' little daughter back wherever the hell she was, and be sure to stay away from that punk Gerald, and I'll get at you soon." He walked off down the alley and Carla shuddered.

She had to find a way to get Penny to take her to L.A.— as soon as possible.

Chapter 2

Food, food and more food. Smells of cinnamon and caramelized brown sugar wafted from the glazed ham and the candied yams. Another whiff of the air, and the homey aroma of melted cheese mixed with butter, milk and pasta baked to perfection assaulted the senses.

Too bad Penny hadn't had a real appetite since she'd gotten the news.

From Tuesday evening, when she got the phone call from Carla telling her Big Mama had passed away, until the Saturday afternoon after the funeral, Penny had pretty much been running on fumes. Sometimes she remembered to eat a bite, but most times not.

Every member of Mount Zion must have brought a dish over to Big Mama's house after the funeral and interment.

And they were all there, milling around, making small talk and sharing memories.

Penny wanted them all to leave, so she could go out into the backyard, sit on the bench under the big oak tree and pretend none of it was happening. She forced smiles and made chitchat, because Big Mama had raised her to be polite. Because of Big Mama, she tried to hold it together.

She could be strong this time. She could prevail over loss this time, especially when she had nothing else to lose. Penny wrapped her arms around herself and closed her eyes for a moment in an effort to push her thoughts back. She couldn't allow herself to dredge up past losses, not if she wanted to make it through the rest of the day.

She let good times fill her mind.

Being back in Big Mama's little yellow and white house on Warren Street brought back all kinds of memories. Memories of roller-skating around the corner and having to come in before the streetlights came on. Memories of playing kickball and tag in the PS School #10 playground. Memories of buying a twenty-five-cent grape juice, a bag of barbecue potato chips, a fat pickle and a couple of packs of Now and Laters from the Puerto Rican–owned bodega on the corner and thinking she had the makings of a queen's meal at her disposal.

Most of all, she had memories of feeling safe and secure.

Standing there in the house she had grown up in, knowing the woman who had loved her and raised her was dead, felt as if someone had pulled the floor out from under her and she was balanced on one beam with a huge black hole waiting to engulf her. It felt as if she stood on the perilous edge of a steep cliff in a pair of stilettos after having one too many mojitos. But at least she was still standing, still balancing. She hadn't caved yet. Big Mama would have been proud of the way she was holding it together.

How did people make it after losing the person who had always been their rock, their advice giver, the person who helped them make a way to the light when darkness threatened? Big Mama had been all those things to Penny, and more. There had never been a time when Big Mama didn't have advice for Penny's life, *wanted or not.*

She remembered when she was twelve and Big Mama sat her under the tree to explain the changes happening to her preteen body and just a little bit about the birds and the bees. Big Mama had been somewhat vague when it came to some parts of the talk. But she had always been the voice of strength and reason, even when Penny messed up and got pregnant at seventeen.

Big Mama was really gone.

In a week or so, Penny would be gone, too. She hated the fact that she'd probably never again see the small three-bedroom, one-bathroom house her grandmother had worked so hard to keep after the grandfather Penny had never had the pleasure of knowing died.

As soon as she settled Big Mama's affairs, she'd say goodbye to Paterson, New Jersey, for good.

But could she really say goodbye to North Jersey *forever?*

She couldn't believe she'd been away for so long. She missed home more than she'd let herself believe. There was really nothing like North Jersey. From the tenements to the fact that you could literally go one block and be in another town—a town that often felt like a different world, North Jersey offered a packed and condensed mix of flavors and cultures different from the equally diverse but much more spread-out and free-flowing Los Angeles she now called home.

Penny was surprised by how she'd gotten back into the flow of Paterson in under a week. The brothers playing c-lo on the corner, the sisters on the stoops gossiping and people watching, the kids running their little behinds in the street, dangerously close to being run over by a car, the storefront churches on just about every block, right next to the liquor stores, the feeling, the flavor, all called out to a part of her she'd thought was gone.

You can take the girl out of Jersey, but you can't take Jersey out of the girl.

Penny shook her head.

"Brat, you gonna be leaving for California soon, huh?"

Penny jumped and her reverie ended at the sound of Carla's voice. She made a mental note not to let her mother get to her. But some things were a whole lot easier in theory.

She didn't need therapy to know that her unresolved issues and textbook abandonment fears all stemmed from the petite, honey-complexioned woman standing in front of her, drinking grape soda as if it were the finest wine.

Penny noted that Carla had taken to calling her by the childhood "endearment" she'd used whenever Big Mama wasn't around. She couldn't remember exactly when it went from shut-up-brat, get-out-of-here-brat, you-make-me-sick-you-little-brat, to just Brat, said in a weird, almost loving way. She only knew it was the name her mother called her by.

Gritting her teeth and counting to ten, Penny responded, "Yes, Carla. I have to go back. I have a business to get back to. The most I can stay is a week or two."

Penny ran an image-consulting firm with her friend Maritza Morales. They were both former video models/dancers, and they'd met on a rap video shoot about twelve years ago. They'd found they were both working their way through school and had developed a friendship. Since Penny had only ever had guy friends, developing a close friendship with a woman had been a challenge. Maritza had had a similar history, since she'd grown up as the only girl in a family of brothers. But they'd worked at their friendship, and it had grown.

Their business, New Images by Keys and Morales, was doing well. Maritza could more than pick up the slack for a little while, in order for Penny to handle her grandmother's affairs. But it took the two of them and their six faithful employees to really make it a work. Even though Penny pretty much made her own hours, she still needed to do her part to make sure the business remained a success.

Panic crossed Carla's face. "But I… Well, I… Well, what am I gonna do? I need somebody to…"

Even though years of hard living had taken a bit of a toll on Carla, she still had the good looks, fair skin, long, wavy black hair and petite but somewhat curvy body that most men found irresistible. She also had a vulnerable, childlike appeal that she seemed to be able to pull out when she needed it. If Penny hadn't seen all the faces Carla worked like a pro—all her multiple personalities, as Penny liked to refer to them—she might have fallen victim to the sad, helpless puppy-dog expression Carla wore at the moment.

Penny knew better, however, and she refused to fall for it.

"Carla, you're a grown woman. You're going have to learn how to take care of yourself, eventually." Penny started walking out of the food-filled dining room, thinking she'd miss Big Mama's cherry stained furniture and her china cabinet full of knickknacks and family photos.

She knew she wouldn't be taking any of it with her. Her memories would have to be enough.

Carla would need a place to stay, and since the house was paid for, she could stay here.

Penny only hoped her mother didn't resort to doing drugs again and end up losing the house and everything in it. But that wasn't her problem. She couldn't be responsible for her grown mother.

She wouldn't be responsible. She refused.

Carla stomped her foot and followed, walking so close she was almost on Penny's behind.

"I do know how to take care of myself, Brat. I just… Well…with Mama gone now, I just don't know if…" Carla gave a helpless shrug of her shoulders. "She was the only one who never gave up on me, and she was helping me to stay clean."

Yet again.

How many times had Big Mama helped Carla get clean and straighten up? And what had given Carla the sense of entitlement that said the whole world had to cater to her needs? Penny couldn't even fathom how a down-to-earth saint of a woman like Big Mama could have given birth to a self-absorbed person like Carla. She hated that she had to steel herself against Carla's pleas, because it made her feel hard and cold. A small part of her wanted to help her mother.

However, given her past with Carla, she needed to protect herself. She couldn't let Carla hurt her again. She wouldn't be able to deal with it, on top of Big Mama's death. She would topple over into the waiting black abyss for sure if she opened herself up to fall victim to her mother's antics again.

"I can't take Big Mama's place, Carla. You're going to have to do it on your own this time." Feeling as if she was being too harsh didn't stop Penny from holding her ground.

All those years growing up with a crack addict for a

mother had made her toughen up. She had spent too much of her life trying to help Carla and waiting for the woman to get it together. All Penny had ever gotten for her trouble was a broken heart and being called Brat.

Stopping midway in the hall between the dining room and the formal living room, Penny let out a soft hiss and a curse when Carla stepped on the back of her foot.

"You wrong for that, Brat. You just won't forgive. That's always been your problem." Carla rolled her eyes in disgust. "You can't go through your life like that. That's why you don't have *nobody* special in your life now! Your heart's hard and cold."

Penny pursed her lips and slanted her right eye slightly.

Carla made it *so* easy not to want to help her.

This would normally be the time when Big Mama would cut in and tell them they needed to treat each other better and remind them of the importance of family. But Big Mama wasn't here anymore. It was just the two of them.

Plastering a smile on her face, Penny started to back away. "Well, Carla…*darling* mother of mine…I suggest you start learning to toughen up. It's a cold world out there, and you need to learn how to face it."

Walking away from Carla proved to be easier than Penny thought it would be. She contemplated leaving for Los Angeles right after the last guest left the house. The fact that Carla could even fix her mouth to talk about help and forgiveness irritated Penny to no end.

"Forgive her, my behind. I can forgive. I already forgave her a million times." Mumbling to herself as she made her way to the kitchen, Penny didn't notice Jason until she walked right into him.

First Carla, now Jason! Lifting her head to the ceiling, she couldn't help but think: *What is it? You just don't like me this week, do you? Is it because I haven't been to church? If I go to service tomorrow, will you cut me some slack? Huh?*

Jason's strong arms embraced and held her. She felt a slight shiver travel its way across and through her body.

Yes, her traitorous body *would* still react to his touch, wouldn't it? Because what else would be more fitting at a time like this than being smacked in the face with the fact that she'd ruined her relationship with the only man who'd ever completed her, mind, body and soul. Yeah. She needed reminding of how much she had loved Jason just as she dealt with the loss of her grandmother and with her crazy, recovering-addict mother. What else would make sure her balancing act crumbled? She took a deep breath and firmed her resolve.

"Sorry," she muttered, trying not to look into his dark, brooding and still very sexy brown eyes. "I wasn't looking where I was going.

"You can let me go now." She tried to pull herself from his hold, but he maintained a grip on her.

"Can I?" Jason gave her a squinting, inquisitive gaze before dropping his arms to his side. "We need to talk, Penny."

Urghhhhhh! Not today. I'm hanging on by a string here. Honest. Pleading with the universe for some leniency probably wouldn't work, given her background, but maybe, just maybe, with Big Mama up in the heavens now, she could catch a break. Unless Big Mama was the one pulling the strings... *Nah...*

"Jason, it was really wonderful of you to come to both the wake and the funeral and pay your condolences. I appreciate it more than you know." *Or would even believe, given our history.* "But we really don't have anything left to talk about.

We said everything we needed to say fifteen years ago. And I, for one, don't feel much like revisiting the past."

"Well, maybe I need to. I lost the two people that meant the world to me—the two people who I thought would never betray me. I think we have a lot to talk about." With his jaw set in an angry and stilted manner, Jason appeared immovable.

"Not here. Not today. Please, Jason." One day she might be able to revisit that moment in her life and try to right the wrongs, but Penny didn't see it happening on the day she had buried her grandmother.

"So when, Penny? When?"

"Goodness, you're being a real jerk right now! My grandmother just died!"

A shimmer of regret crossed Jason's face for a moment and then, just as quickly, turned stony. "And fifteen years ago, a baby I believed was mine died, a baby we were going to raise together. And when that baby died, instead of mourning the loss with the love of my life, I got gut punched by being told that she was in love with the man I thought was my best friend! So forgive me if I still feel like I need to resolve some things and I'm not willing to give you the space to run until you manage to escape town again."

The hot anger in his eyes burned her to her core. Her stomach started to jump until she could feel it in her throat. She knew without a doubt that she couldn't deal with Jason now. She would never be able to maintain her facade when faced with his glare, which mixed hurt, anger, and betrayal.

At least fifteen years ago she'd had Terrill there to stand by her.

Terrill had been there through it all. She had hated having to use her best friend in such a manner. If she had it to do all over again, Terrill and Jason's friendship would be the only thing she would change. She would make it so at least those two could remain friends. Taking a deep breath, she straightened her back and narrowed her eyes, summoning up indignation from somewhere, even though she felt like the person with the least right to any sort of self-righteous stance.

The fact still remained; she had just placed Big Mama in the ground. Jason just showed her once again that, when push came to shove, he really only cared about his own feelings, his own hurt.

She hurt, too. More than she could ever let him know.

"You need to leave, Jason. If you don't leave, I'll call your colleagues in blue and have them come and get you. I don't think you want that. So, just continue to think of me as a whore, a slut, a heartless tramp…whatever you need to do to hold on to your bitterness and make you just stay away from me."

…*A backstabber and a slut… If I would have known you'd become such a slut, I would never have bothered with you in the first place*… She could still hear Jason's cracking voice, filled with tears and raw emotion, as he'd spat his venom at her and Terrill fifteen years ago. Three hearts had been irreparably damaged that evening, and it had all been her fault.

She walked away from him with her head held high. But, it was hard to maintain a dignified pose when she felt lower than a heel.

"You just won't stop, will you? If you can't cut Penny some slack on the day she buried Big Mama, then you need to leave."

Terrill's irritatingly calm and reasonable voice sent an angry chill through Jason's nerves. And watching Penny strut away from him didn't help the steady boiling in his guts.

Why had he even bothered to show up at the house after

the interment? What was this sick, masochistic need he had to be in her presence, even when she had shown him exactly who she was?

He had work he could be doing, cases he could be investigating. He'd taken a few days off when he found out Penny was going to be in town. Now he didn't know why he'd done it. What did he really hope to gain?

He had no idea. It wasn't as if she wanted him around. He could be at the lab now working through the evidence on the newest addition to his cold-case files. He could be interviewing old witnesses to see if time had caused alliances to shift enough for friends or relatives to give up their knowledge about a crime.

A new case had just come up. A man accused of the murder of two community activists and all-around Good Samaritans over thirty years ago had gotten off based on DNA evidence. The real murderer was still out there. As part of the cold-case team, Jason should be out there finding the person who had killed the popular married couple, instead of running behind Penny and begging her to talk to him.

But something didn't seem right. And this time he was determined to find out what it was.

"You need to mind your business, Terrill."

"Penny is my friend. And you used to…" Terrill paused before hissing in disgust. "Jason, this just isn't the time or the place. You should leave if you can't see that."

Jason could literally feel his shoulders rising and his chest bulking up with each word falling out of Terrill's mouth. Spoiling for a fight, he taunted, "You gonna make me?"

Terrill shook his head and turned up his lips. "We're grown men. I'm not going to resort to fisticuffs here."

Pansy. Pretty boy. How did I ever hang out with this guy?

"Why? You scared I'll kick your ass?" Jason leaned forward a little; the urge to give Terrill a physical shove was almost too compelling to hold back.

"No. I don't want to give any more stress to Penny than she has at this time."

"Well, aren't you the perfect little boyfriend?"

"Just lay off, Jason," Terrill hissed.

"Mind your business, Terrill."

Carla came sneaking up on them. "You boys aren't going to start fighting in here, are you?"

Terrill turned toward Penny's mom and answered, "No. We aren't."

Jason felt Terrill might just be wrong about that. Because he needed very badly to lash out at someone, and from where he stood, Terrill, with his I'm-Mr.-Perfect aura, was the ideal candidate.

Turning to face Carla, Jason took a deep breath. Even though she had a thirty-three-year-old daughter, Carla was only forty-seven years old herself. In fact, the entire time he'd known Penny, they'd always thought of Carla as more of an older sister. She'd certainly never acted like a parent, especially not when she was hooked on drugs.

Looking at her now, Jason could see that all those years of addiction had caught up with her a little bit. While she was still a striking woman, she no longer possessed the wholesome beauty she'd had when she was younger. Her once soft looks had a hard and rough edge to them now. Her honey complexion had a dull yellow appearance in spots. Her naturally wavy hair was a tad brittle and had lost its shine. She had a lot of gray hairs mixed in with the black. Her eyes still held the same youthful, wholesome appeal, however. They danced and shimmered with mischief.

Carla opened her mouth in a wide grin, and it became apparent that one of her front teeth was badly chipped. That might have made less brazen women too shy to smile, but not Carla.

"I always wondered what Brat had that made the two of you follow her around like little puppies. Whatever it was, I guess she's still got it. Ha!"

Knowing how much hearing the woman who gave birth to her call her Brat had hurt Penny, Jason felt a strange need to stand up for her that he quickly squelched. He wasn't about to champion her cause. She had Terrill for that. But he reckoned he wouldn't add any more stress to her day. She probably had enough stress, dealing with Carla.

"We were just best friends, Carla. If anything, Penny was stuck to us like glue. We just realized she wasn't going to go anywhere until we let her join the crew." Terrill had an almost wistful sound to his voice.

Jason raised his eyebrow and looked at his *ex*-best friend. No one would have been able to tell him way back then, when they were all eleven-year-olds riding their bikes and skates without a care in the world, that things would come to this. But then, no one would have been able to tell him he would fall madly in love with the scrawny, snaggle-toothed girl either.

He still remembered the first time they had all played together in the small attic apartment on Warren Street where Terrill and his mother lived. Big Mama had had to rush off for some emergency with Carla. She'd had no choice but to leave Penny with Terrill's mom. Jason had come over to play with Terrill, and had been thoroughly disgusted that a girl! was there during their playtime. The horror!

But Penny wouldn't let them brush her off. He still remembered the way she had snatched his Rubik's Cube and snapped, "Let me show you how to do it." She had finished the complicated box that had had he and Terrill stumped for months in no time flat. He wasn't even going to go into all the times she had beaten them in some race or another. She had gone from an icky girl to the coolest girl he had ever met to his second best friend by the end of the day.

"Whatever. A girl could do worse than having two strong, strapping young men such as y'all to look out for her." Carla let out a hooting laugh, and her eyes took in Jason. "I guess you don't really look out for her anymore, since she stomped on your heart. But you're here anyway, huh? You can't stay away, now that she's back. Ha!" Carla laughed so hard she started to cough as she opened the fridge and pulled out a can of grape soda.

Ouch. "I'm just here to pay my respects, Carla."

"Yeah, right. And I can take a hit of crack today and not have to worry about getting hooked. Somebody is swimming in the river of *de-ni-al.*" Carla sang the word *denial* like a song.

"We're all just here to pay our respects. Big Mama always opened her doors to us and made us feel like family," Terrill offered lightly. "We wouldn't want to do anything that would take away from this time of mourning for your family, for Penny." Terrill gave Jason a pointed stare.

Fine.

He would cut Penny and Terrill some slack today. But Penny wasn't leaving town this time until she gave him the closure he needed. She owed him. He had waited fifteen years, but the wait was going to be over.

"I've got to go. Please accept my condolences, Carla. And please, tell Penny I will be back by later to talk with her." Jason thought about saying goodbye to Terrill, but he wasn't feeling *that* amicable. It would take a lot more than conversation for him to reach a point where he could reach out to his old friend again.

With everyone gone, Big Mama's house felt cold and empty. Penny was just happy Terrill was still there and he wouldn't be going back to Los Angeles tonight. Sitting with him in the only room she and her friends had been allowed to hang out in, the only room without some kind of plastic protection covering the furniture, Penny let out a sigh.

As they sat on the worn black pleather sofa that had been the bane of her existence in high school, Penny ran her hand lovingly over rips and large, exposed patches of cotton filling.

Everything about the room said 1980s bad design—from the sofa to the black lacquer, gold and mirrored coffee and end tables.

Penny couldn't help but smile when she remembered how she'd pouted when Big Mama refused to buy cool *real* leather sofas for Penny and her friends to hang out on.

Big Mama had said, "Child, I'm not gonna spend that kind of money just for you and your little friends to eat potato chips and drink soda on it and tear it up. You better get this here! Stuff that you could wipe off when you get a spill!"

Terrill's voice pulled her away from her memories.

"If you need me to stick around a little longer, Penny, I will. I can rearrange some things and do it."

Terrill's willingness to continually be there for her made the ball of guilt in her chest throb. She wondered what she'd done to deserve such a good friend. She knew she'd never be fully worthy of his generosity.

"No, I'll be fine. I'm not staying around here long. Just long enough to settle Big Mama's affairs, and then I'm out.

For good." Letting out an uneasy sigh, she turned to look at her oldest friend. "Thanks for being here for me. You're always there for me, and I appreciate it. I know that you gave up a lot to stand by my side, and—"

Terrill interrupted her. "Don't worry about it, Penny. But a lot of time has passed. Maybe enough time…"

Carla came waltzing in the room, her mouth wide open and spouting her nonsense. "So you ended up sticking around. I would have put money on the other one being here." She gave Terrill her irritating grin.

"No offense, but I always thought he was a better match for Brat, anyway. His folks certainly had more money. But I guess you rollin' in the dough now, too. Big-time record company man and all! Ha! You the one hooked Brat up with them videos?"

An excited gleam crossed Carla's eyes, and she clasped her hands together. "You think you could hook me up? I'm thinking of moving out to Cali with Brat. I need me a change of scenery. I'm getting tired of P-Town. And Cali-for-nia, knows how to par-ty. Cali-for-nia knows how to par-ty." Carla did a little dance as she sang the Tupac lyrics.

Oh, no, the hell you aren't! "Carla, you can give that one up. You are *not* moving to California."

"Why not? Why you gotta be like that, Brat? What did I ever do to you to make you hate me so much, except give birth to your behind?"

"You have got to be kidding me, Carla. Just can it, 'cause I'm not the one. You can't guilt me into taking care of you. You have never taken care of me. I don't owe you anything." Penny shook her head incredulously.

"I'll help you settle Big Mama's affairs and help you out so you can remain here and keep this place. However, when

I leave here, the only thing you're going to see from me is a monthly check. And if you keep tripping, you're going to mess that up."

"What do you think, Terrill? You think it's right that Brat is gonna to throw her mama out to the wolves? She knows I need help. But she's just gonna go on about her little life." Carla had the nerve to let tears come trailing down her face.

"I think if you would stop calling your daughter Brat, she might be able to make her way past all the hurt you've piled on her through the years. And I think the two of you need to talk and come to a space of understanding." Terrill gave Penny a peck on the cheek and placed his arm around her for a quick hug. "I'm going to head out. I'll stop back by tomorrow to see how you're doing. Maybe we can go to service at Mount Zion. Call me if you need anything."

Carla shrugged, and her crocodile tears miraculously cleared up. "Hey, don't forget about the videos. I think I have star potential," she called after Terrill as he made his way out of the room.

Worried that her lips were going to remain stuck in the curled-up snarl she seemed to sport lately from being forced to tolerate Carla, Penny tried to form a smile.

It didn't work.

"You aren't moving to California. I'd move back to Paterson before I let you move with me."

"So I guess you're moving back to Paterson, then. Because I'm moving to California with you when you leave here. The sooner the better."

Penny let out a sigh and threw up her hands. How did one reason with such an unreasonable person?

Chapter 3

The constant pressing buzz of the doorbell interrupted Penny's argument with Carla. Penny made a mental note to thank the person who had the perfect timing to show up just when Carla was trying to figure out a way to make Penny take her to California.

Is it so bad that I don't really want anything else to do with my old life? she thought as she snatched open the door.

Seeing Jason standing there answered her mental plea to the universe. *Screw you, Penny.* She couldn't catch a break.

He'd changed from the suit he'd worn to the funeral into a pair of slacks and a short-sleeved silk dress shirt. Standing there leaning against the doorway, he gave off a definite air of sexiness that made her want to kick herself for even noticing. Even surly and sulking, the man was *fine.*

"Why are you back here?" was what she said. *Why can't*

things be different between us? was what she wouldn't allow herself to think. It was too late for them. There was no sense dreaming things could be different.

"Can I come in?" His square jaw and taut expression told her he wasn't about to leave anytime soon.

That didn't mean she couldn't try. Penny dug in her heels and leaned against the door frame.

Big mistake.

That only brought her closer to him, and closer to his cologne. Musk with a hint of seduction never smelled so good. She moved back a little. But it was too late. The whiff had done its damage.

Dang.

She'd done her best to get over him through the years. She'd had relationships with other guys, but she'd always kept herself protected. She had a wall so thick and so tall around her, no one had been able to penetrate it. She liked it that way. It was so much safer.

The fact that seeing Jason again had the strength to drill holes in her wall and shake her foundation was unsettling, to say the least. She needed to do something to keep him away. She couldn't go through what she'd gone through back then and survive whole. Putting herself back together after she had destroyed their relationship was the hardest thing she had ever had to do. She had to continue to protect what was left of her heart.

"Why? Can't you just leave me alone? I'm truly fine with you hating me for the rest of our lives and us never seeing each other again." Her voice cracked as she said those words, and she barely stifled a wince.

She realized at that moment that she didn't want Jason to hate her. Too bad what she wanted didn't matter. Not anymore…

"Well, I'm not fine with it. You're going to talk to me, Penny. You owe me this." Jason pretty much elbowed his way past the crack in the door and entered the house.

"Hey! The other one is back! You just missed the third wheel. Or are you the third wheel now? I'm having a hard time keeping track of y'all's little threesome." Carla snickered and ran her tongue across her chipped front tooth before smirking.

Honor thy mother.

Penny cut Carla a glance meant to shut her up. But even as she did, she knew it was useless. From the time she was a kid, Carla had been finding ways to torture her and make her life miserable.

No way am I taking that woman back to Los Angeles with me.

The scowl on Jason's face hinted that he didn't find Carla's antics funny, either.

Carla stuck out her tongue at Penny before turning to Jason. "I don't know what you looking at me like that for, Mr. Policeman. I ain't the one that's been stringing y'all around for years. I told Brat she should have stayed with you instead of hooking up with that other one. But hey, he's a big-time music man now, and he's gonna set me up *love-ly*. Ain't that right, Brat?"

Carla danced around and started singing the chorus to Lil' Kim's "Crush on You."

One. Two. Three. Four. Fi— Aw, hell!

"Carla, leave us alone! Go do something with yourself."

"Why you gotta be all—"

"Go!"

"Fine!" Carla turned to Jason. "You see what I have to—"

Penny put her hands on her hips and snarled, "Carla!"

"Fine, Brat!" Carla went stomping off up the stairs. A white slip hung clearly visible under the black dress Carla wore, and her pink house shoes scraped across the wood steps.

Penny watched her walk all the way up and sucked her teeth when one of the family photos fell from the wall as Carla stormed past. Penny would have to pick it up later, *after* she got rid of Jason.

She let out a sigh. "We can talk in the living room." She turned and he followed her.

Too late to ask himself why he'd bothered coming back to Big Mama's that evening. He was here now. Time to get his much-needed closure, once and for all.

Sitting in the room where he'd sipped on iced tea and talked with Big Mama each time he'd visited her, hoping she'd mention something about Penny, Jason started to wonder if he wasn't just a little bit touched in the head. If the stony hostility bouncing off of Penny like shock waves was any indication, she probably wouldn't be offering up what he needed.

If her taking him into the fancy formal living room with the floral, plastic-covered furniture offered any hint, then she had no desire to make him feel as comfortable as he felt when they were teenagers, hanging out in the den with the pleather sofas she hated.

She had her guard up. But what she didn't know was that, as a detective, he'd become a pro at breaking down people's barriers and getting them to tell the truth. It was time for her walls to come tumbling down.

"So, what do I have to do to get you to leave me alone, Jason?" Penny sat down on the sofa, and the plastic squeaked.

He sat next to her and got a strong whiff of her perfume. She still wore Beautiful. He remembered the Christmas during their junior year of high school when he'd given her the perfume for the first time, and his gut clenched. Gritting his teeth, he firmed his resolve.

"You could start by telling me the truth, telling me what really happened fifteen years ago. One minute we were having a baby and planning to get married. The next minute you had a miscarriage and I'm being told you're in love with Terrill. You even went so far as to say the baby wasn't mine."

He felt his voice crack as a sharp pain laced his chest. The raw pain threatening to bubble up in his chest had to be squelched.

Penny's copper eyes looked away and her stony gaze soon found a lot of interest in the shaking hands folded on her lap. "That's pretty much what happened back then. So, again I ask you. What do you want from me?"

"I want you to look me in the eye and tell me what we had was a lie. I want you to look at me and tell me you had sex with my best friend. I want you to tell me the child wasn't mine, that it wasn't our baby. I want you to look me in the eye and tell me you never loved me."

Her hand moved to the tiny scar at the side of her right eye.

Jason knew that she always worried the scar whenever she felt under pressure or up against a wall. His eyes narrowed.

She was definitely hiding something.

Her lower lip trembled slightly, and she let out a soft sigh. "Are you a glutton for punishment or something? Why this sudden need to revisit and relive the past? We've been there and done that. I've told you all of this before. I don't see the point in the constant repeating. So why don't you just—"

He couldn't let her finish, had to cut her off. "Why can't

you do it, Penny? Look at me while you cut my heart out. You owe me that. You didn't look at me then. You kept your face buried in Terrill's chest. I was too angry to think there was a reason why you couldn't look at me."

"There was no reason!"

"Then look at me, damn it!"

She lifted her head, and her ice-glazed eyes were pooling with tears. "You have no right to come in here and try and boss me around. I don't have to answer to you, Jason. Get out of my house. I don't want to see you… Just leave, please."

Her bottom lip quivered again, and this time it was more pronounced. She appeared to be just on the edge of breaking.

He didn't know if he wanted to see her broken. He could clearly see that she was hanging on by a thread.

Leaning forward, he cupped her face in his hand, gently stroking her cheek with his thumb. He had no idea what he was doing or why he felt the need to touch her, to comfort her. But he had to, even though he was the one bringing her the stress.

Her lip shook even more, and the tears that had once been content to remain pooled in her eyes started their way down her cheeks.

His heart started beating faster, causing a powerful thud in his chest. It was official; he was the biggest jerk in the city…probably the state…most likely the entire country….

Letting his hand move to caress her cheek and wipe away the tears, he let out the breath he'd had no idea he was holding. "Put us both out of our misery, Pen, please."

He sighed and placed his lips firmly over hers, kissing her with years of pent-up energy and frustration.

The startled gasp out of her mouth barely registered, and he used it as an opportunity to forge ahead with his tongue. He moved his hands and arms from her face to her back, pulling her over to him and scooping her into his lap. She felt so good against him. Every luscious part of her seemed to be made just for his hands, his only. He continued to taste and touch her even when she started to wiggle and tried to break away.

Penny placed her hands on Jason's chest, pushing him away. Even as she attempted to do so, she couldn't seem to get herself to stop kissing him. His taste was everything she remembered, multiplied over and over again. Lord, she could barely resist him.

Insane.

That's what she had to be. She needed to get her behind on a plane to Los Angeles immediately.

The strength of his hold nearly took her breath away. His thighs felt like the perfect spot to rest her behind. What she wouldn't have given to just be able to nestle closer to his rippling chest. His muscled arms wrapped around her felt so right. Yes, she needed to stop this now.

She made an attempt to close her lips, pursing them as she tried to finesse her way off his lap. All she managed to do was make him squeeze her tighter and cause him to nip and nibble on her bottom lip.

She opened her eyes and kept her mouth closed until he nipped her a little sharper.

His gaze, hooded in desire, said more to her than words could have at that point. And as if trying to prove just that, he only said one word. "Open."

No way. She tried to push away.

He held her and nipped her lip again. His tug softened as he whispered, "Open." It was more of a plea now.

The desire, the plea, they weakened her. Hesitantly, she

yielded her lips to his demand. She wanted to kiss him forever. What did that mean?

It means you need to get your behind on the next plane to L.A.

His tongue plundered her mouth at will as his hands roamed her body. Before she knew it, she was beginning to writhe and moan on his lap. She couldn't help it. Only when he halted the kiss did she get any semblance of control. Except for the panting breaths and the shaking body, she was the picture of poise.

"Tell me."

"Tell you… Tell you what?" she panted.

Where had all the air gone? Why did it feel like such a struggle to breathe? What had he done to her?

"Tell me what I need to hear, Penny."

Only a jerk would make her forget herself, forget she needed to protect her heart, forget it was too late, forget there wasn't a future for the two of them.

Scooting off his lap and standing as best she could on shaky legs, Penny began to back away. She couldn't look him in the eye and say those things. She just couldn't. She couldn't do it then, and she couldn't do it now.

"Please leave, Jason. Now."

"No. Not until you say it!" He stood up, too, walking toward her even as she backed way.

She blinked several times, and the tears really started to fall.

Oh, God, why won't he just leave me alone!

Her eyes went wide, and her mouth opened and closed several times before she covered it with her hands, afraid of what she might say if she risked uttering a word.

She glanced around the room for an escape. Her eyes caught an old picture of herself and Big Mama, taken when she was ten. She was sitting on Big Mama's lap, with two long pigtails and a big space where her two front teeth should have been. The grin on her face and the gleam in her eyes reminded her of the safety she'd always felt in Big Mama's lap.

Her knees gave out from under her, and she collapsed to the floor, sobbing uncontrollably. Her shoulders shook and her body rocked back and forth as she held herself in a tight embrace, all the while keeping her gaze on the huge framed picture on the wall.

Big Mama was really gone.

Gone.

Closing her eyes, Penny let deep, painful moans leave her in quick succession. One after the other, each utterance seemed to carry its own special brand of pain.

Somebody was screaming, "No!" The loud, piercing screams seemed to shatter all the facades around her. For the first time in a long time, all of her shields were down and she felt vulnerable, bare.

The voice wouldn't relent. It kept screaming, "No!"

She felt arms wrap around her, and she realized she was the one screaming. But she couldn't stop.

He had pushed her too hard, and he could feel his heart breaking with each of her soul-piercing cries. He wouldn't have known he still had a heart left to break, if he hadn't felt the sharp shooting pain in his chest when she fell to her knees. He got up from the sofa, got down on the floor with her and wrapped his arms around her. As he held her crying, shaking body, he mentally chided himself for not picking a better time to confront her.

"I'm sorry, Pen. It'll be okay. Just let it out, baby. God, I'm so sorry…"

Even though he figured he was probably the last person she wanted to comfort her, he knew he had to try. To his surprise, she actually leaned into his arms and buried her head in his chest. She was still sobbing, but at least she'd stopped screaming.

Carla came running down the stairs, so fast she almost slid into them. "What are you doing? What did you do to her?"

"I didn't do anything..." *Not exactly the truth.* "I think Big Mama's death finally hit her and she cracked."

The incredulous look on Carla's face spoke volumes. She walked over to them and pushed him away. For a small woman, she packed a lot of punch. Not enough to really move him, but enough to make him get the picture—she wanted him gone.

"Get out of here. Leave her alone." Carla dropped to her knees and reached for Penny. She pulled her until Penny fell into her arms. "I've got her. You can leave now. Get out!"

Penny wrapped herself into Carla's arms. The older woman folded herself around her child and shot daggers at Jason as she did.

Soft, shuddering sobs still heaved from Penny's chest, but it appeared as if she might be all right.

No thanks to me.

He turned slowly and let himself out. As he walked away, he heard Carla cooing and comforting Penny, and he wished it could have been him doing it.

"It's okay, baby. I miss Mama, too. But it will be okay. We'll be okay. We have each other. See, you need me, too." Carla's caressing hand patted Penny's hair, and for several minutes she actually felt as if Big Mama was still there.

Penny's tears had run dry, and she realized that she must have sat there on the floor sobbing for quite some time.

Besides the fact the hard wood was starting to make her butt numb, the lack of feeling in her legs and the ache when she shifted her body clued her in that she and Carla had been there for more than a minute.

"I can come with you to California. Then I can take care…well…we can take care of each other this time, Br— Penny."

What am I doing? Penny scooted away from her mother and looked at the her. As best as she could see with her tear-swollen eyes, Carla was still the same petite and crazy woman. She contemplated telling Carla just how insane she was. But then the press of the doorbell jarred her and her heart started pounding.

Please don't let it be Jason again. She didn't know how he'd managed to almost break her. *Almost? Girl, please! That man broke you all the way down. You better run.*

If she hadn't been trying to be so strong and hold it all in, she might have been able to maintain everything. But he'd kept pushing, and she'd broken. She didn't think she could take any more of him that evening.

"I'll get it. And if it's that ole high-and-mighty Hightower cop, I'm gonna cuss him out! I don't know what you put on that boy, but he is just determined to continue sniffing around you. It's probably best that we move to California instead of staying here the way he's coming after you." Carla just kept right on spouting her nonsense as she trotted off to the door.

Penny got up and followed her, just in case she needed some help turning Jason away.

The man acted as if he'd never heard the word no. He never did like not getting his own way. The baby Hightower boy had been a little spoiled in that regard.

"Oh, hell, no!" Carla's high-pitched yell reached her from

the entryway. "I said I'd call you. What part of I'll call you can't you understand? Why you showing up here now?"

Penny put more pep in her step and raced to the entryway. She figured it wasn't Jason who had Carla yelling like that. When she got to the door, she saw an older man standing there she didn't recognize.

He appeared to be in his mid-fifties. It was hard to tell. He looked as if he had had a rough life, but the only tellers were the eyes. His face was unusually smooth, and his lean, muscled body appeared to be in tip-top shape. His salt-and-pepper hair was cropped close to his scalp, with just a hint of a receding hairline.

He glanced up at Penny, and his eyes actually seemed to brighten. She frowned, because she could have sworn she had seen him someplace before.

Carla placed her hands on her hips and cemented herself between the man and the entrance.

"What's going on, Carla? Who is this man?"

"He ain't nobody important, and nobody for you to be worrying about."

"Oh, now I'm nobody. I ain't important? You just gonna hold a grudge for damn near thirty-something years?" The man took his eyes off of Penny and narrowed them on Carla.

"She don't need to know you. She doing just fine without you. *We* don't need you. *We* fixin' to move to California." Carla gripped the door and started shutting it in the man's face.

"Why don't you let her decide if she needs to know me or not?" He looked at Penny again.

His eyes. There was something about his eyes, the copper color. She had seen them before.

In the mirror.

Oh crap! You have got to be kidding me. Penny raised her head toward the heavens. *Big Mama, are you up there yet? Can you stop whoever it is who seems to have it in for me up there?*

The man pressed against the door. "Can I at least come in and talk to her?"

Penny knew Carla wouldn't be able to hold off the strong, muscle-bound man for long. She was torn between helping her mother shove the door in his face and meeting the man so that they could get this little *ghettofied* family reunion out of the way. It would be one less thing to deal with.

"Carla, just let him in. Let's get this over with."

Carla glared at her and kept trying to close the door. "Uh-uh, Brat. Just like that other one brings out the worse in you and upsets you no end, this fool rubs me *all* the way wrong. I ain't able to deal with him tonight. He gotta go."

Penny walked over to the door.

"She calls you Carla? You're her mother. Why don't she call you Mama or Mom?" The man kept trying to make his way in.

Carla had gained strength of fortitude and mouth. "Same reason she don't call you Daddy or Dad! We ain't never did a thing for her to earn those titles. Now get away from here. I'll call you if she wants to see you. You gave me the number." Carla gave the door a hard shove.

Penny put her hand on the door and started to push with Carla.

"Oh, come on. I just want to meet her." The man looked Penny in the eye. "I just want to meet you. Please. You the only child I have."

"She the only child I have, too. And I'm the only parent she need. You just gonna go back to jail anyway, eventually. Can't nobody depend on you."

"Why can't you just let her decide? She grown now. Let her decide."

"Just 'cause she grown don't mean she know what's good for her. I know best in this regard. You ain't worth getting to know."

"At least I ain't wasted my life as no junkie."

"No. You just a criminal. You wasted yours in jail." Carla gave the door a heaving push and managed to shut it. She wasted no time clicking the locks.

The man started banging and ringing the bell at the same time.

Penny just stared at Carla and then back at the door.

Carla stood there, breathing heavily, and finally leaned against the wall. When the man kept at his assault of the door, Carla yelled, "If you don't leave here, I'm gonna call the cops on your ass. You hear me? The cops! You better run. With your criminal history, you ain't got a strike to play with. Get from round here!"

"I just want to meet my daughter! Why are you being such a bitch?"

"Because I am one. And I'll be the baddest one you ever met, if you don't leave. I told you I'd talk to Brat, and if she wants to see you, I'd call you."

The door actually started to shake then, and if Penny could have managed to move any part of her mouth, she would have said something. But it just hung open, refusing to close. She'd suspected who the man was, and it had been confirmed.

"Brat, stop standing there with your mouth hanging open!" Carla rolled her eyes. "Go and call the cops on this fool. Let them take his behind back to jail!" she screamed at the door.

Penny shook her head. "No."

Squinting, Carla heaved herself from the wall. "Fine. I'll do it."

Penny sighed, opened the door and let her father in.

Chapter 4

Yep. This is my father. Can my little ghetto homecoming become any more stressful?

Peering into the tall stranger's face, Penny sighed, stepped aside and let him in.

He took slightly hesitant steps forward, and soon they were both standing in the den.

"Have a—" Penny started.

"Hi, I'm—" The man edged forward and stuck out his hand before running it across his close-cropped salt-and-pepper hair and giving a nervous chuckle.

Penny found herself giggling, as well. "I'm sorry. Why don't we have a seat? I think I know who you are. I'm just not sure why you're here. Or rather, why you're here *now.*"

Did that sound too harsh? She supposed it did. But really,

what did one say to a father she couldn't recall ever meeting and had no memory of?

Big Mama and Carla had never talked about the man. The times she remembered asking if she had a father, she'd never gotten any clear answers from either one of them.

Big Mama had only said, "Of course, baby. Everyone has a father…"

After Penny got older, she'd just figured if he was worth knowing, they would have mentioned him or told her something about him.

His tall, muscular frame seemed to shrink somewhat as his shoulders hunched and he sank down on the worn pleather sofa. He ran his hand across his head again and looked at her with those eyes, eyes just like her own.

The more she looked at him, the more she could see the other similarities between them. She had always thought she'd gotten her height from Big Mama somehow, because Carla was such a petite thing. But seeing how tall and sturdy her father was, she figured she must have gotten her own tall, shapely build from her father's side of the family. She wondered what the women in his family looked like. It was hard to tell if her own toasted-cinnamon skin was a mix between his mocha complexion and Carla's soft, honey skin tone.

"My name is Gerald McEarly, and I'm your father. You probably don't remember me much 'cause I got sent away on that murder rap pretty soon after you was born. I—I was cleared of those charges. The DNA finally cleared me. That's why I'm out," he started.

Her eyes popped open.

Murder?

He must have sensed from the expression on her face that

she was coming to some less-than-flattering conclusions. He ran his hand across his head again and sighed before finishing. "I might have been guilty of selling a little…hustling a little…but I didn't kill anyone. I would have never killed that couple. But that's not important, really." The commanding, bass-filled tone of his voice didn't seem to match the hesitant and rambling manner in which he spoke.

When Penny looked into his huge copper eyes to see if she could get a read on him, to figure out what he wanted, she saw that they had a pleading expression in them.

Pleading for what? What did he expect from her?

He got halfway up and reached into his back pocket.

Instinctively she jumped back, and a hurt expression crossed his face.

"You're my daughter. The only child I have. I would never hurt you. I just wanted to show you something, show you what I kept."

The tattered black leather wallet looked like it had seen better days. Penny noticed it bulked not with money, but with pictures. He had several small photos in the wallet, some wallet-size and some cut down to fit in the wallet.

"This is you." He handed her a picture of her as a baby. "And this is you and your mama. She used to send me pictures of the two of you all the time for the first few years. Then she stopped." His voice choked. He blinked and ran his hand over his eyes before continuing. "Of course, she was young. I shoulda known she wouldn't have waited all this time… But that's not important. I held on to what pictures I had the entire time. So I could keep focused. I never forgot about either of you."

This is just too much. Or is it too little too late?

Even though her heart went out to him, based on the pain that radiated from him, she had no idea how to respond.

Heck, even if Carla stopped writing him, why had he stopped? Why hadn't he reached out to her sooner?

"I'm sorry, Gerald. But, I mean, well…you never wrote or anything. Or called. So I find it really hard to believe you thought of me all the time you were in prison."

"I wrote you and your mama all the time. I kept writing for a while, even after she stopped writing to me and sending pictures. Even after she started sending the letters back unopened… I thought maybe she would get over her anger. At least bring you to see me or something… But she never did. Then I heard about her being hooked on that crack and seeing…" A pained expression crossed his face.

"What're you doing in here?" Carla shot Penny a glare that screamed betrayal. "Brat! Why did you let him in here? Get out, Gerald! I've called the cops, and they'll be here any minute. They gonna lock you up. *Again.*"

"I just wanted to meet my child, Carla. Damn. You act like I'm gonna hurt her or something. I just wanted to see her. To meet her." Gerald heaved a sigh and ran his hand across his head before glaring at Carla. He placed his photos back in his wallet and put the wallet in his back pocket.

"How am I supposed to know you won't hurt us? You're a criminal. You *did* go to jail for murder." Carla crossed her arms and gave Gerald a pointed look before turning to Penny. "You see what you did, Brat? You let a murderer in the house."

"I was cleared. The DNA cleared me, and you know it, Carla. Why you deliberately trying to poison her mind toward me?"

Carla shrugged, twisted up her lips and slanted her eye before placing her hand on her hips.

If it weren't her life, Penny might have found the entire

display mildly amusing. The two deadbeat parents were trying to one-up one another. In her eyes, neither would be getting the parent of the year award anytime soon.

The doorbell rang and Carla shot off to answer it. She turned slightly. "Too late to leave now. That's the cops. I told you to get out and leave us alone. Oh, well. Too bad, so sad."

Gerald's shoulders slumped, and Penny almost felt bad for him.

She had no idea what the man had hoped to accomplish with his visit. But she was pretty sure this wasn't it. Seeing the way Carla's treatment affected him made her cringe as she thought of how her own funky attitude might have made Jason feel. At least Carla had a reason to be so mean and bitter. She, on the other hand, had no right to treat Jason badly. She only hoped he would stay away so she could leave Paterson without having another confrontation that would only end up hurting him and, most of all, herself.

"I just wanted to see you, that's all. I just wanted to see you before you went back off to California. I didn't come to hurt anybody, just wanted to see you for myself." Gerald's sad voice pulled her out of her thoughts of Jason.

Carla came flouncing back into the sitting room, with Jason following right behind her.

Penny didn't even bother looking toward the heavens. What was the point? Someone up there clearly wanted her to face her past.

Must be Big Mama…. I can't do it, Big Mama. I don't think I can do it….

Carla's smirk let Penny know her mother was relishing every minute of the ex-lovers' tit for tat they were caught in.

"Well, looka, looka who P-Town's finest saw fit to send over and help us get rid of this lowlife. The wonderful Hightower you can't seem to get enough of, Brat. Ain't that a blip? Huh? Ha!" Carla tilted her head haughtily before pointing to Gerald. "That's him, Detective Hightower. That's the criminal that tried to break down my door and who has been harassing me. I'd like him arrested."

Penny glared at Carla, and then shot Jason an angry glare, as well.

Since when did police detectives come and check out random domestic disputes?

"I picked the call up on my scanner and told them I knew you all and I was in the neighborhood, so I could check it out." Jason at least appeared a tad contrite, as if anyone so overbearing could be contrite.

"Well, I'm afraid you've wasted your time, Jason. This man is my father, and I invited him in so we could talk and get to know one another."

Jason's jaw dropped. He eyed Gerald, then looked at Carla. "Did you call in a false report?"

Carla's honey skin seemed to take on red-hot tones as she glowered at Penny. Her shoulders arched, her chest poked out, and her tiny hands found their way to her hips.

Penny could have sworn she saw steam trailing from Carla's nose and ears.

"I didn't call in a false report. I didn't invite this man into my home." Carla pointed angrily at Gerald, and cut her eyes at Penny at the same time.

"No, you didn't, but I did, Carla. So, Detective Hightower, I'm sorry we've wasted your time. I can see you out now, if you'd like. Things are really under control here." Penny stood up from the sofa. She glanced at Carla, and the betrayed look in her mother's eyes almost made her heart turn soft toward the woman.

Almost.

Penny sighed. "And, Gerald, perhaps you should leave, too. It's getting late, and we've had a long day, with the funeral and the burial. If you leave me a number to reach you, I promise to try and meet with you again before I leave town."

"And when will that be, Penny?" Jason seemed to have forgotten he was there on police business and not to get knee-deep in her life.

Penny squinted her eyes and contemplated telling him it was none of his business. She opted for the civil approach, even though her head throbbed and her heart ached. She didn't want to be cruel or mean and evil to this man.

She didn't want to hurt him anymore. Because for some reason it still broke her heart when she had to push him away. And since she didn't want to finish the already emotionally draining day with yet another confrontation with Jason, she painted a pleasant smile on her face.

"I'm not sure exactly when I'll be leaving, *Detective* Hightower. It depends on how long it takes me to settle up Big Mama's affairs." She kept her bright expression firm. "Now, if you gentlemen would be so kind…we're really at the ends of our ropes…." She shot Carla an apologetic glance, but her mother turned away in a huff.

Penny walked off toward the door, fully expecting both men to follow her.

Gerald handed her a piece of paper. "This is my number at the boardinghouse where I'm staying. I, well…I hope you use it. I'd sure like to see you again and talk."

Jason just narrowed his eyes at her and walked out.

She had the feeling she hadn't seen the last of him by a long shot. In fact, given the way her forced trip home had been going, if she was certain of anything at all it was that she would be seeing much more of Jason Hightower. Whether she wanted to or not.

Jason stood in front of Big Mama's house and watched as Penny's father started walking off down the street. The man didn't appear to have a car, and Jason felt an unreasonable urge to find out more about him. He didn't like the recently-released-from-prison aura the man gave off. And he couldn't shake the totally unrealistic desire he felt to protect and watch out for Penny.

"Hey, man, you need a lift or something? I can drop you off." Jason knew there was an edge to his voice that probably didn't sound particularly inviting to the man, especially if he really was an ex-con. But he was doing the best he could.

The man paused and gave him a once-over. "You, uh… You sure? I'm on the other side of town, down the hill…on Temple Street. It's probably out of your way."

"It's cool. I'd like to talk to you for a minute, anyway."

After a few seconds of contemplation, the older man nodded and then started walking back toward him. Jason opened the door to his SUV, and they got in.

"So, you're Penny's dad?"

"Yeah." The man's face seemed to light up at the mention of Penny's name.

"You and Carla?"

A sad sigh escaped the man's lips. "Carla was the love of my life, man. I mean, I was as much in love as a nineteen-year-old young hustler could be. And she was just a little high school freshman."

"That's statutory, man—" Jason began.

"I know. Trust me, her mama threatened to have me locked

up when Carla ended up pregnant. I wanted to do the right thing. Even went and asked if I could marry her." The man chuckled uneasily. "Her mama said hell no, and threatened me with a gun. She said she was gonna have me locked up for messing with her child. And I think she would have, if they hadn't gotten me on that bum murder rap before she got the chance.".

"You did time for murder?" Jason started to get an uneasy feeling. Given Carla's history, he would have pegged the man for a former drug dealer. But murder?

"Yes. But they just let me out after DNA testing proved I was innocent all along. I might just sue. Them damn cops should have looked harder for the real murderer." He must have realized that he was riding with a cop. "I mean, I got nothing against cops and all. I just feel like the whole system did me dirty, you understand?"

Jason could have gone into a discussion on the merits of the Paterson Police Department. But he knew sometimes the wrong people got locked up. Just ask Rubin "Hurricane" Carter… So he nodded to encourage the man to keep talking.

He was beginning to think he knew who this man was— and that there might be a connection between this man's recent release and the newest cold-case file to come across his desk. If there was, then there might be some clues to be gained that could lead him to figure out who the real murderer was.

"Anyway, I realize all cops ain't bad. I mean, you seem like a cool dude. Maybe with some younger cats on there, some *brothers,* maybe the Paterson Police Department has changed some since I been gone." The man glanced out the window as he spoke.

The tone of his voice and the fact that he wouldn't look in Jason's direction, let him know the man hardly believed what he'd just said.

Jason could sniff out a lie a mile away. That's why he wasn't going to let Penny leave again until he got the truth out of her, once and for all.

Jason cleared his throat. "My name is Jason Hightower, by the way."

"Yeah. I'm Gerald McEarly."

Bingo. Gerald McEarly was the man who'd originally been convicted in the case on his desk. He'd recently been cleared of a double murder—a married couple who had been prominent community activists on a crusade to rid the streets of drugs and crime. Now Jason knew he had to try to find out as much about the man as he could. Finding out about him might offer up some clues that would help him solve the case.

"Well, Gerald, welcome back. I grew up with your daughter, and we dated throughout high school before we both went away to college."

"Oh, really?"

Jason could feel Gerald's eyes on him as he drove. He turned quickly and found the man studying him intently.

Jason offered a little of his own history to make Gerald feel comfortable. "We grew up in the same church, and played together as kids. Me, her and our friend Terrill used to be inseparable."

"Umm…what happen?"

"Times change. People change." Jason had no desire to rehash the past with Penny's dad. The point was to get Gerald to open up. It would be nice if he could gather some insight into who might have had the biggest motive to set Gerald up for murder, or who might have had an even bigger motive to commit the crime.

Gerald probably wouldn't offer up that information if he

flat out asked him tonight. But he might offer some insight unknowingly, if Jason could get him talking. It was surprising how many cold cases were solved just by detectives talking to people, reinterviewing old witnesses, that kind of thing. Time could help the truth come out, at least in some cases.

"So when did you get out? And what made you decide to stop by their place tonight?"

"I just wanted to see my daughter. I'd only ever seen the baby pictures and pictures of her as a toddler. And then, for a minute when she was dancing in them videos, I saw some of them when the guys would watch them in jail. But you know, the last thing a guy wants to do is listen to a bunch of horny jailbirds commenting on the video girls and know one of them is his daughter."

Jason nodded. The last thing a college student wanted to do was watch music videos with his new college buddies and listen to them rave about that hottie with the body and the copper eyes. His college years had been rough thanks to Penny's stint as a video vixen.

He pulled up to the address on Temple Street that Gerald had given him and made a U-turn so he could drop him off right in front of the weathered gray house.

"Thanks for the ride, young man. I appreciate it." Gerald opened the door and slowly stepped out. "Maybe I'll see you around."

Oh, you can count on that.

Until Jason found out who had really committed those murders, and whether this man was any threat to Penny, Gerald McEarly would definitely be seeing more of him. He nodded as Gerald shut the door. Instead of heading home, Jason went to the precinct. He had a sudden urge to find out all he could about Gerald McEarly, and to dive into the latest cold case to land on his desk.

The downtown precinct of the Paterson Police Department was unusually busy, even for a Friday night. Jason tried to take that as a positive sign, since it meant many more criminals were off the street, at least for the night. But a crowded precinct meant there was more crime out there to begin with.

Ideally, he'd be home watching a game with his brothers or out on a hot date on his night off. Ideally, he wouldn't even be concerned about the drama going on in the life of his cheating ex-girlfriend. Too bad ideal situations seemed to be lacking, and all he was left with was this obsessive and overwhelming need to protect and serve Penny.

The fact that her father was the man cleared of murder in a just-reopened cold case wasn't lost on him. He didn't believe in coincidences.

"Hey, Jason. What are you doing here tonight? I thought this was your night off." His brother Lawrence eyed him as he chugged coffee out of Jason's Pace University alumni mug.

Jason had gotten his BS in forensic science from Pace's stellar program. Once he was done, he'd moved back to Paterson and joined the Paterson Police Department, like his father and other men in his family—the ones who weren't firemen, anyway. The desire to serve the community just seemed to run through the blood of Hightower men, and he was no different. It had never really occurred to him to do anything else.

He was tempted to snatch his mug away from his nosy older brother, but he decided it wasn't really worth it. "What are you doing here? I thought you all but moved into the satellite trailer on Governor Street since the McKnight twins were released."

It was rare that their paths crossed, since Jason spent the bulk of his time going through old reports, retesting old evidence when newer, more cutting-edge tools became available and interviewing old witnesses for new clues. As a narcotics detective, Lawrence spent the majority of his time in surveillance mode, stalking dealers and getting them off the streets.

Lawrence shrugged. "Somebody has to keep the riffraff in line. But that still doesn't tell me what you're doing here."

"I just wanted to do a little research." Telling Lawrence he wanted to do research on Penny's father would no doubt earn him an earful that he had neither the time nor the inclination to listen to, so Jason left that out. "The release of the guy cleared of the double murder of that community activist couple means more work for me."

Lawrence nodded knowingly. "Pouring yourself into your work might be just the ticket until Penny goes back to Los Angeles. You don't want to end up doing anything stupid."

If by stupid Lawrence meant hounding Penny for answers and digging through her father's records to make sure the man wasn't a threat, he was way too late.

When it came to Penny, Jason realized, he bypassed stupid and went headfirst into crazy.

"Yeah, well, a guy's gotta do what a guy's gotta do." Jason shrugged and started to walk away. "And make sure you clean out my mug and put it back. I don't know why you always take my mug, with all the dang mugs there are in this place—including three of your own."

Lawrence grinned and held up the mug in a mock salute.

Jason kept going and didn't stop until he entered the records room.

After several hours reading up on Gerald McEarly, Jason felt he didn't know the man any better than he had before he started. Nothing in the man's past seemed to scream that he'd be a threat to Penny. But Jason couldn't say for sure he wouldn't be.

And there was also nothing about Gerald McEarly's past that seemed to point to who the real murderer was.

Who had done it? Someone had killed the couple and hadn't had to pay for it. Nothing in the court records, or Gerald's police records, gave any hint of a lead.

Gerald McEarly had made bad decisions in his past. Decisions that would have landed him in jail eventually even if he hadn't been found guilty of the crime he'd recently been cleared of. That meant he had to be watched carefully, as far as Jason was concerned.

If Penny weren't involved, he might not have been so obsessed about Gerald. But she was, and Jason had to come to grips with the fact that it made all the difference in the world.

Jason rubbed his head in frustration and leaned back. There were times when his stubborn streak paid off. Unfortunately, tonight didn't seem like one of those nights.

It took a certain amount of tenacity to be a good detective, and even more to be a cold-case detective. What other kind of person would think he could solve crimes that were sometimes decades old?

He stood and walked over to the only window in the small room. The sounds of the still very busy police department seemed miles away, and the pounding of his heart seemed way louder than normal.

Cars zoomed down Martin Luther King Boulevard. As he watched them, he tried to process his feelings.

Penny was back for a short time. The very beautiful woman was the same very beautiful girl who'd lied to him and stomped on his heart. Why the heck was he spending his Friday night trying to make sure her deadbeat dad meant her no harm?

Because it's related to your case, he told himself. But he knew that was only a fraction of the reason why.

Given Penny's deceit, maybe she and her parents deserved one another. He should really leave them to their sordid little lives….

Then he thought about Penny. *His Penny…* His copper-eyed angel…

She'd been as sweet and innocent as they came back then. She'd given him her heart and her virginity, and no one could tell him they hadn't been soul mates.

So what had made her stray?

And what had made his *other* best friend, the only man outside his family he'd have trusted with his life, the one he'd thought would always have his back, want to destroy him without any regard?

Those questions had overwhelmed his detective's mind for the past fifteen years. Now he had to complicate it with Penny and Terrill's reappearance, questions about Penny's father and the reopened murder case.

He groaned out loud and moved away from the window. Nothing would be solved tonight. But he knew he wouldn't rest until at least one fifteen-year-old mystery was laid to rest. He *would* find out why Penny and Terrill had betrayed him.

Chapter 5

The adult choir always sang on the second Sunday at Mount Zion, and Penny was happy for it. Not that she didn't appreciate the staid and steady songs sung by the elders in the senior choir, which Big Mama used to belong to, but they did seem to make church service drag on just a little bit longer whenever they sang.

And with every single member of the Hightower family, including Jason, sitting in church this afternoon, she wanted the service over quickly, so she and Terrill could get out of there without having to have yet another uncomfortable, awkward encounter.

Determined not to draw attention to herself, Penny didn't even stand up and sing along with the choir.

"Speak to My Heart" was one of her favorite songs. Today,

calmness came over her spirit when she heard the song. It almost seemed as if, by sitting still and listening properly, she'd be able to figure out the right thing to do.

She did manage to clap as the choir finished singing. The soloist had a voice like an angel, and Penny could see the wheels turning in Terrill's record executive head. Since there was no way they'd be able to have him try to connect with the potential next big thing *and* get out of the church without running into the Hightower family, Penny hoped he'd turn his star-finding mode off. She thought about shooting up a silent prayer. But given her track record since she arrived home, she had an inkling of how that prayer would be answered.

She was starting to regret her decision to come to service. She should have been spending the day going through Big Mama's things and deciding what to tackle first at the start of business on Monday morning. The sooner she wrapped things up, the sooner she'd be able to go back to Los Angeles.

The last time Penny spoke to her business partner, Maritza Morales, she had said she had everything under control. However, Penny still felt the need to get her life back to normal as soon as possible. Last night with Jason had been a close call. She didn't think she could take much more of his probing.

Then there was the fact that she was still very much attracted to him…. If that kiss they'd shared was any indicator, the man still sparked her fire.

Lord, look at me lusting after the man. And in church, no less. Forgive me.

She took a small peek toward the ceiling and hoped lightning didn't come down and strike her.

"Ahhh, speak to my heart. Speak to my heart!" The pastor stood behind the podium and pounded it with his hand. "Oh,

some of us bid the Lord to speak to us and tell us what to do,
but we don't listen…. Y'all don't hear me…"

The pastor turned as if he were going to walk away, only
to be called back by the responses of "Preach!" and "Tell it!"
from the congregation.

"It never ceases to amaze me how God's children can see
signs of His desires for them all around them. Know in their
heart what the Lord wants them to do. Hear the soft sweet
voice of *Je-sus* whispering the right thing in their ear, and still
go off and do what they want to do. Still go off and do things
their own way. That's disobedience, church!"

"Sure is! Tell it, Pastor!"

"Mmm…hmmm…. Preach!"

The amen choir was in full form today, ready to amplify
and agree with everything the pastor said. The man had just
started preaching, and already they were dead on with the call
and response.

The sun shone through the beautiful stained-glass windows of the church, each one a superb artistic rendering of a
key moment in Jesus's life, from his birth in the manger to
his death on the cross. The bold colors of the stained glass
refracted the light and dispersed it around the church in such
a way that even the glass seemed to be in accord with the
pastor's powerful voice.

Penny felt an odd stirring deep inside of her, and she
looked down at her hands in an effort to find something to
do besides listen to the pastor. She recognized the feeling
coming over her for what it was.

Big Mama used to say you knew it whenever the Word was
speaking to you, knew it when you came to church and got
the message God was trying to send to you, knew it when the
word was *meant* for you.

"Some of y'all think you know better than the Lord. You think you have a better plan for your life than God does!" The pastor slammed his hand on the podium and did a little spin. "And some of you so high and mighty, you think you have a better plan for others' lives, too. You're not just content to ignore God's plans for you. You're so tough, you think you know what's best for everybody. You're busy messing with God's plans for others. Some of y'all are busybodies, always in other folks' business."

"I know that's right, Pastor! Mmmph."

Was that Sophie's voice? I know *that wasn't Sophie.*

Penny shook her head at the fact that not everyone was ready to hear the message. Truth be told, she wasn't ready to hear it, either. But she wasn't hypocritical enough to act as if she didn't have the faults the pastor was preaching about.

"Preach on it! Preach on it!" One of the deacons waved his right hand in the air in agreement with what the pastor said.

"See, but I'm gonna tell you something you might not know." The pastor leaned forward on the podium, as if he were letting them in on a secret. "You can't mess with God's will." He stepped back and shook his head. "No. What God has planned for a man, no other man can mess with. *His will be done.* On Earth as it is in Heaven." He pointed his finger at the congregation. "You can't mess with God's will!"

"Sure can't!" a younger woman shouted.

Another man clapped and stood. "Tell 'em, Pastor. You betta tell them!"

"And even if you ignore the voice of God, speaking to your heart and telling you the right thing to do, you can't ignore it for long. God isn't going to let you cause havoc and strife in the lives of His children for long, either…"

Penny started thinking about her role in Jason and Terrill's broken friendship. She had decided at the time that deceit was the best route to take, even though everything in her heart told her it was wrong. She had thought it would be best for Jason if she was no longer a part of his life.

She hadn't meant for Terrill to become a casualty of the fallout.

At the time, she'd decided to ignore everything she knew was right, even her own love for Jason. But she'd done it so he could have a better life. Didn't that count for something? It wasn't as if she'd done it to be cruel.

"Not even your *best* intentions can measure up to the Master's plan. And if you *truly* let God work through you, then you'd know that…" The pastor's words seemed to be a direct response to her thoughts.

Well, alrighty then…

Penny wrapped her arms around her waist and pulled herself farther into the corner of the pew. It would have been nice to disappear right into the pew.

"Think about the Lord Jesus before he died on the cross for our sins. Think about what it meant for him to follow God's plans…what God told his heart to do…. Think about what it meant to do his Father's will when it meant his very life on Earth would be lost." The pastor paused and shook his head for emphasis. "And some of us don't want to do the right thing because it's just *easier* to do the wrong thing. We think we can save ourselves some hurt or discomfort. We take the easy way, instead of God's way, and we end up losing.

"And some of us don't want to do the right thing because our material possessions might be at risk. Or our money might be a little lighter if we do. So we don't pay our tithes like we supposed to, even though the Bible clearly tells us *ten percent!* Yes, think about the Savior giving up his life for you and imagine what you might have done in our Savior's place."

The pastor wiped his face with a white handkerchief, even though he hardly seemed to be sweating. He must be giving the congregation enough time to imagine themselves in the place of Jesus.

Penny tried to imagine herself making the decision Jesus had made, but she kept coming back to the decision she'd made fifteen years ago.

It didn't make any sense for her to come clean now.

Did it?

"Would you go to the cross and die for the sins of people who you hadn't even met, folks who you knew going in would ignore your Word, ignore you when you spoke to their hearts? People who just went on ahead and did things their way, because they couldn't be bothered with silly things like right and wrong?" The pastor twisted up his lips in a decidedly disgusted fashion.

"No. No, you wouldn't. You'd work out some kind of a rationalization in your mind about how unworthy some of the people were. How some of them wouldn't even take the balm of salvation you were offering, would never open up their hearts to know God. And how you could really do so much more alive and walking among them, even with your Father whispering in your heart it was the right thing to do…"

Penny lifted her head toward the ceiling.

Oh, yeah, Big Mama was definitely up in heaven pulling strings now.

Penny remembered when she'd lost the baby all those years ago, when she'd made up her mind to break up with Jason and let him think she and Terrill were a couple. Big Mama had voiced her opinion on the matter once, and only once.

Big Mama had said she didn't care how much Penny rationalized things in her mind, her heart had to know it wasn't right. She'd said one day Penny's heart was going to let her know she'd done wrong, and hopefully it wouldn't be too late to make things right.

Too late.

It was really too late. Jason hated her, and he should. He also hated Terrill, and for that she would always feel guilty. But it was too late to do anything about it.

"Maybe…the Lord…is trying…to tell you something. Maybe the Lord is trying to tell you something. Right now…" The pastor started singing, and the choir chimed in.

No, they didn't bust out, "Maybe the Lord is Trying to Tell You Something," Penny thought. There was no way she was going to have a *Color Purple*–inspired, come-to-Jesus moment.

It's too late, Big Mama. Stop it.

As the choir sang the words, they penetrated her heart more than she could have imagined. She felt as if she were inside a pressure chamber and she could feel everything squeezing and pushing in. The steel enclosure she had encased her heart and her feelings in all those years ago wanted to cave in under the strain.

How long would it be before her walls collapsed? She didn't feel she had a lot of time at all.

"Maybe the Lord is putting something on your heart right now." The pastor spoke in a softer voice, and the choir started to hum along. "Maybe you're tired of trying things your way and want to give God's way a chance. Maybe you just need to bring the heaviness in your heart and hand it over to the Lord today. Maybe you just need to sit in a space of silence and listen to His voice this morning. I invite you now to come on up and bring it to the altar. Lay down your burdens. The Lord is thy Shepherd. Let him lead you. Let him help you carry the load if it's too heavy. Bring it to the cross."

Before Penny even realized what she was doing, she stood and started walking up to the altar.

So much for not trying to call attention to herself....

In her heart, she knew there was no way she was going to make it through losing Big Mama, her father's reappearance, Carla's antics *and* Jason's relentless probing without a little help from the Lord.

Jason watched as Penny made her way to the front of the church and wondered what she had done that made her feel the need to head up to the altar. Because of the way Big Mama raised her in the church, he knew, Penny didn't wear guilt easily.

However, he'd only ever seen her go up to the altar twice before. Once was after the first time they'd made love in high school. She'd felt so torn and guilt-ridden about it, and, he'd thought they would never be intimate again. Luckily—or maybe not so luckily, depending—that didn't happen.

Their hormones had continued to get the better of them, and eventually a condom had broken and she'd gotten pregnant.

Then she'd said the baby wasn't his after all.

The memory of those words led him to the only other time Penny had made a trip to the altar of Mount Zion Baptist, right after she got out of the hospital, when she'd lost the baby.

At the time, he could only fathom it was because she had been guilty of cheating on him. Now he was starting to think she might have been feeling guilty about lying to him and making him *believe* she'd cheated.

Watching her kneel in front of the pastor as he prayed for her and the others at the altar, Jason could only frown.

Maybe the Lord was trying to tell him something. Because he knew he couldn't rest until he found out the truth.

He felt Joel's elbow in his side and closed his eyes. Everyone else's heads were bowed in prayer, and he was busy watching Penny and trying to figure her out. Joel's nudge served as a reminder. But Jason couldn't help but wonder what Joel was doing paying attention to him when he should have had his own eyes closed in prayer.

Jason noticed his mother making a beeline over to the pew where Penny and Terrill were sitting instead of lining up to shake the pastor's hand. She practically stepped over his father and anyone else in her way. And Jason could only shake his head in dread as he thought about what his mother's mad dash could possibly mean.

He sincerely hoped she wasn't inviting them to Sunday dinner. And since he knew his mother so well, he could then only hope Penny and Terrill had the sense, the common decency and good taste, to say no. Because if he had to sit through Sunday dinner with the two of them—her in her beautiful navy and cream silk floral dress and him in his navy-blue designer suit, looking like a power couple—he didn't know what he'd do.

Jason decided not to leave his mother to her own devices and followed her over to Terrill and Penny.

"Oh, Mrs. Hightower, I don't think that would be a good idea. Besides, I—" Penny's words were cut off by his mother.

"Nonsense, Penny! Of course you and Terrill will come to Sunday dinner. It'll be just like old times. It's time to let bygones be bygones. I feel it. The Lord put it on my spirit, and after today's sermon, I certainly don't want to go around second-guessing the Lord."

Leave it to his mother to make such quick use of the day's sermon.

Jason didn't want to say for certain that the Lord hadn't put the desire to mend the fences between him and his former best friends on his mother's spirit. But he wouldn't have placed any money on it.

"Now, Mama, if Terrill and Penny have other things to do, then perhaps we should let them do that." Jason knew it would take more than any of them had in them to sway his mother on this.

But perhaps if they all worked together…

"You know I've missed your Sunday meals, Mrs. Hightower. But I'll be flying out on a red-eye tonight, and—" Terrill started in with his gentle refusal, only to be shot down midway in.

"All the more reason for you to come by for dinner, son. We haven't seen you in years, and now you're here. You've moved your mom to California, so you hardly ever come back to visit. When will we see you again?" His mother turned to Penny. "And I bet you'll be moving Carla back to California with you. And *you* didn't even visit when your grandmother was alive. We're likely to never see either one of you again.

"Can't you just grant this old lady one last dinner with you all, now that you've grown up? Penny, you can ride on over with James and me now. That way we can get in the kitchen together, like we used to. I've missed that. And I want to hear all about your life in Los Angeles."

Jason narrowed his eyes. His mother was pouring it on thick, even for her. There was no way either Penny or Terrill would say no to the woman. Heck, he even found himself falling for the line.

"Mrs. Hightower…" Penny began.

"I remember those times in the kitchen with you. It was like I finally had the daughter I always wanted. I've missed you so much. Both of you." Mrs. Hightower put the saddest little expression on her face, and sighed.

Jason heard a groan and realized that it was coming from him. All eyes turned to him, and he suddenly felt as if the walls of the sanctuary were closing in.

Penny took a deep breath. "I don't think that, given the past, everyone would be okay with us coming to dinner. I miss you more than you know, more than I could ever express. But I just feel like we need to be sensitive to the feelings that—"

"Nonsense, Penny. Jason won't have a problem with either of you coming. Frankly, you all need to grow up and let the past be the past. You all were friends. You were close. You loved one another, and in the case of you and Jason, you were *in* love with one another. It's time to put the past behind us. So come on, Penny, James likes to beat the traffic getting out of the parking lot. We'll see you guys later. Terrill, I mean to see you, too."

His mother took Penny by the arm and actually led her out of the church. Jason watched them walk away and wondered how in the heck he was going to get through a dinner with Penny and… He turned to Terrill, who just shrugged.

"It'll be awkward. But honestly, I don't know how to just *not* show up when your mother has made her expectations so very clear."

Jason wanted to tell Terrill he needed to figure out a way. He wanted to threaten him with bodily harm if he dared show up at his parents' home.

But he couldn't.

So he just turned and walked away.

As he headed back over to his brothers, he saw that all three of them were standing there watching everything.

"Mama invited Penny and Terrill to Sunday dinner." Jason stared at his brothers, hoping one of them had some advice on how to handle this one. As the youngest, he normally couldn't stand it when they offered up their two cents on his life. Today, he'd gladly take any advice they had to give.

"You could always not show up. I know I wouldn't if Mama invited my cheating ex-wife to Sunday dinner." Patrick folded his arms firmly across his chest.

"Well, you don't have to worry about that. Mama can't stand your ex-wife. But I think Aunt Sophie still has lunch with her once a month. She's still mourning the breakup of what she called the 'perfect marriage.'" Joel let out a gut-busting laugh, only to stop just as quickly, when he realized there were still some other folks in the church.

Lawrence took off his blazer and slung it over his shoulder. "Well, I think he should definitely come to dinner and face them both. They were the ones who were wrong. And he can't let them run him out of his own mama's house. That's just wrong. I'd have a real problem if he punked out like that."

"Yeah, but if he gets up in there and starts fisticuffs with Terrill at Sunday dinner…" Joel began.

"Jason isn't stupid. He can be the bigger man. He's a Hightower. We're honorable men," Lawrence cut in.

"We don't back down," Patrick added.

"And we always do things the right way," Joel continued.

"*Our* way," Jason finished, and they all laughed.

"That's right. So we'll see you at dinner. And remember, never let them see you sweat." Lawrence loosened the tie he only wore in church and started walking off.

"Yep. Stay cool." Joel winked and followed Lawrence.

"And remember, no woman in the world is worth all this stress. She cheated. It's her loss. You're the bigger man. You're a Hightower." Patrick patted Jason's back awkwardly.

Jason sighed. He must have looked pretty pathetic if his older brother had taken to expressing affection. The move was certainly atypical of the eldest Hightower son, to say the least. Jason decided to brace himself for a stressful dinner. His brothers were right.

He wasn't missing Mama's Sunday dinner for anyone.

After telling Penny she didn't feel like doing the whole church scene, Carla waited for her daughter to leave the house before making her way down the hill to the Temple Street boardinghouse where she knew Gerald McEarly was staying.

She knocked on the door to Gerald's room. She was taking a great risk by coming there. But she had to somehow convince Gerald that it was a bad idea for him to just keep showing up at her place. Even if he wanted to get to know Penny, it was too late for all that. And if Clyde found out Gerald stopped by, then it would make things all the worse.

Clyde "C-Money" Markum didn't hand out idle threats, and she had to convince Gerald to stay away until she could convince Penny to get her out of town.

Gerald opened the door and her heart skipped a beat. How could she possibly be having the same fluttering feelings she'd had when she was just a girl and she saw him for the first time?

After all she'd been through, the rough life she'd had, how could she be responding to him like a young girl in love?

Better yet, how did she turn it off and do what she needed
to do, when the older man was so much bigger, stronger and
finer than the young man had been. And the older man *still*
looked at her with that same sparkle in his eyes.

He smiled at her and stepped aside for her to walk in.

And why the heck was he smiling at her when she'd tried
to get him locked up last night? He wasn't making it easy for
her to do what she needed to do at all, *not at all*.

The small room had a twin bed, a tiny chest of drawers
with a hot plate on top and a corner table with a wooden chair
in front of it. There wasn't much in the way of decorations,
unless you counted the brown blanket and the odd-shaped
yellow crocheted doilies on the table.

"Hey, girl. This is a pleasant surprise. I wasn't expecting
you here, after the way you acted last night." He smiled, and
his whole face lit up.

She loved the way his face brightened when he looked at
her. Nobody had ever been able to look at her and make her
feel more special.

Nope, this wouldn't be easy.

"That's why I'm here, Gerald. You can't come back
over there. Just stay away, please. I'll tell her where you
live and she can come see you here or whatever. But I
can't have you showing up at my place. Okay?" Carla
rushed her words out and quickly did a U-turn toward the
door.

Yep, coming here was a bad idea. But at least she'd said
her piece. Now she had to get the hell out of Dodge.

Gerald's hand reached out and grabbed her shoulder
before she could make her great escape. He spun her around,
and he had that same glimmer in his eyes, that same way of
looking at her that made her heart go all out of whack.

"Baby, what's wrong? What has you all scared? When I first got out and we met up, you seemed open to me getting to know our daughter. And I even thought—"

"There's nothing wrong with me, Gerald. And I ain't scared of anything. I just don't need you sniffing around my place, that's all. The past is the past. If Brat wants to have a relationship with you, then that's her business. But I don't. So stay away."

"I can't do that." He bent his head down and covered her mouth in a hard, soul-penetrating kiss, a kiss that wouldn't yield. One that offered no outs…only ins….

Carla couldn't help it. She opened her mouth and gave everything she felt, everything he made her feel. And feeling again, after so many years, had an amazing effect, took her higher than any drug ever had or ever could.

It wasn't a rush her addictive personality could easily pass up. And as she allowed him to lead her to the bed, she knew she would have to figure out a way to control the situation, and her desire, to get Gerald to stay away. But when his strong hand cupped her breast and his demanding mouth claimed her nipple, she found it harder and harder to remember why she had to let him go.

And after an hour in Gerald's bed and a half hour trying to talk him into staying away, Carla rushed home trying to think of better ways to get Penny to let her come to California. She decided she would show Penny she'd changed by cooking a nice Sunday meal, or at least fixing up some of the many leftovers from all the food people brought over after Mama's funeral so she could have a nice meal after church.

The last thing she expected as she walked up to the house was to find Clyde standing there, with that mean and ugly glare on his face. Something about the way he looked at her told her he knew exactly where she'd just come from.

He walked up to her, grabbed her by the hair and pulled her toward the house. "You have got to be one stupid, hard-headed little slut!"

Chapter 6

Being in the kitchen with Mrs. Hightower again felt surreal and just right, all at the same time.

Stately and opulent, the Hightowers' large Tudor home on Eastside Park Drive in Paterson looked pretty much the same on the outside. On the inside, the decorations and furnishings had changed. But the warm and welcoming aura remained the same.

Penny knew the homey feel of the Hightower minimansion must have been the only thing that saved her from feeling out of place and overwhelmed when she visited as a child. Although class differences weren't as pronounced in Paterson as they were in other places she had lived and visited through the years, they did exist.

The distance between the Hightowers' humongous home with a view of the park and Big Mama's small three-bedroom

Colonial with no view and no park in the heart of the 'hood might just as well have been light years. When it came down to it, their big home, family legacies and community standing made the Hightowers as close to the elite as a small inner city such as Paterson, New Jersey, could lay claim to.

Penny didn't have any illusions that James and Celia Hightower's easy acceptance meant anything more than that they were two really nice salt-of-the-earth folks. She still found herself wanting to bask in the comfort she felt in their home, especially since she had a feeling the easy calm would disappear as soon as Jason and Terrill showed up.

"Here, I'm gonna let you take over the dressing and the potato salad. I know you remember how to do it. I've got to get these pies in the oven. I'm making my sweet potato pie. I wonder if Terrill can still polish off an entire pie all by himself." Celia chuckled softly and shook her head. "I better make a few of them, come to think of it." She buzzed around the kitchen with a bright smile on her face.

Penny got busy breaking up the corn bread Celia had already made and moved on to the slicing and dicing of celery, onion and—Celia Hightower's secret ingredient— bell peppers. Before long the two women had the majority of the spread for the Sunday meal all done.

Penny couldn't help but remember the wonderful times she used to have with Mrs. Hightower growing up. She had really been like another mother figure, next to Big Mama. With Carla constantly MIA, Penny had needed the added attention.

She couldn't believe Celia still made the majority of the dishes exactly the way she'd taught her to make them. Between Celia Hightower and Big Mama's training in the kitchen, Penny could hang with the best of cooks. As she mixed together the fixings for the potato salad, Penny found herself wishing this nice, quiet afternoon with Celia didn't have to end.

"So, when are you planning to head back to California, baby? I hope I get a chance to see you again before you go back."

Celia moved gracefully around her state-of-the-art kitchen. The kitchen had clearly been upgraded, outfitted with stainless steel appliances, marble countertops and beautiful cherrywood cabinets, since Penny had last been there. But even with all the new things, the kitchen still felt as down home as it always had.

"I'm not sure now. I was planning to head back as soon as I settled up Big Mama's affairs. But some unexpected things have come up, and I may stay a week or so longer than that."

"That's good. We can go out for lunch or something. Maybe spend the afternoon at the mall. Remember our trips window-shopping at Garden State Plaza?" A wistful and nostalgic expression crossed Mrs. Hightower's face.

"Yes, I certainly do. Those were some fun times." Penny smiled, remembering the many times Mrs. Hightower's input had saved her from Big Mama's very old-fashioned taste in clothes.

"Yes, indeed they were. Then you had your sweet sixteen and started dating my son and forgot all about me. All your time was spent with *Ja-son*." Mrs. Hightower chuckled, and Penny cringed.

"That's not true. I still hung out with you! And even before Jason and I started dating, he, Terrill and I were always together, anyway."

"Mmmmm… If you say so… All I know is, once you fell in love, you didn't have time to be hanging out with this old lady."

Penny could only laugh. Part of what Celia said was true. Once Penny admitted the feelings she'd probably always had for Jason, she'd been a goner. Thinking about how much she'd loved him caused a tremendous lump to form in her chest.

"What happened, Penny? You could tell me to mind my business if you want. But I've always wondered. Jason said you broke things off with him after you lost the baby and decided to be with Terrill. But something about that always seemed odd to me. I watched you three grow up. And I know you all like the back of my hand. And you were *not* in love with Terrill, Penny. I know that."

Penny could only stand there with her mouth hanging open. She couldn't believe Jason hadn't told his family the entire lie she'd told him, the lie that the baby was Terrill's.

Why had he left that out? Could that be why he was still hounding her to admit it had been a lie?

She closed her eyes and swallowed. Could she lie to Mrs. Hightower, too?

No, she couldn't.

"I did love Terrill, Mrs. Hightower. I still love Terrill."

That wasn't a lie. She would love her best friend forever. The sacrifice he'd made for her was a debt she could never repay. She would always love him for it.

"You're playing with words, Penny. I know you love Terrill. I know you've loved Terrill and Jason from the time you all ran around here in the backyard playing and calling yourselves the Three Musketeers. But you were *in* love with Jason. Something must have happened when you lost the baby. I saw the change in you when you realized you were pregnant. You were scared. And maybe you even thought you dodged a bullet when you lost the child, and you didn't want to chance it happening again…. I don't know your reasons for breaking my son's heart. But I do know you were in love with him and *not* Terrill."

Penny felt her jaw drop even farther, as if it were possible for her mouth to open any wider.

Mrs. Hightower was pulling out the big guns, and she was doing it in her smiling and pleasant way.

Mrs. Hightower continued to move around the kitchen, cooking and humming. "My, my, my, I've got to get these pies out of the oven. Finish up that green bean casserole and then set the dining room table for me, please, sweetie. I'd appreciate it." She gave Penny a hug and a peck on the cheek.

Penny let out a breath she hadn't realized she was holding and finished up her tasks deep in thought. Her hopes of leaving Paterson with her secret intact seemed to be dwindling away right in front of her eyes. Between Jason's pushing and his mother's subtle prodding, there was no way she wouldn't fold. If she were a betting woman, she wouldn't even risk gambling on herself. She didn't like the odds.

Well, that means no lunch and shopping with Mrs. Hightower.

No matter how much she'd missed the woman's company, spending more time with her would be a huge mistake.

After today's sermon in church, her secret was weighing on her more heavily than it normally did. She just didn't know how to go about making things right.

Jason let himself in his parents' home through the front door, and the first thing he saw as he made his way toward the family room was Penny setting the dining room table. The desire to follow his old pattern and help her proved to be one he couldn't resist.

They worked in silence until they'd finished the task. When they were done, she glanced at him with a nervous expression on her face.

She cleared her throat, her eyes shuttered, and her voice took on a husky edge. "Thanks for helping, Jason."

"You're welcome."

He kept staring at her, because he couldn't believe how damn beautiful she still was and how badly he still wanted her. He actually wanted to kiss her right there in the dining room. He had been thinking about the kiss at Big Mama's house and wanting to taste her lips again ever since. It was as if all it took was one kiss to make him want her again with a passion that tripled anything he had ever felt. He still wanted Penny, *bad*.

She let out a sigh. "Look, I know this is really awkward for you. But I just wanted to say I'm glad you're being understanding about things. I hadn't realized how much I missed your mom and—"

"She missed you, too, Penny. You could have come to see her anytime in the past fifteen years and she would have welcomed you with open arms." The edge in his voice would not be contained. As much as he desired her, he realized he was also still very angry with her.

The source of his anger both worried and confused him. Instead of being angry that she might have slept with Terrill or that she'd actually lied about her relationship with Terrill, Jason felt heated because she had stayed away so long, because he hadn't had the pleasure of seeing her beautiful face regularly in fifteen years. How could she have stayed away for so long?

She cringed. "I know, Jason. But you know it wasn't that simple. I—" She paused. "Oh, forget it. You're impossible, Jason." She turned to walk out of the dining room.

Jason reached out and touched her shoulder. He couldn't let her walk away.

She turned and stared at him with those huge copper eyes, and he was done.

He pulled her close and covered her mouth without even thinking someone might walk in on them. He didn't care if they did. He had to taste her again. Her mouth opened and her tongue forged into his mouth and wrapped around his so precisely, it felt as if they had never stopped kissing, as if no time had passed.

The soft, welcoming warm heat of her mouth sent shock waves to his groin. He nibbled and feasted on her lush, delicious lips with all the desire and intensity he felt. Her hands went up to his chest and caressed. His hands moved to her behind and pulled her closer, but she stopped and shoved him away.

The wild expression on her face, a mix between passion and anger, made him think he might have jumped the gun by kissing her again. She panted as she shook her head, spun around and went running from the room.

Not surprisingly, watching her storm out of the dining room only made him feel more confused and frustrated than he'd been before he kissed her.

Something had to give—but what? His detective's brain kept telling him something was wrong. Penny was lying. He could feel it. His heart, the eighteen-year-old heart he had shielded for the past fifteen years, told him she had lied and she really loved him. While he didn't know what he would do if his mind and heart were right, he knew he had to find out.

Soon all of his brothers were there, and then Terrill showed up, bearing flowers for his mother. Looking at his ex-best friend, the suave record executive, made Jason realize the dinner would be even harder than he'd imagined. Being the bigger man was not supposed to screw with his guts and make him gnash his teeth. Wasn't it supposed to be a good feeling?

The doorbell rang as soon as they all sat down at the table. His mother went off to answer the door and came back with his aunt Sophie right behind her. The slight tilt of his mother's nose and the twist of her lips let him know that she probably couldn't think of any person she would less like to have at her dinner table.

He couldn't help but think that his mother was getting her own medicine served back to her. If he had to sit through a dinner with Terrill because of his mother's meddling, it seemed only fitting that his mother should have to deal with her own archrival, Aunt Sophie.

Jason felt a smile take over his face for the first time that evening, and it actually felt good.

Aunt Sophie made herself comfortable at the dining room table. "I figured I'd stop over here and see what you all were up to."

"You know you're always welcomed here, sis." James Hightower smiled at his sister until he caught the sour expression on his wife's face.

Jason didn't envy his father's role as lifetime referee between those two. Although they were subtle most of the time, and their battles had never become knock-down-drag-outs, he had a feeling one day the two women would either come to blows or spontaneously combust.

Everyone ate in awkward silence, the tension almost palpable.

"Mama, you really outdid yourself on this dressing!" Lawrence said as he scooped a second helping on his plate.

"And this potato salad," James added, clearly trying to get

out of the doghouse with his wife. "You know I *love* your potato salad. You make the best, babe."

"I didn't make the potato salad or the dressing. Penny did."

"Mmmph." Aunt Sophie made a show of pushing her potato salad and dressing off to the side of her plate.

Lawrence grinned. "I forgot 'lil sis could cook. I always said, if I couldn't get a hold of my mama's cooking, I'd take a plate from Penny any day. So what you been up to in Cali?" Food was the ultimate bridge over troubled water, and the only thing Lawrence easily succumbed to. Feed the man a great meal and he would be won over for sure.

Jason narrowed his eyes on Lawrence, and his brother shrugged, still grinning his silly grin, and shoving more dressing on his plate.

"I own an image consulting business. I'm a stylist and a publicist." Penny smiled at Lawrence.

"Image? Mmmph. Stylist? Mmmph." Sophie twisted up her face like she was sucking on a sour lemon.

Jason frowned at his aunt. He'd seen her be a snob before, but she was bordering on rude with Penny today. He was shocked by how much it disturbed him and made him want to protect Penny.

His mother rolled her eyes at Sophie and then turned a smiling face on Penny. "I've seen stories in various magazines mention your business. You have a lot of high-profile clients. That must be so exciting."

Terrill added his two cents. "Yes, Penny and her partner, Maritza Morales, have really built an amazing company. Top-notch. Can you please pass the greens and the macaroni?"

Joel's face lit up. "Maritza Morales, the former video girl? Wow. She is one beautiful woman." He passed the bowls to Terrill.

Terrill's face took on an odd expression, one Jason recognized from when they were younger and Terrill had fallen for a woman. "Yes. Maritza did some videos in the past. That's how Penny and she met."

Jason found it interesting that he'd never seen his former best friend get his goofy-in-love look around Penny. *Ever.* Either Terrill hid it well, or he'd never felt anything for Penny.

Penny nodded. "Yeah. I can't remember which one, though. That was a long time ago. Maritza's great."

"She sure is. Thick in all the right places, and fine as she wants to be," Joel agreed.

Terrill's left eye twitched a little, and he gritted his teeth.

"Video hos. Mmmph." Aunt Sophie twisted up her lips as the ugly word left her mouth.

"Sophie!" Celia and James snapped in unison with Jason's outraged "Aunt Sophie!"

"What? That's what they call them, isn't it?" She gave Penny a pointed look.

Penny glared at Sophie for a moment before taking a deep breath. She then pursed her lips and turned her attention to the other people at the table, as if she were forcing herself to remain respectful.

Jason felt a hot, angry heat start to course through his veins. Aunt Sophie needed to stop. Penny didn't deserve to be treated in such a manner, and he was only seconds away from telling his aunt so.

"So you two remained close in California. That's good. You can look out for one another." Joel addressed his words to Terrill, clearly trying to change the subject.

Terrill smiled. "You know I had to look out for our girl. Couldn't just leave her to the wolves in Cali."

Jason had the sudden urge to snap at Terrill, ask him to

leave, something. But he suppressed it. This was no time to start tripping. He couldn't help it if he'd thought he'd always be the one protecting and looking out for Penny.

"Your mother told Sister Robinson you and Penny weren't dating anymore. That you must have broken up with her as soon as y'all got to California, because as far as she knew you two weren't an item." Aunt Sophie had her lips twisted to the side. "And I took that to mean you were smarter than you looked. But I guess if you still messing with *her*—" she glanced at Penny "—then you're not."

Patrick cleared his throat and reached for the potato salad. "So, Penny, you gonna be in town for long?"

"With all due respect, Aunt Sophie, I think you owe Penny an apology." Jason couldn't believe he found himself standing up for Penny, but there it was.

Penny looked up and stared at him with those wide, beautiful eyes, and his heart started racing and pounding out of control.

He wanted to say, *Why are you looking so shocked, baby? Don't you remember when I told you that I'd always have your back when we were kids? What about the time when we were teenagers, before we ever admitted our feelings for one another, and I picked you up from your job at Willowbrook Mall after you missed the last bus and didn't have a way home? Remember I told you I would always be there for you?*

His feelings for her had been so deep that the words *protect and serve* took on a new meaning. The fact that he still felt almost exactly the same need to look out for her didn't shock him nearly as much as he'd have imagined.

"I think you should apologize to all of us for ruining a nice Sunday dinner." James gave his older sister a stern look, and

Jason realized once again why he was so proud of the man who'd raised him. James Hightower might have a quiet manner, but he always stood his ground and spoke up for what was right, no matter what.

Unfortunately, having her baby brother *and* her nephew both chastise her only served to make Sophie angrier.

"Me? Apologize to her? Mmmph." Aunt Sophie let out a bitter laugh and then turned a very hateful look on Penny. "I really hate to be a disruption to Sunday dinner. But someone has to be the voice of reason here. The mere fact that Celia has this little…tramp…at the dinner table and let her come within an inch of the food preparation tells me she isn't playing with a full deck. But I would have thought you would know better, James." Tsk. "And after the way she dropped you for your best friend and a trip to Los Angeles, I would hope you would know better, Jason. *Please* tell me you all know better."

Penny pushed back her seat and stood. "Mr. and Mrs. Hightower, it has been lovely and I really appreciate your invitation." She turned to his mother. "I really enjoyed cooking with you. It was so much fun. I do miss you, but I'm sorry, I can't stay here and be insulted."

Turning to Terrill, she said, "I know you don't want to miss out on this lovely meal, but can you take me home now?"

Terrill placed his napkin on the table, and without a moment's hesitation, he was at her side and they were leaving.

Jason tried to ignore the piercing pain he felt across his chest when Penny turned to Terrill instead of him. When the hell was it going to stop hurting? After fifteen years, he'd have thought he'd be immune to it. Had he really thought because he was stupid enough to take her side and tell his aunt to apologize Penny would see the error of her ways and fall into his arms? If he had, then he needed some serious psychiatric help.

As soon as Penny and Terrill left, Aunt Sophie smiled. "Well, I'm going to head on home myself. Thanks for dinner. And, Jason, remember what I said. She isn't worth it."

Sophie took her leave by offering a smirk to Celia and narrowing her eyes at James. Clearly she wasn't going to get over her baby brother's slight anytime soon. So Jason figured that meant they wouldn't be graced with her presence at Sunday dinner for at least two weeks, if she could contain her busybody nature for that long.

Joel reached for the dressing and the macaroni and cheese at the same time. Smiling, he glanced at their mother. "Honestly, Mama, how did you really expect this dinner to turn out? You had to know it was a disaster waiting to happen."

Patrick smirked. "Yeah, Aunt Sophie probably saved us from an even bigger altercation. I came fully expecting to have to hold baby bro back from fighting Terrill."

Jason cringed. "It would take more than you to hold me back, fireman," he said incredulously.

"Please, the rigors of my job demand I bench-press cops like you—oh, I'm sorry, detectives like you. You might want to hold off on picking fights, anyway. You might not be in shape." Patrick threw back his head and laughed.

Lawrence grabbed a biscuit and chimed in. "Hey, just so you know, detectives get just as much, if not more, exercise than beat cops. Heck, I'm running down drug dealers on a regular basis."

"Yeah, but you're a narc. Baby bro doesn't get nearly as much exercise, do you?" Joel, the other fireman in the family, put in.

Jason figured his brothers were trying to get his mind off

of Penny by bringing up the old Hightower family battle between the firemen and the cops. Since they weren't the first generation of Hightower men to find the honor of working to protect and serve the community through these careers and they wouldn't be the last, Jason was used to this rivalry.

He'd grown up listening to his father and his father's cousins as they argued about which Hightower tradition was more worthy—fighting crime or fighting fires. The debate always started with someone making a slight at the occupation of another, and soon the entire room became embroiled in it.

James Hightower, a highly decorated police captain, now retired, owned a lucrative security business that specialized in all forms of security, from anti-theft devices to fire alarms and even security guards. The elder Hightower often found himself still joining in, even though he no longer worked for the police force.

Glad for the distraction and change of subject, Jason was just about to really get into the fray when he felt his mother tap his arm.

"Jason, can you help me put some things away in the kitchen? I think they'll be just fine carrying on without you. Your dad is there. So there are still two cops and two firemen there to keep it even." Celia walked out of the dining room and into the kitchen.

Jason followed his mother into the kitchen, even though he realized that, since she hadn't taken any of the food back there with her, she probably didn't really need any help putting anything away.

Celia pulled out one of the chairs and sat down. "Let's sit here at the table, Jason."

Nope, no putting away food going on in here.

Jason sat down across from his mother and immediately noticed that she was giving him the all-knowing gaze that had always been able to get him to confess to just about anything when he was a boy.

He straightened up in his chair. Her look wouldn't work today. He had no intentions on letting it. And besides, he had nothing to hide. As far as he was concerned, his mother should have used that expression on Penny.

Now *there* was a woman with lots of secrets and lies around her.

He sat up in his chair, smugly waiting to see what tricks his mother had up her sleeves.

"You still love her, don't you?"

His shoulders slouched, and he winced.

Well, all right then, Mama!

Celia Hightower didn't usually hold back, but Jason thought the question was a bit too direct, even for her.

Speechless, he cleared his throat and stared at her. He let the question move around in his head as he tried to think of how he might respond.

"You really don't have to answer that, especially if you're going to lie. I already know the answer. In fact, while y'all might think the dinner was a bust and mean old Sophie ruined things, I got all the information I wanted and needed tonight. Penny Keys still loves *you* and *you* still love her."

"And what on earth makes you think that, Mama?"

"Oh, I spoke to Penny while we were fixing dinner. I can tell—"

"Did she say she still loved me?" Jason had to stop his mother's delusions. "Nope, I bet she didn't. And I know you didn't hear anything of the kind come out of my mouth. So what are you basing your grand theories of love on, Mama?"

"I'm basing them on what I know, what I've always known. She's the one, Jason. I knew it when you were ten years old and came home complaining about having to share your best friend with some ol' silly girl. And by the time you all were teenagers, I knew it was only a matter of time before you both realized it. Imagine my shock when I realized that my baby boy was the first of my sons to find the love of his life?

"I don't know what happened when she lost the baby. My guess is, she got scared and decided to push you away by faking she'd fallen in love with Terrill. But she has never looked at Terrill the way she looks at you."

Just a few words and he could stop his mother's crazy dreams of happily ever after for him and Penny. All he had to do was tell her what he'd never told anyone in his family— that Penny had said the baby wasn't his. Back then, he'd said it didn't make a difference if his family knew that part or not. They'd all seen her leave for California with Terrill. They all felt enough pity for him as it was.

Now, he had no idea why he didn't just spout out the full story and close the Penny and Jason story once and for all. But he still couldn't tell his mother.

Celia reached across the table and touched his hand. "Don't miss out on the chance to make things right. She's the one. I know it."

"Mama—"

"No, listen. I want you happy, not miserable, like you've been since Penny left. At least make an effort to talk to her and see if I'm right. You know your mama is never wrong."

Jason only laughed. There was no arguing with her.

If she needed to hold on to hope for a reconciliation between him and Penny, for whatever reason, then who was he to steal her joy? She would see soon enough, when Penny left for Los Angeles, that it wasn't meant to be.

"Well, I don't know, Mama… That's not what Aunt Sophie said. To hear her tell it, you're never right. You sure you don't have it confused?"

Celia slapped his wrist playfully. "That old busybody is just mad because she couldn't stop your father from marrying me. And she won't rest until everyone is as miserable as she is. But she has several strikes against her, and she doesn't even know it. First, you and your brothers are Hightower men, like your father. You're men of honor, and you won't be swayed once you realize what you want. And second, your mother is stubborn and crafty. Sophie really doesn't know who she's messing with, poor thing. Now, let's start putting away this food for real."

Chapter 7

"Penny, maybe you should just tell Jason the truth once and for all. It might help both of you to finally clear the air. He should know it wasn't true."

Terrill stared at Penny as they sat in his parked rental car in front of Big Mama's house. She wiped tears from her eyes and shook her head. "It's too late, Terrill. Plus, if he hates me now, he'll really hate me if I tell him the truth. I'm so sorry I dragged you into this back then. You've been a great friend, better than I deserve."

"Penny, I just want you to stop crying. You know I can't stand to see you cry. That's how you managed to talk me into helping you in the first place." Terrill sighed. "Look, I can reschedule some meetings. I don't have to go back to Los Angeles yet. I can—"

"No, I'll be fine. I'm going to settle Big Mama's affairs

and get out of here as soon as I can. I'll have to get to know my father some other time. Maybe I can set him and Carla up on alternating visitation schedules." She cracked as much of a smile as she could and hoped she'd convinced Terrill she was okay. "Plus, I need you to go back to L.A. and keep an eye on Maritza. She's probably bossing around some very important clients as we speak."

Sometimes her business partner got a little heavy-handed with the consulting, and she was known to dig in her heels on occasion. The thing was, when Maritza felt passionate about something, she had a tendency *not* to be open for input. Between Penny's more free-flowing, interactive consulting style and Maritza's trust-me-I-know-what's-best, do-it-my-way demeanor, they managed to fulfill their clients' needs. Still, Penny needed to get back before too many of the clients who were used to her open approach had to deal with Maritza.

"And I'm supposed to help how? Your little business partner can't stand me." Terrill chuckled and rubbed his chin. "Although, if she thinks I'm keeping an eye on her, that should make her good and mad. And I love making her good and mad."

Penny shoved his shoulder. "Play nice, Terrill. I swear, you better not do anything to tick her off, or she'll be blowing up my cell phone."

The rivalry between those two often made her long for the easygoing three-way friendship she, Jason and Terrill used to share. Most times she found herself playing referee to the ongoing Maritza and Terrill battle royal. Maybe without her as the go-between, they'd find a way to make peace on their own.

Yeah, right! That'll be the day.

"Listen, you, just check in on her every now and then until I get back." She reached over and hugged him. "Travel safe, and I'll see you soon. Thanks so much for being here for me yet again. I appreciate it."

"I'll always have your back, until you smarten up and let the guy who's really supposed to have it take over. You need to talk to Jason, Penny. I'm telling you this as your best friend."

"Were you not at dinner? Did you not hear Sophie go on and on belittling me? No way. I did the right thing back then, no need to go back now. The only thing I would do differently is, I wouldn't put you in the middle. I would have made up a random boyfriend. I would have kept you out of it. There was no reason for us both to lose his friendship."

Terrill didn't say anything, and her heart ached with guilt.

Maybe she could write Jason a nice long letter once she left Paterson and confess everything. If she did, and put all the blame on herself, where it belonged, then maybe Terrill and Jason could be friends again. That option held a lot of appeal.

Terrill leaned over and gave her a peck on the cheek. "I'll call you tomorrow night sometime to check up."

"You do that." She got out of the car and headed up the steps.

Everything Mrs. Hightower and Terrill had said to her ran through her head, along with what she was still trying to process from this morning's sermon. It was all too much, and it all seemed to be pointing toward her telling Jason the truth.

She honestly didn't think she had it in her.

The front door was stuck, so she gave it an extra push and was able to squeeze by. What she found once she entered the foyer made her blood freeze.

Nothing could have prepared her. No one could have warned her about the emotions that would overcome her if she was ever faced with the thought of losing her mother. Seeing Carla's still and bleeding body laying on the floor brought it all home in the sound of Penny's bloodcurdling screams.

Penny dropped to the floor and checked Carla's pulse. "Mommy! Mommy! Are you alive? Please be alive! Who did this? Who would do something like this? Oh, my God! What happened?"

The faint heartbeat caused Penny to breathe a sigh of relief. She dumped out the contents of her purse and used her cell phone to dial 911.

She felt tears pouring down her face.

Carla had to live.

She couldn't take it if her mother died. She cared. And the realization that she did care caused a strange sense of peace to cover her heart.

"Mommy, the ambulance is going to be here any minute, okay? Please hold on. Please be okay."

Carla wasn't responding, and Penny wasn't even sure she could hear her. So she used the time to talk to the woman who had given birth to her. She talked to her about everything, and she prayed. She asked God to please spare her mother, so that she could try and make things right between them.

When the ambulance came and the EMTs placed Carla on the stretcher, Penny felt her knees going weak. Just as her legs threatened to give out from under her, strong arms caught her.

She looked up to find herself in Jason's arms.

"What do you do, sit around listening for any mention of this address on your police scanner?" Her words came out in a breathless awe that would have bothered her if she weren't so happy to see him there. Having his arms around her felt so right and so good to her.

He shook his head and smiled. "No. Believe it or not, I was just going to stop by and see if you were okay after your run-in with Aunt Sophie this afternoon. Then I saw the lights from the ambulance. What happened?"

She wasn't prepared for what seeing the slightest twitch of his lips into a smile did to her. It literally stopped her heart and then jump-started it into a fast and frenzied pace. She hadn't seen Jason's smile in so long, she'd almost forgotten what it did to her to see it. She shook her head to clear out the fog and focus.

"I don't know what happened. I came home and found my mother knocked out and bleeding on the floor. Someone must have attacked her. I can't even imagine who would do something like that." She wiped away tears that didn't seem to want to stop. Watching them place Carla in the back of the ambulance, she pulled away from Jason. "I better go. I want to ride to the hospital with her. Thanks for stopping by. I'm fine, though. I have bigger things than your mean old aunt to worry about."

"I'm going to ask the neighbors some questions, to see if anyone has seen anything. I'll meet you at the hospital later." Jason walked over to the ambulance with her. "What hospital are you taking her to?"

"Saint Joseph's," one of the EMTs responded.

"I'll see you later, Penny. Wait for me, please." He didn't even stay put for a response.

Are you kidding me?

She stood there with her mouth open. She wanted to tell him he didn't have to come. Heck, she couldn't concentrate on Carla, deal with Jason and cope with Big Mama's death without having a nervous breakdown.

And God forbid if he smiled at her again. She wouldn't be able to resist....

"You coming, miss?" the EMT shouted as he got Carla strapped in and his partner continued to try and get Carla to respond.

Penny hurried to get in the ambulance. She couldn't think about Jason now. She had to make sure her mother was going to be all right.

Jason spoke with the cops who'd been sent to investigate and gave the house a once-over as they secured the scene. He made sure not to touch anything. But from what he could see, nothing had been stolen and there were no signs of a forced entry. As far as he could tell from a surface investigation, Carla had let her attacker in—or her attacker had had a key.

Deciding it was best to try to see if anyone had seen anything, Jason started with the young boys whose game of football in the street had been interrupted by the ambulance.

He walked up to the four young men, who had moved their game back into the middle of the street. They looked to be about eleven or twelve years old. And instead of giving them a hard time about playing in the street, Jason decided to let it slide for now. There were worse things boys that age could be doing than playing a game of touch football.

"Hello, guys." He flipped his badge. "How long were you all out here playing?"

The young men stopped and eyed him suspiciously.

The smallest of the bunch, but clearly the oldest and most mature, stepped up. "We didn't do anything. We just out here playing and minding our business." The short youngster stood and spoke with the confidence of a much older man.

Jason could always tell when kids had seen too much in their lives. They gave off the same hard edge that the little Gary Coleman look-alike was giving him. Getting information from these kids wouldn't be easy. Jason took a deep breath. Patience had never been his strong suit. However, most times the job demanded it. So he counted to ten often and practiced.

"I didn't say you did anything. I'm asking because I want to know if you saw anything. A woman was hurt, and we'd like to find the person responsible."

The other young men kept their eyes anywhere but on Jason and their friend, and none of them seemed to be in a hurry to offer any information. One focused on a nonexistent spot on his expensive sneakers. Another took sudden notice of the luxury car parked on the street. The other just kept his eyes on the ground.

"Nobody likes a snitch, especially not OGs." The young man turned as if he were done talking.

"What if this person decides to hurt someone you love? Your mother? Your sister? Will you still stand by the don't snitch creed?" It was all Jason could do not to try and shake some sense into the boy.

The street code of silence made his job as a police detective difficult at times, but he dealt with it. This time, however, things were different.

What if Penny had been home? What if she'd been attacked? What if whoever attacked Carla came back and attacked Penny?

The little man-child shrugged. "We ain't see nothing. You might want to ask Old Lady Henderson, though. *She* sees everything." The boy walked back to his friends and started playing with the football.

For a brief minute, Jason contemplated continuing to question the young men. He was pretty sure he could break one of the silent ones if he got them talking. But he realized he'd never be able to do that if their little leader was there. It was clear that they deferred to the smaller young man with the mouth. There were lots of things he could have done to make them talk, all of which would have further ruined their already nonexistent trust of the police. So he decided to leave it alone for now.

He might have a better chance with Old Lady Henderson. She lived right next door to Big Mama's house, and he remembered her well. She'd been the one who always made sure Big Mama knew if Penny had any boys in the house when Big Mama wasn't home. Even when they thought Old Lady Henderson wasn't looking, she was *always* looking.

He walked up to her small brown and white Colonial home, which, except for the color, was the same as Big Mama's yellow and white house next door. He could hear gospel music playing in the house, so he knew she was home. He just hoped she could help.

"Well, hello." She kept the door cracked and eyed him through it. She had shrunk over the years. But she still wore those floral housedresses and kept her hair wrapped up in a color-coordinated terry-cloth head wrap. Today she had on a tropical design with bright oranges and yellows and a bright yellow wrap on her head. She stood about five feet, if that. But she still had a large presence.

He took out his badge.

The door didn't budge. She glanced at the badge over her cat-framed glasses and then looked at him again. Everything in her expression seemed to say, *So what? You have a badge.*

He put the badge back in his pocket. "Mrs. Henderson, I'm here because your neighbor, Carla Keys, was attacked in her home, and I wanted to know if you saw anything, or saw anyone suspicious around the premises."

"Well, with Carla around, you know I have to keep my eyes open…ain't no telling… Especially when she was on them drugs… Things had a tendency to go missing, if you know what I mean. The oddest of things, too—"

"Right. But did you happen to see anyone entering or leaving the house today?" Jason had to cut her off, because he could tell she was about to go off on a tangent and who knew how long it would take him to reel her back in.

She narrowed her eyes at him, and for a minute he felt almost chastised for being rude to an elder.

When she gathered he had gotten the message she intended, she continued. "Well, I saw a man pulling her in the house. One of those boyfriends of hers Doreen had to keep from 'round here years ago. Lord, Carla seemed to pick the worst apples in the bunch to mess around with. They just seemed to get worse and worse. Poor Doreen, God bless her soul, she tried with that Carla. She sure tried. You know Carla was her change-of-life baby? Lord, Doreen didn't think she was gonna be blessed with children, and then she got pregnant at such a late age. That's why Carla is so spoiled. Doreen spoiled her to death, especially once her husband passed. 'Course, now, he was a good bit older than Doreen. I don't suppose he was expecting any children—"

"So, do you think you would be able to pick this man out if you saw him again?" Jason cringed inwardly as he cut Mrs. Henderson off yet again. But he needed to keep her focused.

She pursed her lips and squinted before answering. "Sure would. He done got a little older since the days when he used to hang around here. But I'd know him anywhere. And he's been over here before lately. He came by and saw Doreen before she passed. If they hadn't said it was natural causes,

I would have pegged him for harming Doreen. She used to have words with him, and had to get a restraining order to keep him away, back in the day. But that foolish Carla went off with him anyway. Is she gonna be okay?"

"We don't know yet. We hope so. Do you mind coming with me downtown, to see if you can point out the person who might have attacked Carla?"

"Sure, I'll go. Just let me change into something presentable and turn off my music. I was getting me a little Sunday service. I ain't always able to deal with those folks in the church and keep up with all their foolishness. So I have my Sunday service right here at Bedside Baptist most times."

She gave him a piercing stare. "I guess you can come in and wait. I don't 'spect you'd do nothing to harm me, being a cop and all. And you one of them Hightowers, too. Most of them would rather die than do something less than honorable. You know, I used to know some of your great-uncles, back in the day. Boy, they were something. Mmm. Most girls had huge crushes on those Hightower boys…" She broke off and shook her head as if she was remembering something.

Jason had seen pictures of some of his great-uncles, his father and the cousins from back in the day. He could imagine what Old Lady Henderson was remembering, given the honorable Hightower heartthrob legacy he and his brothers and all the men in his family seemed bound to uphold. It shocked him that the older woman had been a Hightower fan back in the day.

He entered her home and followed her to the sitting room. Taking note of the windows in the house, he saw how she managed to see everything and get into everyone's business. He could see the indentations in the curtains, the lifts in the blinds, and all the spaces for her to peep out and watch. He and Penny had never stood a chance, trying to sneak around with this woman living next door. He shook his head and chuckled. Hopefully, Mrs. Henderson's nosiness would pay off and they'd be able to arrest Carla's attacker.

After a few hours at the precinct, it seemed as if Jason's suspicions about Gerald McEarly weren't going to pay off. Old Lady Henderson seemed quite adamant that Gerald was not the one. Although he was one of Carla's old boyfriends who had started sniffing around lately, he wasn't the one she'd seen dragging Carla into the house.

Jason had her look through a bunch of mug shots. But without something more to go on, they were stuck.

He had a feeling Old Lady Henderson was right. But without another firm suspect to go on, he didn't want to take Gerald out of the running just yet.

Jason dropped the elderly woman back home. Then he made a slight detour on his way to meet Penny at the hospital. Checking up on Gerald McEarly seemed like a good idea. If Gerald wasn't the attacker, then he'd probably want to know what had happened.

The older man was home and let Jason into his small room at the boardinghouse.

As he stepped into the sparse room, Jason did a quick survey. There wasn't much in the way of furniture, and the bed was unmade.

"Hey there, Detective. To what do I owe the honors of a house call? Is everything okay? Is Penny okay?" A seemingly sincere expression of concern crossed Gerald's face when he mentioned Penny.

"Penny is fine. It's Carla who might not make it." He knew he had to play this one carefully. He wasn't ready to read the man his rights and arrest him. But he wasn't ready to give him a clean bill, either.

Gerald's face went pale and he grabbed hold of Jason's suit jacket. "Carla? What happened to Carla? I just saw her earlier today. She was fine. What happened to her?"

Jason slanted his eye and removed his jacket from Gerald's clutches before clearing his throat. "You saw her earlier today? Did you go over there again, starting more arguments with her?"

"No, she came over here. She was trying to get me to agree not to come over there again. But I couldn't do it. I want to get to know my daughter. And I still…" Gerald faltered. "Where is Carla? I need to see her. I need to make sure she's okay. Can you take me to her? And Penny just lost her grandmother. Now she's dealing with this all alone." He rushed toward the door.

Jason had some misgivings about taking Gerald with him to the hospital. If he was the attacker, then he was the last person Carla needed to see. And even if he wasn't, Carla clearly didn't want him around. At least that was what she kept saying….

Yeah, and Penny says the same thing about you, and yet you're going down to the hospital and you don't plan to leave her side until the attacker is caught.

Jason rolled his eyes at the unbidden thoughts in his head. He was not the person to judge Gerald's misguided persistence, not unless he wanted a big old boulder to roll down the hill and shatter his glass house.

"Fine, I'll take you with me to the hospital. But if Carla doesn't want you there, then you will have to leave. And if she says you're the one who attacked her, I'm taking you right to jail."

Chapter 8

When Carla opened her eyes and looked at her, Penny breathed a sigh of relief. They were going to keep Carla overnight, and she had needed more than a few stitches, but she would live.

Thank you, Jesus, Penny thought as she looked toward the ceiling.

Seeing her small, vulnerable mother in that hospital bed really made her question her resistance to moving the woman to Los Angeles.

With Carla's light complexion, every single bruise seemed amplified. And they each seemed to be screaming, *Take care of your mother.*

The thought that her mother could very well have died was not lost on her. In fact, it was the only thing that stopped Penny from thinking about how much she hated hospitals.

She especially hated this hospital, the place where she'd lost her baby and been given an emergency D and C.

She had a general aversion to hospital rooms. And this one, with its stark white beddings and overly antiseptic smells, pushed every one of her buttons.

Penny forced a smile and willed the bad memories to the back of her head. She was not going to start tripping. She refused.

"So, you're awake. How're you feeling?"

Carla winced. "Like a truck ran over me."

Penny reached out and smoothed Carla's soft, curly hair, which had taken on a pretty wild look with all she'd been through. "They can give you some more medicine for the pain. I'll buzz the nurse—"

"No! No more drugs than necessary, please. I can manage. I have to manage. I don't want to risk—"

"But, Carla, if you're in pain, then you need to take them. If you don't take them the way you're supposed to, then the pain will become too much and you'll take them to get rid of it and—"

"Is it time for a new dose yet?"

"No, but…"

"Well, then, I'll wait." Carla winced again, and then she looked at Penny with a devilish gleam in her eyes. "So, it's back to Carla, huh? No more *Mommy?*"

Penny narrowed her eyes. Carla had heard her. Leave it to that woman to use her frantic pleas against her.

"I don't know why you're looking all evil 'cause you love your mother and you don't want her to die. That means you're a good daughter, Brat. And a good daughter would take her mother out of this dangerous environment and move her someplace safe, like California." Carla shut her eyes and plastered a big, cheesy grin on her face.

Penny tried to remember that the woman had been attacked.

Someone had gone upside Carla's head. She had the stitches to prove it. She might very well be suffering from a concussion.

So Penny gritted her teeth.

"It's really no big deal that I called you Mommy. You are my mother. And as for California, let's not go there today. You need to save your strength, and it's an argument you can't win."

She didn't know why she said that, when she'd just been thinking she would indeed move Carla to Los Angeles. It was just another example of the way her mother was able to push her buttons and often get negative and hurtful results.

Carla opened her eyes again and stared at her. There was such a mix of fear and hopelessness present in her gaze for a moment that it gave Penny pause.

What has Carla so afraid? And who did this to her?

Penny didn't know the answers to any of those questions. But she wanted to know. Whoever had done this to her mother had to be caught.

"What happened to you? Who attacked you? Was it one of your crackhead friends?"

"No. I don't have any crackhead friends. How many times do I have to tell you that?" Carla sucked her teeth and then quickly placed her hand on her black-and-blue bruised jaw.

"Then who did it? Tell me."

"That's not important. What is important is, if you really don't want me to die, then you best get me out of Paterson, and fast."

Carla in California…

Penny tried to let the very idea run around in her head. Selling Big Mama's house and setting Carla up in an apartment as far away as one could possibly be and still be in Los Angeles could work.

But without Big Mama as a buffer, the two of them didn't stand a chance in the same city. They had so much healing to do. She didn't know if they could find their way to a sane and normal mother-and-daughter relationship.

"I'll tell you what." Penny sighed. "You tell me the truth about who did this to you, and I'll consider moving you to L.A."

Carla's face lit up, but then went cold. "What's *he* doing here?"

Penny turned around and saw that Gerald had walked into the room with Jason.

"Well, hello to you, too, Carla. I see your mouth is working fine and the attacker didn't mess up your evil streak." Gerald's word sounded warm and friendly, but he had a look of extreme fear on his face. He seemed genuinely concerned about Carla.

Penny couldn't figure out what the deal was between her parents, but she found herself increasingly intrigued.

"Hi, Carla. I'm glad to see you're okay. You had us worried there for a minute." Jason stood beside Carla's bed. "I'd like to take a statement from you about what happened. We need to get the person who attacked you."

Carla bit her lip, and her eyes started dancing around in her head.

Penny recognized Carla's shifty-eyed gaze, and it made the hairs stand up on the back of her neck. How many times had she seen that look when Carla was hooked on drugs?

Oh, please, God, don't let her be back on crack.

"Did you know your attacker?" Jason's eyes darted from Carla to Gerald. "Can you give me a name? Mrs. Henderson from next door said she saw one of your ex-boyfriends around the house today."

Carla rolled her eyes. "That old biddy needs to mind her own damn business."

"Carla, you're being very hostile. You need to stop it. Jason is trying to help. He's trying to get the person who hurt you."

"I ain't asked for nobody's help." Carla glared at Gerald as she spoke and then she turned to Penny. "The only thing I need is for us to hurry up and move to Cali. You're the only person who can help me, Brat. Everything will be fine once we get away from here."

Jason's eyes narrowed. "So, you aren't going to file a complaint or help in any kind of investigation? You're just going to let the person who beat you up get away with it, and possibly come back to harm you again—or, God forbid, harm Penny?"

Penny felt her heart still at Jason's mention of her name. She inhaled and exhaled, then touched Carla's arm. "Mommy, you need to cooperate with the police and tell Jason who did this to you."

"And you need to stop holding a grudge and let me come and live with you. But people never do what they're supposed to do, do they?" Carla shot Gerald another harsh stare. Then she turned to Jason. "Sorry, Mr. Policeman, I can't give you any information. I can't remember a thing. It's all a blur. They say that happens sometimes when folks get head injuries. Can't help you." Carla closed her eyes. "I'm feeling tired. Can you take Penny home and get this man out of my room, Mr. Policeman?"

"I'm staying." Gerald planted his feet in a manner that suggested that nothing short of an arrest would get him to leave Carla's side. "But I'd appreciate it if you could keep an eye on our daughter while I look after her mother. Make sure whoever hurt Carla doesn't hurt Penny, too."

Carla opened her eyes and pinned them on Gerald as he took a seat in the chair next to her bed.

"Urgh! Why are you so hardheaded? I don't need you to look after me. It's too late!" Carla huffed, and then winced. She placed her hand on her head.

"Calm down, I promise I won't bother you. But I'm damn sure not going to let whoever hurt you come in here and finish the job." Gerald sighed. "Just relax. You won't even know I'm here."

"Are you sure it's all right? I can stay here with her," Penny offered.

"No, you go on home and get some rest. You'll need it once they let this one out." Gerald laughed at his own joke.

Penny frowned. Heck, Gerald was right. A sick Carla was worse that a sick child. She would have her hands full, caring for her and settling Big Mama's estate. She glanced at Jason and knew that adding his never-ending presence to the mix would make things all the more taxing.

"You know, Jason, I really appreciate all you are doing to help. I couldn't ask you to trouble yourself and take me home, too. I can catch a cab, if Gerald is going to look after Carla. Carla, I'll go get a rental car and be here in time to get you when you're released tomorrow."

"It's no trouble, Penny. In fact, I plan to stay pretty close to your side until we figure out who did this. So let's go." Jason gave Carla one last look. "Carla, is Gerald the person who attacked you today?"

A shocked expression crossed Carla's face, and then she twisted up her lips and the devilish gleam glazed her eyes again. "What if I said he was? Would you make him leave?"

"I'd arrest him for assault and expect you to press charges and make a formal statement," Jason answered, with a serious tone.

Carla glanced at Gerald. "Y'all don't have no laws against people annoying folks to death?"

Jason shook his head. "No, Carla. Sorry."

"Mmm…like I could count on you to tell me if there was. Look at the way you're going after Brat. Fine, I'll handle Gerald myself."

Penny cringed. Carla was a piece of work. She had half a mind to tell her mother to apologize to Jason. But she remembered whom she was talking about.

"Carla, you should apologize to both Jason and Gerald. They're just concerned about you, and you're acting like—"

Carla cut her off. "Oh, brother! Bye, Brat. I'll see you in the morning." She gave Gerald the side eye. "What time are visiting hours over?"

"Woman, be quiet and get some rest, or at least let us get some rest. Penny, I'll make sure nothing else happens to your mother, even if it kills me. And the way her mouth is going, it just might. I'll be here when you get back." Gerald leaned back in his chair and closed his eyes.

Carla rolled her eyes and turned her head to face the wall.

Feeling adequately dismissed, Penny turned to Jason. "Well, I guess I can take a ride home, if you don't mind."

"I don't mind at all. And for the record, you're getting more than a ride home. I'm hanging around, just in case the attacker shows up again."

Once Penny and Jason left, Carla sat up in the bed. Her entire body ached, and it hurt to move. She guessed she should thank the Lord she was alive. But the fact that Gerald seemed determined to keep showing up meant she probably wouldn't be alive for long. C-Money didn't make idle threats. And C-Money did *not* want her with Gerald.

She glanced at Gerald. Sitting in the chair with his head back and his eyes closed, he looked as if he didn't have a care in the world. Meanwhile, she had to shoulder everything, all the burden of making sure that C-Money never hurt anyone else she cared about.

Sure, she shouldn't have been stupid enough to get involved with Gerald's biggest rival back in the day, when Gerald got sent away on that murder rap. But C-Money had come at her hard. And before she knew it, she'd gotten caught up, first in his game and then in his drugs.

When C-Money struck her daughter, Carla had finally got the strength to leave him alone. But he'd threatened her child's life. So she'd stayed. She'd broken her mother's heart when she chose to stay with C-Money.

Now, if she didn't find a way to get Penny to get her out of town as soon as possible, C-Money might make good on his threat after all.

"You have to go, Gerald. Please."

Gerald opened his eyes and stared at her. He just looked at her for what seemed like forever, and her heart felt as if it were going to explode.

Why did she have to give him up again, when he was back and it seemed as if he still loved her, in spite of everything she'd done? Why did he have to look at her so lovingly?

"Who did this to you, baby? Please tell me what happened. Tell me who hurt you. Let me help you." The earnestness in his voice would have been her undoing, if she didn't have Penny to worry about now.

It was one thing when C-Money was just threatening her,

a whole other thing when it came to her child. She might not be the best mother in the world, but she loved her daughter, in her own way.

"You can't help me, Gerald. The only thing that can help me is if I get out of town. The only person that can make that happen is Brat."

He cringed. "Why do you call her that? That doesn't seem like a very loving nickname for your child, Carla."

Her eyes narrowed. *Here it comes, the guilt and blame.* "I call her Brat because I have always called her that. Believe it or not, I know I can be pretty spoiled and childish. My mother always gave me everything I wanted. Even when I got pregnant at a young age and the father of my child went to jail and I got hooked on drugs, she raised my child for me."

Carla shrugged. "But guess what? Mama spoiled Penny, too. And my child is very smart and can be a bit self-righteous. She always had those traits. When she was a kid, she would tattle and tell Mama everything I did, so I started calling her a brat, because heck, I was still a kid myself. And maybe I was a little jealous of all the attention she got that used to be mine." She sighed.

It sounded bad when she explained it. But it was what it was. He asked, so she answered.

"The name stuck. You know black folks and nicknames," she continued, with a shrug that tested her sore shoulder.

Gerald had a weird expression on his face, and she couldn't tell if he was judging her or not.

She realized then and there she couldn't take it if he was casting judgment. She had dropped the ball big-time when it came to raising their child. But so had he.

He smiled. "She called you Mommy once today."

Carla couldn't believe he actually seemed pleased by that.

She knew it made her heart feel ten times lighter to hear her child call her Mommy, but what did he care for?

"She called me Mommy a few times. I guess finding me passed out on the floor scared her. She didn't want me to die."

"Did she always call you Carla?"

"No, she started that when she was about four or five, around the time she started calling my mother 'the big mama.' She would call out for her mama and I'd come running and she'd say, 'Not you! I want the big mama! Not you, Carla!' The big mama became Big Mama, and I stayed Carla." She turned her head, because she felt a tear trying to escape.

There was no time to be crying over past foolishness, but the memory still bothered her. She realized that was around the time she'd started calling Penny Brat. "I guess even as a kid she knew I wasn't much of a mother."

"She loves you."

"I suppose." Carla thought about the scared look on her daughter's face. "She probably just didn't want to have to deal with more funeral arrangements so soon after Mama passed."

"I'm not leaving you, Carla. I'm going to be here. I love you still. I always have and I always will."

Carla couldn't figure out for the life of her why he had to go and say that for. Why did he have to be all the right things at the wrong dang time? If he had only shown up before C-Money got out of jail, then she would be able to have him, to enjoy his love. Even though her body felt racked with pain, she still felt tingly thinking about the things he'd done to her in his room.

"It's too dangerous. And it's not just me. It could get dangerous for you and Penny, too."

"This person threatened my child?" Gerald leaped up from

his chair, and all of his calm and easygoing nature was gone. The look on his face was a mask of anger and outrage.

"Gerald—"

"Tell me his name, Carla. Let me handle this." He started to pace the floor.

She wanted to tell him so bad. Oh, boy, did she want to lay down the burden and put it on someone else's shoulders. But she knew how dangerous C-Money could be. She had felt his fists. She had also seen him do some pretty horrendous things.

No, she couldn't risk what he might do to Gerald. She already knew C-Money hated Gerald. That was why C-Money had come after her so strong in the first place and made her sever all ties with Gerald all those years ago.

"Like I told that Hightower cop, I don't know. My memory is foggy." She closed her eyes and faced the wall, but not too late to see the look of disappointment crossing Gerald's face.

Oh, well...

Chapter 9

"Look, Penny, either you can spend the night at my place or I can spend the night at Big Mama's house. But trust me, I am *not* leaving you alone tonight. Someone attacked your mother in your house, and she won't tell us who it was. That person is still out there, and I would never forgive myself if something happened to you." Jason tapped the steering wheel as they sat parked in front of Big Mama's house.

Penny nibbled on her lip and eyed him wearily as she rubbed the tiny scar on her right eye in concentration. She wasn't stupid; she realized it probably wasn't safe. But did that mean she really had to spend even more time with Jason? The same Jason who was treating her so kindly right now? The same Jason who'd stood up to his aunt for her this afternoon? The same Jason she'd lied to, who'd probably never forgive her if he found out the truth? The same Jason who was probably using this whole nice act as some sort of "good cop" routine to wear down her defenses and get her to finally tell him the truth about what happened all those years ago?

She turned and faced the window. He wasn't going to take no for an answer. She could see his Hightower stubborn streak bubbling at the surface.

"Why is it such a big deal to you if I'm safe or not? Why do you care?"

"Are you serious? Do you even have to ask?"

"Yes, I have to ask, Jason. I mean, given our history—"

"Given our history, you should know I wouldn't allow you to be hurt…that I'll always be here for you."

Penny took a sharp intake of breath. She remembered the first time the eleven-year-old Jason had said those words to her.

Penny, Jason and Terrill had been racing down a steep hill on their bikes when she took a bad fall, skinning her knees and elbows in the process. Jason had turned around to help her, and she'd teased him about letting Terrill win the race. Jason had told her it didn't matter, because she was hurt and needed his help. The eleven-year-old boy had stated firmly that he would always be there to help her if she needed it, because she was his best friend.

And then there had been the time when she decided she was tired of being friends with boys, just after she turned sixteen. Jason had been very vocal about why she shouldn't be hanging out with the older girls she had met at her job in the mall. When she went with the girls to a club in Newark, Jason had been the one who let her know he thought it was a bad idea. And when she ended up stranded in Newark, with no way back to Paterson, it had been Jason who begged his oldest brother, Patrick, for his car to go and get Penny. He had given her the silent treatment the entire ride back, before reading her the riot act and then surprising her with an atmosphere-altering kiss. If the kiss hadn't already blown her away, his confession of his feelings for her would have toppled her. That night had been the beginning of their move from best friends to boyfriend and girlfriend.

She started to remember all the times he'd been there for her. When he'd been her friend… When he'd been her first love…

It hurt to think about all she had lost…all she had destroyed.

"I can't do this, Jason."

"Why not, Penny? What are you afraid of? Look, I promise I won't hassle you about the past. We can call a truce. For now… At least until we find the person who attacked Carla." He held out his hand.

Penny sighed. She placed her hand in his, and as soon as they touched, she felt a jolt pass through her body, clear down to the depths of her heart.

It was *such* a bad idea to allow Jason to stay the night. But…maybe she'd have an advantage if they stayed at Big Mama's house. At least she would be in her own territory.

"Well, since you seem to be determined to do this, you can stay here. But I still don't think it's a good idea."

Jason smiled at her, and her heart stopped. This was the second time today she'd seen his smile. Why did it still have the power to make her swoon?

She needed air, so she opened the door and got out of his SUV. She took a big gulp and kept walking toward the house. She heard him put the alarm on and knew he was right behind her.

She could feel him.

Once inside the house, she started to rethink her brilliant plan to keep things on her own turf. They had too many memories in this house. They didn't have any memories at his new place.

She should have gone to his home.

How many times had they made out in the den? How many stolen kisses and sweet caresses had they shared here?

She turned to him. "I'm going to change out of these church clothes and heels. I'll bring down some sheets and blankets for the sofa bed. It's not comfortable, but we—"

"It'll be fine. I probably won't sleep much, anyway. I need to be alert."

"Right… Well… I'll be right back."

After putting on some sweats and a T-shirt, she grabbed the linen and went downstairs. Jason was already sitting on the pleather sofa that would serve as his bed for the night.

He looked up at her when she entered the room, and she just stood in the entryway like a dork. He squinted and studied her for what seemed like an eternity before patting the spot next to him on the sofa in invitation.

She sighed and sat down, holding the bed fittings on her lap. "Thanks, Jason, for staying here with me tonight. I know it must be awkward. It really means a lot to me to have you here."

More than you will ever know.

"Why did you leave with Terrill today?"

She turned and stared at him. "What do you mean? You were there. Your aunt was tripping, as usual. And I'm not a kid anymore. I don't have to sit there and take her abuse."

"I know that. I just want to know, why did you have to leave with *him?*"

"Umm…because I didn't have a car and I needed a ride." She knew her voice must have sounded a bit flip and sarcastic. But she couldn't understand where he was going with his questions.

"I would have taken you home."

The calm and earnest nature of his voice made her pulse

quicken. She knew he would have taken her home. She knew he would still protect her in any way he could.

What she didn't know was what it meant and how it would change once he found out the truth.

"Jason…I couldn't ask you to leave your family dinner just to take me home."

"*Yes*, you could have. But you wouldn't, and I just thought I'd ask why. I mean, technically, you had two ex-boyfriends there, and you decided to leave with one. So I just wanted to know why you picked him."

Oh, brother. "You said we weren't going to rehash the past. We have a truce."

"This isn't the past. This happened today."

Semantics. "Yes, it happened today. But don't you think following this line of conversation will lead us down a slippery slope right down to the past?"

Jason's eyebrows scrunched up, and his eyes closed slightly. "I guess my real question is not so much why you left with Terrill, but are you still involved with him? I need to know if you guys are still a couple."

The first thought that came to her mind was, why on earth would he need to know that information? Then she made the mistake of looking in his eyes, and the desire and longing she saw there almost took her breath away.

She couldn't form words, knowing he still cared for her when she'd deceived him the way she had, when she made him believe the worst in her. All she could do was shake her head.

"Is that a no?"

She nodded.

He leaned in and covered her mouth with his.

She took a sharp intake of breath and opened her mouth

to his kiss. The jolt she'd felt earlier, when she shook his hand for the truce, became amplified, and the charge spiraled from her heart to each of her erogenous zones. Her nipples tightened and her sex clenched in anticipation. A soft sigh escaped her lips, and she leaned farther into the kiss.

Jason's hands began to trail her body, lifting her T-shirt and teasing the hardened peaks of her nipples.

"I've missed you, Penny."

Oh, my God, I've missed you, too. So much. More than you will ever know. I've missed you and I've missed this.

Instead of voicing how she felt, Penny thought it would be best to go with gestures.

She could show him how much she'd missed him. And then they could both go their separate ways. Maybe they could find a way to bring some closure to things.

She moaned and let her hands explore his body. Could she have this moment with Jason and still be able to walk away with her heart intact?

Probably not... But could she really pass up the chance to be with him again, to feel his touch?

She broke away from the kiss. "This is probably not a good idea."

He smiled. "Oh, I don't know, Pen. I'm thinking this is just about the best idea I've had in a long time."

Her heart cracked wide open at his devilish grin. That dimple and those perfect teeth would always be her undoing.

Oh, God, please don't start acting like my sweet, silly, sexy Jason. Bring back the jerk with the one-track mind who only wanted to rehash what happened fifteen years ago. I can deal with that *guy.*

"Don't do that." She found her breath enough to speak, but she was sure it sounded more like a pant.

"Don't do what?" He smiled again.

She sighed. "You're making this hard. We can't go back to the past. There's too much baggage there. So the two of us hooking up right now is not a smart move."

He leaned back on the sofa. "So, tell me about your life in L.A. What has it been like for you all these years?"

"It's been fine." *Except for the part where I never really got over you.* "I ended up going to UCLA. I did some music videos to pay my way through school and got a small taste of celebrity through my own calendar."

Her life post-Jason had hollowness to it that she found difficult to talk about. It might have something to do with how she dealt with—or rather didn't deal with—loss.

When she lost her mother to drugs, it had been her first major loss, and she'd never really recovered. Losing her baby and her first love in one fell swoop because she'd messed everything up had left her numb for years. She must have cried continuously the first two years she lived in Los Angeles. Poor Terrill had been so worried about her. But she'd gotten it together. Earned a degree. Earned an advanced degree. Started a business. She'd done what she had to do. She'd functioned. She'd survived, in spite of the loss.

And now Big Mama was gone and she had almost lost Carla again and Jason was here, but he would be gone in a heartbeat if she told him the truth.

Shaking her head, she pushed her anxiety to the back of her mind and begged it to stay put.

"Ah, yes, the calendar. Can I just tell you, when I saw that calendar hanging on the wall of some of the guys in my dorm at Pace, I wanted to hurt somebody?"

"Hey, that calendar paid the tuition my junior year. But it was all a means to an end. I had no desire to be the top video *model.*" She stressed the word *model* because that was what she'd been in spite of Sophie's attempts to besmirch her with the label *ho.*

She'd never had sex with directors or rappers to be in videos. And after being loved by Jason, she hadn't been easily impressed by the men she met on the video shoots. Who could have competed with the love of her life? So she hadn't had to worry about falling victim to the groupie syndrome that a lot of the video girls ended up succumbing to.

"All I wanted was my degree. But I made a lot of friends during my short stint. One of them, Maritza Morales, was another video girl who was finishing up her degree at UC Irvine. We clicked and started our own image consulting and publicity firm, Keys and Morales. She's a wonderful partner—a real cool Latina who acknowledges her African heritage. She calls herself a *Blacktina.* And she's from the Bronx, a *Nuyorican*, so we had the whole East Coast connect happening. We got each other. We clicked."

"Yeah. I've heard a lot about your company. You're doing big things. I'm proud of you, girl."

The sincere expression on his face, along with the adoration in his tone, made her nervous, because it weakened her resistance almost to null. The fact was, all his pride would go away once he knew what a truly horrible person she was, so there was no need to bask in the ill-deserved praise.

"We do okay. Enough about me. What about you? You joined the police force instead of becoming a fireman. I always figured you'd be one or the other, given the Hightower family legacy. But what made you choose the police?"

"I've always been interested in figuring things out. So becoming a police detective just seemed like the way to go. A degree in forensics and a minor in criminology pretty much made it a given." His nonchalant manner of talking about his accomplishments only served to make her swell with happiness and pride for him. He had done what he set out to do, and he was continuing the wonderful rich legacy of service of the men in his family.

"Does your family still have those summer softball games, firemen versus the cops?"

"Yeah, but the younger guys decided to add basketball to the mix." He placed his arm on the headrest of the sofa, and his hand touched her shoulder.

Another jolt of electricity passed through her. "Basketball. That…that…must be fun."

"It is fun. I love beating the firemen in my family at basketball."

"So the cops always win, huh?"

He frowned. "Well. Not always… Actually, we've been having a losing streak. But we're coming back up."

She laughed. He smiled. And her heart stopped and restarted like clockwork.

"You don't know how much I've missed your laugh, Pen."

You don't know how much I've missed your smile. Dang. Does the sexy gleam in his eyes have to surface every time he shows his teeth?

Torn didn't even begin to cover how she felt at that moment. "I need to get out of here."

Oops, did I say that out loud?

"Why do you have to get out of here? I'm on my best behavior." His hand slowly caressed her neck and move up to her cheek.

A moan escaped her lips before she could stop it. Letting Mr. Good Behavior in hadn't been her brightest idea. But she couldn't very well make him leave now. Could she?

He turned her face to his and captured her lips in another one of his mind-altering kisses.

As she let her tongue glide into his mouth and tasted the addictive nature of his masculinity, she couldn't think of one reason she should stop, not one reason she shouldn't kiss him until all of their clothing fell off. Sure, she might think otherwise if she halted their lip and tongue exploration, but why on earth would she do that?

His hand dipped under her T-shirt and cupped her breast. She found herself leaning back on the sofa to give him better access, and was rewarded when he began to rub her nipples.

"Mmmmm…Jason…"

He nibbled on her lips in a seductive manner, taking a small nip before responding, "Yes, Penny?"

She closed her eyes and tried to catch her breath. "What are we doing?"

His left eye slanted. "Rhetorical question?"

She let her hands roam his chest, lingering over the ripples of muscles underneath his dress shirt. She moved to his tie. It hardly seemed fair that he still had to wear his church clothes, when she'd had the chance to change into something more comfortable. The least she could do was loosen his tie, and maybe the first two buttons on his shirt.

His eyes followed her hands, watching as she tossed his tie to the side and arching when she stopped at the second button.

She let her hands rest on his shoulders. "We've got so much history between us, Jason."

"Which we agreed to leave in the past for now." His hands moved from underneath her T-shirt to his own shirt. He finished the job she'd started, and removed his shirt.

"But—"

"Look, Penny, all I know is right here, right now, I feel like I need to connect with you. I want you so badly. And I feel like no matter what happened in the past, you want me, too. Am I right?"

"Yes." She didn't even hesitate, didn't give herself a moment to think about her answer.

Jason let out a sigh of relief. He'd be lying if he said he wasn't still determined to find out what really happened to their relationship back then. But he'd also be lying if he didn't admit he still wanted Penny. He still craved her touch. He still desired her beyond belief.

He leaned forward and gave her a small peck on the lips before removing her T-shirt. The pink lacy bra underneath was one of those numbers that showed lots of cleavage. It looked hot, but he knew what would be even hotter. He reached behind her and unfastened the bra.

He had to take a moment to pause and appreciate all her beauty. She had more curves than when they were seventeen. And yet her thirty-three-year-old body still had the same impact on him as it had in the past. He couldn't keep his hands off of her then, and he couldn't keep his hands off her now. He wanted to see more.

He got up from the sofa and knelt in front of her. Slowly, he let his hands slide to the waistband of her sweats and inched them down her soft and shapely thighs. He placed his head between her legs and inhaled. The heady scent was all woman, with a hint of Beautiful perfume. He wanted to taste. But in order to do that, he would have to remove the cute little matching pink lace panties.

Her eyes were closed and her head was back, but she lifted just enough to aid him in the removal. He positioned her hips on the edge of the seat and spread her legs before diving in for a more thorough exploration.

It was one of the things he hadn't done a lot of when they were teenage lovers, but it was something he wouldn't deny himself now. He let his tongue lap her already wet and slick folds. He teased her pleasure button and grabbed hold of her behind as she started to squirm. He held her hips firmly and fed like a starving man.

"Oh, Jason. Oh, God!" Penny grabbed the back of his head and pulled him into her, even as she tried to move away from the pleasure he was giving her.

He continued to lick and let his tongue travel into her core with all the precision that another part of his body wanted to bring.

Her body rewarded him with the sweet-honeyed flow of her essence, and he gladly took it. He could have tasted her forever, but it had been too long, and he needed to feel her, too.

He took the blanket she'd brought downstairs for him and spread it on the floor.

"I want to make love to you, Penny. I need to. Will you let me make love to you?" He had no idea what he'd do if she said no. He might have to resort to begging.

It might have been a mistake to take a taste of something he thought had been long lost to him. But he had done it, and now she was as much in his system as she was before she broke his heart.

She closed her eyes and then opened them. She stared at him, and it seemed as if time stood still. With her sexy body and her beautiful face flush in the aftermath of her orgasm, it was all he could do to wait for her answer without reaching out and caressing her soft skin.

"I want you, too, Jason. I want you to make love to me."

He smiled as he stood and held out his hand to her. He positioned her on the blanket.

"We can always go upstairs to the bedroom, you know," she said as she gazed at him with the stars in her copper eyes that he remembered from high school.

He started removing his own clothes and chuckled. "Next time. I can't make it upstairs. I need you now." He took protection out of his wallet and then slung his clothes on the sofa. "I've waited a long time for this."

Penny opened herself to Jason in more ways than one as her thighs circled around his back and her arms closed around his neck. His penetration felt like a homecoming. And the way her heart pumped loudly in her chest, she knew she was giving him more than her body. All the feelings she'd thought were long buried seemed to be bubbling up and taking over.

She let her hands roam over his muscular frame, taking in every new bulge and ripple. His broad and expansive chest felt good to her, as did his firm and taut backside. Even though she could tell with his clothes on that he had become quite the man, nothing could have prepared her for the way he felt as he moved his hips in and out of her.

He took one of her nipples in his mouth and began to suckle, causing her back to arch and her hips to rush and greet his thrust. Each piston down by him was greedily welcomed by a push up from her. They moved in unison, and soon his mouth moved from her nipples to her mouth.

His tongue traced her lips and then dived in. The way his tongue mimicked his manhood took her over the edge. Soon she was crying out in pleasure around his scandalous kiss. Her hips bucked wildly, and she felt herself tighten and release as the most ferocious and mind-blowing spasms she'd ever experienced racked her body.

This seemed to make him want to take her higher, and he began to move even faster and harder. She felt slick and wanton as her orgasm crested and moved quickly into another.

"Jason!" What was he doing to her? "Oh…my…"

He threw his head back and called out her name as he joined her in bliss.

Moments later, wrapped in his arms and lying on a blanket on the floor, Penny waited for the feeling of regret to come over her. She waited, but nothing came.

He touched her face. "Let's take this to the bedroom now."

As Jason held Penny in his arms in a comfortable spooning position, he thought it was what he'd always imagined it would be like. When they were two horny teenagers, they hadn't spent a lot of time spooning after sex. Those stolen moments hadn't been conducive to lying in each other's arms and sleeping afterward.

So he appreciated the chance to finally hold her when he woke up in the middle of the night with her perfectly round behind pressed so seductively to his groin.

He glanced around her bedroom and was surprised to see that nothing had changed. Big Mama must have left everything in place, even down to the New Edition posters on the wall. She still had the full-size white canopy bed with gold trimming, with the matching desk and dresser. Even the lilac canopy and bedspread were the same.

He started thinking about all the times they'd spent making out in this room, and realized the trip down memory lane wasn't helping him control his growing erection. He thought maybe he should try to go back to sleep.

Once they made it upstairs to the bedroom, she'd conked out and he'd dropped off sleeping soon after. Then he'd felt himself automatically responding to Penny's sweet body as his sex swelled and jutted out. He shifted a little, trying not to wake her, even though her waking up at that moment would have been a blessing.

Moving again, he was surprised when she turned with wide-open eyes and stared at him.

"I thought you'd never wake up," she said she as reached up and cupped his face in her hands.

He studied her face, checking for any signs of regret, but all he found was desire. He searched his own mind for second thoughts, and even though he still wanted to know what had happened back then, he wanted to be with her in this moment more.

Thinking of the implications of his feelings, he tried to grapple with the fact that, for all intents and purposes, he seemed to be okay with her betrayal.

Had time healed his wounds, or was he just incredibly aroused?

The pressure building in his sex as Penny stroked his cheek answered that question for him. She leaned forward, lightly brushed his lips and tried to pull back. He wasn't having that, so he gripped her shoulders and held her in place, deepening the kiss.

She moaned into his mouth and slung her leg over his hip. He smiled and let his hands roam her body.

Luscious was the word that came to mind as he cupped her behind in his hand and squeezed. *Succulent* jumped forth in his head as he moved higher and teased the more than a handful that made up her breasts. *"Amazing..."* He actually mouthed the word into her mouth as his hand trailed back down her belly and dipped into her wet and waiting sex.

She arched her back and rocked her hips as he added another finger to his task and used his thumb to press and stroke her spot of desire. Pulling his mouth away from hers, he moved to her nipples and tasted them. He could have sworn she tasted like brown sugar.

Penny grumbled in complaint when he broke the kiss, but began to mewl with pleasure when he suckled her.

"Mmmm...Jason..." She started to writhe, her words coming out in a soft pant.

He was too busy moving from one breast to the other to answer her. The only thing he knew for certain was, he had to be inside her soon. Then he remembered he had used his one and only condom. He could have taken the time to curse himself, but that would have meant he wouldn't have the benefit of Penny's sure-to-be-magnificent orgasm. He kept working on her, delving deeper with his fingers and sucking her already tightened nipples to glorious peaks.

A soft and sexy grunt escaped her lips, and her body twisted, almost making his mouth lose its grasp. But there was no way he was letting go when she was so close. She screamed, and her sex grabbed on to his fingers, desperately pulling them up and in, furiously trying to milk them for all they were worth.

Penny pulled his head from her breasts and planted her lips on his, pushing through with her tongue. The kiss was hard and demanding and clearly an attempt to stop herself from screaming again.

Jason could only smile and join the tongue-wrestling match.

Watching her come down was even more fulfilling than

watching her explode. Jason could almost make himself forget about his own growing need. *Almost.* He willed himself to deflate, but it wasn't working.

Penny let out a deep and fulfilled sigh and opened her eyes. When she noticed his erection, she frowned. "Why'd you stop? Aren't you forgetting someone?" She reached down and enclosed his manhood in her silky hands.

"No more condoms, baby. Unless you have some?"

She groaned and shook her head. Then she smiled. "That doesn't mean this guy has to go without." She started to kiss her way down his chest.

When her sweet and sexy mouth covered him, he moaned and almost exploded at her soft, wet touch. The moment she began to suckle it almost did him in.

"Amazing..." he said again, in a voice that was between a grunt and a groan.

Chapter 10

The morning after… Wasn't that always when the postloving panic signs started to surface? Jitters? Postorgasmic awareness? Horror? Stone-cold fear? Penny couldn't believe how much she had let things get out of hand.

She almost dreaded waking up with Jason. *Almost.* Then she felt his strong arms still wrapped around her, holding her close and tight. And she suddenly wished she was having an active enough sex life to keep boxes and boxes of condoms at her disposal.

Talk about wasted opportunity… Urgh! She sighed.

"What's that sigh for?" Jason murmured as he kissed the back of her neck.

A tingle spread from her neck to her toes, and she realized she needed to get out of bed in a hurry. Not only did she have to go get a rental car for the rest of her stay in Jersey, she also had to get Carla from the hospital. Add to that the fact that she had a million errands to run in order to tie up Big Mama's affairs, and she was looking at a very busy day.

But none of those things were the real reason why she had to get out of bed. She had to get out of bed because she didn't trust herself not to make love with Jason, condoms be damned.

"That sigh was because I don't feel like getting up yet. But I have a million and one things to do today, including going to get a rental. So…" She pulled away, got up from the bed and stretched.

The way his eyes roamed her naked body as she stretched would have made her feel self-conscious if he hadn't already kissed every blessed spot on her body and told her repeatedly how beautiful and amazing she was. Her knees started to get weak just from thinking about his homage to her calves, ankles and thighs, to name just three body parts he'd blessed with his mouth. She wasn't even going to think about the arch of her foot and her toes.

Lord, when did Jason turn into such a foot man? Hello—no more condoms, horny girl.

Penny shook her head to clear it. "I'm going to take a shower and get dressed."

Jason got up from the bed and took a stretch, too.

Penny's mouth fell open as she watched his muscles lengthen and move. His biceps… Lord, his biceps… They bulked and pulled, and it was all she could do not to reach out and touch. The six-pack and tightly molded stomach and chest area had her darn near panting. She couldn't help but look down, and in addition to the rippling mountains of his thighs, she got to see another one of his muscles standing at full attention.

Thinking of the way he'd tasted last night caused a small sensation to travel up her thighs. She so wanted to touch and taste him again. But did she dare? She, more than anyone, knew what her obsession with Jason could lead to, especially when a lack of protection was involved.

She had become darn near addicted to making love to him, almost from the very first time. She had wanted him with a passion that refused to be quelled. Once she had gotten over the initial guilt of having premarital sex and let her love for him and her desire and attraction take over, she'd been a goner. She couldn't get enough back then, and that was how she'd ended up pregnant.

"I'll take a shower with you, and then we can kill two birds with one stone. That way, if you don't mind stopping by my place so I can get into a change of clothes, I can take you to get a rental car before I go to work."

"Parts of your plan sound good, Jason…"

Too dang good.

She let her eyes zoom back to his prideful manhood standing tall. "But don't you think it would be a little more than unwise for us to shower together…"

"I promise, anything we do in the shower will be safe." He gave her that wicked grin of his. "I'm sure you remember, before we actually had sex the first time, we found lots of innovative ways to find release. Feel like playing a little bit more?"

Her heart flip-flopped as it always did when he smiled.

Good God, yes!

But did she trust herself to taste and touch but not go all the way? Sure she did. "Last one in the shower is a scrub."

She took off to the door and out of her bedroom, with Jason close at her heels. Their lifelong competitive streak kicked in full blast as they raced down the hall to the bathroom.

* * *

She remembered every moment of that scandalous shower as she stood in Carla's room, waiting for the doctors to discharge her mother. She could still feel the tingles on her skin from every place his tongue had touched. She still felt the heavy thudding in her heart as she replayed his parting words. "Next time, we take this to my place. As much as I loved the nostalgia of Big Mama's house, the thought of making love to you again with Ralph, Ronnie, Johnny, Ricky, Mike and sometimes Bobby watching isn't sexy."

She'd playfully slapped him on the arm when he joked about the old New Edition posters still hanging in her bedroom at Big Mama's. The room had become a shrine to her preteen and teenage years, when she'd had a super crush on the boy band.

However, once she realized her feelings for Jason, there wasn't a thing any pop singer could have done for her, not even Ralph Tresvant. And she had *loved* Ralph Tresvant.

Penny relished the fact that Jason was hinting that there would be a next time between the two of them.

She knew she had to be careful, though. There might not be any after-sex regrets *yet*. But she knew they were coming.

Jason surely couldn't have forgiven her if he thought she had really betrayed him with Terrill. And even if he had forgiven her, once he found out it had all been a lie, he would never forgive her for that.

So why was she grinning like a fool and gazing into space at the thought of him making love to her again?

Her heart was only going to end up broken.

"Why you looking all dazed and confused?" Carla nudged her and gave her a thorough once-over.

Penny cleared her throat. "I'm not dazed, or confused."

"Mmm...hmm...you got that I'm-so-in-love look on your

face." Carla turned up her mouth in disgust. "Aww, man! Don't do it, Brat."

"Don't do what, Carla?"

"Don't go falling for that uppity Hightower boy again. He's out of your league. Even though you have made a success of yourself and all that… In this town, with his family, we *still* the underdogs. You need to be checking for that other one." Carla rolled her eyes and sucked her teeth.

Penny folded her arms across her chest and pursed her lips. Even though Carla was making a huge amount of sense to her at the moment, she found it disturbing that she had sunken to a level where Carla, of all people, had to get her focused and on track.

"What other one?"

"The one in California. Y'all are from the same neighborhood. You both worked your way out of Paterson to Los Angeles…. Plus, he's gonna make me a star when we move there! Focus, Brat! We need to get on out there today or tomorrow, before you get sidetracked and end up in that Hightower boy's bed again. Then you'd probably be trying to stay here or something. We need to cut Paterson loose and start over. California, Brat, me and you. *California.* Focus."

Penny huffed and pointed to the wheelchair. "Get in this thing and let's go home. I've got to get out of here. How do you feel about going with me to handle some of Big Mama's affairs? I'm not sure how I feel about leaving you in the house alone, especially since you won't come clean about who attacked you."

Carla got in the wheelchair. "We need to just leave and go to L.A. You can handle the rest of that stuff by phone. You ain't gotta stay here for that. I don't feel like riding around and sitting in no car."

Penny started rolling Carla's mouthy behind down the

corridor. "Oh, but you're up for a four-hour plane ride to the West Coast?"

"Yep. I thought you'd never ask. When do we leave?"

"*We* aren't leaving. I'm going back when I get done settling Big Mama's estate. And I haven't decided what I'm going to do with you yet."

Carla sucked her teeth. "Well, I guess you'll be coming back to bury me soon enough. But don't worry, you won't be here long settling my affairs, 'cause I ain't got nothing."

Now why did she have to say that? Penny thought of finding Carla on the floor bleeding. She knew she wasn't ready to lose her mother. But was she really ready for Carla to move to Los Angeles?

As they made it to the hospital exit, she saw her father coming in.

"Don't you have work or something? What're you doing back here? We fine. We don't need you, Gerald." Carla's agitated voice held just a hint of panic.

Gerald simply gazed at Carla. "Well, I figured I'd come back and check up on you anyway."

Either he's getting off on annoying the heck out of Carla, or he's really in love with her.

Penny chuckled at her thoughts. The look in his eyes was definitely the expression of a man in love, not a man playing games. Penny couldn't believe the devotion she saw shining in her father's eyes.

The way Carla constantly dissed the man, Penny was surprised he even bothered. Penny decided right then and there that she'd make more of an effort to get to know her father. It was only fair.

"I'm glad you're here, Gerald. I'd love it if you could stay at the house with my mother while I go and handle some errands. I shouldn't be more than a few hours, and I don't want to leave her alone in the house, since she won't say who attacked her and they might come back." She gave Carla a pointed look.

Gerald's face lit up as he nodded in agreement. "That's a great idea, Penny. I'd be happy to stay with her and watch over her."

Carla made a show of sucking her teeth.

"What? Oh, what part of the damn game is this?" Carla hissed before turning her lips up. "How the two of you gonna just gang up on me? Brat, you hardly know this man. You've known me all your life. And yet you side with him? I'll tell ya, the game done changed. No loyalty at all."

"I'm looking out for your best interests. So let's get you home and settled, so I can do what I have to do. The sooner I'm done, the sooner I can be back and relieve you of your torture."

"I don't need him to stay with me. I'll be fine."

"Well, I'll worry less with him there. What if the attacker comes back, Carla?" Penny shuddered at the thought.

The mention of the possibility of another attack must have gotten through to Carla.

"Fine. Fine. It's not like you ever listen to me anyway. Nobody ever listens to me." Carla sulked, but at least she stopped arguing.

Penny gave her father a weary look and almost pitied him until she noticed he still had that awestruck expression on his face as he gazed at Carla. She guessed he was happy any time he could spend time with Carla.

Love must make people crazy! Penny mused as she vowed to try and keep her own ever-growing insanity in check.

Jason spent part of his day at the downtown precinct going through the now reopened murder case that had sent

Gerald to prison for a crime he didn't commit. He also went back over Gerald's record. Even if the man hadn't been the one to attack Carla, Jason had a nagging suspicion Gerald was somehow connected.

The murdered couple had been Good Samaritan community activists. They had been known to call in and report drug deals or any other crimes going on. Technically, any of the criminals they had reported could have been the one to kill them. It just so happened that Gerald had been the last person seen in the area and he'd argued with the husband about their snitching on him. Most of the evidence against him had been circumstantial. But it had been enough to convince a jury to find him guilty.

Lucky for Gerald, both victims had gotten DNA evidence from the real murderer on them. The technology hadn't been as sophisticated then as it was now. But advances had helped to clear him some thirty years later, and the same technology would help the police to find and arrest the real murderer.

Jason couldn't figure out why he had a feeling the two cases might be connected. But he never ignored a hunch. Even if the two cases weren't connected, his feelings about Penny seemed to give both of her parents' cases priority in his mind.

Jason knew Carla's history wasn't squeaky-clean. From what he could remember, she used to run with a pretty wild crowd, especially when she was hooked on crack. But based on what he'd seen of her over the past five years, and his visits with Big Mama, he thought she'd left all that behind her.

Whoever beat her the other day hadn't stolen anything. In his mind, that ruled out any of her junkie friends.

On the other hand, Gerald was a former dealer and street hustler. Based on what Jason had read, Gerald hadn't been big-time, but he'd seemed to be headed in that direction before the murder charge. Maybe one of Gerald's enemies was using Carla to send a message to Gerald. Maybe one of his enemies had set him up for the murder. And if that was the case, how long would it take before he upped the ante and harmed Penny?

Rubbing his head in frustration, he leaned back in his chair. He had to find a way to get Carla to talk. Or maybe he could get Old Lady Henderson back down here to look at some more mug shots. He needed a name and a face. He needed to find the culprit and get rid of any threat to Penny.

Thinking about Penny's mother's case provided a nice distraction from his other thoughts of Penny. He couldn't believe he'd actually made love to her. How had he gone from wanting answers and closure to darn near starting another relationship?

And what would he do if he…no, *when* he got the answers he'd waited all these years for? Because he was just as determined as ever to find out the truth. If anything, making love to her had made him desire the truth even more. But he had said he wouldn't badger her about it until he found out what happened to Carla.

What kind of idiotic promise was that?

The kind you make when you want to make love to the sexiest woman you've ever known, the only woman who ever had your heart. Stupid!

When his cell phone rang, it didn't take much for him to agree to meet his brother Joel for lunch.

Halfway into the lunch, he started to regret his decision.

"Do you really think you're cool with the fact that she was with Terrill? That she left you for Terrill after she lost the baby?" Joel took a bite of his Johnny's Grill Texas-style hot dog. Johnny's was Joel's favorite spot to eat, and talking him into trying another place was always a no-win battle.

North Jersey probably had more spots where you could get a Texas-style hot dog than the great state of Texas. There had to be hundreds of places serving them in Passaic County alone. But, out of all the restaurants, Joel swore by Johnny's Grill.

Johnny's Grill was packed, as usual; the restaurant kept folks coming in for their legendary wieners. The lunchtime hustle and bustle had a crowd of just about every class, creed and color that made up North Jersey's multicultural population. Blacks and Latinos, Italians and Jews, all were packed in at the red and platinum chairs and tables, chomping down the signature dogs.

"All the way-way," could be heard, along with whatever number of hot dogs folks were ordering, as the cashiers behind the counter shouted orders back to the kitchen.

"'Cause I know for a fact that I wouldn't be able to forgive it, man." Joel took another bite, chewed and swallowed. "I'm telling you, man, Johnny's Grill has the best hot dogs in the area, if not the world."

He closed his eyes and smacked his lips in reverence to the deep-fried, chili sauce, onions and mustard-covered tube of beef on a bun. Then he pinned Jason with a know-it-all stare. "I love Penny to death. I still think of her like a little sister, even though she ripped out your heart, stomped on it and handed it back to you. And if it had been any other guy but Terrill, I might even say give it another try. But it was Terrill, man. *Terrill!*" Joel stuck his fork in his cheese fries.

Jason had to laugh at his brother's love for the deep-fried hot dogs and gravy-covered fries. The man was lucky he was in such excellent shape and had such a physically demanding job, because those hot dogs would have a lesser man looking more than a little round, the way Joel put them away every chance he got.

Jason sighed and took a sip of his root beer. "How did we get on the subject of Penny?"

"'Cause you have that same lovesick expression on your face you had at dinner. And since I'm a man who likes to watch out for my younger brother, I have to save you from yourself." He paused and took swig of his root beer before continuing.

"Now, should you put the past behind you and stop letting it get to you? Yes. Should you be cordial to Penny and Terrill and show them their betrayal didn't break you? Damn straight. But getting intimately or emotionally involved with Penny Keys again is a sucker move, baby bro. *Sucker move.* And I can't let you go out like that."

Too late.

"Look, I can appreciate your advice, especially given you're all of two years older than me and have *so* much more wisdom." Jason couldn't contain the sarcasm lacing his tone and he didn't want to. "But my love life is my business."

"Love life? See, I'm too late. Don't say I didn't warn you. Why don't you let me hook you up with someone?"

Jason slanted his eyes. "Now I *know* you know I don't need any help meeting women."

Joel grinned. "All right. So why are you getting caught up with Penny again? She's going back to Los Angeles, right? And who else is in Los Angeles? Let's say you can forgive and forget what happened between Penny and Terrill, and the two of you start something real, right here and right now. Can you honestly say you'd be cool with her living in Los Angeles with the man who broke you guys up before right there? Yeah, right!"

"It's time to change the subject. You've had your say, almighty big brother of mine." Jason pushed away from the table. "Gotta get back to work. Some of us have to protect the streets and keep the riffraff at bay."

"Yeah, one of those cold cases you're obsessed with might get warm while you're having lunch. Here's some more free advice, because I'm feeling kind. A case that has gone un- solved for twenty-plus years probably isn't going anywhere anytime soon." Joel chuckled at his own cleverness.

"Oh, go put out a fire. I'll catch you later. Love you, bro."

Both stood, hugged and gave each other pounds. No matter how much he and his brothers got on each other's nerves, they still made a point of hugging each other goodbye and saying I love you. With the dangerous jobs they held, they knew anything could happen and they didn't want to have their last words to one another be words of anger.

"Later. Love you, too, man."

Penny didn't know who was getting on her nerves more— her spoiled, snotty mother or the father who was overindul- gent and had taken up permanent residence as Carla's doormat. It wasn't so much that he let Carla walk all over him, but he didn't check her at all.

While Penny could appreciate his whole baby-I'm- back-and-I'm-not-going-anywhere routine, when she added Carla's sulking I-don't-care-what-you-do-I'm-not-giving-you- another-chance spiel to the mix, it had all the fixings to drive her crazy and make her willing to do anything to get out of the house.

Anything.

As she sat in the living room, watching the evening game shows with her parents, she sent out a desperate plea into the universe for someone, anyone, to come and save her from the slapstick comedy that her life had become.

She'd never been so pleased to hear a doorbell ring—until she saw it was Jason.

Oh, the tightening of her nipples and the sudden soaking feeling she felt in her panties as she remembered the previous evening signaled she was more than a little happy to see him on one level. But after spending the day going over all the reasons why things would never work between them, and how her mother and his aunt Sophie were right, she wasn't in his league, he was the last person she needed to see.

"Hi, Jason."

"Hey. Can I come in?"

Duh. She was standing there looking like an idiot. The man probably had information about who had attacked Carla.

"Sure. Do you have information about the case?"

"I don't have any leads yet. It would be so much easier if your mother would just talk." He shook his head in frustration and added sarcastically, "Oops, I meant regain her memory." He didn't believe Carla's story any more than Penny did.

Penny and her father had both tried to get the truth out of Carla. But the woman wouldn't budge.

"She still won't talk. I would say just forget it. But knowing Carla, it could be a very bad situation waiting to blow up."

"Yeah. Listen, how about you let me take you out to dinner, and I can run some thoughts I have been having about this by you? Maybe something can trigger your memory. And if that doesn't work, I can always go back to Old Lady Henderson."

"Old Lady Henderson? Oh, my, that woman had to be the nosiest person on the block. I couldn't have you over without her telling Big Mama, 'Penny's fast behind had a boy in the house.'" Penny chuckled.

"Yeah, she might be crucial to finding out who beat Carla, especially if Carla continues to be difficult."

"I'm game to do whatever I can to help." She looked down at her casual light gray linen skirt, which hit just above her knees, and her short-sleeved pink silk shirt. "Should I change?"

He looked her over, his eyes stopping at her legs. "No. You look great."

"Well, I'll just go tell the folks I'm leaving and see if Gerald will stay with Carla until I come back."

Penny walked back to the living room, and Jason followed her.

As soon as they walked in the room, Carla let out an exasperated sigh and rolled her eyes. "Aww, Brat! What're you doing with him? You never listen to me!"

"He's a nice man, Carla. She could do worse."

Gerald nodded a greeting to Jason.

"Who asked you? Did anybody ask Gerald?" Carla looked around the room, pretending she was waiting for an answer to her question. "Nope, nobody asked you anything. Mind your business. I know what's best for my daughter."

If she wasn't so annoyed at how rude Carla was being, Penny might have laughed. "I'm going out to dinner with Jason. Gerald, do you mind staying here with Carla until I get back? Make sure she gets some rest and make sure the person she won't tell on doesn't hurt her again?"

"I don't need no babysitter. I just need to be left alone," Carla huffed.

"Well, you got one, darling, so tough." Gerald didn't even look at Carla. He still seemed unfazed by her antics. "Go on and have a nice time. I'm not going anywhere. And I'm not going to let any more harm come to your mother."

"Thanks, Gerald." Penny sincerely believed the man would fight to the death to protect Carla. She couldn't understand it, based on the way Carla behaved. But she reasoned it wasn't for her to understand.

Riding in the SUV with Jason put her in a whole other state of confusion. She knew she was less deserving of kindness from Jason than her mother was from Gerald. Her lies had cost Jason his best friend. And even if she came clean now, it probably wouldn't change anything. Still, she couldn't seem to stay the heavy beating of her heart whenever he came around.

Making love to Jason Hightower had to have been the most idiotic thing she had ever done. Yet as she glanced at him driving his SUV in silent determination, she knew without a doubt that she would gladly make love to him again and again.

He kept his eyes on the road, but a slow and sexy smile crossed his lips. "What are you looking at?"

The stalled pitter-patter of her heart noted his smile, and was followed by a tightening of her nipples and a clench in her sex.

"I'm not looking at you." She cleared her throat and turned to look out the window.

She took in all the changes that had happened in the city since she'd been gone. The entire stretch of Broadway, all the way up to Elmwood Park, was now Martin Luther King Jr. Way. She remembered when only a small section of the main street was named after the slain leader. Back in the day, they used to joke that only the worst part of Broadway was named after King. She wondered what the joke would be now. Did this mean that the entire city had gotten worse?

It didn't seem as if Paterson was any the worse for wear, at least not to her eyes. So many new buildings had sprouted up, and many of the older ones were gone. But, oddly, it still felt like home.

"You were looking. I could feel it."

"Well, you must be *feeling* things, then, 'cause I wasn't."

"Oh, I'm feeling things, all right. And I intend to feel a whole lot more by the time the night is over."

She burst out laughing. "You're still crazy."

He laughed a little, too, and then his voice went sober. "Yeah, still crazy about you."

By the sound of his voice, Penny could tell he wasn't thrilled about having feelings for her. She couldn't blame him.

They rode the rest of the way up Route 4, listening to the *Quiet Storm* radio programming and letting slow jam after slow jam speak all the emotions neither of them dared to voice.

The Italian restaurant he took her to in Paramus was small and quaint. It was a family-owned business, and it had a classy and intimate appeal. Everything, from the white table-cloths to the candles and the beautiful real floral arrangements on the tables, set the scene for a nice, quiet romantic evening. The smell of lilac, lilies and roses wafted through the air, along with the spicy aroma of tomatoes, garlic, onions and fresh herbs.

After eating their food in relative silence, Penny could no longer take it. If he was having second thoughts about what had happened between them the other night and he wanted a way out, she would give it to him.

When she opened her mouth to tell him he didn't have to feel obligated to take her out and she understood if he wanted to backtrack, the words refused to come out. Instead, she inquired, "So, how was work?"

"Do you mean, have I come any closer to figuring out who attacked your mother?"

"No…well…I wasn't talking about that. I was just making small talk." She grinned. "But have you?"

"No, I haven't. Tell me, do you remember any of Carla's old boyfriends? Old Lady Henderson said she'd seen one of Carla's old boyfriends around the house and she said she'd also seen him the day Big Mama passed. The description she gave seemed to fit your father. But she was adamant it wasn't him. So do you remember anyone who might fit that description?"

Penny closed her eyes in thought. Carla really didn't have a lot of boyfriends, per se. And for a lot of Penny's life, Carla hadn't been around. Right before she got hooked on the drugs really bad, Big Mama had kicked her out.

A flash of one of Carla's boyfriends came to mind, and she automatically raised her hand to touch the tiny, now barely noticeable scar on the side of her right eye. She remembered the day she had gotten it.

The man who'd given it to her was the one boyfriend of Carla's Penny wished she could forget.

She didn't know his real name. But she could still clearly see his mean snarling face as he'd slapped her in front of Big Mama's house and she'd hit the pavement. She had gotten a gash over her eye that needed five stitches to heal. She'd only been twelve years old at the time. And she'd had no idea what she had done that was so bad as to make a grown man strike her.

It was enough to make Big Mama tell Carla she couldn't come around anymore if she was going to bring harm to a defenseless child.

Carla had chosen that man, C-Money, over her own daughter.

Jason watched her rubbing her scar and squinted. He remembered when she'd gotten it. He hadn't been there at the time, but he'd seen the stitches afterward. He knew it had happened when one of Carla's boyfriends hit Penny and knocked her to the ground.

He felt himself getting hot. Back then, he'd had his first

instincts to kill, along with a desire to protect Penny so that no one ever hurt her like that again. It shocked him how prevalent those desires still were.

Penny looked up at him, and he found himself trapped in the bold, round copper pools of her eyes. "C-Money," was all she said.

Jason vaguely remembered him, the drug dealer and pimp who'd gotten Carla strung-out on the crack. He'd only seen him a couple of times, and he'd been a boy then. He remembered enough about the man to know he did indeed favor Gerald.

"Do you know his real name?"

"No, I don't." Penny was still rubbing her fingers lightly across her scar. "I've tried to block that scumbag from my memory." She glanced at him and self-consciously removed her hand from her eye. She sighed.

He wanted to tell her that the little fraction of a scar did nothing to take away from her beauty. He wanted to tell her that he'd never let scum like C-Money get near her to hurt her again. He wanted to tell her he would always protect her. But he knew he couldn't keep those kinds of promises to her anymore. She was about to go back to Los Angeles. And he wouldn't be able to protect her when she left.

"Well, the nickname is something to go on, at least, and I think I'm going to go back down to the precinct and see if I can find out some more information. I don't think your mother is going to talk. But if you think you can get her to talk, try. She doesn't have to be afraid of him anymore."

As much as it killed him to think he wouldn't end the evening with Penny wrapped in his arms, he knew he had to make headway on this case. If C-Money were the attacker, he wouldn't be allowed to hurt Penny again.

* * *

Carla hated stress. She never could handle it, and yet it always seemed to follow her around. She had no idea how C-Money knew to show up every single time she had seen Gerald. The jerk must have been watching her like a hawk. She hated feeling like the scared little mouse. The last thing she even wanted to think about was what he was going to do when he found out that Gerald was at the hospital and the house. He probably already knew.

Granted, she should have never started seeing C-Money in the first place. Her life had pretty much gone downhill from there.

That's karma for you, Carla. Start screwing your man's archenemy and the universe will start screwing you.

She needed a cigarette. Well, she needed more than that…but a stogie would help take down the edge a little, while she tried to think her way out of this mess.

Maybe Gerald would have one. Then he'd be good for something.

Carla rolled her eyes as she thought Gerald was good for a lot of things. That was the problem.

She got up from her bed, put on her robe and went downstairs. Her entire body ached, and she thought about taking one of those painkillers. The doctor said as long as she was careful she should be fine. Given the way her life was going, she didn't want to risk it.

Truth be told, she still hadn't come to grips with the fact that her mama was gone. And adding a daughter who couldn't seem to stand her and two ex-boyfriends with serious issues to the mix made her a candidate for drug therapy, if ever there was one.

Gerald was sitting in the front room watching the news.

She cleared her throat. "Hey, you got a cigarette you can loan me?"

Gerald took out his pack of cigarettes and handed it to her. "Loan you? You gonna give it back after you done?"

"Ha, ha, ha, very funny." Carla looked at the pack and turned up her nose. "Light? What kind of crap is this? Since when you started smoking lights? You might as well not even bother with these."

"Beggars can't be choosers," Gerald offered wryly. "And I'm cutting back."

"Mmm. Whatever. I guess this'll have to do." She took one out of the pack and sat down next to him on the sofa. "Dang, I need to go find an ashtray."

Gerald placed his hand on her knee. "Sit back, relax. Just tell me where to look and I'll go get you one."

"There should be some clean ones in the back of the top kitchen cabinet, over the fridge. We haven't used them in years. Mama didn't allow smoking in the house after Daddy died."

"Okay. I'll be right back."

Carla watched him exit the room and took a deep breath.

Jail had made the man finer, if that was possible. His tall, muscular frame did all kinds of things to her libido. And it didn't help that she had the new memories of making love to him in his room to add to her old feelings. Plus, he was being so nice, so tender, so sweet, so understanding. So *Gerald*.

He came back and sat down beside her, placing the ashtray on the coffee table in front of them.

Carla put the cigarette in her mouth. And before she could reach for some matches, he lit it for her.

"Thanks."

"You're welcome."

"No. I mean thanks for everything. For staying at the hospital, and staying here with me and stuff. I do appreciate it, even if I don't always act like it."

He nodded and turned his attention back toward the television.

She took a long pull and exhaled. If she could just figure out how to get Penny to let her move to Los Angeles, Carla knew things would be fine. Fine, except she wouldn't feel Gerald's touch again. She crossed her legs and leaned back.

Gerald let out a deep sigh and turned off the television. He turned to her with an irritated expression on his face.

"What? What's wrong with you?" Here she was trying to be nice to the man and he wanted to cop an attitude. That's why she should have kept being mean to him.

Men are such a trip. Treat them bad and they can't get enough of you. Treat them nice and they give you their behinds to kiss.

"I just… I just can't believe you're not going to tell me who did this to you. And then you keep pushing me away like it's nothing. Like *I'm* nothing. Like we didn't mean anything to each other. Carla…I let you do that when I was in jail 'cause I figured maybe it was for the best. I mean, it wasn't like I could do anything for you in jail. But I'm not gonna let you do that now."

"*Let me?* Hmph." Carla finished her cigarette and put it out before standing up. "You're not the boss of me. I can do whatever I want. And I can take care of my own problems. I've been doing it for a long time."

"Is that how you got hooked on crack? Handling your own problems by taking them to the pipe?" The edge in his voice let her know he'd had his fill of being nice to her. The kid gloves had come off with a vengeance.

"That's low, Gerald."

His eyes narrowed, and he harrumphed. "No. Low is me finding out my girl is out on the streets, whoring for the man who might have set me up."

Carla swallowed and sat back on the sofa. "I wasn't—"

"You wasn't? You wasn't? You sure you want to keep on lying? Ain't that going against one of your twelve steps?"

Her heart started beating double time in her chest. Gerald knew about her and C-Money, and he was still trying to be with her. The sheer thought of it blew her away. She would never in a million years have considered that he could find out about her transgressions and still love her. That was why she'd thought she had to keep it a secret. She hadn't wanted Gerald to know she had sunk so low.

"If I didn't know C-Money was in jail for selling that crack he got you hooked on, I would know who did this to you. But it couldn't have been him. So who was it? Did he have one of his thugs beat you up?"

Carla tried to think of a reason, any reason, why she shouldn't tell Gerald the truth. The battle between those two had been a long time coming, and honestly, she was tired of being a casualty of their dang war. Hell, she was nobody's dang collateral damage, and neither was her child.

"Can I have another cigarette?"

Gerald handed her the pack but he still had that stern expression on his face. Even in his obvious anger, he still lit her smoke and patiently waited for her to open up.

"C-Money ain't in jail. And for the record, I didn't want to get involved with him when you got locked up for murder. Let's just say he made it hard for a girl to say no." She took a long drag.

The expression on Gerald's face would have stopped anyone in his or her tracks. She had never seen him so angry.

"He did this to you?"

She shrugged. "He doesn't like it when you come around."

"You still messing with him?" His voice choked a little, as his anger turned to hurt.

She wished she could take it all away. The last thing she wanted to do was hurt Gerald.

"Not by choice."

Gerald closed his eyes and clenched his hands so tightly the brown of his knuckles appeared almost white. He snarled, "I'm gonna kill him."

"Then you really will be a murderer, and you'll go back to jail."

"If he was the man who set me up, the man who then started seeing my woman and made her stop me from seeing even a picture of my daughter, then he's the man who stole my life from me, and he has to pay."

"So, you just gonna let him steal the rest of your life, too?"

"You don't understand!"

"Oh, I understand perfectly. It's a man thing, and you want to continue your little pissing contest. All I ask is that you let me and my child get out of the line of fire this time. Help me talk Brat into moving me to Los Angeles with her as soon as possible. 'Cause, honestly, he came at me this time, but he said he might just be coming for her next. Who knows what he'll do when he sees I didn't heed his warning and stay away from you?"

Gerald leaped up from the seat and paced the floor like a caged bear.

Carla put out her second cigarette and reached for another. They were lights, after all, and she reasoned it would take at least three or four to give her the kick she needed to really plot her way out of the C-Money mess.

But if she got Gerald to work with her, then she could get herself and Penny out of there and safe. That was the only thing that really mattered now.

She smoked the third cigarette and watched him pace. Each step his long legs took back and forth around the small room seemed to have an impact on some part of her body. The first go-round made her nipples stand at attention. The second caused moisture to pool between her legs. And then he'd pause and stare at her for a few seconds before stalking around again. She fanned her neck and put out her fourth cigarette before standing up and walking over to him.

She put her hand on his chest.

Rock. Solid. Muscle.

She moved her hand to his tender, caring face.

"You can help me, Gerald. You can help me by getting Brat and me out of danger." She stood on her toes. Her hand trailed to the back of his neck and pulled his head down so his face was directly in front of hers. She let all of her feelings show. Her fear for her child's life…her love for her child's father…all of it.

She needed to barter those feelings for the bigger picture.

Gerald must have believed her eyes, because his started to tear up. She used her hand to wipe away the ones that made their way down his face. She placed her hand in his and led him to her bedroom.

Chapter 11

Peeved? Funky? Irritated? Those words about summed up the reasons Penny was in the kitchen glaring at her mother and twisting her lips in disgust. She tried to tell herself it wasn't because she'd come home and found her parents in bed together clearly postcoital, when she'd had to go to bed all alone.

She wanted to believe she wasn't so small-minded that she'd resent that her mother had gotten some loving last night.

Really, she had no business wanting to share a bed with Jason Hightower again anyway, did she?

And then there was Carla, all bruised and battered but bouncing around the kitchen like a happy hummingbird, cooking breakfast as if she'd done it all her life.

"Since when did you turn into Betty Crocker?" Penny stood in front of the coffeemaker and willed it to drip just a little bit faster. She needed lots of caffeine to deal with her mother this morning, especially if her suspicions about who'd beaten Carla were true.

Because, when it was all said and done, if Carla was protecting C-Money…the man who'd given Penny the scar on her eye…she didn't know how she'd deal with that.

"What do you mean? I could always cook breakfast. Don't you remember those little happy face chocolate chip pancakes I used to make you when you were a little girl?"

"Nope." Penny rolled her eyes and decided to move the coffeepot and let her mug fill up instead of waiting. Once she had a full cup, she replaced the pot and sat down at the kitchen table.

Carla had stopped stirring whatever she was making and turned to glare at Penny with her hands on her hips.

"Your food is going to burn up. You better watch that pot." Penny scooped a little sugar into her coffee and added a touch of cream before taking a sip.

Yes, that's what I need.

Carla pursed her lips and turned back to her pots. "I'm making eggs, grits and corned beef hash. There's gonna be plenty, so I hope you're hungry."

"I don't do red meat. And for some reason, the older I get, eggs don't agree with me anymore. I'll just make some toast or something, thanks."

Carla sucked her teeth. "You just don't want none 'cause I made it, Brat."

"That's not true." *But I do like living…* Penny couldn't remember Carla ever cooking, and frankly, she wasn't in a hurry to be the taste-test dummy for Carla's little kitchen experiment. "I'm not really a breakfast person."

"Mmm hmm. Whatever, Brat! I remember the way you used to dig into Mama's biscuits, ham, eggs and gravy."

"Are you making biscuits, ham, eggs and gravy?"

Carla turned and narrowed her eyes. Then she took a deep breath and plastered a fake smile on her face. "I'm just saying, I cooked breakfast 'cause I wanted to show you I can carry my weight and stuff if you let me come out to Cali with you. You should at least taste some."

Oh, brother. Not this again.

Penny decided to ignore Carla. How many times could she possibly tell her mother it wasn't going to happen? What was it going to take to get the woman to see that?

Carla literally bounced as she turned off the stove and came to sit at the table with Penny. Her eyes looked overly bright, and when she spoke again, her voice got really high and extremely chipper.

"You know, your daddy and I were talking last night, and he agrees it would be best for me to go out to L.A. with you as soon as possible, like yesterday, at least until this situation blows over. You know, with me being assaulted and all that."

My daddy? *Is she for real? Ignore her. She's not all there. You can still love your mother without buying into her craziness.*

Penny got up and refilled her coffee.

Carla got up, too. "I'll just fix you a plate so you can taste—"

"I don't want any. I'm going to have toast. Thanks anyway."

"Brat, when are you gonna get that chip off your shoulder, huh? I mean, you act like you the only person in the world who might have had a less-than-ideal childhood. You turned out fine. Suck it up and deal. Shoot. Some people had it way worse than you. I'm just asking you to help me out this one time, dang!"

Penny arched her eyebrow and started to head for the door.

Carla grabbed Penny's arm and held on. "Just listen to me, Penny. You could at least listen."

It was too much, way too much, especially if C-Money was still in Carla's life. Penny felt the heat rise from her neck to the ends of her sisterlocks.

Carla had some nerve.

"I could at least listen? Why? Why, Carla? Why should I listen to you? It's not going to change anything. Why are you treating me like I owe you something, huh? Yes, you gave me life. Thank you. Does that mean I have to take over where your own mother left off?"

Carla slapped her and she took a step back with tears in her eyes.

Penny's eyes widened, and her hand went to her stinging cheek. It felt as if her chest had exploded as all of the past hurts came flooding to the surface. She took a deep breath. Her hand traveled up her face and landed on her scar.

"How could you, Carla? What made you think it was okay to leave your own daughter for a man? Not just any man, but a man who slapped a child down on the pavement because she accidentally stepped on his freaking sneakers! And you chose him, Carla. I heard Big Mama tell you that if you were going to keep bringing him around here then you would have to leave. And you left. You left me for him!"

"You don't know what you're talking about, Brat. You weren't—"

"I remember everything, Carla. I remember C-Money slapping me. Sitting in the emergency room with Big Mama. Getting stitches. I look in the mirror every day, and this little scar reminds me that my own mother choose a man over me. You chose C-Money, and now you won't even tell the police he was the one who beat you up. Because it *was* him. Wasn't it, Carla? Wasn't it?"

Penny didn't like the sound of her voice. It sounded shrill, harsh and ugly to her ears, but she couldn't stop.

"Is that true, Carla? Did he hit her and leave a scar? You let him hit our daughter, and you stayed with him?"

Penny turned and saw Gerald standing in the doorway. The expression on his face appeared to be a mixture of horror, disappointment and hurt. His anger-laced voice was a far cry from the happy-go-lucky tone she'd heard the past couple of days.

Carla let go of Penny's arm and wrapped her arms around herself. She looked so vulnerable in that moment, Penny wished she could take it all back. But it had all happened just the way she'd said it did. And she needed Carla to say something about why she'd made the decisions she had.

Carla's eyes narrowed, and her chin lifted up defiantly.

"Is it true?" Gerald's voice was shaking with anger.

Carla closed her eyes, then she opened them and glared at Penny. "You don't know the full story, Brat!"

"So why don't you tell me the full story? Better yet, why don't you tell me why you're still protecting that man? I know he was the one who beat you up. Why won't you press charges? Why won't you talk to the police?" Penny tried to keep her voice level and calm, but it was impossible. The more she thought about it, the more upset she became.

Gerald seemed stuck in the same spot. He hadn't moved from the doorway, and he still had a stunned look on his face.

Penny almost felt sorry for him. But the sooner he realized Carla was only looking out for Carla, the better for him. It might hurt a little now, but he'd be saving himself from a world of hurt later. Penny knew about hurt firsthand. She knew because, in spite of all her history with the woman, she felt a sharp pain in her heart at the fact that Carla was *still* protecting C-Money. She was still putting C-Money before everyone else.

Carla's eyes shifted from side to side. Tears welled up in her eyes as she narrowed them, first on Penny and then on Gerald. "Neither one of you can sit there and judge me. I'm doing the best I can. I did the best I could." She glared at Gerald. "You weren't there. So you don't get to point the finger now. If you had been there, none of it would have happened!" She stormed past Gerald and went running out of the room.

Classic Carla. Blame the rest of the world for your mistakes! Penny wiped her eyes and sat down at the kitchen table. This was way more drama than she had coffee for.

Dumbstruck, Gerald continued to stand in the doorway.

"You better sit down before you fall down. You look like you could use a seat." Penny took a sip of her coffee and leaned back in her chair.

She hadn't wanted to get into a full-blown battle with Carla. She had just wanted to find out if C-Money was the person who'd beaten Carla. And she still hadn't gotten her mother to confirm he was the one. Carla hadn't admitted a thing.

Dang!

Gerald pulled out a chair and sat down.

For a while, neither of them said a word, which was fine with Penny. She had filled her ghetto-drama quota for the year, as far as she was concerned. She needed to get on the first plane to Los Angeles.

Carla was right about one thing; Penny could handle everything else via phone. And whatever she couldn't handle that way, Carla could take care of. Because Penny knew she wasn't going to let Carla move to Los Angeles.

If her mother was still messing around with C-Money, then what other bad habits was she holding on to? Maybe it was really time for the two of them to finally go their separate ways for good.

The only thing stopping her from making the call to the travel agent was Jason. Oddly, a few days ago he would have been the last person she wanted to come face-to-face with. But now…

Now what? You still can't have anything with him. It's too late. Take your memories and your behind back to L.A.

She sighed.

"I'm sorry you had to go through that as a kid. Carla was right. If I had—"

Oh, brother.

Penny had to cut the man off. Someone had to help him. It might as well be her. "You didn't make Carla start seeing C-Money. You didn't make C-Money hit Carla and me. And you didn't make Carla choose him over her own child. It's *not* your fault. You have nothing to apologize for."

"C-Money was my enemy. We had a beef before I went to jail. We always had a rivalry. He went after Carla to get to me."

Penny exhaled. "Even if that is true, Carla is a grown woman. She was a grown woman when she made the decision to leave me and Big Mama to go with him. He got her hooked on crack, and she's still protecting him. He might have come here the day Big Mama died. You can't tell me the shock of that didn't send her into a stroke. And Carla is still protecting him! He came in here, and he could have killed her. And she's still—" Penny took a big, heaping breath and wiped her face. Despite her resolve to remain calm, more tears were falling.

She'd thought she was long over shedding tears about her mother's rejection and neglect. But Carla clearly could still get to her. At least in the past she'd had Big Mama.

Now Big Mama was gone, and C-Money's evil ugly mug might have been the last face she'd seen.

Gerald slid his chair over and placed his arm around her.

She tried to maintain her distance at first, but soon found herself placing her head on his shoulder and letting her tears run their course. She'd done more crying in the past three days than she'd done in a long time.

"I know Carla didn't make the decisions we would have wanted her to make, darling. But neither one of us had to walk in her shoes. I still love her. And I love you more than my own life. I want you both safe. And the only way I can see for that to happen is for the both of you to go out to your place in Los Angeles until either the cops get C-Money or I do." As he patted her head and held her close, Gerald's voice maintained an eerie calm.

Penny looked up at him and saw that a stark determination had replaced his earlier stunned expression. Now she was the one stuck on stupid and waiting to get dumber. How in the world did Carla manage to get everyone to come over to Crazyville with her?

The doorbell rang, and Penny wasted no time getting up to answer it. She'd never thought she would be as happy to see Jason as she was at that moment. She needed someone sane to talk to.

"Hey." Jason stepped in the door and pulled her into his arms. "What happened? Why are you crying?"

Penny tried to pull away and wipe her face, but Jason held her tight.

"What happened?" he repeated.

"Nothing. I'm fine. I'm just having a little misunderstanding with the folks."

Gosh, that sounds like high school. I've got to get out of this Twilight Zone version of my life.

Carla came down the stairs, fully dressed in jeans and a T-shirt. "Brat! You called the cops?" she whined as she stamped her slipper-clad foot on the ground.

Penny rolled her eyes. "No, I did not call the police. But you're going to tell Jason everything he needs to know about what C-Money did to you. We need his full name—"

"I've found out his full name, and I've already been in touch with his parole officer to get a lead on where he is. What I need Carla to do is to tell me if Clyde Markum is the man who attacked her. And if he is, she needs to file a formal complaint and press charges."

Jason kept his arm around Penny as he spoke to Carla. Penny felt uneasy about how good it felt to be in his arms and how much she found herself wanting to stay there forever. She barely moved. It felt too good, too right.

Carla stomped her foot again in frustration. "I can't press charges against him. Brat, why can't we just go?"

Penny threw up her arms as she pulled away from Jason and walked toward Carla. "Why can't you do the right thing for once, Carla? Please."

"I'm trying to do the right thing. Honest. I am."

Jason walked over to Carla and put his hand on her shoulder. "The right thing is to help the police put a criminal back behind bars."

Gerald walked into the foyer and nodded at Jason.

They all seemed to be at a standstill, waiting to see what Carla would do.

Carla reached up and touched Penny's cheek. "I'm sorry I hit you, Brat. And I'm sorry, but I can't press charges." She headed back up the stairs. Before she got to the top, she turned. "Don't you have some more of Mama's affairs to settle today? You best get to it. And maybe you should think about either staying with your cop friend or just going on back to Los Angeles. Today or tomorrow. Like I said, this isn't really the best place to be, and it's no need for both of us to be in danger."

"Then press charges!" Penny screamed the words out and it was all she could do not to take off up the stairs after Carla.

Carla shrugged. "No offense, but I don't trust the cops, and I really don't think they can help with this."

Penny turned to Gerald. "What do you think? Please don't tell me you agree with her."

"I told you what I think, Penny. I think you and your mother need to get out of town." Gerald turned and followed Carla up the stairs.

"I swear. This place has turned into the psych ward. They're all crazy. Am I crazy?" She turned to Jason and then shook her head. "Never mind. Don't answer that."

Jason smiled, and she felt her heart stop and restart.

Danger. Danger.

"We aren't going to be able to make her press charges. And she's right about one thing. It will be dangerous for you both in this house with him on the loose. This Clyde 'C-Money' Markum is a pretty nasty piece of work."

"You don't have to tell me. I remember. Boy, do I remember." A chill went through her, and she shuddered and touched her scar.

Jason stepped over and placed his arms around her.

It felt so good.

"Mmm." She didn't realize she'd moaned out loud until his lips brushed her neck in several butterfly kisses.

"I missed you last night." His arms tightened around her, and he held her closer.

"I missed you, too." *Too much... Especially since it's too late for us...* Penny started to pull away, but he pulled her more snugly against his body.

"Go and get some clothes. You can stay with me until we find a way to get Carla to press charges. I'm going to talk with Gerald and see if he can spend more time, at least the time when he isn't working, here with Carla. I'm going to increase patrols in the area. But until she presses charges, I can't order a more permanent watch."

Penny wished she had sense enough to say, *Oh, I won't have to stay with you. I'm headed back to Los Angeles on the next thing smoking.* But common sense escaped her, because Jason's arms felt like all the home she would ever want or need.

Was she wrong to want to bask in them for a little while longer, and have some more memories to add to the ones from her youth?

"I'm really afraid for Carla. I don't want anything to happen to her."

"And I don't want anything to happen to you."

Penny gazed up at him. The sincerity in his eyes made goose bumps pop up on her arms and neck. She felt hot and cold at the same time, as a warm and sexy chill coursed through her body.

"So go and get a few things. And I'll go and talk to Gerald and Carla while you're doing that."

Jason watched as Penny made her way up the stairs. Watching the gentle sway of her hips as she moved made him simultaneously question his sanity for suggesting that she spend some time at his place and wonder why he hadn't thought of the option sooner.

The only thing he was sure of was that he would protect Penny at all costs. He still had no idea why he still felt so compelled to do so. He only knew he wouldn't let anything, not even his own need for closure and information, get in the way of him doing so.

Everything he had discovered about Clyde Markum said the man was extremely dangerous. And if Jason was right, the man was also a murderer.

There hadn't been a person in Paterson thirty-five years ago who stood to gain more with the murder of those two people and the arrest of Gerald than Clyde Markum. Gerald had been one of his biggest competitors as far as the sale of marijuana, and the husband and wife had called and reported Markum more than any of the other dealers they complained about to the police. With everyone out of the way, Markum had been able to become a drug kingpin once crack hit in the eighties.

But all of that was circumstantial, and Jason was a man of science and evidence. That was why he'd requested that several tests be run against the DNA they had on file for Markum and what they had in the cold-case evidence for the murders.

He knocked on Carla's closed bedroom door, hoping he wasn't interrupting something.

Gerald's voice responded to the knock. "Come in."

Jason walked in and saw Carla wrapped up on Gerald's lap with her head buried in his chest. The man looked as if he had the weight of the world on his shoulders, but it also appeared that he wouldn't care to be anyplace in the world other than where he was.

Jason knew the feeling well. That was why he hadn't wanted to let Penny go a few moments ago.

Carla looked up with a tear-stained face, saw him and then laid her head back down.

"She's not ready," was all Gerald said, but he said it with a finality that let Jason know that now was not the time to try and push Carla to do the right thing.

Jason cleared his throat. "I understand that. But she should understand we won't be able to police the way we could if she would press charges. His attacking her violates his parole. We could have him back in jail. At the very least, we'd be able to set up an officer for protection. And she should really think about Penny, too."

Carla sat up. "You gotta make her go back to L.A. You gotta tell her to leave. Or at least make her go to your place. But it's better if she leaves town. She's gotta go."

The panicked, glazed-over stare in Carla's eyes made Jason's heart stop. "Did he threaten Penny?"

"Oh, shoot! Oh, shoot! Oh, shoot!" Carla crunched up her fists and covered her eyes.

Gerald pulled her close. "I hate to have to ask you this. A man should be able to look after his own. But can you look after Penny until she heads back to L.A.? I'll look after Carla. I'll try and get her to see what she needs to do. I can't make any promises. But I'll try."

Jason nodded, left the couple in the room and went to look for Penny.

Chapter 12

After running all of her errands and tying up as much of Big Mama's affairs as she could, Penny headed back over to Jason's place. She saw his SUV in the parking lot and thought about all the reasons she shouldn't have taken him up on his offer to share his space with her.

Technically, she'd handled as much business as she could, and she should head back to her life in Los Angeles.

The sound of Kelis's "Bossy" pulled her from her thoughts and she took her cell phone out of her purse to see what her friend and business partner had to say.

"You need to get back here before I kill your boy." Maritza Morales's voice had a frustrated high-pitched tone to it.

Penny couldn't help but smile. "Well, hello to you, too, *chica.*"

Maritza and Terrill had a love-hate relationship that Penny

tried to stay out of. But her two friends liked to keep her in the middle.

"When are you coming back? Because if your boy doesn't stay away from me, I'm going to have to cut him."

"Now, now, Maritza, you don't have to resort to violence. I'll be back soon. There have been some recent events that might keep me here a little longer. My mother was attacked, and I'm going to hang around just a bit longer to make sure the person responsible is caught."

"Oh, I'm sorry to hear about your mom. Dang, you just lost your grandmother, and now this. Well, I guess I can deal with *el stupido* a little while longer. Business is going well, with the exception of our silent partner feeling like your absence suddenly grants him a voice."

Penny laughed. She was sure any advice or commentary Terrill had to offer Maritza would be met with hostility, no matter what.

"I'm sure he's only trying to help. You should cut him some slack."

"Oh, I'll cut him, all right. Don't give me any ideas."

"Girl, stop. Hey, listen, I've been thinking since I've been out here in Jersey. We should think about expanding and opening up an office in NYC. We need an East Coast presence for Keys and Morales."

Where the heck did that *come from?*

"We should look into it." Maritza sounded excited about the idea.

"Yeah, I'm thinking I'll start running the cost and risk factors when I get back. How did the meeting with Da Stunnas go today?"

"Oh, yeah! You reminded me why I called you. Terrill makes me sick. I prepared the perfect image package for Da

Stunnas, and his A and R idiots are going to ruin everything I'm trying to accomplish. You know how I work. I know what's best when it comes to these things. That's why they pay me, you know… Hold on, Penny."

While Penny waited for her friend to come back on the line, she tried to come up with a sane and valid reason for all of a sudden thinking it would be a good idea to open up a New York office. It made sense businesswise, but Penny knew her mind and her heart were not on business.

"I've got to take this call, *chica*. Listen, take as much time as you need in Jersey. I have things here. Just call your boy and remind him of the *silent* in 'silent partner.' Smooches."

"All right. Later, *chica*."

Maritza hung up. But no sooner had Penny closed her cell phone to put it back in her purse than the melody of Run DMC's "Together Forever" began to pour from her phone. She opened it and sighed. "You know I'm not there to protect you, so I don't know why you're getting Martiza started."

Terrill's soft chuckle warmed her heart, but she decided to remain firm. If Terrill kept goading Maritza, the woman might actually cut him one day.

"How did I know she would have called you complaining already? All I did was make a few tiny suggestions, and she blew up. You would have thought I'd asked her for blood or her firstborn. I don't know how you put up with her." Terrill laughed again, and she could almost see his devilish grin. "So when will you be back here? And should I start looking for a place for Carla in the wonderful condo area where I have my mother?"

"Ha ha ha. Please do not bring up my mother. I don't know what is getting into that woman. Anyway, someone attacked her the other day—"

"Oh, my God. Is she okay? Do you need me to come back out there?"

"No, I don't need you to come back out here. But thanks for offering." Penny couldn't believe how lucky she was to have a friend like Terrill. "Carla's banged up pretty bad. But she's out of the hospital now. Do you believe she won't tell who did it to her? But Jason and I came up with the person we think is responsible. And my father thinks it's the same person. Do you remember that lowlife she used to mess with, C-Money?"

"Okay, slow down, Penny. You have dropped too many things in one breath for me to just let go without at least a *say what?* But I'm going to start with the most shocking one. Jason? As in Jason Hightower? Y'all playing Encyclopedia Brown and Nancy Drew up in that piece." Terrill started laughing again. "Or is there something else you want to share?"

Penny rolled her eyes. "Yes, Jason Hightower. He is a cop, you know. And he's been working the case and offering his help and protection. Because Carla won't just come clean and tell us who—"

Terrill cut her off, full of glee. "So, have you talked with him about what happened in the past? Is that why he's offering his help? I knew he'd under—"

She sighed and cut him off right back. "I haven't told him anything. I don't plan on telling him any—"

There was a tap on her car window and she stopped in mid-sentence as she looked up.

"I've gotta go, Terrill. Jason's here. I'll call you later." She hung up her phone and put it in her purse.

Stepping out of the car, she walked right into Jason's arms.

"I figured I'd come out and make sure you weren't having

second thoughts. You were sitting in the car for a minute. I didn't realize you were on the phone."

Her cell phone started playing "Together Forever" again, and she wished she had taken the time to put the dang thing on silent.

"Just work stuff."

"Your business partner? Maritza, right? Is she holding down the fort all right with you away?" He glanced at the purse with the vibrating, melody-producing phone inside. "Are you going to answer that?"

Penny shook her head. "Nope, the office is now officially closed for the day. I'm all yours."

"Mmm…I like the sound of that."

She felt the heat rise up to her cheeks and felt a warm tingly sensation throughout the rest of her body. "Together Forever" started playing again, and she almost answered it.

"Well, come on inside. I've made you a delicious meal."

They headed into his town house, hand in hand.

His town house was located in West Paterson, near Garret Mountain. The grey and white stone buildings that made up the complex appeared to have been recently built and had a modern design.

It amazed Penny how the sections of North Jersey changed in a matter of minutes, depending on which direction you were headed. The area of West Paterson where Jason lived was a far cry from some of the more urban sections of Paterson where they had grown up.

"You cooked? Oh, my… I don't know about that. As far as I can remember, you couldn't even boil water without burning it."

"Hey, a brother learned a few things over the years."

Penny eyed him suspiciously. "You wouldn't be trying to poison me or anything like that, would you?"

Jason laughed. "Girl, come on in the house."

"Umm…that wasn't an answer, and it certainly wasn't a 'Why, no, Penny, I'm not trying to poison you.'" Penny followed him in the house, giggling at the thought of Jason cooking, and not knowing what to expect.

From the moment she walked into his home, she became more relaxed. Even though the place screamed bachelor pad, it also fit Jason. It fit with everything she'd known about him as a young man and everything she was learning about him as a grown man.

The furniture was sleek and modern, but at the same time comfortable and homey. It reminded her of Jason—cutting-edge but true, fine as all get-out but still down to earth and cool, a smooth player with a true and dedicated heart. The black leather sofas had clean lines, but they also looked like you could curl up and take a nice nap on them. The artwork on his walls had an experimental feel, but it also seemed to speak to her soul. Even the dining table had an artful but still everyday-use kind of feel to it. She loved his decorating tastes, because they made her think of him and all the things she felt about him.

"Nice place," was all she could say as she took in the living room and dining room area when they first walked in.

"I'll give you the grand tour after we eat."

She didn't even want to think about what she would feel once she saw the rest of his home.

The food was magnificent. Jason had prepared fettuc-cine Alfredo and a Caesar salad with the most tender and tasty grilled chicken she had ever had. He had grilled the chicken breasts out on the state-of-the art grill that sat on his amazing deck. Watching him work the grill had an arousing effect on her. He oozed masculinity, and it shot right to her erogenous zones. The way he lovingly prepared her meal kicked her already intense feelings up to something she wasn't sure she was ready to name. So she smiled and figured she'd try to hold her emotions in check and go with the flow.

The chardonnay he picked to complement the meal not only worked well with the food, but also helped to calm her nerves.

"Well, I guess I stand corrected, Jason. You can do a little something in the kitchen. I'm impressed."

"Thanks. I had to learn how to cook something, or I'd end up at my mother's house for dinner every night."

"You could have learned to cook a long time ago. If I remember correctly, you boys would tease me when I would stay in the kitchen with your mother, learning to cook. She would have taught you, as well."

"Please, I tried to get my mother to teach me a few things, and she wouldn't hear of it. She said she couldn't be sharing her recipes with just anybody."

Penny busted out laughing. She could totally picture Mrs. Hightower saying that. The woman was a hoot. Penny knew she would miss her and the entire family.

"It's not funny. I swear, that might be one of the reasons why she'd love to see us get back together. She taught you all her tricks and recipes, and she wants to be sure they stay in the family."

Penny cracked up even more. "You wrong for that. Wait till I see your mama. I'm going to tell her how you were clowning on her."

Jason took a sip of his wine. "Tell her. I bet she won't deny it."

Penny wiped a tear from her eye and held her stomach. She

tried to remember the last time she'd laughed this hard. It had been a while, a long while.

"I love your laugh." Jason had a hooded look in his eyes, and it sent pools of desire to her core.

Her phone started playing "Together Forever," and she excused herself from the table. "Let me get this, or they'll be ringing all night." She answered the phone, knowing it was Terrill. "Yes?"

Terrill had the nerve to laugh. "Girl, you know you can't just leave a brother hanging like that."

"Right, you'll have to deal with my partner on this. I'm out of town due to a death in the family. Please call the office during business hours and someone will be able to respond to your inquiry."

Terrill really busted a gut then. "Okay, I'll call you tomorrow, and by then I want *full* disclosure."

"Right. Call during business hours. Goodbye." Penny made sure she put the phone on silent.

"I can't believe you have 'Together Forever' as your ring tone. Do you remember the summer camp talent show when we lip-synched to Run DMC?"

"Of course I do. I gave up a chance to be in the winning group impersonating Salt-N-Pepa to be with you two, and missed out on my chance to get my very own big trophy. All because you and Terrill both wanted to be Run." Penny shook her head in mock disgust. "When we all know my Run was *way* better than the either of you guys'. But no…I had to be Jam Master Jay because I was a girl."

"Awww…you looked cute up onstage fake mixing and scratching. And my Run put the both of you out of the game." Jason grabbed his fork and got up from the table and recited some lyrics.

"Please." Penny grabbed her spoon and stood with her arms crossed over her chest and her legs spread in a B-girl stance. She twisted her lips to the side and then rapped her favorite Run verse from "Together Forever."

They finished the verse in unison, then broke out in a peal of laughter.

"Okay, your Run might be better than Terrill's, but it can't touch mine."

"Uh-uh, you better recognize!"

Jason pulled her into his arms. "Recognize what? My skills? I already do." He laughed and leaned down just before covering her mouth with his.

If the combination of goose bumps and heat was any indication, her body must have been waiting for his lips to touch hers all day. She wrapped her arms around his neck and let her tongue lick its way to happiness. She moved her hands across his broad shoulders and down his arms.

So many muscles…so little time…

His hands went from her waist to her behind. And as he cupped her ample bottom, she couldn't help but give it a little shake. He groaned and gave her a scandalous squeeze. His firm grip caused her to moan, and her hands found their way under his shirt and fondled his abs and chest.

"Mmm… This feels good," she said, in a voice that was somewhere between a groan and a hiss.

He nibbled her lower lip. "Then don't stop."

"We have to stop."

"No. We. Don't." He started walking her backward to what she could only assume was the bedroom.

"Yes, we do. I need to wash the dishes, since you prepared such a lovely meal for me. And then we need to talk about what's going on with Carla…" The feel of his tongue on her neck and behind her ear made her forget her line of argument.

He leaned her against the wall halfway down the long hallway. Or did it just seem long because she could no longer wait to feel him?

"We can clean up the kitchen together afterward, and I can let you know all about what I found out about Clyde Markum while we clean. Two birds with one stone, and everyone will be satisfied."

Satisfied. Yes.

She tugged at his shirt and lifted it up. It had to go. It was interrupting her view. He lifted his arms and helped her remove the offending object, and she smiled. Her hands lightly brushed over the many hills and ripples, and as she traced his masculine outline, she felt as if she could go on touching him forever.

And she could have, too, if only Jason wasn't ready to do a little stroking of his own. He knelt down and lifted the hem of her dress. His movements were so slow and so focused, she could feel her legs start to shake just from the anticipation of his touch, just from the hint of his breath on her skin. Once he had her dress up to her waist, she instinctively spread her legs and was rewarded with the press of his tongue licking its way up her thigh. When he reached her thong, he seemed content to trail over the material with his caresses for a moment.

The feel of his lips and tongue almost on her sex caused more dampness than she'd ever thought possible. And when he finally got tired of the barrier and ripped it away, Penny could only rejoice, no matter how much the lace thong had cost. It was getting in the way. It had to go.

"I promise, one day we are going to make it to the bedroom," Jason said as he stood, removed his pants and sheathed himself for their protection. "But not right now."

He lifted her up against the wall and entered her as his mouth claimed hers again. She arched her back and tilted her hips to give him greater access. Each stroke of his sex in hers, along with his tongue in her mouth, felt like a mark of ownership, a move in reclamation. She could hardly wrap her mind around what it meant to be making love to her first love against the wall, not when her heart felt as if it were about to explode.

The only thing she could do was open herself. Open to the sensations. Open to the building explosions bubbling under every single one of her cells. And open to the love…

She pulled her mouth away from his probing tongue, turned her head and panted. The palpitations in her chest made it almost impossible to breathe. And the steady, strong, steadfast piston movement of his hips didn't bring any calm. If anything, it stirred the storm inside her to a pitch so high she couldn't imagine bringing it back down. She just rolled her hips and let her pelvis connect with his and gripped his firm, muscular behind with her feet, which were still clad in her strappy sandals.

"Give me those lips back, Penny." Jason licked from the V of her cleavage to her chin and continued to move his hips in and out, faster and deeper.

There was nothing she could do to stop the release of the slowly building tension traveling from her stomach to her heated sex. The explosion splashed forth and continued all the way down to her toes. She still couldn't turn her head as she tightened around him. But she could shake her head, even as her hands gripped his shoulders the way her sex gripped his shaft.

Once her body settled from the most intense orgasm she had ever experienced, she decided to take a chance that her voice might actually work. But when she turned her head and looked at Jason, the thudding in her heart picked up double time.

No... You cannot fall in love with him, she pleaded with herself.

Silly girl, you never fell out of love with him, she mentally chided herself in response.

"Open your mouth, baby. Let me taste that luscious mouth of yours." He had the most seductive look in his eyes, and he seemed so content to just stand there stroking away and bringing her to mind-shattering orgasm after mind-shattering orgasm.

"I could do this all night. I need those lips to finish me off, baby. Give me a kiss. Come on, open for me, baby."

She closed her eyes and tried to block out the feelings stirring in her heart as she pressed her mouth against his. She felt him smile against her lips as he began to mimic stroke for stroke between his mouth and his hips. The kiss became more intense as his hips moved from side to side in all kinds of angles. Her bottom bounced up and down and round and round on his firm thighs.

It felt like the wildest ride she had ever been on, and just like on a roller coaster, she began to get that tingling feeling in her stomach on each trip down. Except this feeling wasn't content to just hang out in her belly. It wanted to put each and every nerve ending in her body on alert, and she let it. Soon she was screaming out his name around his tongue in a muffled and mumbled voice.

She felt him smile again, and heard him groan as he moved in for the kill and sent her bouncing even higher and back down again on his slick, soulful shaft. She grabbed the back of his head and clutched him as her sex wrapped itself around him as if it never wanted to let go. He let out a long and low moan and leaned into her, pressing her against the wall with his hands, firmly holding on to her behind.

"Penny…Penny…Penny…"

Her name sounded like a prayer coming from his lips.

She didn't know when she had ever heard such reverence. But she did know her heart hadn't calmed down one bit. If anything, the aftermath of his lovemaking, and him saying her name that way, sent her heart into overdrive.

How was she going to deal with what would surely only end in heartbreak?

Jason let Penny down from the wall and stepped back. His entire body felt invigorated, and he had a sense of purpose unlike anything he'd felt in years. It all should have been perfect. But as he looked at Penny and realized that he still had feelings for her—feelings deeper than anything he'd felt for her as a teenager, even—he didn't feel the happiness that should have accompanied those feelings.

He'd just made love again to the woman he now knew without a doubt was the love of his life, and he didn't feel an ounce of joy.

He didn't have any regrets, but he wasn't happy.

She pulled her dress down, and without even looking at him, she headed toward the kitchen. That action alone let Jason know she wasn't going to willingly do what she needed to do in order to bring him to a place where he could possibly be happy about their union.

After he got rid of the protection, he found her in the kitchen, talking on her cell phone.

"Call me when you get this message, Carla, please. I don't want to spend the night worried about you. Bye." She hung up the phone, he assumed after turning the ringer back on.

He could tell she was very concerned about her mother, despite the argument they'd had earlier in the day. And he wished he had better news to give her. But after checking in with C-Money's parole officer and doing some more digging on the cold case that had reopened the moment the DNA evidence cleared Gerald, Jason was more and more certain they were dealing with a clever and crafty sociopath. He wished Carla would file a complaint, but even then they'd have to find the man to make sure everyone was safe.

"Is she not picking up the phone?"

Penny gazed up, and once again he found himself almost lost in the copper pools of her eyes. He almost forgot that he was determined to find out once and for all if she had lied to him fifteen years ago. Everything in his cop's instincts said yes, she had.

But what if she hadn't? Would he be able to be with her and trust her again, knowing she'd cheated on him with their best friend? He didn't know if he really could.

"She's not answering. If she doesn't call back—"

Her phone stared playing Tupac's "Dear Mama," and he had to laugh. She clearly had different ring tones for different people, and it didn't take a genius to figure out it was Carla on the other end.

"Where are you? I called Big Mama's line and then I called your cell and I got no answer. You know you need to be in the house until the police find that fool who hurt you. And even then, you need to come clean about who really did it. But that's—"

She stopped talking for a moment, and her eyes narrowed before she rolled them. "I know you're not a child, Carla. I was worried—" She took a deep breath and sighed. "Well, is Gerald still there with you?"

She looked at him, and he could only feel sorry for her. Between Big Mama's death and Carla's attack, she had a lot going on. And Carla being Carla didn't make things any easier. He wished he could back off and not press Penny for the answers he needed.

But he needed them, and he intended to get them. Tonight.

"Fine, Carla. Just stay in the house, please. And think about—" Her left eye slanted, and she hissed before hanging up the phone. "She hung up on me. No, she *didn't* just hang up on me!"

"She'll probably call back. Come here. We can leave these for tomorrow. Let's go to bed."

"Ewwww. Now I *know* Mrs. Hightower didn't raise you to leave a dirty kitchen. You relax. I'll clean up the kitchen. It'll take my mind off Carla, or at least it'll let me think about what I'm going to do. I can't leave her here, with C-Money on the loose. Crazy as she is, she's the only mother I have. I'm going to have to take her to Los Angeles with me." Her shoulders relaxed.

Jason arched his right eye in surprise.

Penny actually appeared to lighten with her statement. It seemed as if at least one weight had been lifted from her shoulders.

"I'll tell you what. We can clean up the kitchen together, and I'll tell you what I found out about C-Money today."

"Okay. I'll wash. You dry."

He nodded, and they started working side by side. The way it was supposed to be, as far as he was concerned.

"Have I told you what my specialty is in the department?" Jason asked. He realized he hadn't really shared a whole lot with Penny about his job, except for the fact he was a cop.

"I know you normally work on cold cases. So, I'm happy you're taking the time to look into what happened to Carla."

Jason wondered where she had heard about him, but

decided to put that aside for now. "Yes, I normally work cold cases. Anyway, your father's case opened up one pretty huge murder case, and I was already looking into it when I found out who your dad was. From what I can tell, there may be a link between the double murder he was falsely convicted of and Carla's attack. The link is C-Money. If it all pans out, then we won't need Carla to testify. There's no statute of limitations on murder. But we need to find C-Money. He's been a ghost. He does have DNA on file, since he was recently in the system, and I have ordered forensic tests that should be back in a week or so. The same DNA evidence that cleared your father should help us put the real killer behind bars, if my hunches are right."

"That's good news. Isn't it?"

"Yes, it is, if I'm right and he's the murderer. Then all we have to do is bring him in. But first we have to find him. His parole officer hasn't seen him since his release. He's been keeping a pretty low profile on the streets, too. I think the fact your father was released around the same time as him has him a little shook. That little bit of time he did for drug dealing won't have anything on what he'll do for a double murder."

Penny shivered. "Carla sure knows how to pick them. Goodness gracious, I don't know how Big Mama did it." She dried her hands on the dish towel and smiled. "See, now we can sleep well, knowing the kitchen is clean."

Jason smiled. He noticed that Penny seemed to be holding her breath.

She placed her hand on her chest and patted it.

He walked over to her and held out his hand. He hoped she was ready to finally come clean, because his good-cop gloves were about to come off.

Chapter 13

While Jason showered, Penny went out into the living room to call Terrill. She said she needed to wrap up some business calls, but what she really needed was a friendly sounding board.

Everything was happening so fast, and she needed some clarity. If she could talk things out with the one person in the world who knew her secret, the one person she trusted more than anyone besides Big Mama and—oddly enough—Jason, she felt like she might be able to gain the courage she was going to need.

Unfortunately, Terrill wasn't answering his cell, and the three-hour time difference meant she probably wouldn't be able to speak with him this evening. She left her ringer on, hoping that he'd call back before Jason was done in the shower. Unfortunately, he didn't, so she left her phone in the living room and took her own shower.

After showering, Penny felt as if she'd cleared her head. Jason had gone above and beyond what he said he'd do, and not only had he found out who might have hurt her mother, he might have found the man responsible for her growing up without a father.

The way he looked at her made her think he wanted something big in return. How could she possibly deny him the truth, after all he had done for her and her family?

Entering his bedroom in the nude, she couldn't help but remember the first time she'd taken her clothes off for him. She'd been so nervous about her first time, and he'd made everything special for her. She couldn't think of anyone she would rather have shared the first time with. And she couldn't think of anyone she wanted to be with more right now. If she could just have one more special night with him, she wouldn't be greedy. She knew it wasn't going to work out for them, but she wanted to take something back to Los Angeles with her.

Like the rest of his home, Jason's bedroom showcased style and comfort. The California king-sized bed was made of the most gorgeous wood platform, with a mix of mahogany, redwood and pine crafted together splendidly in the headboard. The bed, like the man, personified strength, character and beauty. The rest of the furnishings played off the woods represented in the bed. The bedding offered a masculine pattern of bold stripes that seemed to echo the rich browns of the woods.

Jason was sitting on the bed, with his back up against the pillows and the headboard. He wasn't wearing a stitch of clothing, and he looked delectable. She ran her tongue over her lips and took him in. So many scandalous thoughts came into her mind as she took in his perfect form.

His calves and thighs offered just the right amount of bulk

and strength. She got goose bumps just thinking about the way they'd just held her up against the wall and taken her on the ride of her life. As her eyes traveled up his chest and the length of the pipes of steel that made up his arms, she realized she wanted to ride again.

"Are you just going to stand in the doorway, or are you going to come in here and let me make love to you in this bed?"

"Oh, I'm going to come over there, all right." She took slow steps and climbed onto the huge bed. She started from the foot of the bed and did a seductive crawl, wiggling her behind the entire time, until she was right smack dab between his legs.

"But I don't know about letting you make love to me." She took him in her mouth and tasted him. She wanted to remember each lick, each suck, each pull. She wanted to remember the salty masculine flavor for the rest of her life. So she twirled her tongue and savored him.

"Unhhhh… Penny…girl…if you don't want me to make love to you, you better stop what you're doing."

Penny lifted her eyes and saw that Jason's head had fallen back against the headboard as his hips slowly started to move up and down on the mattress. He caressed her face with his hand.

"Penny, let me make love to you, baby, please."

Penny lifted her head. "Nope. You can't do that tonight. Because it's my turn to make love to you." She crawled forward and straddled him, bringing his head to her own for a kiss.

She kissed him hard before reaching for the protection. She stopped the kiss just long enough to cover him and then lower herself onto his shaft. He felt glorious, and she found it impossible not to cry out as he entered her.

"Oh, baby. Oh, Penny. That feels so good." He took her nipple in his mouth and wrapped his arms around her waist, pulling her so close she could barely distinguish where he stopped and she started.

He alternated between her nipples and thrust his hips up to meet her downward strokes. The combination created a quick and almost debilitating climax that made her almost topple off her riding position on his lap. Luckily, he held her tight.

He lifted his head and smiled his disarming smile, and she felt her sex tighten around him again.

Did he just make me come by smiling at me? Surely not...

But she screamed out in release nonetheless, and covered his mouth with hers.

She let her tongue make love to his mouth and opened her own mouth to his probing. She bounced and rotated her hips until she thought she might pass out.

When Jason grabbed her and held her close to him, stilling her hips as he moved his like a hard-striking piston, in and out, harder and faster, she knew he was about to explode again. He called out her name, and his head fell back against the headboard. She kissed his face and trailed more kisses down his chest. Her body was shuddering, and her legs were shaking.

She rolled off him and stared at the ceiling in a daze. She felt the bed shift and figured that he must have gotten up to get rid of the protection, but she couldn't spare the strength to look and see for sure. When the bed shifted again and he pulled her into his arms, she felt those chills that came with the feelings of love and desire mixed to a fever p

His hand trailed down her arm and her ba savored the strength he exuded. How had she n this man go all those years ago? And how would she manage to do it again now? Because it was only a matter of time before everything hit the fan.

Knowing Jason the way she did, she figured his "good cop" routine would be up soon, and he would be back to his tell-me-the-truth and give-me-answers self any moment now. She just hoped she got to spend one more night with him holding her tight before it came to that.

"Penny?"

"Hmm?"

"I know we agreed to a truce until we figured out what happened to Carla, and I know Markum hasn't been arrested yet. But I feel like things are moving really fast between us. And I think we need to talk about the past and get it out in the open, so we aren't taking it with us into the new area we are headed to."

Penny sighed. "Do we have to do it now?" *Can't we do it later? One more night, that's all I ask. Please…*

"Baby, can you turn around and look at me? Please?"

Against her better judgment, she turned and looked at him. His eyes held a sincerity that took her breath away. She placed her head on his chest.

He lifted her chin and stared at her. "Did you love me fifteen years ago? Were you as madly in love with me as I was with you? Was that real, Penny?"

She couldn't look at him and lie. "Yes."

"Do you still love me?"

Oh. God. Yes.

How could he ask her that? How could he expect her to put her bare soul on the line like that? She took a deep breath and tried to turn away, but he held her chin and kept her ̲ng him.

"Yes." Her voice sounded breathless in her ears.

He exhaled. His eyes closed for a few seconds, and then he opened them. She saw so many raw emotions on his face that she didn't dare try to name. She couldn't allow herself to dream big. She couldn't acknowledge she saw his heart in his eyes, love all over his face. She knew he was holding back, protecting himself. And she couldn't blame him.

"You wanna know what I think happened, Penny?"

Did she want to know? Would it change anything?

"I think you lied to me fifteen years ago. I don't think you cheated on me with Terrill. I don't think you were pregnant with his child. I think *our* child died fifteen years ago. And for some crazy reason, you felt the need to hurt me because of it. What I don't know is why. Was it because I was working too much?

"I know after we found out you were pregnant, I started working extra hours and took on a second night shift job to save for when we went off to college. But you were working long hours, too, even though I told you I would take care of things and you didn't have to. Was it the jobs, and the fact that I wasn't there when you lost the baby? What was it? What did I do to make you want to hurt me and lie to me like that?"

Penny took a deep breath. This was so wrong. He couldn't possibly blame himself. It wasn't his fault. It was all her fault.

She closed her eyes.

"Talk to me, baby. I want to know. I need to understand. I know you loved me. You just admitted that. And if you loved me, there was no way you could have slept with Terrill."

"I did—" She stalled and swallowed.

This was the hardest thing she'd had to do since ̲ ̲ told the big lie fifteen years ago.

"I did you wrong, Jason. And I don't deserve yo ̲ ̲ ̲ ̲ ̲ ̲ ness. You shouldn't feel any guilt or blame for a ̲ ̲ happened back then. It was all my fault. I was a horrible person. I'm still a horrible person. There's no going back from what I did to you…from what I did to your friendship with Terrill. He was your best friend, too, and I was wrong." Her words came out in a rush, and her eyes filled with tears. She looked at Jason and saw his face fill with horror as she spoke.

He pushed away from her and got up from the bed.

"You… I don't… Damn… Penny…"

He backed away, and the expression on his face broke her heart. He looked as if someone had stolen his puppy and kicked him.

She had no idea why he was backing away from her as if she had the plague. But she figured it was only right. Maybe he finally saw what she'd known all along. She was no good for him, and she would only ruin his life. That was what his aunt Sophie had said when Penny lost their child. And if she finished telling him how awful she'd been back then, he'd probably take off running. But she needed to tell him the entire truth. She owed him that much.

"Jason, let me explain. Let me tell you why—"

"I don't want to hear why, Penny! That you could do something like that and claim you loved me… I can't even look at you right now!" Jason stormed out of the room and slammed the door behind him.

The floodgates opened, and tears poured from her eyes. Her heart felt a hundred times worse than it had when she let him go the first time. Crying hadn't made her feel any better then, and it probably wouldn't help now. But that didn't stop the waterworks.

Jason went into the living room and sat on the sofa. How could he have been so wrong about Penny? He'd have bet his life that she hadn't slept with Terrill. In fact, he'd spent a good part of his life post-Penny believing that if he ever got her face-to-face and looked her in the eye, she wouldn't be able to lie to him about what had happened. He had felt so close to her when she admitted she loved him. She still loved him. And then she'd looked him in the eyes and said she did it.

She did it.

Talk about a blow…

He ran his hand over his head and closed his eyes. He'd been kidding himself when he said he'd be able to forgive Penny for sleeping with Terrill. That would take more work than he was capable of.

How could he do it? Then he thought about how right she felt in his arms, how his love for her had never really gone away. And he thought, how could he not?

The sound of Run DMC's "Together Forever" jolted him and he saw that Penny's cell phone was sitting on the coffee table, ringing. He picked it up, curious to see who had that ring tone, and saw Terrill's name on the caller ID. Even though he knew it was an invasion of privacy, he answered her phone.

"Hello, Terrill."

"Hey…Jason… What's up, man? Er…is Penny there? She called me a little while ago, and I'm returning her call."

"She's here. She's not available at the moment. But I wanted to talk to you for a moment, if you don't mind?"

"Sure. I guess. What's up, man?" Terrill's voice sounded hesitant, but there was no way he was going to let the man off the phone.

"I just got Penny to look me in the eye and tell me the truth about what happened all those years ago."

Terrill's sigh of relief was audible. "She did? Finally!

That's good, man. I hated lying to you back then. But she was so distraught after the miscarriage. And she seemed to get it in her head that it was her fault and she didn't deserve you and she would only ruin your life. It was crazy, man. I was so afraid for her. Man, I never saw her cry like that. I kept hoping you would show up soon. And when you did and she dropped that big lie and told you to leave… I was so torn. I would have come clean. But you took it so hard you became unreachable. I mean…you said some pretty harsh things to us… Some stuff you just can't come back from…"

There was a pause, and it gave Jason a moment to remember how harsh he'd been to Terrill and Penny back then. No one could have told him he'd ever have said some of those things to the two people who had been the closest to him. But then, no one could have told him he would have been so hurt by his two best friends.

"But I understood, Jason. The way you loved Penny. I know how you must have felt, and I know that's why you said that stuff. So I backed off. But it killed me to lie to you. And for the record, Penny never really got over it. She must have cried for the first two years she was in Los Angeles. It wasn't pretty, man. She never really got over you…." Terrill spoke at such a breakneck speed, it left Jason stunned.

"Whew! I'm glad you finally know the truth. I hope it's not too late for you two, even if it might be too late for us to ever be friends again." There was a hopefulness in Terrill's voice that gave Jason pause.

Jason's head felt as if it were about to explode. The information was coming at him too fast, and there was too much conflicting information for him to process, at least if he wanted sane and reasonable answers.

"Penny looked me in the eye and said she did it. She said she had sex with you."

"Oh…oh…" Terrill sighed. "She's going to kill me, then. Either she's gonna kill me, or I won't have any best friends left when it's all said and done. I guess she's still lying, and she must have figured out a way to lie while looking you dead in the eye. She never used to be able to do that."

"Are you saying you didn't have sex with her? Ever?"

"Never, man. Penny is my dearest and oldest friend, and I love her like a sister. But that's it. Listen, man, can you just tell her I called and I'll call her back later?" Terrill broke off the call.

Jason couldn't believe it. Somebody was lying, and he was determined to find out who it was.

His mind went back to fifteen years earlier, when they'd just graduated from high school and their friendship had come to an end….

He'd come home after a ten-hour shift at the car dealership where he was working, tired and ready for bed.

His boss had needed someone to drive a car down to Delaware and bring another one back. Ever since he and Penny found out she was pregnant, he'd been picking up as many hours as he could.

He wanted to do the right thing by her, and he wanted to take care of his responsibilities. Even more, he loved her and he knew she was the one he wanted to spend the rest of his life with. If a baby meant things would happen sooner than he'd expected, he was cool with it.

As soon as he walked in the house that Saturday evening, he knew something was wrong. His parents were both sitting in the front room. And his mother looked as if she'd been crying.

"Penny lost the baby, son. She's at St. Joseph's Hospital. We had no way of reaching you to let you know." His father's rich baritone voice sounded heavy with sorrow.

Jason felt his knees give out.

Both his parents rushed over to him.

He heard them saying things like "Everything happens for a reason" and "You need to get to the hospital and be strong for Penny." But his heart felt as if it were going to explode. Everything seemed cruel and pointless. How could their baby be dead?

Somehow he made it to the hospital and found his way to Penny's room. The guilt from the thought that she'd had to go through it all alone tore at his soul. He should have been there. When he saw Terrill sitting on the edge of her bed and heard Penny's body-racking cries, the guilt multiplied.

He walked over to the bed with tears coming down his face. His girl was in pain. He had never heard her cry like that, and he never wanted to hear it again.

"Hey, Jason." Terrill's somber voice matched the expression in his eyes.

Jason nodded. He didn't trust himself to talk.

Penny didn't look at him at all. She held on to Terrill and sobbed.

Terrill shot Jason a pleading look. They both seemed at a loss to know what it would take to make Penny stop crying.

"Penny, baby—" Jason started.

"Leave. I want you to leave, Jason. The baby is gone, so you don't have to hang around and do the right thing anymore. It's over." Penny's voice had a gravelly texture and seemed to be laced with pain.

"Penny, I'm sorry I didn't get here sooner. Baby, I'm sorry. Babe, look at me, please…" Jason pleaded.

She kept her head nestled in Terrill's shoulders.

"I don't want to look at you, Jason. I don't want to… I can't be with you anymore. It's over. Leave me alone. Go on with your life and leave me alone."

Her words felt like a hot knife slicing through his heart. Jason stared at Terrill, who seemed just as shocked as he was.

"I'm not leaving. Look, I know you're mad. You have every right to be upset. But I would have been here if I could have. Terrill, man, can you leave us alone for a minute? We need—"

"No! No, I don't want Terrill to leave. I want you to leave, Jason. What is it going to take to get you to see that it's over? I'm not the right girl for you."

"You're talking crazy, Pen. I love you. You're the love of my life."

"I want out of this relationship. I want to be with… I want to be with Terrill now. He's the one I want now. He's the one who should mourn the loss of my child with me. We're a couple now, Jason. Terrill and I will mourn the loss of our child together."

Jason took a step back. He hadn't thought she could say anything more hurtful than the things she'd already said.

Stunned, he grabbed the railing of the bed for support.

"You're with Terrill? You've been with Terrill? What do you mean? Are you saying Terrill was the father? What are you saying, Penny?" The questions tumbled from his mouth in a fast-paced rush. He felt the circulation giving out in his hands, but he couldn't loosen his hold on the bed. He didn't trust what he might do if he did.

Terrill's eyes were wide. But he didn't say anything.

"Yes. Is that what you need to hear in order to leave? Yes. I slept with Terrill and he was the father. Will you leave now?"

Jason let go of the bed rail and snatched Terrill off of the bed. Before he even realized what he was doing, he'd punched his friend in the face twice.

Terrill was down on the floor, glaring up at him, his expression a mask of shock, anger and sadness.

Penny buried her head in the pillow and started sobbing again.

"You want me to leave? Fine. I'm out. The two of you deserve each other, a backstabber and a slut. I can't believe I ever trusted either one of you. My aunt Sophie was right all along. You're both ghetto-gutter trash, and neither one of you is good enough to call a friend." The ugly words caused a trickle of pain to run through his heart. But he couldn't stop. He wanted to hurt them as much as they had hurt him.

"Like mother, like daughter, huh? If I would have known you would become such a slut, I would never have bothered with you in the first place. *The both of you can go to hell.*"

The creaking of the bedroom door let Penny know that Jason had entered the room again. But she wasn't in any frame of mind to face him. She'd spent the past hour tossing and turning, torn between wanting to go after him and wanting to go home. It had turned out worse than she thought it would, and she hadn't even given him her full confession. She'd been crying her eyes out from the time he left the room, and she knew she wasn't done.

She figured if she stayed really still, he'd just go to sleep and she could get out of there in the morning. When the light came on, she knew that wasn't going to happen. She felt the bed bounce, but she didn't look up from her pillow.

"Penny?" His voice had a firm and slightly irritated tone. She could tell he wanted to talk. But how in the world was she supposed to do this? Yes, she'd messed up. She was more than willing to admit that. But her heart was on the line now.

She still loved him. There was no denying it anymore.

"Penny, I know you're not sleeping. We need to talk."

She sat up in the bed and tried to wipe her face. It was no use. She could feel the clamminess the tears had left, and she figured her eyes and nose were a big, red, puffy mess.

His eyes seemed to soften for a moment, but then they took on the same determined gaze of steel he'd had a few days ago, when she saw him at the wake.

"I spoke to Terrill. He called your cell phone and I answered it. And I've been sitting in the living room for the past half an hour trying to figure out which one of you is telling me the truth and which one of you is lying. He says the two of you never had sex. And you just sat here in this room and told me you did."

Penny eyes went wide. "I said I did you wrong. I didn't say I had sex with Terrill. I did you wrong when I lied to you about it. I caused you to lose your best friend. I'm a horrible person, and I know that. And I know saying I'm sorry isn't going to change what I did. But I'm sorry. I'm so sorry."

Jason squinted and leaned forward. "You're admitting it was a lie?"

She nodded. "Yes. I'm sorry."

"Why? Why did you lie?"

She took a deep breath and kept her focus on him. He deserved to hear the truth, all of it. It didn't matter if he never forgave her or he decided to kick her out of his home in the dead of night. It was time to come clean.

She swallowed and twiddled her hands.

"When I found out I was pregnant, I was so scared. I was seventeen and went from having my entire life in front of me to having to put off college for a year, maybe more—"

"You were going to be able to go to school. We were going to work it out so that I would start first. You'd have been able to take classes in a year or two, once we saved some more money and the baby was old enough for day care."

"*We* didn't make those plans, Jason. *You* did. You made all the decisions, even down to deciding we were ready to have the baby, that we would have the baby and keep it. You had it all figured out, and I was starting to feel trapped. I knew I wasn't really ready.

"But rather than be a woman about it and let you know, I just worked as many hours as I could at the boutique so I could save money and have enough before it was too late… So I could really make the decision based on all of my options… I was saving money because I didn't want to have a child just because I didn't have any other choices open to me…"

The disgust and horror on Jason's face almost made her want to stop talking. It was the same look she'd been so afraid of seeing when she was seventeen. She'd known even back then how ready Jason was to be a father, to do the right thing. She'd known he wouldn't really understand her fears. She hadn't been ready to become a mother. She let her fear keep her from being honest about her feelings then; she couldn't do that now.

"I was seventeen and I was scared. And I thought about abortion." She let the words settle. She had thought about it. She didn't know if she would have gone through with it. She'd never know because the decision had been taken away from her.

"I was working hard to save money, and I wasn't taking proper care of myself. Between working that summer job, the stress and fear of being a teenage mom and ruining my life the way Carla used to say I ruined hers, the fear of thinking

I might one day resent my child and say some of the jacked-up things my mother had said to me to my child…I ended up having a miscarriage."

She took a deep breath and started to rub her scar.

The confession was even harder than she'd thought it would be. "When I lost our child, I felt so much guilt, and then I felt a little bit relieved, and then I felt even more guilt about my relief. At the time, I felt as if I had killed our child by working too much and not eating right."

Jason sighed. "It wasn't anyone's fault, Pen. It just happened. No one was to blame."

"I know that now, but at the time, I felt like I was to blame. Then, after I'd had the emergency D and C and they took what was left of our child from me, I had to listen to your aunt— a freaking *nurse*, no less—standing outside of my room, telling one of her colleagues how glad she was I lost the baby, because I wasn't good enough for you and I would only ruin your life. She actually stood right outside my door and went on and on about how the only way a silly little slut like me could hold on to a fine young man like you would be to trap him by getting pregnant. She said she hoped you wouldn't be so foolish and allow me to trap you again.

"She was glad I lost the baby. And then I thought, well, Penny, you're no better. You're sort of relieved. You're thinking, well, I can go to college now. I can have a life now. You're a selfish and awful person. And you really *aren't* good enough for Jason."

"That's ridiculous. How could you even think something like that? And how could you let anything Aunt Sophie said get to you? Why do you let her get to you? Who is she to judge anyone?" Incredulous, Jason just shook his head in dismissal.

But he wasn't the one who'd had to grow up listening to jokes about her crack-whore mother and being made to feel small because she was being raised by her grandmother and not by two loving parents in a traditional family. Saying she shouldn't have let any of that get to her was fine in theory. But the cruel things she'd heard growing up had left scars on the psyche.

Penny rubbed her fingers back and forth over the tiny scar above her eye.

She was through pretending she wasn't damaged. Frankly, it was just too darn tiring. Yes, she had issues. How could she not have them, given all she'd seen, all she'd been through?

"She was your aunt. And she had been making snide comments about Terrill and me from the time we were kids and playing at your house. She always said things to make us feel that we were not fit to play with her nephew."

"But you two were my best friends. And *you* were my *girl.* Mine. I never made you feel like that. *Ever.* I loved you. And Terrill? I would have laid down my life for him. He was like another brother to me. I don't understand why he would do this. Why didn't he try and talk you out of it?"

"But when you thought we had betrayed you, you repeated just about every vile thing your aunt ever said about us, Jason! I know you were hurt, and I know I pushed you away. But hearing those things from you made me feel as if I had made the right decision… That you would have thrown me away eventually anyway, because I wasn't good enough. And no matter how much I wanted to call after you and admit I had lied, I couldn't after that." Penny sighed. She had to finish her confession now, or she never would.

She also had to try to make things right between Jason and Terrill again. If nothing else, she had to do that.

"When Terrill showed up at the hospital, he found me in a horrible state. My hormones were so out of whack, and I was crying hysterically. I guess I must have told him what your aunt said…I don't know. I felt like I was going crazy at the time. The guilt and sorrow just seemed to be beating at me. I do remember I asked for his help, and he said he'd do anything for me if I'd just stop crying. And then you showed up. And I told you to leave, that I didn't want to be in a relationship with you anymore—"

"And I thought you were just mad because I hadn't made it to the hospital sooner. I was working, and by the time word got to me that they had to rush you from your job at the mall…"

Penny sighed.

So much hurt, so many wrongs.

"For what it's worth, Terrill wanted to tell you the truth. He's wanted me to tell you the truth for years. Even after I told the lie, and the way you reacted…your striking him… God, the way I made you treat your best friend… I don't blame you if you can never forgive me. I don't think I'll ever really be able to forgive myself.

"If you'd like, I can leave now. I can go on back to Big Mama's house until I get a flight out of here. I just wanted you to know, even though I hurt you worse than anyone ever could, I didn't mean to initially. I was just trying to let you go, because the guilt was too much and I felt so unworthy of your love. And once I grasped what I'd done, I couldn't figure out how to go back, how to undo it. But if you can, don't blame Terrill anymore for it—"

"Don't blame Terrill? I blame you both! He was my best friend. He of all people knew how much I loved you. He didn't have to even look me in the eye to know how what you said would break me. And he let me go on for fifteen years…

Both of you robbed me of not only my best friends, but the chance to properly mourn my child." Jason let out a hiss of frustration. He eyes showed heated anger.

"Do you realize what that was like? What it has been like to know you lost something and feel the loss so intensely? To feel that you can't mourn because you'd been told it was never yours? I loved that child, Pen. From the moment we took the home pregnancy test in the bathroom at Big Mama's house, I loved our child. And when you told the lie, it became a double loss."

"I know. I'm sorry." Penny moved to get out of bed. She had to grab her clothes and get out of there.

"Where are you going?"

"I'm leaving. You know the truth now, and I was right all along—you hate me, and it's too late for us."

"I don't hate you, Penny. I could never hate you. That's the problem. If I could hate you, this would be so easy. I would have been able to say goodbye to you, to us, a long time ago." He paused and shook his head. "And I don't want you to leave. I said you can stay until we get Markum behind bars and you sort things out with Carla. I'm not going back on that now."

"Do you think you'll ever be able to forgive me?" She realized as soon as the words exited her mouth that it was too much. She had no right to ask such a thing for herself. But she knew the least she could do was to try to right the other wrong she had done. "At least can you see your way clear to forgiving Terrill? He got caught in the middle of all this, and I know for a fact, losing your friendship took a lot from him."

Jason opened his mouth but then pursed his lips in thought.

Penny was glad for the hesitation. She had a feeling that if he was to go with his first mind on this, he'd say something that would crush her heart. And she wouldn't be able to fault him for it, either.

"I honestly don't know, Penny. For the past fifteen years, I've been telling myself all I needed was to find proof that you'd lied. I kept thinking, if you had lied and you really still loved me all along, then things could be fine between us again. And now that I have exactly what I've wished for all these years, I'm still plagued by the fact you lied to me and the two of you stole something very precious from me. The memory of my child, and the right to properly mourn him or her."

Penny's heart broke, and tears started to fall down her cheeks again. But her chest felt ten pounds lighter with the truth out. And she supposed that was more than she deserved.

She nodded. "I understand."

"I think I'll sleep in the guest room tonight, Penny. I need to sort some things out. I'll see you in the morning."

Penny felt a small gasp escape her lips, and she balled up into a knot on the bed. She curled up tight, trying to hold it all together on the outside when she was falling to pieces on the inside.

Chapter 14

The next morning, Penny and Jason went through the motions of being cordial. He gave her a key. That way, if she had to go out and run errands, she wouldn't have to wait for him to return from work to get back in.

The tension of the lie was gone, but it had been replaced by another tension. The truth had done exactly what she'd thought it would do.

Jason hated her now.

Oh, he said he didn't. But his distance and disappointment were palpable. After taking a shower and making a series of business calls, Penny decided to call the airlines and see about getting an earlier flight back home to Los Angeles. She purchased a ticket for Carla, too. She was able to get them both out on a red-eye that evening.

Things were going to work out fine.

She was about to call Carla to let her know she had gotten her wish and would be moving to Los Angeles, when the doorbell rang. She looked out of the peephole and saw Jason's aunt Sophie standing there. In spite of her desire just to let the evil woman go away, Penny decided at least to see what she wanted.

"Jason's not here right now." *Might as well cut to the chase,* Penny thought as she opened the door without so much as a hello.

Sophie came in anyway, seeming to turn her nose up as she walked past Penny.

"Then why are you here, Penny? Are you trying to ruin his life yet again? No doubt you've used your sluttish ways to woo him back into bed. I hope you haven't picked up any diseases from all those rappers and musicians you've been messing with. At least I hope you're using protection this time. Surely you don't need to trap him by getting pregnant now. You must have plenty of other men out there in California who can pay you child support. What about Terrill?" Sophie kept talking as she walked into the town house.

Stunned, Penny closed the door and followed her in. "We used protection back then, Sophie. The condom broke."

"You shouldn't have been having sex, then. And you certainly shouldn't be having sex now. Didn't your grandmother just die? Shouldn't you be grieving, or at least paying attention to that crackhead mother of yours, so she doesn't have a relapse in this time of loss? I mean, really, Penny, your priorities have never been great, but this is, well…" Sophie had the nerve to have an expression of concern on her face.

"Jason's not here, and I don't have to listen to your insults. So you need to leave."

"You can't make me leave my nephew's home." She

paused for effect and puffed out her triple-D chest. "In fact,
I think you should leave."

"I'm not going anywhere. Jason wants me here."

*Okay, that is a bit of an overstatement. But she doesn't
know that...*

"He's even given me a key. So I'll ask you again, nicely,
to leave."

Sophie harrumphed, glared at her and then kept walking,
right on into the living room.

Penny followed her and folded her arms across her chest.

"Maybe I should call the police," Sophie said. "There are
so many family members on the force, it would be fairly
easy to have you locked away like the trash you are."

"That's your prerogative, but I can tell you this much.
There won't be too much more name-calling from you."

"Are you threatening me?"

"Call it what you want, Sophie. But I'll say this, even
though my dear sweet grandmother raised me right and taught
me to respect my elders. I'm still my mother's daughter, as
you are so fond of bringing up every chance you get. And just
how long do you think she would sit up here and make nice
with you while you hurled insults at her?"

"Gutter trash! I always knew it!" Sophie hissed.

"Gutter trash that is about five seconds off of your old evil
behind. Now, keep testing me..." Penny counted to ten
because, no matter how much she felt the old miserable
woman deserved a butt-kicking, she knew she was not going
to stoop to that level.

But she was only human, and the restraint required to deal
with Sophie Hightower was more than she had in reserve. She
counted to ten again.

"You know, you have been looking down your nose at me

from the time I was a kid. You always made snide comments about me and Terrill and how we weren't good enough—"

"You weren't. You little no-class street urchins *weren't* good enough! He picked up all kinds of bad habits hanging out with the two of you. That no-class, common-behind sister-in-law of mine allowed you two to come over and practically become part of the family. And then the unthinkable happened and his head was turned by that slutty little body you started to get. And I know you tried to trap him… But God is good and thank the Lord you lost that baby. Jason's life would have been ruined."

"Get. Out. I don't believe you have the nerve to repeat those horrible words again!"

"No, I—"

Penny grabbed the older woman by the arm and started to pull her toward the door.

"Let me go. I'm going to press charges."

"Be my guest! But you are about to leave here. Now." Penny opened the door. "Get out!"

Sophie's back straightened and she threw her head up as she walked out of the door. "I'm going to tell my nephew how you treated me, and believe you me, missy, you will be out of here before—"

Penny slammed the door in her face and slouched down in front of it. She let out a heavy sigh and waited for the tears to come.

When they didn't, she got up, brushed herself off and got ready to leave before being thrown out. Because she was certain that when Jason heard she'd bodily put his aunt out of the house, he'd really be through with her.

It was time to go get her mother and get out of Jersey once and for all.

* * *

Jason sat across from Joel, unable to believe that his brother—no, make that his *former* brother—was laughing at him. He'd just told him about all the lies and deception his two former best friends had put him through. He'd just bared his soul about how he'd spent the past fifteen years hoping for exactly this and how he felt so confused now that he'd gotten what he'd hoped for.

And his brother was just cracking up. When he finally finished laughing, Joel actually had to wipe tears from his eyes.

"You mean to tell me you came down to the firehouse to tell me you finally got what you wanted and you don't know what to do? I mean, seriously, bro, you have been pining for Penny since she left here, and now she's back and she even said she still loves you…and you don't know what to do?"

"I have not been pining. I have dated plenty of beautiful women."

"Yeah, yeah, you're the player of the year. Blah. Blah. Blah. But you're also on some ole Michael Jackson tip right about now."

Jason frowned. He had no idea what Michael Jackson had to do with anything.

Joel started singing "Never Can Say Goodbye" off-key.

"Whatever, man. I don't know why I even bothered coming to talk with you," Jason said.

"Because you know after I finished laughing at you, I would give you great advice," Joel replied. "Lawrence would just laugh at you and tell you to stop acting like a chump. And Patrick would laugh at you, call you pathetic and tell you love is for suckers."

"Well, when are you going to get to the part where you give out the good advice?" Jason frowned. "I don't have all day."

"When I'm done laughing." Joel burst out laughing again, slapping his knee. "Nah, seriously, bro. Here's the thing. She messed up *big*-time. But it sounds like she did it for reasons she thought were right. She thought she was doing it for you. She loved you. She still loves you. How can you walk away from that, especially when you love her, too?"

Jason's cell phone rang and he answered it. It was just the call he'd been waiting for. He finally had a lead on Clyde Markum.

The man had been sighted a little too close to Big Mama's neighborhood for his taste. But at least Penny was at his town house and not in any danger.

He paused at the realization that he truly cared about what happened to her. He wasn't exactly ready to face what Joel was talking about. But he figured he would have more clarity once he got rid of the Markum threat.

"Gotta go, Joel. I'll see you later."

"Yeah, baby bro. Just remember, I'm the best man at the wedding. I don't care if you and Terrill are cool again. I'm your brother and I'm the one who talked some sense into you."

Jason shook his head and decided to ignore Joel. He didn't know if there would ever be a wedding. And he certainly didn't know if he and Terrill would ever be cool again. All he knew for sure was, he had to do what he could to protect Penny and make sure she was safe. That meant getting Markum.

Penny entered Big Mama's house and searched every single room. Carla and Gerald were nowhere to be found. She had no idea where they could be, and she was starting to get worried.

She was on her way back out of the house, calling Carla's cell phone, when she ran smack into a hard muscular form.

"Seems like I lucked out and found the little baby slut instead of the mama slut. You'll make the perfect lesson to send to that druggie whore and punk father of yours."

Penny looked up into the glaring face of Clyde "C-Money" Markum, and a cold jolt of fear ran through her body.

Chapter 15

Carla didn't even know why she'd let Gerald talk her into going to the Puerto Rican restaurant on Lafayette Street for a bite to eat. She guessed she must have been getting a touch of cabin fever.

Not that she didn't like being hauled up in the bedroom with Gerald making love to her the way he did. A woman could get used to that kind of loving, *real* quick.

But when they weren't making love, he wanted to talk. And when they talked, he wanted answers.

She was tired of everybody blaming her, especially since she'd already confessed to the fact that she'd made a mess of things.

She wanted to make a new start. But it didn't look as if that was going to happen. If it was then God wouldn't have let C-Money get out of jail at the same time Gerald was cleared.

When she was with Gerald, it was easy to make herself believe they could have a future.

But C-Money wasn't going to let that happen.

So she had to put distance between them.

Gerald didn't like the distance; it put him on edge. His being on edge caused him to snap at her and say some stuff you just couldn't apologize for and take back.

So she left his behind in the restaurant and walked home alone. He could sit there mad forever, for all she cared, and she didn't even care if C-Money was waiting at the house to finish the job he started. At least she wouldn't have to deal with Penny and Gerald and their accusing copper eyes, their mean words.

She looked behind her, didn't see Gerald or C-Money and let out a sigh.

So maybe she wasn't in *that* much of a rush to run into C-Money's fist again, but still.

The door to Big Mama's house was open and she knew she'd locked it. Her first instinct was to run as fast as her feet could carry her. Then she saw those fancy strapped sandals Penny always wore dangling, and she screamed.

C-Money had her baby up against the wall, clutching her by the throat.

Penny was pounding at him with her hands, but she was gasping for breath and it didn't look good.

Carla didn't even think about what she was doing. She leaped onto C-Money's back and started striking him in the head and neck. She clawed at him with her nails and raked as much skin and meat as she could.

"Not my child, you asshole! Not my child! I told you never to touch her again." She struck him with her fists, but he hardly seemed to notice. It was only the second time she'd ever had the courage to fight back against him. And she was determined the outcome would be different this time.

She'd tried to leave him when he smacked Penny all those years ago. She'd slapped him across the face and told him he had better never touch a hair on her baby's head again. She'd told him her child's father would come out of jail to see about him if he did.

That was when C-Money told her if Gerald ever got out of jail he was a dead man. He'd smoke Gerald the way he did that nosy snitch couple. And she wasn't going to be able to do anything about it.

He'd beaten her pretty badly that night, and even threatened her mother and her child. That was why she'd decided to just leave her mother's house and move in with Clyde for good. She hadn't felt as if she had had a choice.

But now she did have a choice, and she was going to go down fighting. She'd die before she let him hurt her child again.

He slung Carla off his back and let Penny slide to the ground.

Carla could tell Penny was still breathing, and she thanked God.

The girl was coughing and holding her neck. But she would live. If it was the last thing Carla did, Penny was going to live through this. She picked herself up off the floor and glared at Clyde.

"You are one stupid little whore." He ran his hand across the scratches she'd left on his face. Both of his cheeks wore matching red angry lines. He took a step toward her, but she held her ground, not moving an inch.

He backhanded her, and she stumbled but tried to maintain her balance. The second blow had her on the ground, and before she could get up he was kicking her.

Carla looked up and realized that Penny must have taken

a page from her book, because she'd caught her breath and was up and on Clyde's back, pounding away.

Penny's fist flew and pounded him in the head as her other arm grabbed him in a choke hold. She was hanging on for dear life.

"Leave my mother alone, you bastard! I hate you! I hate you!"

Carla slid away on the floor and tried to get out of Clyde's reach. She was starting to think they might just be able to take him together. She stood up and took a deep breath. His kicking had aggravated her already sore ribs, but she didn't let that stop her. She hauled off and kicked him in the groin as hard as she could, and he toppled.

Penny fell with him, but luckily, she fell on top of him, and she continued to pound him in the head and neck.

Clyde was cursing up a storm, but it didn't matter.

Carla added her kicks to Penny's punches, and soon Penny was up and kicking him, too. That was how Gerald and Jason found them when they burst into the foyer, a day late and a dollar short.

Carla and her baby girl were kicking C-Money's old mean, evil behind.

Penny looked in the mirror and frowned at the black-and-blue ring around her neck. One thing was certain—if Carla hadn't come back when she did, she'd have been in some serious trouble. She went into Carla's bedroom and got on the bed with her.

Jason had arrested Clyde and taken him downtown to be booked. Carla was going to press charges, and so was Penny. And if Jason was right and the DNA proved that Clyde had actually been the one who murdered those good people, then they wouldn't have to worry about C-Money for a good long while.

Penny curled up next to Carla on the bed. For the second time in just four days, she'd come too close to losing her mother. She wasn't going to let any more bad blood fester between them. She hugged her mother the way she'd always hugged her grandmother, the way she had always wanted to hug Carla. "I love you."

"I know. I love you, too." Carla hugged her back and wrapped her in her arms. "I never chose any man over you—"

"It's okay, Carla. It was the past. We don't have to rehash that. You were right. I had a good childhood with Big Mama. You did the best you could. Let's just start fresh, huh?"

"But you need to know this. Now, the drugs did have me trippin'. I'll admit that. But the only reason why I just went on ahead and stayed away is because C-Money threatened you and Mama. And I wasn't that messed up on crack to risk y'all."

"It's okay, Mommy. It's fine. We're going to be fine. In fact, we can start our new lives out in L.A., just like you wanted." Penny hugged Carla tighter.

"L.A.? Chile, please, I said I didn't choose a man over you in the past…" Carla started giggling like a little schoolgirl. "But I'm staying right here in P-Town with my man Gerald. Girl, I love your daddy so-oo much, and now we can *finally* be together. I'm like Diana Ross in *Mahogany*, girl. I got my ole man back!"

Penny sat up and stared at Carla. "Unh…unh… You mean to tell me that you've been nagging me to move you to California since I came back, and now you don't want to go?"

"That was only because C-Money was threatening Gerald,

and you and me, too. Heck, now that he's behind bars, I'm straight." Carla smiled and then touched Penny's face. "Don't worry, Brat. Me and your daddy will come and visit you in L.A. But shouldn't you be thinking about moving closer to home to be with your man? What's up with you and Mr. Po-Po?"

Penny sighed and gave her mother the quick-and-dirty version of how she'd messed things up with Jason, not just once, but twice.

Carla listened, nodded and wiped away Penny's tears when they fell. And Penny felt mothered by her for the first time.

"Well, I guess you take after me more than we knew. You made some wrong decisions when it came to love, too. But, I'll tell you this—if that Hightower boy loves you half as much as your daddy loves me, and I think he does, then you can make your way back from this. All you have to ask yourself is, do you really want it? What're you going to do now? Are you going to run again, or are you going to face your heart?"

Penny sighed.

Why did Carla have to pick now to start giving sane and logical advice?

She had no idea if she was going to be brave enough to face her heart this time. Her cards were on the table, and Jason knew how she felt about him. She guessed she could either wait and see if he could ever forgive her, or go on her merry way, back to Los Angeles.

Decisions… Decisions…

Chapter 16

When Jason rang the doorbell to Big Mama's house, Penny was sort of shocked to see him. It was late, and she was about to go to bed. She hadn't even changed into her pajamas. But after spending most of the evening and into the night talking, laughing and joking with her parents, and after almost having the life choked out of her earlier, she figured she was just going to drop off with her clothes still on, anyway.

Dry cleaning is such a wonderful thing…

Jason stepped into the foyer and wrapped her in his arms as soon as he stepped in. He kissed her on the cheek and inhaled.

"You're not at my place." He kissed her full on the lips. "I need you at my place. We have to talk."

She didn't dare hope that his "need" meant he had forgiven her. But she wasn't about to argue with the man, either. If there was any a chance he could forgive her, she'd take it.

She told her parents she was leaving with Jason, and Carla gave her the thumbs-up.

Once they got outside, Penny wasn't sure if she should drive her rental or not.

Jason told her to leave it, and they drove off in his SUV.

They made it to Jason's town house in record time and with very little conversation. They just listened to the slow jams on the radio and rode.

And it seemed like every song played had a message for her. First they played Babyface's "Never Keeping Secrets." Then they played Stacy Lattisaw's "Don't Throw it All Away." Denise Williams's "It's Gonna Take a Miracle" was the last straw. The soulful tune about how Williams did her man wrong and will never find another man like him made Penny tilt her head toward the sky and mouth, *Okay, enough already. I get it.*

By the time they started playing Heather Headley's "In My Mind, I'll Always Be His Lady," Penny's nerves had almost balled up in knots. She self-consciously rubbed the little scar on her eye and thought about leaping from the car. Thankfully, they were already at Jason's place.

Once inside, they sat in the living room, and Jason just looked at her. After what felt like forever, but couldn't have been more than a couple of minutes, he spoke.

"You scared me to death today, Pen. Here I was thinking you were here, perfectly safe, and you were in danger." He reached out and touched the angry bruise on her neck. "I could have lost you today, and you wouldn't even have known how much I love you."

Penny let out a breath and opened her mouth before she realized she had no idea what to say or how to respond.

Jason loved her.

But could he forgive her? Did they stand a chance?

"I know I hurt you, Jason. I hurt you so bad. And I will never forgive myself for that. But—"

"I forgive you. I love you."

She knew she'd never get tired of hearing that. "I love you, too."

He kissed her. And of all the powerful and passionate kisses he'd laid on her since she'd been back home, this one struck her to her core. Emotions she'd thought she'd never feel again burst forth from her. She felt like she had felt the first time he kissed her.

Wild, untamed and finally free.

He stood, held out his hand and walked her to the bedroom.

Jason had the woman he loved in his home and in his arms. Admitting he loved her made it feel as if a heavy load had been lifted off his shoulders. When he ran into Gerald and realized Carla was alone and could be in danger, he'd rushed off to save Penny's mother. Nothing could have prepared him for seeing Penny there and in danger, as well.

Markum had been carrying a gun. Luckily, he'd been too cocky to think he needed it with two women. And by the time he might have realized he needed it, the two women already had him at a disadvantage. But he still could have pulled that gun at any moment.

The thought of it gave Jason considerable pause.

The fact that the pimp had had the crap stomped out of him by women—one of whom he'd gotten hooked on drugs and degraded for years—was a case of stunningly perfect karma, as far as Jason was concerned.

Every time he looked at the bruises on Penny's neck, he

wished he'd been the one to stomp the man. It was all he could do to arrest him and not use excessive force.

Jason slowly took off all of Penny's clothes and searched her body for any more bruises. There were a few on her back. And as he kissed each one, he silently thanked God they were only minor. Placing her on the bed, he paid homage to every inch of her curvy body with his lips. He couldn't kiss her enough to make up for all the time they'd lost. But that wouldn't stop him from trying. By the time he made his way up her body to her beautiful face, he found that tears were falling down her cheeks.

"What's wrong? Are you in pain?"

She shook her head. "I'm just so happy. And at the same time I'm so scared I'm going to wake up and find none of this is real. That I really messed up, and it really is too late… I don't want to lose you, Jason. I love you so much, and I wasted too much time."

"This is real, and it's not going anywhere. I want you to be my wife. And I sure hope you are ready to be a mother soon, because I want you to have my babies, Pen. I love you, and I want to marry you as soon as possible. So we will have to figure out how we're going to do this. I've waited fifteen years. I don't think I can wait much longer."

Penny smiled at him and let her hand caress his head and the back of his neck, causing sweet seductive chills to cover his skin.

"I'm ready to have your babies, and *so-oo* beyond ready to be your wife. I think it's time for Keys and Morales to open up an East Coast office. I can commute to the city from North Jersey pretty easily."

"Now that's what we like to hear." Jason reached for the protection and covered himself, longing for the day when they wouldn't need it.

But the next time she carried his child, she'd be Mrs. Jason Hightower.

He entered her in one full stroke, and the soft, heated core of her womanhood took his breath away. He covered her lips with his own and started the slow, seductive dance he was happy they would have the rest of their lives to continue.

Penny couldn't help but smile as she arched her back and moved in tandem with Jason's sure and solid strokes. Every time Jason had made love to her in the past few days had been special but this…after he'd professed his love…it felt magical….

She swiveled her hips to match the angles and dips of his. When he moved, she moved, and each time their pelvises connected she felt shock waves of pleasure pulsing through her.

"Feels so good, Jason. I love you so much." She thrust her hips upward and let out a sharp cry. The climax rippling through her body caused her to see stars.

He nibbled on her neck and inhaled. "You are the most amazing woman I know. I'm so glad to finally have you back where you belong."

He began to piston his hips back and forth, harder and faster, and she bounced up to meet him, plunge for plunge.

"Jason! Jason!" she screamed as another orgasm ripped through her.

"You're amazing. You're my heart. Let it loose, baby, and open your luscious mouth so I can taste of your sweetness." Jason smiled, and Penny's heart stuttered in the way she had come to expect every time the man showed that beautifully dimpled grin.

She came apart then, but she felt a startling sense of completion as she writhed on the bed and her sex clenched his for all it was worth. Her climax triggered his, and soon he was calling out her name and holding her tight.

It wasn't too late.

And as Jason wrapped her in his arms, she'd never felt more protected or more loved.

Epilogue

The wedding had been about fifteen years in the making for Mount Zion, but finally Jason Hightower had the love of his life right where he wanted her.

Well, he would, once she made her way down the aisle.

The church looked lovely, all decorated in beautiful bronze and off-white. The creamy floral arrangements had the sanctuary smelling heavenly, and the pews were filled with family and friends. Everything was perfect, except for the fact that the bride hadn't made it down the aisle yet.

Jason glanced over at his new best man and took a deep breath. If anyone had ever told him he and Terrill would be friends again, he'd have laughed in his face.

Luckily, Terrill had been willing and able to stand in for him when Joel got called away to fight an out-of-control warehouse fire in downtown Paterson.

They'd thought about holding off on the wedding when Joel had to leave, but Joel had reminded them of how long they'd waited. And he'd promised to try to make it back for at least some of the reception.

Jason only hoped his brother would be okay and was happy his oldest brother, Patrick, wasn't on call and could be there to share their special day.

Terrill winked at him and smiled. "You're not getting cold feet, are you?"

Jason shook his head. "No, man, I've never wanted anything more in my life."

"He's just scared Penny might have changed her mind and decided she could do better." Patrick smirked and elbowed Lawrence.

"She can do better. There are three other Hightower brothers who are just as deserving of a woman who can cook all of Mama's signature dishes," Lawrence joked.

Patrick laughed. "All you think about is food." His face turned serious. "Baby bro, maybe you should be getting a little nervous. I mean, she is taking a minute to make it down here. And where are Mama and Aunt Sophie?"

"I don't know." Lawrence glanced up the aisle and then stared at Jason with a teasing glint in his eyes. "But it can't be good. See, baby bro, you should have picked me as your best man... No offense to Joel or Terrill. But we are brothers in blood *and* brothers in blue. I can't believe you picked Joel! And then you went with Terrill when Joel got called away. You know I bring the good luck, man."

Terrill just laughed. Clearly, he remembered enough about the Hightower brothers to know this was not an argument he wanted a piece of.

"Who said you would have been the best man, Lawrence?

Please. I'm the oldest. I'm the one who taught you guys the airtight game you need to be able to even…" Patrick started talking, but Jason blocked him out and kept his eyes on the door.

What is taking her so long?

Carla glared at Sophie. "All I know is, somebody needs to tell her to keep her thoughts to herself before I break my foot off in her behind. That's *all* I'm saying."

Penny was torn between helping her mother put the older woman in check and pulling Carla back. She decided to just pull her back. "Not today, Mommy. We're going to have to learn how to ignore miserable people."

"Penny is right." Celia Hightower rolled her eyes at her sister-in-law and started to help Penny with her dress so that they could exit. "Besides, if anyone is going to have the pleasure of breaking her foot off anywhere, it will be me, if Sophie does anything more to put a blemish on the wedding I have been waiting for since these children were ten years old." She patted Penny's cheek. "What do you think I gave you all my recipes for, girl? You have to marry my son to keep that kind of info."

Sophie started to speak up. "I didn't even say anything wrong. I simply—"

"You talking slick! And I'm not gonna have much more of it. This is my baby's big day, and *you* ain't gonna ruin it, you old bat. You need to go on ahead and get out of here while you can still walk. I might be small, but I pack a mean punch." Carla balled up her fists and placed them at her side.

"Well, I never!" Sophie huffed and left the dressing room.

"Well, that's obvious for the world to see. And with your attitude, we can all see *why* you never!" Carla hollered after Sophie.

Penny couldn't help but laugh. She hugged Carla, and felt nothing but joy and warmth flood her body when Carla wrapped her arms around her and hugged her back.

If the love of her life wasn't waiting for her, she might have stood there soaking up her mother's love forever. It felt good to know she had had it all along.

"Okay, let's go and make an honest woman out of me. I've kept this man waiting fifteen years, and I don't want to keep him waiting one minute more." She walked out and placed her hand in her father's hand.

"You look beautiful, Penny."

"Thanks, Pops. You ready to give me away?"

Gerald shook his head, and a hesitant smile crossed his lips. "No. I feel like I just got you. But I like this Hightower guy… So, I guess I can let you go."

"I can promise I'll never be far away. I'm glad you're in my life now."

A tear fell down Gerald's cheek, and he nodded.

Once they entered the sanctuary, Penny's eyes went immediately to Jason's. He was there waiting for her, and looking as handsome as ever in his tux. The gleam of happiness that flooded his eyes when he saw her was something she knew she would never get tired of seeing.

When he smiled and those perfect teeth and that sexy dimple made their appearance, her heart stopped and restarted in a quick and steady pace that left her breathless. She hoped she could get used to that sudden stilling of her pulse, because she intended to keep her man in smiles for a long time to come.

* * * * *

Praise for Edward Bloor's
Crusader

"This novel is deeper, denser and more complex than most YA fare, and serious readers will appreciate it."
—*Publishers Weekly*

"Loaded with moral and ethical concerns, Bloor's novel offers a palpable atmosphere and a fascinating range of undeniably human characters."
—*Horn Book Guide*

"Many sections [of *Crusader*] force readers to address their preconceptions and consider complicated issues—about the way another ethnic group might view history, who the real enemy of civilization is, and what true redemption might look like. . . . This is a stretch book in the truest sense; it will challenge young adults—and you."
—*Booklist*

"Roberta's transformation from androgynous geek to self-sufficient, truth-seeking heroine is believable throughout. . . . Roberta emerges from her war a contemporary crusader, strong and whole and sure."
—*Kirkus Reviews*

CRUSADER

✝

CRUSADER

EDWARD BLOOR

✝

SCHOLASTIC INC.

New York Toronto London Auckland Sydney
Mexico City New Delhi Hong Kong

For Pam, Mandi, and Spencer
In loco temporis

ISBN 0-439-22160-9

Lyrics from the Live song "Lightning Crashes" from the album THROWING COPPER courtesy of Radioactive Records, lyrics written by Edward Kowalczyk © 1994 Loco De Amor Music/Audible Sun Music/BMI.

12 11 10 9 8 7 6 5 4 3 2 1   1 2 3 4 5 6/0

Printed in the U.S.A.   01

First Scholastic printing, April 2001

Lightning crashes, an old mother dies.
Her intentions fall to the floor.

—Live, "Lightning Crashes"

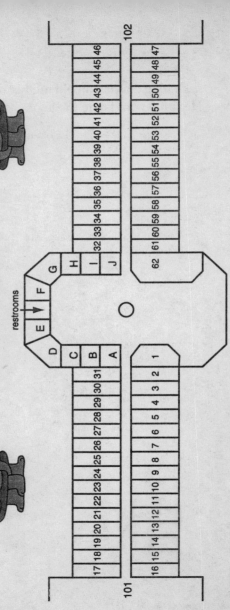

The West End Mall

Route 27 & Everglades Boulevard
Atlantic County, Florida
"The end of high prices."

restrooms

101

102

Specialty Stores

Slot#	Name
32	Arcane—The Virtual Reality Arcade
52	Army/Navy Supply
16	The Bible Outlet
30-31	BioMed Labs
18	Blockbuster Video
17	Body Art
20	
6	Candlewycke
10-12	Crescent Electronics
37	
58-59	Eyes and Ears
19	Family Dentistry
4	Figaro Fudge
7-8	The Gap
53	Gepetto's Toy Store
26-27	The Gold and Diamond Source
36	Guns and Knives
43	Hair Cutz
60	Isabel's Hallmark
14	
44-46	Lombardo's Drugs

Slot#	Name
34	Love-a-Pet
1	Mall Office
57	The Necessary Room
41	On the Beach
50	Outlet Shoes
9	
22	PIP Printing
24-25	Sans-a-belt
13	The Shoe Emporium
56	
33	SpecialTees
35	Sports Authority
38-39	
23	SunBelt Savings
62	
61	Tan & Nails
29	Today's Woman
54-55	Underground Sound
15	Walden Books
5	
48	West End Big-and-Tall
21	West End Dermatology Center
2-3	

Food Court

Slot#	Name
G	Brother's Pizza
B	
J	The Chili Dog
I	
E	El sandwich Cubano
F	
D	
A	The Garden of Eatin'
C	Soft Swirl Ice Cream
H	Taco Stop

Anchor Stores

Slot#	Name
101	Anchor Store
102	Anchor Store

CRUSADER

✝

August

FRIDAY, THE 18TH ❧ I don't usually look in mirrors because I don't need to. I don't style my hair; I don't use makeup. Most days I couldn't tell you what color clothes I have on. Kristin says that's because I don't have a mother to teach me about such things. Kristin is usually right.

I stood in the bathroom staring at my face, studying it, trying to decide if it looked older, when I heard Hawg's booming voice. It was coming from the mall parking lot.

I opened the back door to watch Hawg and Ironman for a moment. What a pair they were. Hawg's burly frame was packed into his red Arkansas T-shirt, the one with the charging pig on it. Ironman was wearing his usual black T-shirt. Either it was two sizes too large or he was two sizes too small. The shirt had a death's-head, a snake, and the word IRONMAN on it.

Hawg was yelling about his one obsession, football. "Whompin' on 'em, man! We was whompin' on 'em. Upside their heads and down. No lie. They'd like to have quit at halftime, we whomped 'em up so good."

I don't know how much of this football talk Ironman understands. He usually just stands there grinning.

I quietly joined them. Hawg and Ironman seemed hard at work with cans of spray paint, red Glidden spray paint. They had our portable TV stand lying on the ground between them, like a patient on a table. Hawg was leaning backward and squirting at the stand awkwardly, like you'd squirt poison at a big bug. I finally said, "What are you guys doing?"

They both turned in surprise, then exhaled in relief that I wasn't Uncle Frank. Hawg answered, "Your uncle told us to paint the Sony stand. He wants her to be red now."

"Really? Why?"

"Damn if I know." Hawg picked up the stand and flopped it over. Then he held up his hands to show Ironman. They were now streaked bloodred from the paint. I went back inside as Hawg resumed his story, "Second half started, brother, and we dogged 'em good. *Whomp! Whomp!*"

I had no sooner gotten back to the bathroom mirror than I heard the same ringing of the bell. I opened the door again and saw the UPS guy standing there in his brown shirt, shorts, and socks. I see this guy at least once a week, but I honestly don't know if he remembers me from one visit to the next. If he does, he doesn't let on. He looked down at his clipboard and told me, "Two packages. Nine hundred ninety-nine dollars COD."

I said, "I'm sorry. What does that mean?"

He looked up. "It means you have to give me a check for that amount, or you don't get your boxes."

"Really? Is this from Arcane?"

He checked his paperwork and confirmed, "Arcane — The Virtual Reality Arcade — Antioch, Illinois. Two packages. COD. Cash on delivery."

I stood there dumbly. I finally said, "We've never had to do that before."

"You would have to take that up with the sender. I either deliver it or I don't deliver it."

Just then the door to the arcade opened and Uncle Frank came in. Uncle Frank used to be an army officer. He still has the crew cut and the military bearing. The UPS guy practically snapped to attention. He even said, "How are you today, sir?"

I said, "He wants a check for nine hundred ninety-nine dollars."

Uncle Frank sputtered, "What?"

The UPS guy repeated his COD story, but this time he told it like he was on our side.

Uncle Frank told him coldly, "They've been sending packages to me for three years now. Never COD. This is a mistake."

The UPS guy suggested, "Why don't you call this Arcane company in Illinois?"

Uncle Frank stared hard at the UPS guy, who got very uncomfortable. Suddenly we all swiveled at the sound of the register buzzer. My cousin Karl had pressed it from up front. Uncle Frank looked at me. "See what he wants, will you?"

I walked out onto the floor of our family arcade and stood for a moment surveying the hardware. We have twelve different Arcane "experiences" set up in our arcade. The less bloody experiences are placed up front; the more violent and weird ones are in back. Each experience costs $4.95 for two minutes of "nonstop virtual reality excitement."

I spotted a Japanese family. They were wandering my way, right toward Mekong Massacre. This was why Karl had hit the buzzer. We don't let any Asian customers have the Mekong Massacre experience. We don't let Asians have the Halls of Montezuma experience or the Genghis Khan Rides! experience, either. Uncle Frank calls this our Asian Policy. Some Asians take these games so seriously that they get emotionally upset. Then they want their money back. We're instructed to tell all Asians that those three games are "experiencing technical difficulties."

I don't personally believe in the Asian Policy. I don't see any harm in letting a Japanese customer pretend to kill a Viet Cong guerrilla, or a Korean customer pretend to slice up an invading Chinese Mongol. Then again, I can distinguish between Japanese and Vietnamese, and Korean and Chinese, and so on. Uncle Frank can't. That's why we have an Asian Policy.

The family wandered all the way around the arcade in a circle, then left, so I returned to the UPS guy COD scene. Hawg and Ironman were back inside now, listening to Uncle Frank angrily growl, "Forget it," and slam down the phone.

I asked him, "It wasn't a mistake?"

Uncle Frank answered, "Apparently not," and wrote out a check.

The UPS guy tore off a receipt. It looked like he was about to say something else, but Uncle Frank shooed him out the door. Then we all turned and looked, with great interest, at the two cartons that had cost us a thousand bucks. Uncle Frank shook his head in utter disbelief. He turned to Hawg and Ironman, finally acknowledging their presence, and ordered, "Wash that paint off your hands before you touch this. It's worth more than you are." Then he asked me, "What did Karl want?"

I said, "Japanese. Looking at Mekong Massacre."

"Did you head them off?"

"Yes."

Uncle Frank thought for a moment. "Mekong Massacre's been marginal for a long time. What kind of numbers does it have?"

"About twenty-five customers a week."

"Is that all? Maybe we should get rid of it. I hate to, though." Uncle Frank pointed at the two new boxes. "But we have to make room for this one. He'll be right up front. And he comes with a promo display."

"Oh, good. What's he called?"

"Crusader."

I walked over to the boxes. Hawg and Ironman, now with clean hands, followed me and began to extract the pieces of the promotional display. Hawg pulled out a jewel-handled metal sword and held it up to admire. Then he unwrapped a gorgeous metal shield with a coat of arms that bore a lion, a snake, and a chalice. Even Uncle Frank was impressed by that and came over to check it out, too. He reached in and unfurled a white linen tunic with a big red cross sewn on the front. He nodded admiringly. Then he said, "Come out front, Roberta. I need to talk to you."

I followed Uncle Frank up to the front register. Uncle Frank and his two children — my cousins, Karl and Kristin — all work at Arcane. Karl is eighteen, tall, and scary looking. Kristin is seventeen, tall, and gorgeous looking. Uncle Frank asked Karl, "Where's Kristin?"

Karl answered, "I think she's out with Nina."

"Oh? That's good. That Nina's a good girl."

Karl looked over at me, sneakily, and rolled his eyes. I rolled mine back. Nina is not a good girl.

Uncle Frank went behind the counter and pulled a green bank deposit bag from the floor safe. He told me, "Roberta, you're in charge of assembling this new display. I don't want any mistakes."

"Okay, Uncle Frank."

"It could be the last one we get for a while."

I returned to the back room and pushed open the door, expecting to see a mess, but the guys seemed to be handling the assembly okay. The Crusader had no real body. He had an open wire frame shaped like an upside-down cone, so large that a person could fit inside it. And that's where Ironman currently was. He said to Hawg, "There's gotta be a metal bar for the shoulders."

"There ain't no metal bar, Ironman. I told you that already."

"There's gotta be."

"There ain't. Now, don't make me hurt you, boy."

I said, "It's probably in this other box." I opened the second box and saw the CD-ROM to run Crusader, and the legend card that explained the experience. The card said:

> God's champion against medieval evil!
> He battles the bloodthirsty infidel
> across the scorching sands of Asia Minor,
> to reclaim the Holy Land for God.

The shoulder bar was also in the box, as were a pair of chain-mail boots and a pair of chain-mail gloves.

The three of us spent the next half hour putting him all together. He was a magnificent sight to see. Those boots of his attached to the base. They stuck out from under the white-and-red tunic, which stretched upward six feet to the broad shoulder bar. A pair of hollow arms, capped by the chain-mail gloves, curved out of the midsection and met in the front, clasping on to the handle of that jeweled sword. The sword and the shield were both held steady by a wire attached to the base. The Crusader was topped by a heavy metal helmet, through which peered a pair of bright blue battery-operated eyes.

Hawg, Ironman, and I were so impressed by him that we nearly overlooked a final piece, a chain-mail collar that attached to the helmet and circled his neck. A series of black links were embedded in his collar, forming symbols inside the gray links. I pointed out, "Look, the collar says something."

Hawg and Ironman came behind the display. Hawg ran a stubby finger over the black links, tracing their lines. He said aloud, "Deuce volt."

I said, "What does that mean?"

"Damn if I know. Some Spanish or somethin'."

"Well, how do you spell it?"

"D-E-U-S and V-O-L-T."

"Volt?" I asked. "Like an electric volt?"

Hawg nodded. "Must be. Yeah. Like it needs a two-volt battery when his eyes stop blinking."

The door opened behind us, and Kristin strolled in. We all turned to look at her. Kristin is pretty close to perfect. She's blond, and beautiful; she's an A student, and popular, and athletic. Uncle Frank is as proud of her as he is ashamed of Karl.

Kristin usually says hello to me when she arrives, but today she was distracted by the Crusader. "Excellent. Most excellent," she commented. "What's his name?"

I answered, "Crusader."

"Hmm." She checked him out like he was a potential boyfriend.

Kristin headed into the arcade, so I followed. A group of young guys were now gathered around Vampire's Feast, watching another guy flail away with the white plastic wand. One of them spotted Kristin and said to her, "Hey, aren't you from Lourdes Academy?"

Kristin kept walking, but she turned and asked him with mock enthusiasm, "Hey, aren't you from Loser Academy?"

The guy took a step back. His eyes registered hurt and embarrassment, but Kristin didn't care. She's absolutely ruthless when it comes to guys.

Kristin looks a lot like the pictures I've seen of her mother, my aunt Ingrid. Aunt Ingrid lived in Germany when she married Uncle Frank, and when she had Karl and Kristin. And she lives in Germany still.

The Crusader remained in the back for the rest of the evening. Uncle Frank was so pleased with the job Hawg and Ironman had done assembling him that he actually smiled in their general direction.

Unfortunately his good moods never last for long. When I went into the back room with the garbage, Uncle Frank was sitting at his desk, frowning and counting the receipts for the day. He never looked up, but he said to me, "Does your dad know he's covering Sunday?"

"Yes. He knows."

Uncle Frank and my dad are partners in the arcade, uneasy partners. He punched some numbers into a calculator, then continued, "So where is the surfer dude off to today?"

"I think he's out shopping for boats, with Suzie."

This made Uncle Frank frown even more. "So he's out looking at boats while this boat is sinking." He finished his calculations and looked up at me. "Do you need a ride home tonight?"

"No, thanks. I'm going to walk."

"No, you're not. It's dangerous enough crossing that road in the daytime. We'll drop you off."

We finished the closing checklist by nine-fifteen and trekked to Uncle Frank's white Mercedes. Uncle Frank also has a silver Volkswagen, which Kristin drives. Karl has a driver's license, too, but I've never seen him use it. We pulled out of the mall parking lot and crossed Route 27, heading for my duplex in Sawgrass Estates, about a half mile east. I spotted two dark shapes on the right-hand side of the road and knew right away who they were.

I said, "It's Hawg and Ironman."

Karl stared hard through the window. He asked, "Can we pick them up?"

Uncle Frank just said, "No room." When we passed them I could see Hawg talking in an animated way to Ironman, who was grinning.

When we got to my house, the driveway was empty and the windows were dark. Nobody was home. Kristin said to no one in particular, "So where's Uncle Bob?"

I said, "He'll be here in a minute."

Uncle Frank asked me, "Do you want to come back to the house with us?"

"No. It's okay."

Kristin leaned over and insisted, "Go inside and check all the locks. Then come back and wave to us. We'll wait."

I did just what she said. Then they pulled away.

Inside I got a Coke and opened a can of barbecue Pringles. I noticed that Dad had left a bag from Block-buster Video on the counter by the door. This was

Dad's way of telling me that he wouldn't be back until late.

Dad often stops and gets two or three videos, which he leaves in the same spot by the door. I never open the bags. I don't even know what the videos are. I use the same spot, though, for my own purposes. I put papers that Dad has to sign there, on top of the Blockbuster Video bag. The system works well.

After a short stack of Pringles, I flopped down on the couch and turned on *CNN Headline News*. I watched the thirty-minute roundup. I saw many different people in many different news stories, but they all seemed to be surrounded by the same mob of reporters. "Jackals," my journalism teacher, Mr. Herman, calls them. "The jackals of carrion journalism."

I then flipped to Channel 57, an independent local station. Every Friday and Saturday night at ten o'clock, they have a two-hour show called *The Last Judgment*. It's hosted by Stephen Cross.

Stephen Cross looks like a statue of Jesus, like the ones they have in the Bible Outlet in the mall. He is skinny, and he has long brown hair and a beard. He even wears sandals — black sandals — with black pants and a pure white shirt. His face, though, is lined and weathered, like it was left out in a desert for forty years. It's a face that has lived a hard life, a face that has sinned.

The choir members and musicians on the show change, but Stephen Cross is always the same. And he always says the same thing. He testifies about his sinful life as a teenager and young man, and he preaches "the gospel of redemption." He talks to troubled teens and young adults — in psychiatric wards, in halfway houses, in boot camps, and in other places where they send bad kids.

Tonight he ended with a familiar quotation. It is the essence of his preaching, and he always says it exactly the same way: "Admit the truth; ask forgiveness; find redemption."

I've been tuning in to watch Stephen Cross every Friday and Saturday night since summer began. Here's why: A few months ago, I had a short, horrible dream. In the dream my dad said to me, "Your mother is in your room." Naturally I went in to look. My mother was indeed in there. She was lying on the bed, just like it was her bed. But she was, without doubt, dead.

I woke up shaking violently, unsure of where I was. I didn't even know if the dream had ended. I turned on the light, half expecting to still see her there. But I was alone.

I dared to crack open the bedroom door. Then I crept out of my room into the living room and turned on all the lights. I sat down on the couch, in that horrible midnight silence. I grasped at the remote and clicked on the TV, just to hear a sound, and I heard Stephen Cross. Then I saw him snap into view. He seemed to be looking directly at me; he seemed to be talking directly to me. When he asked me to kneel down and pray with him, I slid off the couch and onto my knees. I never spoke a word, but after a few minutes

I felt like I had been pulled back from that terrifying place.

In the daylight the whole thing seemed kind of silly. When I told my dad about it, he laughed and said, "Remember, honey, it wasn't real. You should stop watching scary movies."

But I don't watch scary movies. I don't watch any movies. That dream was real enough to me.

SATURDAY, THE 19TH ⤳ While waiting for Arcane to open today, I noticed something: The mannequin had moved.

The mannequin sits in the empty storefront across the mallway, in what used to be La Boutique de Paris. It is always leaning to the right, against the wall the now-empty store shares with Isabel's Hallmark. But today the mannequin was leaning forward, its plastic face pressed against the glass, like it was trying to get a better look into the center of the mall.

So, after months of leaning to the right, why did the mannequin suddenly move?

I walked across the mallway and stood with the back of my head pressed against the glass, just a windowpane away from the mannequin. Now we saw essentially the same thing: Leo, from mall maintenance, had placed his yellow sawhorse, the one with DANGER emblazoned on it, on a spot in the dead center of the rotunda, right where the fountain used to be.

I made a note to question Leo about this. The explanation could be a simple one. Leo could clear the whole matter up with a quote like, "Some kid puked." But there might be more to the story. There might be news that I could use for the mall newsletter, or for my portfolio in Journalism II.

I looked back across the mallway to our slot, Slot #32. It's the first one north of the rotunda, right next to the food court. From where I stood I could see my cousin Karl. He was on the other side of the sliding Plexiglas door, polishing the glass vigorously with a roll of paper towels and a bottle of Windex. Behind Karl, I could make out the dark shapes of Hawg and Ironman.

I heard some huffing and puffing, then I saw an old couple power-walking by. These old people are a common sight in the West End Mall. The doors here open every day at seven to allow the residents of Century Towers to come in and power-walk.

Karl seemed to be waving at that old couple. But they took no notice of him.

Thirty seconds later another old guy came along. This time Karl stepped forward and waved something at him. It was a square white card with big black lettering on it. Karl held it up, chest high, to let the old guy read it. It said YES, WE'RE OPEN. The old guy seemed to notice it, but he continued walking past.

Karl turned around toward Hawg and Ironman, shaking his head. Then he turned back and scanned the mallway like a sentry. He saw something to his left that made his eyes bulge out. An old lady was approaching. She wasn't power-walking, though. She appeared to be window-shopping, like she was waiting for the stores to open.

She noticed Karl, stopped, and looked up at the Arcane logo with a puzzled expression on her face. Then she seemed to make up her mind. She set off, on a beeline, toward Karl and his sign.

Karl started to gesture frantically, with his free hand flopping behind him, trying to get the attention of the other two guys. The three of them watched as the old lady quickly closed the distance to the entrance and then smashed, face first, into the Plexiglas. The glass bowed slightly and then snapped back, like the invisible barrier to another dimension. The lady's hand shot up to her forehead. She stared for a stunned moment at Karl and his sign. Then she spun around and hurried off back the way she came, her hand to her forehead.

Karl was nearly doubled over now, facing back toward the other guys. His body was convulsing, jackknifing up and down in uncontrollable laughter. I could see that Hawg was laughing, too, but not nearly as merrily. Ironman had on a nervous grin, as he always does.

Then, suddenly, they all reacted to the same sound, and the smiles vanished from their faces. Hawg and Ironman backed away. Karl, clutching the sign tightly to his chest, darted quickly behind the cash register counter.

Uncle Frank emerged from the back. He walked

stiffly to the front, like a G.I. Joe action figure. He unlocked the door and slid it along its runner until the three big glass panes were stacked together, like cards in a deck.

I leaned and looked down to the right, trying to spot the lady, but she had disappeared. The mallway was now completely empty. It was the calm before another busy day at the West End Mall.

When I looked back, Karl, Hawg, and Ironman were setting up our new promotional display, the Crusader. Hawg and Ironman knelt before him and billowed out his white robe so that it fell precisely onto the chainmail boots, while Karl crouched behind him at the floor plug. Suddenly the two piercing blue eyes lit up inside his silver helmet. The three guys got up and stepped backward, into the mallway. The Crusader was indeed a dazzling sight. He was tall, over seven feet tall, and broad shouldered. His tunic was pure white, except for the bloodred cross over his midsection. His jeweled sword jutted out before him, irresistible to any passerby.

Hawg remarked simply, "Damn, I know where I'm spending my minutes tonight."

Hawg and Ironman don't technically work at Arcane. They don't have name tags, and they're not on the payroll. They started out as regular customers. Before long, they were hanging out here all the time. At first Uncle Frank kicked them out when they didn't have money. Then he realized that they would work for nothing, just to do the Arcane experiences. Now Hawg and Ironman each get five experiences a night, in exchange for about five hours of work. Depending on how you look at it, that's either $4.95 per hour (which is bad) or two minutes per hour (which is worse). Most of what they do is maintenance, like taking out the trash, cleaning the wands, and spraying the helmets for head lice. Head lice are a big problem here.

I watched as Karl, Hawg, and Ironman wheeled out our big Sony TV monitor, with its newly painted red stand, and parked it just outside the entranceway. Karl plugged its cord into a floor outlet. The monitor flickered on immediately, and its stereo speakers crackled to life with a five-minute promotional video called "Arcane — The Virtual Reality Arcade."

The video showed heroes battling dragons with spears, and battling pirates with swords, and battling space aliens with light sabers, all in very cool, very spooky virtual environments. The special effects were awesomely realistic, with heads and arms flying off, bloodcurdling screams, and pulsing, creepy music. Then the video showed some happy people taking part in the Arcane experiences. It showed teenagers, parents, grandparents, even some little kids, standing in the black plastic circles, wearing the black plastic helmets, and hacking away with the white plastic wands.

On a good day, like a day when a tourist bus comes in, we might get two hundred paying customers. On a bad day we might get only ten. You can't have too many bad days, or you won't be able to pay your bills. That's what happened to Dad and me with our last arcade franchise.

Seven years ago, after my mom died, we moved from our old location on the Strip into this new one at the West End Mall. We used the money from Mom's insurance policy to buy the only arcade franchise in the mall.

Things went okay for the first few years, but it seemed like our receipts got a little smaller every month. The franchisors started to get nervous. Dad told them not to worry about it, that everything was going to be fine, but they didn't see it that way. The day we missed our third monthly payment, they sent two big guys out with a truck and carted away all of our gaming equipment — the tables, the terminals, everything. Dad and I were left sitting here on the floor in an empty store.

That's when Dad called his brother, my uncle Frank. Uncle Frank had just retired from the army as a colonel and was looking for a job up in Washington. Dad talked him into traveling to Atlanta and checking out an Arcane franchise. I guess Uncle Frank liked what he saw. Before the month was over, the two brothers were in business. Legally, Colonel Frank Ritter owns the franchise and pays the franchise fees; Bob Ritter owns the mall slot and pays the rent and the employees' wages.

We've been in business as Arcane for three years now. At first there were a lot of good days. There were even some great days. During one stretch we set records of 240, 255, and 288 customers in one day. Customers were truly "amazed and delighted," as the franchise brochures said they would be. People had never seen anything like the Arcane experiences; they would try four or five of them in a visit.

But then the theme parks picked up on the idea. And then some of the big hotels put Arcane-type experiences in their kids' arcades. We stopped having great days. Still, things were going well enough until the Gold Coast Mall opened just fifteen miles east of here. That has hurt everybody's business. Now it's rare for any store here to have a good day.

I watched the guys finish setting up the displays and go back inside. It was exactly 10:00, time for me to go to work. I left the mystery of the mannequin in Slot #61 for now and crossed the mallway.

I walked in, went behind the counter, and fished my name tag out of the drawer. The name tags are all we wear to mark us as employees. At our old arcade Mom, Dad, and I used to wear uniforms, matching royal blue smocks with big pockets for holding change. We don't need those here. The Arcane experiences aren't coin operated. We start them like you would run a computer program, and everybody pays at the register.

I picked up the phone and buzzed to the back. Uncle Frank picked up with an abrupt and ugly "What?" like he thought I was Karl.

I said, "It's Roberta, Uncle Frank."

"Oh. Sorry."

"It's dead up here. Do you mind if I go deliver my newsletters?"

"No. Not at all. Go ahead."

"Thanks." I ran back out and hurried down to the mall office. Suzie Quinn, the mall manager, was already there, seated at her desk. She was putting on mascara. My dad was there, too, seated in a chair in front of her. He swiveled around and said, "Hey, honey. Sorry I didn't call this morning. I didn't want to wake you."

"That's okay."

"We got a loaner boat from the Sea Ray salesman. Wound up all the way up in Boca." Dad grinned. "Didn't get the boat back to the marina till dawn."

Dad and Suzie exchanged a secret look. Dad and Suzie seem like a couple. They're both tan, and they both have blond hair. But I don't think Suzie's hair color is real.

Suzie pointed to a pile of papers on her desk and smiled. It was this month's edition of the mall newsletter, still in its PIP Printing wrapper. She said, "Here you go, Roberta. The August issue. Thanks for all your help."

I told her, "Sure. I was glad to." I unwrapped the pile and handed the top copy to Dad. I pointed out, "Here's my article, Dad, on the front page."

He said, "Great, honey. That's great. I'll read it right now."

Because I'm a journalism student, I volunteer to help Suzie lay out the newsletter, proofread the type, bring the disk to the printers, et cetera. This issue contained my first full-length feature. It was about Toby the Turtle, the mall's mascot, whose cartoon image appears on the parking lot banners and on all official mall advertisements.

Neither Suzie nor Dad said anything else, so I figured they were waiting for me to leave. I lugged the pile out to the mallway and turned left, beginning my clockwise delivery route.

I've delivered the newsletter ever since the first issue, back in January. Twenty of the slots in the West End Mall are currently empty, like Slot #61, the mannequin window. But fifty-two slots remain occupied.

Most of the people who saw me just said, "Thanks," or "Hi," or "Hi, Roberta." Devin at Candlewycke tried to get me to come inside, but I wouldn't. Devin is a weird guy. He's old, like in his fifties, but he looks like a cross between a goth and a skinhead. He wears black all the time — black hip-hugger jeans and a long-sleeved black shirt. Creepy. His gift shop has beautiful hand-carved candles up front, but it has weird stuff, like Nazi daggers, in the back. No way I'm going in there when it's not open.

Slots #10, #11, and #12 belong to Crescent Electronics, the most successful store in the mall. They started out in #12 only, but they tripled in size and now are talking about taking over one of the empty department stores. Crescent is run by a nineteen-year-old guy named Samir Samad, who everybody calls Sam. Technically, Sam's father is the owner, but he lives in Los Angeles, and he leaves all the decision making in Florida to Sam.

Sam takes courses at the University of South Florida, which is where I would like to go for my undergraduate degree. I try to speak to him whenever I can. I wanted to point out my feature to Sam, but he was involved in a heated discussion with Verna, the mall security guard.

A Crescent employee slid open the door and came out. He had an open can of turpentine in one hand and a brush in the other. I watched as he bent down and started to dab at drops of red paint on the mallway floor. I decided to slip inside, holding up a copy of the newsletter in case anyone wondered what I was doing. Once in there, I could hear Sam. "I'm telling you, this is a racist attack. Whoever did this knew it was my car, and knew that I am Muslim."

Verna sounded puzzled. "Why would they paint a Star of David on your car, though? Isn't that for Jewish people?"

Sam explained patiently, "Precisely so. Yes. It is an insult for a person of the Muslim faith to have to drive around with a Jewish religious symbol on his car."

Verna nodded sympathetically. "I understand that now, once you've explained it to me. But couldn't there be another explanation?"

"Like what?"

"Like it was random. Someone was going to paint that star on that particular car no matter who owned it? It was a random act of vandalism?"

Sam shook his head. "No. I do not believe in random things. Not with the hang-up phone calls we've been getting at the store. Not with the red crosses painted on the store windows. Not with that rebel flag crap. No. There is a clear pattern here. I would hope that you, Verna, being African American, would be sensitive to the racist nature of this attack."

"Sam, if I could see this 'racist nature' thing, I'd be all over it like a rash. But I'm not prepared, at this point, to go down there with you and accuse this guy with no evidence."

Sam exhaled. He turned, saw me, and pulled back, surprised. "What do you want?"

I was still holding a newsletter in my hand. "Here's your newsletter. I wrote a feature in it."

"Just put it on the counter."

I mumbled, "Sorry," and backed out, dropping the newsletter where he had said to. I heard Sam say one more thing to Verna: "I wonder how long she was standing there."

I delivered the rest of the newsletters as quickly as possible, not making eye contact with anyone. The encounter with Sam made me feel terrible, like I was a criminal. And what was the story there? What was going on with Sam's car, and the "racist nature" of something?

I slid a newsletter through the open door of Love-a-Pet, in Slot #34. Then I turned and nearly bumped into Ironman's mother, Mrs. Royce, as she unlocked the door of SpecialTees, Slot #33. SpecialTees is a shop that puts your name or message on different styles of T-shirts, and hats, and sweatshirts. I guess Mrs. Royce doesn't always get the right message on the right shirt. People are always complaining. Ironman and his little sister, Dolly, both wear SpecialTees reject shirts with misspelled words on them, or wrong names, or wrong messages.

I hurried away, completed deliveries to the north-end stores, and came to my last stop, Isabel's Hallmark. I couldn't see Mrs. Weiss inside, so I propped a copy against her door.

I walked into Arcane, past the three guys at the counter. They didn't say anything, so neither did I. I continued into the back room to start spraying helmets.

Uncle Frank was seated there at his desk, looking at invoices. The phone rang, but he made no move to answer it. After the third ring he looked up at me and said, "Would you mind getting that?"

I pressed the blinking button and said, "Arcane — The Virtual Reality Arcade. Roberta speaking."

"I know who it is, honey. This is Isabel."

"Oh, hi, Mrs. Weiss."

"Congratulations to you! A front-page feature. I am going to go hang this up by the register."

"Thanks."

"Did you eat breakfast this morning?"

"Yes, ma'am."

"What did you have? A chili dog?"

"No, ma'am. A Pop-Tart."

"What's that? Some kind of doughnut?"

"No, it's a breakfast food. It has fruit in it."

"I'm sure. Look, honey, I need to speak to your uncle right away."

"All right." I covered the mouthpiece and told Uncle Frank, "It's Mrs. Weiss for you."

He pointed toward the front. "From the card shop?"

I nodded. He took the phone and said, "Hello, Mrs. Weiss. What can I do for you?"

I picked up a can of disinfectant, but I stayed where I was. It was unusual for Mrs. Weiss to call Uncle Frank. It was potentially news. I watched Uncle Frank tighten his grip on the phone, like he was holding a saber. He finally replied, "Yes, Mrs. Weiss, I will take care of this matter immediately. And I thank you for calling it to my attention."

Uncle Frank slammed down the phone, rose, and bolted through the door. I followed him up to the counter. Karl was opening a roll of nickels and placing them carefully in the register. Uncle Frank waited for him to finish before he asked, "Karl, do you know anything about an accident in front of our store this morning?"

Karl looked at the coins, then up at his father. "No."

"You didn't see or hear anything unusual?"

Karl shook his head from side to side. "No."

"Because a woman named Millie Roman has just filed an accident report, and she claims the accident happened right here, in front of you."

Karl started to fidget. He answered defensively, "It might have happened, but I didn't see it."

Then Uncle Frank asked him, with chilling slowness, "You didn't stand behind our door, with a sign that said YES, WE'RE OPEN, and entice her to walk into the glass?"

Karl's head started to bob up and down. "No. No, not deliberately."

Uncle Frank took a deep breath. He asked, "Where is the sign now?"

"I don't know."

Uncle Frank repeated in that same, almost hypnotizing, voice, "Where is the sign now?"

Karl squeezed his eyes shut. Then he reached under the counter, pulled out the sign, and handed it over.

Uncle Frank took it and stared at it long and hard. When he finally spoke, it was still in that slow voice. "Here's what you're going to do. You're going to walk across to that card shop. This Millie Roman is over there now. You're going to apologize to her. Furthermore, you're going to pay for any damages that might arise out of this complaint. Do you understand?"

Karl's eyes were open now, but he was looking at the cash register. He whispered, "Yes, sir."

Uncle Frank continued. "Karl, do you understand that this is the type of behavior that will land you back at the Positive Place?"

Karl looked up. The fear was visible in his face. He answered, "Yes, sir."

"And do you want to go back to the Positive Place?"

"Oh no, sir."

When Uncle Frank spoke again, it was in his normal voice. "Did you miss a medication today?"

"No, sir."

"No? Are you sure?"

Karl nodded. Uncle Frank studied the back of the sign. He said. "I wish you had. I wish I had some simple reason to hang this on. I wish to god I did."

"Yes, sir."

"Now, get over there and apologize to that poor woman. Roberta, you go, too, and see that he does."

Karl shambled around the counter and out into the mallway before I could react. I ran behind him, catching up just as he reached the entrance to Isabel's Hallmark. He cocked his head to the left and right, looking for the old lady.

I spotted her first. She was sitting on a chair behind the cash register counter. Mrs. Weiss was standing next to her, waiting. I touched Karl on the arm and pointed to them. He strode directly to the counter, put both hands on it, and shouted, "I'm sorry!" Then he spun around on his heel and stalked out.

The old lady looked like she had just been hit again. Mrs. Weiss put a comforting hand on her shoulder. Her other hand pointed up at me. She said, "Millie, this is Roberta Ritter. Roberta, this is Millie Roman."

The old lady, Mrs. Roman, looked up at me with a wary expression. I said, "It's nice to meet you, Mrs. Roman. I'm sorry about what Karl did. Please don't take it personally. He's like this for medical reasons."

Mrs. Weiss quickly picked up on this theme. "That's right. That's exactly right. It's medical. If it hadn't been you, Millie, it would have been the next person along. He was just set to blow." Mrs. Weiss looked at me. "Roberta, what is wrong with that boy?"

"I don't really know, Mrs. Weiss."

"Has he always behaved this way?"

"I've only known him for three years. He's been like this for three years."

"What's wrong with his face? Is that a rash?"

"No, I think that's just what his skin looks like, Mrs. Weiss. He's had that bad skin for at least three years, too."

Mrs. Roman spoke up. "He shouldn't eat potato chips. Those are very greasy."

Mrs. Weiss and I both looked at her, waiting, but she didn't say anything else. I finally said, "Sorry, Mrs. Weiss, but I really need to get back."

"Oh, of course, honey. You go on. Are you coming to the cemetery tomorrow?"

"Yes, ma'am." I said to the old lady, "It was nice to meet you, Mrs. Roman." But she didn't respond.

Uncle Frank asked, "Did Karl apologize okay?"

"Yes, sir. He did it."

"Good. That's good." Uncle Frank shook his head, slowly and sadly. "You know, Roberta, the doctors have been telling me since Karl was seven years old that he's going to outgrow this. Well, it hasn't happened yet. I'd hate like hell to send him back to that Positive Place. I know they scared the pants off him there, but it just might be what he needs. I don't know."

I wanted to answer Uncle Frank, but I couldn't think of anything to say. I know that Karl has ADHD. And I know what the letters stand for, attention deficit hyperactivity disorder. But that's about it.

Suddenly Uncle Frank's eyes brightened. He said, "Hi, Kitten." I turned and saw that Kristin had arrived.

Uncle Frank calls Kristin "Kitten." He calls Karl "Karl." Then I watched Uncle Frank's eyes veer off to follow someone behind me, entering the arcade. He whispered, "AAs, Roberta."

AA is the code for African Americans. We also use an A-code for Asians and an S-code for Spanish, any type of Spanish. We should probably have a code for Native Americans, too, in case they get too close to Custer's Last Stand, but we don't.

I looked toward the back and saw an African American father and son. They were getting dangerously close to King Kong, an experience in which you battle prehistoric dinosaurs and spear-carrying natives. I said, "I'll take care of it."

Uncle Frank mumbled to me, "The dad looks like he might be a vet. See if you can steer him to the Halls of Montezuma."

"Okay." As I closed in on them, I saw what Uncle Frank meant. The dad had muscles, very good posture, and a shaved head.

But before I could say anything, his kid noticed Galactic Defender. It's one of our most popular space-alien experiences. He decided. "Daddy, I want to do this one."

I said, "Can I help you, sir?"

The dad pointed a big finger at Galactic Defender. "What happens in this one?"

"You fight space aliens."

"Uh-huh. Is it real bloody?"

"No, sir. I don't think the aliens even have blood."

"Okay. Let's do it." I opened the black plastic circle and helped the kid step up onto the round platform within it. Then I picked up the electronic wand from its sheath, stretched out the wire, and handed it to him, saying, "Squeeze this handle at the bottom whenever you want to slice. Otherwise you'll just be hitting them and they won't die."

The kid said, "Okay." I helped him put on the helmet, adjusted the viewer over his eyes, and stepped out of the circle, clicking it shut. I ripped out a ticket from my book and handed it to the dad. "You pay up front."

I keyed in a code and announced, "Here we go." The kid crouched down, ready for battle. As he struck out against the first wave of aliens, the dad asked, "What's that King Kong game like?"

"That's currently experiencing technical difficulties."

"Oh? What kind of technical difficulties?"

"Software."

That seemed to satisfy him.

I changed the subject. "Sir, were you a veteran?"

"Pardon?"

"Were you in the Marines? Or the army or navy or anything?"

"No, I wasn't. Why do you ask?"

"Well, if you were, the Halls of Montezuma is pretty good."

"Yeah? Who do you fight in that one?"

"The Japanese."

He looked at me questioningly. "Is that right? Because, you know, the Halls of Montezuma, the real ones, are in Mexico."

"Uh, no, I didn't know that."

"And the shores of Tripoli, of course, are in Africa."

"The what?"

"It's the second line of the Marine Corps song: *From the Halls of Montezuma to the shores of Tripoli.*"

"Uh, no, I didn't know that, either."

We stood in silence for a few seconds, watching the kid hack against the black plastic ring. Then the dad said, "But if it's a Marine thing, you're probably right. You're probably fighting the Japanese in World War Two. Maybe on Iwo Jima. Or Guadalcanal."

I shook my head and pretended to check my ticket book. Finally the kid's two minutes were up. I opened the ring and helped him step down. The dad said, "How was it?"

The kid's eyes sparkled. "I killed six aliens."

"Cool."

"Can I do it again?"

"No." The dad turned to me and smiled. "Thank you, now."

They walked up toward the counter to pay. I stood there feeling stupid.

I took my break at three and walked around the corner into the food court. As usual, I checked out the first slot on the right, the Chili Dog. I eat there as often as I can, depending on who is at the counter. If it's Gene, the owner, I get something. If it's Betty the Goth, I keep on walking, either to the Taco Stop or to El sandwich cubano.

Betty the Goth is short and thin and as white as a zombie. She dyes her hair with a black dye like shoe polish. She paints her nails black; she uses black lipstick; she wears nothing but black. She makes it really hard to think about food.

Fortunately Gene was behind the counter, so I ordered a Coney Island dog. Gene likes to pump me for information about the mall. A lot of the owners do that. They figure I have the inside scoop because (1) I write for the newsletter, and (2) my dad is dating Suzie Quinn, the mall manager.

Gene asked, "So how's business, Roberta?"

I said, "A little slow." No one at the West End Mall ever admits they're doing well. "How about you, Gene?"

"It stinks." Gene speared a twelve-inch hot dog and put it on a ten-inch bun. "Hey, I heard the Shoe Emporium is pullin' out. Is that true?"

"No. It's Outlet Shoes, the one in Slot Number Thirteen."

"Is that right? What're they gonna do?"

"They're trying to refinance their loan so they can move to the Gold Coast Mall."

"Ha! Fat chance. Hey, I just had a gig at the Gold Coast Mall. They had one of those celebrity look-alike days. Guess who I was."

"I don't know. The Cat in the Hat?"

"What? No. These were real people."

"I don't know, Gene."

"Okay. Okay. I was Oliver Hardy. There was supposed to be another guy there, and we were going to be Laurel and Hardy, but he never showed."

"I don't know who that is."

"No? The fat guy and the skinny guy? They were very funny comics, a long time ago?"

"Sorry."

"Well, I was the fat guy. Now I gotta find a new skinny guy to work with. I oughta do the act here. The old people would know who Laurel and Hardy were. It'd go over better here than at the Gold Coast Mall." Gene dipped into the chili pot and ladled some onto my Coney Island dog.

I said, "That's plenty. I'll see you later, Gene."

When I got back from break Kristin was behind the counter. She muttered, "Pinheads at ten o'clock." Pinheads is her name for skinheads.

I looked to the left and saw who she meant — two white guys with shaved heads. They were wearing green army fatigues and high boots. One was doing the

Viking Raid experience; the other was watching him. They were both really into it. The guy in the circle was grunting and screaming with each swat of the wand. The other guy was cracking up, laughing and carrying on with a big, green-toothed grin.

Uncle Frank stuck his head out of the back to see what was going on. He came out and stood by them, but he didn't say anything. When the time was up, Uncle Frank helped the first guy down. The green-teeth guy said to him, "Hey, did you ever hear of White Riot?"

Uncle Frank looked surprised, like he didn't think the guy could speak. He answered, "No. Is it an Arcane experience?"

The guy paused for a second, and straightened up. He answered, "Yes, sir. They got it up in Atlanta. It's awesome."

The first guy added, "Awesome, man. Ultraviolent."

Uncle Frank said, "Well, they have a lot of things in Atlanta that we don't have down here. We're a much smaller operation."

The green-teeth guy said, "You oughta get it." Then he added, "Sir."

Uncle Frank examined the helmet carefully for lice. "I oughta do a lot of things." He regarded the guy warily. "What's this White Riot about? Who do you fight in it?"

"The Mud People, sir. You eliminate as many Mud People as possible in ten minutes."

Uncle Frank thought about this. Then he asked, "Ten minutes? You mean two minutes?"

"No, sir. Ten minutes."

"For how much?"

"Sir?"

"How much do you pay? Is it twenty-five dollars for ten minutes?"

The first guy answered, "You pay for the party, man, then you're in. You do whatever you want." He turned to Green Teeth. "It's, like, forty bucks a head, right?"

"Right. Sometimes, if they got a really primo experience, a real hardcore one, it's fifty bucks. But once you pay, that's it. You can rock all night."

Uncle Frank seemed genuinely disturbed by this, the way he gets if Karl doesn't follow the opening or closing checklists. He asked, "How can they do that? They're in a mall like we are?"

"Yes, sir. They are. But the mall closes at nine, and the party doesn't start until nine-thirty."

"And what are these hardcore experiences you're talking about?"

"It's like the ones you got here, but the violence is much more primo. And let's just say, sir, it's a lot clearer who the enemy is."

Uncle Frank looked appalled. "Is that what this White Riot thing is about?"

The first guy practically shouted, "No, man! White Riot's not even hardcore. It's PG compared to some of them. Ever hear of Lynch Mob? Or Stormtrooper?"

Apparently Uncle Frank decided right then that guy's helmet needed delousing. He marched into the back with it without another word. The pinheads watched him go, then they walked up to the register. The guy who had done the experience handed his ticket to me. The other one asked Kristin, "Did you ever hear of Stormtrooper?"

Kristin regarded him coldly. "Did you ever hear of toothpaste?"

It turned into a busy Saturday night. Some goth kids came in and hung around Vampire's Feast. More pinheads came in; they stood in a noisy circle around King Kong. And, of course, the Head Louse arrived.

The Head Louse is a stocky guy, like Hawg. And he has a crew cut, like Hawg. But he also has long blond hairs hanging from the sides of his head down over his neck. Kristin named him the Head Louse because, she suspects, he doesn't wash that long hair very often.

Like a lot of the guys in the arcade, he's always looking at Kristin. And when he wants a ticket, he always seeks her out.

Thanks to Crusader, we had our first big day in months. Our shiny new knight attracted fifty customers all by himself, for a total of $250.

Dad dropped me off at home at ten, saying, "I'm going to Suzie's, honey, but I'll be back early."

I did some homework, and then I tuned in to *The Last Judgment*. Stephen Cross, as he often does, got right up to the camera lens and spoke directly to me. His head was so close, and the backlighting was so intense, that he looked like a talking skull. It made me feel very creepy, and very alone.

I clicked off the TV and went into my room. I went to sleep with the light on, hoping it would keep me from dreaming. It didn't work.

In this dream, I was sitting on a plastic chair against a wall in a hospital emergency room. I was watching a group of doctors and nurses in blue masks and blue scrubs. They were gathered around a bloody patient on a high stretcher, working furiously.

A policewoman walked over to me and said, "What are you doing here? You're too young to be in here by yourself."

I pointed to the patient on the stretcher. I answered, "My mom. She had a heart attack." The policewoman started to write that down in a notebook. But she stopped when a doctor turned away from his work, looked at us, and said, "No she didn't. You're lying again."

Then I woke up.

SUNDAY, THE 20TH ❧ Dad still wasn't in when I walked out to get the Sunday paper. I read it over breakfast, a Pop-Tart, before taking a quick shower and getting dressed. Then I put a folder on top of the Blockbuster Video bag. It contained a permission form for a field trip I'm very excited about. My journalism class is going to visit a TV newsroom. I hope to see the kind of job that I'll be doing one day.

I still had some time to spare, so I switched on the local news. I switched it right off, though, when the weather came on. I can't understand why there are more than ten seconds of airtime devoted to weather. Today they said, "There's a thirty-percent chance of rain," which was ridiculous. They must announce that every day to fool the tourists.

The fact is, there is a two-hundred-percent chance of rain every day during the rainy season, which is now. It will definitely rain twice — around eleven A.M. and around four P.M. Twice a day, every day, a storm like the end of the world hits. Huge black thunderheads, as tall as skyscrapers, rumble in from the west, from the Everglades. They pelt us with rain, like from huge fire hoses. It happens like that every day, twice a day.

Because of that, I always time my walk to reach the mall before eleven o'clock. Today I was hoping Dad would stop by and give me a ride. It is a short walk to the mall — two blocks down to Everglades Boulevard and then about a quarter mile west to Route 27 — but there aren't any sidewalks.

By ten o'clock, though, I had to figure he wasn't coming. I locked up and set off.

I was sweating by the time I got to Everglades Boulevard. Before I turned right, I noticed two familiar bodies coming up from 110th Street. Hawg seemed to be demonstrating some kind of football move to Ironman. All I could hear was "Whomp! Whomp!" I stood on the corner and waited.

Hawg called out to me, "Roberta, your daddy ain't bailin' on us today, is he? 'Cause I count on him bein' there on Sunday. Sunday's our day of rest. Right, Ironman?"

Ironman grinned nervously. I could see that both these guys still had on yesterday's T-shirts. In the harsh morning sun, the black made Ironman's face look even more shriveled and pasty; the dark red made Hawg's look rounder, and made his pimples look more erupted.

Hawg continued, "What if your daddy didn't show up? Would we have to call your uncle?"

"Yeah, I guess so. Somebody'd have to open the safe."

"Damn!" Hawg pointed at Ironman. "If that happens, we head up to Crescent and watch football. I need a day of rest."

Ironman said, "They won't let us into Crescent."

"I know. That damn A-rab'll kick us out. He hates my guts. No lie. But we don't need to go in. We can watch through the window." He suddenly turned to me. "Roberta, did you see the Hawgs last night? On ESPN? They whomped up on Ole Miss real good."

"No. I never watch sports. Or weather."

"You missed it last night. They ran that power-I right down their throats. Them Mississippi boys was roadkill." Hawg turned back to Ironman, assuming I wasn't interested. He told him, "That's what I love to play, the power-I. They don't do that down here. They run that damn pro-set all the time. But in the power-I, the center is the main man."

I asked, "What does all that mean? What's a power-eye? Is it like a telescope?"

Hawg stopped still. He looked at me like I had just asked what planet we were on. But then he seemed pleased to be able to explain, "A power-I, my darlin', is a football formation. The center — which is me — the quarterback, the fullback, and the tailback all line up in a straight line, like a letter I. It's smash-mouth Southern football at its finest."

We reached the intersection of Everglades Boulevard and Route 27. Route 27 is a four-lane highway with a thin grass median. It was once the western end of Atlantic County, and of civilization, until the Lyons Group built the West End Mall and Century Towers.

I stopped and checked the traffic to the south. Suddenly, Hawg spun around and yelled, "Here's how she works, Roberta!" He looked around him at some imaginary teammates. "The center hears the play and the count. Then he breaks the huddle." Hawg clapped his hands together once and spun around, like he was doing a comical dance step. "He leads 'em all up to the line." He strode forward three paces, to the edge of the highway, and crouched down with his rear end facing us. "He snaps the ball, and he fires out!" With this, Hawg exploded out of his crouch like he had been shot from a cannon. He sprinted blindly, faster than I ever thought he could, running recklessly across all four lanes, and into the mall parking lot, where he slowed and stopped.

A white station wagon in the northbound lane, and a U-Haul truck in the southbound lane, whizzed by right after Hawg's sprint. The truck leaned on its horn. I waited with Ironman while a stream of other vehicles raced by. I asked, "Does he do that a lot?"

Ironman grinned nervously. "I've seen him do it before. When he's showing off for somebody."

"Why would he show off for me?"

"I don't know. People don't usually ask him to explain football stuff like you did."

We waited until the light changed, and crossed to the parking lot. Hawg yelled out to Ironman, "Hey! What took you girls so long?"

We walked together across the nearly empty parking lot, toward the tall glass doors of the mall entrance. It was already hot, Florida-asphalt hot, and the parking lot was a shimmering mirage. I noticed Dad's Chevy Malibu parked next to Suzie's Miata. Hawg noticed it, too. He looked at me and pumped his fist. "All right! Won't need to watch Mr. A-rab's damn TV today!"

We parted company at the mall office. Suzie was already seated behind her desk. She had Dad's copy of the newsletter in front of her, and she didn't look happy. She snapped at me right away, "Roberta, what is this turtle thing that you wrote?"

I sat in one of the two seats in front of her desk and looked at her, confused. I finally said, "You know. It's the feature you asked me to write. About the mall's mascot."

Her mascara'd eyes narrowed. "Roberta, this is not the feature I asked you to write. I asked you to write up something about how Toby the Turtle came to be our mascot." She held out both hands toward me, as if they contained a crystal ball. She spoke like she was seeing back into the past. "There was a contest. Hundreds of kids entered this contest. One kid sent in the name Toby the Turtle and a cute drawing of a turtle. That kid won the contest. End of story."

I sat up. "No, that's not the end of the story. And that's not the real story."

My dad came in with two Danish pastries. He walked around behind the desk and handed one to Suzie.

I told them both, "Ten years ago this area was a big turtle habitat. Hundreds of alligator snapping turtles lived here. An environmental group from Brevard County called Save the Turtles got an injunction against the Lyons Group and stopped the bulldozers from rolling and from plowing them all under. It was a big news story."

Dad said, "I never knew about that."

At that moment I realized that Dad hadn't read my feature after all. I answered, "Mr. Lyons agreed to donate another parcel he owned as a wildlife sanctuary. The environmental group rejected the offer, but an Atlantic County judge overruled them. One day later the bulldozers started to roll. They entombed all those turtles."

Dad said, "That's awful."

Suzie slammed her pastry down on the desk, scattering crumbs. She rounded on Dad. "Will you help me out here, please? I have to explain to Mr. Lyons why we're digging up some ten-year-old dead turtles in his newsletter when we're supposed to be spreading positive news about the West End Mall!"

Dad looked from Suzie to me. He finally said,

"Well, Roberta, I guess what Suzie is saying is that this turtle business is really water under the bridge. You know? Part of the past. The newsletter is strictly for good stuff."

Suzie interrupted. "Strictly for good stuff, from now on. And from now on, Roberta, I need to see every word that you write before it goes into the newsletter. Do you understand?"

I meekly said, "Yes."

Suzie wiped up the crumbs on her desk and dumped them into the wastebasket. Then she took a deep breath, stretched her lips around to her ears, and smiled. She said, "Good. I appreciate your help on the newsletter. You know that. But Mr. Lyons is very sensitive about this turtle stuff. Especially since he's running for the state senate. He could read this at the wrong time, on the wrong day, and I'd be fired on the spot."

Something outside the glass caught Suzie's attention. She said quickly to Dad and me, "Oh no! I forgot about the steering committee meeting."

The door opened behind us, and I turned to see Sam and Mr. Lombardo. Mr. Lombardo is a real old guy, about seventy-five, and he looks it. He owns the drugstore in Slots #44 through 46. He, Sam, and Suzie make up the steering committee of the West End Retailers Association.

Sam said, "This is going to be a quick one. Right, Suzie?"

Suzie smiled. "Right. It should take about five minutes."

Mr. Lombardo demanded, "Is this about the fall slogan?"

Suzie tensed up. "No, Mr. Lombardo, as I told you on the phone, this is about capital improvements. We need to approve the funds for the new fountain."

"What fountain?"

"In the rotunda."

"There's no fountain in the rotunda. There's just a bunch of loose tiles lying out there, waiting to trip somebody."

"There is a fountain under the tiles, Mr. Lombardo. There always has been. You've been here long enough to remember it. They say it was a very beautiful fountain, and we now want to bring it back to life."

Mr. Lombardo held up his newsletter. "I want to talk about this slogan." He pointed a long finger at the banner headline above and to the left of my turtle feature.

Sam protested, "I'm here to talk about capital improvements."

But Mr. Lombardo ignored him. "'Fall in the Mall.' What kind of cockamamy slogan is that? 'Fall in the Mall.' Like, 'Come in here and pretend to slip on a floor tile and sue us'? 'Take what little money we have left'?"

Sam rolled his eyes.

Suzie explained, as if to a child, "Mr. Lombardo, I think you know that the slogan means it's *fall* in the mall. Like *autumn*. Except that *autumn* doesn't rhyme with *mall*, but *fall* does."

"I don't care if it rhymes. It stinks."

"You're entitled to your opinion, Mr. Lombardo. It

happens to be the same slogan the Gold Coast Mall used last year, and I don't recall that they had any lawsuits."

"No. They didn't have loose tiles piled up in their walkway, either, I'll bet."

"Mr. Lombardo, we are fixing the floor. We are making capital improvements to the rotunda. Do you understand that? We're restoring its beautiful fountain. People are going to remember that fountain, and they're going to want to come back to the West End Mall to enjoy another look at it."

Mr. Lombardo looked at Sam. He said, "Great. Maybe they'll throw some pennies in it, and we can divvy them up."

Sam stood up. "Sorry. I don't have time for this today. I have a business to run." He said to Suzie, "I vote in favor of the fountain. Does it take a simple majority to approve this?"

"It does."

"Then it's approved. Let's go for it." Sam exited as quickly as he had entered.

Mr. Lombardo stood up. "I haven't approved anything!"

Suzie offered, "If you wish to vote against the fountain, your vote will be duly noted."

"Yeah. I vote against the fountain, and I vote against that slogan, too. And that Arab boy isn't the only one who has a business to run around here. I've been running a business in this mall since he was in diapers. If those people even use diapers." Mr. Lombardo started to stalk out, but he suddenly stopped and looked over at me. He reached into his pocket, pulled out a folded newsletter, and pointed it at me. "Oh yeah, and I remember this turtle thing, too, little girl. Mr. Lyons wants to be a senator? I wouldn't vote for him for dogcatcher." He stomped out.

Suzie waited until she was sure he wasn't coming back before she smiled at us and said, "It's official. The fountain is approved."

Dad went up to Suzie and gave her a big hug and kiss. I moved back up to the desk. Suzie disengaged from Dad and said to me, nearly in tears, "Do you see why I get so upset about little things? There are some real nasty people around here." She picked up the newsletter, came around the desk, and playfully banged me on the head. "Listen, Roberta, Mr. Lyons himself wants to be the feature in October's newsletter, right before the election. Do you think you can write a little something about him?"

I nodded nervously.

"Without putting anything about dead turtles in it?"

I laughed, although I wished I hadn't. I said, "Yes. I can do that. What should I write?"

Suzie put her arm around Dad. "Explain what a recapitalization is, very simply, for people like Mr. Lombardo. Explain that the bank has to reapprove the mall's loan every five years. It's important that the merchants here get a personal statement from Mr. Lyons so they know he's behind them and the recap. We need something to buck up the troops here! This place is so depressed, my god!"

Dad sympathized. "Yeah. That old Lombardo's a fun guy."

Suzie answered, "Sam can be just as bad, in his own way. He sends in these Arabs, with pushcarts, to talk to me about renting mallway space. I have to tell them no. That's only going to scare away our remaining white customers. What we need are upscale businesses — boutiques, salons, bistros. I'm not turning this place into some Arab bizarre."

I corrected her. "It's bazaar."

"What?"

"B-A-Z-A-A-R. It's not 'biz,' it's 'baz.'"

Suzie snapped at me, "Roberta! What on earth are you talking about?"

Dad said, "Honey, I think Suzie needs a little quiet time."

"Oh. Okay." I exited the office. By the time I passed by the window, Dad was already kissing Suzie again.

All the stores were open now, but the mallway was practically empty. Karl was alone in the arcade, standing behind the counter. I went around to get my name tag and was surprised to hear him ask, "So how's it going, cuz?"

I looked at his eyes. Karl seemed in focus and very relaxed. This happens sometimes when his medication is just right. Kristin calls this Karl's "window of opportunity," when you can talk to him for a while like he's normal.

I said, "It's going okay, Karl. How about you?"

By way of reply, he handed me a note and commented, "I guess this is for you."

The note was in Uncle Frank's handwriting. It said, *Roberta, take the Wizard dummy to the trash trailer. Ask our own dummies to help you.* I reread the note, puzzled. Was he trying to be funny?

Karl eyed me curiously. "I'm not one of those dummies, am I?"

"No."

"Good. Good." Karl returned to his magazine, his brow furrowed in concentration.

When I opened the back door, I saw that the guys had dismantled the Wizard already. The Wizard had been our mallway display dummy for the past three months. We all thought he looked pretty cool, with his star wand and his pointy blue cap, but the Crusader made him look like a garden gnome. Now, Hawg and Ironman had stuffed his various parts into two large garbage bags. I said, "Are you guys ready for the trash trailer?"

Hawg was sweating from his exertions. He grunted, "Yeah. Hell, it'll be nice goin' someplace cool. Right, Ironman?"

Ironman grinned. He didn't have to say anything. I knew that he, too, really liked this part of the job. He and Hawg each grabbed a bag. I grabbed a fast-food drink cup that Karl had left behind and led them out the door, across the back parking lot, to the trash trailer.

The trash trailer is a long rectangular box — ten feet high, ten feet deep, and fifty feet long. It is actually a walk-in refrigerator. The temperature inside is a constant twenty-nine degrees Fahrenheit. All trash from the West End Mall has to be stored in the trash trailer overnight and picked up first thing in the morning. It's the law. Ray Lyons got the law passed shortly after the mall opened and his Century Towers condos were overrun by rats.

I pulled on the big metal handle and opened the door. Hawg and Ironman pushed past with their bags, eager to get into the cold air. They carried them down to the far end and placed them next to some barrels marked FOOD COURT ONLY. Then Hawg reached up and pulled the string on the overhead lightbulb. I let the door close behind me and followed them down there, laying my cup in the barrel. Then I said, "Come on, guys, it's freezing in here."

Hawg said, "Well, it's a damn refrigerator, ain't it?"

"Are you coming?"

"Naw, we're gonna chill here for a little while. Right, Ironman?"

I didn't need to look at Ironman to know he agreed. Against my better judgment, I said, "All right. But don't tell Uncle Frank I let you. And don't forget to turn the light out when you leave."

I left the back door of Arcane unlocked for Hawg

and Ironman, something I would never have done if Uncle Frank were there, and walked up to the front of the arcade. Dad was out in the mallway looking at the Crusader, so I joined him. He pointed at the Crusader's chain-mail collar and asked me, "Are those words there? Is something written on his collar?"

I looked at it again and answered, "Yeah. We think it means 'two volts' in Latin. He has one of those battery-operated heads. Like the Wizard."

Dad said, "Cool. People are going to love him. Who do you fight?"

"I don't know." I called inside, "Karl, has anyone done Crusader yet?"

Karl looked up from his magazine. "Yeah, I did it this morning. It's awesome. Real kick-ass."

"Who do you fight against?"

"I don't know. Some guys with turbans on their heads."

I said, half serious, to Dad, "We might think about an Arab Policy." He just laughed and walked off toward the food court.

I looked around the arcade. Not one customer was in there, so I sat down on the Crusader platform to rest. It was shaping up like a bad day, financially speaking. Sundays often are. That's why Uncle Frank usually takes Sundays off. Kristin does, too. Karl, on the other hand, never takes a day off. He comes in every day, seven days a week, fifty-two weeks a year. At least he did for his first two years. Last year he stopped taking his medication for a while. He went nuts one night and started smashing windows with a tire iron. He got sentenced to ten days in the Positive Place, so he messed up his perfect attendance.

I never work the whole day on Sunday because I ride with Mrs. Weiss out to the cemetery. She visits her husband's grave; I visit my mom's crypt. Today, Mrs. Weiss had invited Mrs. Roman to join us.

Dad was behind the counter when I went to turn in my name tag. He asked me, "Are you going with Mrs. Weiss today?"

"Yes."

He shook his head and sighed. "You know, sweetheart, I would like to go with you. I just can't take it."

"I know. That's okay."

"I do stop at Mommy's grave on my own, when I get my courage up."

"You do?"

"Yes, of course. More than you might think." He managed to smile. "I sit by that statue of Jesus, and I look up where Mommy is, and I pray."

A voice interrupted him. "That's not a statue of Jesus!" Dad and I turned and saw the short, skinny body of Mrs. Weiss on the other side of the counter. She added, "That's an angel. I'm Jewish and I know that."

Dad laughed uncomfortably. He said, "Yes, of course. I guess it is."

"It definitely is. It has wings. Did Jesus have wings?"

Dad shook his head. "No, I don't think so."

"And it has a big sword. Did Jesus carry a big sword?"

Mrs. Weiss lifted her right arm high enough to show me what she was carrying. "I brought the stepladder from the store for you, Roberta."

I took the stepladder from her and we started out together. Dad called, "Have a good time, you two."

We both stopped and stared at him. Dad got flustered and added, "I don't mean it like that. I mean, have a good, safe trip."

Mrs. Weiss walked away ahead of me. When I caught up to her in the rotunda, she said, "Maybe if they served beer and had dancing girls, he'd go to the cemetery."

I said, "He goes to the cemetery, Mrs. Weiss. More than you might think."

Mrs. Weiss made a small snorting sound. She pointed ahead, to the entrance door. "There's Millie. I told her to meet us here. Her dead husband's out at the cemetery."

Mrs. Roman had on a dress and panty hose and a rain hat. She called out, "I didn't know whether to bring a raincoat. Do I need a raincoat? I have an umbrella."

Mrs. Weiss told her, "No, you'll die in the humidity. We're never more than a short walk from the car. You'll be fine."

The three of us hurried out into the parking lot. A strong gust of air, thunderstorm air, hit us just as we reached Mrs. Weiss's Lincoln Town Car. It's a really big car, and really white, with a red leather interior. We pulled out of the mall parking lot just ahead of the black wall of storm clouds.

Mrs. Weiss talks more than I do, but she is no match for Mrs. Roman. Mrs. Roman did most of the talking on our ride. I sat in the backseat and listened. Every few minutes I leaned my head back and looked out the window at the swiftly moving storm in the west. The sky seemed to have a green tint.

I was surprised when Mrs. Roman turned around and asked me, "So, Roberta, how old are you?"

"I'm fifteen."

"And you go to high school?"

"Yes, ma'am. I just started my junior year."

"Your junior year! You look so young."

"Actually, I am a little young. My mom started me a year ahead of time. She thought I was ready for kindergarten when I was four, so she put me in Montessori school."

"Is that right? . . . Now, is fifteen old enough to drive?"

"No, ma'am. I can get my learner's permit when I turn sixteen. I've already taken driver's ed, though, so I do know how to drive."

She said, "Good for you. I have a license, but I don't drive. I never have. My husband made me get one for identification purposes and for emergencies. But I've never had to use it, thank god."

We reached Seventy-second Street and turned north. Now the storm clouds were out the left-side window. They were gaining on us fast.

Mrs. Roman looked at me again. "So, Roberta, who do you have buried here at the cemetery?"

"My mom."

"Oh no. Oh, that's sad. Now, what happened to her?"

"She died when I was eight." I should have left it at that, but I never can. I added, "Of a heart attack."

"Oh, how tragic. That really is. My Joe died when he was sixty-nine years of age. But you can't call that tragic, not when you almost make it to seventy. Not when you were a man who both smoked and drank." She asked Mrs. Weiss, "Did your husband smoke?"

"He smoked. It helped kill him."

Mrs. Roman turned back to me. "I hate to tell you how my husband died. He died during a medical procedure." She leaned toward Mrs. Weiss and half whispered, "I don't know if it's appropriate to tell a young girl about this."

"You can tell her. She's a news reporter. She needs to hear."

"Well, he died during a barium enema. Do you know what that is, Roberta?"

"I think so, ma'am."

"I hope to god you never learn about it firsthand, because it is a horrible thing. It is a horrible thing even to talk about. Joe had problems, intestinal problems, and the doctors said he needed to get this barium enema so they could get a good look at his colon. Well, they never got their look, because his colon exploded with all that barium in it." Mrs. Roman paused, her voice quickly filling with emotion. "And Joe died. Just like that. It was a routine procedure, they said."

We drove on in silence for a minute.

Then Mrs. Roman resumed her story. "Right away, my son and daughter said, 'You sue them, Ma. You get a lawyer. You get an autopsy before Papa's body ever leaves that hospital.' So I did. And do you know what they found? Joe even had barium in his brain." She paused for emphasis. "Anyway, long story short, they settled out of court for eighty thousand dollars, and the lawyer took ten thousand. I sold the house and bought a condo at Century Towers. I couldn't believe the deal! They were practically giving them away. Long story short."

I felt the big Lincoln turning right and realized we were at the Eternal Rest Cemetery. We pulled up to our usual spot and prepared to get out, but suddenly Mrs. Weiss screamed, "Look! Look at that! I caught him!"

A young guy in a groundskeeper's shirt was walking toward us with a golf club and a bucket of balls. When he saw Mrs. Weiss he froze in his tracks.

She rolled down the window and leaned out. "You get off these graves! Do you hear me? If I ever catch you again, I'll wrap that club around your scrawny little neck!" The guy spun around and started off at a brisk walk. Mrs. Weiss rolled the window back up and assured us, "That infuriates me. I need to talk to the manager."

Suddenly the storm that had been stalking us closed

in and struck. The day turned as dark as nighttime. The winds howled, pelting the car with such force that it bounced up and down on its springs.

All we could do was sit in the driving rain, in the noise and the dark. Not even Mrs. Roman spoke. The storm battered us for fifteen minutes. Then, as quickly as it had hit, the storm moved on, to do the same thing to the people east of us. The sun came out, and steam started to rise. I grabbed the stepladder, opened the door, and got out.

The cemetery roads were puddled, and the grass was wet, but the air was rosy all around us, and fresh to breathe. We set out on our separate missions. Mrs. Weiss walked up and to the right, to an all-Jewish section of the cemetery.

Mrs. Roman and I walked to the left, to the Guardian Angel section. I watched her kneel down on the soggy grass of a grave, panty hose and all, and start to pray.

I kept walking another twenty yards, past the statue, to the walls of the mausoleum area. My mom is in the first section, in Crypt #109E. The walls are fifteen feet high, and they are covered with polished black marble. You can have a crypt placed in the wall at five different levels — A, B, C, D, or E, in ascending order. That means my mom's crypt, #109E, is on the level that the cemetery calls the Heaven Level. And that's why I needed the stepladder.

Unfortunately, just as I got to Mom's wall I felt big, cold raindrops on my back. The main storm had passed on, but some straggler clouds were still raining on us. I heard a car horn and turned around. Mrs. Roman was on the blacktop road, hurrying back toward the Lincoln. Mrs. Weiss was already in the car. She gestured through the window at me to get over there, but I didn't. I had something I was determined to do. I'd failed to do it last week, using a rickety garbage can, but I wasn't going to fail this week.

Most of the nameplates on the mausoleum walls are made of bronze. Many have little angels or crosses carved in them. The nicest have a long bronze vase sticking out, parallel to the wall, like a Statue of Liberty torch. Mom's doesn't have any of that. It's just a plastic rectangle.

I opened the stepladder and set it in front of Crypt #109A. I climbed to the fourth, and top, step, balancing myself against the black marble facade of 109C. I slid my hand up the wall and stretched up on my tiptoes.

I could just reach it. I ran my right index finger inside the plastic grooves and, slowly and carefully, traced the letters of her name: R-I-T-T-E-R. When I was finished, I placed both hands against the wall, on either side of her nameplate. The rain was coming down harder now, wetting my hair. I looked at my face in the black mirror of the marble. Who did I look like? The dead woman lying on the other side of this wall? She had plain brown hair, and brown eyes, like I do. In pictures she always looked pale next to Dad. Of course, most people look pale next to Dad.

I started to think about my mom's death, but I forced myself to stop. The rain dripped out of my hair and onto my face, like a sudden flood of tears. I took a last look at myself and climbed back down the ladder. I folded it up and walked quickly to the car, soaked to the skin.

I got into the back, dripping on the floor mats. Mrs. Weiss eyed me angrily in the rearview mirror. Mrs. Roman said, "Roberta, I thought you were a smarter girl than that. Standing out in the rain? In Florida?"

Mrs. Weiss dropped the Lincoln into gear and pulled out. I said to both of them, "I'm sorry I kept you waiting. There was something I had to do."

Mrs. Roman said, like it was the last word on the subject, "What? Catch your death of pneumonia?"

Mrs. Weiss shot me a glance in the mirror. "Roberta, there's an old expression: Have sense enough not to stand out in the rain."

I said, "All right. I'm sorry."

It was a little after six o'clock when Mrs. Weiss finally turned down 111th Street. She asked me, "Roberta, do you have anything to eat for dinner?"

"Yes, ma'am."

"What? What is it, Sugar Pops?"

"No, we have a couple of Kid Cuisines in the freezer."

"What's that? More junk?"

"No. They're frozen dinners. Complete dinners. They have vegetables in them."

"Frozen junk. Do you want to come back with me?

I made tuna fish, with the applesauce and raisins in it, the way you like it."

"No, thank you, Mrs. Weiss. That's okay. I have homework."

"Bring your homework. I'll help you with it."

"No, that's okay. Not tonight."

"All right. Suit yourself."

We pulled into the driveway. Mrs. Roman had gotten quiet right after we turned into my neighborhood. I thought maybe she was crying. But she turned to Mrs. Weiss and said, in a half whisper, "This is it? This is where she lives?"

I was surprised. I wondered just what she had seen to make her say that. I slid over until I was directly behind her seat. Then I looked through the front window and tried to see our house through her eyes.

It's a Florida duplex — two small houses connected together. It has two front doors in the middle. It has one covered carport on each side. True, the brown trim around the top is cracked and peeling off. And the poles that hold up the carport are bent and rickety. But it didn't look that bad to me. Believe me, there are much worse houses on our street.

"This is your last chance. Are you sure you don't want to stay with me tonight?" Mrs. Weiss explained to Mrs. Roman, "My second bedroom is for Roberta, whenever she wants."

"That's nice."

I said, "I'm sure. Thank you for asking. And for the ride."

"You're welcome, dear. You be careful."

I could hear my feet squishing on the driveway as I walked through the carport and let myself in the kitchen door. Right away I saw the blinking light on the answering machine. There were two messages. I pressed the button and listened while I got out a macaroni-and-cheese Kid Cuisine and put it in the microwave. The first message was from Dad: "Hi, honey. It's me. Pick up if you're there." After a pause, he resumed, "Will you be okay there for a couple of hours? Me and Suzie have to stop by the Marina Bay Yacht Club. She's invited to a big reception for Mr. Lyons. I put a ten-dollar bill on the fridge if you want to call for a pizza. You lock up, and call me if there's any problem. See ya."

The time of the call was 6:05. I must have just missed him.

The second message was from Suzie, but it definitely wasn't for me: "Hi, I know you're there. Pick up." There wasn't much chance of that. My dad never answers the telephone. Ever. It's like a phobia with him. I guess Suzie hasn't figured that out yet. She paused to wait for him, then continued, in a low whisper. "You must be in the shower. I wish I was in the shower with you. Cleaning you up." Then she switched to a monotone, like from *Mission: Impossible*. "This tape will self-destruct in ten seconds . . ."

I deleted the message.

After dinner I got my favorite photo of Mom and me and placed it on the coffee table. Dad took this photo.

Mom and I are standing in front of the high counter at our old arcade, both of us in our blue smocks. Mom has her arms around me from behind, enveloping me. I'm not smiling, but she is.

I studied her face in the picture, wondering what she would think of me now.

I'd never spent much time missing Mom. Not in seven years. But lately I've been thinking about her a lot. I felt like I nearly touched her today, through that plastic nameplate, through that black marble. That sounds silly, but I really felt that way.

I slid off the couch and rummaged through the wire magazine rack next to the TV. I reached underneath a pile of *Times* and *Newsweeks* until I felt it. A hardcover book. I pulled it up and read the title aloud, *"The Sneetches and Other Stories* by Doctor Seuss." This was my favorite book when I was little. I guess it still is. I think it was Mom's, too. At least she told me it was.

I can remember this scene so clearly: Mom would come home from work. It would be past my bedtime. The sitter would leave, which was my cue to walk out of my bedroom with the book. Then Mom would walk me back into the bedroom, and we would read one story. Then I'd go to sleep.

I carried the book into my room and set it on the bed. I looked at it, thinking, *This is the book. It is not a copy of it. This is the actual book that my mother held in her hands as she sat next to me, those many nights, those hundreds of nights, when she was alive.*

But that was a long time ago. That was before I was

allowed to stay home by myself. It was before I was allowed to eat whatever I wanted for dinner. It was before I was allowed to stand out in the rain.

MONDAY, THE 21ST ↝ Ever since that first horrible dream, I have lived in fear of having another one. I actually hate to go to sleep. Whenever I have a dream now and the first hint of my mother shows up in it, I snap awake. So I only have fragments of dreams. Here's the fragment that I had last night:

My mother appeared in a totally unfrightening way, wearing the blue smock, looking exactly as she does in our arcade photo. She smiled and said, calmly and caringly, "Do you need to talk to me?"

This time, when I sat up in bed, I knew it had only been a dream. The room was already lightening; it was nearly time to get up. So that question my mom asked me stayed inside my head all day — as Mrs. Weiss would say, "like a nourishing breakfast." I repeated Mom's words over and over on the bus ride up Route 27, past the Atlantic County Landfill, to Memorial High. Once I got into school, though, I had to concentrate on school things.

My day at Memorial basically revolves around two subjects — broadcasting and journalism. Last year I picked Journalism I as an elective, and it was great. My teacher was Mrs. Knight. We mostly studied the newspaper, which was delivered every day. But we also managed to put out an issue of our own school newspaper,

The Spartan, in November. We had an April issue all ready to go, too. But the principal, Mr. Archer, told Mrs. Knight that there was no more money available for paper or printing. She got so mad at him that she quit. She got a job writing news in the news department at Channel 57.

But before she left, she brought in her own replacement. He was a thin little man whom she introduced to us this way: "This is Mr. Peter Herman, an old colleague of mine from the newspaper trade."

He really isn't that old, although he is bald and he is slightly stooped over when he stands. Mr. Herman took over Journalism I and II this year.

Mr. Herman is my favorite teacher now. I get to see him before the morning announcements, during fifth period for journalism, and during seventh period for study hall. Most teachers can only talk about the questions that we'll be asked on standardized tests. Mr. Herman isn't like that. He talks about the importance of journalism in a society. He talks about high standards and ideals.

My day begins in the guidance office, which is actually the main office of the school. I run the televised announcements, the Pledge of Allegiance, and "The Star-Spangled Banner." Last year Mrs. Knight's students did that job and got credit for TV production. I volunteered to do it this year, hoping to learn some camera work, copy writing, and tape editing. Unfortunately, it didn't turn out that way. Mrs. Knight, as I said, left, and Mr. Herman isn't at all interested in TV. So now I go in every morning, pop a video of the Pledge and "The Star-Spangled Banner" into the VCR, and rewind it when it's done playing.

Mr. Herman, however, is still technically in charge of the TV stuff, so he and I must meet in the office each morning. We check with Mr. Archer to see if he has any special announcements for us. If he does, we videotape him saying them. Then we run the Pledge and the "Banner."

Mr. Archer is very nice. He has been the principal of Memorial High School for about twenty years. He has a big red face, and he drives a big red Cadillac. I know, from my mornings in his office, that he takes medicine to keep his blood pressure down. Mr. Archer has his official office; he also has a "time-out office" next door, where he keeps the kids who are waiting to be punished. He has a sign on that wall that reads, *If you're so smart, what are you doing here?*

Occasionally a teacher makes a videotape at home and wants us to play it on the morning announcements. When that happens I put the tape in for Mr. Archer to inspect and approve. Mr. Herman has to stand there with me while this goes on, which I don't think he likes very much.

Mr. Archer tends to tell the same stories over and over. This morning, after he approved a videotape for the cheerleaders' fund-raiser, he retold one. He said, "Just let that tape play for a few more seconds. Once a teacher brought in a tape from home, and he had taped over some video from the Playboy Channel. Soon as his announcement ended, the kids were staring at a naked lady on a motorcycle."

He told the same story last week. But then he looked at Mr. Herman and added, "Buck naked on a Harley." This week he didn't.

When morning announcements were finished, I wheeled the TV and VCR back into the time-out office. Mr. Herman pointed at the sign on the wall and muttered. "That should be the motto of this school."

We walked out of the office together. Mr. Herman said to me, "Here's a tidbit I picked up in the teachers' lounge. Did you know that this high school, in its thirty-year history, has never had a National Merit Scholarship finalist?"

I said, "What's that?"

Mr. Herman expelled a short laugh. "Perfect. Perfect rejoinder, Roberta. Right on cue. Now tell me you're joking."

"I'm not."

He winced. "National Merit is a test that you take your junior year. I know they give it here. I've seen it advertised."

"Oh. I guess I'll be taking it."

"Of course you will. And you will be the first to be a scholarship finalist."

"Me?"

"Yes."

"I'm not in advanced placement."

"Why on earth not? And if you are not, then who is?"

"The kids who have time to be, Mr. Herman."

Mr. Herman arrived at his classroom. But before he went in, he said, "As God is my witness, Roberta, you will be in AP classes this year. And you will take that test, and do wonderfully well, and destroy this dubious distinction."

I headed off to my first-period class, PE. I don't like it much. Most kids really, really hate it, but I don't. I just don't like it. Second period I have Mr. Archer, Jr., for history. He's the principal's son. He teaches American history, and he helps coach the football and baseball teams. The football and baseball guys, and anyone else who wants to, call him Archie. I don't, though.

My English class is pretty boring. Junior year is American Lit. So far all we've read is stuff by Indians and Pilgrims. Third and fifth periods are when juniors are called down to guidance for RDT, random drug testing. I haven't been called yet. I think they're doing it in alphabetical order. Betty the Goth is in my English class. She sits in the back and twirls that black hair around her finger. She got called down to RDT last week.

Spanish is the hardest class I have. It's hard for me, anyway, and the three other kids who weren't born speaking Spanish. I like it, though.

Lunch is lunch. It's quick, crowded, and a little dangerous. Lunch is when kids who are going to get beat up get beat up. We had racial incidents last year that have carried over to this year. Some black guys jumped some white guy. Then some Spanish guys jumped a black kid. I think Hawg got into one of those fights. Then we went on alert. Sheriff's deputies were in the cafeteria and in the halls every period, so things calmed down.

Anyway, we only get twenty minutes for lunch. I spend them standing in the lines in front of a long row of vending machines, near the cafeteria entrance. I get in a line for chips, and then eat them while standing in a second line for a soda, which I drink while waiting in a third line for a Snickers, which I just stand there and eat. By then, our twenty minutes are up, and it's time to go.

Fifth period, Journalism II, is my favorite class. I sit in the first row, right in front of Mr. Herman's desk. He keeps a wooden podium on top of his desk. He always stands behind that podium and delivers a lecture, from notes, for the first twenty minutes of class. Then he gives us an assignment from an old workbook called *Journalism Today*. Sometimes it's a writing assignment, sometimes an editing assignment, sometimes a page-layout assignment.

I should say, he does that for the kids who sit up front, like me and Betty the Goth and a few others. The kids who sit in the back are pretty much on their own. For some reason beyond my comprehension, about ten football guys signed up for Journalism II, Hawg among them. For all the attention Mr. Herman pays to them, that football group may as well be out on the practice field. Mr. Herman addresses his lectures, and gives all his personal attention, to whoever sits in the first two rows.

Today's lecture was about the muckrakers. They were a group of American journalists who worked on different newspapers in the early 1900s. They wrote about poor people getting exploited and killed by greedy rich people. Back then the rich people didn't care about the conditions in the factories and the mines and the slums. They could do whatever they wanted, and no one stood up to them. Except the muckrakers.

Mr. Herman said that the most famous muckrakers were named Upton Sinclair and Lincoln Steffens. He shot a glance at me and added, "But there was a woman muckraker, named Ida Tarbell." I heard some loud sniggering in the back of the room. The rude noises had come, no doubt, from Hawg and some other football guys. But Mr. Herman didn't let on. He never does. He resumed his lecture as if nothing had happened.

On the way out of class, I handed Mr. Herman a copy of the mall newsletter. I said, "There's a feature by me on the front page, Mr. Herman. And a short one on the back."

He took it and smiled at me, weakly. I think teaching takes a lot out of Mr. Herman. By the time my class gets here, he has already taught two Journalism I classes and another Journalism II.

Math class is easy. Algebra, analytic geometry, calculus — it's all easy for me. It always has been. Betty the Goth is in this class; I think it's easy for her, too. She finishes her work in half a period, then spends the rest of the time touching up her black nail polish.

My last period of the day is study hall, which is the wimpiest elective of them all. A lot of the college-prep students take Latin as their third elective. Not me. I get all of my homework done in seventh period, which is important to me timewise. I'm working my shift at Arcane when those other kids are home studying their Latin.

Today I was hoping that by seventh period Mr. Herman would have read my article. He came into study hall, sat down at the desk, and opened his briefcase. He pulled out his copy of the newsletter and looked at me sternly. Then he broke into a big smile. "You little muckraker, you. It's quite a story, Roberta. And I assure you, I shall never set foot in that mall again." He pulled a blue pencil from his briefcase, then asked, "Tell me, how did this go over with that Suzie creature?"

"She didn't like it."

"I didn't imagine she would."

"She told me I have to run everything past her now. I think if my dad wasn't standing there, she'd have fired me."

He grinned devilishly. "Excellent. Excellent." He wagged that blue pencil at me and asked, "Do you want me to be brutally honest?"

I didn't know what to say to that. I answered, "Okay."

"Good. Then here it is: You meander in this feature, my dear, like a lost little turtle on the beach. Then you bury your readers with details, like you're a big bulldozer. Extraneous details." He started to make deep blue marks on the article, swiftly and surely. "We don't need to know the name of every person who ever had a passing thought about this issue, do we?"

"No, sir."

"We just need two people — the David and the Goliath. The good guy and the bad guy. Do you follow me?"

"Yes, sir. I think so."

"So who is David here?"

"Uh, I don't know. The turtles?"

He looked at me unhappily. He thought for a moment, then said, "Perhaps. Perhaps. But you only need one. Two good guys make a crowd. Perhaps this Toby the Turtle fellow could be the good guy, the David here. What do you think?"

"Uh, okay."

"Toby will personify all that is good and noble on the environmental side." Mr. Herman made another series of swift pencil strokes. "Now, who will personify all that is evil and avaricious on the developers' side?"

"I'm sorry, what?"

"If Toby is to play David, who will play Goliath? Who will be the bad guy?"

"I guess that would be Mr. Lyons."

"Yes. Excellent. I think Mr. Ray Lyons will do nicely. In fact, it's a masterpiece of casting." Mr. Herman finished editing the article with a flourish of his hand. He turned the newsletter around and held it out to me. It looked like some kindergartner had scribbled on it with a blue crayon. There must have been a hundred separate edits; just about every line had been changed somehow. He said, "Now, that's what a newspaper editor would do to you, my dear."

I must have looked pretty shocked, because he softened his voice. "Please. Please. Don't take this so personally."

I shrugged. "No, I'm not."

"This is what an editor would do to you ten minutes after hearing that you had just won the Pulitzer Prize for journalism."

I shrugged again. "It's okay. Really."

I turned the article facedown. I pointed to the back of the newsletter. "Did you look at my short feature?"

"This 'People Pieces' thing? No, that's trivia. I'm only interested in the journalism."

"Okay. Thank you, Mr. Herman. Now what should I do with this?"

"Type it up, with my changes, and give it back to me. I'll put it in your portfolio."

"Okay."

Mr. Herman looked away, into his briefcase. He pulled out a pile of journalism class papers and started to mark on them. I got out my math and Spanish books and set to work finishing my homework assignments. But my mind drifted — first to my mom, then to Arcane, then back to the mall newsletter. I was still trying not to take Mr. Herman's critique personally.

A strange sight greeted me when I got to the mall entrance. In the mallway, directly opposite Suzie's glass window, was a pile of television sets. The sets were stacked up three high and three wide, forming an almost perfect square. Once inside, I could see that all nine sets were turned on to the same channel, Channel 57. I could see nine separate images of Angela del Fuego, Mr. Herman's least-favorite television journalist. The sound was off, but that didn't matter. Today's topic on *Angela Live* was pretty obvious. She was interviewing a row of men who were dressed like women.

Suzie was watching the TV wall from her desk as I walked in. She said, "I wish the sound were on. I want to hear what those guys have to say."

I said, "Can I use the computer? I have to revise my feature."

Suzie looked alarmed. "What for?"

"For class. Mr. Herman wants to put it into my portfolio."

"Will anybody else see it?"

"No."

"Okay, then. Go ahead."

I logged on and located my document. Suzie called over to me, "Hey, you know what? *Angela Live* has its own web site. I got onto it today. And guess what? You can see what her topics are going to be up to a week in advance. I'm glad I looked. I have a bus full of Brazilian teenagers coming in here on Friday. And guess what the topic is?"

"What?"

"'Teenagers in Brazil'! I couldn't believe my eyes. I called Sam up at Crescent and asked if I could borrow a big-screen TV for Friday. He didn't want to risk put-

ting a big screen out in the mallway. He thinks somebody's gonna vandalize it. But he offered this — nine
portable TVs. What do you think? I like it even better."

"Yeah. It looks pretty cool."

"I'm going to take the teenagers on a tour of the mall
at three. It'll give me a chance to use my Spanish. I'll
get them all back here at four, gathered around the TV
wall, so they can watch Angela."

"Sounds okay. But, you know, they don't speak
Spanish."

"Who don't?"

"The Brazilians. They speak Portuguese."

Suzie didn't want to believe me, I could tell, but she
finally did. She said, "Is that right? They must understand it, though. If everybody else down there speaks it,
they must understand it."

"You could give it a try." I looked back through the
window. Angela del Fuego was feeling a guy's fur collar.

Suzie turned her attention to a FedEx envelope on
her desk, so I got back to work on my feature. I quickly
made about a dozen edits before she interrupted me
again. "I helped organize a big fund-raiser last night at
Marina Bay, a big political fund-raiser. People came to
meet Mr. Lyons and to give him their support. You
know he's running for the state senate? He has some famous campaign manager from Washington helping to
get him elected. Your dad and I met him last night. His
name is Philip Knowlton."

Suzie paused, as if waiting for me. I said, "Was he
nice?"

She looked at me like maybe I was putting her on. But I wasn't. She answered, "He's not here to be nice, Roberta. He's here to get Mr. Lyons elected." Suzie opened a Twix bar. "But I guess he was nice enough. Basically, the more money you had to contribute to the campaign, the nicer he was to you."

"That's pretty creepy."

She gave me that same look. "No, that's just the way it is." Suzie bit the Twix in half. "He wants to schedule Mr. Lyons for an 'event' here in September."

"What event?"

"The new fountain. Mr. Lyons will be here to turn it on and to give a speech. Channel Three will definitely be here to cover it, and maybe Channel Fifty-seven and the Sunshine Network.

"'National attention' is the word they were using last night. Mr. Lyons needs to get 'national attention.'"

I started to point out to her that that was two words, but I caught myself. I got up to leave, but there was something about Suzie's look that made me stand still by the desk. She seemed to be struggling with something. She finally said to me, "Roberta, you know your dad and I are getting pretty close now. Right?"

"Uh-huh."

"I just want you to know that if you ever need to talk to me for . . . girl talk? You know. I'm here for you."

I flashed back in horror to Mom's words from the dream, *Do you need to talk to me?* I wanted to shout at Suzie, *No! I don't need to talk to* you. *I need to talk to my mother.* But I only shouted to myself.

Suzie must have noticed the change in my face. She quickly added, "Of course, if you'd rather talk to someone else, that's fine, too. I'll understand. Okay?"

"Okay."

I hustled out of there.

WEDNESDAY, THE 23RD ~ As I passed the rotunda today, I heard a loud clanging sound. I looked over and saw Leo kneeling behind the DANGER horse. He looked up and saw me, too, which was bad, because I was already late.

He yelled, "Hey, Roberta! Come over here."

Leo is a skinny, wiry guy. He has one of those bodies that could be anywhere from thirty to seventy years old. He has a square head and big false teeth. His teeth are so big that they look like a mistake, like he got some big guy's teeth instead of his own. I called back, "I can't, Leo. I'm late. Can I talk to you on break?"

He yelled, "Come over here!" again. I looked ahead at Arcane, then I detoured over to the rotunda. Leo gestured around him. "Look at this, will you?" I guessed he was talking about the big hole and the loose tiles. "You got to tell your dad's girlfriend" — he bugged his eyes toward the office — "Suzie the Floozy over there, that this ain't gonna work."

"What isn't going to work, Leo?"

"This new fountain scam they got going now. They're telling everybody we got a new fountain. Do you see anything new here?"

"No. I guess not."

"I'm hooking up the old fountain. There ain't one new thing under here. Just an old pump, an old motor, and some very old pipes. They need to rip it all out and start over."

"But, Leo, isn't the whole point that they want the old fountain back? So people can remember what it was like ten years ago?"

"It broke ten years ago! That's why we shut it down and capped it."

"Oh." I looked nervously at Arcane.

Leo took pity on me. "Go on. If you gotta go to work, go on. But remember to tell her what I said."

I half ran the remaining twenty yards to Arcane. Kristin was alone behind the counter.

I said, "I'm sorry I'm late."

She said, "You're late?"

"Yeah. Is my dad here?"

"He's in the back, eating."

On weekdays Uncle Frank usually works from ten to five, and then Dad takes over from four to nine. Sometimes it's the opposite. Either way, that one hour when they overlap is uncomfortable for everybody.

Someone who looked at our business from the outside, like the mannequin in Slot #61, might think that Uncle Frank does all the work and Dad does nothing. That's probably how Karl and Kristin look at it. That's definitely how Uncle Frank looks at it. But the fact is my dad has been in the arcade business for twenty years. He really knows what he's doing. Uncle Frank has been in the arcade business for three years. He only thinks he knows what he's doing.

Uncle Frank soon came walking up the mallway from the north side. He was carrying some weird type of vacuum cleaner. Kristin greeted him with, "What's that, Daddy?"

"It's a shampooer. I rented it from Lombardo. I'm having nightmares about what's living in this carpet." Uncle Frank looked around the arcade, probably for Karl. He told Kristin, "I want Karl and the two stooges to do this, but I want you to supervise them. Okay?"

"Okay, Daddy."

"The two can move the furniture. Make sure they don't break anything." He studied the machine. "Karl can run the shampooer." He looked over at me and said, with a touch of pride, "Karl can run any machine." He looked back at Kristin. "But make sure he's thinking clear."

"Okay."

Devin walked by and stopped to look at Crusader. Uncle Frank said, so only Kristin and I could hear, "Look at that dirtbag, will you?"

Kristin agreed, "Gross."

"Somebody needs to tell that guy it's two more months till Halloween."

I told him, "He was in here last night with the goths. They were doing Vampire's Feast."

Uncle Frank told Kristin, "You call me if he even looks at you."

I followed Uncle Frank to the back, where he deposited the shampooer. Dad was leaning against a carton, eating a meatball sub. Uncle Frank didn't look at him, but he did ask, "So how did it go yesterday?"

Dad answered, "Not bad. A little slow."

"Slow? Then I hope you sent the useless twins home."

"No. I let 'em stay."

"You let them sit around on their butts all day?"

Dad winked at me. "I like to keep them around in case we get busy. You have good days and bad days in this business. You never know which one it is until the day is over."

Uncle Frank stepped into the open bathroom and started washing his hands.

I handed Dad my revised feature. He asked, "What's this, honey?"

"This is an improved version of my feature about the turtles. Mr. Herman's going to put it into my portfolio."

"Great. I'll read it right now. What's your portfolio?"

"It's a folder where you keep samples of your schoolwork. Your best work."

"Uh-huh. Now, tell me, is that something you can send to a college with your application?"

"I don't know. I guess so. If they want it."

Dad addressed Uncle Frank. "Roberta's going to the University of South Florida for a degree in journalism. It's all set. We bought that prepaid college plan for her when she was little. Now all she has to do is get decent grades." He looked at me. "Like she has been."

Uncle Frank said, "Good. That's good. I looked into

that plan for Kristin, but we weren't even Florida residents till last year, not officially. So it wasn't worth it."

Dad said, "You gotta buy it when they're young. Roberta was only eight when Mary Ann got hers."

I couldn't believe my ears. Dad and Uncle Frank were having a real conversation! Uncle Frank asked him, "How much a month was it?"

"We didn't do the monthly plan. We plopped the whole thing down at once. That's the cheapest way to go. You pay five grand one time. It was all the money we had in the world. But now, ten years later, she's got a free ride to college." Dad looked away. He always gets a sad look when he tells that prepaid college plan story.

Hawg, Ironman, and Karl arrived right at seven o'clock. Kristin put them to work with the rug shampooer. Hawg dragged the black platforms aside, Ironman picked up the trash under them, and Karl followed with the rug shampooer. It was a very efficient operation. It was also a very noisy operation, and the place looked like it was turned upside-down. Not too many customers ventured in.

Nina stopped by at about seven-thirty. Nina is Kristin's best friend. She's as glamorous as Kristin is, only in a darker, Latin kind of way. They both attend Our Lady of Lourdes Academy. It's a private school, mostly for rich Catholic girls. Nina is both rich and Catholic. Kristin is neither. Uncle Frank sent her there after he visited Memorial High and saw what the kids there look like.

Nina doesn't need to work. Her father is Dr.

Navarro. He's the occupant of Slots #2 and 3, Florida Dermatology. It's one of three medical offices that he owns. Nina comes in whenever she feels like it to help him with the computerized billing. Tonight she didn't feel like helping, so she was hanging out at Arcane.

Uncle Frank never gives her a hard time for hanging out, like he does Hawg and Ironman. Uncle Frank thinks Nina is some kind of super-good, role-model girl. Maybe it's because she wears crosses around her neck. Or because she goes to Lourdes Academy. Or because her father is rich. Anyway, he's very much in favor of Kristin hanging out with her.

Whenever Nina is there, she and Kristin stand at the register and crack on guys mercilessly. They'll smile at a guy when he comes up to pay. Then they'll mutter "loser" and "scumbag" and stuff like that as soon as he turns around. It's pretty funny, if you're not the guy.

Hardly any guys came in tonight, so Nina turned her attention to the shampooing project. Nina asked Kristin, "What's the fat one's name again?"

"Hawg."

"Why do you call him that?"

"Why don't you ask him?"

"Maybe I will." Nina called over the whirring of the shampooer, "Hey, Hawg!"

Hawg stopped dragging the Galactic Defender unit and turned to her. "What?"

"How come they call you that name?"

Hawg looked suspicious. He knew she was putting him on. "What name?"

"That nickname of yours."

"You mean Hawg?"

"Yeah. Other than the fact that, no offense, you kind of look like a pig. Why do they call you that?"

I don't think Hawg took offense. He answered seriously, "You ever hear of the Arkansas Razorbacks? The Razorback Hawgs?"

"No. Never did. What's that, a football team?"

"Yeah. I come from west Georgia, but that's my team. Always has been."

I think Nina would have been satisfied if the explanation had ended there, but it didn't. "A lot of Georgia boys root for the Bulldogs, from the University of Georgia in Athens, but not me."

Nina turned away and looked out into the mall, signaling that the conversation was over. But Hawg wasn't finished. He redirected his attention to Ironman and continued, "I ain't rootin' for no University of Georgia Bulldogs, and I ain't goin' there, either. I'm goin' to Fayetteville, Arkansas, home of the Arkansas Razorbacks."

Kristin actually seemed interested. She asked him, "So what are you doing down here?"

Hawg didn't like that question, even though it was Kristin who had asked it. He didn't look back at her. He looked at Ironman and said, "But first I gotta whomp on some of these sissy Florida boys and make a big name for myself. Then I can get me a football scholarship back up to Fayetteville."

Nina rolled her head and shoulders at Kristin, indicating they should take a walk in the mall. Kristin asked me, "Roberta, will you watch the register?"

I said, "Okay."

They headed out and immediately started to laugh about something, probably Hawg, as he went back to dragging furniture out of the way.

I took my dinner break at eight o'clock. I spotted Betty the Goth's black hair at the Chili Dog, so I cut over to Burger 'n' Fries. An old Greek couple owns the place. They don't speak very good English, but they're really nice. Most of the words that we say to each other are from their menu. I got the cheeseburger basket with a Mountain Dew and carried it to the nearest table without trash on it. But it turned out to be sticky. I checked the other tables around me; they weren't any better.

I sat and watched Leo work on the fountain until Verna the security guard turned into the food court. She saw me and came right over.

"Hello, Roberta. Can I interrupt you for one minute?"

Verna sat across from me. She started to place her hands on the table, thought better of it, and folded them across her chest. "Do you mind if I ask you a question?"

"No."

"That tall boy at Arcane is your cousin, right?"

"Right. My cousin Karl."

"Okay. Now, is there something wrong with Karl?"

I took a bite of my cheeseburger. Then I answered, "He has a hyperactivity disorder, ADHD."

"I see. That disorder, is that where you can't pay attention?"

"Sometimes. And sometimes he can't stop moving and doing stuff. Weird stuff. It's a chemical imbalance. The doctors give him other chemicals, to balance him out."

"Uh-huh. Karl had an incident last year, did he not? Some car windows were broken?"

"Yes, ma'am."

"And he was sent to an institution of some kind?"

"Yes, ma'am. The Positive Place. It's a behavioral hospital for teenagers."

"I see. Does he ever hang out with those skinheads?"

"No, I don't think so. He might talk to them in the arcade. But I've never seen him with them outside of the arcade."

"Uh-huh. Do you keep any red paint at Arcane? Any red spray paint?"

I thought about the Sony stand, but I told her, "No."

"Now, what about that stocky boy? What's his name?"

"Hawg?"

"Yeah. What's his real name?"

I took another bite and glanced at my watch. Verna was eating up my break. I answered, "I'm not sure."

"So what about him? Does he ever hang out with the skinheads?"

"No. Same as Karl. He might talk to them at Arcane, but that's about it."

"And does he have that chemical imbalance thing?"

"No, I don't think so."

Verna nodded. I took the opportunity to say, "Hey, Verna, why are you asking me all this?"

"I promised Sam I'd ask around a little for him. Maybe find out who's been messing with him."

"Sam from Crescent?"

"Yeah. Somebody messed up the side of his car. They painted a big red Star of David on it."

"That's terrible. That's really creepy. He's such a nice guy."

"He is a nice guy, when nobody's messing with him. Right now he's not feeling too nice." Verna got up. "So if you hear anything about Sam, or about Crescent Electronics, or any of that bad stuff, you let me know."

Verna left. I dumped the rest of my food and hurried back to Arcane. I turned my head to avoid eye contact with Leo and wound up looking right at the deathly white face of Betty the Goth. I cast my eyes down at the floor and walked straight ahead.

I didn't see anybody when I got into Arcane, but I saw that the guys had finished their shampooing project. I followed a set of wet parallel wheel tracks to the back, through the office, and out into the parking lot.

The three guys were at the faucet behind Special-Tees, Slot #33. Hawg and Ironman were dumping the dirty water out of the shampooer while Karl looked on. Hawg was doing all the talking. I gathered from what I heard that he had been called down to guidance for RDT, random drug testing, that morning. He looked over at me, then continued, "Ain't nothin' to it, Ironman. You wait in line there, and that fat lady — what's her name, Roberta?"

"Mrs. Biddulph."

"Yeah, Mrs. Bit-off, she hands you a cup with your name on it and a screw-top lid. She sends you into the toilet to do your business, then you give it back to her. They've already tested most of the football team."

Ironman was grinning. Karl was just staring off into space. I thought to myself, *I know these guys. These guys wouldn't do anything bad. Not the kind of stuff that Verna was talking about.*

I went back out to the front and joined Nina and Kristin near the Crusader experience. My dad was standing inside the circle, gearing himself up to use it. Soon he was thrashing the air with the wand and whooping, just like a teenager. Nina and Kristin exchanged a look, like *What's wrong with this guy?*

We all watched Dad for a little bit, then Nina asked me, "So, Roberta, what guy do you like?"

I said, "Me? I don't know."

Nina looked at Kristin. "It's that Sam guy, isn't it?"

"I told you, I don't know."

"You mean, you don't know because you don't have those kinds of feelings? Like, you don't have any hormones?"

"No, I mean I don't know because I don't know. I have as many hormones as anybody else."

"Then tell me some guy you like. Some movie star or somebody who gets your hormones moving."

Kristin, as usual, moved to rescue me. "Drop it, Nina."

But I wanted to answer for myself. I pointed my right arm straight ahead, and told her, "Him. I have feelings for him."

Nina was appalled. "Not your father!"

"No. No, next to him. The Crusader. That's who I have feelings for."

Kristin agreed. "Good choice. He's hot."

Nina asked, "You're talking about the statue?"

Kristin continued, "He's tall. He's strong. He's a man of war, but he's a man of God, too."

I added, "And he has blue eyes."

Nina said, "I don't like blue eyes. A lot of psycho killers have blue eyes."

Dad's two minutes were over. As he was taking off his helmet we all heard Suzie yell to him from the rotunda, "Oh, my god! What are you doing?"

Dad laughed happily and pointed at the Crusader legend. "What's it look like I'm doing? I'm killing — I don't know what I'm killing. Turks or something." Dad stepped down from the platform. For some reason he called over to me, "Honey, you really ought to try this."

I shook my head. "No, thanks."

Suzie came up and took my arm in hers, but she spoke to Dad. "You nut! You'll break a leg. Won't he, Roberta?"

That reminded me of something, something I hadn't

thought of in a long time. I told her, "It wouldn't be the first time."

"Oh? Do tell. Spill it."

"Dad did break his leg. I remember him on crutches."

Dad interrupted, "Yeah, that's right. I broke it at the beach. The surf was up."

Suzie looked at me. "He is a big kid, isn't he?" Then, apparently, Suzie remembered something, too. She broke away, spun around, and directed two of her long red nails at Nina and Kristin, like the prongs of a fork. "I want to talk to you two about an idea I had. You always look so gorgeous, and I think, *We have our own super-models right here at the West End Mall. Why not use them?*"

Nina looked genuinely interested. Suzie continued, "I'm looking for girls to model for the new Fall in the Mall promotion. We have a little money to give you — fifty dollars for two hours. You can borrow any outfit from any store in the mall to wear. What do you say? It'll be a chance to see what real modeling is all about."

Nina didn't hesitate. She said, "That sounds great to me. I'm there."

Suzie continued, with rising enthusiasm, "We did this at my last mall and it was a lot of fun. The models get up in the windows of the stores. People don't know they're real, you know? And they freak when they find out!"

Kristin wasn't so sure. She asked, "So, you mean, there's glass between us and the people staring at us."

"Yes."

Kristin said to Nina, "Okay. That might not be so bad."

Nina replied, "That would be great! Everybody would come to see us."

Suddenly, for some reason, Kristin asked, "What about Roberta?"

Suzie squirmed uncomfortably, trying to think of what to say. But then she got an idea and smiled brightly. "Yes, of course. There is a part that would be right for you, Roberta."

Kristin looked at me. "There you go!"

Suzie added, "If you wouldn't mind doing a little acting."

I was in shock. I would mind. I definitely would mind.

Kristin smiled at me. "Did you hear that, cuz? You're in."

"I don't want to be in."

"Come on. It'll be fun. And it'll be fifty bucks."

"I don't want to stand like a dummy in a store window."

Nina bristled. "I'm not standing like a dummy. I'm posing like a supermodel."

Kristin gestured toward Nina and said to me, "There you go. Do you hear that?"

"But I'm no model. I don't want to be a model."

"All right. So don't be a model," Kristin challenged me. "Be a reporter. An investigative reporter. You know?

You're going undercover to explore the glamorous world of the supermodels."

Nina smiled. "Yeah, I like the sound of that."

Suzie took Dad by the arm. "Great. Then we're all set. You girls go pick your outfits. Try the Gap. You can tell them I sent you. Then report to me at eleven on Saturday." She started to tug Dad toward the food court. "Come on. I came to steal you away for a cappuccino."

Kristin and Nina started yakking about the modeling. I started feeling sick about it. I walked off by myself, sat down on the Crusader platform, and waited for customers.

A few of the regulars showed up. So did a group I had seen once or twice before. They were four guys from Saint Francis Xavier Prep, the brother school to Lourdes Academy. It's for the rich Catholic boys. The group followed Kristin and Nina to the counter and stood there with them for about an hour.

The Head Louse came by, too. He checked out the Crusader in the mallway and came in to read its legend. Then I watched him glance at the counter two or three times, seeing if he could get Kristin's attention. He couldn't. He finally gave up and looked over at me.

I said, "Can I help you?"

The Head Louse had done hundreds of Arcane experiences in the past month, so he didn't need much help. He hopped up onto the platform and put on the helmet as I clicked the plastic circle closed around him.

The Head Louse had very strong arms, and he moved

well. He reacted to the sights and sounds inside the helmet with quick and precise movements of the wand, smacking it against the black surface of the circle. His mouth never made a sound. When his two minutes were up, he tossed down the wand and removed the helmet. He looked at me and said, "Not bad."

I let him out of the circle and handed him his ticket. He took another glance at the counter, saw that the Xavier boys were still there, and said, "Can I just pay you?"

I said, "Sure."

Then he added, "Where are Karl and Hawg?"

"They're out back. They're cleaning out the rug shampooer."

"Oh. They're here tonight, though?"

"Yeah."

"They're here until closing time?"

I hesitated. I thought about all of Verna's questions in the food court and said, "Why? Why do you want to know?"

"No reason. I just wanted to say hey." He handed me a five-dollar bill and said, "You keep the change. I wouldn't want to interrupt all that hard work going on at the cash register." He smiled weirdly. He walked out into the mallway and turned toward the food court.

Dad and Suzie returned at about eight-forty-five. They each had a soft-swirl ice-cream cone. I didn't want to watch them carrying on, so I walked into the back room.

Ironman was seated at Uncle Frank's desk. He was

hunched over and shivering. Hawg was standing over him, rubbing his back vigorously. He said, "Hey, come on, Ironman. We was just messin' around. We weren't gonna leave you in there. Honest. Were we, Karl?"

Karl just stared.

I said, "What's going on? What did you do?"

Hawg answered, "Hey, we had worked up a big ol' sweat. We went to cool off in the trash trailer. Ironman just decided to stay a little overtime."

Karl looked at me creepily. "He decided to stay in there in the dark."

Ironman managed to blurt out, "No, I didn't. You wouldn't let me out."

Karl answered, "That door doesn't lock."

Ironman bleated, "You were holding it!"

Karl looked at me and explained, "No way."

Hawg shook him by the shoulders. "We was just horsin' around, buddy. We was just holdin' it for a minute. Of course we was gonna let you out."

I said, "You'd better not let Uncle Frank hear about this."

Karl shot me an angry look. "He's not gonna find out, though. Is he, cuz?"

"He's not going to find out from me, but I don't know who else saw you out there. Mr. Lombardo? Verna? Mrs. Royce?"

Karl's eyes clouded over with worry.

Kristin came through the door. She asked Karl, "Where's that rug shampooer?"

Karl's face was now a blank wall. Then his head

snapped up and he blurted out, "It's outside. It's out back."

Kristin looked him in the eyes. "Karl? You left it outside?"

Karl was thinking as hard as he could. He said, "Just to dry out. That's all. We rinsed it out with the hose." He turned and darted through the door. Kristin called after him, "It had better still be there."

It was.

The five of us went through the closing checklist. Ironman had a long sneezing fit, ten sneezes at least. Then he reverted to his old self, trailing along after Hawg. He seemed to forgive Hawg and Karl completely. But I found myself thinking harder about them.

At 9:10 I was standing next to Suzie in the mallway while Dad put the cash drawer in the safe. I took the opportunity to say, "Leo asked me to tell you that the fountain won't work because the parts are too old, and also that it wasn't working ten years ago when they shut it down."

Suzie smiled. "That's Leo, isn't it? You ask him to put in a lightbulb, and he'll give you twenty reasons why it can't be done. The county has already inspected that plumbing. It works fine." She touched my arm. "But thank you for telling me, sweetie. If he doesn't have the fountain going by tomorrow, I will call somebody else in. We have to make sure everything is right for Mr. Lyons's visit."

Dad locked the sliding-glass doors. Kristin took Karl home in the Volkswagen. I guessed Dad had offered

Hawg and Ironman a ride, because they stayed with us all the way to the car and hopped into the back.

Suzie got into her little Miata and drove away. After we dropped the guys off, Dad looked over at me and said, "Suzie's coming over. Okay?"

"Okay."

"First she's gonna stop at Taco Bell and get our dinner. It's Mexican night at Sawgrass Estates."

Suzie's Miata was already in our carport when we got home, so we pulled in behind her. Once we got inside she and Dad pulled out the blender to make margaritas.

I checked inside the Taco Bell bag. Suzie had gotten me my usual, a Mexican pizza. I took it into the living room, sat on the couch, and clicked on the local news. A weather girl announced that there was a thirty-percent chance of rain tomorrow.

Dad and Suzie never came in to join me. They sat in the kitchen and drank their margaritas, laughing at stuff that I couldn't hear. At eleven-thirty I clicked the TV off, muttered, "Good night," in their direction, and went into my room. My *Sneetches* book was on the dresser. I tossed it onto the bed. Then I searched in my closet until I found an old box of stuff. I reached in, felt around, and pulled out another book. It was *The Cat in the Hat*, another early favorite. I pressed it against *The Sneetches*, making a kind of Dr. Seuss sandwich. I turned off the light, lay on the bed, and clutched the books to my chest, like a hard, flat teddy bear.

I squeezed the books tightly and tried to summon up

a real, nondream picture of my mother. I tried to picture her right there, in the bedroom. Again, I had to wonder: What would she think of how we lived? What would she think of what was going on out in the kitchen? What would she think of me?

FRİDAY, THE 25TH ✦ The first thing I noticed at the mall today was that Leo had placed two DANGER horses between Suzie's window and the wall of TVs. He had also set up about two dozen food court chairs in front of the TVs.

I slipped around the first DANGER horse and entered the office. Suzie was gone. A copy of *Teach Yourself Spanish* was left open on her desk. I supposed she was out giving a tour to that group from Brazil.

Suzie's phone rang. I picked it up and answered, "West End Mall."

"Hey, cuz. It's Kristin."

"Hey. How did you know I was here?"

"You're not at Arcane; where else would you be? Listen: I just talked to my dad. He said he'll cover for you tonight so you can come with Nina and me to the Gold Coast Mall."

"What for?"

"For our modeling clothes. For tomorrow. What, did you forget?"

"No."

I heard a loud burst of static, then, "We're the supermodels. You're the undercover reporter. Remember?"

"Aren't we supposed to model the clothes they sell here? Isn't that the idea?"

"The idea, cuz, is for us to look professional. We're not standing up there in some Kmart blue-light-special stretch pants. We're gonna look good." There was a pause and another burst of static. "Nina says, 'Looking good is not good enough.' You might want to write that down."

"Nina? Where are you?"

"We're in Nina's car. We're still at Lourdes, trying to get out of the parking lot. Nina's surrounded by boys."

"Look, uh, Kristin, I don't think we have the money for me to go shopping at the Gold Coast Mall. Not when Suzie said we could get the clothes for free, right here. I mean, that's the whole idea."

I could hear Nina yell in the background, "Don't be such a loser, Roberta!"

But Kristin didn't repeat that. She said, "All right. Look, just come with us and window-shop. Then you can write the whole thing up for the newsletter."

I could hear Nina again. "Don't do us any favors, Roberta."

Kristin ignored her. She said seriously, "Come on, Roberta. I got you a night off. What else are you going to do?"

What could I say? I muttered, "All right."

"All right! We're going to leave at six. You be ready."

"I'll be ready." She hung up, and so did I.

I left the office, detoured around the chair area, and started up the right side of the mallway. There was a guy working in the rotunda, a big burly guy. Definitely not

Leo. The words ACE PLUMBING were printed across the back of his shirt. Had Leo been replaced? I guessed so. I hoped he hadn't been fired.

I entered Arcane just as Uncle Frank was finishing up with two freaky-looking guys at Crusader. I said, "Uncle Frank, are you sure you don't need help tonight? I'll be glad to stay."

He shook his head. "No. No problem. I'm closing tonight, anyway. I've got Karl here if it gets busy. I've got the morons, too."

"You're sure?"

Uncle Frank thought about it. "It'll be good for you to get out. You and Kristin. And that Nina's a nice girl. A real religious girl."

I didn't say anything.

He changed the subject. "Say, Roberta, what's the slowest night here?"

"The slowest night? For money, you mean?"

"Money, traffic, everything."

"That would be Tuesday."

"I thought so. Okay." Uncle Frank walked away toward the back. I watched him go. He was really behaving oddly.

Karl and I stood together in silence for a long time. No customers came in. I finally said, "I'll be right back, Karl. Okay?"

Karl didn't answer, but he seemed alert enough to cover the front. I walked across the mallway to Isabel's Hallmark. On the way I looked over at the mannequin. Its forehead was no longer pressed straight against the glass. It had slumped to the right and was now wedged, skull first, into the corner. *Why does that thing keep moving?*

Margaret was standing behind Mrs. Weiss's cash register. She's currently "the girl." Mrs. Weiss always has a girl working for her. It doesn't seem to matter how old she is — if she's younger than Mrs. Weiss, she's "the girl." Margaret has been the girl for about two weeks. She's one of the ladies from Century Towers — an old lady, but not as old as Mrs. Weiss.

I looked down the first aisle and spotted Mrs. Weiss. She was setting up a display beneath a cardboard banner that said NEW FAMILIES.

Mrs. Weiss reads every card that comes into her store. She turned, saw me, and pointed quickly at a stack near her feet. "Will you look at these cards, Roberta? This whole pile of cards, there must be twenty-five of them, is for parents to tell their children that they can't be with them — for their birthdays, their graduations, even their weddings!" She pointed up at the banner. "That's what we used to call a broken home. Now we're calling it a 'new family'?" She kicked at the pile. "Let me tell you, honey, if your family isn't working any better than this, it's broken."

Mrs. Weiss worked her jaw for a moment. Then she said, "Margaret just gave her notice. Why don't you come over here and work for me?"

"I can't, Mrs. Weiss. You know that. They need me at Arcane."

"Yes, of course they do. You're exactly what they

need. Tell me, how much does your father pay you to run that place?"

"I don't run it."

"Bah! How much does he pay you?"

"Well, you know, I'm only fifteen. He doesn't technically pay me. He gives me money, though, whenever I ask for it."

"You don't have to tell me what you work for. I already know. You work for nothing." Mrs. Weiss studied the cards at her feet for a long moment.

Then, through the window, I caught sight of a bright yellow sign. It was bobbing up and down, coming down the mallway. It was a square sign with green letters that spelled out BRASIL TOURS. I walked around a card rack to see who was carrying it.

Mrs. Weiss looked up, too. She said, "What is that?"

A tall woman in a brown wool suit was at the head of a double line of teenage girls. The woman bore the sign before her like the first flag in a parade. She was about fifty years old, with gray-and-black hair pulled back in a bun. Suzie was walking next to her. She was talking and carrying on about something, but the woman didn't seem to be listening. Behind them walked sixteen girls arranged in eight pairs. The girls all had on matching outfits — khaki shorts and white sneakers, and yellow shirts with BRASIL TOURS printed in green. The words looked funny to me, like SpecialTees mistake shirts, but I guessed that was the Portuguese way of spelling *Brazil*.

Mrs. Weiss and I watched as the parade turned right, into Arcane.

I said, "Karl's going to need some help. I have to go, Mrs. Weiss."

By the time I had cut back across the mall, all those girls in the yellow shirts were gathered around the tall lady, who, I could now see, wore a tag that said DONA CLARA. Dona Clara lectured them sternly in Portuguese. She held up a five-dollar bill. I guessed she was telling them not to spend any more than that.

I stood in front of the counter. One girl leaned forward and stared at my name tag. Her long red hair hung way down her back. She had white skin with a few freckles, and green eyes. She sure didn't look Spanish. I smiled at her, so she said, "Roberta? May I try my English on you?"

I said, "Sure."

"I am Gabriela," she said. She held out a white hand for me to shake, which I did.

I heard myself talking very slowly. "Do you want to try one of the Arcane experiences?"

She said, "What is your favorite one?"

"My favorite what?"

She pointed at Crusader. "Your favorite . . . experience."

"I don't know. I've never done any of them."

Gabriela thought about this. "You are not permitted?"

"Oh, I'm permitted. I just don't want to."

"Why?"

There was no way Gabriela could understand this, but I said it anyway. "These experiences aren't real. I only like things that are real."

She stared at me for a moment. Then she held up a five-dollar bill. "What do I do?"

I demonstrated with the Crusader gear. "You put this helmet on, and you pick up the wand. A movie comes on inside the helmet. You see it and hear it. As you turn, the movie turns. As you move this wand, you stab people and cut their heads off."

Gabriela held up the hand without the money as if to stop me. She repeated, "You cut their heads off?"

"In some of the experiences. Like this one. In Galactic Defender over there, the enemies are aliens, so it's like you're cutting off their space helmets."

Gabriela walked over to Galactic Defender. She turned and handed me the money. "Okay. I'll try it."

As I helped her get set up, I noticed that the tour group kids had spread out all over the arcade. Uncle Frank and Karl were helping girls at Custer's Last Stand and King Kong. When the Galactic Defender CD started, I moved over and helped another girl at Crusader; then another one at Dragon Slayer.

When I got back to Galactic Defender, I could see that it was not going well. Gabriela's head was twitching, like she was having a seizure. She stumbled backward a couple of times, but she never raised the wand. It remained frozen at her side. When the experience was finished she stood still until I climbed up and got her out of the helmet. After I helped her step down, she whispered, "I did not like that."

I said, "Oh, I'm sorry." I really was. I added, "I'll tell Uncle Frank. He won't charge you."

Gabriela shook her head several times, as if to shake off the experience. "No. I want to pay. That is what our money is for today. To spend here."

I took her money and stepped quickly over to Crusader, which had just ended. That girl seemed to have liked it. She made a funny face at Gabriela and said something in Portuguese. I took her money, too. Then I helped the girl at Dragon Slayer.

Suzie walked by and pinched my arm. She said, "I brought you a lot of business. Didn't I?"

I took my three five-dollar bills to the register. Gabriela followed and stood before the counter. She pulled out a pen and one of Suzie's business cards. She scribbled something quickly and pointed at Suzie. "Roberta, do you know that lady?"

I said, "Yes, I do."

Gabriela stifled a laugh. "That lady speaks some really bad Spanish."

I laughed, too. "I'll bet."

"Some of the girls know only the Portuguese. They understand some Spanish. And they understand some English. But this lady, it's like she is not speaking any language." Gabriela held the card up for me to see what she had written. It looked like, *O que.* I tried to pronounce it and messed it up, so she pronounced it for me, "Okay." She pointed at it and explained, "*O que* is the Portuguese for 'What?' You say it when you don't understand. This lady keeps asking them stuff in Spanish, and they keep answering '*O que*' like they don't understand. But she thinks they're saying 'Okay.'"

That cracked me up. Uncle Frank and Karl both came behind the counter with bunches of five-dollar bills. They stared at me, like they had never seen me laugh before. Weird.

I slipped back down to the floor. I asked Gabriela, "So why are you all dressed alike?"

She answered, "We are from the same *colegio*." She thought about that and explained, "The same high school. When a girl at school has her birthday, fifteen years old, she takes a trip. We all took the Florida trip. Twenty-eight girls and Dona Clara. Dona Clara is one of our teachers."

"I counted sixteen girls. Where are the rest?"

"They are at the hotel. They are all sick."

"Oh no."

Suzie called over to Dona Clara. "It's almost four o'clock. *Vamanos!*" She held up her wristwatch and smiled enormously. Dona Clara got the message, but she had obviously stopped smiling back at Suzie a while ago. She pumped the green sign pole up and down a few times, and the girls all reassembled in their pairs.

Suzie took me by the arm. "Roberta, come watch the show with us. Walk over with your new friend."

I looked at Dona Clara. She didn't seem to mind, so I stood outside the line, next to Gabriela.

Gabriela introduced me to the girl next to her, saying. "This is Monica. *Monica, issa é Roberta.*"

Monica smiled and shook hands.

Dona Clara walked by the girls and tapped on the tops of their heads. She counted aloud in Portuguese, sixteen heads. She pumped the sign one more time, and we took off.

We had already walked straight through the rotunda before I realized that the mess was all gone. No DAN-GER horses, no loose tiles, no Leo, no Ace Plumbing guy. The fountain job appeared to have been completed.

Suzie guided us into the area in front of the TV sets. Gabriela, Monica, and I took seats in the back. Dona Clara arranged the other girls' seats, separating some of them, like all teachers do. She looked right at me and thought for a moment. Then she smiled slightly and turned her attention to someone else.

Suzie took a remote from the top of the TV wall. She came behind me and pressed the volume button until we could hear.

Somebody patted me on the shoulder. I turned and saw Kristin. She was panting, like she had been running. She said, "We just made it. The storm's about to hit."

Nina was behind her. She was staring at the TV wall. "Hey, it's four o'clock. Are you watching Angela?"

Suzie answered her, "You bet."

Nina gave two thumbs-up. "All right! Angela's my girl. What's the topic today?"

Suzie said, "Brazilian teenagers," and pointed to the tour group.

Nina looked puzzled. She said to Kristin, "What kind of topic is that?" Nina and Kristin took chairs next to me, on the far side of Gabriela and Monica.

Suzie called out to everyone, "Shh! *Andalay! Andalay!* Here we go."

The nine screens filled up with pictures of Angela del Fuego — her bright red nails, her long red hair, her shiny white teeth. It was her usual opening — a montage of scenes from past shows. Then a voice-over from Angela began: "When you think of Brazil, you think of Rio de Janeiro, Brazil's most famous city and main tourist destination. You think of its world-renowned beaches — Copacabana and Ipanema. What you try not to think of is this: A stone's throw from all this wealth and glamor are the *favelas*, the brutal slums in which as many as two million Brazilians eke out a miserable, violent, and brief existence."

The voice-over paused while the screens filled with pictures of people living in lean-to shacks and poking through piles of garbage. The last picture was of a little girl with a bloated stomach. She was naked, standing ankle-deep in the mud, and crying. The voice-over resumed, "What happens when children such as this one survive until their teenage years, and try to leave the *favelas*, will shock you. Today on *Angela Live*."

A series of commercials began, during which we sat in uncomfortable silence. Suzie attempted to smile at Dona Clara, but Dona Clara was staring out through the glass doors at the raging thunderstorm.

Gabriela leaned over, pointed to Kristin and Nina, and asked, "Roberta, are these your friends?"

I said, "Yes," and introduced them. "This is my cousin Kristin and her friend Nina. This is Gabriela."

Kristin took Gabriela's outstretched hand and shook it. She said, "Hi."

At first Nina didn't move. The she stared at Gabriela for a moment and said, "You got nice hair."

Gabriela muttered, "Thank you," and sat back in her chair.

A few seconds later Angela del Fuego returned. This time she was live, standing in her studio. She had on a two-piece black suit with a white blouse, and lots of gold jewelry. She had three guests sitting behind her on a stage — a South American priest in a priest's collar, a young black lady in a blue dress, and a white-guy lawyer in a gray suit.

The camera zoomed in on Angela as she spoke to the audience. "Are there areas in your city where you won't go to shop because of street kids? I know there are for me. As a woman alone, I don't feel safe there. So I spend my money somewhere else. Shopkeepers in those areas might not like it, but there's not much they can do about it. Shopkeepers in Rio, on the other hand, *can* do something about it. They can have the street kids murdered."

The TV screens filled with a picture of a row of bloody bodies, dead teenagers' bodies, lined up on a sidewalk. Angela continued, "These teenagers were shot as they lay sleeping outside a cathedral. They were shot by a death squad of off-duty police officers hired by the local shopkeepers — hired as we might hire someone to sweep the sidewalk, or to clean the windows."

I looked at the girls from the tour group. By now even the ones who didn't speak English had gotten the message. They were obviously uncomfortable, shifting around in their seats. Some were looking over at Dona Clara, whose mouth was hanging slightly open. I watched as, suddenly, she snapped her mouth shut, stood up, and picked up the green pole. She shoved the DANGER horse out of her way and stepped out into the mallway. The girls all got up, with a loud scraping of chairs, and fell into two lines behind her.

I turned toward Suzie. She seemed to be struck dumb, like she had forgotten how to speak entirely.

Dona Clara quickly counted the girls. Then she pointed angrily at the wall of TVs and said to all of us, in unaccented English, "Tell her to talk about Miami." She called to the girls, "Vamos," which, I figure, is Portuguese for "Vamanos."

They started forward. Gabriela looked over her shoulder and raised her free hand, the hand that wasn't holding Monica's, to wave good-bye. I waved back. They marched straight out the glass door and into the thunderstorm. They must have drowned on the way to their bus.

Suzie came up next to Kristin, Nina, and me. She sighed. "That's what I get for going out of my way."

We all looked back at the screens. The woman in blue was saying, "In the last year alone, more than twelve hundred children were murdered in Rio. That's about four children a day, just in that one city."

I said to Suzie, "Do you want us to take these chairs back?"

Nina answered, "Hey, don't take mine. I want to see this."

Suzie said, "No, that's all right, Roberta. Leo will come and get them." She sat down with Nina and Kristin. "I want to see the rest of this, too."

I worked my way out of the chair area and started back toward work. The last thing I heard as I circled behind the TV wall was, "It's happening in South America today. Will it happen in North America tomorrow?"

When I entered Arcane, Uncle Frank seemed surprised to see me. He said, "What? Is the show over?"

"Let's just say the tour is over." I joined him behind the counter.

I spotted Hawg and Ironman coming in from the north side. They had stopped to talk to the Head Louse. They all looked very serious. As usual, I could only hear Hawg's end of the conversation. He told the Head Louse, very emphatically, "That's right! I don't like him. Somebody don't want me in his store, and kicks me out just for trying to watch a damn football game on TV — I don't have to like him. Do I?"

Uncle Frank gestured toward them and shook his head. "Sounds like I'm the only one who doesn't kick them out."

Uncle Frank knelt down and opened the floor safe. He pulled out a handful of coin rolls and started to sort them. I looked up as the Head Louse approached the counter. He asked, "So where's Karl?"

I told him, "I don't know. He might be down at Love-a-Pet; he might be at the food court."

Uncle Frank stood up. He locked eyes with the Head

Louse, who took a quick step backward. Uncle Frank demanded, "Why do you want to know where Karl is?"

The Head Louse gulped. "He's a friend of mine, that's all."

"He's on break. When he's on break, we give him a break."

The Head Louse took another step, spun around, and left the arcade. Uncle Frank watched him go.

Nina and Kristin arrived with Karl just after five. They were talking about the Brazilian kids on the TV show, but not the Brazilian kids in our mall. It was like they had missed the real story — that the Brazilians had marched out of the mall in disgust.

Kristin said, "All right, Roberta will know." She turned to me, "What language were they speaking?"

I said, "Who, the Brazilians?"

Nina sneered. "No, the Munchkins."

I answered Kristin anyway. "They were speaking Portuguese."

Nina sounded triumphant. "See, I told you that wasn't Spanish."

Kristin answered, "I didn't say it was Spanish. I said it sounded more like German."

"Girl, that's not German!"

"Right, like you would know."

"I know it wasn't Spanish." Nina turned to me. "Roberta, you missed a really good show." She turned back to Kristin. "Did you see Angela's nails today? They were so perfect, you know? So long, it's like they're not even human.

"My aunt says that Angela del Fuego goes to her salon, like, every Saturday and spends at least five hundred bucks in one hour. They all start working on her at once — manicure, pedicure, mud pack, facial. Like that scene in *The Wizard of Oz* when everybody's working on the Cowardly Lion. You know, when they get to the Emerald City, and they all go inside, and they're all getting their hair done and stuff?"

Kristin said, "Yeah, I remember that. They're doing Toto, too."

"Yeah, that's it. Toto, too. Angela always looks so fine." The two of them settled into their usual spots behind the counter.

Suddenly Nina got very excited. "Oh! Oh! Did you see the show yesterday?"

Kristin answered, "No. What was it about?"

"Guess."

"No, I'm not going to guess."

"No, really. I'm serious. See if you can guess. This is too weird. You'll never guess it."

"Then I give up."

She poked at Karl, rousing him from a magazine. "How about you, big guy?"

I figured Karl hadn't been listening, but I was wrong. He came up with a guess right away. "Teenage psycho zombies from hell?"

"No. Listen to this: These kinda dumpy-looking women were all married to serial killers, and they didn't know it." She looked from me to Karl to Kristin triumphantly. "But they all said, like, afterward, 'Oh yeah,

I wondered why he had that bloodstain on his socks.' Or 'I wondered why he would never let me open the trunk of his car.' Stuff like that. It's like they all had little pieces of the puzzle, but they couldn't see the whole thing."

I understood immediately. I added, "Or they didn't want to see the whole thing."

"Yeah. There you go." Nina looked hard at me for a moment, like she was waiting for me to say something else. But I didn't.

Dad appeared from around the corner with a slice of pizza and a Coke. He stopped by the side of the counter. "Hey, honey. Suzie said that tomorrow you should wear what you would normally wear. Just come to the mall office at eleven and she'll fix you up."

"Okay. Thanks, Dad."

Nina waited until he left to say, "You know she's gonna send you to the Gap."

I shrugged. "That's fine with me."

Nina looked away. "Whatever."

Kristin said, "Roberta, there's still time to get something with us tonight. Your dad will give you the money."

"No. That's okay."

Uncle Frank came back from dinner early, at about five-thirty. He looked agitated. Right away he called over to us, "Go on. Go on. I'm back now."

Kristin came around and took him by the elbow. "Daddy, I'll need some money for the mall." Uncle Frank took out his wallet and gave her a twenty-dollar bill. Kristin just stared at it. She looked embarrassed.

"Uh, Daddy, I'll need a lot more than this tonight. We're going to the Gold Coast Mall." Uncle Frank looked at her and then at Nina. He seemed trapped. He looked through his wallet again. He pulled out his American Express card and handed it to Kristin, saying, "You girls be careful over there."

"We will. Thanks, Daddy." Kristin and Nina hurried out.

I felt really bad about leaving him. But I said, "Good night, Uncle Frank," and ran to catch up with them.

As we hurried through the rotunda, I saw a couple standing by the south anchor store, arguing. It was Sam and Verna. I heard Sam say, "I was at my car an hour ago, and it was fine. So now you know who did it! If you don't believe me, ask Griffin."

I knew right away what had happened: Sam's car had been vandalized again. And I knew I had to see it for myself. As soon as we got through the door, I practically yelled at Nina, "We have to drive around back. Somebody's car got vandalized!"

I thought Nina would give me a hard time, but she agreed right away. "Yeah, sure. Okay."

We ran all the way out to the perimeter parking spaces. Nina's car is a black Corvette convertible with red leather seats. She has license plates that say NINA 1.

Nina turned the engine on with a loud roar. "Where are we going?"

I squeezed into the back. "Go around the south anchor store, the one that used to be Burdines."

"Okay."

We zoomed around to the back of the mall. I spotted Sam's car right away. It was parked against the building, about twenty yards up from the trash trailer. It was a brand-new white BMW with a brand-new paint job. But it now had a deep, ragged scratch running from the back bumper to the front bumper, like a long appendix scar.

Nina called out, "Oh, man! That's cold. That's real cold. Look, they keyed that beautiful Beemer."

Kristin said, "I don't think a key did that. That scratch is too deep and wide. That looks like a tire iron."

Nina asked me, "So whose car is it?"

"Sam's."

"Oh yeah?" Nina whipped the Corvette around. "That's a nice car, and he's very foolish. If you have a nice car, you don't park it out back. There's too many scumbags around here. Like my father says, 'If you go looking for trouble, you're sure to find it.'"

I thought about Sam as we pulled out of the parking lot. Sam wasn't a fool, and he wasn't looking for trouble. Just the opposite. Why would somebody hate him?

FRIDAY NIGHT ⟿ I've never been in a car traveling as fast as Nina's Corvette did down Everglades Boulevard. It was frightening. The wind blew so hard into my face that my own words could not get out. They blew right back down my throat.

However, I could still hear voices from the front seat.

They came hurtling past me clear and loud. So I listened, like I was supposed to do.

Kristin asked, "Is Carlos going to be there tonight?"

Nina sneered. "Carlos? What do I care where he is?"

Kristin laughed in disbelief. "So you're not going to the cotillion dance with him?"

Nina shrugged. "I might. If I don't get a better offer. Like, from a real man."

Kristin laughed again. "If Carlos only knew how you talk about him."

"What? I talk about him the same way when he's there. I tell him, 'Carlos, you got two chances with me: no way and no how.'"

"So why do you go out with him?"

"Because he begs me to. And because he takes me to nice places."

"Isn't he in love with you?"

Nina hesitated, like she had never thought about that. Then she said, "Yeah, of course he's in love with me." She thought about it a minute more. "It's like, he's in love with me, but he knows he shouldn't be. Like, he knows he's out of his league and he's never gonna get loved in return, but that's okay. He's happy just to be where he is."

Kristin held up her thumb at a right angle to her index finger, forming the letter *L*. She and Nina said in unison, "Loser."

We finally slowed down for a red light at Seventy-second Street. I took the opportunity to lean forward and ask, "If you think he's such a loser, why do you go out with him?"

Nina looked surprised to see someone in the backseat. But she answered me seriously, "There was one moment in time when he had potential. When I first met him, he was sitting in the parking lot at Xavier in this blue Jaguar XKE convertible. Beautiful car. He asked me out to the Marlins game that night, and I was real excited to go. I was even standing out in the driveway with my sister, like, waiting for him, so she could see the car. And what does he do? He pulls up in some little pickup truck. Like a Toyota or something. My sister started laughing so hard she had to run inside.

"He gets out and says to me, 'So you ready to go?'

"I said, 'Not in that thing. What do you think I'm gonna do, go pick sugarcane? Where's the XKE?'

"He says, 'Oh, that's my dad's car. He's using it tonight.'

"I said, 'Well, you can go get your dad's car, or you can go to that baseball game by yourself.'"

Kristin interjected, "So what did he do?"

"I don't know what he did. But he came back, like, two hours later, with the Jag. We made it to the game around the seventh inning."

I said to her, "So what if he had refused to go get that car? What if he had said, 'Take it or leave it'?"

Nina thought for a long time. "I guess I'd have had a little more respect for him. But he didn't say that. He went and got the Jag."

The light changed and we roared off, but we soon

got caught in the eastbound traffic. I leaned forward again. "How about you, Kristin? Who are you going to this dance with?"

Kristin curled up her lip. "Greg Vandervelt."

"Who's that?"

"Just some guy who asked me."

Nina scoffed. "Oh yeah, just some guy." She yelled back to me, "He's, like, the king of the Anglos. He's a captain on the baseball team, president of the student council, straight-A honor roll. He's, like, perfect."

It was Kristin's turn to scoff. "He's not perfect. He's boring. He's a stuffed shirt. All he can talk about is himself and how great he is."

Nina disagreed. "Well, he sure looks good." She yelled back to me, "All the little blond girls want Greggie for their own. But he has chosen Kristin. Together they shall be king and queen of the Anglos."

Kristin said, "He's Dutch and I'm German. How's that make us king and queen of the Anglos?"

"Because you're all Anglos to us."

I said to Nina, "It sounds like you don't approve of Greg."

"Hey, I don't care about him one way or the other. As long as he treats my girl here good, he's okay with me."

We drove straight east, toward the Atlantic Ocean. After we crossed the Intracoastal Waterway, Kristin turned and pointed. "That's the Gold Coast Mall, Roberta. You've never been there, have you?"

"No." I looked ahead, on the right. It was enormous, at least four times the size of the West End Mall. It took up most of the land between the Intracoastal and A1A, the beach road. Each corner of the mall had a spiral parking ramp attached to it. One was pink; one was orange; one was pale green; one was pale blue.

Nina turned right and drove around to the back. There weren't any trash trailers back there. The back of this mall was as immaculate as the front, and as luxurious. Nina said, "Let's park in Avocado. I have avocado eyeliner on tonight."

We took a glass elevator to the ground level. Nina knew right where to go. She said to me, "Roberta, are you watching my every move for the newsletter?"

I said, "Yeah, I guess."

Nina led us to four chiseled glass doors with brass frames and handles. She pushed them open, and I quickly found myself inside the Gold Coast Mall.

It was a beautiful, beautiful place. Nina and Kristin had to wait for me because I was stuck in one spot, staring. The floor was made of pink-and-white marble. The storefronts had wooden planters attached above them, with lush plants hanging down. The music and the lighting were both very soft and elegant. There was an oasis in front of us, with mahogany benches and a babbling brook. I felt like I had stepped into a rich person's mansion, not a mall.

Kristin said to me, "It's hard to believe the same guy owns our mall."

"Who? Ray Lyons?"

"Yep. If I were him, I'd be ashamed to admit it."

Nina tugged on Kristin's arm. "You tell me, girl-friend. Tell me what guys we're gonna see tonight." Then she turned to me. "I should say, 'What guys are going to have the privilege of seeing us tonight?'"

I asked Nina, "Are a lot of guys from Xavier going to be here?"

"For sure. This is a big Xavier hangout. Xavier and Lourdes. We'll check out Bloomie's first. There'll be some girls in there getting their colors done. There always are."

I asked her, "What's that?"

"Makeup? Finding out the best color of makeup to use? What, you never did that?"

"I never heard of it."

"*Madre de Dios.*" She shot a disbelieving look over at Kristin. Then she said, "Roberta, you need a makeover. You need one in the worst way."

I wasn't interested. "I don't want a makeover."

"I didn't say you want one. I said you need one. Bad."

We turned into the golden-framed entrance of Bloomingdale's. It looked fantastic. It smelled fantastic. There were high stools and counters all around us, showcasing different brands of makeup. Nina stopped next to a girl on a white stool who was staring hard into a round mirror. She was drawing a purple line under her eyelid with a pencil. Nina winked at me and then said, "Oh! That color looks so good on you, Lisette."

The girl looked further into the mirror until she spotted who was speaking. She said, "Ninaaaa," in a drawn-out way. Then she went back to her purple line.

We continued on. Nina turned to Kristin and said, "She stuffs."

Kristin nodded in agreement. "Most definitely."

I asked Nina, "Stuffs what?"

"She stuffs her bra. You can see it." She turned to Kristin, disgusted. "God! You know, if you're gonna stuff it, have a little class. Use some shoulder pads or something. This girl, you can see wadded-up Kleenex sticking out of her blouse."

We went to another counter, which said CLINIQUE. This time Nina and Kristin made me sit on the stool. They started moving bands of color on a color chart, like a slide rule, trying to figure out my colors. Kristin said, "I think she's earth tones."

Nina said, "I think she's hopeless."

"Cut it out, Nina."

"I'm joking. Lighten up. I'd go with pale greens and yellows. She's more like forest tones."

They went on like that for about ten minutes, with me sitting there silently, like I was in the dentist's chair. Then Nina bought a couple of bottles and tubes and said to me, "Okay, Roberta. We're all ready for your makeover. We'll do it tomorrow morning."

Kristin asked, "Where do you want to do it?"

Nina started to answer, but Kristin interrupted her. "I was asking Roberta!"

I said, "I don't know. My house, I guess."

"What time?"

"We have to be at the mall office at eleven. Is ten o'clock enough time?"

Nina said, "Girl, there is not enough time in all of —"

Kristin interrupted her again. "What she means is that we'll be there at ten."

Nina frowned, but she said, "Sure, whatever," and led us off in a new direction. We stopped at a set of red-and-gold doors that said BLOOMINGDALE'S BOU-TIQUE. She said to Kristin, "Here it is, girlfriend. The dress you want is right through that door."

Kristin didn't seem so sure. She said, "No, I want to look out here, in the petites."

Nina shook her head. "Whatever. To each her own and all that. Roberta, who you hanging with?"

I said, "I don't know."

Nina decided. "You'd better come with me, then."

I looked at the red doors. "Am I allowed in there?"

Nina laughed out loud. She shouted, "Allowed? You come with me. And you take notes."

We burst though the red doors and entered a circular room with dresses displayed around its perimeter. Two ladies in what looked like French maids' outfits approached us. They looked like they were going to ask me what I was doing there, but Nina jumped all over them. She started to order them around like they were her personal maids, and they took it from her! It was a little nasty, and a little embarrassing. But it didn't last long. When the maids found what she was asking for,

Nina announced, "I'll take it," without even trying it on. We were back outside the red doors, purchase in hand, in ten minutes.

Nina said, "What did you think of that, huh? That has to be a new record."

I said, "That was really fast. How much did you pay for that dress?"

Nina shook her head for a few seconds, like she wasn't going to answer. Then she said, "I'll tell you, but don't you put it in the article. Okay? My dad would go nuts."

"Okay."

"It was eight hundred and fifty dollars."

I laughed. "You're kidding. Right?"

"No, I'm not kidding. That's how much a dress like this costs."

"No dress I've ever heard of costs that much. I bet that's more than I've spent on clothes in my entire life."

"Yeah, well, where do you shop, at Kmart?"

"Yeah. Or Wal-Mart. Or Target."

"I believe it. Did you know that all those clothes are made by child slaves?"

"Not all of them."

"Do you know which ones aren't?"

"No."

"There you go. If you want clothes made by grown-ups, and by people who understand fashion, you have to pay for them."

We both spotted Kristin up ahead of us. She was near where we had left her, standing by those high white stools, and she was talking to three guys. Nina told me, "Look, that's Greg. Do you see what I mean? He's, like, the super-Anglo. And he's always prepped out like that."

Greg and the two guys with him were all dressed basically the same, in tan slacks with polo shirts. When we got closer, I heard Greg ask Kristin, "So you really know karate?"

Kristin answered matter-of-factly, "I really know karate."

"Do you think you could take me?"

"I could take all three of you losers." She turned and saw us. Right away she said, "I'd like you to meet my cousin, Roberta."

Greg turned, but he looked right past me until he focused on Nina. He said, "I should have known your partner wouldn't be far away."

Nina smiled brightly. She said to the three of them, in a perky voice, "Hey, you guys need to come to the West End Mall tomorrow at noon. Kristin is going to be modeling."

Greg said, "Swimsuits?"

Kristin elbowed him in the side, which I think hurt more than he let on. He looked at Nina. "You know, she never mentioned that to us."

Kristin told the three guys, "Nina will be modeling tomorrow, too. And Roberta."

Greg took a deep breath. "Okay. Maybe we'll check it out." He looked at Kristin. "Noon, right?"

But it was Nina who answered him. "That's right. You tell all the guys you know to be there."

Greg looked at his friends, who were already drifting away. He said, "Yeah, okay. Maybe we'll see you there."

Kristin lifted the wrapping from around Nina's dress. "This is spectacular."

Nina took her by the arm. "Come on. There's one for you in there, too."

Kristin resisted. "No. That's super-expensive. I can't go that way."

"You *can* go that way. Believe me." Nina took Kristin's arm and pulled her back toward the Boutique. They went quickly through the red doors, without me. I hung back for a few minutes, not wanting to walk through by myself. But I didn't want to stand in the aisle by myself, either. I finally opened the door, cautiously, and peeked in.

Nina and Kristin were already at the cash register. I hurried over to join them before one of the French maids could see me. Kristin was saying, "I don't know. Maybe I ought to try it on."

Nina was adamant. "If you're truly a size seven, then you're a size seven. Trying things on is for people who don't know what size they are. Or who are always changing sizes. Bingeing and purging people."

Kristin stared at the dress doubtfully. She finally said, "Well, at least it's on sale. Right?"

Nina assured her, "That's right." She snapped at a French maid who was passing by. "Hey, come here and take her money. This girl is a supermodel."

The woman did as Nina said. She even answered,

"Yes, ma'am," meekly and politely. Like she didn't really mind the way Nina was speaking to her. Like she was only acting in a play. She took the black dress, and Kristin's credit card, and began to ring it up.

Kristin asked, "How much is it?"

The woman punched some keys on a little credit card machine. She never looked up. "Four hundred and ten dollars."

Kristin bent backward about six inches. She shot a glance at me. Nina, of course, thought nothing of it. Unless she thought it was a great bargain. I couldn't tell either way.

Kristin was struggling to say something, but she never got the chance. The French maid came back from around the register. She wasn't meek anymore. She said, "The cardserver refused payment. Do you have another card?"

Kristin looked sick. She shook her head and said, "No."

The French maid smiled slightly, and coldly. She asked, "Will you be paying cash, then? Or will you be writing a check?"

I thought Kristin was going to break down and cry. She took the credit card back from the woman and just stared at it. Nobody said anything until Nina finally broke the spell. She snapped at the woman, "She's not doing either one. She's gonna go someplace else where the credit card machine works."

Nina led Kristin out by the elbow, and I followed. We

were all the way back in the mallway when Nina asked, "So where do you want to go now? How about Saks?"

Kristin still had her head down. She muttered, "No, I'd better not. I can't charge four hundred dollars on this card, and I don't have anything else." She looked up at Nina. "This is crazy, anyway. I don't want to spend that much money on an outfit that I'll wear one time. That's crazy."

Nina said, "I agree. I don't want to do that, either."

I said, "But you just did. You spent twice that much."

Nina waved her hand in dismissal. "Nah. I didn't spend anything. It's a loaner."

Kristin demanded, "A what?"

"A loaner. I'm bringing the thing back tomorrow afternoon."

Kristin shook her head. She was as confused as I was. "How are you going to return it? What are you going to say is wrong with it?"

"Wrong with it? I don't know. 'It didn't match my lipstick.' 'It made my Lhasa sneeze.' Whatever."

Kristin was outraged. "That's dishonest!"

"Oh, please."

"No. No, I'm not going to do that. I'm going to find a hundred-dollar dress, and I'm going to wear it tomorrow, and then I'm going to keep it."

"Hey, whatever. You do whatever you want."

We started down the mallway. Nina turned to me. "Okay, reporter girl, I guess you think she's right and I'm wrong. Huh?"

"Yeah."

"That figures. But I want you to listen to me, and I want to read this part in your newsletter story." Nina held up her $850 dress in its garment bag. "I am doing this store a favor, and I am doing this designer a favor, by wearing this dress tomorrow. Girls, and young women, and even older women who keep themselves in shape, will come to this store and buy their over-priced dresses. But they will not return those dresses, because theirs will not be loaners. And that will all be because of me." Nina reached over and tapped her finger against my head. "This is what you call thinking like a supermodel. You don't think Alek Wek buys her own clothes. Do you? Or Rebecca Romijn-Stamos? Designers are lined up, begging them to wear their clothes."

Kristin made a sudden, sharp right into Petite Sophisticate. Within five minutes she found a black dress for $100. To me, it was just as nice as Nina's, and I told her so. But when Kristin went to pay for it at the cash register, it happened again. The girl behind the register said, "Sorry, it won't take your credit card. Do you have another one?"

Kristin was humiliated. Her neck and face turned pink. Nina came over and rubbed her arm gently, like she was a little kid. She said, "Hey, girlfriend, don't worry about it. I'll put it on my card, and you can pay me back." Nina handed over a gold credit card, and the transaction was quickly completed. Kristin took the dress and walked, with her head even lower than before, back out into the mallway.

Nina tried to reassure her. "Don't worry about it. It's probably some kind of technical difficulties, like they get on cable TV. Those green cards get all messed up. I think it's because too many people have them. The wires get overloaded or something."

Kristin said, "I'm going to pay you back tonight."

"Don't worry about it."

"I am worried about it. I'm going to pay you back tonight."

We stopped at an ice-cream stall in the middle of the mallway, called Gelato. Nina got us all free samples, and then we left.

I was eager to get home. But as we turned out of the parking garage a big white convertible pulled up even with us. It had three guys inside. One guy riding in the front seat looked over and yelled, "Nina! Hey, Nina!"

Nina answered, "Yo! What's up?"

I looked over at them. The guy who'd yelled to Nina, and the driver next to him, looked scary to me. Like guys who start fights. The third one, in the backseat, was a smaller guy with blond hair in a bowl cut.

The first guy said, "Nina, I've been thinking about you lately."

"Yeah? Then you've been dreaming lately."

"Come on, I'm serious. I want to talk to you."

"Yeah? So talk."

"How about taking a ride with us. Just for fun. We're cruising the Strip tonight."

Nina didn't check with Kristin or me. She just said, "Okay."

The driver peeled out in front of us and turned east. We followed, speeding right behind them toward A1A.

Kristin asked Nina, "Who are they?"

"I don't know."

"Then why are we following them?"

"I know the one in the front seat. He's on the football team. He was dating that Theresa girl from algebra class, the one with the big nose. You know who I mean?"

"Yeah. But I don't remember him."

"She really ought to have that thing fixed."

"What about the rest of them?"

"I've seen the driver around. I think he's on the football team, too."

After we had raced all the way to A1A, we followed them on a slow cruise up the Strip. The Strip is a stretch of hotels, restaurants, and other tourist businesses that runs along A1A. It's a weird mix of sunburnt tourist families on the one hand, and street kids, prostitutes, and drug dealers on the other.

Seven years ago my mom, dad, and I owned an arcade on the Strip. That was back in the days of Mario Brothers and Street Fighter. It was before there was virtual reality. We did a good business in the daytime with the tourist families. We did an even better business in the nighttime with the teenagers, and the bikers, and all sorts of weirdos. We were open seven days a week. I always got to go in with Mom on Saturday and Sunday. I used to make change for the tourist families.

But that was a long time ago. As we sped along the

Strip in the Corvette, I couldn't recognize anything from those days. The further we went, the harder I strained to catch a memory. I remembered that our business, which was called the Family Arcade, was just south of Ocean Boulevard. I yelled up to Nina, "Where's Ocean Boulevard?"

"Ocean? It's the next light."

I looked closely at every business, trying to pick out our old spot. I saw the Greek Isles Family Restaurant, and a T-shirt shop, and a tattoo and piercing parlor. I didn't remember any of them. I didn't remember anything at all, until I saw the 7-Eleven.

Nina slowed down and turned left into the 7-Eleven parking lot, following the guys' car. All at once I remembered everything about the place.

I remembered the row of telephones across the front. And the surveillance camera bolted over the front door. And the Slurpee machine inside the window. My mom used to let me walk next door to the 7-Eleven to get a Slurpee, a cherry Slurpee, every Saturday and Sunday.

So I looked back one space to the left, at the tattoo and piercing parlor. That had to be it. That had to be our arcade.

The guys parked in front of the telephones, so we parked in the space to the right of them. Kristin said, "What are we doing here, Nina? I don't like this."

Nina told her, "I don't know. I guess they're going to the store."

We sat there for an uncomfortable minute or two,

looking at some creepy guys who were hanging around the telephones. The parking lot on either side of us seemed to be filled with kids just wandering around. Street kids. Kristin said, "I don't see anybody going in the store. Let's get out of here."

Nina called over to the guy in the front seat, "Hey, what's going on?"

The blond one from the backseat got out and walked up to the telephone bank. The guy in the front seat said, "He needs to make a phone call. So, Nina, you want to join the party tonight?"

"I don't know. Where's the party?"

"I guess it's right here."

"In the parking lot?"

"No, no. Maybe out on the beach."

Nina switched off the car. Kristin hissed at her, "What are you doing?"

"I'm saving some gas. Chill out."

The guy said, "You are really looking fine, Nina."

It sounded like we were going to be there for a while, so I hopped up and vaulted out of the car. Kristin shouted at me, "Roberta! What do you think you're doing?"

I pointed toward the tattoo parlor. "I think that was our arcade. The one we owned before Arcane."

"Yeah? So what? Get back in the car."

"I haven't seen it in seven years. I want to take a quick look."

"No way! Get back in here."

Nina said, "Chill out, girlfriend. Everything's cool. We got all these big, strong guys to protect us."

Kristin and I both looked over at the telephones. The blond from the backseat was talking to some little guy with a metal chain around his neck. He was real creepy looking. So was his partner, a tall guy with long arms and longer hair. When he saw us looking at him, he put a can of beer on top of the pay phone and took a step forward, into the light. All he had on was a tight pair of cutoffs and some thongs. I could see that he had tattoos on both arms. His partner said something to him, so he turned back.

I told Kristin, "I just want to take a quick look, Kristin. Really, just thirty seconds."

Kristin shook her head back and forth, like she couldn't believe any of this. She said, "Yeah, why not. Whatever."

As I walked behind the guys' car, I saw the big creepy guy step forward again. He said to Kristin, "Hey, are you ladies here for spring break?"

Kristin answered, "It's August, you moron."

I walked toward a pair of dirty-looking kids — a skinny boy with a shaved head and a chubby girl with long curly hair. They looked like they were about twelve years old. They also looked sickly, really pale, like they had just donated three gallons of blood. The girl stepped in front of me. I looked into her eyes for a moment. She asked me, "You got some change?"

I shook my head no. I wanted to say something to her, but nothing came to mind, so I continued on toward the wide front window of the tattoo parlor. The window had the words THIRD EYE TATTOO AND BODY

PIERCING PARLOR painted on it in gold. Beneath the name was the image of a golden globe, with a big eyeball in the middle of it.

I pressed my face up against the glass and stared in. A woman was sitting behind a card table, reading a paperback in the dim light. She took no notice of me. I scanned the whole place, remembering everything that I could. I saw where the pinball tables used to be, and the air hockey, and the cash register.

Then, I don't know why, I spun around to look at the Corvette. That creepy guy was now standing right over Kristin. What happened next was unbelievable. The guy reached down and grabbed her. Then Kristin's right arm shot upward, like a rocket. The heel of her hand caught the guy under his chin and snapped his head back. And then he kept going back, like a falling tree, until his head smacked onto the asphalt.

Nina screamed and cranked the ignition key. The Corvette roared, squealed backward, then shot toward the exit. Nina was all the way out on A1A when Kristin grabbed her arm and shouted, "Roberta!"

Nina slammed on the brakes as Kristin waved at me frantically. "Roberta, run! Get in the car!"

I took off and ran past the chubby girl and the skinny boy. I ran as fast as I could. The big creepy guy was already back up on his feet, stumbling over to his partner and shouting, "Give me the piece! I'm wastin' her. Give me the piece!"

When I was close enough to the car, I dived over the side and crashed in the back. Nina floored it and we peeled away. We hit Ocean Boulevard at about sixty miles per hour. Somehow Nina managed to make the turn.

We continued to accelerate all the way down Ocean Boulevard. Nina was scared, and her driving showed it, but Kristin was freaking out. She yelled, "He grabbed me! That disgusting pig! He grabbed me!"

Nina yelled back, over the wind and the revving engine, "What do you mean? Who grabbed you?"

"You saw him! That creep! He was standing right over me, drooling."

"Oh, that scary dude?"

"That beer-breath scumbag! You didn't know he was there?"

"I was talking to the guys. I didn't know what he was doing."

"He was standing there looking down my blouse the whole time. You knew I wanted to get out of there!"

"I didn't know. I was talking to the guys."

I leaned forward, as best I could, and yelled, "What did he do?"

Kristin pulled her lips back, baring her teeth. "He said, 'Are those real?' and he reached down and grabbed me."

Nina shouted, "He grabbed you how? Like he choked you?"

"No! He grabbed my breasts! Aren't you listening?" Kristin unbuttoned her blouse and folded down the side of her bra. "Oh, my god! I have red marks from his hand on me. Oh, my god!" She rolled her head back, like she was going to pass out from disgust.

Nina finally slowed down. I have no idea if we had been running traffic lights, but if we did, we got away with it. She asked, "So do you need to go to the hospital?"

"No."

"How about the cops. Do you want to call the cops?"

"What for?"

"To report that guy?"

Kristin said, "No, what I want to do is kill him. I want to go back there and kill him with my bare hands."

I spoke up. "I heard him say he was going to kill you."

"What?"

"When I was running for the car, I heard him. He was asking for a piece. That's a gun. He said he was going to waste you."

Kristin sat back and rebuttoned her blouse. When she finally spoke, she was calm. "Perfect. The perfect ending to a perfect night. I'll go back and get in my karate stance, and he'll shoot me."

Nina said, "That's a real bad idea."

Kristin sneered at her. "It's called sarcasm. The real bad idea was to follow those guys."

"Oh yeah. Right. Like I knew something like this was going to happen."

Kristin leaned toward her. "No? Okay, tell us. What did you think was going to happen?"

"I don't know." Kristin didn't say anything else, just stared at her, until Nina added, "Maybe I thought they'd get some beer and we'd all go out on the beach."

Kristin nodded, slowly. She spoke in slow disbelief. "The three of them. And us. And beer. On the beach."

"Yeah. I don't know. Whatever."

Kristin turned to include me. "First of all, I don't do that."

Nina rolled her eyes. "Oh, right. You're too good to do that."

"I'm too smart to do that."

"Okay. So now you're smarter than me."

"I'm too smart to do that. And so is Roberta."

"Roberta?"

"Yeah. She's sitting in the backseat. Remember? You tried to leave her at the 7-Eleven?"

"I didn't try to leave her! I didn't even know she was out of the car." She looked at me in the rearview mirror. "Roberta, I swear I didn't know. I thought you were still sitting there."

Kristin ripped into her. "What else did you think tonight, Nina? Tell us what your great brain was thinking."

"Hey, what are you talking about?"

"Did you really think those guys were buying beer?"

"Yeah."

"Well, that would have been bad enough. That would have been enough for me to want to get out of there. But that's not the half of it."

"What are you talking about?"

Kristin was now speaking to her like she was a moron. "Nina, they keep the beer inside the store. In a big refrigerator. Those guys were outside the store."

"So what?"

"So they were buying dope! Could you possibly not know that?"

"Dope?"

"What did you think those scuzzy guys were doing on the phone? Calling home to their parents?"

"You don't know this. You're just saying this."

"Oh, I don't? I know what happened to me tonight, and now I'm thinking that I was lucky! I can just imagine the rest of it. Those Xavier guys with their drugs, and those scuzzy guys with their guns, and you, me, and Roberta out on the beach. That's how girls disappear. That's how they get killed. That's how they wind up in a swamp somewhere with nothing left to identify them but their teeth."

Nobody said anything after that until Nina finally said, "That's sick."

"That's true."

"No, I mean about those Xavier guys. I don't know any guys there who are into drugs. That's so low-class, you know? What were they buying, like, crack cocaine?"

"How am I supposed to know?"

We drove on in angry silence. Finally, at Ocean and University, Nina asked, "So, okay, where are we going?"

Kristin told her, "To my house. I'm going to give you a hundred dollars."

"Okay." Nina turned left. Kristin, Uncle Frank, and

Karl live in a really nice house in a neighborhood called Alhambra Estates. I think it's really nice, anyway. Kristin complains that they don't have a swimming pool. Uncle Frank complains about everything else.

Nina told Kristin, "Look, I want to apologize. I'm sorry you got hurt. I had no idea things would turn out this way."

Kristin mumbled, "Forget about it. I just want tonight to be over."

"No. It's not over yet. It's not even ten o'clock. My little sister's still awake. No way I'm going to bed. Do you want to come over for a while?"

"No."

"Just for a few minutes. We have to try on the dresses. We have to plan our colors for tomorrow."

The Corvette turned onto Kristin's street. I saw Uncle Frank up ahead, standing by the open trunk of his car. Nina turned sharply into the driveway, startling him in the headlights. He threw something into the trunk and closed it.

Nina waved and called, in her phony voice, "Colonel Ritter! How are you doing?"

Uncle Frank squinted past the headlights, trying to see us. A look of recognition came over his face, and he said, "Hey, girls, how did your shopping trip go?"

Kristin got out, slammed the door, and stomped up to him. She pulled his American Express card from her pocket and snarled, "I'll tell you how it went. Your stupid credit card didn't work!"

Uncle Frank's face registered hurt — hurt about the

credit card, and hurt that Kristin would speak to him that way. He took the card from her meekly and answered, "I'm sorry. It should have worked." He looked over at Nina. "It's not like I don't pay the bill."

Kristin started to let him have it. "It didn't work for four —" But then she stopped herself. I could see her thinking about the money she almost spent tonight. As she finished the sentence, her voice kept losing air, like she was a punctured balloon. "It didn't work for a hundred dollars, and that's what the dress cost. I'm going to go in and get my money and pay Nina back."

Uncle Frank nodded somberly in the headlights.

Now Kristin looked like she was going to cry, and I don't think it was about the credit card. She said, "I'm sorry I yelled like that. I was embarrassed."

"Sure, Kitten. I understand."

Kristin hurried inside. Uncle Frank remained. Nina, in her phony voice, called over to him. "Your place is looking real nice, Colonel."

He answered, "Ah, this whole neighborhood's going to hell — pardon my expression, Nina. We need to find a new neighborhood."

Kristin came right back out and got into the car.

Nina told Uncle Frank, "Yeah, I hear that, Colonel." She threw the car in reverse. As soon as we cleared the driveway, Nina informed me, "Roberta, we're going to drop you off first." The fun was definitely over. Nina kept messing with the radio. She finally turned it off, announcing, "This all sucks. This really sucks."

We pulled up in front of my house to find it dark and

empty. Kristin turned and looked at me. "Where is your father?"

"I don't know. I was with you."

"You shouldn't be going in there by yourself."

"He'll be here."

"Okay. We'll wait until he gets back."

Nina broke in, "Hey, come on! It's bad enough I gotta come back here tomorrow."

Kristin pointed at the house. "It's an empty, dark house."

Nina answered, "Yeah? So what? Every house is an empty, dark house until somebody gets home and turns the lights on. Am I right? So Roberta got home first. So what?"

"So we're not leaving."

Nina asked Kristin, "Do you think I'm never home by myself? Are you never home by yourself?"

Kristin answered, "I've never spent a whole night by myself. Have you?"

"No." Nina turned to me. "Your father's not coming home? What? Is he sleeping with that Suzie chick? Please tell me he's not."

"No, he's not. He's coming home. And I'm getting out of the car now."

I climbed out and started up the driveway. Nina had backed out and was peeling away before I reached the carport. But I heard Kristin yell, "We'll be here at ten!"

I let myself in and turned on the lights. Dad had left a note on the Blockbuster Video bag saying, *Roberta, We'll be back after dinner. Page me if there is any prob-*

lem. There wasn't any problem, so I got undressed and ready for bed. I turned on Channel 57.

I perked up when I saw what was on. It was a *Last Judgment* special about the Crusades. A voice-over intoned, "The Holy Land was overrun by the infidels, people who hated Jesus. The Christian pilgrims who tried to visit the Holy Land were robbed and beaten and murdered. So some brave men of God took up the cross, wearing it on their tunics and vowing to keep it on until the Holy Land was freed."

The clip ended, and I was once again looking into the eyes of Stephen Cross. He told me, "At some moment in your life, God may challenge you to take up the cross. It may not be for a battle with horses and swords, but it may be for a battle just as strenuous, and just as important. Will you be ready? Will you pray with me now to be ready for that moment?"

Stephen Cross then asked me to kneel before the set, so I did. He ordered, "Pray with me now. Any prayer you know, and I know you know one. Everybody knows one. Pray that prayer with me now."

As Stephen Cross closed his eyes, I whispered, "Now I lay me down to sleep. I pray the Lord my soul to keep. If I should die before I wake, I pray the Lord my soul to take."

A few moments later, Stephen Cross opened his eyes and thanked me for praying with him. It's funny, but I hadn't been scared before I said that prayer. Now I definitely was.

I turned off the TV, went into the bedroom, and lay

down. I thought about paging Dad. But instead I turned the hall light on and left my door cracked open. I fell asleep in that twilight, and that's when I had this dream.

Mom was sitting at a folding card table, under a lightbulb that was hanging from a wire. She looked scared. She held out a dollar bill and said to me, "Take this, Roberta, and go get a Slurpee. A cherry one."

I said, "No. No, I don't want one."

She leaned forward. She looked as white as a ghost, like all the blood was drained from her body. She insisted, "Do as I say. Now."

But I wouldn't. I wouldn't take the money. Because I knew if I did, and if I left her, that I would never see her again. We stood frozen for a moment. Then she said sadly, "Roberta, you know the truth. And you know where you have to go."

That's when I sat up, wide awake. I heard Dad's voice down the hall. I listened to him for several minutes. I wanted to go talk to him about the dream, but I didn't. I didn't because he wasn't alone.

SATURDAY, THE 26TH ❧ Suzie was gone when I walked outside, into the humid dawn, and picked up the newspaper. I ate breakfast, showered, and read until ten o'clock. Then I heard the Corvette pull loudly into the driveway. Nina and Kristin glided through the kitchen door looking like supermodels. They were carrying their garment bags — Nina's from

Bloomingdale's; Kristin's from Petite Sophisticate. Their hairdos were already in place, and their faces were already made up. Heavily made up.

Nina's dark brown hair was brushed straight back, and it had a gold comb in it. Dark gold paint on her eyelids swept back across her temples. She looked like Cleopatra from a storybook.

Kristin had her hair curled and hanging down in tight ringlets, like Shirley Temple. She had sky blue paint on her eyelids, but not nearly as much as Nina. She looked super-healthy, like an athlete or an astronaut.

Nina looked around uncomfortably and then said, "This place is like when I went to Havana to visit my mother's relatives. They lived in houses like this. It was unbelievable." She draped her red garment bag over a kitchen chair. She also had a plastic supermarket bag with her. She dumped its contents out on the table and said, "Okay, Roberta, sit down. We'll do what we can do."

I sat in a kitchen chair while Nina and Kristin stood in front of me, studying my face. Nina took a handful of my hair. "What do you wash this with, a Brillo pad?"

"What do you mean?"

"Feel this, Kristin. It's like it's not even hair."

Kristin took a handful, too. She said, "Let's start with the volumizing mousse."

Nina said, "Come on, share with us, Roberta. Who does your hair?"

"Hair Cutz. In the mall."

"Uh-huh. And exactly what do you do there? You give them five bucks and say, 'Make me look like a boy'?"

Kristin told her, "Cut it out, Nina."

"No, I really want to know. Hair like this doesn't just happen."

The two of them proceeded to put stuff in my hair and on my face. They worked in silence for a while, spraying and smearing. Finally Nina said, "Hey, you guys, I'm sorry I was acting a little weird last night. I woke up at, like, three o'clock this morning because I got my period."

Kristin said, "I'm surprised I slept okay. I was sure I would have a nightmare, but I didn't. Before I went to bed, though, I took a long shower, until all the hot water ran out. I had to wash that pig's hand off of me."

Nina rummaged through her plastic bag and announced, "Oh no, I forgot tissues. You got tissues in this house, Roberta?"

"No."

"Then what am I gonna use to put this makeup on?"

"How about toilet paper?"

Nina looked up at heaven. She said, "They have tissues in Havana, Roberta. Okay, where do I find that toilet paper?"

Kristin said, "I'll find it," and walked down the hall.

Nina bent in front of me and started to outline my eyes with a green pencil. She said, "So, Roberta, Kristin told me about your medical problem."

"What problem?"

"'What problem'? You've never gotten your period. Right? She said you're like one of those little Olympic ice-skating girls, like one of those gymnastics freaks."

Kristin came back and handed over the toilet paper. She told her, "I'm sure I didn't say it like that."

"Whatever. It's true, though. Right?"

I answered, "It's true that it hasn't happened yet. I don't think that makes me an ice-skating freak, or whatever you're talking about."

"Hey, girl, all I'm saying is that it's not normal. You need to go see a doctor."

"I do see a doctor."

"Yeah? What does he say? Or is it a she?" Nina turned to Kristin. "I have to go to a woman myself."

Kristin agreed, "Me, too."

I said, "The last one I saw was a he. And he asked me about it. About menstruation. And he told me there is a wide range of normality."

"A who?"

"A wide range of normality."

"Yeah? Sounds to me like you got some free advice at the free clinic. They do a lot of that down in Havana, too. But let me tell you something, girl, there ain't nothing normal about it. Not at your age." Nina stopped penciling and pulled back. "How old are you?"

"I'm fifteen."

Kristin added, "She's almost sixteen. Next month."

Nina went back to work. "Roberta, you need to get

yourself a real doctor. One real female doctor that you keep going back to." She stood up and said, "All right. That's it. You're done. You're looking the best you're ever gonna look."

Kristin held up a compact mirror for me. My hair now rose up around my face and fell back, a darker shade of brown than before. My eyes shone out from the eyeliner like dark glass. I didn't look like Cleopatra. And I didn't look like an astronaut.

No. I looked like my mom.

Dad chose that exact moment to come out. He started to say something to the girls, but he caught sight of me and stopped still. For a long, freaky minute, he stood there looking at my dead mother, at his dead wife. An emotion flickered in his eyes and twitched at the corners of his mouth. It looked like fear. Then he turned, without a word, and walked back out of the kitchen.

I'm not sure the girls even realized he had been there. Nina was busy picking up her beauty supplies, and Kristin never pays any attention to my dad. So I acted like nothing had happened. I put my hand up to my face and said, "You guys, this feels weird. It feels like Halloween."

Nina snapped, "Don't touch that. Don't even think about it. And don't touch your hair, either."

I looked back in the mirror, at that strange yet familiar face. I asked Nina, "So . . . how do I change myself back?"

"Why would you want to do that?"

"After the show is over, I'll want to get back to normal."

"You will?"

"Yeah. How do I get this stuff off?"

"You don't. Once you start using makeup, you never stop. Not until you're dead. It's part of your daily routine, like breathing."

But Kristin reached into Nina's bag, pulled out a jar, and handed it to me. "Here. You use this cold cream. It'll take it right off."

Nina added, "Yeah. Just be sure to use lots of toilet paper." She picked up her garment bag and said to Kristin, "Let's see how these dresses look with our makeup and hair." She turned to me. "Do you have your own room, Roberta?"

"Yeah. Down the hall."

Nina took her garment bag down the hall, into my room. Kristin held up the powder, lipstick, eye shadow, and so on, and said to me, "In case you ever want to look like this again, I'm gonna leave all this stuff in your bathroom." She then took out two tortoiseshell clips and tried them in different places on my hair.

Nina came back quickly. She was four inches taller, in super-spiked high heels. She looked fabulous. Kristin and I told her so at the same time.

Nina smirked, but she was obviously pleased. "Yeah, yeah, what do you two skanks know about it?" She tossed Kristin's garment bag to her. "Come on, we're running out of time."

Kristin went down to my room next.

Nina leaned against the sink, shifting around in her heels. We had absolutely nothing to say to each other. That was okay with me, but she had to say something. "So how long have you been living in this place?"

"Seven years. Ever since my mom died."

"Oh yeah?"

"Yeah. She had a heart attack."

Nina nodded understandingly, but I'm not sure she believed me. She changed the subject. "So I hope you have enough quotes and stuff for your newsletter article, because this is gonna be it."

"I'm sure I do."

Kristin returned in her dress and stood next to Nina. She was wearing two-inch heels, so Nina had gained a net total of two inches. Side by side, they did look spectacular, both in their black strapless dresses. I'd say Nina looked fifty dollars more spectacular, but not seven hundred and fifty dollars more.

Nina said, "All right. Let's go." She looked at my clothes. "Get something on, Roberta. You're not wearing that."

I looked down at my clothes. I had on brown corduroy pants, a white T-shirt, and white sneakers. I said, "Why not? It's just until we get to the mall. Then Suzie's going to pick out an outfit for me."

"Still, people are going to see you between here and there."

Kristin grabbed her by the elbow. "Come on, I thought you were in a hurry."

"Girl, I'll never be in that big a hurry. My house could be on fire, and I wouldn't go outside in that."

I opened the kitchen door to leave. Nina and Kristin reached into their shopping bags and pulled out two pairs of sandals. They put their high-heeled shoes back into the bags.

Dad came in the kitchen. He wouldn't even look at me. He said, to no one in particular, "Looks like we're all leaving together."

The four of us walked out to the carport. Nina unlocked the Corvette and said to me, "Roberta, do you want to ride with your dad?"

Kristin answered pointedly, "No. She doesn't."

Nina told her, "Hey, you know, it's not like I have a real backseat here. That's all I'm saying."

I looked at Dad's beat-up Malibu. I told him, "I guess I'll ride with them."

He said, "Okay, honey. You're going to go to the mall office, right? I know Suzie has something to tell you about the big show today. All three of you." Dad looked Nina up and down. "The way you girls look, it makes me wish I were sixteen again."

I squeezed into the back. Kristin muttered disgustedly, "Yeah. I bet it does."

We rocketed up Everglades Boulevard and stopped at the light at Route 27. Just to our right, five yards from the intersection, a family of three — a father, a mother, and a little girl — was erecting a homemade shrine. The shrine consisted of a framed picture of a young man in a high school cap and gown, a bouquet of white flowers, and a small white cross. The father solemnly hammered the cross into the ground. The photo and the bouquet were attached to it.

Nina said to Kristin, "You know what that is, right? That's a Spanish thing. They're making a shrine to that dead boy, probably their son."

"Why do it there?"

"Because that's the spot where his soul departed this earth."

"What?"

"That's where he got killed. He probably got hit by a car. Or he got killed driving his own car."

I said, "That happens here a lot, Kristin."

She sounded genuinely surprised. "It does?"

"Oh yeah. I see them when I'm walking to work, families like this, and they're not only Spanish. All kinds of people do this. They come to the spot where the accident happened."

The light changed, and Nina roared across Route 27. She parked diagonally, across two spaces, right near the front of the mall. As I got out of the car, I saw Sam standing at his vandalized BMW. He was just across the row from us, hoisting a video camera. He walked in a slow circle around the car, videotaping the damage.

I stood watching him while Nina and Kristin gathered up their stuff. Sam must have sensed that I was standing there, because he lowered the camera and looked over at me. That gave me a funny feeling. He stared at me intensely, trying to figure out who I was. I almost yelled, "Trick or treat," but I contained myself.

Sam was still staring when Nina and Kristin started off toward the mall. Kristin yelled, "Come on, Roberta."

Nina jerked her head in Sam's direction. "That's the guy who runs Crescent, right?"

I said, "Yeah. That's Sam. Samir Samad."

"What is he? An Arab or something?"

"I think he's from California."

"No, no, no. Look at him. He looks like he ought to be wearing one of those sheets. You know what I mean?"

"No. Not really."

"Like he's an Arab. In the desert."

Kristin said, "You heard her, Nina. He's from California. That makes him an American."

"Hey, my mother's from Havana. She doesn't care if you call her a Cuban. She calls herself one." She turned to me. "Anyway, Roberta, whatever he is, he was checking you out."

"He was?"

"Are you blind, girl? He was checking you out big time. His tongue was practically hanging down to the ground."

"It was not."

Kristin looked in my eyes. "Do you like him?"

"I don't know."

Nina asked, "Well, do you like that type?"

"I don't know. I guess so."

"Because, you see, I do not. I like a hard-body type. I don't like guys who have that soft-body type. You know? Like that Pillsbury Doughboy look? Kristin, what's the word I'm looking for?"

"I have no idea."

"Pudgy? Is that a word?"

I said, "Yeah. That's a word."

"Well, he looks pudgy. Like he's got too high a percentage of body fat, you know, for his height."

I defended Sam. "He's not fat."

"Maybe not now, but he's gonna be. He's gonna be, like, some big fat Arab camel trader."

Kristin said, "I don't believe you, Nina. You are such a racist. You're like Hitler."

"What are you talking about? No way I'm a racist!" Nina paused and then added, "You're the one who lived in Germany. So don't go calling me Hitler."

"So don't go calling people fat Arabs."

"I'm not. I'm just stating a fact. Okay? A biological fact. I say the same thing about Carlos. It's his body type. In ten years Carlos is going to be a fat Cuban. He's got that body type, that pudgy body type. That's all I'm saying."

People entering and leaving the mall spotted us and stopped to stare. Especially the men. Even little boys and really old men. Nina and Kristin ignored them all. They leaned against the glass of SunBelt Savings, Slot #62, to switch their sandals for their high heels. Nina took out a handkerchief and dabbed her face. Then her jaw dropped. She pointed across the mallway to the office and gasped. "*Madre de Dios!* What is that?"

I looked over there, too. Suzie was holding up a posterboard and talking to someone who, even from this distance, could only be Betty the Goth.

Kristin asked her, "What? What are you talking about?"

"That thing over there, with the witch makeup. What is that supposed to be?"

I said, "That's Betty the Goth."

"The who?"

"Goth. You know, the goth kids?"

"No."

Kristin said, "You've seen her around. She works in the food court."

"Hey, if I ever saw her, I must have blocked it out."

The three of us started across the mallway. Kristin needled her. "At least she's not an Arab."

Nina shot her a look as she pushed open the glass door.

Suzie shouted out, "Ah! Here come the other models now. Look at you two! You look fabulous." Suzie's eyes fell on me. A puzzled expression came over her face. "Roberta? Uh, you look very different today." The three of us joined Betty and stood around Suzie's desk. "Uh, Roberta, didn't your dad tell you what the story is today?"

I said, "The story?"

Suzie looked at me, troubled. "Yes, we have a story

for the modeling show today, if you want to call it that, or a theme, or whatever. It's all about Before and After." Suzie held up four white posters. Two had BEFORE printed on them, and two had AFTER. She told me, "You and Betty are going to be the Befores, and Nina and Kristin are going to be the Afters." She looked at all of us in turn. "Do you understand? It's 'Before and After you go shopping at the West End Mall.'"

Suzie stepped quickly over to the window and started banging on the glass. Dad was across the mallway with Hawg and Ironman. Suzie gestured impatiently for him to come join us.

Kristin leaned toward me and whispered, "Did you know anything about this?"

Before I could answer, Dad burst through the door, grinning. Suzie spoke to him sharply. "Bob, didn't you explain the story to Roberta?"

"What story?"

Suzie's jaw clenched. "The story about the modeling show. The one that I spent all that time last night explaining to you."

Dad stopped grinning. "No, I was going to leave that up to you. Why? Is there a problem?"

Suzie's eyes rolled up to the ceiling, where they stayed for several seconds. Then they rolled back down to Dad. She said sarcastically, "Okay. Here is an explanation of the problem then, just for you: Roberta is supposed to be a Before." Dad narrowed his eyes at her. He clearly did not like being spoken to this way, especially not in front of us. Suzie, sensing this, backed off a little.

She tried to smile at me. "Roberta, sweetie, you look great. But, the fact is, you look too great. You look so great that I now have one Before and three Afters in the modeling show. Do you understand?"

I understood perfectly. I said, "Yes."

"I need you to look the way you looked when I picked you for the show. The way you always look."

Kristin spoke up. "This stinks, Roberta. Don't do it."

Dad, to everyone's surprise, agreed. "Roberta, you don't have to do this if you don't want to." He looked hard at Suzie. "Does she, Suzie?"

But Suzie was ready for him. "No, of course not. If Roberta doesn't want to do it, then she doesn't have to do it. But I need to know that right away. Somebody has to play this part in the show, and it is fifty dollars for two hours' work. I need to go over to the food court and get somebody else, if that's what Roberta wants."

I answered her immediately. "No, that's not what I want. I want the fifty dollars."

Suzie contorted the left side of her face in a combination of a wink and a smile. "Of course you do." She came around the desk. She walked over and put her hand through Dad's arm. "It really doesn't matter to me who plays what. You can switch roles if you want to."

Nina scoffed at that suggestion. She looked at Betty and addressed her for the first time. "I'll tell you what, I'll be the Before, and you be the After. Okay? I'll be *Before* you lose your mind, and you be *After*."

Betty, calm as always, replied, "Fine with me."

Kristin was still shaking her head back and forth, like

she was thinking of bailing out. I told her, "Kristin, it's okay. Give me that cold cream and I'll get this junk off my face."

Kristin sighed deeply. Then she took me by the elbow and led me into Suzie's bathroom. There was a big box of tissues in there. She told me, "Close your eyes. And don't open them for a long time. Not until I say so."

Kristin dipped tissues into the cold cream (which really was cold) and started to smear it around my eyes. She worked at removing all the makeup that she and Nina had just put on me. She kept muttering, "This stinks, Roberta. This really stinks. You don't want fifty dollars this bad."

"Yes, I do."

"Then I'll give it to you. I'm serious. I have it in savings. I'll get it out today and give it to you."

"Don't be ridiculous. This is no big deal."

I heard Suzie come in. She asked Kristin, "Now, what are we going to do about her hair? We need to do something about her hair, too."

Kristin didn't answer her. I could feel Kristin's strong fingers making circles around my eye sockets, removing all the green shadow. But then I could feel another pair of hands. They had to be Suzie's. Her hands started to push and pull at my hair. Then I felt a comb tugging at it.

Suzie said, "If we can just pull this hair forward and then run it straight down at the sides, like Roberta usually wears it. You know, flat, and straight down. That'll be okay."

Suzie's hands finally finished flattening my hair. She went away. Kristin finally told me, "Okay. You can open your eyes."

I looked into the mirror. I was pretty much back to my old self. Though my hair did look a little bit better than usual.

We went back out and joined the others at Suzie's desk. She visually examined the four of us. "I want one of you on each team to be the timer. Nina and Kristin, it should probably be you two. Every five minutes you should change your position. People love that! They're watching you stand perfectly still, wondering if you're a mannequin or a real girl, and then suddenly you move! So when the timer sees that five minutes have passed, she moves, and the other model moves with her. You both, very smoothly, change from one pose to another." Suzie demonstrated by assuming a mannequin position. "Like, from this" — she slowly changed from that pose into another one — "to this."

Suzie picked up the posters. "I have Nina and Betty starting out in the window of Slot Number Nine, next to Crescent Electronics. You'll be there for the first hour."

Nina protested, "Wait a minute, I want to be with Kristin."

"No, no. You girls are both Afters. Each pair needs a Before and an After. I have you and Betty together because you both have dark hair and eyes, and other similar features."

"Similar?"

"I have Roberta and her cousin together, too, because, you know, they're related. Kristin and Roberta, I have you in the window of Slot Number Sixty-one, right across from Arcane. Then, after one hour, the two teams will switch locations. Empty stores are on the master key, so each team gets a master key." Suzie handed a key to Betty and one to me. "Okay? It's almost twelve o'clock. High noon. Showtime."

Nobody except Suzie seemed eager to begin, but we all picked up our poster signs and walked to the door. Suzie added, "Let's have fun doing this, girls. I know the customers are going to have a lot of fun watching you."

Nina and Kristin led the way out, in their high heels, with their AFTER signs. Betty and I followed with our BEFORE signs. When we reached the rotunda, Nina said, "Later," to Kristin and turned left. She and Betty headed off toward Slot #9.

Kristin and I walked up to Slot #61. I used my master key on the sliding-glass door. I pulled it open a foot, and we both slipped into the abandoned store. Once inside, Kristin stepped carefully over the mannequins and climbed up onto the window platform.

I remained staring at the mannequins for a moment. Someone had pushed them off the platform. They were lying stiffly and awkwardly, like they had been murdered here, like they had been struggling the very moment rigor mortis had set in.

Kristin said, "Come on up. Let's get this over with."

I slid the doors closed and stood next to Kristin. I saw that she had leaned her sign up against the glass, so I did the same. Kristin said, "Let's start with one of these." She stood with her right leg and right arm back, her left leg bent slightly, and her left hand on her hip. I mimicked her. No one walked by for a long moment. Kristin whispered to me, "I hate this. Do you hate this?"

"No. What's to hate about it? It's fifty dollars."

"I hate what she did to you."

"What?"

Kristin sighed, a stiff mannequin sigh. "Never mind."

Our first audience member had a familiar face. It was Mrs. Roman. She walked by and recognized me. She stopped and stared, clearly clueless as to what was going on. She tapped on the Plexiglas, and said very loudly, "Roberta, what are you doing in there? What does this sign mean?"

Kristin spoke out of the side of her mouth, like a ventriloquist. "Don't answer. You're an actress. An actress who's playing a mannequin."

An old couple joined Mrs. Roman at the window. They both carried flyers that explained the "story." They were soon joined by about ten other people, all carrying flyers, all eager to see us in action . . . or in inaction. Most of their attention, of course, was on Kristin — on her clothes, and makeup, and hair. A couple of them, though, pointed at me, and at my sign, and laughed.

Mrs. Roman left, but she came right back with Mrs. Weiss. Mrs. Weiss did not look confused. She looked angry. She never even looked up at me. She read my sign. She read Kristin's sign. Then she shook her head and left.

In my pose — head up, eyes straight ahead — I could see directly into Arcane. Karl was at the register, reading. After about ten minutes Hawg and Ironman strolled out and stopped in the middle of the mallway to look at us. Hawg stared intently at Kristin. Ironman seemed to be staring at the floor.

We heard some noise, and then a group of loud teenage boys appeared in front of us. I recognized them right away — the skinny blond kid and the two football guys from last night. They were acting obnoxious, and the blond kid was the worst one. He started showing off for the other two. He had on a blue dress shirt. He started unbuttoning the shirt, stroking his chest, and making sounds like striptease music. The guys with him began laughing, while the older customers all edged away.

Kristin muttered to me, "Do you believe this?"

I said, "Do you want me to go get Uncle Frank?"

"What for?"

"I don't know. To protect us?"

"Don't worry about it."

The three Xavier guys pressed closer. The blond kid positioned himself right in front of Kristin. He stuck his tongue out as far as he could and pressed it against the glass. Then he started moaning.

Kristin said, "Okay, that's it. Time to change positions." Kristin turned slowly and delivered a solid karate kick to the Plexiglas. The window bowed outward and smacked into the blond guy's teeth. He yelled and snapped his head backward, covering his mouth with his hand.

The remaining old people covered their own mouths, as if in sympathy. But Hawg didn't. He laughed, long and loud. He bellowed, "Good kick, Kristin! That's a three-point field goal."

The two other Xavier guys rounded on Hawg and Ironman. It looked like a fight was about to break out. One of them, the driver from last night, was about a foot taller than Hawg. He walked up to him, looked down, and pulled back his fist as if to punch him. Hawg caught him in the stomach with a quick right jab, doubling the guy over. The remaining Xavier guy, the one who had been talking to Nina, took a step toward Hawg, but then he thought better of it and stopped. He took his two wounded comrades by the elbows, and the three of them started backing away. He yelled at Hawg, "You're dead! You know that? You're dead when you try to leave here tonight, fatso."

Hawg answered calmly, "I ain't leavin'. I'm here right now, son. Come and get it."

"You're the one who's gonna get it. Tonight!"

"I'm here right now. Come on and give it to me."

"We know where to find you, cracker boy."

"Yeah, right here. You can find me right here. Right now."

The Xavier guys soon disappeared from our view. Hawg remained standing in his same spot for a while, as if to prove a point. Then he and Ironman walked back into Arcane.

More people stopped to stare at us, but without further incident. After about ten changes in position, Kristin announced, "Okay, that's it. That's one hour."

We climbed back down and exited Slot #61 carefully. We turned left and immediately saw Nina and Betty the Goth coming across the rotunda. Nina was in her stockings. A guy was walking behind her carrying her shoes. Betty was behind him.

Nina looked at Kristin, but neither of them said anything. Betty smiled at me and asked, "How's it going?"

I said, "Okay."

Our time over in Slot #9 was very different. People didn't pay much attention to us there. I guess the novelty of the live modeling had already worn off. Sam walked by once. He stopped to look at us. Kristin muttered, "There he is."

I said, "I know."

At about one-forty-five, we were both surprised to see Nina in front of the window. She rapped on it once and shouted, "Come on. This show is over."

Kristin and I looked at each other. By this time we had no audience at all. Kristin said, "Okay. Let's knock off. We can walk over to the office slowly. My feet are starting to hurt, anyway."

We left our signs in the window, exited Slot #9, and followed Nina and the shoe guy around the corner. Betty was already standing by the wall, right before the glass window of the mall office. She said, "I don't know about this, you guys. We still have ten minutes."

Nina fiddled with her watch. She announced, "Not anymore, we don't. I'm the timer. And my watch says two o'clock. The show's over."

Kristin agreed. "That works for me."

Nina told the guy, "Wait here with the shoes." She walked, in her black stockings, to the office door. The rest of us followed. As I passed him, I said to the guy, "You must be Carlos."

He nodded.

As we trooped through the door, Suzie looked up from her desk and called brightly, "Here they come. My supermodels. How was it?"

Betty answered for us, "It was great. Can I get my money?"

Suzie pointed to four envelopes that she had fanned out on the edge of her desk. "You sure can."

Betty picked hers up, checked it, and started out. For some reason, she said to Nina, "So long, Nina. That was pretty cool."

Nina seemed surprised. She just said, "Yeah," in return.

Betty opened the door and added, "Maybe we'll do it again." She continued out and walked back past the window, toward the food court.

Nina muttered, "Uh, yeah. We'll be doing a lot of

stuff together. Right. Like if I ever need to polish my shoes in a hurry, maybe I can use your head."

Suzie laughed. Kristin and I did not. We all picked up our pay envelopes and left.

Carlos was waiting by the mall exit. Nina and Kristin turned right to go with him. I didn't know what to do, so I just stood there. Nina decided for me. "Roberta, we need to go get changed. You don't. So you stay here. We're going to my house."

I said, "Okay," and walked to the food court. I peeked around the counter at the Chili Dog to see if Gene was working. But suddenly Betty tapped me on the shoulder.

"Hey, so what did you think of that modeling?"

"It was okay. I don't think I'd like to do it again. How about you?"

"I really liked it." She narrowed her eyes at the Chili Dog. "It sure beats working there."

"Yeah? What? You don't like it there?"

Betty looked at me like I was crazy. "Come on. That place is an armpit. And it's bad karma. You know? I have to serve people food that is poison for them, all day long, every day. I'll have to pay for that somehow." Betty looked right into my eyes. "Did you mind being a Before?"

"No. Did you?"

"No. Because I don't think I was the Before. I think Nina was, only she didn't know it."

I had to disagree. "I don't know. Nina's a real After, if you ask me."

Betty shook her black hair with conviction. "No. Don't you see? She's only imitating others now. She dresses herself and paints herself to look like others. Like these fake women that she sees on TV. Not like her real self."

"I don't know. Nina works real hard on her looks, all the time."

"Maybe so. But she's never seen *herself* in the mirror. Not once. I guarantee it."

I didn't know what to say to that. I don't like to say *Whatever*, so I muttered, "Maybe you're right."

I headed over to Isabel's Hallmark. Mrs. Weiss saw me coming. I know she did, but she acted like she didn't. I must have stood in front of her at the register for half a minute. Then she finally said, without looking up, "I hope you got paid a lot of money for that stunt, Roberta."

"Fifty dollars."

"Yes? Whose idea was it to put that sign in front of you?"

"Suzie's."

She snorted. "*Humph.* Like I needed to ask."

I said, "Anyway, it was only a show. I was an actress. I was playing a part."

Mrs. Weiss said, "Fine. Do what you want. But be careful about the parts you agree to play, Roberta. You never know when one is going to stick."

A strange quiet had settled over the mall, strange at least for a Saturday afternoon. No one came into Arcane; no one even walked by. Karl, Uncle Frank, and I stood by the counter, silent and motionless.

Kristin returned from Nina's at four-fifteen. Her hair was still in the ringlets, but she had removed most of the makeup, and she now wore just jeans and a plain white blouse. Maybe I was imagining it, but she seemed to be avoiding me.

Then Hawg showed up and stood outside Special-Tees, waiting for Ironman. Uncle Frank remarked to me, "Look at this. This is great. When the other loser gets here, we'll have six people to take care of zero customers."

As if to prove him wrong, a family with two teenage girls walked in, followed by some younger boys clutching ten-dollar bills. Soon six of the twelve Arcane experiences were in use, and the time started to pass quickly.

Hawg remained near the front, giving advice to the Head Louse and two pinheads about Mekong Massacre. If he was concerned about that gang of Xavier guys coming back, he certainly didn't act like it. I walked a customer back to Vampire's Feast, and I heard Hawg saying, "Could be trouble tonight. I may have to whomp on some preppy boys."

The Xavier guys never did show up. Hawg did get his trouble, though, in an unlikely form.

Sam arrived at about eight-thirty, looking as mad as I have ever seen him. He stood by the Sony monitor for a minute, staring down the mallway like he was waiting for someone. I said, "Hi, Sam."

He looked right through me, like I was a stranger.

Verna appeared at his side. "Sam, what are you doing here? I told you I would talk to him, and I will."

Sam shook his head, indicating that wasn't good enough. He told her, "So go ahead and talk to him."

Verna warned him, "You keep out of this."

Sam turned toward Hawg's group, but Verna held him by the arm. She spoke with authority. "This is my job. Based on what I hear tonight, it may become the detective's job. But it is not *your* job. Do you understand?"

Sam nodded quickly, like he understood. Then Verna walked over to the group and started talking very low to Hawg. Hawg listened, shaking his head back and forth. I could see his lips moving, saying "No. No."

But Sam had no intention of keeping out of it. He walked up next to Verna and demanded of Hawg, "I have a question for you: Did you vandalize my car? And my store?"

Verna held up a big hand. "Hold on, Sam. I'm talking to this man."

"Right. Well, I'm talking to him, too." He suddenly exploded, "You did it! I know you did. The police know you did. And you're going to pay."

Hawg turned so that he had his back to Verna and Sam. This enraged Sam further. Sam walked around the group until he stood right in front of him. Hawg finally looked up. He said matter-of-factly, "You want to fight me? Okay. But you got to get in line."

Sam snarled at him. "No! I'm not going to fight you.

I'm going to have you arrested, you . . . you trailer trash, you redneck moron! So you had better be very careful what you say or do next. You got that?"

Hawg answered him slowly and evenly, "I'll tell you what . . . I don't think I need advice from no sand nigger."

Sam's jaw opened involuntarily. "What did you call me?"

"You heard me."

Sam looked over at Verna. "Yeah. Yeah, I think we all heard you." Sam stood in his place, trying to decide what to do next. I think he might have gone after Hawg, even though Hawg is bigger than he is, but then Uncle Frank intervened. He took Sam by the arm and steered him out into the mallway, talking very earnestly to him.

The Head Louse did the same sort of thing with Hawg, walking him out, too, but in the opposite direction.

And that's how it ended.

By now it was nearly closing time. The customers who had been in the arcade had all stopped to watch the ruckus between Sam and Hawg. Once that was over, they all left.

Kristin reappeared at the register. I called over to her, "Hand me the trash bag. I'll start the closing checklist."

She reached down, pulled up the bag, and handed it to me, without saying a word. I hauled the bag into the back room and dumped the contents of Uncle

Frank's trashcan into it. I unlocked the back door and started out with the trash, but as soon as I hit the humid air, I heard a sound, the sound of gushing water.

I looked to the right, behind Slot #33, SpecialTees. Ironman was kneeling down, in the dark, with his back to me. He had his head under the outside faucet. He was completely soaking his hair, his shirt, and his pants. The gushing water puddled up around his knees and started running in a stream toward me. I watched it until it reached my feet.

Ironman finally turned off the faucet. But he continued to kneel there, on all fours, shaking his head and squeezing his hair. I stepped over the little river of water and approached him. "Hey, are you okay?"

Ironman turned and faced my way. With his hair wet, he looked even smaller, like some dogs do. I repeated, "Are you okay?"

He pulled two handfuls of scraggly hair back until they were behind his ears. Then he squeezed some more water out of them. He managed about half of his nervous smile. "I guess so."

"What happened?"

"I got swirled."

"What?"

"Those guys? The one that Kristin kicked? And the others? They swirled me."

"What's that mean?"

Ironman looked surprised that I didn't know. He explained, "They grabbed me in the men's room, at the food court . . ." He stopped there, leaned forward, and blew some water out of his nose. "They held my head in a toilet and started flushing it."

I screamed, "No!"

Ironman looked alarmed. He shot a glance at the back door of SpecialTees, then at the back door of Arcane. I dropped the trash bag and said, "I'll go get Uncle Frank."

Now it was Ironman's turn to scream, "No! No!" He struggled to his feet on the sloppy asphalt. "You don't get anybody! You don't tell anybody!" He slogged toward me as fast as he could. When he got close to me I could see real terror in his eyes. Terror and pain. He yelled, "And you can't ever tell Hawg! Ever! He's in enough trouble already. You gotta swear you will never tell him."

I nodded my head rapidly. "Yeah, okay. I swear. I won't tell Hawg."

"You won't tell anybody."

"I won't tell anybody."

"Not your uncle, or your father, or Kristin, or Karl."

"I won't tell anybody."

Ironman backed off a step. He tried to smile. "Anyway, it's no big deal. It's just a joke." He twisted his head to one side, trying to get water to drain from his ear.

The door to SpecialTees opened, casting a rectangle of light onto the watery mess that Ironman had made. Mrs. Royce emerged with a trash bag, stepping carefully over the water. When she spotted us she stiffened in fright. But then she recognized us and said, "What are you doing out here?"

I waited for Ironman to answer his mother, but he just stared at her dumbly. Mrs. Royce took a wary step toward him. "And why are you all wet? Look at you, you're soaked."

I heard myself saying, "I did it, Mrs. Royce. I'm sorry. We were messing around with the hose, and I got him all wet."

Mrs. Royce stared at me curiously. "That doesn't sound like you, Roberta. That sounds like something those boys would do, but not you. I thought you had more sense."

"I'm sorry, Mrs. Royce."

She pointed back toward the open door and told Ironman, "Get out of that wet shirt before you catch pneumonia. Take a shirt from the mistake pile."

Ironman set off obediently, peeling off his black T-shirt. His mother caught his arm as he passed by. "And give me that filthy thing. That's going into the trash right now."

He dropped the shirt onto her arm, without even looking, and shambled toward the lighted doorway. Mrs. Royce held it with two roly-poly fingers to put it into her trash bag, like it was a dead skunk. She looked at me. "You just got the one trash bag?"

"Yes, ma'am."

"Well, let me have it. I'm going there anyway."

"Thank you. I'm sorry again about the water."

"That's all right." She looked at me sadly. "That's not the worst thing anybody's ever done to him. Good night, now."

"Good night." I went back into the office. The bathroom door was cracked open slightly. I thought about it for a moment, then I slipped inside. I found myself staring into that mirror again.

Suddenly I was startled by the sound of someone rushing in from the arcade. I leaned closer to the mirror, so that I could see out. It was Uncle Frank. I thought about clearing my throat or turning on the water, to alert him that I was there, but I didn't.

Uncle Frank never even looked in my direction. His actions were very fast, almost frantic. He sat down hard in his chair. He poked at his desk lock with a key, got it in, and yanked the drawer open. Then he pulled out a clear glass bottle, opened it, and took a long drink. It looked like plain water, but why would he lock away a bottle of water? It had to be liquor. A clear liquor, like vodka.

The door opened again. This time it was Kristin. Uncle Frank must have hidden the bottle under the desk, because she didn't say anything about it. He sat looking up at her, the drawer wide open, until she spoke.

"Dad, do you know what Roberta tells people about her mother?"

Uncle Frank answered her evenly, "What, Kitten?"

"She tells them that her mother died of a heart attack."

"Is that right?"

"Yes. That's right. That's what she told Nina today."

Uncle Frank shook his head, confused. "Okay. What about it?"

"Well, isn't that a little sick?" Kristin shot a look toward the back. "Where is she now? At the trash trailer?"

Kristin walked out of view. This gave Uncle Frank a chance to stash his bottle and relock the drawer. Then he told her, "Kitten, let's let Roberta handle it in her own way. She doesn't have to go into the gory details for everybody she meets. Does she? Let her say what she wants."

Kristin reappeared. "Sure. She can say what she wants. I'm just worried that she actually believes it."

The two of them exited together, leaving me alone. Leaving me motionless, like a mall model. Like a mannequin. I stared again at my face in the mirror. Whose face was it? Without the makeup, it was no longer Mom's. And how could it be? Mom was lying in Crypt #109E at Eternal Rest Cemetery.

I wanted to feel something at that moment, but I couldn't. If I felt anything, it was stupidity. I felt like one of those lonely women on *Angela Live*, the ones who lived with the serial killers and didn't know it. And didn't want to know it. I was stupid and lonely enough to tell myself that Mom died of a heart attack. But I knew it wasn't true. I'd known it all along.

I remembered the policewoman in our kitchen. And I remembered Dad. He was holding on to a kitchen chair like he might tumble over. He was crying so hard that he was slobbering. Stuff was coming out of his mouth and his nose and his eyes, all at the same time. He told me, "Roberta, your mommy's heart stopped beating."

And we left it at that. We never talked about the facts of her death again. That was the one story I never investigated. But then, I didn't have to. I already knew the facts. They were right there in the newspaper. They were on the local TV news. My mother didn't die of a heart attack. My mother was murdered. She was stabbed to death during a robbery at the Family Arcade on the Strip.

And her murderer was never caught.

September

SUNDAY, THE 17TH ❧ I read the Sunday *Atlantic Times* from cover to cover. Then I locked up and headed out into the morning heat. I made it from our carport to the glass doors of the mall in fourteen minutes. That was a fast time, and I was really sweating because of it.

I used my key to unlock the office door. Suzie had told me that the September newsletter would be sitting outside the mall office in its PIP Printing wrapper, and it was.

The newsletter had a different look. Suzie had warned me about that. She said the old one was too depressing. The first thing I noticed was that the lead article was not written by me; it was written by Suzie. And it was not about the live models in the mall. It was about the rededication of the fountain. State senate candidate Ray Lyons was coming on September 25. He was to be the guest of honor, but there would be other special guests, too, including TV personality Angela del Fuego and West End Mall mascot Toby the Turtle. There would also be gigantic sales throughout the mall.

I had written up our modeling adventure, just like I promised Nina. It had taken up two full newsletter columns. Suzie had hinted that she had to cut back the modeling story to make room for "some last-minute stuff," but this was ridiculous. She had butchered it, trimming it down to a boxed feature at the bottom of the right column. It was like a joke. Or a contest, to discover how little of an original story you could possibly use.

I checked the back. My "People Pieces" feature had survived. The back page also had an article about Ray Lyons's "lifelong dedication to the environment." It said, "Not an environmental crazy, but a true nature lover, Ray Lyons grew up here, and he remembers how it was. . . ." I read as much of that one as I could stand, then I picked up the newsletters and set off to deliver them.

It was now eleven-forty-five, and employees were starting to arrive. I ran into Betty outside Candlewycke. She was staring through the window, looking for someone in the darkness. She said, "I'm looking for a new job. Are you guys hiring?"

"Are you kidding?"

Betty peered more intently into the gloom. "The only offer I have so far is from Devin, but this is where I started out two years ago, you know? I hate to go backward."

"Two years ago? How old are you?"

"Fifteen." Betty saw me calculating. She said, "I lied about my age. I still do."

"Do you lie on your income-tax form?"

"I don't pay taxes. I don't believe in them."

"How do you get away with that?"

"I don't get a paycheck. Never have. I work strictly for cash." I must have looked shocked, because she added, "A lot of kids here do that."

Devin appeared, spooky and evil looking, behind the glass. He started spraying Windex on a Nazi dagger case. Betty continued, "I hated working at the Chili Dog, anyway. Do you know what Gene does?"

"Do I want to know?"

"Probably not." But she continued, "He takes the dirty plates that people leave behind, and he scrapes off the chili and puts it back into the chili pot."

"Oh, god!" My stomach turned.

Betty looked toward the food court, shaking her jet black hair. "That Gene is a weird guy."

Upset as I was about the chili, I heard myself saying, "Oh, right. And Devin isn't?"

"Hey, let me tell you something about Devin: Devin is who he appears to be."

"Yeah. That's what I'm afraid of."

"I guess I have to work for him for a while, until something new opens up." Betty knocked on the window. Devin straightened himself up, like a vampire after a long night's sleep.

I said, "I have to deliver these." I handed Betty a copy and took off before Devin could reach us. I delivered most of the newsletters quickly, slipping them through the open cracks of the sliding-glass doors.

When I got back to the mall office, Suzie was on the computer, staring at the screen. She had a Danish in a

Styrofoam container on her lap. As soon as she saw me, she hurriedly clicked out of her document. "Oh, hello, Roberta. Did you deliver the newsletters?"

"Yes."

"What did you think?"

"About what?"

"The exciting news! Mr. Lyons will be here in a week. I'm planning a huge event. I want all the merchants to take part. This new fountain could turn things around for the West End Mall."

"Will the fountain be ready?"

"The fountain has been ready. Don't listen to that Leo. I have a real plumber coming here now."

Suzie brushed some crumbs into the trash. "Tell your uncle Frank I'm getting a tour bus to stop here today. A big Asian tour group."

"What kind of Asian?"

"I don't know. Does it matter?"

Just then I saw Dad through the window. He was getting cash at the ATM at SunBelt Savings. I watched him walk across the mallway, counting the bills.

He opened the door, and Suzie walked over to kiss him. "Mister Moneybags, are you taking me to breakfast?"

"You haven't had breakfast?"

"No."

"Let's go."

As soon as they left I got back on the computer. Suzie had clicked out of her file, but she had not clicked out of Word. I pulled back up the last document. It was her résumé.

Suzie Quinn has worked for the Marriott hotel chain at three different hotels. She has been a banquet manager and a convention hostess, whatever that is. She left Marriott to become the assistant manager of a mall in Miami, a mall owned by the Lyons Corporation. Then she became the manager of a mall in West Palm Beach, also owned by Lyons. It seemed like she changed jobs every six months.

I logged off and left the office. I still had no inclination to go to work. Instead I detoured into the card shop. Mrs. Weiss was alone behind the register. She looked at me and said, "Did you have breakfast?"

"Yes, ma'am." I lied, "My dad bought me a Danish."

"A Danish? Bah. He may as well buy you a cupcake."

"Why are you sitting?"

"Why shouldn't I sit? It's my store." She sighed. "It's all mine; I don't have any help today. I don't even have anyone to cover for our cemetery trip."

"That's okay," I said.

"Why haven't you gone to work yet?"

"You noticed that?"

"I notice everything. Have you finally had enough? Have you stopped working for nothing?"

"No. I'm just feeling . . . I don't know, like I don't want to go in yet."

"You *are* sick of it. Tell me, Roberta, what do people

do over in that nuthouse? What does five dollars buy them?"

"Oh, you know. They put on the helmets, and they swing the wands. They have the different experiences."

"Experiences? Those aren't experiences. Experiences are real life. Those are TV shows."

"Well, it's just pretend."

"What? They pretend they're somebody else. Some big hero instead of some miserable little nobody."

I didn't know what to say to that. Mrs. Weiss was in a bad mood. When she gets like this, there's no talking to her.

I finally wandered into Arcane and stood next to Karl. Karl didn't even acknowledge me. We stood in silence until Kristin came out of the back. She wasn't much more talkative. All she had to say was, "I feel lousy. Weird-lousy."

I said, "What did you have for breakfast?"

"It's not my stomach. It's all over. Like I'm getting my period. But that can't be. I just had it."

"I can't help you there."

"Maybe I'll take some Motrin."

Karl suddenly said, "Couldn't hurt."

Kristin went into the back for the Motrin. I spent a minute watching Karl. He appeared to be reading a magazine, yet he never turned the page. His eyes weren't even focused on the page. Instead his head was rotating slowly and purposefully, like a radar dish. Karl was taking in everything around him — by sound, and feel, and smell.

His head snapped back, and mine did, too, when Nina burst in, shouting, "Hey, what's up, you losers! Where's my girl Kristin?"

I said, "She'll be out in a minute."

"A minute's too long. I got things to do. How you doing, big guy?"

Karl muttered, "I'm here."

"Yeah, you are that, Karl. You got that 'here' thing going for you."

Kristin came out, so Nina immediately forgot about Karl and me. "Hey, girl."

Kristin answered weakly, "Hey."

"I was just up at the food court. Did you see that chick from the Taco Stop? She's got some guy's name tattooed on her thigh."

Kristin perked up a little. "Really? What's his name?"

"I don't know. I couldn't bear to read it. She had a big glob of cellulite, like, right next to it. It grossed me out. That whole idea grosses me out."

Karl said, in what I guess he thought was a Cuban accent, "You're not gonna get a little C for Carlos? In some special place?"

Nina wasn't amused. "Back off, crazy man."

Kristin said, "Anybody who gets a tattoo is crazy. And if you get some guy's name tattooed on you, then you're crazy *and* you're stupid. What happens when he dumps you? What do you do then?"

Nina knew. "You go see Dr. Navarro. My dad used to remove tattoos all the time, for two hundred dollars a pop, back when he had an office on the Strip. He used to do a dynamite business. Guys and girls would break up, get back together, break up again. I told him he ought to have a tattoo parlor attached to the office. Then he'd get them coming and going."

I said, "Then he'd be like Sylvester McMonkey McBean."

"Huh?"

"From Dr. Seuss? *The Sneetches?* Sylvester McMonkey McBean put the star tattoos on the Sneetches, and then he took them off again. And he kept charging them more each time."

Nina rolled her eyes at Kristin. "We can always count on you to contribute to the conversation, Roberta."

Then Nina pointed into the mallway at some approaching teenage boys. "Oh, my god, look at these scuzzbags! What is this, some new promotion — Scuzzbag Sunday?"

Nina and Kristin turned their attention to the boys. I picked up an aerosol can, walked out onto the floor, and started to spray the helmets. When I finished I went into the back to see Uncle Frank. He was just sitting at his desk. He wasn't writing anything, or talking on the phone, or even thinking, as far as I could tell. I said, "Uncle Frank, did you hear that a tour bus is coming today?"

"No. What flavor?"

"Suzie said they're Asian. She didn't know which country."

"We'll be lucky if she got the continent right. Here. Take these and put them out." Uncle Frank reached down into his bottom drawer and pulled out three signs. They all said OUT OF ORDER. "Put one on Halls of Montezuma, one on Mekong Massacre, and one on Genghis Khan Rides!"

"Okay."

Before I could leave, Kristin came into the back, took Uncle Frank's hand, and placed it on her forehead. "Daddy, I feel warm."

Uncle Frank turned his complete attention to Kristin, as I went out into the arcade. Just as I had put up the third sign, I heard a loud thud over to my left. I went to check it out and saw Hawg sprawled on the ground next to Vampire's Feast. I crouched next to him. "Are you okay?"

"Sure thing, little lady. I just chopped so hard at that damn thing I fell right off. Whew! That was scary. Listen to that sound!"

Hawg held the helmet out toward me; I shrank back. "No. No, I don't do that."

"You don't do what?"

"I don't put those helmets on."

"You don't have to put it on. Just listen to that sound she makes." Hawg continued to hold the black helmet out. I could hear the sound, and it was horrible. It was a high-pitched shriek, like a woman scared beyond mortal terror, screaming like she wanted to rip out her vocal cords.

I stammered, "What is that?"

"That's the banshees of hell. They're comin' to get you, if you don't get them first."

"Is that what they all sound like?"

"No, just this one. I never had it turned so loud before. It scared me right off the damn platform."

I tried to shake the sound out of my head as I walked up to the front.

Suzie's tour bus never materialized, but customers came in and out all afternoon, so many that we took the OUT OF ORDER signs down to give them more choices. It was one of our busiest days in months. I finally took my break at three and ate a quick *combinacion* plate at the Taco Stop. I was only gone for about fifteen minutes, but after I dumped my tray and turned the corner, I beheld a very different scene. An ugly scene.

A tall guy in a dark blue turban had Karl pinned against the Crusader experience. Karl seemed stuck to the black ring, like a refrigerator magnet. The guy was stabbing Karl with his index finger, hard, like he was trying to hurt him. He was yelling, "You think this is funny? Do you?"

Karl's face was not smiling; it was zoned out. Maybe the guy mistook that for smiling. At any rate, he yelled even louder, "This is not funny! This is racist! This is evil!"

Karl seemed to shrivel a little with each poke of the finger. He didn't look like he could take much more of it. I started toward him, but Hawg got there first.

He came up quickly from behind Crusader, thrusting himself between Karl and his attacker, forcing the turban guy backward. The guy aimed a big finger at Hawg, but before he could use it, Hawg took another belligerent step, forcing the guy out into the mallway. Hawg yelled back, "You got a problem here, Karl?"

Karl remained shriveled, stuck against the Crusader ring. The turban guy looked from Karl to Hawg. He sputtered out, "This is racist, and you are profiting from it. There is blood on your money." He made a spitting motion on the mallway, although I don't think anything came out, then he stomped angrily away.

I hurried over to Karl. Hawg and I each took an arm and pried him away from the black ring. Karl's elbow felt bony and surprisingly light, like a bird's. We walked him slowly into the back room. Karl stayed there for about an hour. When he finally came out, though, he was fine. He seemed to have forgotten all about it.

Near closing time Kristin got a call from the franchise guy. Dad never answers the store phone, in case it's the franchise guy. Now Uncle Frank is getting the same way. I guess the guy asked for Uncle Frank, because Kristin covered the receiver and pointed to him. "Daddy, it's a guy from Antioch, Illinois. From Arcane."

Uncle Frank shook his head. "Tell him I'm not here."

Kristin spoke into the phone. "He's not here right now." Her face hardened as she listened; then she hung up.

Uncle Frank asked, "What did he say?"

"He was rude. He implied that I was lying." Kristin looked him in the eye. "Of course, it's true. I was lying."

Uncle Frank said, "I'm sorry, Kitten. Don't pay any attention to him."

She muttered, "I won't," but it was clear from the way she banged the change drawer around that she did.

Dad dropped me off at home a little before ten. Suzie's car was right behind ours. Dad said, "We're going over to the beach. Want to come?"

"Do you want me to come?"

"Sure."

"Does Suzie?"

"Of course she does."

"How about if I ask her?"

Dad looked nervously at Suzie, idling in the Miata. "Sure, honey. If you want to come, just ask her."

I told him, "I don't want to come. I have school tomorrow."

"Oh yeah. Right. Well, you go ahead and beep me, for any reason. Good night."

I went inside and got a Fruit Roll-Up. Just as I stuffed it in my mouth, the phone rang. I had a quick thought that it might be Dad calling me from Suzie's car, but it wasn't. A deep, all-business voice demanded, "Is Robert Ritter there?"

"No."

"Is this his phone number?"

I called on a lifetime of training for dealing with strangers. I asked, "Who is this?"

After a pause, he answered stiffly, "This is Mr. Lewis. I am calling from Arcane Industries in Illinois. Mr. Ritter left this phone number on his franchise application. Is this his phone number?"

"I'm not allowed to give out that kind of information."

"I see. Do you know when I can possibly reach him at work?"

"No."

"How about Colonel Frank Ritter? He's the one I really need to speak to. Can you be of any help in putting me in touch with him? Either at home or at work?"

"No."

"How old are you, miss?"

"I'm eighteen."

"Then you are the person I will have to deliver this message to. Colonel Ritter must call me within the next twenty-four hours or I will begin reclamation proceedings against his franchise. Do you understand?"

"Yes. I'll tell my father to tell my uncle to call you." I already knew the answer, but I asked him, "Mr. Lewis, what are reclamation proceedings?"

I don't think he wanted to tell me, but he did. "It's a legal process. At the end of that process I send a truck down there and reclaim our equipment."

"I see. How far behind are we?"

"Your uncle has defaulted on two payments, August first and September first. That's six thousand dollars. Should that figure reach nine thousand I will pull your franchise so fast your head will spin. And the cost to me of doing that — the movers, the shipping, the cleanup — will eat up your collateral down payment in its entirety. Do I make myself clear?"

"Yes."

"And ask him one more thing for me. If he's a military man, what's he doing hiding behind teenage girls? That's who I get at the work number, and that's who I get at this number. Why won't he talk to me himself? Will you ask him that?"

"Yes, sir."

"Thank you." Mr. Lewis hung up. I punched in the number of Dad's beeper. I got a recording, punched in our home phone number, and waited.

I waited until bedtime, but he never called back.

MONDAY, THE 18TH ✤ Today was the day of the journalism field trip to Channel 57. It was a chance to see Mrs. Knight again, and I was very excited about that.

In the morning I waited outside Mr. Archer's office for Mr. Herman to arrive. There were no extra tapes to run or announcements to make, and that gave me time to ask, "Mr. Herman, did you get a chance to read the draft of my article?"

"Your article? What was it about?"

"It was about modeling. And shopping."

"Ah yes. Yes. A very amusing feature, Roberta. Even touching in parts. I nearly wept when the credit card didn't go through."

I held out a copy. "Here's what made it into the newsletter. Suzie chopped it down to nothing."

Mr. Herman raised one eyebrow and scanned the little boxed feature. "I really must meet Suzie someday. Someday, perhaps, when I have a very nasty, very contagious disease."

"Do you think it's a good article?"

"Yes. For a lightweight feature. It shows that you have range. Range is absolutely essential for a reporter. It shows that you can cover a bloody mass murder in an orphanage on one corner and a kitten rescue from a tree on the next."

"So you really think I can be a reporter?"

"How can you even ask me that, Roberta? Have you ever seen me waste a moment of my time on a child who lacks potential? Or ambition?" He stopped still and looked at me. He gestured toward my nose, and my eyes, and my ears. "Listen to me: You have a nose for news. You have an eye for detail. You have an ear for dialogue." He grasped the pointer finger of my hand. "You have a feel for the topic." He counted off on his own fingers: "Smell. See. Hear. Feel. All right. And when that Suzie creature got into in a snit over Toby the Turtle, you got a taste of what real journalism can do."

Mr. Archer emerged from his office. He looked very red, like his blood pressure was too high. He nodded at us to get things started. I popped in the tape and we all stood around the VCR for the Pledge and the Banner.

Afterward, as Mr. Herman and I were walking out, I told him, "I've been trying to get *The Muckrakers*,

Mr. Herman. I ordered it through Waldenbooks, but it never came in."

Mr. Herman made a sniffing sound. "You may as well have ordered it through Taco Bell. Have you tried ordering it online?"

"No, sir. We don't have a computer at home. I guess I could use Suzie's, but —"

"Tut-tut. Here." He reached into his briefcase and pulled out his copy of the book. "If you really want to read it, you can read mine."

"I really want to read it."

"All right, then. Here it is." He shook his head from side to side. "I think you could get anything from me simply by invoking the name of Suzie."

I slid Mr. Herman's copy of *The Muckrakers* carefully into my backpack and went to my first class.

At noon I got outside early and stood in the shade next to the only bus in sight. The rest of the students in the journalism class started to gather behind me, including Hawg and some of his teammates. I turned around and smiled at him. He said, "Hey, Roberta."

When the bus door opened, I climbed on and sat in the first seat. Hawg and the football guys continued on to the back.

When Mr. Herman got on, he sat right next to me. He said, "I just spoke to our mutual friend Mrs. Knight. She informed me that Channel 57 picks students to be interns. Would Roberta Ritter be interested in learning the news business?"

I nearly shouted, "Yes!" Then I immediately thought of work and asked, "But I have a job."

"Yes, of course you do. What is it again?"

"I work at Arcane, in the West End Mall."

"And that is why you are hesitating to accept an internship that could set you on your path in life? Because you work in a mall?"

I added weakly, "It's my family's business." I felt awful. I started babbling, "But I can do it, Mr. Herman. My uncle Frank is very good about changing the schedule around. My dad, too. And my cousins won't mind."

"Good heavens! Is this some sort of family sweatshop?"

I repeated, "It's our family business."

Mr. Herman muttered, "I see," and pulled out some papers to grade.

I didn't say anything else as we drove in the blazing sun, down Everglades Boulevard, to Fiftieth Street. Then I blurted out, "I'm sorry, Mr. Herman. I know there are a lot of other kids who would be better. I don't look like a newsperson. I don't act like a newsperson. I'd better say no."

Mr. Herman continued to look at his papers. But then he sighed deeply and said, "I am racking my brain, trying to think of who you remind me of. Perhaps Jane Eyre. Or Little Orphan Annie. Or that poor-yet-plucky little girl who Shirley Temple played in that movie where her father gets amnesia." He turned and looked right at me. "Understand, Roberta, the very reason I see potential in you is that you are not an attractive airhead whose involvement with a news story begins and ends with reading the TelePrompTer. No. I believe the internship belongs to you."

I nodded vigorously. "Thank you, Mr. Herman. Thank you. So I'll be working with Mrs. Knight again?"

"Yes, I'm afraid so."

"Afraid so? Isn't that a good thing?"

"Mrs. Knight is not my favorite person. In fact, she may not even be a person."

The bus driver pulled up in front of the Channel 57 studios, a low white building that looked like it had been built with Legos. "Did you two have a fight?"

"Professionals such as Mrs. Knight and I do not have fights."

"So what happened?"

"What happened? Let me see. I had already been here on the job, the job that she recruited me for, for two weeks, before I learned that you never actually put out a newspaper because you did not possess any paper. I had to learn that absurd fact from a student, of all things. That one who looks like a witch."

"Betty?"

"Is that her name?"

Mr. Herman and I got off the bus first and started toward the Lego building. A darkly tinted glass door opened, and we saw Mrs. Knight. She looked very different. She was about thirty pounds lighter, and she had short, frosted hair.

Mr. Herman spoke up immediately, in a friendly voice, "You look so thin, darling."

She gave him a huge smile. "Why, so do you."

"That's just my hair."

Mrs. Knight held the door, smiling, while about twenty of us piled into the lobby. Then she stood with her back to the door and announced, "I am so excited to see all you students from Memorial High School down here. It's like a homecoming for me. And a family reunion." Mrs. Knight went on like that. I looked around and calculated that she only knew about four of us from last year.

We walked farther into the building and encountered two people standing next to some very expensive-looking equipment. One was a nerdy guy with a red tie and a white shirt. The tie was loosened and the shirtsleeves were rolled up, like he was working very hard. Next to him was a pretty teenage girl with white-blond hair pulled back in a ponytail. Mrs. Knight said, "I'd like to start the tour with Bill and Lori. We like to call Bill, Oscar the Grouch."

Bill did not seem to like that.

She asked him, "Bill, can you tell these students from Memorial a little about this first piece of equipment?"

Bill didn't actually look at us, but he did say, "This piece is called a remote soundboard. We just got it in. We take it with us for remote shows."

Mrs. Knight explained, "Meaning shows not shot here in the studio."

Bill added, "This board cost nearly a hundred thousand dollars, so please do not touch it."

Mrs. Knight said, "Next to the remote soundboard is another interesting piece of equipment. It's called a video dubbing board." Mrs. Knight picked up a camera that was attached by wire to the board. She aimed it at a couple of the football guys and said, "I need a volunteer to say his name and school."

Surprisingly, Hawg's hand went up. His big face filled the monitor as he said into the camera, "I'm Hawg. My school is the University of Arkansas in Fayetteville, Arkansas. Home of the Razorback Hawgs."

Mrs. Knight loved that. She turned the camera toward me. "Okay, Roberta. Now you."

I didn't want to do it. I looked away from the camera and mumbled, "I'm Roberta Ritter, from Memorial High School."

Mrs. Knight yelled, "Good!" even though it wasn't. Then she said, "We'll come back to this area later to see what Lori can do with the videotape we just shot."

Mrs. Knight opened another door and gestured to the football guys to start filing through. She called over to me, "Roberta, you might want to stay here and talk to Lori about the internship."

I said, "That'd be okay, but I want to see the studio."

She smiled brightly, "Oh, you will. You'll see a lot of it." When the last journalism class member filed through, she hooked her arm through Mr. Herman's and said, "Come on, you'll be my escort. We need to talk."

Mr. Herman looked over his shoulder at me as if he

were about to say something, but then he disappeared quietly down the corridor with her.

I was left looking at Lori. She looked like a cheerleader. She spoke intelligently, though. She asked me, "You're Roberta?"

"Uh-huh."

"Tell me something about yourself, Roberta."

"I want to be a reporter. A journalist. Maybe even a muckraking journalist."

I don't think Lori knew what that meant. She said, "I see," then added, "I want to be a TV newscaster, maybe do the weather."

"Uh-huh. So what do you do now?"

"For now, I'm an intern."

"Yeah? I might be an intern, too. But it will be in the news department."

Lori looked puzzled. She told me, "There's only one intern job that I know about, and this is it." She pointed to the video dubbing board. "Mrs. Knight said I'm to show you how this works. Okay?"

"Okay."

Lori picked up the video camera, like Mrs. Knight had done. "You shoot people with the video camera. Their faces and voices are recorded here, on Tape A. Then you use this keypad to copy Tape A onto Tape B."

Lori then pointed to a small monitor set inside the board. "Now, here's the fun part. You run the video from Tape A on the monitor and stop it when somebody is about to speak. Then you run the audio from

Tape B and stop it when you find a funny match. Like this." Lori rewound Tape A until Hawg's face appeared. The she ran Tape B until we heard my voice. She punched some numbers on the keypad, and the monitor played Hawg's face while my voice said, "I'm Roberta Ritter from Memorial High School." I had to laugh. Lori laughed, too, even though she'd probably done this a hundred times.

Suddenly that Bill guy appeared. He scowled at Lori and said, "This isn't a toy. It's an expensive piece of equipment."

"Mrs. Knight said to train Roberta to use it. She's the next intern."

"Are you training or playing?"

Lori seemed to fear him. "Training."

"Then do it, please." Bill continued on through the door.

Lori said, "Bill really freaks out when kids get near the equipment. Whenever you have a tour, you have to watch the kids carefully and make sure nobody touches anything."

My classmates returned quickly. They didn't look at all interested, but Mrs. Knight was still perky. She gathered them around the video dubbing board. She told them, "You always hear that seeing is believing. Well, remember those statements you saw before? Let's look at them now. And listen to them."

Mrs. Knight nodded at Lori, who hit a button. Everybody watched and listened as my voice came out of Hawg's mouth. A couple of the football guys laughed. The rest of the class didn't seem to get it. Mrs. Knight said, "Seeing is not always believing, is it?"

Then Mrs. Knight led us to the third and final console. It was basically a computer with two screens. She said, "We have one last piece of equipment to show you today. One last treat. How many of you were born here in South Florida?"

About half the class grudgingly raised their hands, although I bet most of the rest had been born here, too. Mrs. Knight continued, "If you were, or even if you weren't, you will find this fascinating. We call this the video vault. We have a database of newscasts from the past twenty years. Each of you can instantly access the evening news for the day you were born simply by typing in your birthday on the keyboard. The broadcast will come up on the screen, with sound and video."

Mrs. Knight pushed some buttons on the keyboard to boot it up. "We have to limit everybody to two minutes, so you can use the arrows on the keyboard to fast-forward to a section you like, such as sports. Or even the weather. You know? What was the weather like on the day that you were born?"

Hawg again volunteered to go first. He announced, "I wasn't born in Florida, but I was born in November, and I bet the Hawgs was in the sports news."

Lori showed him how to access his birthday, saying, "Type it in here. Okay, here we go, sixteen years into the past." They quickly located the newscast and fast-forwarded to the sports. I didn't hear anything about the University of Arkansas. Hawg growled, "What kinda sports news is that?" Everybody soon had the idea, so Lori wasn't needed. Two kids at a time stepped up, punched in their birthdays, and watched part of a newscast.

I hung back, standing near Mr. Herman. Mrs. Knight, who had mysteriously disappeared for a while, returned just as mysteriously and said to him, "You're all set," which he seemed to understand.

After about twenty minutes, I saw that no one else was waiting to use the video vault. No one was hanging around it, either, so I stepped up and typed in a date. But the date was not my birthday. Instead, I typed in October 31. And it was not sixteen years into the past. It was seven.

The broadcast came on immediately. The news anchors had dated hairstyles and clothes. The opening graphics looked dated, too.

I listened to the lead story. It was about the weather. The anchorman said, "Our lead story this evening: Thunderstorms threaten Halloween revelers." I fast-forwarded through footage of lightning and heavy rain. I stopped when I saw a picture. It was my mom's picture. She was the second story. The man read off the TelePrompTer: "Thunderstorms were deadly for a local businesswoman tonight. Police say she was stabbed to death; that a large amount of cash was stolen from the Family Arcade near Ocean Boulevard; and that the storm provided cover for her killer to get away. We have live coverage at the site."

The screen filled with the image of the Family Arcade, exactly as it used to be. The Arcade came back to me in a flood of memory. I took in every detail of the facade as the camera zoomed forward. Yellow police tape blocked the sidewalk in front of the store. The camera panned downward and focused on a stain on the sidewalk, a long, dark smear. A voice said, "This is where store owner Mary Ann Ritter's life ended early this evening. She is the latest victim along a block that has seen more than its share of violence this year."

I couldn't focus on any more of the words as the camera remained, relentlessly, on that stain. Finally it cut back to the studio, where the anchor said, "Police are hoping for help from a store surveillance camera, or from a passerby, or from someone who might know the killer, to help crack this case. If you have any information about tonight's grisly murder-robbery, please call the Sheriff's Department Crimeline."

The newscast moved on to a lightning strike, so I logged off and rejoined the class.

I vaguely remember Mrs. Knight saying good-bye to all of us, and climbing back onto the bus. I had hoped to be alone for a while, but Mr. Herman again sat with me.

I tried hard to focus on what he was saying. It was something like this: "Mrs. Knight should be renamed; she should be Mrs. Queen, shouldn't she? She's the queen of the phonies. Her exalted TV journalism job turns out to be on a tabloid trash show."

I couldn't think of a thing to say. I couldn't even move. He added, "Now she wants to make it up to me about your phony newspaper class that never puts out a newspaper. She informed me that the news department is looking for an acid-tongued commentator. She has arranged an audition for yours truly."

Mr. Herman finally picked up on my state of mind. He asked, "Roberta, are you all right?"

I managed to say, "I'm sorry, Mr. Herman. I have something that I need to think about."

"Of course." He let me ride in silence the rest of the way.

I got off the field-trip bus just in time to catch my regular bus. Then I went home and did something I had not done in years. Probably in seven years. I cried. I sat on the couch in the living room, clutching a pillow, and cried for about thirty minutes. They say that's supposed to make you feel better, but it didn't work for me. I felt sick inside, like I had eaten poisoned food.

It was time for me to start walking to the mall, but I couldn't. I could barely move. I didn't know what to do. Dad sometimes calls Uncle Frank and lies to him, saying he is too sick to go in. I figured I could try that, too.

I called him and, I must admit, I really sounded sick. "Uncle Frank, it's Roberta. I'm not feeling well."

"You don't sound well, Roberta."

I lied to him easily. "I think I had better take the night off."

"Absolutely. Do you need us to come over? To bring you anything? Do you need to go to the doctor?"

"No. No. Nothing like that. I'm just really worn-out

and feeling under the weather. Dad can take care of me if I get worse."

"He's there?"

"Yes."

"I thought I just saw him up by the office."

"He's been in and out, taking care of me."

"Okay. Take as much time as you need."

"Okay." I was about to hang up when Karl picked up the phone at the front. He said, "You sick, cuz?"

"Yeah."

"Kristin is, too."

"Oh yeah?"

There was a long pause, like Karl had forgotten I was there. But then he said, "Hey, some guy from Antioch keeps calling for my dad, but my dad said he's not here. What do I do?"

"Act like you're crazy."

"Okay."

Karl hung up, and I just sat there, unmoving. I sat for hours, trying to get back to this morning, to the time before I had seen that stain. The phone rang at 8:30. It rang again at 8:35, and again at 8:40. I finally picked it up and heard Mrs. Weiss's voice say, "I asked your uncle where you were. He said you were sick."

"Yes, Mrs. Weiss. But I'm feeling better now."

"You should stay with me tonight. You can't be by yourself if you're sick."

"My dad is here."

"Oh? Is that right?"

"Yes."

"Put him on."

"I — I didn't mean right now. He will be here."

"Pack an overnight bag. I'll come pick you up after I close."

"I don't know, Mrs. Weiss —"

"Roberta, I don't want you alone when you're sick. You need to be over here."

I didn't know what else to say, so I said, "Okay."

"I'll be there at about nine-fifteen."

"No. No, don't come here. I want to walk. I need to walk."

"Nobody needs to walk. Not down here. It's too dangerous."

"But I really need the air."

"Fine, then, walk. Pack a bag and start walking now, though, before it gets any later."

"I will." Mrs. Weiss hung up, and I set about gathering what I needed for tonight and tomorrow. I put it all into a plastic supermarket bag and started off. I walked west down Everglades Boulevard into the last light of the day. Night had fallen before I even remembered the video vault. It had slipped clean out of my mind, the way Mrs. Knight had slipped out of the studio lobby today, without me noticing. And, like Mrs. Knight, it suddenly returned. I continued to walk quickly, with a purpose, but the image was back in my mind. It would not be denied. The image of a discolored sidewalk in the rain sickened me all over again.

I stopped at the Route 27 intersection, standing still,

with my head drooping down. I listened to the dangerous whir of the traffic just two feet away. It was a terrifying chaotic sound. I sensed when the light changed,
and I started to cross. Then I sensed movement, a men-
acing white blur to my left. A white station wagon
turned onto Route 27, and I was right in its path. I
stopped and looked at it, waiting for it to hit me. The
woman behind the wheel reacted frantically, slamming
on the brakes, her headlights stopping just inches from
my knees. The woman threw both hands outward,
bugged her eyes at me, and screamed out the window,
"What's wrong with you? Are you crazy?"

I met her stare and held it, then I screamed back,
"You have no idea what's wrong with me!" The woman
rolled her window up and looked away. I continued
across the highway.

Most people do not walk to Century Towers, they
drive. Pedestrians have to walk up to the guard booth,
tell the guard their name, and say who they're visiting.
The guard on duty tonight was an old guy with a name
tag that said GEORGE.

I stood outside the open window of the guardhouse
until George finally acknowledged me. "Are you here
to visit somebody?"

"Mrs. Weiss, in three-oh-three."

"Who?"

I repeated, "Mrs. Weiss, in three-oh-three," and he
buzzed up to Mrs. Weiss's. I added, "Tell her it's
Roberta."

"Who?" he snapped at me again, like I wasn't speaking loud enough to suit him. I thought, *He would never talk like that to a grown-up*. I repeated, "Roberta."

"Roberta what?"

I heard Mrs. Weiss's voice shriek at him through the speaker, "Your job is to tell me that it's Roberta, you lunkhead. If I want to know more about her name, I will instruct you to ask. Let her up this instant."

George bristled, but he didn't say anything else. He pointed toward Building 1, the only building there was, and I walked the twenty yards to the outside elevator. I rode up to the third-floor landing. The elevator opened onto an outdoor walkway with a red railing. From this height, I could see the land that had been cleared for Buildings 2 and 3 ten years ago. It had long since been overrun by weeds and palmetto grass.

Mrs. Weiss opened her door right before I got there. "Roberta, dear, are you all right?"

"Yes, Mrs. Weiss."

"I shouldn't have let you walk here."

"I didn't have any trouble."

"Only with that Nazi downstairs."

"Right."

"Come on, get in here. You're letting the air-conditioning out." She stood back to let me enter.

All Century Towers condos are set up the same way: You enter through the kitchen. Beyond the kitchen is the living room, and beyond that, the balcony. The bedrooms and bathroom are off to the right.

Mrs. Roman was in the living room, watching TV. I said, "Hi, Mrs. Roman."

"Roberta, darling. You're sick? You don't eat right."

"I'm feeling better. What are you watching?"

"Me? Nothing." She pointed over my shoulder at Mrs. Weiss. "She watches these nature shows. She watches to learn about fish. When I watch a show about fish, it's a cooking show."

Mrs. Weiss guided me to the couch. She sat next to me and took hold of my hand. "I watch to learn about life. What else is there that's worth learning about?"

Mrs. Roman winked at me. "Fine. But fish? Salmon?"

The fish show ended, and a show called *The World at War* came on. I concentrated on it, trying to block out the images from the video vault. The screen showed a man in a hall, making a speech. It sounded like German.

Mrs. Weiss perked up. "Look, Roberta. It's Hitler! This is why I watch the nature shows . . . Watch this now. This is man's way, right here. These Nazis passed laws making it a crime to be a Jew. Not to kill a Jew, mind you, but to *be* a Jew. So much for man's laws. Nature's laws alone are real."

Mrs. Roman commented, "Isabel loves to watch these war movies, too."

Mrs. Weiss corrected her, as if she'd had to before, "These aren't movies. This is real."

A few minutes later some grainy black-and-white footage came on, and Mrs. Weiss's comforting grip suddenly turned into a tight fist. She whispered, "Maybe you shouldn't look at this part," almost as if she were talking to herself. Anyway, I looked at it. About twenty naked men came running out of a wooden shack. They lined themselves up along the side of a ditch. Then a line of machine-gunners opened fire and killed them all. The men fell into the open ditch. Then another line of naked men came running out, and the same thing happened. My mouth must have dropped open. I had come here to get away from a horrible video, and I had found another one.

Mrs. Roman must have seen my expression. She yelled to Mrs. Weiss, "Look now. You're upsetting the girl. She shouldn't be watching this!"

I said, "Who are those men?"

"They're Jews. From a Nazi concentration camp. The Nazis made them dig their own grave and line up beside it, then they shot them. The camp commander made home movies of it. Nice, huh?"

Mrs. Roman protested, "Nobody should be watching this, Isabel. It's too horrible."

But Mrs. Weiss disagreed. "No, I think she should see this." She looked at me intently. "This is not ancient history, Roberta. This happened just a few years ago. Just a moment ago in time. This happened to my family."

Mrs. Roman left when the show ended. Mrs. Weiss and I got glasses of iced tea and moved out to the balcony. I stood next to her and looked out over the darkness. After a few minutes I asked, "How can people possibly do that? How can they kill someone and go on living themselves?"

"Are you talking about the Nazis?"

I wasn't, but I answered, "Yes."

"People have been killing each other for thousands of years. There are people, lots of them, who feel nothing about taking another life. When I was your age, Roberta, the entire world was at war. Everybody was trying to kill everybody else."

We each sat in a folding chair and looked out over the sawgrass.

I said, "That was World War Two?"

"That was World War Two."

"I asked Archie if we were going to cover World War Two in history. We're not."

"Archie? Is that a teacher?"

"He's my history teacher. And he's a football coach."

"Bah. They don't teach you history. Believe me, I know. They teach you social studies. I taught it myself."

I didn't know that. I said, "Really?"

"Yes. I taught for twenty years, up in Nassau County, New York." Mrs. Weiss thought for a moment. Then she asked me, "So tell me, what have you learned from all your years of public school social studies? Never mind, let me guess: that Indian Squanto helped the Pilgrims to plant corn. Am I right?"

"Yeah. He told them to plant a little dead fish with each kernel."

"I knew it. You'll never learn any history in that place. What did you learn about World War Two? Let me guess: that Hitler and the Nazis were bad, and that the Americans were good?"

"Yes."

In the near-darkness, Mrs. Weiss became very animated. "Hitler the Boogie Man?" She began thrusting her arm straight out and retracting it, over and over, like the pinheads' Nazi salute: "Bad Hitler! Bad Hitler!"

I had to laugh. But I *was* puzzled. I asked her, "He *was* bad, wasn't he?"

"Of course. He was evil. So what? Lots of people are."

"So how did he get all those people to follow him?"

"Because he had a vision. He had a dark vision of who he could be. And he pursued that vision with all his might. He pursued it until he made it come true."

Mrs. Weiss got up with her empty glass. She took my glass, too, and went inside. She returned with a tube of Ritz crackers. She set down two saucers and laid some crackers out for us to share. Then she said, "So what else did you learn about the war in your history class?"

"That we won?"

"Okay. That's true enough. Who was our leader?"

"Roosevelt?"

"Which one?"

"Franklin?"

"Good guess. Did you know that he pretended, until his dying day, that he could walk? Whereas in fact he couldn't, because he had polio."

"Come on. Nobody knew he couldn't walk?"

"Nope. His sons were always standing next to him, propping him up."

"That's pretty weird, Mrs. Weiss."

"Sure it is. History is weird when you get past that Indian Squanto stuff they feed you. History doesn't smell very good, Roberta. History stinks. And United States history stinks right along with it. You know what they ought to put in that textbook of yours? You know those perfume strips that they put in the magazines, where you tear it off and smell it? They ought to put a strip in that book, so you could tear it off and smell all the rotting corpses. Then maybe you'd remember some history."

Mrs. Weiss gathered up the crackers. "That's enough for tonight. It's late, and you have school. You have to go learn lots of new history tomorrow. Anyway, the Nazi Holocaust is old news now. There have been so many holocausts since then. They don't even make the front page anymore. They're on page six."

We walked into the kitchen and put our saucers in the sink. Mrs. Weiss opened a drawer and pulled out an envelope. She handed it to me. "Listen, Century Towers has very strict rules about children. If you're going to stay over here regularly, you have to get your father's permission. It's a liability waiver. Have him sign it."

I slid the paper into my backpack. "Okay, I will."

TUESDAY, THE 19TH ❧ This afternoon, at the beginning of Mr. Herman's lecture, a boy walked into class holding a green guidance department form. I knew what that meant right away. Someone was being called down to Mrs. Biddulph's office for RDT.

Mr. Herman gets very angry at interruptions. He stopped speaking to stare coldly at the kid, then he demanded, "What do you want?"

The kid held out the form, and Mr. Herman snatched it. He read it and said, "Roberta Ritter. You're wanted in guidance. There's an ironically named place." He handed the form back to the kid as I stood up.

Mr. Herman was about to resume speaking when the kid said, "What about the other one?"

Mr. Herman arched one eyebrow and snapped. "What other one?"

The kid pointed at the form. "The other name on here."

"I don't know who that is." Mr. Herman directed his eyebrows into the distance, like he was exercising them. "It could be one of them in the back, I suppose. Why don't you go ask them?"

I followed the kid back to the group of football players. He said, "Any of you named Hugh Mason?"

Hawg looked up and said, "Yeah. Who wants to know?"

I was surprised. I was surprised to hear that Hawg had a real name, and that Hugh Mason was it.

"The two of you have to go to guidance."

"What for?"

"I don't know."

Hawg shrugged and got up. On the way out, he said to me, "I guess anything's better than listening to Mr. Homo."

I followed Hawg and the boy into the corridor. I found myself walking next to Hawg, so I took the opportunity to say, "Can I ask you something?"

"Will I know the answer?"

"Yes, I think so."

"Then shoot."

"Why do you football guys take journalism?"

"That's an easy one. The guys on the team, the ones that took it last year, recommended it highly. They said you don't even put out a damn newspaper."

"That's true. But things are different this year. Mr. Herman is a much tougher teacher."

"Yeah, well, that's just my luck."

"What'd he put on your progress report?"

"My what?"

"Your progress report. It comes out halfway through the term? It tells you what grade you have?"

"Is that what that paper was? Hell, I threw it away."

When we got to the guidance office, Mrs. Biddulph handed me a clear plastic cup with a label on the side and a lid on the top. She said, "Take this black pen and write your full name on the label. Take the cup into the bathroom, fill it to the label with urine, secure the lid tightly, and leave it on the tray in there. Then wash your hands and go back to class."

Hawg added, "I hope you drank your orange juice this mornin'."

I started toward the bathroom and heard Mrs. Biddulph say to him, "All right, Hugh. You are here as a callback. Do you know what that means?"

I locked the bathroom door and carefully followed all the instructions. By the time I had washed and dried my hands and opened the door, Hawg's mood had turned angry. He was practically yelling at Mrs. Biddulph. "What? It took you two damn weeks to find one micromilligram?"

"Young man, watch your language, please."

Hawg struggled to control his temper. "Listen, ma'am. I don't smoke no damn reefer. I hate that stuff. That stuff ruined my mama's life."

Mrs. Biddulph said, "I am only telling you the result of the test. The rest is up to Mr. Archer. You can explain the situation to him."

"No, I'm gonna explain it to you right now, 'cause now I got her all figured out. Here's what happened. I rode home from practice with a buncha Florida boys, and one of them lit up a damn marijuana cigarette in the car. I didn't have nothin' to do with it. I was just sitting there breathing the damn air, and that's the god's honest truth."

Mrs. Biddulph said, "You'll have your chance to speak to Mr. Archer."

"You talkin' about the principal? Or Archie?"

"The principal."

"Damn."

"And please watch your language in here."

Mrs. Biddulph handed us each a guidance pass. Hawg and I walked back to class together, but he didn't say a word. I risked a quick sideways glance on the stairs. I couldn't tell for sure, but he appeared to have tears in his eyes.

I was hurrying through the rotunda at four o'clock when I spotted Uncle Frank. I couldn't believe my eyes.

He was standing there talking to Devin. They looked like one of Suzie's Before and After poses.

When I got into Arcane, Dad was alone behind the register. I asked him, "Where's Kristin?"

He said, "I don't know, honey. I think they're doing something mysterious in the back."

"Who?"

"The two girls."

I walked back through the empty aisles and opened the office door. Kristin's voice yelled, "Who's that?"

I said, "It's me."

Nina answered, "Oh, good, Roberta, get in here."

I peered into the bathroom at the two of them. Kristin had her blouse unbuttoned. She was twisted around, trying to see her own back in the mirror.

Nina ordered, "Come in here and lock the door, Roberta. Now, tell me, what's that look like to you?"

I stared at Kristin's back and saw two circular red splotches behind her bra strap, like a pair of quarters. I said, "A rash?"

Nina agreed. "Yeah, that's it. You got some kinda rash goin' here."

Kristin was upset. "What are you talking about? A rash? What does that mean?"

I added, "Like a poison-ivy rash."

Nina smiled evilly. "Yeah, that's it. Looks like you've been rolling around outside with your blouse off, in some poison ivy."

Kristin snapped at her, "Shut up, Nina. What is it really?"

Nina said, "I'm not the doctor. We could ask my father, but he's at the Sunrise office today."

Kristin rebuttoned her blouse. Then we all piled out of the bathroom and went out front. Kristin told me, "I need to find my dad. Right away."

I heard Hawg and Ironman coming toward me from the SpecialTees side of the store. Hawg was deep into an explanation of his trip to the guidance office. They came to a stop in front of the counter, so he included me in it. "Hey, you know them boys I was riding with after practice? They was already called down for RDT the first week of school. So they knew they wasn't gonna be called again for the rest of the year. Hell, half the football team's already been called down — now they can do whatever the hell they want.

"Then, to top her all off, Mr. Homo gave me an F on that progress-report thing. Damn guidance mailed a copy of it to my house. Archie told me Mr. Homo failed the whole damn offensive line. But I'm the only one who had an F from him and a damn RDT report, so I'm the one they're trying to kick off the team."

Even Ironman looked shocked. He actually said something. "What are you going to do?"

"If they don't keep me on that team, I'll tell you what I'm gonna do, I'm goin' back up to Georgia."

I suggested, "Can't your father — I mean your stepfather — talk to Mr. Archer?"

"Sure he can, but he won't. I went home and told him the truth about them Florida boys and their reefer in the car. And he knows it's the truth. He knows I don't mess with no drugs. But he won't do a damn thing about it. So I told him, 'That's it. I'm goin' back up to Georgia. I'm gonna go play at my old high school up there, where they don't make you piss in no damn cup.'"

I said, "Well, you're only a junior. Can't you just wait and play next year?"

"Next year!" Hawg looked at me in amazement, like I had suggested something truly and impossibly bizarre. "There ain't no next year. I'm in my prime now, girl. I am college draft material right now. I aim to play football now, or die tryin'."

Suddenly Kristin, followed by Uncle Frank, hurried into the arcade. Uncle Frank announced, "I'm taking Kristin to the walk-in clinic." They continued on to the back. We didn't see them again after that.

At seven o'clock I took a break and walked up to the mall office. I opened the door as Suzie was telling Dad, "I've checked and rechecked the fountain. It's ready to go. I have Gene appearing as Toby the Turtle. Kids will like that. I have Channel Fifty-seven and Channel Three coming, and a reporter from the *Atlantic News*."

Dad threw out his hands. "So now you can relax. You're ready."

Suzie shook her head angrily, flopping her blond bangs. "That Mr. Knowlton can be very rude. Let me tell you something — I've only known him for a month, and I've already had it up to here with his faxes, and his phone calls, and his FedEx deliveries. I'm doing everything I can for 'the candidate.'"

Dad said, "I know you are."

The door opened behind me, and Suzie's face lit up with a smile. She cried out, "Mr. Knowlton! So good to see you."

Philip Knowlton entered and set a leather briefcase on the floor. He appeared to be about forty, although his bald head made it difficult to tell. He was mostly thin, except for a very unhealthy-looking stomach protruding over his belt. He looked around the office without actually seeming to see us.

Once she realized he wasn't going to say anything, Suzie continued, "We're all ready to go on our end."

Mr. Knowlton finally looked at her. "That's good. We have six days until the candidate appears. How big a crowd are you expecting?"

"Probably about a hundred people."

"Demographics?"

"Pardon me?"

"What kind of people will make up this crowd?"

Suzie seemed confused. "Shoppers, mostly."

Knowlton pursed his lips. He spoke more slowly. "Old shoppers? Young shoppers? Males? Females? Middle class? Upper middle?"

"Oh, I'd say young females and their kids. Mostly middle class. Maybe some retired people."

Knowlton actually smiled at that. "You're kidding? Retired people? In South Florida?"

Dad and Suzie laughed.

"I want to do a man-in-the-street ad for Mr. Lyons.

I'll need a young person, an old person, and some sort of minority."

Suzie assured him, "No problem." She looked over at me. "We'll get Roberta here, old Lombardo, and, uh, Sam. Sam's an Arab."

"Fine. And how exactly are you going to attract this crowd?"

Suzie had an idea. "Tell you what — I'll show you how exactly." She picked up the phone, dialed a number, and said, "Gene? It's Suzie. Can you come to the mall office right away? There's somebody here I'd like you to meet."

She hung up and said, "We will actually have two things to attract people — a costumed character for the little kids, and the rededication of the fountain for the grown-ups."

Knowlton corrected her, "Mr. Lyons will be the main attraction. Mr. Lyons is the reason we are here."

Suzie agreed, "Of course."

Gene burst through the door, wearing his Chili Dog top. Suzie pointed and said, "Gene, this is Mr. Knowlton, the man I told you about."

Gene stuck out his hand enthusiastically. He said, "Toby the Turtle, at your service."

Knowlton's hand stopped halfway to Gene's. His jaw dropped. "What did you say?"

Gene continued smiling. "Of course that's not my real name. I'm Gene. I'm playing Toby the Turtle on Monday." He turned to Suzie. "It is Monday, right?"

Suzie replied, "Right. Monday the twenty-fifth."

Knowlton turned to her. "Is this some kind of joke?"

Suzie smiled nervously. She shook her head no.

Knowlton looked up toward heaven, as if looking for help. He asked Suzie, "I did put you on Mr. Lyons's routing system, did I not? You do receive the e-mails?"

She nodded.

"Do you ever read them?"

Suzie continued nodding.

"Then you are aware that Mr. Lyons has a problem on environmental issues, a problem mostly brought on by an unfortunate entombing of turtles?"

Suzie stopped nodding and looked down.

Knowlton held both hands out, as if measuring one foot's worth of stupidity. "So what would be the stupidest thing we could possibly do? Wait a minute, I know! We could schedule the candidate to appear here, at the scene of the crime, with a man wearing a turtle costume!"

I looked over at Dad. He was looking away, as if this really didn't affect him. He obviously had no intention of standing up for Suzie.

Knowlton picked up his briefcase. "I am going out now to examine the area where the candidate will be speaking. It should take me about ten minutes. If you come up with another idea by then, one that does not automatically cost the candidate the election, I will listen to it. If you do not, I will hire my own people to stage this event." He cast a withering glance at Gene. Then he told Suzie, "This is not *The Amateur Hour*.

Mr. Lyons is poised to become a national figure. Let's treat him like one." And out he went.

Suzie had to have been devastated. But she didn't fall apart, she sprang into action. She shouted, "Gene! What other character could you do?"

"Uh, Oliver Hardy."

"Who's that?"

"From Laurel and Hardy?"

"No! What else?"

"Lou Costello. From Abbott and Costello."

"Gene, who can you do by yourself? Just you!"

"Uh, I got my Santa suit in the van."

Suzie stared at him intensely. Then she sat down and started scribbling madly on a legal pad. By the time Knowlton returned, she was ready for him.

Knowlton was in a calmer mood after visiting the rotunda. He said, "Okay. What do you have for me?"

Suzie read off the legal pad. "We have the biggest attraction in the world — Santa Claus. It's an early visit from Santa. He wants to get a head start on the kids' Christmas lists. Mr. Lyons is coming on September twenty-fifth, so it's 'Buy on September twenty-fifth and you can relax on December twenty-fifth.' We have great layaway sales at all the stores. 'Get your shopping done now so you can enjoy the holidays. Get great prices now, too.' The mothers will love it, and the kids will love it."

Knowlton asked, "What about the retired people?"

"The retired people are going to be here, anyway."

Knowlton thought for a long moment. He finally answered, as if to himself, "It's a dumb idea, but at least it's not fatal. I can work with this as long as I can keep Mr. Lyons separate from Santa Claus. Mr. Lyons can't be associated with giving people things that they haven't worked for."

He looked up at Suzie. "All right. You do the Santa bit early, to get the kids and moms in here. Mr. Lyons can tape a man-in-the-street session while all that nonsense is going on. Then Santa disappears." He pointed an accusing finger at Gene. "I mean, I want you out of here. I want no photos showing the candidate and Santa Claus in the same universe. Then Mr. Lyons comes out for the fountain bit. He throws the switch, he gives his speech, he endears himself to young and old alike." Mr. Knowlton snapped the locks on his briefcase. "All right. I think that will work. You'll get your final schedule from me tomorrow."

Knowlton picked up the briefcase and started out. Suzie, still holding her legal pad, followed him. But he walked straight through the mall exit without looking back.

I felt a great sense of relief leaving with Mrs. Weiss and Mrs. Roman for dinner. I felt like I was with normal people for a change. We piled into the white Lincoln and headed south, up and onto the cloverleaf highway at the edge of the Everglades. Mrs. Weiss said, "I don't like driving up in the air like this. It upsets my stomach."

I told her, "This reminds me of the Zax, on the prairie of Prax."

"What? Is that a children's book?"

"You know, the Dr. Seuss story? There's nothing out in this prairie, then, all of a sudden, a big cloverleaf highway starts coming through, and they build it right over the Zax?"

Mrs. Roman said, "I remember that book. I used to read it to my grandson."

The Hollywood Cafeteria is only one exit south of us, down Route 75. We were there in less than ten minutes. It's an old people's restaurant, with an early-bird special, a blue-plate special, and an after-hours special, which is what we were in time for.

Somewhere near the end of our meal, we started talking about Mr. Lyons. Mrs. Roman said she liked him, because "He sticks up for the old people."

But Mrs. Weiss sneered, "Bah, he sticks up for anything that'll get him a vote. He'd be for shooting the old people if that got him votes. Believe me, he's an empty suit. He'll say anything."

"He's running against a man who left his wife when she had cancer. Do you believe that?"

"Of course I believe it. He probably kicked his dog, too."

I said, "Kicked his dog? Really?"

Mrs. Weiss and Mrs. Roman both laughed. Mrs. Weiss said, "Don't take things so literally, Roberta."

"What? Did he kick the dog or didn't he?"

"We'll never know. And it doesn't matter."

"Why doesn't it matter?"

"Listen: Let's say you and I are running for office.

Nobody knows either one of us. Nobody really wants to know us, because they're sick to death of listening to politicians. So I let it be known that my opponent, Roberta Ritter, kicks her dog."

"But I don't own a dog."

"Doesn't matter. A lot of voters do own dogs, and they don't want to vote for anybody, like you, who kicks dogs."

"But it's not true! Can't I hold a press conference and say it's not true?"

"Yes. Of course you can. But that's exactly what a lying dog-kicker like you would do. Hold a big press conference and lie about it."

"Mrs. Weiss, how do you know all these things?"

Mrs. Weiss laughed. "I'm old. That's how."

"You're elderly," Mrs. Roman assured her.

"That's right, Roberta. And don't mess with the elderly. We know all the tricks. We know all the salesmen's tricks, and the doctors' tricks, and the politicians' tricks. Especially the politicians'. We're the only ones who have the time to go vote for the politicians. So if they fool with us, we, the old people, will get them."

They kept talking, on and off, about Ray Lyons all through dinner and all the way back in the car. When we pulled into Sawgrass Estates, however, my neighborhood once again had a silencing effect on Mrs. Roman. She didn't even say good night. Mrs. Weiss, of course, did. I got out and waved as they drove away.

I watched them cruise up the street; then I walked slowly up the driveway. It was a walk I had made hundreds of times in the dark. I was never afraid, but tonight something about it was spooky. I paused at the first pole of the carport, sensing someone's presence.

My sense was right.

The figure of a man stepped out between me and the door. He was a burly man, and he was so close that I could not run away. I felt my mouth opening slowly, but there was no way I could scream. The man came toward me, reaching into his pocket.

I just stood still and waited, with my head drooping forward, for him to close the final few feet between us. But he didn't. He stopped. And he said, in a voice that I did not know, "Roberta?"

I tried to regain control of my eyes, and my neck. I pulled my head backward until I could see who it was.

It was someone I knew. I had heard about that; a rapist is often someone you know. He was from Arcane. He was the guy with the long hair down his back and the stocky body.

He said again, "Roberta?"

The Head Louse. It was the Head Louse. Had he been having thoughts about me? Had he stalked me? And waited out here in the dark carport, when there would be no one to help me?

He spoke again. "Roberta, do you hear me?"

But something was odd. This wasn't the Head Louse's voice. It was an intelligent voice. "Roberta? Do you know who I am?"

I looked up at him. He pulled something black out of his pocket. A gun? A knife? He pointed it at me and snapped it. It fell open, showing a picture ID and a piece of gold metal. He took another step forward and held it out to me, so close that I could see it. He said, "Do you know what this is?"

Dimly, I could read a name: *Griffin*. I finally looked right at him. I heard myself say something really stupid. "A sheriff's star?"

He nodded, not smiling. "It's an Atlantic County Sheriff's Department badge. It's my identification. Can you read the name?"

I looked hard at the picture and read the name aloud, "Griffin."

"Right. I'm a detective. Do you understand that?" He waited patiently for an answer that did not come. He continued, "I've been working an undercover job at the mall. Do you understand?"

I did not. I whispered, "I thought you were that guy who came to Arcane."

"No. I'm not that guy. Not really. I thought maybe you had figured that out by now."

"No."

"I never was that guy." He pointed to the badge. "I'm this guy."

I started to get some control back over my brain. I asked him, "What do you want?"

"We need to talk. But first, I want you to do something for me. Go inside, pick up the phone, and call nine-one-one. Tell them it's not an emergency, but you need to talk to the platoon sergeant. Okay?

"Tell the sergeant who you are. Ask him if it's safe to

let me in. If he says it is, then open the door and let me in. I have some questions I need to ask you."

I did exactly as I was told. I crossed in front of him, unlocked the door, and entered the kitchen. He did not follow. I stood with my hand on the Blockbuster Video bag, steadying myself as I dialed. I heard myself talking to a Sergeant Fisk. He told me that Detective Griffin was working a case and needed to speak to me about it. I listened quietly, and then I hung up. I opened the door and let Detective Griffin in.

He was upset, too. I could tell. He said, "I'm sorry about this. I know I scared you."

"No. That's okay."

"It's just that . . . There's an element of secrecy to this case, so I have to talk to you without other people knowing. Again, I apologize for what happened out there on the driveway. If it's okay with you, I'll say what I have to say and be going."

"Okay."

We remained standing by the kitchen door. "I've been working a case for two months now. The state's attorney and some other very important, very influential people are concerned about certain events at the West End Mall, events that fall under the state's hate crimes law. Someone at your mall has been the victim of racially motivated crimes."

I said, "Sam?"

"That's right. Sam. What do you know about them?"

"Nothing. I saw that his car got keyed."

"That's right. It did. But that's just the tip of it. He's

been finding rebel flags, Nazi daggers, graffiti on a weekly basis. All of it seems to be because he's of Arab descent. That's what makes it a hate crime. Are you following me?"

I was gaining more control. "Yes."

"Sam has spent many nights, on his own time, hoping to catch somebody red-handed. That hasn't happened. But he and I have built up a strong circumstantial case against an employee of your arcade." He waited for me to respond, but that wasn't going to happen. He finally came out and asked, "Have you ever seen any racist actions or heard any racist statements from Hawg?"

I felt a moment of relief that it wasn't Karl. Then I felt bad for Hawg. I answered, "No."

He flipped open a small notebook. "Does anything like this sound familiar? He once told me this: 'Buncha niggers tried to mess with me in the cafeteria. I got up in the biggest one's face. I said, "You think I'm scared of you because you're black? Well, I ain't. Let's go, boy."'"

"No, I've never heard him say anything like that."

I don't think Detective Griffin believed me, but he did take a step back toward the door. He said, "Well, if he does, or if you think of anything that might help Sam out, or help me out, you can tell me in confidence. I won't reveal that you're my source. Until that time I'll leave you be. Again, I'm sorry that I startled you."

He let himself out and disappeared into the night. I locked the door behind him. Then I walked like a zombie to the couch and fell onto it.

I needed some time to think, but I didn't get it. The portable phone started ringing right next to my head. I picked it up heavily and croaked, "Hello?"

"Oh, my god, Roberta. Do you have it, too?"

"Kristin? Is that you?"

"Yes. Are you sick, too?"

"I . . . I don't think so."

"Listen: We just got back from the doctor. That rash? It's not poison ivy. It's the chicken pox."

"Really? You never had the chicken pox?"

"No. Did you?"

"Yeah. I thought everybody did."

Kristin exhaled loudly. "No, Not everybody. I guess I don't need to warn you then."

"No."

"Okay. Good-bye."

"Good-bye." Kristin sounded mad. Like I hadn't given her any sympathy.

It was true. I hadn't. I had my own problems to worry about.

WEDNESDAY, THE 20TH ❧ This afternoon I got off the school bus at Everglades Boulevard and crossed to catch the county bus on the other side of the road. The heat was painful. It was one of those days when you can't touch anything metal or you'll get a third-degree burn. I remembered that when I tried to unbuckle my backpack to pull out *The Muckrakers*.

Two buses drove by before one pulled up. It said

CITY HALL CIRCLE in electronic letters across the front. I'd been on plenty of school buses, and YMCA and church buses, but I had never before ridden a county bus. I climbed up the black stairs and asked the driver, "How much does it cost?"

He was a fat guy with thick tortoiseshell glasses. He told me, "Seventy-five cents."

I handed him a dollar. He pointed to a sticker attached to a metal-and-plastic change box. It said, *Driver does not make change*. I guess he thought I couldn't read, because he added, "I don't make change."

I reached into my pocket and felt around. I told him, "Well, I don't have any coins. What should I do?"

"You'll have to pay a dollar. Or you'll have to get off."

I stuffed the dollar into the box. I turned and walked down the aisle as he pulled away. I counted a dozen people on the bus — ten women and two little boys. Six of the women wore uniforms of various kinds, from either a hotel, a fast-food restaurant, or a theme park. Nobody was talking. But if they had talked, I had the feeling it wouldn't have been in English.

At least it was cool in the bus. The air-conditioning worked, and the windows were tinted. Everything we passed outside had a cool blue coloring. I watched as we drove past a blue sign for Seventy-second Street, the site of the cemetery. Then I settled back to read my book.

Before I knew it, we were driving past the Channel 57 Studios. I hopped up and hurried to the front. I told the driver, "I had to get off back there."

I expected him to say something mean, but he said, "Where?"

"The Channel Fifty-seven studios."

He pulled over in the middle of the block and opened the door. He said, "Let me know next time. I'll stop at the door."

I hopped off and walked back to the white studio building. I pushed open the door of the reception area. Then I followed the same path that I had taken on the class trip. I opened the door of the interior lobby and walked inside, where I heard Mrs. Knight's bubbly voice. "Roberta! You're here."

Mrs. Knight grabbed my elbow as she hurried by, pulling me along with her. She brought me up to Lori again, introduced me again, and told her again to train me on the video dubbing board. Then she disappeared. Lori said, "Do you remember what I showed you before?"

"Sure."

"Why don't you go ahead and mess around with these tapes? You can get a feel for how to do it." She stood watching me for a minute, then she said, "I'm really sick of that machine. Believe me, the trick gets old."

"But are you sick of being a TV intern?"

"I'm not a TV intern. I'm a TV slave. I'm less-than-minimum-wage labor."

"Didn't you learn anything?"

"I learned that Bill is a jerk." Lori watched me for a while and commented, "You already run that thing better than I do."

I answered, "Thanks."

The door flew open and we both turned, expecting, I think, to see Bill. But instead we saw Mr. Herman. He looked awful — pale and pain filled, like he was about to cry. He froze in the doorway, as confused by the sight of me as I was by the sight of him.

Lori said, "I'm going to take off now, Roberta. Good luck."

I waved to her and then looked back at the doorway. "Are you okay, Mr. Herman?"

"Yes, of course, Roberta. I was just looking for Mrs. Knight."

"She was here a few minutes ago. She'll probably be back."

Mr. Herman was perspiring so much that it showed through his suit jacket. I said, "Can I get you a soda?"

"No. No, I'm quite all right." He breathed deeply and seemed to regain some of his composure. He asked me, "What are you doing here?"

"The internship. Remember? Today is my first day."

"Ah yes. Good for you."

I told him, "I'm reading *The Muckrakers*."

"Good. Good." Neither of us spoke for a moment, then he asked, "So what do you think of them?"

"I think they're great. They really helped the poor people."

"Yes. It's curious, though. They were not poor people themselves, were they? They only wrote about them. They did not want to actually be poor . . . Nor do I."

Mrs. Knight came up behind him. "So how did it go?"

Mr. Herman cast a nervous glance at me; then he answered, "They said I sounded good but I looked shiny. Now, what does that mean?"

"Shiny? Like, your nose? Or the top of your head?"

"I don't know. They didn't elaborate."

The two of them walked out together. I hung out by the video dubbing board for another fifteen minutes, messing with Tape A and Tape B, until Bill came through and asked me, "What are you doing?"

I said, "I'm the new intern."

He shook his head, annoyed. "There's nothing for you to do here. There's no tour today, so you can leave."

I said, "Okay. Should I come back tomorrow?"

Bill nodded grudgingly. Then he watched me walk out — to make sure I didn't damage any equipment. I crossed the street and walked for two blocks until I found a bus stop. When the bus pulled up, the same driver was sitting behind the wheel. He didn't say anything, but I could tell that he recognized me. I stuffed another dollar into the box and rode west to the mall.

I had crossed the parking lot as far as the first Toby the Turtle banner when I noticed something odd: The glass entrance doors were wide open. As I got closer to the doors, I could tell why. A horrendous smell, like of rotting food, was pouring out of the mall. I covered my nose and continued inside. When I got about halfway to the rotunda, I could see three large fans whirring behind the fountain area. They were blowing the smell away from the food court and toward the mall entrance.

I saw Suzie standing in the middle of the fountain. She was arguing with Leo. Some of the merchants were drifting around, talking to each other in the area behind the fans.

When I got close enough I could hear Leo say, "I don't want to be here when you turn that thing on."

Suzie didn't answer. She just stood there, with the fans whipping her dress and hair.

I asked Leo the obvious question. "What's that smell?"

"It's a leak in the pipe. That's swamp gas leakin' in here. Nice, ain't it?"

Suzie said to Leo, as if I weren't even there, "Leo, can you please just help me to solve the problem? That's our job here. Yours and mine. We need to solve this problem today so that it's gone by tomorrow."

Leo said, "This problem ain't gonna be gone tomorrow. This system was bad ten years ago and it's twice as bad now."

Suzie snapped at him, "That is not true! You listen to me: I have had a real plumber in here, someone who actually knows what he's talking about. Someone who actually started the job and got it done in the same day, if you can imagine that. He checked out this system, and he said it was working fine."

Leo winked at me. "Yeah. That's why we got all the doors stuck open and the fans on."

Suzie threw up her hands. "Forget it. Just forget it. I can't talk to you. Go back and do whatever it is that you do."

I arrived at Arcane and immediately froze. Sam was there. I watched from the entrance, and Uncle Frank watched from the register, while Sam read the Crusader legend. He must have sensed our eyes on him because he looked up, pointed at the legend, and asked Uncle Frank, "Do you know what this is about?"

We moved toward him until Sam, Uncle Frank, and I were all gathered around Crusader. Uncle Frank answered, "It's about the Crusades. Isn't it?"

Sam shook his head sadly. "It's about somebody's version of the Crusades, yeah."

Uncle Frank asked, "What are you saying?" From his tone, he seemed ready for an argument.

Sam paused for a long moment. I expected him to say, *Forget it*, and walk away, but he didn't. He told Uncle Frank, "I know something about the Crusades. Do you?"

Uncle Frank eyeballed him. "A little bit. I've read some history. I know that it was a just war."

"Meaning what?"

"Meaning we had the right to fight it."

"'We'? Who is 'we,' Colonel? Americans didn't fight in the Crusades. America wasn't even a country then. It wouldn't be for many centuries." Uncle Frank didn't respond. Sam asked, "Have you ever read the histories of Omar Abu-Rishe?"

Uncle Frank stood up even straighter than usual. "No. I can't say that I have."

"What about Shafiq Jabri?"

"No. Why? What did they have to say?"

"They said that the Crusades raised the human atrocity level to a new high. They said that the Crusaders were incredibly bloodthirsty."

"I guess that kind of thing could be said for both sides."

"Not really."

Uncle Frank blinked. "Well, it was another era. It happened a long time ago."

Sam repeated, "Not really. In Arab history, it was just a moment ago. In fact, in Arab history, the Crusades haven't ended."

"How's that?"

"The Christians are still fighting the infidel, Colonel, and it's still in the name of the cross."

"All right. What do you mean, the infidel? Define your terms."

"The non-Christian people. The Japanese. The Vietnamese. The Iraqis."

Uncle Frank took a breath, held it, and let it out. "We had reasons for fighting against all of those people. Good reasons."

"Yeah? And they had good reasons for fighting back." Sam pointed at the Crusader legend. "The infidels sometimes fight back. But they can never keep up with the atrocity level. Can they?" Sam ticked off items on his finger. "The atomic bomb. Agent Orange. Depleted uranium. There's always something new. Right, Colonel?"

Uncle Frank answered tightly, "Right."

"But you don't use the new weapons in Europe, against Christians. Do you?" He started ticking on the fingers again. "The Christian Germans don't get the A-bomb. The Christian Russians don't get Agent Orange. The Christian Serbs don't get depleted uranium. No. We save that stuff for the infidel. We can raise the atrocity level on him, because he is less than human, he is the infidel."

"You're entitled to your opinion, Sam. I don't think history would back you up."

"Whose history?"

"The history of the atomic bomb, for one thing. It wasn't ready for Germany."

"No? But it was miraculously ready for the infidel three months later?"

"That's right."

"Do you know, Colonel, that the Japanese were trying to surrender to us? We nuked them anyway. Twice. Just to scare the Russians."

Uncle Frank smiled knowingly. "At least you said 'we,' Sam. You're part of this country, aren't you? You seem to be doing okay over here."

"Sure. I'm doing okay, for an infidel." Sam looked at me briefly, as if to acknowledge that I was there. Then he abruptly took off, leaving Uncle Frank to chew over his parting words.

I didn't see much of Uncle Frank for the rest of the evening. But after we had finished the closing checklist, he did come up to ask, "Roberta, have you had the chicken pox?"

I nodded. "Yes."

"Can you ride home with us tonight? I want you to visit Kristin."

When we got to the car, Uncle Frank told Karl to sit in the back. Karl didn't like that, but he obeyed. Then Uncle Frank explained to me, "Kristin is really heartbroken. And that Nina girl isn't helping matters. She's telling Kristin she's going to need 'acid peels,' or a facelift, or some such nonsense. Kristin's convinced that she's ugly, and that she's never going to be anything else." Uncle Frank's voice thickened. "I tell her it's only temporary, that those red spots will all go away. I have to tell you, though, Roberta, that it's a really bad case. The doctor says she will have some scarring."

We soon pulled into the driveway. Karl hopped out, but Uncle Frank stayed seated, so I did, too. Uncle Frank didn't look at me, but he started talking to me like he never had before. "That's my beautiful girl sitting in there. I can't believe this is happening to my beautiful girl." Suddenly he hit the steering wheel with the heel of his hand. "Those damn Europeans. They think they're so advanced! So superior! I left these kids with their mother for years at a time. Do you think she ever had them vaccinated for anything? Or inoculated? No!" He finally turned and looked at me. "You don't think Kristin would ever . . . try to hurt herself, do you?"

I didn't. I said, "No. That doesn't sound like Kristin."

Uncle Frank nodded in agreement. But he added, "I'm worried, though. She doesn't sleep. She doesn't eat. All she does is cry. Try to feel something for her. Okay?"

I was confused. "What do you mean 'try,' Uncle Frank? Of course I feel something for her."

"I mean, try to show it. She needs to know that you feel for her."

"What? I don't show it?"

He looked surprised. He told me, "You don't show anything, Roberta. You never have."

Once inside, Uncle Frank led me to Kristin's darkened room. She was sitting up in her bed, watching a TV set with the sound off. In the video glow I could clearly see her many pustules and the shadows that fell from them. It looked like ants were crawling across her face. Kristin saw my reaction. She said, "You didn't expect this, did you?"

"It's not so bad."

"Don't lie, Roberta. I have them everywhere. They're all over my face; they're all over my back. I have them all the way up my tongue." She began sobbing. She applied a towel to her back, like she was patting it dry.

Uncle Frank spoke from behind me. "Remember what the doctor said, Kitten. Try not to scratch." Then I heard Uncle Frank close the door.

Kristin hung her head in absolute misery. I stood for a few minutes in the semidarkness. The room smelled stale, like someone had been imprisoned in it for years.

I couldn't think of anything to say. I finally thought of, "What do you hear from Nina?"

Kristin spoke softly, and in dead earnest. "What do I hear from Nina? I hear, in her voice, and in her words, how the world is going to look at me from now on."

I stood for a little while longer. I dared ask her, "Kristin, you wouldn't hurt yourself, would you?"

Kristin asked, as if to clarify the question, "What do you mean? Kill myself?"

"Yeah. I guess."

She shook her head no. Then she added, "I feel like I'm dead already." After another long pause she told me quietly, "I called my mother."

"Oh yeah?"

"Yeah. She's in Munich now. She's training for a new job. She wants to come over as soon as she's done with the training."

"That's great."

"Yeah." Kristin strained to see me better in the darkness. She seemed to stare at me for a long time, very intently. Then she said, "What did you do after your mother got killed?"

The question stunned me. All I could manage was, "Huh?"

"After her murder, Roberta — what did you do when you didn't have a mother anymore?"

"I still had Dad. He kept the arcade going for us. Before we lost it."

"But what about you?"

I took a step back, toward the door. "What do you mean? I was in school, Kristin, where do you think I would be?"

"What about after school?"

"I was in an after-school program, like a thousand other kids."

"Where?"

"The Y for a while. The Baptist church for a while."

"When did your father pick you up?"

"Right after he closed up."

"When was that?"

I put my hand on the doorknob. I hated this. I wanted to ask the questions, not answer them. But I finally said, "He closed early — seven on weekdays, nine on weekends."

"So then what did you do? You and your dad?"

I tried to be casual. I held up my hands and shrugged. "We got something to eat, and we went home."

"Uh-huh. And then did he stay there with you?"

"Sure."

"He never went out?"

I felt like I was pinned against the door, like a pin-the-tail-on-the-donkey. I admitted, "Yeah. He went out sometimes."

"And who stayed with you then?"

"I don't know. A baby-sitter. A neighbor. I don't remember."

"What was your neighbor's name?"

"Kristin! What's the matter with you? I don't remember the name of every neighbor, or every baby-sitter, that I ever had."

"Okay. Just name one."

I shouted at her, "Stop it! I don't want to do this anymore."

Kristin paused for a moment. She shook her head slowly in the gloom. "Don't get upset. Just tell me: Do you think this . . . routine of yours was normal?"

I tried not to sound upset. "Why are you asking me all these questions?"

She sat back against the bed's headboard. She stretched her neck and dropped her head down as it had been before. "Because I miss my mother."

THURSDAY, THE 21ST ✢ When I came into the kitchen this morning, I found an envelope on the counter that said *To Roberta*. I put a Pop-Tart in the toaster, sat down, and opened it. The front of the card featured the words *To a Special Daughter* in red letters. The cover art showed a box wrapped in silver paper with a red ribbon. Inside the card the box was opened, and the words *A Special Birthday Wish* were spilling out, again in red letters. At the bottom, written in Dad's large handwriting, was *Love, Dad and Suzie*.

The Pop-Tart popped up. I grabbed it with a paper towel and sat back down to examine the card further. It had probably come from Lombardo's Drugs. Neither Dad nor Suzie would ever go into Isabel's Hallmark. If they had, though, they would have found cards like this in the juvenile section.

I heard a noise in Dad's room. I listened and caught a trace of Suzie's voice. This was way too early for either Dad or Suzie to be up. I had hoped to get out the door without seeing them, but apparently their plan was to get up early and catch me.

Suzie stumbled into the kitchen wearing a pair of jeans and a Marriott T-shirt. Her hair was pressed to one side of her head; her face looked really pale. Dad followed in his cutoff shorts. He looked fine, like he was ready to go, ready to pack up his board and go surfing.

Dad smiled and said, "Happy birthday, honey!"

"Thanks."

"Listen, there's been a slight change of plans. I hope it's okay. Suzie just got a call about another fund-raiser for Mr. Lyons tonight. What we would like to do, if it's okay with you, is go out and celebrate on Sunday night at any restaurant you like. Anywhere at all."

I surprised myself with my answer. "I know where I want to go."

"Where?"

"The Greek Isles Family Restaurant."

Suzie covered a yawn. "Where's that?"

"It's on the Strip."

A brief flicker crossed Dad's eyes. He said, "Sure, honey. I think I know where that is. Why do you want to go there?"

"I'd like to try Greek food."

Suzie said, "Greek sounds good."

"All right!" Dad clapped his hands together. "Sounds like we're all set."

When I got home from school I found two more birthday cards in my mailbox, but these were nice ones. Mrs. Roman had sent a Hallmark card with a cool red sports car on the front. Inside was a ten-dollar bill and the words, *Happy Birthday, Roberta Darling, Love, Millie Roman.* Mrs. Weiss sent a Hallmark, too, with a white dove on the front. It had a hundred-dollar bill in it and the words, *Spend this on something important, like yourself. Happy sweet sixteen. Love, Isabel.*

I stared in wonder at the hundred-dollar bill. I had seen such bills at Arcane, but I had never owned one. It looked like play money.

Once I got into the kitchen, I folded the hundred-dollar bill several times and stuck it inside my wallet. I set the two expensive cards out on the table, next to the cheap one from Dad and Suzie. Then it was time to leave. I picked up my backpack and headed out to the bus stop for another day as a TV intern.

I had only been waiting at the bus stop for a minute, absently watching the traffic speed by, when I spotted a familiar car. It was Uncle Frank's silver Volkswagen. Apparently the driver spotted me, too. The car stopped suddenly, and dangerously, in the left lane. Then it whipped around in a U-turn and sped back in the other direction. Now I could see who was in it: Karl was at the wheel, and Hawg was next to him. The car repeated the same U-turn maneuver down the road and pulled up right in front of me at the bus stop.

Karl called through the passenger-side window, "You want a ride, cuz?"

I looked in at Hawg, but he wouldn't look back. He said to Karl, "We gonna go or ain't we, Karl?"

Karl told him, "Yeah. Yeah. We're going. I just have to help my cousin out here." He looked back at me. "Where are you heading?"

"I'm going to the Channel Fifty-seven Studios. It's straight down Everglades to Fiftieth Street."

"Well, hop in!"

Hawg had to lean forward so I could squeeze into the backseat. I could tell he didn't like that much. Karl pushed down on the accelerator and we sped off.

We careened down Everglades Boulevard. Karl yelled back to me, "I bet this beats taking the bus."

I tried to catch Karl's eye in the rearview mirror, but he didn't seem to be using it. I yelled up, "So where are you guys going?"

Hawg looked over at Karl. Karl answered, "Let's just say we got a plan, cuz."

I saw the studios ahead. I told him, "Here. Drop me off at this light."

Karl squealed around the corner, turned the wheel hard, and jammed to a halt. Hawg leaned forward again to let me squeeze out. I turned to thank Karl, but he accelerated away before Hawg could even get the door closed.

I found myself on the side street next to the studio's

parking lot. I noticed a large sand-colored structure on the other side of the lot. I could see from the high pitch of its roof, and from its size, that it was a renovated church. The sign over the front door made me stop still in amazement. It read, THE ETERNAL WORD STUDIOS — HOME OF *THE LAST JUDGMENT* TELEVISION SHOW. I'd never expected that Stephen Cross broadcast from there, so close to me. I said, "Huh," out loud.

Arcane was dead when I got there today, and it didn't get much livelier at night. Neither Karl nor Hawg showed up, so Ironman kept away, too. Uncle Frank and I took care of the few scattered customers. Most of them did the Crusader experience. Uncle Frank asked me, "What are the numbers on Crusader?"

"Eighty-five customers last week."

"Is that right? God, if it wasn't for him, we'd be out of business."

"Really?"

"Pretty close. I'm packing up three more losers this week. At this point, if it's not a top moneymaker, it's going."

At eighty-thirty, Uncle Frank asked me, "Do you want to leave early?" I shook my head no, but he insisted. "Go on, Roberta. I can stand here and go bankrupt all by myself."

I asked him, "What about the closing checklist?"

"Let's not worry about that tonight. Why should we vacuum the carpet if nobody's walked on it?"

I was eager to finish *The Muckrakers*, so I agreed to

go. When I got home I put a Kid Cuisine macaroni-and-cheese dinner in the microwave. There was one message on the answering machine: "Roberta? This is Kristin. Call me back."

I decided to eat first. I ate at the kitchen table and started to leaf through my birthday cards. But Kristin called back right away. She said, "Roberta? Thank god."

"Kristin? I was going to call you."

She was all business. "Listen: I have to tell you a bunch of stuff. The phone's been ringing like crazy here. Karl ran off with the Volkswagen today. He took that Hawg guy with him. I think the plan was to go to Georgia."

"Georgia?"

"That must have been Hawg's idea. I don't think Karl even knows where Georgia is. But anyway, they never got out of the county. They got arrested up in Atlantic Beach."

"What happened? Did the police call you?"

"No, Karl did. He was really spaced. He didn't even sound upset. He talked about going to Georgia like it was around the corner. But they stopped off at some place called the Bodacious Barbecue. Then they realized they didn't have enough money to pay, so they tried to sneak out. The waitress followed them and wrote down the tag number. And as she was doing that, Karl backed into a van."

"He had an accident, too?"

"Yeah. He smashed in the back of the Volks. It can't even be driven now. And, to top it all off, he was driving after dark on a restricted license. Dad's gone up there to bail him out. He's really pissed."

"I bet. What about Hawg?"

"I don't know. I think he's on his own. There's no way Dad would pay his bail, too."

I shook my head. "Is that all?"

"Isn't that enough?"

"Yeah." I paused to let all of it sink in. Then I asked her, "How are you feeling?"

"I feel sick, but I think it's getting better."

"That's good."

"I'm thinking about a lot of stuff, you know?"

"Like what?"

"Like who I am, like who I want to be."

"That's good. I guess."

Kristin paused. "It's good if I can think of somebody I want to be. Somebody, you know, with really bad skin." She sighed deeply. "Okay. I better get back to my cave."

"Thanks for calling, Kristin. I hope the guys get home tonight."

She said, "Yeah. Me, too. But I wouldn't bet on Hawg."

FRIDAY, THE 22ND ↢ I detected a new smell when I got to the mall today — a sulfurous smell, like a wet match. From a distance I could see three people at the open plumbing grate. Suzie, of course, was at the center of it. Leo was on one side of her and the Ace

Plumbing guy was on the other. The first thing I heard was from the Ace Plumbing guy. "What you smelled was *not* a dead animal; it was methane gas."

Leo answered, "I know it was methane gas. I said an animal got in there and died and *that* caused the methane gas to back up."

The guy said, "We have no idea what caused it."

Suzie added, "We don't *care* what caused it."

The guy continued, "I've sealed all the pipe joints. Now no more gas can escape."

"But that's dangerous," Leo told him.

Suzie yelled, "Enough! I don't smell anything. The problem is solved. Let's just make sure we keep it solved."

The Ace guy said, "For safety's sake, ma'am, let's keep the tiles off the grate area. Let's leave it easy to get at in case we have to get down there and seal it again."

Leo grinned in disbelief. "So you want to just leave a hole in the middle of the mall floor?"

Suzie walked over and straddled the grate, like a storybook giant. "Problem solving, Leo. Have you ever heard of that? Problem solving? That's when you don't just stand around saying negative things. Instead you think of a solution. Here's a problem-solving idea for you: You place the Santa seat over the grate. Like this. No one will be able to see the grate. And if you have to get at a pipe, you just tilt up the seat. Okay? Problem solved."

Suzie stalked away toward the office. Leo was still grinning, like he was the only one who got the joke. I headed toward the card shop. I waited for Mrs. Weiss to finish with a customer, then I said, "Thank you, Mrs. Weiss. That was a great present. I can't believe you gave me that much money."

She shook her hand, like she was clearing away crumbs. "What else am I going to do with it?" Then she held a manila envelope toward me. "Here, Roberta. Have your father sign this. It's for my car insurance, so I can give you driving lessons."

I took the envelope. Another customer came up, so I said good-bye and slipped out.

Dad and Suzie were standing in front of Arcane, probably because no one was inside. Dad told me, "Your uncle Frank has been gone all day. And guess what?"

"What?"

"The business ran just fine without him."

"Where has he been?"

"Down at the county courthouse. They have Karl down there. He tried to walk out on a restaurant check, and then he got into an accident. Oh yeah, and he was driving on a restricted license."

"I know. Kristin called me last night."

"She didn't come in, either."

"She has the chicken pox."

"You're kidding."

"No. You didn't know that?"

"No." Dad seemed upset at that. He added, "Everything's a big secret with your uncle."

Just then, as if on cue, Uncle Frank walked in. He

definitely heard Dad. He demanded, "What's a big secret with me?"

Dad tightened up, but he answered smoothly, "That Kristin has the chicken pox."

Uncle Frank told him, "That's no secret. It's just that — I've had more important things to do than to call you."

Dad smiled. "Fine. No problem. Do you know where she caught it?"

Uncle Frank took a deep breath. "No. I have no idea."

Suzie spoke up. "Well, that's an easy one. She caught it from those Brazilian girls."

Uncle Frank looked at her. "What?"

"Yeah, I was expecting thirty of them, but only half showed up. The rest were sick."

Uncle Frank stared at her, stupefied. "So you thought, *Why not bring them in here? To infect us?*"

Suzie tried to defend herself. "No! Who hasn't had the chicken pox?"

"Kristin! That's who."

The two of them stared at each other. Finally Dad tried to break the tension. He asked Uncle Frank, "So how's Karl?"

By now Uncle Frank was totally frazzled. He muttered, "I have to go to the bathroom. I'll be back out in a minute."

Suzie took off right away, without another word. Dad and I waited a lot longer than a minute, but Uncle Frank did eventually emerge from the back. He seemed a lot less frazzled. He joined us in the entranceway and started to talk.

"I had to go get Karl out on bail last night."

I asked, "What about Hawg?"

Uncle Frank winced. He shook his head and answered abruptly, "Nah. They wouldn't let him go."

Dad said, "What? He was there, too?"

Uncle Frank answered, "Yeah. He talked Karl into going joyriding. They'd be up in Georgia now if this hadn't happened." He got back to his story. "So I drove Karl to the county courthouse this morning for arraignment. We stood up there when our time came. The judge looked over the charges, and he looked over Karl's record. He was good. He was a real *judge*, you know? He gave Karl a real good tongue-lashing, which is just what he needed. He told him that it would be entered into the police computers, from this day on, that Karl Ritter was to be taken directly to the Positive Place for ten days' treatment if he ever got picked up for anything. Even littering. Well, Karl just about fell on his knees crying. He promised everything under the moon. So the judge dismissed the case."

Dad said, "Well, I guess he learned a lesson."

Uncle Frank said, "Yeah," and started off, but I called after him. "What about Hawg? What happened to him?"

Uncle Frank stopped; he came halfway back. "I don't know. I don't really care." Uncle Frank brooded for a moment. His face hardened; his voice turned cold. "I ran into lots of guys like that in the service. A fat slob like that would bring the whole squad down. Get everybody punishment detail until they got fed up with him. Then his folks would get a letter telling them that he'd been killed in a training accident. Of course, it wouldn't really be an accident, but no one would ever know. It happened all the time."

Uncle Frank went back to the office, leaving Dad and me looking at each other in disbelief.

I was amazed, then, by what happened just a half hour later. Hawg walked in from the mallway and went into the back room, with Ironman trailing right behind him. I was back near Vampire's Feast, so I drifted over to the door and waited for the explosion, but it never came. Uncle Frank never said a word to him.

Uncle Frank did come out into the arcade, perhaps to get Hawg out of his sight, so I slipped into the back. I asked him, "Did everything go okay at Juvenile Justice?"

Hawg looked at me quickly, then looked away. He muttered, "It weren't nothin' to me. Shouldn't be nothin' to you, either."

I told him, "It is, though."

He and Ironman started to crush up a small stack of cartons. Hawg addressed Ironman, but I could tell he was including me. "Well, let me tell you about Juvie. They put you in a big damn cage. You have to stand right out there in the open, like a gorilla in a zoo. And they make you wear one of them orange suits, like a damn orangutan. And you got one toilet sitting there, right out in the open, in the middle of the cage. Then what do they do? They bring in a damn school field trip to look at us."

I said, "No!"

"Yeah. A lady came in and hollered, 'I'm bringing in a group of fifth graders. How about you boys talk to them about staying off drugs and staying out of trouble?' Then, sure enough, a minute later she came back with a big line of fifth graders, about forty of 'em, and their parents, staring at us like we're a buncha monkeys. And that lady started in again, 'Some of you boys tell these kids how to stay out of trouble.'

"Well, right about then, that Bodacious Barbecue where me and Karl stopped, it started to kick in wicked fierce. It was all the beans you could eat, and brother, I ate my share. All of a sudden I felt like my insides was gonna explode. I yelled out, 'I got something to say to your kids, lady. Ya'll better run for your lives!'

"I dove for that toilet like it was fourth and goal from the one. Right in the middle of that cage, I yanked them orange pants down and let her rip. Those fifth graders all started runnin' and screamin'. They took off outta there like they had seen damn King Kong bustin' loose from his chains."

Hawg started laughing jovially. Ironman was grinning wide. I didn't know how to react. I just shook my head and asked him, "But what happened in court? What did the judge say to you?"

"Nothin'. It was a whole lot of talk. He tried to scare me, telling me I'm getting house arrest or a probation officer. But weren't none of it true. The cops had already dropped the charges. That waitress wasn't comin' all the way down here to make one dollar. And that van that Karl hit? It took off. It probably didn't have no insurance, or it was stolen, or it was carrying drugs. The cops was just bluffing us all along. I'm afraid old Karl took it pretty hard, though."

"And what did your stepfather say?"

"He said, 'Don't do it again, or you'll find yourself out on the streets like your mama.' I said, 'I am doin' it again. I aim to go back to Georgia. One way or the other.'"

Dad left early, so I wound up walking home with the two guys. Hawg seemed to be back to his normal self, talking about football and whompin' on Ironman. When I got in I saw that Dad had dropped off another Blockbuster Video bag. I guessed that meant he wasn't coming home.

At ten I switched on the TV just in time to catch Stephen Cross. He was speaking at a prison, and he was just great. He said, "My past is a nightmare that I carry around with me, a reminder of the abyss that can open up under us anywhere, at any time. I truly did not know what was nightmare and what was real in those days. You folks sitting out here tonight know the living hell I'm talking about."

Some of the men in the prison audience started shouting out, "Amen!"

Stephen Cross told them, "Near the end of my days of darkness, I was living in hell. Sick at heart. Sick in body. Sick to the soul. And then one day the Lord said to me, 'Wake up, sinner!'"

"Amen!"

Stephen Cross paused; his lined cheeks ran with tears; his chest heaved with emotion. He looked up, and his eyes blazed into the camera lens. "I am not some TV preacher in some expensive suit, standing up here to recite my best sermon that I learned in a prestigious Bible college. No! I am the lowest of the low. I am a drug addict. And a thief. And a whore. And yet God spoke to me, and showed me the way out of hell." He held a Bible high in the air, held it like a shining sword. I could hear the commotion in the audience — men leaping to their feet and crying out.

"The Lord spoke to me, in a jail cell. In a cell like yours. Right here, in hell's waiting room. He said, 'Your name shall be Stephen Cross. And you shall bear witness to me all the rest of your life. You are to tell my children three things: *Admit the truth; ask forgiveness; find redemption.*'"

Stephen Cross opened his arms to the audience. Many men rushed forward to embrace him. Then they all knelt down in a big circle on the floor, like a football huddle, and they prayed.

If I were there, I would have, too.

SUNDAY, THE 24TH ❧ It was a slow Sunday at Arcane. Uncle Frank followed up on his threat to pack up the experiences that were financial losers. His beloved Halls of Montezuma, Custer's Last Stand, and Buccaneer Battle were dismantled and packed into cartons for the UPS guy. I passed the day cleaning, delousing helmets, and taking care of the few customers who came in.

I was relieved when four o'clock came. Today Mrs. Weiss was leaving Mrs. Roman in charge of the store for the first time. I walked over to the shop to thank Mrs. Roman for my card and gift. She seemed distracted, but she did mutter, "It's nothing, dear. You're a lovely girl."

Mrs. Weiss came out of the back, smiling. She didn't seem at all concerned about leaving Mrs. Roman in charge. Her great mood continued out into the parking lot and all the way to Eternal Rest Cemetery. As usual she parked by the guardian angel. She popped the trunk open so I could get out the stepladder. But today she walked along with me. She said, "I want to see where your mother is. Is that all right?"

I assured her, "Of course, Mrs. Weiss. Of course it is."

We walked for a minute, and she commented, "This is nice. This is very nice."

I asked her, "What's the Jewish part of the cemetery like?"

"It's nice, too. Just like this. Of course, we don't have the big statues and angels and things."

"What do the graves look like?"

"Like these. Some headstones. Some wall slots."

"Do they have bronze nameplates and vases outside for flowers?"

"Some do."

"Do they have any stuff that we don't have?"

"Sometimes they have spray paint on them."

That took a moment to register. "What?"

"That's right. Sometimes I go over there and find that someone has vandalized the graves."

"Why?"

Mrs. Weiss answered matter-of-factly, "Because they're Jewish." We walked for another few seconds. Then she asked me, with nothing more than curiosity, "What kind of activity is that, I ask you? What kind of human being spends his time vandalizing graves?"

"I don't know, Mrs. Weiss."

"I don't know, either. I don't know how people like that can look in the mirror."

We reached Mom's area. I placed the stepladder against the wall. Mrs. Weiss looked up at her crypt. That really bothered me. I had to say, "I hate it that my mom has a plastic nameplate instead of a bronze one, and that it's way up there, instead of in a place where I could put my hand on her."

"We could speak to the cemetery manager. We could find out what it takes to . . . upgrade. Or whatever they call it."

"I don't know. My dad doesn't have much money."

"Maybe it doesn't take much." Mrs. Weiss shook her head emphatically. "I don't trust a man who outlives his wife. I never did. The husband should go first, like mine did, like Millie's did. They do the smoking and the drinking, they should die first." She looked up at the wall sadly. "It's funny, Roberta. My husband liked to travel. He would go just about anywhere. The only place he really didn't like was Florida. He always said it was too hot. So he winds up living here."

"Yeah. And dying here."

Mrs. Weiss stared up at my mom again. She told me, "We all travel different routes, Roberta. And we travel to many different places. But we all wind up here in the end. You have to make the most of your travels." She looked away. "I'll leave you alone for a while."

Mrs. Weiss shuffled off. I climbed up the ladder and stretched my hand up until I could feel the letters of my mother's name. It was a little easier this time. Maybe I was growing taller. I held my hand on that name for a long time, with my face pressed against the black wall. I felt like I was waiting for a message, a message that didn't come.

I finally gave up, climbed down, and dragged the ladder back to the Lincoln. Mrs. Weiss was sitting inside, with the air conditioner running, but she was on the passenger side. When I opened the door, she said, "Put that thing in the trunk and get behind the wheel. It's time to practice driving, if you don't mind an old-lady car."

"It's a real nice car."

"You'd like a car like this?"

"Sure. Everything works in it. My dad's cars always have things that don't work in them."

For the next twenty minutes Mrs. Weiss let me steer the big car all over the lanes of Eternal Rest Cemetery.

She hardly spoke. Just once to say, "Go easier on the brakes," and another time, "Try not to overturn." She wouldn't let me drive out of the cemetery, though.

We switched places at the front gate. Mrs. Weiss turned left onto Seventy-second Street, smiling. "So what do you say we go out to dinner? A birthday dinner."

"I'm already going out to dinner. A birthday dinner."

Mrs. Weiss must have been surprised, but she tried not to show it. "Oh? With whom?"

"Dad and Suzie."

"Yes? And where are they taking you?"

"The Greek Isles Family Restaurant."

"Where is that?"

"It's over on the Strip."

"The Strip? What? Where the drug dealers are? Where the prostitutes are? He's taking you there?"

"It's not that bad, Mrs. Weiss. Anyway, it was my idea."

"What would give you an idea like that?"

"I wanted to go back. You know, I practically grew up there. Our first business was right on A1A. Right on the Strip."

Mrs. Weiss paused. Then she said kindly, "I know, dearie. I know all about it."

Now I was surprised. "You do?"

"Of course. I remember when it happened. A terrible thing. Your poor mother."

I thought, *I remember when it happened, too — when I let myself.*

"I was a woman alone, just like your mother. What happened to her made me think twice about where I wanted to open my store. That's how I wound up out at that mall. I had to have the security."

We turned right, into my development. Mrs. Weiss added, "You need security, too, Roberta. You're not safe here. You're a girl alone here."

"I'm not alone."

Mrs. Weiss snapped at me. "Don't tell me that! I know he leaves you here alone. Don't tell me he doesn't."

"Sometimes he —"

"And stop making excuses for him. He's not worth making excuses for. Roberta, if anything happened to you, I would just die. Do you know that?"

She stared at me intensely until I answered, "Yes, ma'am."

"But do you know what your father would do?"

"No, ma'am."

"He would buy you a cheap funeral, then he'd go water-skiing with his girlfriend. It's all about him. Him and only him. That's why I want you to move your things into my guest room."

I didn't know what to say. I got out the passenger side and told her, "Thanks, Mrs. Weiss. I'll think about that."

"I want an answer soon, Roberta. The right answer." She stayed and watched as I walked up the driveway, under the carport, and in through the kitchen door. Then I heard the big Lincoln pull away.

I started to get a soda, then I noticed a note on the

refrigerator. It said: *Roberta, We will pick you up at 7. Expect a nice surprise. Dad and Suzie.*

It was already after six. I took a quick shower, then I found a pair of black slacks and a wrinkled white button-down shirt. I pulled out the ironing board and ironed them both.

After I got dressed I had a strange notion. I went into the bathroom, opened the cabinet under the sink, and took out the bag of makeup that Kristin had left behind. I thought about using it, but I chickened out. I was liable to dab something on wrong and look like a clown. Instead I combed my hair straight down, like I always do. I stood and stared at myself in that mirror for a long time until I heard Dad and Suzie come in. Then I went out to the kitchen.

Suzie greeted me with, "Oh! You look nice!"

Dad smiled. "Come on, birthday girl. Let's go."

Since there were three of us, we had to take Dad's Chevy Malibu. I sat in the back. With the top down and the radio on, I may as well have been sitting in another car. Dad drove to the Strip from the north, down Ocean Boulevard. He turned right just before the 7-Eleven, the tattoo parlor, and the restaurant.

The scene was just the way I remembered it. The same people were hanging out — the same sickly look-ing kids; the same bad guys in front of the 7-Eleven.

Dad couldn't find a space in front of the restaurant, so he parked in the tattoo parlor's lot. It was close enough to the 7-Eleven that the tall scuzzy guy could call over to him, "Yo! Hey, you here to party?"

Dad winked at me. He lowered his voice and answered the guy, "Yeah. We're here for a birthday party."

The scuzzy guy held up his palms. "Cool. If you want to do some real partying later, you come see me."

Dad smiled at him. He answered, "Cool." Then he rolled his eyes at me, like it was funny.

I hated the way he dropped his voice to match that scuzzy guy's. And I hated the way he said "Cool." There was nothing cool about it. That was the guy who had grabbed Kristin, the guy who was going to shoot her just for fighting back.

When we entered the restaurant, the owner came right up to Dad like he was a long-lost friend. He practically shouted, "Look who's here!"

Dad said, "Hey, man, good to see you."

"What's the occasion?"

"A very special occasion, in more ways than one. Do you remember my little girl?"

The guy's eyes bugged out. "Of course I do! Look at you. You always had the red around your mouth, right? From the Slurpees?"

"Right," I said. But I had no recollection of him at all. He turned back to Dad. I wondered, *Does he know about Mom? He must.*

Dad spoke quickly. "And this is Suzie. She's the other part of the very special occasion."

Suzie gave him a wide smile. The guy said, "That's wonderful. Come in. Come in." He grabbed three menus and walked us to a table by the front window. I was glad of that, because I wanted to look out.

Dad sat next to Suzie, across from me. She scooted her chair closer to him so that she could hook her arm in his. Dad and Suzie exchanged a look. Then Dad smiled at me. "Well, Roberta, happy birthday."

Suzie said, "Yeah. Happy birthday."

Then Dad said, "Don't you want to know what the other special occasion is?"

A teenage girl came up and set down three glasses of water. "Can I get you anything from the bar?"

Dad said, "Do you still have those split bottles of champagne?"

"Yes, sir."

"Okay. I'll take one of those. Roberta, how about you?"

I said, "Seven-Up."

The waitress jotted the drink orders down and left.

I tried to look out the window, at the action outside the 7-Eleven, but Dad drew me back. "So where were we? Oh yes, the other special occasion. Can you guess what it is?"

I answered, "No."

"Maybe I should let Suzie tell you."

Suzie didn't like that idea. "No. You tell her."

"We'll both tell her." Dad stopped smiling for a moment. He nodded gravely. "Roberta, maybe it's time we were a family again. Maybe it's time you had a mother again."

If I had been eating any food, I think I would have choked. I must have looked pretty shocked, because

Suzie jumped right in with, "Of course, I could never replace your real mother."

The two of them stared at me uncomfortably. I finally said, pretty much for my own benefit, "So you two are getting married?"

Dad seemed relieved that I understood. He smiled again. "That's right."

As usual, I couldn't think of anything else to say. So I asked, "Where?"

Dad looked at Suzie mischievously. Suzie didn't respond. I think she was disappointed in my reaction, but Dad pushed on. "I don't know. Maybe on a boat."

That was unexpected. I said, "Whose boat?"

He pulled Suzie over. She flopped against him like a marlin. "Our boat. Suzie only wants two things in the world: me and a boat. Pretty soon she'll have both."

I couldn't look at either one of them. I looked outside and asked, "How can we spend money on a boat now?"

Dad was ready with an answer. "Did you ever hear the expression 'Two can live as cheaply as one'? Well, it's true. Suzie and I will have two incomes, but we'll only be paying one rent. That's a great savings."

The waitress came back with our drinks. She said, "Mr. Anthony suggests the leg of lamb for you tonight. He said he would make it special."

Dad held up one finger. "That's his name: Mr. Anthony." He looked at Suzie, then me. "Sounds good. Let's make it three."

The rest of the dinner went a little better. The food was really good, and we kept away from the topic of their marriage. Instead we talked about the West End Mall.

Mr. Anthony stopped by once to ask about the lamb. Then he came back with the waitress and a small cake with a lit candle. Mr. Anthony and the waitress started to sing "Happy Birthday." Dad joined in. Suzie, I think, lip-synched. After that Mr. Anthony said to Dad, "I know about this special birthday occasion. Is this beautiful lady the other one?"

Dad said, "Yep."

"You're . . . you're what?"

Dad laughed and completed Mr. Anthony's thought. "Getting married. Yes."

"Ah! Congratulations." He told the waitress, "Let's have more champagne here. And whatever you're drinking, Roberta."

I was surprised that he remembered my name. I said, "Seven-Up." I added, "Can I ask you a question, Mr. Anthony?"

"Yes. Of course."

"Do you remember our old arcade?"

His smile became tense. "Sure I do."

"It's that tattoo parlor now, right?"

"Right."

"Do you know the owner?"

"I do know her. Her name's Connie. She comes in here. Real nice. But guess what?" He smiled. "She doesn't have a tattoo on her."

Dad laughed. "Is that right?"

I continued, "Do you think this Connie lady would mind if I stopped in there to look around?"

Mr. Anthony thought for a moment. "No, I'm sure she wouldn't."

Dad looked disturbed. He asked me, "Roberta, honey, why would you want to do that?"

"I've been thinking about it a lot lately. I have to see it."

"Why now? Why spoil tonight?"

"It's not spoiling anything. And when else will I ever get down here?"

Dad didn't know what to say. He turned to Mr. Anthony. "How long has it been a tattoo parlor?"

"A couple of years. It was a jewelry store before that, but it kept getting robbed." Mr. Anthony paused. He suddenly looked sick. "I'm sorry. I shouldn't have said that."

Dad reassured him. "It's okay."

Mr. Anthony turned to me. "You tell Connie that I said you should come in and see your old store. And you have a happy birthday."

Dad and Suzie drank their champagne. Then Dad paid the check and we left. Outside, Dad unlocked the car door for Suzie, who slid into the front seat. I kept walking, around the car and up to the door of the Third Eye Tattoo and Body Piercing Parlor. I peered in and saw the same lady as last time sitting at a card table. It looked like she was playing solitaire.

I looked back at Dad. He wanted no part of this. He

was staring at the ground, but then he looked up at me. "Roberta, I don't know what's going on here, but there's no way I can walk back into that building. Do you understand?"

"Sure, Dad. I don't want you to. This is something I want to do. For me. For my birthday."

Suzie said something to him, and he relayed it to me. "We'll sit in the car. Okay?"

"Okay." I looked closely at the frame of the doorway. I thought, *This is how people used to enter the arcade. This is how the killer entered, too.* I took a deep breath and pushed open the glass door. The woman at the table looked up at me. I could see now that, although there were cards on the table, she was actually filing her nails. I wouldn't call her look friendly. She said, "Did you want a tattoo? You'll need an adult with you."

"No. No, ma'am. Mr. Anthony said I could come in and look around."

"Who's Mr. Anthony?"

"He owns the restaurant next door."

The woman nodded. She lightened up a little. "Oh yeah. I forgot his name." She put down her nail file. "What do you want to look at?"

"This was our family business. We had an arcade in this building about seven years ago."

"Really? I heard there was a jewelry store here."

"We were here before them."

The woman thought harder. "Was that the woman who was —" She stopped before she said the rest.

I answered, "Right. My mother."

"Oh? Oh, I'm sorry. I didn't know."

"That's okay. Can I look around?"

"Sure. Suit yourself. But please don't touch anything sharp."

"I won't." I walked slowly through the room, concentrating on the past. I wanted to remember the place exactly as it was — bright, neon, crowded with machines. I looked at the back wall. That was where my mother would stand, so that was where I chose to stand.

I tried to reconstruct where the cash register had been, where the safe had been, where the security camera had been. Then I tried to imagine the killer entering. Did he burst in? Or did he come in casually, posing as a customer? Was my mother afraid when it happened? Or was she too surprised, too stunned to be afraid? I stared at the door. I imagined him entering and closing in on me quickly. I imagined him pulling out a knife. I imagined the knife punching into my stomach, doubling me over.

I clutched my stomach and lurched across the room toward the door. Connie didn't look up. I pulled the door open and staggered outside. My eyes fell immediately on the spot, ten feet in front of the door, where my mother had fallen. I fell, too. I lay there, doubled over, with my hand plugging the imaginary hole in my stomach. I studied the sidewalk in front of my face. Was this the last thing she ever saw? I listened to the blood rushing in my ears. Was that the last thing she ever heard? I felt the grit of the sidewalk. I smelled the asphalt of the parking lot.

Suddenly a face was leaning over, looking down at mine. I knew the face. It was that street girl, the chubby one. She whispered, "Hey, are you okay?"

I unclenched my fist and pulled it back from my stomach. I stretched out, facedown. Then I got up to my knees. I told her, "Yeah. Yeah, I must have slipped."

The skinny boy was standing behind her. I looked from one to the other. Neither one believed I had slipped. The girl asked me, "Are you wasted?"

"Am I what?"

"Are you loaded?"

"What?"

The girl looked at me like she thought I was stupid. She tried, "Do you need some help?"

"No. Thank you. I'm okay now. I slipped."

"No, you didn't."

A car pulled into the space right in front of us. Its headlights made the street kids squint like moles in the sunlight. I was blinded, too, but I realized that it was Dad's Chevy Malibu. He yelled at me, "Come on, Roberta. That's enough now. Get in!"

I didn't react right away, so he yelled again, "I mean it. Get in the car!"

The street girl took a step toward the headlights. She asked me, "Is this guy after you?" But before I could answer, she whipped out a small metal cylinder and yelled back at the car, "Get outta here, you creep. I got Mace. I'll Mace you!"

I hopped up to my feet. "No! No, it's okay. It's my dad."

She remained standing between the car and me. "Are you sure?"

"Sure I'm sure. He drove me here."

"Do you want to go back with him?"

"Yes. Yes, I've been waiting for him."

"No, you haven't. He's been parked right there all along."

"I mean . . . I don't know what I mean. But I want to go with him now."

The girl stepped back, joining the boy. She put the cylinder away. "Okay. It's your funeral."

I walked to the passenger side of the car. Suzie opened the door enough for me to squeeze in. I looked back to thank the girl, but she and the boy had disappeared.

Dad pulled out with a squealing sound, just like Nina had. Maybe he thought that girl might still try to Mace him. He yelled back to me, "What were you doing lying on that sidewalk? What's the matter with you?"

I thought for a moment. Then I yelled into the front seat, "I think it was the lamb. I never had lamb before. I think it gave me cramps."

I guess Dad accepted that explanation. He didn't say anything else about it. We drove back with the radio on and no conversation. By the time they dropped me off at the bottom of the driveway, all was forgiven. Dad just said, "Do you have your key?"

"Yeah."

"Okay. You get to bed. I'll be back soon. I just need to drive Suzie home."

The Chevy Malibu started to back away. Suzie hadn't said anything all the way back, but now she called out cheerfully, "Good night. Happy birthday."

I crawled into bed and tossed all night. I know I had several jagged, dark dreams. But there's only one I can remember now, and only a few seconds of it: My mother sat at the table of the tattoo parlor, where that Connie lady had sat. She looked up at me when I came in. She spoke to me very calmly, without a trace of pain: "Roberta, I told them I didn't want one of these. I never wanted one of these." I looked at her arms. In my mind, I knew she was talking about a tattoo. Her voice was calm, even peaceful, but her actions were anything but. Her right arm was busy doing violence to her left. She had a knife in her right hand, and she was scraping the skin away on her left forearm. The blood from this crude operation was running in a narrow stream, across the card table, onto the floor, and right out into the street.

MONDAY, THE 25TH ✴ Today is a teacher workday. That means that no kids in the county have to go to school. Only teachers.

I took advantage of this to get to the mall in the morning. When I got to the rotunda, I saw that Leo had pulled all the Santa's Workshop stuff out of storage and hauled it in there. He appeared to be having a problem with the Santa seat. Suzie, as usual, was on his case. She was staring at the Santa seat with alarm. "Leo? Why is that chair moving?"

Leo explained without looking up. "It's that pump under the grate. It's making the grate vibrate. So the seat moves a little."

"Does it move when somebody is sitting on it?"

"I don't know."

Suzie looked up to heaven, as if asking for help. She said sarcastically, "That's okay, Leo. I'll do it." Suzie walked over to the Santa seat and sat lightly on it. It stopped moving. She said, "Is this all it takes to hold it still?"

"I guess so."

"So there won't be a problem when Gene is sitting here? He's a big guy."

"Problem? How could there possibly be a problem?" Leo displayed his oversize teeth.

Suzie looked at me for sympathy. "Cut it out, Leo." She got off the seat, which started vibrating again. She walked past me and said, "Roberta, do you have any idea what Sam wants to talk to me about?"

"Sam? No."

"He's got a bug up his behind about something. He's waiting in the office."

I said, "No. I don't know."

Suzie hurried up to the office, so I followed after

her. Sam was sitting in the chair across from the desk. Suzie sat in front of him and unfolded her hands as though to say, *Okay, what is it?*

Sam spread out a newspaper on her desk, the campus newspaper from the University of South Florida. He said, "I picked this paper up today, after my accounting class."

Suzie looked at it without much curiosity. Sam pointed to one part of it and asked her, "Have you by any chance read this article?"

"I don't read campus newspapers, Sam. I'm real busy in here."

"I'm real busy, too, but I read this. It's an interview with the coach of the golf team."

"Is that right?"

"The coach of the golf team pals around with Ray Lyons's son, Richard. They can often be seen playing eighteen holes together on our lush fifty-acre campus."

"You're losing me here, Sam."

"The coach told the student reporter the following: 'I expect this area to have a major PGA golf course within two years.'"

Suzie flopped her hands outward this time, as if to say she had had enough. "Please, Sam, I have a big event to plan."

"He expects this golf course to be, quote, 'on the site of the old West End Mall,' unquote."

Suzie's head snapped up. She looked startled. Sam continued, "Now, to my recollection, the West End Mall is still here. In fact, we're sitting in it right now."

"Yes. Yes, of course."

"So why would he make such a bizarre statement?"

She looked at the article. "Well, it's just stupid. It's a stupid thing to say."

"So he just said it because he's stupid?"

"Sam, I don't know."

"Well, I know. He said it because he believes it to be true. He believes it to be true because he heard it directly from his pal Richard Lyons. The Lyons family has plans for this mall, all right. Demolition plans."

Sam got up dramatically. He told Suzie, "You can keep that and read it when you get a minute. I have my own copy."

I followed Sam up to the rotunda, hoping to hear more about Richard Lyons and his golf course. But that wasn't to be. He didn't say a word to me.

When I finally got to Arcane, I was surprised to see Kristin behind the counter. Right away, I noticed the red splotches across her face, those ant bites. I stopped short and sputtered out, "Kristin, I didn't think you were coming in."

I know my reaction must have hurt, but Kristin didn't flinch. She looked me right in the eye and said, like from a prepared speech, "I realized that I was feeling sorry for myself, and that that was a loser attitude. I decided to do something about the problem instead."

"That's good. What are you going to do?"

"Nina is taking me to see her father this afternoon. I want you to come, too."

"You do? Does Nina want me to?"

"Probably not. But I want you to. For me." Kristin's emotionless expression stretched into a weird smile. "Roberta, today is the beginning of my life. My real life."

I nodded like I understood, but I really had no idea what she meant. We hung out at the counter for a while, not talking. The silence didn't seem to bother Kristin in the least, but it made me squirmy. I finally asked, "So where's Karl?"

"He's still at home. He's not coping well."

"Is he sick, too?"

"No. He's totally freaked out, though. You know, like he was when he went to the Positive Place? I think he's afraid they're going to send him back."

"Who could send him back there but your father?"

"The juvenile courts can, I think. They act in loco parentis. That's what everybody keeps saying, 'in loco parentis.'"

"What does that mean?"

"I don't know. It's Latin. I think it means he's crazy, you know. He's *loco*, so they can put him away."

MONDAY AFTERNOON ⚬ At around four o'clock, I looked up and saw Nina standing before the counter. She was staring at Kristin, like at a train wreck. She didn't say hello; she went right into, "How come you're not wearing any makeup?"

"I have to see the doctor. I can't have makeup on my skin."

Nina nodded uncertainly. "Oh yeah." She came

around and stood with us, as in the past. But now three of us were standing in silence. After about a minute she said, "So are you ready to go?"

Kristin answered quietly, "We have to wait until Roberta's dad arrives."

"Why can't Roberta cover?"

"She's coming with us."

"What for?"

"Because she's family. I need her to be there."

Nina glanced at me disapprovingly. She shook her head. "Girlfriend, let me tell you something, what you need is makeup. At least a little foundation. You can take it off when you get to the office."

Kristin answered quietly again, "No."

This plunged us back into silence. Nina finally said, "So are you coming back to Lourdes?"

"No."

"No? What are you going to do?"

"I'm going to work here. I'm going to help my family."

Nina asked her, "Are you still going to the cotillion?"

"No. That's a waste. It's a waste of my time and a waste of my father's money. He doesn't have to work himself to death in this place just so that I can parade around like some princess."

Nina looked at me like, *What's wrong with her?* She thought for a moment, then asked Kristin, "So what about Greggie?"

"Oh, I called him today. I told him I wasn't going. I told him I wasn't going anywhere with him. Ever."

Kristin paused, then asked, "How about you? Are you going with Carlos?"

"I might. I gotta weigh my offers."

"Offers?" Kristin smiled for the first time. "What? Did you go out with that football guy?"

"Which one?"

"There's more than one?"

Nina got offended. "Why do you say it like that? There's two. Okay? I guess that's more than one. It's not like I'm dating ten guys."

"But are you still dating Carlos?"

"Yeah. He's still around. He'll always be around." She paused and then added, "He asked me to marry him."

"Really? He proposed to you?"

"Oh yeah. Big time. With a big ring."

We both looked at her finger. Kristin asked, "Where is it?"

"I'm getting it reset at Mayor's, over at the Gold Coast Mall."

Kristin seemed puzzled. "So you're going to do it?"

"Sure. Why not?"

"When?"

"He says after he finishes college but before he graduates from medical school. My mother thinks it's a good idea. That gives her five years to plan the wedding."

We both stared at her in amazement.

"That sounds like a lotta time, I know. But some of these nice reception places, like the best hotels and the best restaurants, they gotta be booked years in advance. Especially if you want to get married in June. Even the church, you know, for a June wedding, they want two years' notice."

Kristin looked at me, then back at Nina. She asked her point-blank, "Do you love Carlos?"

Nina answered, "No. Not really."

"Then why marry him?"

Nina explained to us, as if it made perfect sense, "By then, five years from now, I'll feel different about him. We'll both be older. I'll have gotten to do a lot more stuff. You know? Come on, what have I ever done? Gone down to the beach with some football guy? So what? I gotta have some fun. I gotta have some wild times in my life while I can. Someday I'm gonna be driving around a car full of Munchkins, wishing I had done something when I could. I want to, like, get it all out of my system. Then, when I'm twenty-two, I'll be ready to get married."

Kristin added, "And Carlos will be there."

"Without question. I'm the best he's gonna do. Carlos will be there. It'll all be there. The church will be reserved. The reception hall will be booked. Everything. You gotta plan for these things now if you want them to happen."

Just then Dad walked in with a bag of food from the Taco Stop.

I asked him, "Can you cover the front, Dad?"

He answered, "Absolutely." I think he was going to say something else, but the three of us took off too fast.

Kristin led the way to Dr. Navarro's office. Nina and I had to hustle to keep up with her. The office closed at four on Mondays, but Nina used a key to unlock the sliding-glass door. She called out, in a little-girl voice, "Papi?"

Dr. Navarro answered through an open office door, "In here, Princesa."

We followed Nina past the reception area and into an examination room. The first thing I noticed was an antique wooden sign, hung on a wall as a decoration. It said, TATTOOS REMOVED EXPERTLY.

Dr. Navarro nodded hello to me. He smiled at Kristin and said, "Ah, Kristin. What has that evil pox done to you?"

She answered, "I guess that's what I'd like you to tell me, Doctor."

Dr. Navarro has white hair but a very young face. He has a very bright smile, too, like my father's. He indicated that Kristin should sit on the examining table. He put on a strange set of magnifier glasses. They stretched around his head, and they projected an intense light, almost like a laser. He peered intently at Kristin's face and muttered, "*Varicella.*" Then he explained to her, "That's the Latin name for your affliction."

Dr. Navarro looked carefully behind her ears and along her scalpline. As he worked, he chatted with Nina. "Princesa, where have you been? Have you been out with that rogue Carlos? I'll kill him."

"No, Papi. Kristin had to wait to get off work."

"I need you to find some records for me in that infernal database. It won't even let me in."

"Okay. Let me check it out. I may need to go to my backup files."

"Yes, my darling. That's what I wanted to hear." He addressed Kristin. "Is this the worst part? Here on your face?"

"Yes, sir."

"The pox can be a cruel disease. Fortunately, there is much we can do for you now."

Kristin answered hopefully, "There is?"

"Yes. Yes. We live in a time of great advances. Be grateful we do not live in a time of ignorance. Then, a pox was thought to be a sign from God that a person was evil. It was thought to be a mark of the devil, of an inner corruption."

This obviously intrigued Nina. She stopped working on the computer and asked him, "What would happen to the people who got it?"

"Do you mean, if they didn't die?"

"Sí, Papi."

"Ironically, they might get stoned to death by their neighbors, in the name of God."

Dr. Navarro indicated that Kristin should roll up her sleeves more. He continued his answer to Nina, "In superstitious times, people who were different, people like your new friend Betty, would wind up getting tied to a stake and burned alive. Murdered."

Nina seemed disturbed. "Why would people murder someone like Betty?"

"Because people did not understand microbes,

viruses, bacteria. They had to blame someone, so they blamed those who looked different."

Dr. Navarro indicated that Kristin should pull up the back of her shirt, which she did. As he focused his laser goggles on her back, Nina brought up a new example. "Papi, what about a girl who looked like a boy? Who didn't have a female body? Maybe who didn't menstruate?"

Kristin immediately knew what she was talking about. She snapped to my defense. "Nina! Cut it out!"

"What?"

"Stop putting Roberta down. I mean it."

But Nina answered her, "I'm not dissin' the girl. This is for me. I really want to know."

Dr. Navarro kept examining and talking. "It can be dangerous to be different in any way. If you look hard enough, anything can seem like a sign — a sign from God, or a sign from the devil."

Nina concluded, "So this girl might get stoned to death, too?"

"That is possible. Just thank God we live in a time of science, when superstition is confined only to the ignorant."

Dr. Navarro pulled off the goggles, signaling that he was through with the examination. He looked hard at Kristin and asked her, "Tell me this: How has this pox affected you psychologically?"

Kristin thought about it and said, "It was horrible at first, but now I've accepted it. In a way I've embraced it."

He said, "Good for you. Do you remember, just a

month ago, when you and Nina got dressed up for the modeling? You came to our house, and you did your hair and makeup? I looked at you when you were leaving. Remember? And I said, 'I could not imagine two more beautiful girls.' Kristin, you are still that beautiful girl. But you have been attacked by a virus."

Kristin continued to stare straight ahead. Dr. Navarro finally prodded her, "Do you understand what I'm saying?"

"Yes, I understand what you're saying, Doctor. But I disagree. I am no longer that girl."

Dr. Navarro's brow furrowed. He walked over to a high white cabinet and started fishing around inside. He muttered, "I just got some samples, some new vitamin E ointments. Very effective." He asked Nina, "Princesa, do you know the ones I'm talking about?"

"No, Papi."

"Ah, here." He pulled out two tubes, each about the size of a large Tootsie Roll. "Now, Kristin, apply this to every affected area three times a day for ten days, or until it runs out. You'll see a big difference yourself. Then you'll come in and show me. Okay?"

Kristin took the tubes. "Okay. Thank you. Now, how much do I owe you, Dr. Navarro?"

Dr. Navarro looked upward, thinking. Then he answered, "Two thousand, three hundred dollars." He cocked his head and said, "I'm joking, Kristin. I'm only joking. Of course there is no charge for you."

Kristin exhaled. "Thank you, Doctor, but I insist on paying."

"Nonsense. They're free samples. You don't think I pay for them, do you?"

"Then I want to pay for your time. And for your . . . diagnosis."

Dr. Navarro pointed at the wall clock. "Sorry. You're too late. The office is closed."

Kristin slid off the examining table. She tucked in her shirt. Then she walked over and pointed at the antique TATTOOS REMOVED EXPERTLY sign. "Nina said you used to do this for two hundred dollars."

Dr. Navarro was no longer smiling. He looked at Nina, "Princesa, what is going on here?"

Nina rolled her eyes from her father to Kristin. "Girlfriend, what's the matter with you? We're not charging you. Now deal with that."

Kristin looked back. She answered her slowly. "Deal with this: I am not a charity case."

Nina's jaw fell open. She sputtered, "No, you're not. Who said you were? You're a friend of the family."

Kristin shook her head. "No, I'm not that, either. Let's be real. I'm a former classmate. And I work with you here at the mall." She reached into her shirt pocket and slid out some money. She unfolded two hundred-dollar bills. Then she laid them down on the examining table. "I hope this covers it."

Dr. Navarro stared at the bills. He spoke in a low, puzzled voice. "Kristin, do you realize that you are insulting me?"

"No, sir. I don't see it that way. My father is in business here, just like you are. We do not want charity. We want to pay. You, sir, are insulting us."

The hundred-dollar bills remained sitting there for several long moments, looking up at us like a pair of unwanted children. Nina finally reached over and scooped them up. She carried them over to the receptionist's desk, opened a drawer, and pulled out a pad. She wrote out a receipt and handed it to Kristin. Then she walked to the glass door and unlocked it. Kristin and I followed. As we slipped through the opening, Nina said coldly, "Next time, please come during normal office hours."

Kristin took off ahead of me down the mallway. I didn't try to catch her. I couldn't see her face, but I could tell by the set of her shoulders that she was crying.

I stopped at the southern edge of the rotunda and surveyed the scene. It looked like Suzie's Christmas layaway promotion was off to a good start. Mothers with small children had begun to gather, forming a loose line to the Santa chair. Suzie, wearing a red elf hat, was smiling and greeting them. Leo, of all people, had volunteered to take pictures of the kids on Santa's lap. He had brought in his own Polaroid camera and tripod, which he was now fiddling with nervously.

I looked toward the Chili Dog and saw Gene waiting to make his entrance. He was a very convincing-looking Santa. Then, everyone in the rotunda, including me, turned to watch a great commotion near the entrance. The front end of a big RV appeared in the door-way; it rolled past SunBelt Savings and the mall office. I looked at the driver's seat and saw Bill's grim face. He was hunched over, clutching the wheel like a sea captain in a storm. The RV finally came to a halt just short of the food court.

A group of people gathered immediately to gawk at it. The RV was about thirty feet long, nearly as long as a county bus. The words ANGELA LIVE and CHANNEL 57 were painted on it in several spots.

Bill opened the door on the passenger side, the side toward us. He left it open for a couple of minutes, like he was getting some air. I thought about approaching him, maybe even stepping inside since I was an intern, but there was something about Bill's posture in the driver's seat that told me to stay away. Then I heard a murmur from the crowd. People started to point toward the mall office. I turned with them in time to see Angela del Fuego, in a red pantsuit, walk in. She was with Mrs. Knight and a big blond guy with a portable TV camera.

Betty walked by me, drinking a smoothie from the Garden of Eatin'. She said, "Who's that?"

I told her, "It's Angela del Fuego."

Betty scoffed. "Oh. What a joke."

"What do you mean?"

"Those phony nails? That phony hair? Come on."

I couldn't believe she had said that. I asked her, "Well, what about your hair?"

Betty seemed surprised at the question. She replied,

"Black is not phony. Black is not anything. It is absence. Bright red is presence. A phony presence."

I had no idea what to say to that. I heard the sound of someone clearing his throat loudly and deliberately. I turned toward the sound and met Bill's stare. He was now standing on the tile of the rotunda, holding the remote soundboard in front of him like a basket of eggs.

He asked me, "You're the intern, right?"

"Right."

"Start interning. I need to set up the soundboard right here, in front of the truck, where I can protect it."

I said, "Okay."

"Get the stand and the hardware. They're right inside the door."

I stepped up into the RV. I turned to the left and saw a packet of iron legs and clamps, neatly bound with black electrical tape. I picked it up and went back out to Bill.

Bill was looking very perplexed. He clearly didn't want to set the expensive soundboard down anywhere inside the West End Mall. I asked him, "Where do you want me to set this up?"

The question seemed to surprise him. He stated, "You couldn't set this up," but then asked, "could you?"

"Why not?" I peeled off the tape and laid out the four legs on the rotunda tiles. After all my Arcane promotional display assemblies, this was simple. I clamped the legs together in the only way they could possibly be clamped, and I stood the stand upright. Bill examined it for a moment, trying to decide if it would hold or collapse. Then he delicately placed the soundboard on top. I handed him two remaining clamps, which he used to attach the board. Then he pressed a pair of plugs into the floor outlet.

Bill stepped back. He said, "Okay. I need you to stand here and make sure nobody touches the board. That's all you have to do. Just stand here and —"

I interrupted him, "I can't do that. I'm part of the man-in-the-street interview, up at the mall office."

"No, you're not. Not if you want this internship."

Maybe Bill thought that was a scary thing to say to me, but it didn't scare me a bit. I thought of a couple of things to say back to him right away. The best one was, "That's what Angela told me to do. Do you want me to tell her that you said I can't?"

Bill blinked rapidly. He backed off immediately. "No. No." He muttered, "Just stay here for two minutes while I call McKay."

He spun around and got back into the truck. I could hear him call the studio and ask for Mr. McKay. They started talking about the broadcast, the director's cues and stuff. Stuff that I wanted to learn about. I listened as best I could, until I heard, "Hey, cuz! What're you doing?"

I turned and saw Karl. He was standing dangerously close to the soundboard. Uncle Frank was right behind him, but he was looking at the Santa setup. I said, "I'm just watching the equipment for a minute."

Karl said, "Cool." Then he reached a long white finger over, touched a sound-level button, and slid it upward. An earsplitting shriek flew out of the mall public-address system.

Bill bounded angrily out of the truck. He yelled at me, "What was that?"

This time I couldn't think of an answer. But Karl could. He said, "That . . . was feedback, dude."

Bill rounded on him. His eyes darted to Karl's finger, still poised criminally close to the sound-level button. "Don't touch that again! Ever! That thing's worth more than you are!"

Uncle Frank turned around. He walked slowly past Karl, right up to Bill. He stared directly into Bill's eyes for several long, intimidating seconds. Bill tried to return his stare, but his shoulders began to sag. And then he took a step backward, as if he was going to fall. His voice croaked out, "Please do not touch anything out here. It's very valuable." He retreated back into the truck.

Uncle Frank turned toward me. "Who was that?"

"That's Bill. He does the remote broadcasts for the studio."

"You're working for him?"

"Partly. I'm supposed to watch the equipment, but I have to be in the mall office, too."

Uncle Frank nodded. "I see. Well, go ahead down to the office. I'll watch the equipment for you." I must have really reacted to that, because Uncle Frank actually smiled. "It'll be okay. Bill and I have an understanding now."

I ran down toward the mall office. Angela was talking to the blond camera guy about how to shoot the interview. I waited until they finished their planning. Then she turned to me. "Hey, you're the intern, right? You ready for the show?"

"Yes, ma'am. I'm really looking forward to it."

"Good. Stand over there by the old guy." I took my place by the back wall, next to Mr. Lombardo. Then I heard Angela whisper, "Here they come."

We all craned to look at the mall entrance. Philip Knowlton appeared first. He stood just inside the entrance doors, looking out. Then a stocky, red-faced guy walked in. I said, "Is that Mr. Lyons?"

Mr. Lombardo snorted. "No. That's gotta be a bodyguard."

I felt dumb. A tall man came in next. He had a full head of gray hair, and he was wearing a very expensive-looking blue suit. He also had a great tan. I ventured to say, "That's him, right?"

"Right. That's Mr. Big Shot."

Mrs. Knight led the group of three men toward the office. Once inside, she introduced Philip Knowlton to Angela. Angela flashed a particularly dazzling smile. "I know Mr. Knowlton. How are you, Phil?"

Mr. Knowlton smiled back as best he could. "Not bad, Angela. How are you? Let me introduce you to the candidate. This is Ray Lyons. Ray, this is —"

Mr. Lyons took an energetic step forward and extended his hand. "You don't need to tell me who this lovely lady is. My wife watches you every day. My daughters, too."

Angela put on a pretend pout. "What? You don't watch me?"

Mr. Lyons put on a pretend look of his own. He said in a low voice, like it was a secret, "Don't tell anybody. But sometimes I do."

Angela laughed politely. Mrs. Knight laughed loudly. Then Mr. Lyons turned and pointed to the red-faced guy. "And this is Joe Daley. Joe was a Florida state trooper for twenty years. Now he's with us, and we're real glad to have him aboard."

Mr. Daley waved bashfully at Angela. She put him at ease with, "How you doin', Trooper?"

Sam walked in wearing a SAVE THE MALL T-shirt. Philip Knowlton stared at the shirt and snapped, "Wait a minute, who are you?"

When Joe Daley heard that he got up and took a step toward Sam.

Sam answered, "I'm Samir Samad. Man on the street. I'm supposed to be here for an interview."

Knowlton shook his head slowly. "Not in that shirt, you're not."

Sam feigned innocence. "What's wrong with the shirt?"

"It's this simple: Either you get another shirt, or I get another minority."

I thought Sam would get angry at that, but he didn't. He looked at Mr. Lyons. Then he answered, "If the shirt offends anyone, of course I'll change it." And he went back out.

Angela said to me, "You're part of the man-in-the-street thing, too, right?"

"Right. I'm the young person."

Mr. Lombardo growled, "I guess we know what that makes me."

Sam returned two minutes later, wearing a black sport jacket buttoned up over the shirt.

Angela concluded, "Okay. Everybody's here. Let's do it."

It was hard to tell if Angela or Philip Knowlton was running the show. They were both telling people what to do. Angela finally asked him, "Are you ready to tape?"

Knowlton answered, "We can begin, but I reserve the right to interrupt this at any time. The candidate is not here to talk about mud wrestling, or cross-dressing, or anything like that. He's here to talk about the issues. Understood?"

Angela was cool. "Of course I understand. Anyway, you can edit out anything you don't like, Phil. You know that."

"It needn't get to that point." Knowlton added, "Those who do not abide by the rules stand outside, thrusting their microphones at the candidate and shouting questions that never get answered. Understood?"

"Of course."

The cameraman positioned himself in front of Angela with a big camera sitting on his shoulder. He said, "Can I get an ID, Angela? From both of you?"

Angela looked at the camera. "I'm Angela del Fuego."

The cameraman turned to Mr. Lyons. He followed her example. "I'm Ray Lyons."

The cameraman said, "Thank you. Ready."

Mrs. Knight stood right next to him and started to count backward, "Five, four, three . . ." She mouthed the last two numbers silently, then Angela began to speak.

"Welcome to *Meet the Candidates*, Channel Fifty-seven's exclusive look at the men and women running for Florida's top offices. In this segment, we will meet Florida Senate candidate Ray Lyons." The cameraman turned and focused on Mr. Lyons, who smiled easily, showing his white teeth. "Ray Lyons is one of Florida's most successful developers. His projects include the Gold Coast Mall, the West End Mall, which is where we're meeting today, and the Century Towers community."

Angela turned and flashed a dazzling smile at the candidate. "Ray, I'd like to start with a personal question. Where did you get that gorgeous tan?"

I could almost feel Philip Knowlton tighten from his perch behind the camera, but Mr. Lyons handled the question well. He laughed openly and told her, "Thank you, Angela. That's a Florida tan. I got it from growing up here and living and working here my whole life. Can I ask you, where did you get yours?"

Angela shot a sly look at the camera. "A tanning parlor on Las Olas Boulevard." Mrs. Knight laughed loudly. Angela continued. "Mr. Lyons —"

"Call me Ray."

"Okay. Ray, like many Floridians, I'm a transplant from another state. So tell me, what was it like growing up here?"

Suddenly Philip Knowlton walked from behind us right into the picture. Angela gave the "cut" sign to the cameraman, drawing a finger across her throat like she was slashing it. She looked at Knowlton. "Was it something I said?"

Knowlton explained to her, "I don't want Ray to sound like some old geezer who lived here during the Civil War. We want to stress that Ray is youthful and energetic."

"Okay. How about if he talks about raising his family here?"

Knowlton smiled. "All right. That's good. Are you comfortable with that, Ray?"

Mr. Lyons told him, "Sure. How about if I tell the story about Richard and the golf clubs?"

Knowlton thought for a moment, then decided, "I don't think so, Ray."

Mr. Lyons said, "Why not? What's wrong with that?"

"Nothing. But I need to think some more about Richard and the golf stuff."

"What? Is there something wrong with golf now?"

"No. I just don't know how well your voter base relates to it. Let me get some stats. For now, why don't you go ahead and say something about your other kids."

Mr. Lyons didn't look happy. He paused for a moment. Then he shrugged and looked at Angela. Angela asked him, as an aside, "What's your wife's name, Ray?"

He told her, "Estelle."

Angela made the "roll tape" sign to the cameraman, twirling her finger like a fork in spaghetti. She said, "How many children do you and Estelle have, Ray?"

Mr. Lyons smiled broadly. "Three children. All born and raised in Florida, and all still living here. Richard's the oldest. He went to Saint Francis Xavier Prep here, and then to the University of South Florida. Then there's Christie and Annie."

Knowlton interrupted, "Shouldn't that be, 'Then there are Christie and Annie?'"

Mr. Lyons stopped smiling. He clenched his jaw. "I don't talk that way, Phil."

Angela added. "Yeah, Phil. You don't want him to sound like some college professor."

Knowlton nodded his agreement. Angela signaled the cameraman, whispering, "Pick it up where you were, Ray."

Mr. Lyons resumed smiling. "The girls both went to Our Lady of Lourdes Academy. Christie married a Florida Gator, and Annie married an FSU Seminole, so we got it covered in our family."

Angela laughed. "It sure sounds like it." She looked over at Knowlton, who smiled. Then she looked into the lens and switched tones to say, "Now I'd like to bring in our man-in-the-street segment for today."

She turned to look at us. "Folks, thank you for coming." Angela smiled at us as the cameraman turned. We all stared blankly into the lens. "Please introduce yourselves and ask your question of the candidate."

Mr. Lombardo took the lead. He said, "I'm Tom Lombardo. I run the drugstore here in the —"

But Philip Knowlton interrupted him. "We don't need that."

Mr. Lombardo glared at him. "What?"

"Just ask your question. You're a man in the street."

"No, I'm not. I'm Tom Lombardo. I'm not a man in the street. I run the drugstore here in the mall. I have for ten years. Don't interrupt me again." He looked back into the lens and asked, "Mr. Lyons, what are you going to do about Century Towers? That's my home. That's the home to a lot of elderly people. You said you were going to develop three buildings in the community. We've had one building put up in ten years. Where are the rest?"

The cameraman swung back to Mr. Lyons. He answered, "Sir, it's a market economy. The plan for Century Towers remains in place. When demand goes up, the next building will go up."

The cameraman swung back to us, so Sam took a step forward. He said, "I'm Samir Samad."

Knowlton prompted him. "Say your nationality."

"My what?"

"Your nationality."

"Okay. I'm an American."

Knowlton threw up his hands. "Fine."

Sam looked into the lens. "What are you going to do to save the West End Mall from bankruptcy?"

The cameraman did his swivel back. Mr. Lyons answered, "I will continue to support its recapitalization, and try to do some innovative things to widen its customer base, like bringing back that beautiful fountain."

The cameraman swiveled back once more, and I knew it was my turn. I decided to skip the first step and talk to Philip Knowlton directly. "Do I have to say who I am?"

He said, "No. You're a young person. That's obvious. You're here to ask a young-person question. Right?"

"Right." I looked into the lens and asked something dumb. "What are you going to do for young people?"

The cameraman went back to Mr. Lyons. His answer to me was this: "I will try to give them the kind of childhood that I had, the childhood that they are being denied. Denied by crime, drugs, poor schools, and irresponsible parenting. You know, young man, I grew up right near here, and it was a great place to grow up. Can you say that now?"

I had hoped my part was over, but Mr. Lyons's question caused the camera to swing back to me. I told him, "No, sir." But then I said to Angela, "I want to point out that I'm a girl. Is that okay?"

Angela joked, "You go, girl."

Mr. Lyons looked at me and smiled. "Sorry, miss." He asked Angela, "Should I redo it?"

Knowlton answered. "We'll edit it out. I like this

topic, Ray. Give her a little more about what Florida was like before all the problems."

Mr. Lyons nodded. He looked into the lens. "I used to go fishing right on this spot when I was your age. This was a Seminole Indian fish camp. I had this old leaky johnboat that I used to go out in. If I didn't catch a fish in ten minutes, I'd have to turn back empty-handed because the boat was filling up so fast with water. I hated that boat. I kept telling the other fishermen, 'One of these trips, I'm going to let it sink back into the swamp.' And one day, that's exactly what I did."

I was expecting to hear Mrs. Knight laugh. Instead I heard Sam speak up again unexpectedly. He spoke quickly and directly to the candidate. "Mr. Lyons, why did you apply to rezone the mall from commercial to recreational?"

The cameraman swung back. "That's an easy one. I didn't. I did no such thing."

"Then why is your son, Richard, soliciting investors for a golf course and spa on this property?"

"My son, Richard, isn't here to defend himself —"

"What might he say if he were here?"

"— and I don't want to speak for him."

Knowlton seemed shocked by the exchange. He finally managed to say, "You were to ask one question. Mr. Lyons has given you all your answers. Now, thank you. You can go."

Mr. Lombardo left right away. Joe the bodyguard stepped between Sam and Mr. Lyons, just in case he was planning on asking another question, so Sam left, too. Mr. Knowlton told the bodyguard, "Thanks, Joe. Go ahead and pull the car up to the entrance. After the fountain dedication, we have to haul out of here."

The door opened and Suzie entered. I wondered who was watching the Santa line. She smiled shyly and waved at Mr. Lyons as she slid along the wall toward her desk. She whispered to Mr. Knowlton, "So how did it go?"

"It went very well. How is it going outside?"

"Great. The place is packed. The kids are happy. The moms are happy."

Mr. Knowlton looked at his watch. "Okay. Let me check it out now." He turned back to Mr. Lyons. "Just relax here for a few minutes, Ray. I want to make sure Santa is well on his way to the North Pole before we start. I'll be back in a few."

Mr. Knowlton left for the rotunda. As soon as the door closed behind him, Angela made the spaghetti motion at the cameraman. He hoisted up the camera and started to tape.

Mr. Lyons looked at the cameraman curiously, but he didn't object. Angela smiled at him brightly and said, "We need to get a few reaction shots, for the final edit: me laughing at one of your jokes, you looking thoughtful, and so on. Do you mind if we chat a little more, without your manager? You can cut out anything that you don't like."

Mr. Lyons smiled back. "No, I don't mind at all." He pointed to the mallway. "In fact, I've been speaking all by myself, without anyone's help, for most of my life."

Angela laughed. So did Mrs. Knight. Then Angela said, "Just say something funny, Ray, and I'll laugh at it."

Mr. Lyons again looked out at the mallway. He said, "Something funny? Like a joke?"

"Yeah. Anything. Let's get a shot of you and me relaxing and laughing. We'll run it at the end of the interview, over the credits."

Mr. Lyons nodded. "Okay. Let me tell you what Phil said on the way over here. He was telling me about the West End Mall. He said, 'Every time I go there I see nothing but old people. If you want to make money at that mall, open up a Depends undergarment outlet.'"

Angela laughed uproariously. Mrs. Knight did, too. The ex–state trooper walked back in. He looked for Mr. Knowlton. Then he said, "Mr. Lyons, I have the car at the front."

Mr. Lyons pointed at the cameraman. "You're on live TV, Joe. Say something."

Joe turned beet red. He sputtered, "Hey, I'm sorry. I didn't know."

Mr. Lyons laughed and quickly assured him. "We're just kidding around, Joe. It's not live."

He smiled nervously. Mr. Lyons told Angela, "Joe's only been with me for two days. He doesn't know when I'm kidding yet." Joe shrugged good-naturedly. Mr. Lyons continued. "I didn't even know Phil had hired him. I came out to the car yesterday morning, and I saw this guy standing there. I didn't think anything of it. I put my foot up on the bumper to tie my shoe, and he yelled at me, 'Hey! You can't do that. That's Mr. Lyons's car!'

"I yelled back, 'Hey! I am Mr. Lyons. I can do whatever the hell I like!'"

Everyone laughed at that one. Angela looked out the window just in time to see Knowlton. She whispered, "Here he comes," to the cameraman, who turned off the camera and started to stow it.

Knowlton entered and announced, "I'm giving Santa five more minutes. Then we go."

I asked Mrs. Knight, "Should I go help Bill now?"

She said, "If you want to."

I hurried out toward the rotunda. The crowd had changed from earlier. It was no longer a line. It was more of a blob, gathered around the dead center of the mall, where the fountain would soon spring to life. I spotted about a dozen Crescent Employees wearing SAVE THE MALL T-shirts. I also spotted two people with bright yellow shirts that said SAVE THE TURTLES.

As I got closer to Gene and the Santa seat, I understood why Suzie had been able to slip away. Betty was now at the red velvet rope. Betty even had the red elf hat stuck on top of her shoe-polish black hair. Only two mothers with children remained in line to see Gene. I got into line behind the last lady.

Betty looked nervous. She was even paler than usual.

Gene forgot he was playing Santa and yelled out, "Hey, I'm not kidding, Leo. This seat is really shaking."

Leo said, "It can't be. The finest plumbers in Florida have certified it to be perfectly safe."

"Come on, Leo. This is no joke."

The next-to-last woman stepped forward with a little boy, but instead of smiling or *ho-ho-ho*-ing, Gene told her sternly, "You better back off, ma'am. Something's wrong here."

The woman asked him, "What's wrong? What's that shaking?"

He answered, "I don't know, but get these kids back. It's getting stronger."

The little boy in front of me screamed, "Oh! Gross!" and covered his mouth and nose.

Then the smell hit me, too. It was like rotten eggs. Like a whole truckload of rotten eggs. We all backed away, including Betty and Leo, leaving Gene sitting alone on top of the Santa seat. I called to him, "Gene! Maybe you had better get off —" But I never finished that sentence.

Both Gene and the Santa seat started to levitate, like a magician in a magic chair. He leaned forward slightly, to look underneath it, and that was when the pipes exploded. The concussion from the explosion hurtled Gene forward like a swift kick in the pants. He landed on his face at the foot of the tripod. Then Gene and the camera equipment slid across the tiles for another five yards. The ornamental Santa seat flew straight up into the air, riding atop a thick brown geyser of putrid water. The seat balanced momentarily on the vertical stream, then it crashed back down. It half covered the hole, causing the water to squirt higher and wider, like when you put your finger over the end of a running hose.

Gene managed to stagger to his feet. His beard was half ripped from his face; his red pants were soaked with swampy water. Leo scrambled to save his camera equipment. People everywhere started screaming in panic. The smell quickly filled up the rotunda, and parents and children rushed desperately toward the exit. Chaos reigned. Some mothers hoisted up little kids and threw them over their shoulders, running with them like screaming sacks of potatoes. I spotted Ray Lyons running down the center of the mallway. His blue suit jacket was pulled up over his face, forcing him to run blind.

Suddenly I became aware of Philip Knowlton. He was scurrying around the rotunda, oblivious to the smell, screaming orders at everyone. He yelled at Suzie, "Get that Santa out a back door!" Then, "Angela, get your cameraman on Ray. I want shots of Ray helping kids to safety!"

Bill appeared from the truck. He screamed at me, "Grab an end!"

We picked up the soundboard and carried it toward the truck. The putrid water was still squirting high in the air; the kids were still screaming. I saw Suzie pushing Gene toward the Chili Dog, yelling, "Go in the back! Go in the back! You'll be okay."

Bill and I carried the soundboard swiftly and carefully up the three steps and into the truck. We laid it on a couch. Bill pointed to a small rest room in the back of the truck. "Grab me some paper towels." I did, and then stood there while he dabbed at the board, examining it for damage. I looked out through the wide glass windows. Uncle Frank was now standing next to the squirting stream of swamp water. Suzie ran over from the Chili Dog to the same spot.

Even from inside the truck, I could hear her bellowing hysterically at Uncle Frank, "Do something! Do something!" He reared back and kicked hard at the Santa seat, dislodging it and immediately reducing the ten-foot-high spray to a low, steady flow.

Then Leo reappeared holding a large wrench. He paused a moment to knowingly shake his head back and forth at Suzie. Then he bent over and thrust the wrench into the water.

I abandoned Bill and bounded down the truck stairs. By the time I crossed the rotunda, Leo had the stream turned off completely. Uncle Frank said, "Good going, Leo."

Suzie hesitated, then added, "Yeah, Leo."

He looked up at them. "Well, it's the best I can do. You should call that Ace Plumbing guy to really fix it up."

MONDAY EVENING ❧ Just beyond the front entrance, about fifty kids and their parents had packed themselves into a circle. As I walked closer I could see the cameraman moving among them, filming everything. Ray Lyons stood in the center of the circle, listening to the people and looking really concerned. When the cameraman finished, he gave a thumbs-up sign toward the black limo. Philip Knowlton leaned his head out and called, "Okay, Ray! Ray, let's go."

Mr. Lyons shook hands with a few people in the crowd and then pushed through them and got into the car.

Five minutes later news trucks from two networks pulled into the parking lot, but Mr. Lyons and his limo were gone. An on-air news personality jumped out of each van and began interviewing people. I wanted to watch the reporters at work, so I mingled with the parents and kids. They were actually giving credit to Ray Lyons for "fast thinking." Had I missed something?

But then I spotted Griffin. He was leaning against the outside wall, to the left of the entrance. I walked over toward him and he asked me, "What in the world happened in there?"

"I'm not sure. I think it was a plumbing explosion."

The cameraman walked past us. Griffin said, "You see that guy? He was following Ray Lyons all around. By the time this thing makes the news, Lyons will be the hero. He will have snatched all these children from the jaws of certain death."

"Oh, brother."

"Did Lyons do anything in there at all?"

"I don't think so. He didn't make his speech. He didn't turn on the fountain."

"I don't suppose he really saved any kids' lives."

"No."

Griffin laughed ruefully. "He'll do anything to make the news, won't he? Saving small children. Prosecuting hate crimes. Whatever it takes."

I thought about his words for a moment. Then I asked, "Prosecuting hate crimes? What do you mean? Like Hawg's?"

"Yeah. Like Hawg's exactly. He's the very important person I told you about. Ray Lyons made the state's attorney go after Hawg so that he could have a campaign issue. It'll be something like this: Ray Lyons is against committing hate crimes; Ray Lyons is for saving small children."

I stood with him for another minute, watching the on-air news people do their remote broadcasts. Then I told him, "I don't think Hawg did it."

"No? Why?"

I didn't know why, but I came up with this answer: "Because I don't think Hawg is capable of being sneaky. Whoever did it is very sneaky."

Two guys from Crescent, still wearing their SAVE THE MALL T-shirts, propped the entrance doors open with folding chairs. I walked back inside. In the distance I could see Leo setting up some big fans to blow the smell out. Mr. Lombardo, Mrs. Weiss, and at least ten other people held wide brooms and were pushing the remnants of the brown water toward the grate in the rotunda.

Everybody froze for a moment as the Channel 57 truck suddenly roared to life and started to move. I stood aside, by the mall office, and watched it roll toward me. Bill was again at the wheel.

The truck halted right next to me, and the cameraman reached out a long arm holding a videocassette. He said, "Here's the tape for Knowlton."

"What am I supposed to do with it?"

"I don't know. Angela said he has to preview everything we filmed. It's one of Knowlton's rules. Tell him to FedEx it to the studio when he's done."

"Sure. Okay." I took the tape, the door closed, and the truck rolled on. I went into the mall office and stashed the tape in the mall newsletter drawer.

Between the commotion outside and the lingering smell inside, there were zero customers left in the West End Mall. I walked back through the rotunda, past the blowing fans, trying to breathe only through my mouth.

Suzie positioned herself in the middle of the rotunda. She turned to the south and then to the north, yelling the same message down each line of the mallway. "Go ahead and close! No one is coming in here tonight."

I walked into Arcane to tell Uncle Frank what Suzie had said. I passed Hawg just as he was stepping into the Crusader circle. I said, "Do you want me to start it for you?"

"Nah. I got it." He picked up the helmet. But before he put it on he said to me, "You ever try this one, Roberta?"

"I've never tried any of them. You know that."

Hawg looked at me curiously. "No, I didn't know that. I figured you was just sick of 'em all. You know, with you growin' up in an arcade."

"No. I'm not sick of them all. That's not it."

Hawg shrugged and pulled on the helmet. "Well, if you ever get the notion to, I'd recommend this one. It's kick-ass."

"Okay." I left Hawg to his Arcane experience. I walked to the back and opened the office door. Uncle Frank wasn't in there. I heard a hose running, so I continued outside. I looked to the left and saw Uncle Frank rinsing out the bristles of a pushbroom. I called over, "Uncle Frank, Suzie says we should all close up. No one's coming in tonight."

He turned off the hose. "Suzie's right." He didn't say anything else, so I assumed that he meant for us to close. I went back inside and told Karl the news. He didn't seem to hear me, but a few seconds later, he put down his magazine and started the closing checklist.

Hawg was still inside the Crusader ring, hacking at imaginary Arabs. I stopped for a moment and watched him. Was he really hacking at Sam? His teeth were set and showing through his lips. The sides of his mouth, however, were curving upward — not in a snarl, but in a smile. A delighted smile.

Hawg finished the experience and pulled off the helmet. Karl yelled to him, "You'd better spray that helmet. You got lice."

Hawg joined Karl to help wheel in the Sony monitor. He said, "Back home, son, we call 'em cooties."

Griffin knows more about these hate crimes than I do. He has evidence, and his notes in his notebook. But he has also seen Hawg in moments like these, when he is just a big kid playing an arcade game. For me, that's evidence, too.

Karl and I stood together in the mallway watching Uncle Frank lock the sliding-glass doors. It was only eight-fifteen, but here we were, locking up. Uncle Frank turned and said, "Come on, Roberta, we'll give you a ride."

I lied. "No, thanks, Uncle Frank. I have a ride with Mrs. Weiss."

"Okay." He set off, all business, toward the entrance. Karl scrambled along behind him.

I walked over to Isabel's Hallmark and peered through the doorway. It was dark inside. Mrs. Weiss was already gone. I stood still for a moment and listened up and down the mallway. I listened for quiet. When I was sure no one was watching, I walked slowly to Slot #61, took out my master key, and opened the front door. La Boutique de Paris was even dustier than the last time I had been there, when Kristin and I were models. I slipped inside, sat in the window, and hid behind the mannequins' unclothed bodies.

Nothing stirred. I watched and listened for footsteps anywhere on the mallway. The place was completely deserted. That's why I was so startled when the sound came. It was a sharp click, followed by a door opening. Someone had just entered La Boutique de Paris from behind me, from the outside. I looked at the sliding-glass doors in panic. Was there time for me to get out?

The intruder moved quickly to the front of the store. He would have seen me no matter what I did, so what I did was stand up and face him.

It was Sam.

He hopped up onto the wooden platform quickly and confidently, like he thought he was alone. Then he skidded to a halt. He gasped at the sight of me, and his face drained of blood. We stood staring at each other until he croaked out, "Roberta? What are you doing here? How did you get in?"

"I got a key when I was modeling. How did you get in?"

"I got a key from Verna."

Sam sat down heavily against the wall, right where the mannequin once stood. My eyes opened wide. So, that was why the mannequin had moved. Sam had moved it.

I sat down, too. I explained, "Griffin told me what's going on."

Sam was cagey. "Griffin?"

"Yes. Detective Griffin."

"I see. What did he tell you?"

"He told me you've been the victim of hate crimes."

Sam stared into my eyes, but he didn't say anything.

"And that you've been trying to solve them yourself."

Sam looked off down the mallway. He didn't say anything else, so I settled into a comfortable position. I couldn't stand the silence for long, though. I whispered to him, "Why do you sit here and look? Why don't you just use a video camera to catch him?"

Sam answered sadly, "I have used a video camera. I've used every gadget at Crescent. I've had some kind of camera up and running every night this month. It hasn't caught anybody."

"Why?"

"Why? Because 'the alleged perpetrator,' as the detective calls him, knows it's there. He works here in the mall. He sees it sitting there."

"How do you know it's a he?"

Sam scoffed. "I know exactly who it is."

"Who?"

"You know who. The redneck."

"Hawg?"

"Exactly."

"Why are you so sure he did it? Couldn't it be someone else?"

Sam's eyes narrowed angrily, but he admitted, "For a while there, I thought it was someone else. I thought it was Devin. I got into a big hassle with him about the Nazi stuff in his store window. I told him I didn't want my customers walking past that. I told him I'd get his rent raised if he didn't move it. Anyway, I spent some nights in Slot Number Nine figuring I'd catch Devin with a paint can, but it didn't happen."

"So now you're sure it's Hawg?"

"Yeah. And this time it's not just me. It's Griffin and Verna, too. They've both seen him with the red paint, the same stuff that was on my window and my car. And they've heard him threaten me, more than once." Sam turned and asked, "Did you know he tried to flee the state?"

"Yes."

"That's because we finally have him."

We both heard a sound and froze. It was footsteps. In a moment, though, we saw Leo walking down the mall-way with his camera equipment.

I realized that I had leaned closer to Sam. I also realized that I liked it.

We sat like that for two hours. Sam talked about a lot of things. He told me about the University of South Florida and the classes he was taking there. He told me a little about his family.

During one lull, I decided to talk some myself. I asked him, "What is your brother's name?"

He seemed surprised. He answered, "Samir."

"Your brother is named Samir, too?"

"Yeah. We're Samir Abdul and Samir Ahmad."

"You even have the same middle initial?"

He laughed. "Yeah. I guess we do."

"Wow. That's like *Too Many Daves.* Do you know that story?"

"I don't think so."

I started to quote it. *"Did I ever tell you that Mrs. Mc-Cave had twenty-three sons and she named them all Dave?"*

"No, I guess not."

"Well then, do you know this one? It's from a Dr.

Seuss story, too: *That Sam-I-am. That Sam-I-am. I do not like that Sam-I-am!*"

"Oh yeah. I do know that one. *Green Eggs and Ham*, right?"

"Right."

A silence followed that exchange. I started to feel really self-conscious. I figured Sam now thought I was an idiot. I figured he wanted to leave, but to my relief, he launched into a new topic. He asked me, "So what did you think of Mr. Ray Lyons?"

"He seemed nice."

Sam scoffed. "Yeah. And he saved all those kids' lives, too." Sam added bitterly, "Just like he's saving us."

"What do you mean 'saving us'? Do you mean with the recapitalization?"

"Listen: The recap is a fantasy. It's not going to happen. Ray Lyons doesn't want it to happen. Lyons will force us all into bankruptcy, and then young Richard, the golf pro, will get the property cheap. It's a done deal. The bulldozers will roll again, and we'll all be entombed." Sam looked at his watch. "Okay. That's it for me. It's eleven o'clock."

Sam got up to leave, so I did, too. He asked me, "How are you getting home?"

"I'll call home for a ride."

"Yeah? Somebody will come and get you?"

"Right. My dad."

Sam looked suspicious. "How about if I give you a ride?"

"No. He wouldn't like that. Thanks anyway."

Sam unlocked the back door to Slot #61, and we found ourselves in the front parking lot. Sam said, "I'll be here tomorrow, if you want to try again."

I said, "Yeah. I definitely do."

"Come to this door. It's less obvious."

I walked off toward the pay phones by the entrance. Sam said, "Would your father mind if I waited until he picked you up?"

"Probably. He thinks I'm working on the books. He doesn't know what I'm really doing. It'd be better if you left."

"You sure?"

"I'm sure. Thanks again."

Sam waved and headed off toward his BMW. I hoped no one had vandalized it tonight. Apparently no one had, since he pulled away immediately. Then I was free — free to stop pretending about my dad, free to walk home in the dark alone.

TUESDAY, THE 26TH ❧ I was standing with Mr. Herman outside the office this morning, with the Pledge and Banner video in my hand, when I heard Hawg's voice out in the hallway. He sounded very agitated, like he might be near tears. I could hear someone answering him briefly and quietly.

I watched the doorway for a few seconds until they appeared — Hawg and Archie. Hawg was appealing to

Archie to help him get back on the football team. Archie was clearly uncomfortable with the conversation. He was trying to inch away.

Then Hawg caught sight of Mr. Herman. I'm not sure if he saw me or not. He quickly looked back at Archie and told him in dead earnest, "I can't be off that team. You understand? That can't happen."

Archie assured him, "I'll see what I can do."

Hawg took off, muttering under his breath. Archie waited until we had played the Pledge and Banner tape. Then he knocked on his father's door and went inside — I guess to see what he could do.

Mr. Herman's fifth-period lecture today was on the power of journalists. "Edward R. Murrow and his colleagues invented the live broadcast. News that is broadcast live is a dangerous thing, Roberta. Why?"

I thought about it and answered, "Because no one has a chance to change it before you see it. It's what's really happening."

"Precisely so. Because it can show you reality."

Betty raised her hand. "So who changes the news before we see it?"

"Why, the government, of course. Any government. Including, boys and girls, the good old USA."

We heard a stirring from the back of the room. I turned around. The football guys were actually listening, and they didn't like what they had heard.

Mr. Herman continued, "The German people

thought, until the very end, that they were winning World War Two. That is what they read and heard every day, so naturally they believed it. The German government controlled the press.

"Are we any different? Yes and no. The American government did not control the press in Vietnam. Because of free journalists, the American people saw the horror of the war in Vietnam, and they insisted on putting an end to it. But the government learned from that mistake. No journalists were allowed near the fighting in Operation Desert Storm. Was that a good thing?"

Hawg, of all people, answered. "I'd say so. What good are the damn reporters, anyway, if they ain't even on our side?"

Mr. Herman addressed him, probably for the first time all year. "But they aren't supposed to be on 'our side.' They are supposed to be on the side of truth."

"They're on their own damn side. That's all. They're just out for themselves."

Mr. Herman looked at me for a comment, but Hawg wasn't finished.

"The way I see it, if America's in a war, I'm either fighting to win it, or I got no business being there."

Mr. Herman responded tersely, "Unless your business is to report the news as a member of a free press."

"Well, the way I see that one, all we have to do is lose one of them wars and there ain't gonna *be* no more free press."

Mr. Herman shook his head at that, but no one else

did. Hawg's remarks turned the discussion around. Even I had to agree with him. Some of the football players and some of the other students started to speak up, and everyone who spoke supported Hawg.

Mr. Herman didn't like that one bit.

When I got to the TV studio, I walked into a frenzy of activity. Outside, Bill and Mr. McKay were wheeling equipment to the RV. Inside, Mrs. Knight was on the phone, speaking very tensely to someone named Veronica.

I stood in front of her and waited. She hung up, rolled her eyes, and told me, "Roberta, we need somebody to assist Bill on a remote."

Bill and Mr. McKay raced back into the lobby. Bill called over to me, "You! Look in the back of the RV. Make sure we have the hundred-foot spool of cable!" I took off for the RV and did what he said. Then I ran back in and Bill shouted another order at me.

Fifteen minutes later Bill, a cameraman, and I were strapped into our seats and heading north, toward the Gold Coast Mall. Neither of them said a word all the way there.

Somehow Mrs. Knight arrived ahead of us with Angela. The two of them held the mall doors open as we drove in with the RV. We stopped almost immediately, though, in front of a place named Bangles Boutique.

A woman, who must have been Veronica, hung up a computer-generated banner that said ANGELA LIVE —

MAKEOVER MADNESS. Bill pointed at a headset on a console. He told me, "Put that on and listen for Mr. McKay."

I did what he said. Bill and the cameraman went outside and set up. About five minutes later I heard the director through the headset: "Bill? Do you read me?"

"It's not Bill, Mr. McKay. It's Roberta. The intern."

He actually seemed to know who I was. "Oh yeah. Hi, Roberta. Where's Bill?"

"He's setting up outside, sir."

"Good. Don't waste any time calling me 'sir.' Things happen very quickly on these remote broadcasts. Every millisecond matters."

"Yes, sir. I mean — Yes, Mr. McKay."

"Just say 'yes.' While we're waiting, check the top video slot on the console. Make sure the emergency tape is in there."

I looked at the top slot. I pulled out a videocassette from it and read its title aloud to him: 'Angela Live Promo Tape.'"

"That's the one. Good."

Mr. McKay didn't say anything else, so I ventured a question. "What's the emergency tape for?"

"That's in case something goes wrong. We always need a backup tape on a remote broadcast."

"What kind of things go wrong?"

"When we're live? Anything and everything. Sometimes we have technical problems, like a broken cable. Sometimes all hell breaks loose, you know, and we don't want the audience to see what's really going on."

Bill came huffing back up the steps. I removed the headset and handed it to him. He and Mr. McKay worked out director's cues and commercial breaks. I looked out the big window and watched while Mrs. Knight, Angela, and the cameraman prepped the employees of Bangles Boutique and three women volunteers. Each of the volunteers would be given a complete makeover.

About five minutes before the broadcast, Bill realized that I was just sitting there. He ripped off the headset and pointed outside. "Do you see that soundboard?"

I stood up to see it. "Yes."

"Go out there and watch the decibel meter. Signal me with your fingers: one finger for one hundred, two fingers for two hundred, three for three hundred, you get the idea?"

I said, "Four fingers for four hundred?" to see if he would laugh.

He didn't. He answered seriously, "Right. You got it. Now go. And don't take your eyes off that meter."

I did just as Bill said. I stared at the soundboard the entire time and held up my fingers. I never saw any of the show.

When I got to the mall, I was surprised to see Nina inside Suzie's office. She seemed equally surprised to see me. Nina and Suzie were leaning over the desk, signing a paper. I was going to leave without bothering them, but Nina called to me, "Wait up, Roberta. I'm outta here, too."

Nina preceded me out the door. Then she turned and said, "Don't tell anybody what you saw in there, okay?"

"What did I see?"

"You don't know?"

"No."

"If I tell you, do you promise not to tell anybody? Not Kristin, or any of those loser guys at Arcane? And especially not any adults?"

"I promise."

"That crazy lady at the Beauty Supply called Suzie. She told her I took stuff without paying for it. She filed a complaint. She's nuts."

"Why? You didn't take it?"

"Yes, I took it. But I was gonna pay for it. I looked at my watch and saw I was ten minutes late for work. I'm in that Beauty Supply place all the time. I'm their best customer. I was gonna pay for it on my break." Nina shook her head at the injustice of it. "She ought to pay me to shop in that dump. Instead she does something like this."

We stopped for a moment in the rotunda, about to part ways. But first Nina took a strand of my hair in her hand. "You still need that makeover, Roberta. You should have seen *Angela* today. They were doing makeovers at the Gold Coast Mall."

I broke off and started to walk away. But before I did, I said, "I know. I was there."

Nina's eyes got wide. "What? You were what?"

"I work on the show."

Nina ran after me. "Why didn't you tell me? I'd have gone there. I'd have gotten a makeover. I'd have met Angela!"

"What's the big deal? I see her all the time."

"You see Angela del Fuego all the time?"

"When I'm at the studio, yeah. I usually see her."

"Can I come to the studio?"

"Sure. They give student tours."

"Really? Would they give me a student tour?"

"No. But you could go with your journalism class, or your communications class, or your honors English class. Just call them up. Actually, you should have your teacher call."

"I will. I will. I'm telling Sister Ann tomorrow: 'Call Channel Fifty-seven and get us the *Angela* tour.'"

I corrected her, "The student tour."

"Yeah. Whatever."

We walked into Arcane like that. Kristin looked up, surprised to see us together. I don't know how anyone can still be surprised by anything Nina does. She acts like the incident with her father never happened.

Nina reached into her pocket and pulled out a newspaper clipping. She stood in front of the counter, unfolded it, and said to Kristin, "I just wanted to show you what you missed. These are pictures from the cotillion."

"Why would I want to see those?"

"I just thought, you know, since you couldn't go, you'd like to see what it was like."

"Why would I want to do that?"

"Like I said, because I was there, and you weren't."

"I didn't want to be there."

"Right. What? You wanted to be here?"

Kristin clenched her teeth. "Just put it away, Nina."

Nina refolded the paper. "Okay. Sorry. I understand, with your face and everything."

"If you think this is about my face, then no, you don't understand." She added, "And neither does your father."

I thought Nina would go stomping away at that, but she didn't. She walked around, stood next to Kristin, and stared out at the mallway, just like old times.

I studied the two of them. They used to be so much alike. Tonight they were near opposites. Kristin was wearing a plain A-line denim dress. She had no makeup on. Nina had on a white silk blouse, cut low in front. She had lots of makeup on.

Barely a minute had passed before Nina said, "You know that chick Cynthia? She's in honors English?"

Kristin still sounded a little angry. But she, too, was willing to change the subject. She answered, "Yeah. I know who you mean."

"She's having breast enhancement surgery. She's already got it scheduled, for, like, the week after graduation. That way she'll be ready for college."

Kristin said quietly, "That is so sad."

"What? It's not sad if she's doing something about it. She's got, like, nothing there. Me? I'd do it if I had to. Fortunately I don't."

Kristin shook her head slowly.

Nina continued, "I need, like, leg enhancement surgery. I need to be about six inches taller."

Kristin didn't respond.

"I wonder if they can do that. You know? Like, take the bones from some girl who just died and graft them onto somebody else's legs. Make them taller. Why not, right? They can do everything else."

Kristin finally said, "I thought Cynthia had more sense than that. And more character."

"Character? Hey, chill out, girl. She's just trying to be all that she can be."

"By mutilating her body so she can attract boys?"

Nina finally gave up. "Maybe we ought to talk about something else."

At break time, I walked outside and turned toward the rotunda. I noticed Uncle Frank out of the corner of my eye. He was standing behind the Sony monitor, like he was hiding. As soon as he saw me, though, he seemed to get an idea. He said, "Hey, Roberta. Do you know Devin, the manager at Candlewycke?"

I said, "Yes." I couldn't help but ask, "Why? Do you?"

Uncle Frank shot me a look filled with resentment, but he continued, "Do you think you could deliver this envelope to him? It's just some paperwork."

I took the envelope from his outstretched hand. "Paperwork for what?"

Uncle Frank explained, "To make us some extra money."

At Candlewycke I waited outside until Devin drifted like a black specter into the back. Then I hurried in and handed the envelope to Betty. "That's from my uncle. It's for Devin. It's some paperwork."

Betty looked doubtful, but she took the envelope. There was no sign of Devin returning, so I decided to stay for a minute. I said, "Hey, Betty, does Devin wear that same shirt every day?"

Betty thought about that. "I don't think it's the same shirt. I just think he has a lot of them."

"Yeah? But long sleeves? In Florida?"

Betty turned the question back on me. "What do you care? Why can't people wear what they want?"

"I'm just curious."

Betty backed off a bit. "I think it's because of his tattoos. He has lots of them, all over his body. If you look down the back of his neck, you can see them."

We stood over the Nazi dagger case for a minute. Finally Betty asked me, "So . . . what are you guys doing tonight?"

"Hanging out. Why don't you stop by on break? Nina's there. It looks like she's sticking around."

"Yeah, okay. Maybe I will."

I took off back to the arcade. Karl greeted me right away with, "Hey, Roberta, AAs tonight."

"Are you sure, Karl?"

"Yeah. African Americans. Right?"

"Right."

"A busload of them. They're down here for a gospel-singing thing."

"How do you know?"

"My dad wrote it on this paper." Karl held up a page from a loose-leaf binder. "He wants us to put an OUT OF ORDER sign on King Kong. He doesn't want anybody to get offended by those natives."

"Okay. What time are they coming?"

"I don't know. When they get here."

Karl sounded like he was getting agitated. I think he just wanted me to be impressed that he knew what AAs were, and to leave it at that. I went into the back to make the sign.

Hawg and Ironman were sitting on a pile of cardboard boxes. I found a piece of white paper and wrote OUT OF ORDER on it.

Hawg said, "What's that for?"

"King Kong. If we need it."

Hawg nodded like he understood, and I'm sure he did. I told him, "I liked what you said in journalism class today."

"You did, huh?"

"Yeah. I thought you put it really well."

Hawg gave me the strangest look. "Yeah. So did Mr. Homo. That's why he gave me that F."

I wasn't surprised, but I said, "What do you mean? For what you said in class?"

"For the whole shootin' match, darlin'. Now tell me somethin' — how's that fair?"

I knew he didn't really want me to answer that question. But he stood there like he was waiting for some reply, so I decided to tell him the truth. I said, "Well, if you didn't do the classwork for six weeks, what did you expect?"

Hawg's eyes blazed up with instant and frightening fury. He leaped to his feet. Ironman backed out of the way, but I stayed put.

Hawg pointed a big, accusing finger at me and cried, "What did I expect? I expected to get a C, that's what. I read that damn boring muckraker book. I ain't gonna sit up front like you butt-kissers do every day and tell him how 'interesting' it was. I ain't gonna do that. But I still don't deserve no damn F. I don't deserve to get kicked off the football team! What did I expect? I expected things to go right! Like they always did! I was never in no damn trouble until I got sent down here. I expected things to be . . . like they were."

Hawg panted, out of breath with the effort that had taken. He calmed down very quickly. He said almost apologetically, "Well, that's my second speech today, isn't it? How'd you like that one?"

I said, "I'm sorry. I hope you can keep playing football."

"Forget it. Go put your sign up."

I hurried out and taped the sign to King Kong. Uncle Frank walked by the platform as I did, and he nodded approval.

The busload of AAs arrived right after that. Suddenly everybody but Nina was busy. Fortunately for her, Betty dropped by to keep her company. It was comical to me to see the two of them at the counter, standing there like a Before and After rerun.

I guess Karl found it funny, too. He walked up to them and said to Betty, "What's with all the black? You're scaring the customers away."

Betty gave it back to him. "Oh? And you're not?"

Hawg got a big laugh out of that. He called over to me, "Hey, Roberta! Who is that?"

I don't know why I did it. Maybe I was tired. But I just said it out loud, "Betty the Goth." Then I froze, realizing I had never called her that name to her face.

Betty came down from the counter. I tried to drift away, but she followed me. She confronted me in front of Vampire's Feast. "My last name is not 'The Goth.' Do you understand? That is stupid. I've heard you say that about me before, and I want you to stop. Do you understand?"

"Yes."

"Those words do not describe me. They do not define me." She looked at me with ghostly black anger. "What is my name?"

I had to admit to her, "I don't know."

"How can you not know? I'm in two classes with you. You should know my name."

"Sorry."

"I know your name. It's Roberta Ritter. I don't call you something else, do I? I don't call you Roberta the Androgyne. Or Roberta the Hermaphrodite. Do I?"

I had no idea what she was saying. I was just really sorry I had insulted her like that. She got out of my face, walked back to the counter, and announced to everyone, "My name is Elizabeth Lopez."

Nina perked up at that. "Really? You're Cubana?"

Betty told Nina, "My father is."

"I never would have guessed that. What's your mother?"

"French Canadian."

"Oh yeah. What, are they really white up there?"

Betty clenched her jaw. "Some of them."

"So do you speak Spanish?"

"No."

"No? Your father doesn't speak it at home?"

"No. My father doesn't speak at home. Listen: This is stupid. You're all stupid. I'm leaving." Betty shot one more angry glance at me and walked out.

I felt like I needed to get out, too. I ducked over to the card shop, feeling very embarrassed and very stupid. Mrs. Roman was at the register. She told me, "I'm covering so Isabel can get some extra rest. She's not feeling well."

"Oh? What's wrong?"

"She says 'nothing in particular.' She just needs to sleep."

"Is she coming back to make the night deposit?"

"No. I'll have to do that alone, unless I can convince a big strong man like Leo to help me."

I turned and saw that Leo had followed me in. Leo spoke right up. "So, Millie, did you see the big show yesterday?"

"What show?"

"The flying Santa Claus?"

"No. But I heard about it from Isabel. You saw it?"

Leo winked at me. "Yeah, you could say that."

"So what happened?"

Leo chuckled mirthfully. "Nothin' too much. Let's just say old Santa got hisself a swamp-water enema."

Mrs. Roman's eyes narrowed. "Don't joke about that, Leo. An enema is nothing to joke about."

I said, "Excuse me. I have to get back to work."

Uncle Frank came out front at eight-forty-five. He called everybody together and announced, "We're going to close the doors now. Here, Roberta, put this sign out." He held a homemade sign up so we could all see. It said CLOSED FOR PRIVATE PARTY.

I taped it on the glass door. I saw that he had made it on the back of Karl's YES, WE'RE OPEN sign. Then Uncle Frank told me, "Thank you. Now you can go. Kristin, you should go, too. Give Roberta a ride home."

Kristin looked puzzled. She told him, "I don't want to leave, Daddy. I want to know what's going on."

Uncle Frank answered flatly and efficiently, "What's going on is that the arcade has been rented for a private party. The people who have rented it wish to try some Arcane experiences that are not available to the general public. That's all I care to say about those experiences."

"Who rented it?"

"Devin. And some invited guests."

"Daddy, why are we doing this?"

"We're making five hundred dollars for this one-hour party. And we're being paid in cash."

"So why can't I stay?"

Uncle Frank swallowed hard. I could see that he absolutely hated this. He finally answered, "You'll be the only girls here. But I guess it's all right if you stay. I'll leave it up to you."

Uncle Frank handed a pile of new CDs and legend cards to Karl. He told him, "These are for the party only. At the end of the night we'll change them back to the regular experiences. Devin wants these four, and him." He pointed to Crusader. Then he spun around and walked into the back. We all gathered around Karl to read them.

There were four new experiences. They were titled Klan Ride, Lynch Mob, Krystallnacht, and Martial Law. The legends described them as providing *ultra-action and over-the-top thrills*. Two of the experiences, Klan Ride and Lynch Mob, featured blacks as the enemy. Krystallnacht had Jews. And Martial Law had *a horde of white America's enemies*.

We all looked at each other. Kristin said to me, "Maybe we'd better go. I don't want any part of this."

I said, "You go ahead. I'd like to stay."

"Why?"

"Because I'm a reporter."

Kristin gritted her teeth. "Then I'm staying, too. But this is wrong. Nothing is worth this."

The back door opened. Devin walked in, followed by a line of young guys. I recognized one or two as Memorial High kids who had graduated, or who had dropped out.

Karl said, "Here, let's put these in." He gave a CD

and a legend to Hawg, Ironman, and me. We each changed out an experience. I replaced Vampire's Feast with Martial Law.

Hawg sidled up to me after finishing with his. He muttered, "I'm not sure how many of these boys would pass Mrs. Bit-off's Random Drug Test."

Uncle Frank emerged from the back. He said to the entire room, "I want to lay down a few ground rules. First, no one is to leave these premises for any reason. The doors will remain locked at all times. The party will last one hour. There is to be no drinking, eating, or anything else." He looked at Devin. "That's all." I'm not sure how many of our guests were listening.

Devin looked at Kristin and me. He said, "You might want to send the chicks home. Things could get out of hand."

Uncle Frank leveled a stare at him. "No. Things are not going to get out of hand."

Devin held his bony hands up in surrender. He selected a helmet and stepped up onto Galactic Defender's black circle. It was now programmed for Krystallnacht. Karl walked over and started it for him. Then the other guests did the same thing. Soon all five experiences were going full swing.

Kristin whispered to me, "This is too creepy, Roberta. This is evil. Let's get out of here."

"No. I want to be here. But you go ahead. You should do what you think is right."

Kristin thought hard about it. "All right. I'm leaving. See you tomorrow." She let herself out the front door.

I heard a strange voice behind me. "So . . . we've had our first casualty of the evening?"

I spun around to see Devin standing there, staring at me. He said, "Don't you worry. You're perfectly safe with me."

I lied, "I'm not worried."

He took a step closer. He seemed to be scrutinizing my face. "I knew you when you were a baby."

"You did?"

"Yes. Back on the Strip. I knew your dad and your mom." He moved even closer. "That's who you look like. You look like Mary Ann."

I hated hearing him use her name. I said, "You knew my mom?"

"Sure. We used to party together."

I didn't believe that for a minute. I told him, "Well, I sure don't remember you."

"No. You were too young. And right after you were born, your mom got super-straight. She wouldn't party at all."

"Oh no? What about my dad?"

"Your dad? Hey, your dad's another story. Didn't he ever tell you about me?"

"No. What's to tell?"

Devin smiled creepily. "Not a thing. But even if there was something, you wouldn't hear it from me."

I said, "Excuse me," and walked up behind the register. I observed the rest of the party from there, from afar. It was a bizarre and frightening scene. The guests, except for Devin, were all the same. They were all white, teenage males. Each had paid fifty dollars to attack and kill nonwhites, and they set about it with grim determination. Except for the swishing and hacking of the white wands, they made no sound. It was almost silent.

After about forty-five minutes, Uncle Frank came out and watched. He stood impassively, with his arms folded across his chest. He signaled me to come over. "Roberta, we'll give you a ride home after."

"That's okay, Uncle Frank. I'm staying with Mrs. Weiss tonight."

"How are you getting there?"

"I'm going to walk."

"Through that dark parking lot?"

"They have a security guard."

Uncle Frank shrugged. "All right. If you think it's safe . . ." Uncle Frank held his watch up to Devin. He said, "That's it. The hour's up."

The guests were definitely ready to leave. An hour of Arcane experiences is a very long time. They cleared out quickly, leaving us to restore the CDs and legends of the four altered experiences.

At ten o'clock, Hawg, Ironman, and I exited through the back door. I turned left and started walking toward Century Towers. But when those guys were out of sight, I took off running. I circled the south anchor and ran up to a small metal door near the front. I banged on it and slipped in as soon as Sam cracked it open. He said, "Did anybody see you?"

"No."

We crept up front and reclaimed our spots in the window of La Boutique de Paris. As soon as I sat down, I noticed a big mistake on the Arcane closing checklist. The Crusader statue was still out in the mallway. His unblinking blue eyes were aimed right at us.

Sam said, "How was the party?"

"How did it look from here?"

"Pretty sick. What was it about?"

"It was a party to try some Arcane experiences that are . . . hardcore. That are worse than the usual ones."

"Worse than Crusader?"

"Yeah. Crusader was one of them, but I think the others were worse."

Sam shook his head sadly. "Who were the victims?"

"Blacks, Jews, and some assorted enemies."

"There always has to be an enemy, doesn't there?" Sam nodded thoughtfully. He told me, "I've been thinking about Crusader. I went home and did some reading. Do you want to hear about it?"

"Yeah. What were you reading?"

"Let's just call it the Arab version." Sam leaned forward and checked the mallway in both directions. Then he sat back and said, "There are at least two versions of what happened anywhere at any time. Usually more. On the Crusades . . . If you listen to western historians talk about it, it was a holy war. Listen to an Arab historian and you'll get a truer picture of what happened." He asked me, "What do you think it was about?"

I answered, "Freeing the Holy Land."

"Really? Freeing it from whom? From the people who lived there?"

I added, "And helping the Christian pilgrims who were getting attacked."

"In Europe those pilgrims couldn't get a mile out of their home towns without getting attacked. Europe was a violent, lawless cesspool. Its roads were full of armed bands of thieves and murderers. So the Pope and some of the kings decided to export their problem to the East. The pope convinced some prominent thieves and murderers that the rewards were much bigger in Jerusalem, and the victims were much richer. So the crusaders put on the cross and headed for the civilized lands of the East. They set upon peaceful towns like vicious animals. They beheaded thousands of innocent men and paraded around with the heads on stakes. They roasted little children alive and then ate them."

I shivered and screamed, "Get out!" Then I caught myself and peered carefully into the mallway. Nothing stirred.

"Hey, don't take my word for it. It's all in the histories. The Arab histories."

I whispered back, "Yeah? Where am I going to find those?"

"Waldenbooks." Sam paused and added, "I'm joking."

"I know."

We sat still for a half minute. Then he asked me, "So

tell me, Roberta, what were they? God's own army of righteous pilgrims? Or a rampaging mob of bloodthirsty cannibals?"

I was ready for him. "It all depends on who's telling the story."

"You got it."

"But I believe that your version is just as prejudiced as mine."

"Believe whatever you want. Any way you look at it, it was a bloody mess. And it was all in the name of the cross."

I had heard enough. I mumbled, "Like Uncle Frank said, that was all a long time ago."

"Do you really think so? Do you know about your uncle Frank's Desert Storm? Do you know what happened in that?"

"Please, Sam. That's enough."

"You don't want to hear the Arab version?"

I looked at him. I thought to myself, *I'm a reporter; I need to hear things.* I said, "Okay, what?"

"Remember what Mr. Lyons's bulldozers did to Toby and his fellow turtles?"

"Yes."

"Well, the American army did the same thing to the Iraqis in Desert Storm. They trapped them in their desert trenches and then came at them with huge bulldozers. If the Iraqis ran, they got shot. If they didn't run, they got entombed under the desert sand. That's where they still are, I reckon. Just like old Toby."

I said, "I don't believe that."

"Okay. Don't."

After that we sat in stony silence for about five minutes. Now I felt anger at Sam — a patriotic American anger. I was trying to formulate something to say back to him, something about how he should be grateful to our soldiers, when I heard the noise.

Sam heard it, too. Footsteps. And they were hurrying our way. I felt my neck and my head moving forward. Sam's was moving the same way. We both pressed our faces against the Plexiglas, fogging it slightly, but not enough to obscure what we both saw. A figure was hurrying down the mallway, a man's figure.

The figure walked briskly up to the Crusader statue. He stopped and looked at it, as if wondering what to do. He was carrying a can. Was it spray paint? Yes, definitely. The figure set the can down on the mallway, and I could clearly read the words GLIDDEN and PAINT. The man unlocked the door. He pushed the Crusader statue inside. Then he scooped up his can and backed in. Before he relocked the door, he peered out to see if anyone was watching.

Someone was. Sam and I. We both inhaled with a sharp sound as we saw his face. It wasn't Hawg. It wasn't Devin or Karl, either.

It was Uncle Frank.

No question about it.

Sam and I sat there paralyzed. Finally Sam could whisper, "I was ready for that Hawg guy. But not this. If it was that Hawg guy, I was gonna go after him tonight. Now I don't know what to do."

I said, "Let's go down to Crescent and see if anything happened. Let's see if he painted anything."

"Yeah. Yeah, that's a good idea."

We unlocked the door from within and ventured out into the silent mallway. We ran down to Crescent, our adrenaline pumping, but there was no vandalism to be seen. The windows were all free of paint. Sam unlocked the door and went straight to a video camera that was trained on the front window. He removed its tape, stuck it into a VCR, and pressed Rewind.

I was glad Sam didn't ask me to help him, because I would have been useless; I was in a state of shock. He turned on a big TV, set it on Channel 3, and pressed Play.

The tape showed a still mallway, and the bottom part of PIP Printing across the way. Sam pressed Fast Forward until he got to the most recent part. Then he slowed it down.

It all happened very quickly. A man with a hat appeared in the frame. If you looked really hard at him, you could tell that it was Uncle Frank. He stopped right in front of the window and looked into the lens of the camera. Then a look of horror came over his face. He jerked himself backward, out of the frame, and disappeared.

Sam announced, "Okay. We got him. I got Griffin's beeper number. I'm calling him right now."

I followed Sam back to his office. He punched in Griffin's beeper number on the store's phone. He got a call back in less than a minute, but it wasn't from Griffin. It was from his sergeant. I heard Sam say, "No. No. It can wait until tomorrow. Thank you, Sergeant."

Sam looked at me. "Griffin is off tonight. That was Sergeant Fisk. He said we could call nine-one-one if it's an emergency. Otherwise Griffin will call back tomorrow."

"Well, that's good."

Sam nodded happily. "Yeah. That's good." He tightened his mouth up, as if he was trying to hold back something. But he couldn't. His eyes became pools of water. Then two lines of happy tears started to roll down his cheeks.

WEDNESDAY, THE 27TH ❧ That same kid from the guidance office came into Mr. Herman's room just before class started. This time he kept his distance from the podium. He held up a small sheet of paper and pointed to the back of the class. Mr. Herman nodded curtly and then looked back down at his lecture notes.

The kid approached Hawg and said, "They want you down in guidance again."

Hawg snarled at him. "Yeah? Who's 'they'?"

The kid looked at the paper and read, "Mr. Archer."

"So why does Mr. Archer want to see me?"

"I don't know."

"What's it say on your damn paper?"

The kid read the contents of the paper word for word, "Hugh Mason. Journalism Two."

"That's it?"

"That's it."

Mr. Herman looked up at them. He cleared his throat and said, "This is fascinating, but it needs to end now. Leave, both of you."

Hawg sat still for a moment longer, defiantly considering his options. I could tell what he was thinking. I know he thought this was about RDT, but I had a bad feeling that it wasn't. So when Hawg finally got to his feet and started out, I got up with him. Mr. Herman noticed me just as I slipped out the door, but he didn't have time to say anything.

Hawg stomped away ahead of the guidance kid and me. I didn't catch up to him until we were right outside of the office. I tapped him on the back and said, "Hey, wait a minute."

Hawg turned around, surprised. "What are you doing here?"

The guidance kid continued into the office without us. I said, "I don't think you know what's going on."

Hawg looked at me suspiciously. "The hell I don't. They kicked me off the football team, but I ain't goin'. I talked to Archie about it."

"Look, this may not be about any of that — the RDT, or the F in Journalism, or the football team. It may be about something else."

Hawg stared at me blankly, his back to the office. He

didn't see Griffin come out the door, or Mr. Archer, or Officer Dwyer, our permanent deputy. But he could tell by my expression that something was happening behind him. He spun around and regarded them all, one by one. He pointed at Griffin and spoke to him familiarly. "What are you doing here?"

Griffin held out his sheriff's department badge, just as he had that night in the carport. "I'm Detective John Griffin. I've been working undercover at the West End Mall."

"What? You're a damn cop?"

Mr. Archer said, "Can we take this into my office, please?"

Griffin and Officer Dwyer each took a giant step backward, cutting off any plans Hawg may have had for running. Hawg looked sideways at me. His face was frightened, anguished. He walked numbly behind Mr. Archer into the office. Everybody in guidance stopped what they were doing to stare.

Nobody told me to go away, so I followed them all the way in. Mr. Archer closed the door behind us. He indicated that Hawg should sit on a chair in front of his desk, but Hawg remained standing.

Mr. Archer looked at Griffin, who cleared his throat and spoke in a formal way. "Hugh Mason, I am arresting you under the Florida Hate Crimes Statute." Griffin pulled out a small laminated card and started to read him his rights. "You have the right to remain silent —"

But I interrupted. I nearly shouted at him, "Wait a minute! He didn't do it."

Griffin looked at me in surprise, then his eyes narrowed. I think he was about to go back to reading from his card, but then Mr. Archer broke in, "Yeah. Wait a minute, fellas. I want to say something, too."

Griffin put the card down. Mr. Archer held up a manila file. "Hugh? I have your records here, from your time with us. They're not much, but they do tell me something. Also, I have talked with my son about you." He looked at Griffin. "My son is Hugh's history teacher and his football coach."

Mr. Archer came around the desk and stood next to Hawg. Hawg was blinking, like a trapped animal in a cage. Mr. Archer told him, "Hugh, my son said you were a real honest kind of guy. He didn't think you would be involved in criminal activity."

Hawg answered in a quavering voice, "No, sir, I would not."

"I asked him about African American members of the football team, and he said you got along with them very well."

"Yes, sir. That's a fact."

"But I must inform you that I'm releasing your file to the sheriff's department, and it does contain a racial incident."

"What?"

"You did get into a fight with black students on your first day at our school. And you did use racial slurs."

Hawg thought back. He asked Mr. Archer, "You talking about that thing in the cafeteria?"

Mr. Archer peered through his bifocals at the file. "I believe that's where it happened. Yes."

Hawg's voice got stronger. "I was standin' in line at the soda machine. These boys figured they didn't have to wait in line like me. I told 'em they did."

"Well, Hugh, apparently you told them some other things, too."

"Hey, they think you're supposed to be scared of 'em because there's four of 'em and because they're black. Well, that don't happen where I come from. They got all these white boys down here runnin' scared. I ain't scared of 'em. I said I'd take 'em one at a time or all at once. I hit one, and the other three jumped me. Then the damn dean came around the corner, grabbed me, and let them go."

Mr. Archer listened closely. He answered, "All right. But whatever happened, it's classified as race based in our file."

"It was race based, all right. They jumped me because I was white."

"That was a very serious incident, Hugh. I nearly had to put the whole school on alert, and you know what that means."

"Yes, sir."

I don't think Mr. Archer knew what to do next, so he looked at Griffin. Griffin said, "We can read Hugh his rights in the car, sir. Or at the station, if you would prefer that."

Mr. Archer was clearly upset now. He said to Griffin

and Officer Dwyer, "No. We need to step next door and discuss this."

The three men stepped out. Hawg looked at me and hissed, "Roberta, what the hell's going on here?"

"They think you've been doing stuff to Sam, and to Sam's car, and to Crescent Electronics."

"What? Why?"

"Because you had that fight with him at Arcane. You called him that racial name."

"He called me a race name, too. Or don't nobody remember that part?"

I held up my hands, shoulder high.

Mr. Archer opened the door. "Hugh, we're telephoning your father right now."

"My stepfather."

"Yes, of course. He will meet us at the police station."

"What for?"

Mr. Archer looked pained again. "Hugh, you will have a chance to present your side of this case. I promise you that. Your stepfather needs to know that there are two sides to this story."

"Sir, my stepdaddy don't want to hear my side of nothin'. He knows I'm tellin' the truth, but he don't want to hear it. He's got a new wife down here, and she don't want me around. That's the whole damn deal right there. That's why I gotta get back up to Georgia."

Mr. Archer's big head tilted to one side. He turned around and called over to Mrs. Biddulph, who was watching the proceedings from the front desk, "Mrs.

Biddulph, I'll be accompanying Hugh this morning. Take over for me, please."

She answered, "Yes, sir."

Officer Dwyer approached Hawg with a pair of handcuffs. Mr. Archer asked him, "Now, is that really necessary?"

"It is, sir. It's regulations. I'd get written up if I didn't do it."

Griffin told Officer Dwyer, "Go ahead to the car, Deputy. I'll be another few minutes in here." Griffin caught my eye and jerked his thumb toward the time-out office.

I walked in, and he closed the door behind me. He stood in front of the sign that reads, IF YOU'RE SO SMART, WHAT ARE YOU DOING HERE? and waited for me to speak.

I demanded to know, "Didn't you get our page? We paged you!"

Griffin shook his head. "No, I didn't get any page. And who is 'we'?"

"Sam and me. We know who did it. We saw him from the window of La Boutique de Paris." I lowered my voice instinctively. "It was my uncle Frank."

Griffin's mouth twisted up into a disbelieving smile. "Your uncle Frank?"

"We saw him, Detective! With our own eyes."

"Saw him do what?"

"He had a can of red spray paint. He was sneaking around the mall with it. And . . . and! Sam caught him on videotape."

"Caught him doing what?"

I stopped. I felt myself getting flustered. "He . . . he was about to spray paint on Sam's window. That's what."

"Did he?"

"No. He saw the video camera and he ran away."

Griffin looked down at the ground, thinking to himself. Then he started thinking out loud. "So your uncle was outside Crescent, after hours, with spray paint."

I answered triumphantly, "Yes!"

"That changes things."

"Yes!"

Griffin looked me in the eye. "But, Roberta, it doesn't prove anything. There's a difference." He explained, "You saw your uncle last night, but no crime was committed last night." He suddenly glanced at his watch.

I said, "No. Not last night, but —"

Now Griffin was all business. "But nothing. Listen, Roberta. Here's how it works: The department spent the time and money to place me in the mall, and they expect a result. This is the result. An arrest. That's a serious thing, but it's only a part of the process."

"But . . . how can you arrest the wrong guy?"

Griffin pointed a big finger at me. "You know that Hawg has been the prime suspect from the start. He got into it with some blacks at Memorial. He called one the *n*-word. He got into a shouting match with Sam, with witnesses, where he used a racial slur. He even purchased red spray paint from Lombardo's. Hawg has placed himself in this predicament. He has made himself the prime suspect."

"But Hawg didn't do it. Don't you know that now? Uncle Frank did it."

He chose his words very carefully. "I now believe that that is possible. And if Hawg didn't do it, I will find that out. Once he's indicted, I can do a full investigation — physical evidence, fingerprints, alibis, witnesses. All of that. If there's no real case against him, the department will not proceed."

"What about Uncle Frank? Will you proceed against him?"

Griffin's eyes took on an odd expression. He said, "That's tough to say. Colonel Frank Ritter has never been a suspect at all. He's an army veteran, an officer, a business owner. The only thing we have against him is that his niece and Sam were alone in a dark spot in the mall one night and thought they saw him."

"Yeah?"

"Yeah. And maybe the windows were a little foggy."

"What? What are you talking about?"

"Maybe the windows were foggy because things were getting hot between you two."

"Cut it out!"

"Hey, that's nothing compared to what a lawyer would do to you in a courtroom."

I told him, "You are sick." I looked away, embarrassed, but I guessed that was Griffin's point. I pulled myself together and asked him, "So what's going to happen to Hawg? Is he going to get hurt?"

"Come on, Roberta. What do you think we have down there, a medieval torture chamber? I'm gonna take him to a nice office building. I'm going to buy him a soda, give him a doughnut, and let him tell his side of the story. He'll go before a judge, he'll be arraigned, and he'll make bail. He'll be home before supper. Heck, he'll probably be back at the mall."

"Then what?"

"I don't know. Maybe the judge will slap a peace bond on him."

"What's that?"

"It's a court order. He won't be allowed to go within a certain distance of Sam. Like a hundred yards. They use peace bonds a lot now — for stalkers, wife beaters, things like that. They might fix an electronic device on him, too, to make sure he keeps away." He held up his watch to me. "I have to take him in now. I will talk to you again as soon as I can."

I stayed in the time-out room for a few minutes after Griffin left, trying to make sense of his words. When I was ready to go back to class, I walked out into the office. That was when I saw Ironman. I immediately thought, *Oh no. Did he see all of this?*

I stopped and regarded him closely. He seemed the same as always, just sitting there grinning nervously. I concluded that he hadn't seen anything. I said, "Hey, what are you doing here?"

"Waiting for Mrs. Biddulph."

"Are you here for RDT?"

"No. My PE teacher says I got head lice."

"Oh no. Where did you get that?"

"I got no idea."

Mrs. Biddulph hurried back into the office from somewhere, so I said, "See you," and left.

I went back to Journalism II. Mr. Herman was speaking about the Pulitzer Prizes. I slipped in quietly, just as I had left. If he noticed me, he didn't let on.

WEDNESDAY AFTERNOON ❧ I brought an overnight bag with me to work. Ever since Griffin's appearance in the carport, I've been afraid to be at home alone. Tonight I was planning to have dinner with Mrs. Weiss and to stay over there, but first I had to make it through five hours of work with Uncle Frank.

I hung out at the register with Karl for a while. Uncle Frank stayed in his office, as he's now accustomed to doing. At around five, Ironman walked in wearing a black baseball cap. The cap had the words BITNER FAMILY REUNION on it.

Karl looked up from a copy of *PC World* and asked him, "What's with the hat, dude?"

"It was two *t*s."

"Huh?"

"*Bitner.* It was supposed to have two *t*s in it. *Bittner.* They wouldn't take the hats."

"No, doofus. I mean, why are you wearing it?"

"I had to have my head shaved. They said I got head lice."

This bit of information spurred Karl to immediate

action. He dropped the magazine and hurried into the back to tell his father.

Uncle Frank burst out through the office door. He honed in on Ironman like a guided missile, barking at him, "No way you got head lice here."

Poor Ironman shriveled under the power of this accusation. Karl came up behind him and pulled off his cap. Ironman's head was completely shaved. He looked like one of those concentration-camp victims in the old newsreels.

Karl stuffed the cap back onto Ironman's head. "Whoa. Keep that thing on, dude. At all times."

Uncle Frank stared at Ironman's head with extreme distaste. He added, "It didn't happen here," then turned and walked slowly back to the office.

I took a break at five o'clock and walked down to Crescent. As I had hoped, the early news was playing on their wall of televisions. Several employees were gathered around the VCR. I joined them and asked, "Is Sam here?"

A guy answered me enthusiastically, "No. Sam was on the local news. On Channel Fifty-seven. We got it all on tape. Watch."

He walked over to a VCR and pushed in a tape. The wall of TVs filled with images of Sam. He looked upset. He was busily dodging the microphones thrust into his face by reporters.

I asked the guy, "Can you turn the sound on?"

"Sure." But by the time he did, the scene had shifted. Ray Lyons was on the screen. He told a girl reporter, "I deplore these hate crimes. As soon as I heard that an African American businessman was being harassed at one of my malls, I got involved. I demanded a full investigation from the state's attorney. And as a senator I will push for tougher legislation against such crimes."

I didn't know Sam was African American. I'm sure he didn't, either. I was hoping for him to come back on the videotape when, miraculously, he appeared "live" at my elbow. He said, "We need to talk." Sam took off into the mallway, so I followed. He turned and said, in a low voice, "I had a chat with Griffin today."

"So did I."

"When?"

"This morning."

"Okay. I just got off the cell phone with him. This is the latest: Your uncle had an alibi ready about last night."

"He did? What?"

"He said he was making a bank deposit."

"But that's a lie."

"It is and it isn't. It seems he slipped over to the ATM right before we saw him. And he has a deposit slip to prove it. " Sam looked at me knowingly. "For one hundred dollars."

I stared at him for a moment, then finally admitted, "I don't get it."

Sam pointed inside Crescent, at the line of people at the cash register. "Is your business really that bad? I don't make deposits under a thousand dollars. And I sure don't make them alone, in the middle of the night. I think your uncle came up to the Crescent window ready to spray the paint. Then he saw the camera, and he switched to Plan B. He went to the ATM and deposited what he had in his wallet."

"Yeah. Yeah, that makes sense to me." Sam started to walk off. I asked him, "So what happened with Hawg?"

Sam looked like he didn't want to talk about it, but he said, "The judge barred him from being within a hundred yards of me or my place of work, and that means within a hundred yards of the mall. They're putting an ankle bracelet on him in case he tries to come here. Basically, he's under house arrest. He can only go to school and back home until the trial."

"That's terrible."

"It could have been worse. Ray Lyons didn't want to let him out at all. He told the reporters he wanted to see Hawg in adult prison. 'So he can get what's coming to him.'"

"Oh, my god."

Sam looked back at the line at his register. "Listen, I have to get some work done. This has been driving me nuts. I can't let my business fall apart."

"Okay."

But Sam felt compelled to say one more thing. He added, "I'm going to try to see that justice gets done here, Roberta. I believe in justice."

I walked back to Arcane. Now I was more determined than ever to avoid Uncle Frank. That wasn't hard, since he stayed in the back for the rest of the night. Griffin was wrong about Hawg, though. He never showed up at the mall.

When nine o'clock finally drew near, I asked Kristin, "Can you cover for me tonight on the checklist?"

"Do you think that's a good idea? After the head lice business? My dad will be mad."

"I don't care."

Kristin looked at me, genuinely shocked. "Roberta, what has come over you?"

"Nothing. I just want to get out early tonight."

Kristin held up a can of lice spray. "Yeah, sure. Go for it."

I wound up back at Mrs. Weiss's condo, watching the Travel Channel with her. It was a program called *Europe's Capital Cities*. About ten minutes into it, Mrs. Weiss commented, "Those cities are still there, Roberta. Berlin, Vienna, Warsaw. Maybe you'll get to visit them."

"I hope so."

"You won't see many Jews, though. In that sense, Hitler succeeded. He set out to rid his society of us, and he pretty much did it."

After the program, Mrs. Weiss continued on this theme. "My mother and father found themselves in a society that didn't want them. I was eight years old, but it didn't want me, either. I had an aunt in New York, so they sent me with a one-way ticket to visit her. They had no intention of bringing me back.

"Letters started coming to my aunt — *Can you keep*

Isabel for a while? The Nazis are causing trouble. And then, *Can you keep Isabel for a while longer? We might be losing our business.* And finally, *Isabel has to stay there. We have no house now.* The bottom line was that I never saw them again."

"What happened to them?"

She muttered, "What happened? My father took the path that a lot of Jewish men in Germany took. He shot himself through the head."

I gasped. "Oh, my god."

She explained, "There was a government riot against Jewish shops called Krystallnacht, the Night of Broken Glass. It was November 9, 1938. They smashed the glass of Jewish-owned businesses all over Germany. That made my father sick to his soul. He never recovered. He shot himself a week later."

"What about your mother?"

"My mother was the stronger one. She would not give up. She wouldn't do the Nazis' dirty work for them." Mrs. Weiss looked up proudly for a moment, but then she started to cry. "The truth is, they never did kill her. They probably would have. Near the end they were killing every Jew they could get their hands on. A frenzy of murdering. But they didn't get to kill her."

I asked a stupid question. "Were you lonely without her?"

"*Pshht!* Lonely? I cried myself to sleep for five years. I dreamed of her nearly every night. All I had of my mother was her letters. Her letters and her recipes! She wrote out a favorite recipe, by hand, in each letter. When the recipes stopped coming, I knew."

"You knew she'd died?"

"Yes. I knew when it happened. I just knew it, inside me. It would be years before I found out how it happened."

Mrs. Weiss paused. I didn't know if she wanted to go on or not. I asked, "Do you want to tell me about it?"

She did. Mrs. Weiss leaned forward and whispered dramatically, with her eyes open wide, "A person is not really gone until everyone who knew them is gone. I got a letter one day, when I was still living in New York. Harry and I had just gotten married. A lady named Mrs. Freund said that she knew my mother."

Mrs. Weiss sat back and continued quietly, "This woman knew her at Bergen-Belsen, the camp where my mother died. She asked if she could meet with me and talk. Of course I said yes. We met in the city, at a restaurant. I was very surprised when I saw her. Mrs. Freund was about my age. She had been just a little girl in the camp, like I would have been. And she survived.

"She was very gracious, very European. After a few pleasantries, she told me this: She said, 'Your mother did a brave thing. She had a friend in her cabin who got sick with the typhus. Your mother, instead of keeping away from her, nursed her day and night. The two of them died together, of typhus, while the guards watched and did nothing.'"

Suddenly Mrs. Weiss got to her feet. "Come with

me, Roberta." She clicked off the TV. "Enough television."

I followed her to our seats out on the balcony. She resumed her story. "It had been more than twelve years since I had seen my mother, and eight years since I had gotten her last letter. But when this Mrs. Freund told me that story, I felt like I had a mother again! Not only that, but I had a mother who was a hero. A woman who died in a death camp. Defying the Nazis. Helping others. She never gave up on life. And she never gave up being a good person.

"I carry that image of my mother with me to this day. That image has inspired my life. Roberta, I do not even have a real picture of my mother, and yet I carry such a vivid image of her in my heart. Still, to this day, when I have an important decision to make, I look inward, at that image, and ask, *What would my mother do?*"

Mrs. Weiss touched both hands to her heart. "Anyway, I heard Mrs. Freund's words, and I broke down crying, right there in that crowded restaurant. I was inconsolable for many minutes. I finally managed to say to her, 'I'm too late. I'm too late. I can never tell my mother what she means to me now.'" Mrs. Weiss opened her eyes wide again. "And do you know what she did? She put her hand on mine and said, 'Yes, you can. Why don't you write her a letter, today, and tell her how you feel?'

"Of course, I wrote the letter. That day. But I did more than that. I made Harry take me to Europe. We went all the way to the gate of that camp, that Bergen-

Belsen. And do you know what I did then? I left a memorial outside the gate of that horrible place."

"A memorial?"

"Yes. A letter, a bouquet of flowers, and a pack of her recipes, all neatly tied up. I left it there at the gate. I just laid them down and walked away. Wasn't that silly? I made Harry take me halfway around the world, and that's all I did."

"Did Harry think it was silly?"

"No."

"Neither do I."

Mrs. Weiss looked out over the dark swamp for a long time. Then she concluded, "I always thought that some passerby, some poor woman, picked up those recipes, took them home, and used them. Then she passed them on to her daughter, and that daughter is still using them now. That probably didn't happen. Some fat guard probably came along and tossed the whole thing in the trash. But I'd like to think that's what happened."

I told her, "I'd like to think that, too."

Mrs. Weiss leaned back to peer at the kitchen clock. "Eleven o'clock. What kind of mother lets her child stay up until eleven o'clock on a school night?"

"I stay up that late a lot."

"I'm sure you do." Mrs. Weiss got up, so I followed. We stopped at her bedroom door. She said, "So now you know my sad life story. I had no parents. Neither do you."

I started to speak, but she stopped me. "Roberta, life

is hard when you have no one to stick up for you. People push you around, purely because there's no one to stop them from pushing you around. That's just the way it is, and you're going to have to take it." Mrs. Weiss looked at me curiously, like she was about to share a secret. But she didn't. She just said, "For a while, anyway. For a while. Good night."

SATURDAY, THE 30TH ✺ I stayed in my old bedroom at Sawgrass Estates last night, over Mrs. Weiss's objections. Dad and I had Burger King after work, then he went out with Suzie. I read a news magazine and went to bed early. I wasn't afraid until then. I turned the kitchen, living room, and hall lights on before I got into bed. They were still on in the morning when I got up because Dad and Suzie hadn't come back.

There wasn't any milk, so I ate handfuls of dry cereal while I watched CNN. I left the house at ten-thirty, walking as fast as I could through the thick air. It looked and felt like a bad storm was building.

Ironman turned onto 111th Street almost in step with me. He actually said something. He said, "My mom must have left without me."

"Uh-huh," was the best I could manage. We walked quickly, in silence, sweating along through the morning heat and humidity. We made the turn onto Everglades Boulevard a few minutes later.

There was a lot of traffic whizzing by, more than

usual, and it seemed to be going faster than usual. I looked up at the Route 27 intersection. I saw a black pickup truck parked next to a white car. Off to the side, to the north of them, I saw a distinctive red T-shirt. It was Hawg.

As we got closer, I could make out the words ATLANTIC COUNTY JUVENILE JUSTICE written on the side of the car. A guy in a white shirt was talking to another man by the truck.

I asked Ironman, "Is that Hawg's stepfather?"

Ironman jerked his head up and down, up and down, in a sweaty nod. He smiled nervously.

"What are they doing there?"

"I don't know."

Hawg had positioned himself off to the right of the two men, about ten yards away from them. He clearly was not listening to their conversation. He seemed deep in his own thoughts. Ironman and I reached the intersection. The two men took no notice of us, but Hawg snapped his head back, smiled, and said loudly, "Hi, I. M. Hi, Roberta. Y'all on your way to Arcane?"

I answered, "Yes." But then I couldn't think of anything else to say. The scene was too confusing. Ironman and I just stood there, stuck in our spots.

I tried to tune in to the man in the white shirt. He was now pointing down toward Hawg's foot. I looked down, too, and saw a small, round device, like an oversize wristwatch. It was strapped around the sweat sock on Hawg's right ankle.

The man in the white shirt pointed to the traffic on

Route 27. He spoke in a flat, legal voice to Hawg's stepfather. "The boy's parameters end right here." He tried to include Hawg in the conversation. "This is the end of the earth for you, son. At least until we take off the monitor. If you attempt to cross Route Twenty-seven, an electronic signal will go off. If I am in the car, I will hear a loud buzzer."

The man opened his car door and leaned in. "It sounds like this." He pushed a button and turned up the volume until it made an earsplitting sound, like the sound of the banshees of hell from Vampire's Feast.

The man turned it off and explained, "If I am in my office, I will receive a signal on a beeper. I will dispatch a sheriff's deputy to come and get you immediately. Your probation period will then be over, and you will be locked up in a cell. Do you understand?"

Hawg still wasn't listening. He was again staring off, like a statue. Staring north, up Route 27.

The man turned back to the stepfather. "That's what the judge stipulated, sir. Your son is not to —"

"Stepson."

"Pardon me."

"My stepson. He's my ex-wife's boy."

"I see. Well, your stepson was released by the judge with the stipulation that he not go within one hundred yards of Mr. Samir Samad. That means the West End Mall is out of bounds. That means that this spot right here is the end of the earth for him. I hope he understands that."

Out of the corner of my eye, I saw the statue move.

Hawg had suddenly snapped out of his trance. He called over to me, in a clear and loud voice. "Hey, Roberta. Do you remember the power-I?"

I still didn't know what to say. Or do. He turned to Ironman. "How about you, I. M.? You remember how she goes?" He moved toward us, along the edge of the road, until he had formed the three of us into a loose triangle. He bent forward, his hands on his knees, and called out, "The center breaks the huddle." He slapped his hands, gave a little jump, and turned in the air. "He leads them up to the line." Hawg strode quickly to a spot exactly between Ironman and me. I suddenly became aware of the roar of the traffic. My heart started to rise up in my throat.

Hawg crouched down, in a football stance. He yelled out, "He sets. He snaps the ball. And he fires out!" I saw the whites of Hawg's eyes roll up as he sprinted forward, at full speed.

I opened my mouth and yelled, but I couldn't hear the sound. All I could hear was a horrible shrieking, like the banshees of hell, as Hawg tripped off the buzzer in the white car.

Hawg sprinted quickly across the northbound, outside lane, but a red car in the inside lane hit him with a sickening slap. The blow knocked him up into the air, all the way into the first southbound lane, in front of a black van. The van smacked him back in the other direction, twisting his body in a way that a human being cannot be twisted. The driver mashed on his brakes, swerved to the right, and skidded for twenty yards. All the cars around him swerved and braked and blared their horns, trying to avoid a pileup.

I watched Hawg's body fly through the air. But I knew, already, that he was no longer in it. I knew by the way he landed on his face and skidded across the asphalt, finally stopping with his backside stuck up in the air. It was undignified. It was nothing Hawg would have ever done. We all remained rooted in our spots. Finally, the Juvenile Justice guy stepped cautiously across the northbound lanes.

I looked over at Ironman. He was staring at Hawg's body. He had that awful grin on his face. The buzzer in the white car continued to blare its horrific sound. The traffic had now skidded to a halt in every direction.

The Juvenile Justice guy worked his way between two diagonal cars. He reached the bloody spot and looked down. He said something to the body. But, of course, he got no answer. He got no answer because Hawg was no longer in there.

OCTOBER

MONDAY, THE 2ND ✦ Mr. Herman was already in the guidance office this morning when I arrived. I could tell right away that he had heard the news about Hawg. He looked guilty. As soon as I got near him, he asked, "Did you hear about any funeral arrangements for that boy?"

I thought about making him use Hawg's name, but I didn't. I answered, "It was in the paper yesterday. In the obituary section. There's a service tonight at the Eternal Rest Chapel."

After that, Mr. Herman and I waited in silence for the morning announcements. Mr. Archer walked out of his office with some white index cards in his hand. He waved them at us and said, "I've got a few words to say. Wheel that camera into my office."

Mr. Archer sat behind the desk and looked into the camera lens. When he saw the red light, he started to speak. "Good morning, students." He glanced down at the white cards. "I want to say . . . we lost a fine young man in a tragic automobile accident on Saturday morning, right out on Route Twenty-seven. Hugh Mason. A fine young man. A member of the football team. A member of the journalism class."

I shot a look at Mr. Herman. He was staring down, with no expression.

"I ask you all to be extra-careful when you're walking and when you're driving around here. And I ask you to remember Hugh and his family in your prayers." He looked past the lens at me and said, "That's it. Run that first."

"Yes, sir." I rewound the tape and wheeled the tripod back to its spot. When the second bell rang, I inserted Mr. Archer's tape and played it through. Then I ejected it and popped in the Pledge and Banner tape.

I didn't see Mr. Herman again until fifth period. He just handed out worksheets from the *Journalism Today* textbook. He never looked up for the entire class. He appeared to be studying the *Atlantic Times*. In a way he was. I could see from my seat that he was reading the want ads.

The phone was ringing as I let myself in the kitchen door. I didn't want to answer it, but I thought it might be Dad calling about the funeral service. It wasn't. It was Mr. Lewis from Arcane, in Antioch, Illinois. He said, "Hello. Is Robert Ritter there?"

"Who's calling?"

He growled, "You know who this is."

"I'm afraid I can't give out any information."

There was a long pause. Then Mr. Lewis said, "Listen, miss. I need to speak to your father tonight. Not tomorrow, tonight. I will call back at eight P.M. eastern time. If he wishes to keep his franchise, he needs to be there to take that phone call. Understand?"

"He won't be here at eight. We have to go to a funeral."

"Right."

I held the phone out from me and looked at it. Then I asked him, "What do you mean, 'Right'?"

"It means I've heard enough lies from you, miss."

"It's not a lie."

"Look, I know what your father is doing. And your uncle, the colonel, too —"

I held the phone out again and yelled into it, "There is too a funeral!" Then I hung up on him.

I got to Arcane at four o'clock. I walked behind the counter and said, to no one in particular, "Are any of you going to Hawg's service?"

Kristin seemed insulted by the question. "Of course we are."

"Well, can I have a ride?"

"Of course you can."

Ironman was listening, but then he slunk away. I pinned on my name tag and followed him. I caught up with him next to Viking Raid. "Aren't you going?"

"No. I don't think so."

"You can get a ride with us."

"No. I'll get a ride with my mom if I go."

At seven-thirty, Uncle Frank came out of the back

and told us, "If any of you want to go to that funeral thing, you can go now. I'll close up."

We all hurried outside immediately and got into the banged up Volkswagen. Kristin asked Karl, "Do you think Dad's coming?"

"He told me he was."

"But the service is over at nine."

"He told me he was, that's all I know."

No one said anything else all the way to Seventy-second Street. We followed the cemetery road around, past the Jewish section, past the angel, past my mom's wall, until we saw a small building and a parking lot. The lot had a sign, CHAPEL PARKING, so we pulled in. A minute later the three of us walked into a room containing Hawg's body.

I don't know about the others, but I had never been to a funeral service. The only person I ever knew who died was my mom. I don't remember her having a viewing, but I suppose she did. I suppose I got left with a sitter. Anyway, I didn't know what to expect.

A few people were standing around in a small room about the size of my living room. Hawg's body was lying in a casket to the left, over against a wall. He had a harsh spotlight shining down on him. Nobody was anywhere near him until I wandered over to take a look.

I peered down at him quietly, like I was afraid he would wake up. Hawg's face had makeup on it to cover the scrapes and bruises from his skid across Route 27.

I heard a low commotion outside. Then Archie came in with about ten guys from the football team.

They were a mixed group of white guys and black guys. They all had big necks — big white necks and big black necks. They went straight up to Hawg's body, approaching the casket nervously, reverently. Archie knelt down and prayed, so the others bowed their heads and prayed with him.

I kept my distance, but I stayed close enough to hear what they were saying. It was football talk, stuff Hawg used to say, like, "Yeah, he'd put a hurtin' on you."

One guy asked them all, "What's that thing he said? 'Whompin' on ya.' He'd start to whompin' on ya." The others remembered that and smiled.

I spotted Sam as he entered the room. He turned to the right and stood in a short line of people who were waiting to meet Hawg's stepfather. I went over and did the same.

I had only seen Hawg's stepfather that one time — last Saturday, standing out on the highway median strip. I got a closer look at him now. He looked like a regular guy, like a guy who'd come and fix your air conditioner. He certainly didn't look a thing like Hawg. But then again, they were not really related.

When the people in front of us moved on, Sam and I approached him. He asked Sam, "Are you Mr. Samad?"

Sam answered with something peculiar. "No, sir. I am here representing Mr. Samad. Mr. Samad is my father."

Hawg's stepfather looked confused. He muttered, "I see. Well, all right."

Sam walked over to join Karl and Kristin by the casket wall. I found myself in a group with two new arrivals, Mr. Archer and Mrs. Biddulph.

Mrs. Biddulph said, "Our sincere condolences to you and your wife, sir."

Hawg's stepfather looked confused again. He said, "Well, my wife's at home with her two girls. She didn't want them comin', them being so young and all."

Mrs. Biddulph agreed. "No. Of course not."

"And his real mama, well, there ain't much chance of her showin' up. Not as destitute as she is."

"I see." Mrs. Biddulph looked really sorry she had brought up the topic.

Hawg's stepfather explained to Mr. Archer and Mrs. Biddulph, "His mama's still up in Georgia. We were only married for two years. She'd already had him back when she was sixteen. But she got so messed up on the drugs and the liquor that I finally had to kick her out of the house, for everybody's sake. No way we could go on like that. I let her boy stay behind with me. He wasn't even mine, you understand, but I let him stay. He was a sure sight better off with me than with her."

Mr. Archer and Mrs. Biddulph had stopped nodding. Now they were just staring at him. He summed up: "I guess we have to accept that it was God's will. We don't always understand it, but we have to accept it."

Mr. Archer asked, "Where is Hugh to be buried?"

"Georgia, sir. Up in west Georgia, where he came from."

Mr. Archer's big face expressed surprise. He said,

"Well, we were planning on attending the funeral. A delegation of us. Mrs. Biddulph and me and some student leaders."

Hawg's stepfather told them, "Well, sir. Here's what happened. I got a call yesterday from the man at the funeral parlor here. He said they had a benefactor who was gonna pay for the boy to go back home to Georgia, if it was all the same to me. I said it was. I don't have the money to do that myself. His mama certainly don't. And his real father ain't about to show his face now, after all these years — even if he's still alive."

Mr. Archer looked amazed. "May I ask . . . Who is this benefactor?"

"He gave the name of some Arab gentleman, a Mr. Samad. He said that this Mr. Samad wanted to take care of the whole thing."

"Why?"

"Mr. Samad said it's 'cause the boy worked at that mall, out at Route Twenty-seven there."

"I see."

"So I said to the man, 'That's all right, so long as he gets a decent Christian burial. Don't want no Arab burial for him.' He said, 'No, it'd be a Christian burial.'"

Mr. Archer nodded cautiously.

As soon as I could get away, I joined the others by the wall. Kristin was telling Karl, like he was a little kid, "Do you see what Roberta just did? That's the right thing to do. We have to go talk to that man."

Karl looked sick at the prospect, but he said, "Okay," and followed Kristin toward Hawg's stepfather.

I was glad to get Sam alone so I could ask him about that "Arab gentleman" story. I said, "Is your father paying for Hawg's funeral? Up in Georgia?"

Sam swallowed hard. He spoke softly, "Yes, he is."

I looked over at Hawg's stepfather. "Is that why he asked if you were Mr. Samad?"

"That's right."

I didn't know what to say next. I tried, "Your father is very generous."

That made Sam smile, a sad smile. He said, "It's not easy getting money out of my old man. He makes my brother and me work for everything we have. But I told him what happened here, you know, over the past two months, and he insisted on doing this. To him, it was a matter of family honor."

"Why?"

"I accused a man falsely. I set events in motion, and he wound up dead. I'm responsible for that."

"You're not responsible for what Hawg did. He did that to himself."

"No. But I'm responsible for what I did. I accused him, and I was wrong." Sam struggled with the explanation. "I accused him because I had stereotyped him. To me he was a dumb, prejudiced redneck. I assumed that he had stereotyped me, too — because of the color of my skin, because of the sound of my name."

Sam hung his head down. "So tell me, Roberta, who was the prejudiced one?" He walked slowly over to the casket, so I turned back toward Hawg's stepfather.

Kristin and Karl were standing with him in a circle

formed by Mr. Archer and Mrs. Biddulph. I'm sure they had no idea who Mr. Archer and Mrs. Biddulph were. I watched Kristin's eyes drift toward the door. Then I watched them grow wide.

Uncle Frank had appeared in the doorway. And Uncle Frank was drunk. He was standing with a funeral home guy, following the direction of the guy's pointing finger. He started toward Kristin and Karl, walking with a rolling gait, like a sailor on a ship.

Kristin and Karl backed away instinctively as he approached. But Uncle Frank didn't address either of them. He pulled himself upright before Hawg's stepfather and said, "We're truly sorry about your loss."

Hawg's stepfather answered, "Thank you, sir."

"I am, uh, Frank Ritter. Your son worked with us at Arcane."

"My stepson."

"Yes." Uncle Frank and the man stared at each other for a moment. Then Uncle Frank asked, "So have the arrangements all been made?"

"Yes, sir. The boy's going up to Georgia tomorrow."

Uncle Frank repeated, "Georgia." Then he told him, "I lived in Georgia. Up above Atlanta."

Hawg's father said, "Uh-huh."

Mr. Archer and Mrs. Biddulph peeled away from the group. I watched them walk directly to the door and leave.

After another awkward pause Uncle Frank said, "Atlanta. Good hunting up there."

"Yes, sir. There sure is."

"I hunted some boar up there, I remember." Suddenly he started to laugh. Everyone in the room became aware of him then. "Let me tell you something about hunting boar down here in Florida. First of all, there's no such thing."

Hawg's stepfather kept looking at him, respectfully but with growing discomfort.

Uncle Frank smiled wide. "I went up to this boar farm up near Lake Okachobee, Florida. You know what the hunting was like up there? It was like shooting somebody's pet. It was like I took you into my backyard and said, 'There's my dog. See if you can pump a few rounds into him.' In fact, it was worse than that. They drive you out to this blind. You don't even walk, they drive you. Then they pull a chain, and all these ears of corn come plopping down onto the ground, and the boars come trotting up for their breakfast, you know. Like friggin' Lassie. And you're supposed to shoot one, like you're the great white hunter. It's not even hunting. It's the hunting 'experience.' And you're guaranteed a kill or your money back. You're guaranteed to bring home the bacon."

Hawg's stepfather quickly scanned the room for an escape route, for someone else to talk to. But Uncle Frank wasn't finished with him. He stood as erect as he could and said, "You know, I fought in Desert Storm. But I never killed anybody. Most soldiers don't. They go through a twenty-year career, and they never kill anybody. I never did."

Hawg's stepfather answered him nervously, "Yes, sir."

Uncle Frank's horrible smile spread farther. He said very seriously, "You don't have to call me 'sir.'"

Hawg's stepfather said, "Excuse me. I got some new people to greet." He moved swiftly toward the door.

Uncle Frank turned to Kristin and Karl. Kristin whispered, "We have to get you home, Daddy."

Karl wound up driving me home in the Volkswagen. He drove like a maniac — even though he was driving illegally after dark on a restricted license, even though he was already in trouble with the law. I don't know what it takes to reach some people.

I got out of the car in my driveway and hopped out of Karl's path, just in case he tried to run me over in reverse. Dad's car was parked in the carport.

I let myself into the kitchen. Dad was seated at the table looking at a wide, colorful brochure from Sea Ray Boats. He said, "Hey, Roberta."

I asked him, "Why didn't you go to Hawg's viewing?"

"Oh, honey. I'm going to go. I'm going to go to the funeral, instead."

"Well, then, you're going to go to Georgia."

"What?"

"The funeral is going to be in Georgia."

"You're kidding me. I figured it'd be local. I figured I'd go there tomorrow and pay my respects."

"No. Sorry. You're going to have to think of some other way to pay your respects."

He looked at me sheepishly.

I added, "By the way, Mr. Lewis called from Arcane Industries."

Dad pointed at the answering machine. "Yeah, I know. He left another message at eight. I already erased it."

"You didn't talk to him?"

Dad looked surprised. "No."

"He said you had to talk to him tonight, or we'd lose our franchise."

Dad smiled. Then he chuckled softly. He said, "Come on, Roberta. You don't believe everything that people tell you, do you?"

SATURDAY, THE 7TH ⌘ I was late leaving for work today because of a morning thunderstorm. Huge black clouds rose up out of the Everglades, crackling with lightning bolts. The rain pounded deafeningly on the carport and on the roof of the house. The lightning flashed and the thunder boomed, rattling the windows. It went on like that for thirty minutes, a storm like the end of the world.

When it finally stopped, I walked outside. The floodwaters were already receding from the street. Steam began to rise from the black asphalt as I hurried along through the clean, wet air.

As I turned onto Everglades Boulevard I spotted Ironman up ahead of me. He was already at Route 27. I squinted and tried to focus on him. It seemed like an optical illusion, seen through the watery layers of air, but it looked like he was kneeling down. I was still a hundred yards away from him when he got up and scurried across the highway. I could see that he had left something behind him. And I could see what it was — a white cross.

As I got closer, I could see it more clearly. The cross was made from two pieces of white Styrofoam, the sturdy packing kind that comes in UPS cartons. A one-foot piece was glued across a three-foot piece, forming the cross. The bottom part of the long piece was stuck deep into the muddy ground.

I looked around me and studied the spot. As I did I heard again the murderous rushing of the northbound cars, and I realized where Ironman had set his cross. It was on the spot where Hawg had spoken his last words to us, the spot where Hawg had begun his last desperate run.

I touched the top of the cross lightly with my fingertips. I swallowed hard. I felt something welling up in me, welling all the way to my eyes. They filled quickly with tears that overflowed and ran down my cheeks. I looked around again, embarrassed, wondering if anyone had seen me.

The light changed and I ran across, fixing my gaze on the Toby the Turtle banner in the distance. I ran all the way to the mall entrance, stopping at the front door to wipe my fingers across my cheeks. They were still wet. I was still crying. I veered off quickly and walked along the wall, breathing in and out of my mouth, deeply and slowly. I thought about Griffin, and Ray

Lyons, and Angela, and anything else that might distract me. After about five minutes I wiped my cheeks again. They were dry. I had stopped.

I went directly to Arcane. Kristin and Karl were standing behind the register. They looked sad, like two little kids who'd been put in time-out. I stood next to them and affixed my name tag.

Kristin said, "My dad's not here. He wasn't feeling well enough to come in."

I said, "It's not the chicken pox, is it?"

"No. He has a headache. He'll be back tomorrow."

A minute later Karl asked me, "Do you remember your aunt Ingrid?"

Kristin reminded him, "She's never met her."

I looked from one to the other. "Why? What's going on?"

Karl raised his eyebrows. "She's coming."

Kristin added, "We don't have all the details yet."

I said, "That's great. Then I will get to meet her. Finally."

Kristin smiled brightly. "Yeah."

Karl, Kristin, and I ran the arcade all day. Ironman helped out a little, but not much. Ten minutes before closing time Kristin gathered our drink cups into a Taco Stop bag and carried it into the back room. The bag was still sitting there at nine-fifteen, which was unusual.

Kristin remarked to me, a little annoyed, "Why is this bag still here? Doesn't that guy live to take out the trash?"

"Ironman? Yeah. Usually."

Kristin said, "And Karl is gone. Well, forget it. It can stay here until tomorrow."

"Karl is gone?"

"Yeah. We brought both cars today."

"I guess Ironman left, too."

"Maybe he left with his mother. She's been closing early."

When we finished with Kristin's shortened version of the checklist, we walked out into the muggy night. Kristin had parked the Mercedes in the north parking lot, outside the empty anchor store. All the way to the car, though, I found myself looking east, troubled by some thought.

I tried to find the spot where Hawg had died. Then I squinted at the grass beyond that, and I could just make out, in the passing glow of headlights, the shape of a white cross. For some reason, I stopped walking.

I became fixated on that white cross. The harder I looked, the closer it seemed to get, like I was slowly turning a zoom lens. Suddenly a shiver went right through me, and my blood turned cold. An awful picture came to me, clear and distinct. Like a vivid dream. But I knew, without a doubt, that it was real.

I turned and screamed, "Kristin! Come on, follow me!"

She looked at me, puzzled. "What?"

"Come on!" I took off running around the perimeter of the north anchor store. I heard Kristin yell behind me, "Roberta! I can't run in these shoes!"

I yelled back, "Kick them off!"

"Where are we going?"

"The trash trailer. I know where Ironman is!"

Kristin did kick off her shoes. She can run faster than anybody when she wants to, and now she wanted to. She rounded the corner of the empty store and sprinted ahead of me like I was standing still. She reached the trash trailer, grabbed the handle, and yanked it open. I got there in time to see the look of horror on her face.

"Oh, my god, Roberta! He's dead!"

Kristin stood, trapped in the doorway by the sight before her. I pushed past her and looked, too. Ironman was seated with his back against the wall. He was an inhuman color — blue, like a fresh bruise. I insisted, "We don't know that he's dead. It takes a long time to freeze to death."

"He's dead. Look at him. People don't look like that."

"We have to get him out of here."

"I'm not going to touch him. I'm sorry, Roberta. I can't."

"I can." I shoved her aside and stepped up to Ironman. I grabbed his body by his two shoulders and pulled him toward me. His shoulders were cold and slippery, and I lost my grip. He slumped over sideways onto his face.

I yanked on him until he was back up in a sitting position. I got a better grip under his armpits and started to pull. Then I felt Kristin's arm in between mine. She grabbed hold of his shirt, in the middle of his back, and pulled, too. We dragged him steadily toward the door. Kristin stumbled outside and landed, sitting, on the blacktop. I heaved one more time, and Ironman's body slid out, landing on the ground next to her.

I yelled, "What do we do?"

"Get help."

I looked around, thinking, *Should I scream?* I ran to the door of SpecialTees and pounded on it, but no one answered. So I took off running again, back the way we came.

I rounded the north anchor corner and saw Verna's car moving slowly up a row in the parking lot. I tried to scream at her, but I was out of breath. I tried to run toward her, too, but by then I was only lurching along, waving my arms.

Verna drove all the way down the end of one row, turned, and came back up. She clicked her high beams on me, so I finally stopped. She accelerated to my spot, rolled down the window, and yelled, "Roberta? Is that you?"

I stammered at her, "Ironman — the trash trailer."

"Who?"

"Mrs. Royce's son. The owner of SpecialTees."

"What about him?"

"We think he froze to death. We pulled him out. He might not be dead."

Verna told me slowly, with authority, "You calm down. Don't panic." She called 911, identified herself, and gave them a special security code. She told them to send an ambulance to the back of the West End Mall for "a possible freezer death." She hung up and said, "They're on their way. Come on, hop in."

I ran around and got in the passenger side. Verna looked up something in a notebook as we started rolling. She punched in another number. "I'm calling that Royce woman at home. I know she's there. She doesn't even wait until nine to close anymore."

She held up a finger to indicate she had an answer. "Mrs. Royce, this is Verna from mall security." She listened for a second. "It's Verna, the security guard at the mall. The West End Mall." She listened for a few seconds longer this time. "This is Verna, from mall security. I know you understand that much. Now understand this: You need to get back here. Your son has been in an accident, and an ambulance is on the way."

Verna listened to a reply. "Then you need to pack up your daughter and bring her with you." She paused very briefly. "No. Right now. That's all you need to know."

Verna pressed a button and disconnected the call. Now I could see Kristin and Ironman in the headlights. We braked to a halt by the back door of SpecialTees and ran out to them.

Kristin was sitting up, right where I had left her. But Ironman had moved. Or he had been moved. Kristin had pulled him over to her and was cradling him like a baby. She had her right hand on his heart. She had her mouth inside the back of his shirt, blowing warm air down his spinal column.

Verna asked her, "Is he breathing?"

Kristin looked up. Her eyes sparkled like I had never seen them before, like I had never seen anyone's before. She whispered, "His heart is beating, I can feel it."

An Atlantic County Medical Center ambulance pulled up with its lights flashing. Three people got out — a muscular woman with short red hair, a tall, skinny girl, and an older guy.

The woman with the red hair took charge. She pointed at the trash trailer and hollered over to Verna, "What is this contraption? A Deepfreeze?"

Verna said, "Yes, ma'am."

"How cold does it get in there?"

I said, "It maintains a steady temperature of twenty-nine degrees Fahrenheit."

The woman turned to me. "Did he get stuck in there?"

I didn't know how to answer that one. Kristin spoke up. "Yes, ma'am."

The woman leaned over Ironman and examined him quickly. She said, to no one in particular, "How long was he in there?"

I stammered, "I — I don't know." I asked Kristin, "When's the last time we saw him?"

"It was before seven-thirty."

The woman looked back at me and waited, but I had nothing to add. "So he could have been in there for two hours?"

"Yes, ma'am."

She started to bark orders at the other two. Kristin finally let go of Ironman's body as the three paramedics flew into action. Ironman wound up strapped to a stretcher inside the ambulance, hooked up to a monitor with a green screen.

Mrs. Royce squealed up in her Ford Escort wagon. She parked next to Verna and got out. Verna called over, "Your boy got caught in the freezer. They're taking him to the hospital for observation."

Mrs. Royce sputtered, "I have to get Dolly back home. She has allergy-induced asthma. She can't be out in the night air." She walked over to the back of the ambulance and peered in. "William, how do you feel?"

Ironman opened his eyes and grinned weakly.

Mrs. Royce told Verna, "Let me get him home. I'll observe him at home."

Verna's voice hardened. "No, ma'am. They are taking him to the hospital."

Mrs. Royce whispered, "We don't have insurance. I will take him to the hospital if he needs to go. He seems fine now." She told the paramedics, "This is a false alarm."

Verna blew up. "False alarm! I called in the alarm, and there was nothing false about it. You're paying for this ambulance, so you may as well let the boy ride in it."

The lead paramedic approached Mrs. Royce with a clipboard, but then she thought better of it and turned to Kristin. "What's his name?"

Kristin thought about that. She finally answered, "His name is William Royce."

"Will anyone be accompanying Mr. Royce to the hospital?"

Kristin answered without hesitation, "Yes, I will." She told me, "Roberta, you call my dad. All right? Tell him what happened, and tell him where I am."

The paramedic instructed her, "You can go ahead and get in the back." Kristin climbed aboard, sat on a bench, and took hold of Ironman's hand.

Mrs. Royce explained to the paramedic, "It's not that I don't want to go. My daughter has allergy-induced asthma. I have to get her back home."

The paramedic ignored that. She hopped up into the driver's seat, and the ambulance pulled away immediately. Mrs. Royce hurried back to her car and pulled away, too, but she went in the other direction.

Only Verna and I were left in the parking lot. I told her, "Thanks, Verna. Thanks a lot."

"Hey, no problem. Thanks to you, too. It's a good thing you were here. That boy would have been inside that thing until tomorrow morning."

I shivered and said, "Can you imagine finding him then?"

Verna told me, "It wouldn't have been my problem then. Tonight is my last night on the job."

"No! Why?"

"Because there ain't no more job. You guys are on your own now."

"Oh. I'm really sorry, Verna."

"Hey, ain't no thang. Don't worry about it. I'm not."

"What are you going to do?"

"Griffin told me there's plenty of jobs down at the County Services building. He said he would introduce me around. He said I could get into Juvenile Justice and make a lot more than I'm making here."

We walked back toward the car. Verna said, "Come on, Roberta. I'll give you a ride home."

"Are you allowed to do that?"

"No. But what are they going to do, fire me?"

I got back into the mall security car. Verna reached under the seat and fished out her cell phone again. She handed the phone to me. "Here."

"What's this for?"

"You're supposed to call your uncle Frank."

"Oh. Thanks." I dialed the number and put the small phone up to my ear. It was still ringing.

Then I heard a slurred voice. "Hello."

"Uncle Frank? It's Roberta."

"Who?"

"Roberta, Uncle Frank. Ironman got hurt. He went into the trash trailer, and he didn't come out."

"Who is this?"

I stared at the little phone, then I put my mouth up to it again. "Uncle Frank, it's me, Roberta." I looked over at Verna. She was looking straight ahead. I tried, "Uncle Frank, Kristin is going to be late. She rode to the hospital in the ambulance with Ironman."

"Kristin's in the hospital?"

"No, sir. She went to the hospital, but she's okay. She rode with Ironman so he wouldn't be alone."

In the background I heard him yell, "Karl! Come here! Take this. It's about Kristin."

Karl got on. He sounded like a frightened child. "Hello."

I felt a great sense of relief. "Karl, it's Roberta."

I could hear his relief, too. "Oh, hi, cuz."

"Listen: Ironman tried to freeze himself to death in the trash trailer, but Kristin and I pulled him out. Kristin rode with him to the hospital."

"Wow."

"They're okay, though. Kristin's okay, anyway. I think Ironman will be, too."

"Unbelievable. Why did she go with him?"

I didn't know. I said, "She saved his life. She made his heart beat again."

"Wow. So the plan was he was gonna just sit in there till he died?"

"I guess."

Suddenly I heard Uncle Frank again. "Karl! What's going on?"

Karl muttered quietly, "I gotta get off." He hung up.

We pulled into my driveway. I said, "I appreciate the ride, Verna."

"No problem, kid."

"I hope you like your new job."

"Thanks, Roberta."

Verna waited until I got safely inside. I saw one blinking light on the answering machine: "This is Detective John Griffin calling for Roberta Ritter. Please call or page me as soon as possible." I pressed the Erase button right down, thinking, *Why should I talk to you? To make you feel better about Hawg?*

It was so late that I decided to just grab a bag of Doritos and eat them in front of the TV. I switched the set on and moved up the dial until I found *The Last Judgment*. Tonight Stephen Cross was speaking to a studio audience composed mostly of parents. Here is what he said: "You know, the devil does not sit in his headquarters in hell. The devil is a better businessman than that. The devil long ago franchised his operation. Now the devil has branch offices in every city in America.

"Do you know where they are located? You may not. Or you might say, 'Times Square, New York.' But you would be wrong. You most likely could not name the devil's local branch office. But your teenage son or daughter could. Even if that son or daughter is a good, God-loving, Christian child, that son or daughter knows where to go. It is no secret among the young. The information is whispered among them during sleepover parties, and on three-way-dialing phone calls, and in on-line chat rooms."

This audience was not nearly as emotional as those prison guys, but they started to react. I heard a few *amens*. He continued, "We have made it very convenient for our children to go to the devil. We have provided them with cars to get there. We have provided them with money to buy drugs, the coin of the devil's realm. And worst of all, we have let them come to believe that the world of the devil is preferable to the world they live in."

Stephen Cross looked into the camera lens. "Ask yourselves now, and admit it to yourselves if it is true: Is there a young person in your life who would prefer living in hell over living with you?"

WEDNESDAY, THE IITH ~ When I arrived at the studio today, Mrs. Knight informed me, "You have a tour group coming through. They're from Lourdes Academy, so it'll be a nice group. We won't have to worry about them damaging anything."

I hung out in the lobby next to the video dubbing board. Soon the outside door opened and a group of about a dozen girls from Lourdes came in. They were dressed in the uniform that Kristin used to wear. It's a white blouse with the choice of either a maroon skirt, shorts, or slacks. A heavyset nun in a long gray dress was at the lead.

Mrs. Knight appeared and held out her hand, saying, "You must be Sister Ann." The nun admitted she was. She had a deep, flat voice.

I saw Nina right away. She was in the middle of the pack, talking to another girl. The girl looked familiar, too. Then I remembered where I had seen her — at the makeup counter at Bloomingdale's, getting her colors done. She was the one who stuffed.

Mrs. Knight did her introduction and then brought

the group over. Although I had spotted Nina, she apparently had not seen me. When she got close enough, I called over to her, "Hi, Nina."

Nina didn't actually look at me, but she muttered, "Hey, how's it going?"

The girl with her looked at me and made a face, like she had seen something weird. She asked Nina, "Who's that?"

Nina muttered, "That's some chick who works at the West End Mall."

"You're kidding. You shop at the West End Mall?"

"No! My dad has an office there."

It sounded like Nina wanted to drop the subject, but the girl kept on, "So she works for your dad?"

"No, she works at that virtual reality place they got there. Do you remember Kristin? The chick with the bad credit cards? She's Kristin's cousin."

The nun finally interrupted them. She said, "Nina. Lisette. Attention over here, please."

Lisette said, "Yes, Sister Ann."

But they both continued to banter.

Mrs. Knight gave her speech about the expensive equipment. Then she picked up the camera from the video dubbing board and trained it on Sister Ann. She said, "Come on, Sister. State your name and your school, and then make a brief comment."

Sister Ann growled, "A comment?"

Mrs. Knight pressed the button. "Yes. Anything. Anything at all."

"How about, 'Be quiet, Nina.'"

Mrs. Knight giggled. "No. No. Say something about you."

The nun faced the camera. "I'm Sister Ann. From Lourdes Academy."

Mrs. Knight said, "That's it. Now make a comment."

"And I hate this stuff."

Mrs. Knight laughed appreciatively. "Thank you." Then she turned her camera on Nina. Nina was ready. She made a little speech: "I'm Nina Navarro, and I want to have my own TV talk show, like my homegirl Angela del Fuego."

Mrs. Knight said, "Terrific! Thank you." She taped two more girls, then announced, "Okay. Let's start the studio part of the tour."

Nina asked her, "Will we meet Angela del Fuego?"

"Yes, if you like."

"We would like. And I'd like to get her autograph."

Mrs. Knight told her, "Oh, sorry. Angela doesn't do autographs."

Nina's face fell. "Oh no! Why?"

"She has those long nails. She does what she can to protect them."

Nina nodded sympathetically. "Oh yeah. I can see that. When are we going to meet her?"

"After the studio part of the tour."

Nina said to Lisette, "Cool. This is so cool." But Lisette did not seem at all interested.

I had an idea right after the group took off. I made a

copy of Sister Ann's segment and used it to splice in a new tape. I switched Nina's face and Sister Ann's voice. If you looked closely, you could see the blips, but it was still effective.

The Lourdes girls returned. Mrs. Knight arranged them around the video dubbing board for the replays of their tapes. I ran a generic one first, mixing one girl's face with another girl's voice, just so they could get the idea. Then I cued up my special project. Nina's face came up, but Sister Ann's voice came out of her mouth. In that deep growl, she proclaimed, "I'm Nina. And I stuff."

Everyone stared at the screen dumbfounded. Then Lisette started to laugh. In fact, she laughed so hard and so long that she nearly choked. The other girls all got the idea, and they started cracking up, too. Nina looked from me to the screen and back again. I smiled. Nina was shocked at first, but then she gave me the strangest look. It definitely wasn't anger. I think it was respect.

Mrs. Knight needed Sister Ann's help to finally regain order. Then she did her "So you see, seeing is not always believing" line.

Afterward, Mrs. Knight disappeared mysteriously for about thirty seconds. When she returned, she was with Angela del Fuego. Most of the girls regarded Angela with cool curiosity.

Nina once again changed moods with amazing speed. She was ecstatic.

Angela said, "Hello, girls. You are all girls, right?"

Mrs. Knight said, "Right."

"It's great to see you here. Can I answer any questions for anybody?"

None of the girls said anything. It was an awkward moment, but Nina soon rescued it. Her hand shot up, and she practically shouted at Angela, "You got the most beautiful smile."

Angela laughed. "Thanks. So do you."

"Oh, thank you. Are you Cuban?"

"No, sweetie. I'm from L.A."

"Your name, though. Is that Cuban?"

"I don't think so. I just made it up."

Nina was as excited as a little kid. "How could I get started, you know, being like you?"

Angela laughed, but with a trace of worry. She answered, "Well, you could go to Arizona State and major in communications, like I did."

"Then I could have my own show?"

"No. Then you could be a weather girl on a news show."

"Come on! No way! Angela del Fuego was a weather girl?"

"No. But Angela Martinez was — at KTUL in Tulsa, and at WJXX in Jacksonville. Then, one day, she decided she had done her last five-day forecast. She became Angela del Fuego. Now she has her own show, with over two million viewers across Florida and the Southeast."

Angela then turned to Mrs. Knight, who stepped in front of the group and announced, "Okay! We have one final stop on our tour that I know you're going to love!"

Angela made a quick exit as Mrs. Knight led the tour off to the video vault.

After she ushered the Lourdes group out of the building, Mrs. Knight came back and told me, "I'm meeting Mr. Herman down at Angela's dressing room. He's getting a makeover for his second audition."

"Oh yeah? What are they going to do?"

"Make him less shiny." Mrs. Knight winked at me. "I think that means he's going to grow some hair."

I knew Mrs. Knight hadn't come back just to chat with me. She quickly got to the point. "Roberta, I was thinking about your arcade at the West End Mall. Isn't that where those hate crimes happened?"

"Yes."

"Have they solved those?"

I thought about Uncle Frank's face in the dark mallway, but I answered, "No."

"Because I was thinking, maybe some of the kids there got too excited about the arcade games and crossed the line. You know — from virtual reality into reality? Is that possible?"

"I guess anything's possible."

"Do you have a lot of really freaky-looking kids there?"

"Yes."

"Hmm. I think there's a show in there somewhere. What do you think?"

"I don't know, Mrs. Knight."

"It could be good experience for you, too. You could prepare the guests with me."

"What's that?"

"Train them to answer clearly, to stay focused on the topic, to look at Angela. That sort of thing."

Mrs. Knight thumbed through her wallet. "Here, let me give you my card. It has my home and work numbers. You think about what I said, okay?"

Mrs. Knight took off, leaving me alone at the video dubbing board. I remained standing there for several minutes, thinking hard, because another idea was forming in my head. A plan. A plan that soon made me gasp out loud. A plan as simple and as stupid as my internship at Channel 57. I put Mrs. Knight's card in my wallet and left.

I got a burrito and a Coke from the Taco Stop and sat at a sticky table in the food court. After a couple of bites, Betty walked up with a smoothie and sat down. I figured that was a good sign, a sign of truce.

I asked her, "Are you at Candlewycke today?"

"Yeah. Have you heard of anything else?"

"No."

"Me neither. I heard Gepetto's is gonna close."

"Really? When did you hear that?"

"When I went in there for a job."

"Oh." I wondered if they were just trying to get rid of her. I told her, "I saw Nina today at the TV studio."

Betty took a swig of her smoothie. "She is one weird chick."

"How do you mean weird? Weird-looking?"

"No. She's great-looking. Guys follow her all around. She's weird-thinking, weird-acting."

"Like what? What does she do?"

Betty looked around to see if anyone was eavesdropping. "For one thing, she shoplifts. Did you know that?"

I played dumb. "No."

"Yeah. Be careful. Anything she gives you could be hot."

"But she has lots of money."

"I'm sure she does. She has lots of guys, too. But that doesn't stop her."

"God. Do you two hang out a lot?"

"No. She invites me out sometimes. She drives. She pays."

"Why? Why you?"

"I'm not sure. I think I make her feel normal."

We had an exceptionally slow night at Arcane. Kristin and I wound up closing by ourselves. Uncle Frank and Karl just took off. I asked Kristin where they were, and she jumped all over me. "Why shouldn't they take off early for once? They do all the work around here!"

I wasn't about to argue with her, although I do some work, too. We rushed through the closing checklist, then Kristin offered me a ride in the Volkswagen. The car didn't look as bad as before. The back had been hammered out pretty smoothly, though there were some spots with paint missing.

I didn't want to risk another flare-up, so I didn't mention Uncle Frank or Karl again. Instead I asked her, "How is Ironman?"

She said, "He's okay. He's evolving. We both are."

She didn't elaborate, so I followed up with, "He's not suicidal anymore?"

"Oh no. Not at all. In fact, he told me he never intended to kill himself. He just went into the trash trailer, like always, and sat down." Kristin turned into Sawgrass Estates. "And then he couldn't think of any reason to get back up."

We pulled in under the carport. Kristin added, "I felt the same way three weeks ago. I couldn't think of any reason to leave my room. Of course, my room wasn't twenty-nine degrees Fahrenheit. Have you ever felt that way?"

I told her, "No."

Kristin stared at the dark kitchen window. "Do you want me to walk in with you?"

"What for?"

"In case there's a bad guy in there. I'd kick his butt for you."

I looked at her with real affection. "I know you would. But there's nobody in there."

Kristin stopped smiling. "That's right. There's nobody in there. But there should be."

SATURDAY, THE 14TH ⭑⭓ The ringing telephone woke me up at nine. "Hello. This is Vicki at Sunshine Realty. Is your father there?"

"No, ma'am."

After a delay, she said, "I'm calling because your rent at 10021-111th Street is now two weeks overdue."

I didn't say anything. She asked me, "How old are you?"

"Sixteen."

"Can you take a message, then?"

"Yes, ma'am."

"Tell him he will have to pay the late fee, which is an additional fifty dollars, and it is due immediately. Thank you." The woman hung up.

Not five minutes later, Dad breezed in through the kitchen door. "Hey, honey. How's it going?"

"Dad, the lady called from the realtor's office. You have to pay a late fee on the rent. Fifty dollars."

"Don't worry about that. I'll take care of it. Hey, listen to this! We have our new apartment, and it's right on the beach. It's really cool. You will love it."

I didn't say anything, so he continued, "It's on the third floor, so it's safe. It's got a big parking lot, so we can park the boat and keep an eye on it from the balcony. Did I tell you it has a balcony?"

"I don't know."

"And remember, we'll be saving money every month. That's money we can spend on other things, like clothes for you. Like a car for you. Would you like that?"

I shrugged. "Yeah, I guess." I pulled out a Pop-Tart and started to eat it untoasted.

Dad didn't see or hear the shrug. "And wait till you see this boat we're getting! Forget the car, you'll be after me to borrow the boat. You can take a boat out by yourself when you're fifteen. Did you know that?"

I asked him, "Why would I want to take a boat out by myself?"

Dad continued talking. Nothing reached him. "Or you can take it out with me. Or with Suzie and me. It's an awesome experience. When you're out there in a boat, a mile out, two miles out, you're in your own world."

"So are you definitely buying a boat?"

"Yeah, we definitely are. We have it all picked out. It's my wedding present to her. And we're gonna name it after her, the *Suzie Q*."

I mashed the rest of the Pop-Tart into my mouth. Still chewing, I asked him, "Where's the money coming from?"

Dad smiled. "It's rent money. It's money that we're now throwing away on two rents." Dad reached over and took my hand. I hated how it felt, but I didn't pull away. "Honey, I know this is tough for you. I will never, ever, forget your mom. I knew your mom better than anyone on this earth. And I can tell you, without a doubt, that this is what she would want. She would want your life to get back to normal. A normal life, with a mother and a father, and a nice place near the beach. Healthy ocean air."

We both heard a knock at the back door. Dad didn't move to answer it, so neither did I. Then we heard Kristin's voice. "Roberta!"

Dad smiled. He got up and opened the door to Kristin and Ironman. "How are you doing?"

Kristin muttered, "Hello," and walked in.

Ironman followed. He didn't say anything, but he looked at Dad. Ever since that night in the trash trailer, Ironman has looked people in the eye.

The two of them sat in the living room with me.

Dad announced, "I'm gonna go in and crash. I'll see you all at work."

Kristin waited for him to leave. Then she started asking Ironman a series of personal hygiene questions. They've been doing this daily. To everyone's astonishment, they've developed quite a relationship in the past week. She asked him, "Did you floss?"

"Yeah."

"Did you brush with the whitening toothpaste and use the plaque rinse?"

"Yeah. Yeah."

Kristin ran her fingertips lightly over the fuzz growing back atop Ironman's head. She said to me, "Shaving his head was the best thing that ever happened to him. All that gross, greasy hair is gone. Now I'm working on his teeth. And his skin."

I noticed that Kristin had a touch of makeup on. She reached into a Marshall's bag and pulled out a red plaid shirt. She said, "Here, Will. Take this into the bathroom and try it on. I think it will look good on you."

Ironman took the shirt and walked dutifully into the bathroom.

I said, "Will?"

Kristin nodded. "Yes. I'm going to call him Will."

"Kristin! It's not like you found a dog. You can't just rename him."

"I'm not renaming him. William is his real name. Will is a diminutive of William. Like Kris is a diminutive of Kristin."

"I see. So what's my diminutive?"

"For Roberta? I don't know. Bobbi?"

"Yikes."

"Don't worry. You're not a Bobbi."

"Thanks."

"But that boy in there is not an Ironman, either. He's a Will."

"Okay. 'Will,' it is."

Kristin rummaged in the bag and pulled out an amazing array of beauty products.

I said, "God, Kristin, where did you get all this stuff?"

"Most of it came from Nina. Every time she'd come over, like, for a makeover, she'd bring about a hundred dollars' worth of makeup. And then she'd leave it all."

I thought, *Well, it didn't cost her anything.* But I didn't say it. I said, "Her father just hands her money."

"I know."

"Of course, so does yours."

Kristin looked embarrassed. "That was before."

Will came back wearing the shirt. Kristin reacted, "Wow! I knew you'd look great in that." She handed him a tube of gel. "Here, take this in and rub some on top of your head. You don't want your scalp getting too dry. We need to take care of those baby follicles coming up."

Will again did as he was told. As soon as he was gone, Kristin turned to me. "Oh yes, Roberta . . . Will told me something very interesting on the way over here."

I had a funny feeling. A nervous feeling. "Oh? What?"

"He said he was sitting in the guidance office at your school on the day Hawg got arrested."

Now I knew why I was feeling nervous. "Yeah?"

"Yeah. He said you were there, too. Is that right?"

"Right. I was."

"So you can tell me now yourself: Who arrested Hawg?"

"I'm not sure. Technically, I think it was Officer Dwyer."

Kristin focused a laserlike stare at me. "And who else?"

I said quietly, "The Head Louse."

"The Head Louse. Now, isn't that newsworthy? Isn't that the kind of interesting fact that a good reporter would pick up on?"

I admitted, "Yes."

"So why didn't you tell me? What's the big secret?"

"There's no secret." I volunteered, "His real name is Griffin. He's a detective."

"Why didn't you tell me who he was?"

I lied, "I didn't know. I didn't know until Hawg got arrested."

Kristin looked like she might not believe me. In a way I hoped she wouldn't. I was getting away with too many lies. I was getting too good at them. But she said, "So why didn't you tell me *after* that?"

"Because he made me swear I wouldn't. He said he might get killed, like in revenge. He's an undercover cop. He has people out for revenge against him all the time."

"So you were just being loyal to him?"

"Yes."

"Instead of being loyal to me? To your own family?"

I felt awful. I mumbled, "I'm really sorry, Kristin." And I really was.

The arcade was as quiet as a graveyard; so was the rest of the mall. I took a long dinner hour, which was more like two hours, and sat reading in the empty food court. Kristin, Will, and I had the closing checklist completed by five after nine.

As I was walking home across the near-empty parking lot, I became aware of a car following me. The driver accelerated, drew even, and shouted, "Roberta!"

I remembered my safety training; I kept walking. The car could contain a pervert who had, by chance, heard my name. But then I heard "Roberta!" again, and the voice sounded familiar. I turned and looked at the driver. It was Griffin. He was behind the wheel of a black Ford Taurus.

"I need to talk to you. It's about Hawg. Can I give you a ride to your house? Can we talk there?"

I felt a little creepy about that. I didn't want to see him in that carport again. But I decided, "Yeah, okay. I guess."

I got into the passenger side, and we started off. I didn't feel too good about my decision when Griffin remained silent all the way to 111th Street. He parked the car in the driveway, short of the carport, and we walked in through the kitchen door.

I sat down on the living room couch, but Griffin remained standing. He had a briefcase with him, a square black one with a brass combination lock. He set it down on the floor and started talking. "I tried to explain to you before that I'm just a part of a larger process. I'm not the judge; I'm not the jury. I'm just the cop they sent in and asked, 'Is there any evidence there?' I reported back, 'Yes, sir. There is some evidence.'"

He started to pace, his voice rising, "You know, if Hawg hadn't bolted across the road like that, everything would be okay now. That was a bad thing to do. It made him look guilty. Now everybody figures he *was* guilty."

Griffin fixed an angry stare at me. "This should have ended another way. I talked to Hawg for two hours at the station. He knew what the deal was. He knew he wasn't going to take the fall for something he didn't do. And that's the god's honest truth, Roberta. I wasn't going to let that happen."

He clenched both fists and glared at me. "Hawg knew that. I even made him repeat it back to me, word for word, so that *I* knew that *he* knew." Griffin paused. He sat down heavily on the couch. His eyes became moist, then he whispered, "So why did he do it? Why did he run out into that road?"

I knew why, and I told him, "He didn't care. He didn't care about any of that stuff you just said. He just didn't want to be here anymore."

Griffin didn't believe me. "What? He'd rather be dead?"

I didn't say anything else, which made him get agitated again. He hopped up and started pacing as before, shaking his head vehemently. "I didn't do this to him. He did it to himself. I didn't kill him."

I assured him, "Of course you didn't."

My response seemed to make him feel a little better, or calmer at least. He sat back down and opened that black briefcase. "Anyway, Roberta, I know you tried to help."

I interrupted him, "You asked me to help."

"Yes, I did. And you wound up doing a better surveillance than I did. I appreciate that, and I'm real sorry about what happened." He reached into the briefcase and pulled out a big brown envelope.

"I know what happened to your mother. I've heard your uncle and your cousin talk about it. I called down to a buddy of mine at the administrative offices. Sure enough, he was holding some stuff from that case that you're entitled to."

I stared at the envelope. It had the word EVIDENCE stamped on it in big red letters. I asked him, "What is that?"

"It's, uh, your property. Your family's property. Once

your case is classified as inactive, any property that we seized as evidence gets returned to you. Provided, of course, that it's not forensic evidence. You never know. We might get a break in this case someday, and we'll need the forensic evidence."

I began to feel frightened. I asked, "What is forensic evidence?"

Griffin shifted on the couch uncomfortably. "It's, uh, stuff we would have to produce in a court of law. A weapon, or an article of clothing with, uh, blood on it."

I stared hard at the envelope, wishing I had X-ray vision. "So what's in there?"

"It's personal effects of your mother's. Her wallet. Her checkbook. Some children's books. A watch. Some papers."

I reached out for the envelope, and he handed it to me. I weighed it in my hand. "And where did this come from?"

"The sheriff's administrative office, down at the County Services building."

"So how did you get it?"

"That buddy of mine back-doored it. I told him you were good for this signature." Griffin held out a paper to me. "You just get your dad to sign it, and I'll get it notarized." He stopped to explain, "Another buddy does that. Then I turn it in tomorrow. Okay?"

I felt stunned, but I said, "Okay." I breathed deeply a few times. Then I asked him, "Griffin . . . could I have gotten this package myself?"

"No. Only your dad could have."

"So why didn't he?"

He answered me very kindly. "A lot of people don't. There's nothing on this earth worse than the murder of a loved one. People want to close the door on that as soon as they can. I never would have opened this one up if I didn't know you, if I didn't think you would value these things. Am I right?"

I told him, "Oh yes. Yes."

I bent back the brad and opened the envelope. I reached in and pulled out two blue vinyl smocks — a small and a medium. I remembered them well. One was mine, and one was my mother's. Then I pulled out a wallet, a watch, a booklet for a prepaid college plan, and *How the Grinch Stole Christmas*.

Griffin pointed to it. "Tell me about the book."

I answered flatly, like I had told the story too many times, "Some days my mother would pick me up at the sitter or at extended-day. She'd always have a book with her. I'd hold the book on the way home. We'd read it when we got there."

"Was it always Dr. Seuss?"

"Between Mom and me it was. On my own I read older stuff. I started reading chapter books when I was five."

Griffin stared down at the floor for a moment. Then he clapped his hands on his knees and stood up. He said, "Well, I wanted you to have these things because you're entitled to them, but now I'd better get back to work." He walked through the kitchen and straight out. I hurried to lock the door behind him. Then I gathered up all the evidence, carried it into my room, and spread it out on the bed.

Mom had two pictures of me in her wallet, but no money. She had an old American Express card, an Atlantic County library card, and a Florida driver's license. The picture on the license resembled me a little. I read the information about the Florida Prepaid College Plan. I saw that Mom had circled the "lump-sum payment plan" description.

I thought the envelope was empty then, but I stuck my hand inside to make sure. It wasn't. I pulled out a small piece of paper, about the size of a dollar bill. It was very thin paper with a perforated edge, and it had the word RECEIPT printed across the top. Below that, seven years ago, a clerk had typed in: *Surveillance videotape — Family Arcade, October 31, Mary Ann Ritter, homicide investigation.* It was a receipt for a videotape. There was a receipt but no videotape. Griffin hadn't mentioned this.

I then turned my attention to the smocks. I tried my old one on, but it was nowhere near large enough. I couldn't fit both arms in at the same time. I tried my mom's on, and it fit perfectly.

I took it off and laid it down on the bed with the other long-lost possessions. I turned off the light and curled myself around them to sleep. But I had another dream: In the dream, I was in my room, in this room, asleep. I woke up when I heard the sound of the TV in the living room. It was blaring, impossibly loud, like the volume had been turned up all the way. There were no words to the noise, just static, like the sound from the void.

But I knew that if I went out to turn it off, I would be killed. I knew that there was a killer sitting in the living room, watching the blank screen, with the volume turned all the way up.

The dream was so real that I woke up still inside it. I found myself sitting bolt upright, listening for the TV sound. But there was only silence. Still, I was terrified, trapped between reality and the dream. I cowered in my bed, desperate for help. I tried calling out in a timid voice, "Dad." Then I tried it in a louder voice — "Dad" — never really expecting him to be there. But to my surprise, I heard a short knock on the door, and then Dad opened it.

"What is it, honey? What's wrong?"

"I — I had a dream. A nightmare."

"Oh. Oh no. Well, it's okay now. It wasn't real. Can I get you a drink of water? Or a soda?"

"No. No." I saw his eyes flicker to the evidence on my bed, but there was no sign of recognition. He didn't say anything about it. Instead he asked, "Do you want me to sit with you for a little bit?"

"No. No, I know you're here. So I'll be okay."

"That's right. I'm here. Don't you be afraid."

"Okay."

After he left I bound up all the evidence inside the two smocks. I stashed it all in the back of my closet, with my Dr. Seuss books.

But I put the videotape receipt in my wallet.

MONDAY, THE 16TH ✣ Dad came out while I was eating breakfast. He had on a bathing suit and a Marlins cap. He looked like he might be going out on a boat.

He said, "Good morning, Roberta."

I held out Griffin's form to him. I said, "Dad? Can you sign this before you go?"

"Sure. What is it?"

"It's for a field trip. We're going down to the County Services building."

He signed the evidence request form. "That should be an interesting trip. I'll see you at work, then."

My first stop after breakfast was Isabel's Hallmark. I told Mrs. Roman the same story I had told Dad — that I was going to the County Services building on a field trip. That much was true. Then I told her I needed to get the field-trip form notarized.

At that point Mrs. Weiss would have asked me, "Since when do you need to get a field-trip form notarized?" But Mrs. Roman didn't know any better. She dug out the box and put the raised seal on the form, just like I showed her. I took a pen and filled in the signature part while she returned the seal to the drawer.

She did ask me, "So why aren't you in school?"

I said, "I'm on my way. I just forgot to get this done last night."

Mrs. Roman was distracted, of course, since she was worried about running the store alone. She muttered, "Okay. I'll see you later," and walked off to straighten a display.

The County Services building was a sprawling red brick structure stuck in the middle of a gigantic traffic circle. I got off the bus in front of its main entrance.

I walked inside and over to a ceiling-high, glass-encased directory. There must have been a hundred office names in it, all spelled out in white rubber letters against a black background. I found a listing for the Atlantic County Sheriff's Department administrative office. It was in Room 102. I set out walking and did almost a complete lap around the first floor until I came to it.

Room 102 was big — as big as Crescent Electronics. A lot of people were sitting in different-colored plastic chairs. Most were busy writing on clipboards. I figured they were filling out job applications.

I saw a guy who looked familiar. It didn't hit me for a moment, but then it did. He was Hawg's Juvenile Justice guy. Maybe he'd had enough of that and was applying for a new job.

Beyond the rows of chairs was a high white counter. An older woman was working behind it with six people lined up in front of her. I got in line behind them and inched forward.

Just before I reached the front of the line, a younger

woman walked up, said something to the first lady, and then took her place. By now I had told so many lies that new ones were coming to me on their own. Like the Grinch in *How the Grinch Stole Christmas*, I thought up a lie, and I thought it up quick. As soon as the younger woman looked up at me, I said, "I was here before. That other lady told me to go get this form notarized and she would give me this package."

The lady took the receipt and the form and read them. "What kind of package is it?"

"It's personal belongings. It should be a small package with this number on it."

The lady read the ID number. "Okay. Somebody's going to have to go back and find this." She looked around but didn't see anyone who might be inclined to help her. Seeing that there was no one in line behind me, she said, "I think I know where they keep these. Let me take a quick look."

She was gone for about five minutes. One of the job applicants got in line behind me. The lady came walking out of the back section of the big room. As soon as I saw the package, I knew what was in it. So did she. She squeezed it as she handed it to me and said, "It feels like a videotape. Is that right?"

My heart started to pound wildly. All I could do was nod vigorously. I practically snatched it away from her, muttering a low, "Thank you." Then I walked quickly out of the sheriff's department administrative office, like I had just robbed the place.

I couldn't read on the bus ride home; I couldn't

even think. I stashed the evidence package in my backpack and stared out the blue windows.

A storm was gathering in the west. As soon as I got to my stop, it began thundering and lightning and pouring. I had to jump off the bus and run. By the time I reached the carport, I was soaked to the skin. I unlocked the door and squished through the kitchen and living room. Then I peeled off all my clothes and wrapped myself in a towel.

I put on a pair of long pajamas, went out to the kitchen, and made some hot cocoa. The red light on the answering machine was blinking. I waited until the cocoa was ready. Then I clutched it in my shivering fingers as I listened to the message.

It was actually a prerecorded announcement from Mrs. Biddulph. "This is Linda Biddulph at Memorial High School. I am calling to inform you that your child is not in school today. Please furnish your child with a note explaining this absence so that it will not be marked as unexcused."

I drank the hot cocoa down as fast as I could. It made me shiver. Then I spotted my wet backpack, and I remembered what was inside it.

I zippered it open and pulled out the videotape. I carried it into the living room and set it on the coffee table. But I didn't put the tape into the VCR. I couldn't. I just sat on the couch and stared at it.

I was still sitting there at noon when the phone rang. This time it was Dad. "Roberta! You're home. Are you okay?"

"Yes."

"I got paged today by a Mrs. Biddulph from your high school. She said you weren't in school."

"No. I'm not, Dad. I cut."

"You what?"

"I cut school. I ditched. I didn't go."

Dad seemed confused. "Oh?"

"You used to do that. Right, Dad?"

"Well, yeah, actually. The truth is, I did, honey. But I never knew that you did."

"Well, I do."

"So where did you go?"

"The beach."

"Yeah? That's where I used to go. So, uh, I guess I'll see you at work?"

"No, I think I'm going to cut that, too. Okay?" He didn't answer. I added, "You won't tell Uncle Frank, will you?"

"No. No, of course not."

"Okay, then, maybe I'll see you later."

"Okay." Dad hung up.

I continued to stare at the videotape for about another hour. Then I carried it into the bedroom and stuck it in the back of my closet, next to the rest of the evidence.

SATURDAY, THE 21ST ᜡ I have now possessed the videotape for five days. For five days it has been in the back corner of my closet, radiating at me like a chunk of plutonium. At times I had the opportunity to watch it but not the courage. Other times I had the courage but not the opportunity.

Dad came out and had breakfast with me this morning. I took the opportunity to inform him, "I've been moving my things into Mrs. Weiss's condo, over in Century Towers."

"Oh?"

"Yeah. I don't like being here alone. I've been feeling creepy."

Dad nodded knowingly. "Have you had more nightmares?" He shook his head in regret. "Roberta, I'm sorry. I know I've been away too much. It's just that Suzie and me, you know, we're moving into a new phase of our lives. And you're moving with us. We all just need to hang in there until the first of the month. That's when we'll be at our new place."

I waited for a minute. Then I told him, "But I've been thinking about that, too. I think it would be easier for me if I had my stuff at Century Towers. That way I could walk to the mall."

"The mall? But I was thinking that you and I could have the same schedule. We could drive together."

"That wouldn't always work. Anyway, another thing, a bigger thing, is this: If I move out of the school district, I have to go to another school."

Dad looked like he had never even thought about that. "They wouldn't just let you stay there and graduate? You know, since you've been there all along, they wouldn't just let you graduate with your class?"

"No. If we moved from this district, I'd be out. That day."

"Well, okay then, but what if you wound up at a better school? You know, a better place to get ready for college?"

"Dad, I'm fine where I am. I don't want to start all over at a new school."

"No. I can understand that." Dad thought out loud, "Yeah. And that way you could have two places. You could have your real room at home, and you could have a pretend home at Century Towers. I like that. I think that's a good plan."

I did, too, but I had my doubts about which would be my "real" home.

Mrs. Weiss was not in the card store at opening time. She called me at Arcane, though, to claim that she was not really sick. She said, "This is just a test, Roberta. I want to see if Millie can handle a Saturday by herself. Check in on her, will you?"

So I took a ten-minute break to watch Mrs. Roman wait on customers. When I got there she was ringing up a sale for a young black guy. She gave him change and thanked him, but he didn't say anything back.

He walked out, and Mrs. Roman rolled her eyes at me. She said, "Did you see that, Roberta?"

"See what?"

"How that young man was dressed?"

"Yes."

She shook her head. "It used to be, if you were walking around with your underwear sticking out, you'd want someone to tell you. Now they get all offended."

I tried not to laugh. I asked her, "So how are you holding up?"

"I'm fine; it's Isabel I'm worried about. She says she's fine. Then, in the next breath, she says the doctor wants to send her for tests. All I have to hear is the word 'tests' and I worry. I went in with my Joe for tests, and he never came out. Did I tell you what those doctors did?"

I only had ten minutes. I said, "Please, Mrs. Roman. Not the enema story. Not now."

She looked at me with hurt in her eyes. "What? You don't want me to talk? I won't talk."

"No. It's just that I have a lot to do today."

"Oh? And I don't? God forbid you should have to go through what I went through in that hospital."

"I'm sorry, Mrs. Roman. I didn't mean it like that." She sulked in silence for a minute, adjusting the register tape, until Leo walked in. Then she perked up.

Leo was carrying a rolled-up parcel, like a wall poster. He said, "I got that architect's plans here."

Mrs. Roman smiled. "I'll tell Isabel when she calls. I know she wants to see them."

I had been gone longer than ten minutes, so I left them to themselves and went back to Arcane.

Sam stopped by at around four o'clock. He stood by

the Sony monitor, beckoning me to come out. As soon as I joined him, he broke into a you're-not-going-to-believe-this smile. "Guess who just stopped by?"

"Who?"

"Philip Knowlton. And he wasn't alone. He had a TV crew with him."

"Lucky you."

"Oh yeah. I was standing there with a customer. He walked right up and said, 'We want you to thank Mr. Lyons for what he did for you.'

"I said, 'Wait a minute, what did he do for me?'

"He said, 'You know, he stood up for you when you were getting attacked by those hate groups. Here's what we want you to say.' And this sound guy actually held up a cue card for me to read. I started cracking up."

"What was on the cue card?"

Sam was just tickled. He had to compose himself. "Hold on. Let me think a minute. All right, here it is —" Sam switched into the voice of a TV pitchman. "When I was targeted by hate groups as a minority business owner, Ray Lyons heard about it, and he got involved. Thank you, Ray Lyons."

I laughed along with him. "So what did you say?"

"I told him to get lost."

I must have looked doubtful, because he added, "Okay, so I told him nicely. I said, 'Tell you what — I'll thank Mr. Lyons when he announces the recap. Okay?' So he got mad and left."

I loved that. And I wanted to keep talking, but Sam

looked into Arcane and said, "Heads up, Roberta. You got a customer."

I turned and saw a teenage boy at the counter. He was looking all around and holding a ten-dollar bill. "Oh. Okay."

Sam said, "I'll let you go," and took off.

I had a late dinner with Mrs. Weiss. She made tuna fish and applesauce sandwiches on toast. She looked pale, but she sounded like her old self. After dinner we sat out on the balcony with glasses of iced tea.

I said, "Where's Mrs. Roman tonight?"

"Poor thing. She's exhausted. She's had to learn the card business practically overnight."

"How's she doing?"

"You tell me."

I thought of the young black guy. I said, "She's very helpful to her customers."

"That's good. That's hard to find nowadays." Mrs. Weiss gazed out over the Everglades. "Millie is a good soul. She just talks too much for my liking. Do you know, she never worked a day in her life. Not until this."

"That's unbelievable."

Mrs. Weiss rested her hand on top of mine. "Not everybody grows up with a full-time job, Roberta. For someone like Millie, that sort of thing was unimaginable. She grew up in a nice family. Then she married her sweetheart. She had a boy and a girl. Nothing bad ever happened to her until she was old.

"You and me, though, Roberta, we're the opposite. All the bad stuff happened to us when we were young. What worse thing could happen to me after the Nazis? Huh? After a father's suicide, after a mother's death, what am I going to get devastated about? That some loverboy doesn't have the hots for me? Bah!"

I added, "We both lost a mother."

"Yes. And I wouldn't count that father of yours, either. You are basically alone, Roberta. Some children have to raise themselves. I had to. So do you."

I asked her, "How did you raise your child?"

"We raised her to have an easy life. Harry and I both doted on her. She never had a job, except some on-campus thing at college, in the registrar's office. She got married right out of college. She married a man who I did not care for. Fifteen years her senior. A heart surgeon. Divorced. Not Jewish. She never worked again.

"Suddenly she didn't need our money; she didn't need our advice; she didn't need our anything. We went in different directions. Sometimes that's best. I haven't heard from her since Harry's funeral."

"She came down for that?"

Mrs. Weiss looked at me oddly. "Oh, right. Of course, dear." She got up to go to the kitchen. When she returned, she had Ritz crackers and some Velveeta.

I made up my mind, and then I said, "Mrs. Weiss, I met an undercover cop. He knows something about my mother's murder."

Mrs. Weiss seemed to freeze. "Who is this? Do I know him?"

"I'm sure you've seen him. He's been at Arcane a lot, working undercover."

"Squat body? Looks like a little fireplug?"

"Yes. A little."

Mrs. Weiss held up the knife triumphantly. "I knew that one did not belong. He looked out of place." But then her face got a worried look. "So what did he tell you?"

"He told me that we were entitled to some evidence. Some things that belonged to my mom."

"Okay. So did you get this evidence from him?"

"Yes."

"And what was it?"

"Some books and clothes. Some good stuff."

She knew that wasn't all. She added, "And some not-so-good stuff."

"Yes."

"What was it?"

"A surveillance tape."

Mrs. Weiss stopped and put the knife down. "Oh no."

"This tape was from our arcade on the Strip. It was running the night our store got robbed."

"Oh no, Roberta. You don't need to see that. Never in your life do you need to see that."

I said quietly, "I think I do."

Mrs. Weiss practically jumped to her feet. "No! You don't! You give that thing to me, Roberta. That is an evil thing! That stupid cop ought to be fired for that. People weren't meant to watch murders! That's a sick, sick thing."

I pointed inside, at her TV. "But, Mrs. Weiss, we watch murders, don't we? We watched all those Jews getting shot by the Nazis. How is that different?"

She answered, angrily, "Listen to me! You don't know; I do." She clutched both hands and spoke as if she was reciting. "All I needed was an image of my mother, a bright image of a helping angel. It carried me through life. I didn't need to see all the bloody details."

Mrs. Weiss stopped and stood in front of me. "And neither do you. Swear to me that you will not watch that tape."

I said, "Okay."

"Swear that you will give me that tape."

"Okay."

"Are you just saying that? Or do you mean it?"

"I mean it."

She stared at me for a long time. She spoke in a voice I had never heard before. "I mean it, too. You will disappoint me greatly if you do not."

"Yes, ma'am."

"We'll go to your house tomorrow and you'll give it to me."

"Yes, ma'am." I had pretty much destroyed our nice time on the balcony.

Mrs. Weiss pointed weakly to the crackers and asked, "Do you want any?"

"No. Thanks."

"Me neither. I'm tired. I'm turning in."

I helped clean up the balcony. Then I went into the guest room and got changed for bed. Mrs. Weiss came by to say good night. She pointed around the room and said, "This is your room now, Roberta. It's not a guest room anymore. It's your room, and everything in it is yours. Understand?"

What could I say but, "Yes, Mrs. Weiss. Thank you." I felt really bad about upsetting her, about ruining our evening. Her voice had a sharp edge when she told me, "I'll see you in the morning."

I looked around the room. It was clean and new, the opposite of my room at Sawgrass Estates. Despite Mrs. Weiss's insistence, I still felt like a guest in it. I lay down on the large, comfortable bed. I fell asleep quickly but I didn't stay asleep. I was awakened sometime after midnight by the most horrible dream I have ever had.

In the dream I was my present age, but I was very small. I was sitting on my mom's lap, holding a book. We were in our reading chair, back at our old place, but we were not reading. I could not see her face. I could only see her midsection, from her waist up to her neck. I could feel that her midsection was wet. I didn't want to move my head to look, but I knew I had to. Then I could see that it was wet and red. She was leaking red blood, in a straight line, from her neck to her waist.

I woke up with my mouth opened wide in horror. I looked around frantically. I was completely disoriented in that strange room, utterly lost and falling into the void. I tried to understand what was happening, to separate reality from dream. But when I started to do that, things got even worse.

Because in reality, I *was* lying in a pool of blood. It

was dark red and wet. I reached down and pulled up a smear of it on my hand. I lurched out of bed, fell to the floor, and began crying hysterically, "No! No! No! No!"

Mrs. Weiss appeared, blinking and frightened, in her white robe. Then her eyes opened wide and she gasped, "Good god, Roberta! What has happened?"

I started babbling to her, "They — they stabbed her! They stabbed her!"

"What? Who stabbed her? Who stabbed somebody?"

"I — I don't know."

"What crazy thing is this? You didn't do anything to yourself?" Mrs. Weiss switched on the bedroom light. As her eyes adjusted she looked at the bloody mess all over me. She took my face in her hand and asked, "Roberta, is this your time of the month?"

I stared at her blankly. I breathed in and out. That question seemed to bring me back from the dream. I told her, as reasonably as I could, "I . . . I don't know. I've never had one. This has never happened to me before."

I felt Mrs. Weiss's grip on my face tighten. "This has never happened to you before! At your age? Why didn't I know about this?"

She saw how wretched I was, though, and she softened her tone. "Oh, I'm sorry, darling. Here. You sit here. You keep the sheet between your legs, just like this. Eckerd Drugs is open twenty-four hours. I'll be back in twenty minutes. You just sit there like you are. Okay?"

I whispered, "Okay." I sat with the bloody sheet, on

the bloody floor, leaning my head against the bed. I drifted in and out of sleep, like in a delirium. I saw my mom's face. I saw other things, weird things, lines and shapes that added up to nothing. It was like I was drifting in a sea of chaos. Out of control. No up or down, or backward or forward, or right or wrong.

Then Mrs. Weiss was back, handing me an opened box with MAXIPADS written on it. She had taken out a sheet of directions, and she proceeded to read them to me. Then she led me, with the box, into the bathroom. She leaned me against the wall and ordered. "Stay put."

She hurried out and returned with a pair of my underpants, some dark blue shorts, and a T-shirt. She turned on the shower and asked me, "Tell me the truth now, Roberta. Are you okay to stand?"

"Yes, ma'am."

"Are you sure? Because I'll stay in here with you."

"I'm okay."

"I'll give you some privacy, then."

I took a quick shower. I noticed that the bleeding had stopped. I stuck the maxipad on the underpants as best I could, and then I squeezed into the shorts and shirt.

When I walked back into the bedroom, Mrs. Weiss was dumping the bloody sheets into a big plastic bag. I said, "I'm so sorry, Mrs. Weiss. I ruined everything in here."

"Honey, you ruined nothing. This will all wash out."

I knew better. "Not the mattress. The mattress won't wash out."

"I'll clean it up the best I can, then I'll flip it over. It'll be fine. This is your bed, anyway."

"Oh, god, Mrs. Weiss. I'm so sorry."

"Don't you be sorry. This happens to girls. To every girl. This happened to me. Don't you worry about it. I'll tell you, Roberta, I'm glad it happened. Now you're like everybody else. You don't have that secret to carry around with you. You did something normal. You need normal."

I looked at the awful mess. "I don't need this. I hate this."

"Bah. You'll get used to it real fast. Believe me, it'll never be like this again. You'll know what to do next time. It gets easier and easier."

"Oh, god."

"Tell me, darling. Are you having any cramps or pain?"

"No."

"So you're actually lucky. Maybe you'll be a lucky one."

"Lucky?"

"That's right. Maybe someday people will think you were lucky. Now come in and sleep in my room. I have to get my rest."

SUNDAY, THE 22ND ～ I couldn't sleep at all in Mrs. Weiss's room. I lay there for two hours, then I got up and sat by myself on the balcony. At 5 A.M., I went into the guest room and got my sneakers. Then I slipped out of the condo and walked quickly across the empty mall parking lot.

Route 27 was a strange sight at that hour. Only an occasional truck rumbled by to disturb the quiet.

Everglades Boulevard had a little more traffic. I worried that a strange man might stop his car next to me and try to pull me in, but none did. Still, I covered the last three blocks to my house on the run.

The house, of course, was empty. I went right into my bedroom closet and got out the videotape. I brought it into the living room, took it out of its sleeve, and placed it on top of the VCR. Then I went and sat on the couch.

I sat there for a good fifteen minutes staring at that tape. That evil tape. Finally the moment of truth came, as I had always known it would. I could no longer resist the dark pull. I clicked on the TV, got up, and slid the tape into the VCR. Then I pressed the Play button and sat back down on the couch to watch. To watch my mother being murdered.

The video blipped to life right away. The surveillance camera must have been a cheap one, because the images moved slowly and the action had a jerky quality to it. But the extraordinary and miraculous thing about it was this — I saw my mom.

There she was, like I had never seen her before. I sat up, thrilled and delighted. Mom was not wearing her blue vinyl smock, just a white polo shirt, like she was ready to leave for the night. Her hair was pulled back in a tortoiseshell clip. The camera was above her, to her right, taking in the cash register and the counter area. She was staring out of the window, looking bored. It was storming hard. Lightning flashes illuminated the bare wall behind her.

The storm was keeping all the customers away from the arcade. I smiled to think of that. There was Mom, just like me, a clerk waiting for customers to come.

And then a customer came.

Mom turned her head toward the door and froze. The top part of a man entered the frame rapidly. He had on a Halloween mask — a rubber voodoo-head Halloween mask. Mom shrank back against the wall with fear in her eyes. The man's arm reached across the counter, curled around, and grabbed a deposit bag from below. He knew just where it was. His arm had a tattoo of a snake on it, a snake wrapped around a wooden pole.

I expected Mom to stay frozen there, like I was frozen in my seat, but she did not. She pushed away from that wall and took off around the counter. That was the last I saw of her.

I sat watching that surveillance tape for another forty-five minutes, watching the wall illuminated by countless lightning flashes, until I saw a sheriff's deputy come behind the counter. He looked at the camera and said something to somebody else. Right after that, the picture cut out.

The videotape, however, continued to run for a few more minutes. When it finally reached the end, it re-wound itself with an awful whirring. It clacked to an abrupt stop, and an early-morning kids' show popped on. I stared at it with my mouth open, feeling like I wanted to throw up. I was sick to my soul. I felt poisoned inside. I felt a horror, black and bottomless, inside of me.

At some point — I don't know how long after — I stood up and walked to the kitchen door. I went out into the carport and continued down the road, walking in the relentless, glaring sun. I squinted at the objects to the left and right of me. I was surprised to see that everything was still there, just as it had been. That the world outside had not been changed in any way.

I passed like a ghost down 111th Street. I managed somehow to cross Everglades Boulevard. I stood at wobbly attention at the bus stop, barely a foot away from the dangerous traffic.

A bus pulled up. I climbed on and took a seat. I never paid. I never looked at the driver, either. It might have been the usual guy, but I don't know. Whoever it was didn't say anything to me, and the bus started to move. Just before my stop I stood up and moved to the front. The driver stopped and opened the door.

I walked down Seventy-second Street, past the chain-link fences and the palmettos, to the cemetery. I remember feeling the heat pressing down on me. I remember feeling the crack of the lightning close by. And I remember a sudden cold wind making the palm fronds blow upward in the trees.

I passed through the cemetery gates and followed a familiar path toward Slot #109E. The sky got darker.

The wind got stronger. I made it as far as the lawn of the angel statue before the first drop hit me on the back of the neck. It hit with great force, like a stone thrown from a high building. A hailstone.

I lurched ahead. The stones were now striking at my head and my back. I staggered a few feet more and fell. I spread my arms and legs out on the grass and waited for death. I surrendered to the wind and the rain and the hail, letting them beat down on me, letting them stone me to death.

I lay there for several minutes, listening to the winds as if they were the last sounds I would ever hear. But then I heard something else. A sound out of the void. I raised up my head, turned my face into the rain, and stared.

A woman appeared before me. A ghost, wet and wavering. Mom? I couldn't recognize her. And then I could. It was Mrs. Weiss. She was still dressed in her white robe, which was now soaked through. She had on no makeup, and her hair was matted back against her head.

She opened her mouth and railed, but her words were carried off by the howling wind. Then the wind changed direction, and the words came to me: "I thought I had taught you one thing, Roberta! Maybe I was wrong. I thought maybe I would tell you one more time."

She clutched her robe and took a step away from the car and toward me. I saw the white Lincoln appearing and then disappearing in the rain. She balanced herself ten feet from me and screamed: "You have to survive! Do you hear me? Even though they line you up at a ditch, and make you dig your own grave, and strip off your clothes, and pull out your fillings, and point a machine gun at you. You cannot give up! You can never give up! You have to survive because you are too damn stubborn not to survive. Do you hear me? Do you understand, little girl?"

She turned and staggered back to the car, moving as if in slow motion. I strained to watch her through the sheeting of the rain. She pulled open the door and got inside. The reverse lights flashed on, and the big car shot backward. It flew off the roadway and crashed into the angel statue. The statue wobbled once, then tilted forward onto the Lincoln, its stone sword shattering the glass of the back windshield into a spiderweb of jagged lines. Then the statue scraped down the trunk with a horrible noise and broke apart on the ground.

I pulled myself up and stumbled to the car. I yanked open the driver's side door, reached in, and pushed her small body gently but firmly to the right. Then I fell into the seat and slammed the door.

Mrs. Weiss seemed stunned, but she was able to sit upright. I leaned over and clicked the middle seat belt around her. Then I clicked on my own, put the car into Drive, and stepped on the gas. The back tires spun and squealed in the muddy grass, but they finally caught and propelled us onto the roadway. I found the wipers' knob and turned them on. Then I hunched up against the steering wheel and drove slowly along the cemetery road to the exit. I said, "I think I'd better drive it all the way, Mrs. Weiss."

She didn't answer, so I turned left on Seventy-second Street. Mercifully the rain started to let up. I concentrated totally on driving the big car to Everglades Boulevard.

When I turned right, I found myself caught up in the morning traffic.

Mrs. Weiss didn't speak for a long time. Then she whispered, in an exhausted voice, "You have to fight. You have to fight to save what's yours."

I said, "You rest, Mrs. Weiss. I'm going to get you home."

I guided the big car all the way back to Mrs. Weiss's space in the carport. I opened the passenger side door and helped slide her out. She walked unsteadily, but she refused to hold on to me through the elevator ride and the walk down the outside corridor. Once inside the condo, I said, "I'm going to call your doctor, Mrs. Weiss. Where is your doctor's number?"

She answered, much stronger, "I don't have a doctor. Who has a doctor anymore? I have an HMO."

"Where's the number?"

"You're not calling anybody about me. I'm all right. I'm not the one who's dying. I should call about you. You kids, you're the ones who are dying."

Mrs. Weiss pointed into the bathroom. "I have another robe in there for me." Then she pointed into the hall closet. "And I have a thick pool robe in the closet for you. Go put it on."

Mrs. Weiss went into the bathroom and closed the door. I walked to the closet and found a thick white terrycloth robe. I peeled off my wet clothes and covered myself. Mrs. Weiss came out of the bathroom in an old red robe. She told me in a strong voice, "Take those wet clothes and throw them in the tub for now."

I did as she said. When I got back she was in her room, already under the bedspread. She had a faraway look in her eyes. I said, "Mrs. Weiss, I'm sorry. I'm so sorry that I did this to you."

Mrs. Weiss opened her eyes and turned toward me. "You didn't do this to me. I did this to me. You did something much worse to yourself. You watched that tape. Try feeling sorry for that." I looked away in shame. "Promise me, Roberta. Promise me you will get rid of that evil thing."

"I promise."

"Do you mean it this time?"

"Yes, ma'am. I do."

Mrs. Weiss closed her eyes. I thought about tiptoeing away, but she suddenly opened them. "When you weren't here this morning, I knew. I knew right then where you had gone."

All I could do was nod.

"Did you go there to die?"

"I don't know. Maybe."

Mrs. Weiss rolled over and propped herself up on an elbow. "I don't want you to die, Roberta. I have made it my business to see to it that you are one of the survivors. Do you understand?"

"Yes, ma'am."

"I wonder." She explained, like she was talking about one of her TV shows, "Too many children get born. Too many fish get hatched. Too many acorns fall to the ground. A hundred, a thousand times too many. Just to ensure that a few will survive. All of you children, you're all bunched together now, moving down the road in a big mob. None of you knows which way to go. But one day, Roberta, you'll look around, and that mob will be gone. You'll find yourself alone on the open road. You will be the survivor, because you will have learned what it takes to survive."

I felt very strange — cold and hot at the same time. I reached up and felt my face. I was crying again. I gathered tears on my fingertips and held them out for Mrs. Weiss to see. But, to my surprise, she had fallen asleep.

I changed again quickly and walked back down into the parking lot. All signs of the storm were now gone, but I knew it had been real. I knew by the shattered glass of the Lincoln's window and the long granite scar across its trunk.

I trudged through the punishing heat all the way back to my house. The door was still wide open. The TV was still on. I went right to the VCR and popped out the videotape. I never even looked at it, I just slid it into its case. Then I carried it into the bedroom and stashed it in the back corner of my closet. As I did, I said aloud, "I'm sorry again, Mrs. Weiss, but I might be needing this."

I walked back out, turned off the TV, and then called Arcane. Dad answered. "Dad? It's Roberta. I'm not coming in today."

"Oh. Okay, honey. Are you sick?"

"No. I'm just going to cut again."

"You are? Well, it is really dead here, so I guess that's okay. Hey, you're not going to make a habit out of this, are you?"

"I have to go." I hung up before he could say anything else.

MONDAY, THE 23RD ✵ During third period today, Betty told me, "They just had a big fight out on the PE field. We all had to come inside."

I said, "Who was fighting?"

"A black guy and a Hispanic guy. I didn't know either one."

"What was it about?"

"I have no idea."

So what happened right before fifth period wasn't surprising. Mr. Archer came on the P.A. system. He said, "I want all members of the student council to report to the guidance office immediately."

Everybody who had been at Memorial for more than a year knew what that meant. We were going on alert. By the time we got out to the bus stops, there were sheriff's deputies all over the place. They even brought the K9 corps. By the next day there would be metal detectors at the entrances. It was all standard operating procedure. Anybody who causes any trouble in the next few days goes straight to Juvie.

I don't think Mr. Herman knew any of that. I don't think he cared, either. He was standing at his podium as usual, getting ready. He waited for Mr. Archer's announcement to conclude, then he looked up to begin.

But today he did not begin.

Mr. Herman looked around the room, particularly at the kids lounging in the back seats. He picked up a handful of hall passes, walked to the back, and handed them out like tickets to a ride. "Here. Here you are, all of you. Take a hall pass and go. Go do whatever you want, with my blessing."

The football players looked at each other suspiciously. But one by one, they reached out and took the passes. The girls and boys who sat near them did the same. They gathered up their stuff and filed out, grinning disrespectfully.

Mr. Herman held up the passes to the kids in front, too. "Anyone else? This offers expires immediately. Going once; going twice."

Once he was satisfied that everyone remaining really wanted to be there, he returned to the podium. Then he delivered this lecture: "I have talked to you in the past about careers, and about standards. I have tried to show you how high standards developed in the career of journalism, and about how these standards have slowly been eroding. Let me talk to you today about life itself, and about something higher than the highest standards. About ideals.

"The Greek philosopher Plato spoke of ideals twenty-five centuries ago, and his words still apply to us today.

"Plato said that the highest expression of anything — love, truth, friendship — lies in its ideal. But here's the problem: That ideal does not exist here, in reality. It does not exist in our grimy little world. It exists high above it; it can never be reached. It is the standard against which all love, truth, friendship, and so on are to be measured. You must say to yourself, 'Do I really love this person? Let me see. Let me measure my love against the ideal of love. How does it measure up?'

"Now you, as a young person, may have no faith in your country, or in your church, or in your family. But you can still have faith in an ideal. If you have an ideal in front of you, you will never get lost on the journey of life. It is, after all, the journey that matters. So I wish all of you a safe one. Good-bye."

Mr. Herman gathered up his belongings and left the room.

He didn't come back. I waited along with the others for thirty more minutes, until the period ended. Then I went to math. Mr. Herman did not show up for study hall, either. We sat there, unsupervised, and did homework.

After seventh period I headed out to the bus stop. A Channel 57 News truck was parked by the school's front door, along with trucks from the local network stations. I walked over to check it out.

The reporters were packed tightly around Mr. Archer, thrusting microphones in his face. Mr. Archer's face seemed fuller and redder than usual. He looked like his blood pressure was running very high. The reporters were really rude, shouting out things such as, "How do you keep your job? Why is Memorial still open? Don't you have the lowest test scores in the state? Why can't you control your students?"

Mr. Archer listened to the reporters for a long minute, getting redder and redder. He listened until the barrage of shouted questions subsided. Then, to their surprise, he answered one of them. "You really want to know why I can't control my students? I'll tell you. After they leave this school, and for the rest of their lives, the whites stick with the whites, the blacks stick with the blacks, the Spanish stick with the Spanish, and so on. That's what people do. They stick with their own kind.

"You people don't know a thing about education. You have no idea what's going on in public schools. You expect us to mix all these kids together and to have them live in peace and love and harmony. Well, that's a crock! It's never been that way, and it's never going to be that way. These people don't like each other. They don't like each other when they're teenagers, and they don't like each other when they're adults, either. That's just the way it is. There's your answer. Now leave me alone."

Mr. Archer broke out of the circle and lumbered

into the building. The reporters started shouting and running to their trucks. They were all really pumped up, like something great had happened. I had the distinct feeling it wasn't going to be so great for Mr. Archer.

At the studio today I ran the video dubbing machine for a tour group from the University of South Florida. The students were pretty good. They asked smart questions, and they responded to things the way Mrs. Knight expected them to. When Mrs. Knight took them to the video vault, I was alone in the equipment area. I practiced with Tape A and Tape B for a long time, refining my plan to save the mall, trying to convince myself that it could work.

Mr. Herman opened a door behind me and hissed, "Roberta? May I speak with you?"

I told him, "Sure."

He came in and stood next to the machine. He got right to the point. "What happened after I left today?"

I shrugged. "Nothing."

Mr. Herman nodded. "Yes, I suppose the day drones on, regardless of whether the teachers are there or not. That's some commentary about education, isn't it?"

He had asked me a question, so I asked him one, "Mr. Herman, why did you leave today?"

Mr. Herman set his briefcase down. He thought for a moment, then told me, "I think the question is, Why did I ever enter that place? It was a mistake, a mistake that I have now rectified."

"Do you mean you're not coming back?"

"Yes. How long do you think it will take for them to figure it out?"

"You're not even going to tell Mr. Archer?"

"No. Why should I? The man is a moron."

Those words made me angry. I thought, *What did Mr. Archer ever do to you except give you a job?* But I didn't say it.

Mr. Herman must have known how I was thinking, because he launched into an explanation. "I was called down to Mr. Archer's office at lunchtime. He told me I had given out too many Fs."

"How many?"

"How many deserved them?"

"You gave out *that* many?"

"Yes. I thought I could." He shrugged. "It turns out that I couldn't. Therefore, I would like you to do something for me. Can you do me one favor?"

"Sure. I guess so."

Mr. Herman reached into his briefcase. He handed me a padded envelope. I thought, *Oh no, another video-tape,* but I took it from his outstretched hand. "I would like you to play this for me tomorrow. Will you do that?"

I said, "With Mr. Archer's permission."

"Yes, of course. With Mr. Archer's permission."

When my break time came at Arcane, I walked up to Slots #2 and #3, Florida Dermatology. I opened the door to the reception area, walked in, and asked a lady behind the counter, "Is Nina Navarro here today?"

The lady yelled behind her in a Cuban accent, "Nina! You have a friend here."

About two seconds later, Nina popped out of the back. She looked at me and her face fell. I said, "What's wrong?"

"Nothing. I just thought you were some guy. So what's up?"

"I have a favor to ask of you."

"Me?"

"Yeah. I was wondering if you could check your records for something."

Nina looked worried. "Oh, I don't know. Medical records are a private thing."

"I just wanted to know about a particular tattoo. An evil tattoo."

I could see Nina's curiosity starting to rise. She glanced over at the receptionist, then she said, "Come on back."

I followed her into a small office with a desk, a chair, and a PC. Nina closed the door and sat behind the desk.

She said, "Now, what's this about?"

"I wanted to know if you kept records of tattoos that you removed."

"Yeah. But like I said, that would be part of that private medical stuff."

"Can I just ask you some general questions, then? Questions that aren't about people?"

Nina thought about it. "Yeah. I don't see why not."

"Okay. In general, then, if somebody came in to you

to get a tattoo removed, what information would you take down?"

"The usual personal stuff."

"What about a description of the tattoo?"

"For sure, and I'll tell you why. They might come back and try to sue us. They might say, 'Hey, I told you to take this chick's name off my arm, but not the American flag. You messed up my arm.' And we say, 'No, you wrote it right here on this paper, *Take off the chick's name and the American flag.*'"

I had never trusted Nina for a moment, but I had to trust her now. I decided to tell her the truth. "Listen, Nina. I just saw something evil."

"I'm listening."

"It was a surveillance tape, and it was taken the night my mother was murdered."

"Madre de Dios!"

"On the tape I saw the murderer's arm. It had a tattoo. A tattoo of a serpent wound around a wooden pole."

Nina's eyes were fiery. "You didn't see his face?"

"No. It was Halloween night. He had on a mask."

She leaned forward. "This is incredible. I feel like I'm in a movie and we're actors and you're telling me this."

"But like I said, I did see his arm, and his tattoo."

Nina punched excitedly at the computer keyboard. She said, "I am all over this."

"You can help me?"

"I am helping you right now. The records weren't so good back then, but I've keyed in a lot of them since. I'll do a search with the word *snake*. That might turn up something. If not, I'll try *serpent*. It could take a while."

Nina stopped typing and looked up at me. "Hey, I gotta see that tape, though."

I told her simply, "No, you don't."

"I gotta see that arm. It could help me."

I repeated, emphatically, "You don't need to see it. This is not *Angela Live*." Nina looked hurt. I added, "Anyway, the tape is gone."

Now she looked crushed. "Gone?"

"Nina, it nearly killed me to watch it. It's gone." She nodded like she understood. I added, "That thing was evil."

"Yeah. Yeah, I hear that."

I hurried back to work, but there was no need. Everybody was just hanging around.

Mrs. Roman walked across the mallway at seven o'clock. I asked her, "Is Leo minding the store?"

"Yes, the dear man. He'll do anything for anybody. And he's very handy, too."

"Have you heard from Mrs. Weiss?"

"Yes. She says everything is fine. Of course, she would say that. I felt like saying, 'Everything is so fine that you're still not able to get out of bed?' But I didn't. I didn't want to upset her. Will you be with her tonight?"

"Yes. I live there now."

"Good. That's real good. I better get back over to Leo."

I turned toward the counter and was surprised to see

Nina standing there. She was chatting with Kristin like nothing was different. Like I hadn't just asked her to do something that was extremely important to me. To make it worse, much worse, she called right out, "Hey, Roberta, I couldn't find that thing for you."

I joined them at the counter. Kristin was looking daggers at me. I asked Nina, "You couldn't find anything about a serpent or a snake?"

"That's right. I searched the files for both words. *Nada.*"

Kristin locked eyes with me. "What is this?"

Nina answered, "It's a secret."

Kristin remarked coldly, "Another secret, Roberta? You're telling things to Nina now that you don't tell me?"

That made me feel terrible. "It's not a secret, Kristin. I had an idea, but I didn't know if it would work. It didn't work. So it was a bad idea, not a secret."

"Okay. So what was it?"

"I was hoping Nina would have information about my mother's murderer." Kristin's eyes opened wide. "There. Now you know."

Nina said, "The killer had a snake tattoo."

Kristin nodded. "And that's why you searched your files?"

"You got it."

"But, Roberta, how do you know that?"

Nina answered, "Because she saw the video, girl. She saw the murderer — at least she saw his arm. It was on the video."

Kristin got very upset. "Roberta, is this true? Have you told the police?"

"I got the tape from the police. I got it from Griffin."

Nina added, "Yeah. And it was so evil that she destroyed it."

I told Kristin sincerely, "I'm sorry I didn't tell you about it before. You should have known about it before Nina."

Now Nina looked offended.

Kristin put her arm around my shoulder. I don't think she had ever done that before. I don't think she had ever touched me before.

After closing, Mrs. Roman and I walked back to Century Towers together. She was very tired, but she wanted to say good night to Mrs. Weiss, so we both stopped into #303.

Mrs. Weiss was up, sitting in the living room, watching TV. She had a green plaid blanket over her legs. Mrs. Roman called to her from the kitchen door, "Hi, Isabel. We had a great day at the card store."

Mrs. Weiss turned and smiled at her weakly.

"I'm not going to stay tonight, if it's okay."

"It is okay, Millie. You go get your rest. Thank you for everything."

Mrs. Roman left, and I joined Mrs. Weiss in front of the TV. She pointed at it and told me, "It's the History Channel. It's about Egypt tonight."

"How are you feeling?"

"Not bad at all. I had a very restful day. A peaceful day."

"That's good. Can I get you anything?"

Mrs. Weiss waved the offer away. We watched a camera pan down a wall of hieroglyphics. A commercial came on, and I said to her, "I've been thinking about that memorial you left to your mother." Mrs. Weiss cocked her head at me. "I've been thinking . . . maybe I'll do the same."

Mrs. Weiss thought about that. "Sure. Why not? It's no dumber than anything else, right?"

"It's not dumb at all."

"No. But it is . . . temporary. It's all temporary, Roberta. We're all going to be dead someday."

I didn't like the sound of that. I wanted her to stop talking that way, but I answered, "I guess so."

"So what does it matter if you have a big memorial? Or a little one? Or none? You're just as dead."

"I guess."

"Look at these pharaohs of Egypt. They spent all their lives, and all their money, building monuments to themselves. Bunch of fools. Before they were even cold, robbers were in there looting them. Now, three thousand years later, we're parading their bones around the world in a freak show. So what was it all for?"

"I don't know."

"Better someone should look back on one kind deed you did, than look at a big pile of stones."

I nodded in agreement. I wanted to say something — anything — positive to her. I finally thought of this: "I think the bleeding has mostly stopped."

It took a moment for her to figure out what I meant. "Oh? Good. That's good. Next month, you'll be ready. It won't be so bad."

"It's going to take me more than a month to be able to handle this."

Mrs. Weiss shrugged. "You have no choice. When you have no choice, you just handle it." She clicked off the TV. "I'd better get to sleep, darling."

"Can I help you get in there?"

Mrs. Weiss stood up straight. "No. What for?"

I said, "All right, then. Good night." And I watched her walk slowly but steadily into the bedroom.

TUESDAY, THE 24TH ~ Today after I got off the school bus, I had to pass through a double line of deputy sheriffs just to get to the front door. Then I had to pass through a metal detector.

When I got inside the office, I saw Mrs. Biddulph standing next to the video equipment, looking very harried. As soon as she saw me, she cried, "Roberta! Are you in charge of this equipment?"

"Yes, ma'am. Along with Mr. Herman."

Mrs. Biddulph didn't say anything else, so I asked her the question that was on my mind. "Is Mr. Archer coming in this morning?"

"He's working at home today. I will be doing the morning announcements." She thought for a moment. "Are there any?"

"Well, that's up to you, ma'am."

"You don't have anything for me to read?"

"Me? No. All I have is a tape from Mr. Herman. He asked me to play it." I pulled the video from its envelope. "Do you want to preview it?"

"What does Mr. Archer do?"

"He has me play the tape on the monitor, and he previews it. Do you want to do that?"

"Yes, please. Quickly, though."

Mrs. Biddulph stared at the dead screen while I set up the TV and VCR. Then we both watched as Mr. Herman's face appeared onscreen. I could tell where he was sitting — at the news desk in the Channel 57 Studios. He looked at the camera and said this: "I had a notion that I wanted to give something back. To teach. That's what I came here for."

Just then Officer Dwyer came in and beckoned to Mrs. Biddulph. She half turned to me and said, "That's fine." Then she went to talk to the officer. I stopped the tape and rewound it. About two minutes later the first bell rang. Mrs. Biddulph came back and said, "I want to say a few words to start the day. Where should I stand?"

I looked around quickly. "How about in front of Mr. Archer's door?"

Mrs. Biddulph walked over there obediently. She said, "Just tell me when to start." I nodded.

The second bell rang; I pressed the button and pointed at her. Mrs. Biddulph said, "Good morning, everyone. Officer Dwyer just informed me that no student had any trouble of any kind entering the building today. I think that's great. Let's keep it that way. Let's all do our part to make this a completely trouble-free day. And if trouble finds you, just remember the Lord's example — that it is better to turn the other cheek and walk away. Have a great day, everybody!"

Mrs. Biddulph turned her eyes toward me, so I shut off the camera. She walked back to the officer while I cued Mr. Herman's tape and pressed the Play button on the VCR.

I was soon sorry I had.

Mr. Herman's speech began as before: "I had a notion that I wanted to give something back. To teach. That's what I came here for." But then he continued, "But you just sat there, staring at me. I told myself that it was not your fault, that you had been raised by parents who don't value education; who actually resent it; who desperately do not want you to be better educated than they were.

"What I did not realize is that it was I who did not get it. In fact you are supposed to be just as dumb, uncurious, and cretinous as you are. You are supposed to get out of here equipped to be no more than a member of the servant class. Pardon me — I believe they call it the 'service class' now.

"You are destined to serve the small percentage of people whose families did value education, and who made their children's futures their priority and their pride. It is you who have it right, and I who had it wrong. So I bid you good-bye. I hope you all get what you want and what you deserve, and I look forward to tipping you well someday, for services rendered."

The video went black. I couldn't bear to look around me, but I finally did. Fortunately, Mrs. Biddulph wasn't there. I guessed she had left with Officer Dwyer. I popped out Mr. Herman's tape and put in the Pledge and Banner one. After that ended, I turned everything off and hurried to first period.

During second period, a kid arrived with a guidance pass and a slip of paper with my name on it. I figured this was it. I was going to get suspended, or taken to Juvie, for playing Mr. Herman's video. For inciting to riot, maybe.

But I was wrong again. Mrs. Biddulph was standing in her old spot behind the guidance desk. She looked at me with no apparent knowledge of the video incident. She told me, "Roberta, there's a police officer in Mr. Archer's time-out room. He has asked to speak to you. I called your father, and I paged him, but he hasn't answered. So I'm going to leave it up to you. Do you want to speak to him?"

I looked into the room and saw Griffin. I said, "Okay."

I walked into the office. He looked up and said immediately, "Someone signed out the surveillance tape. That wasn't supposed to happen."

I replied, "You could say that about a lot of stuff, couldn't you?"

"That tape was forensic evidence, Roberta. It belongs with the victim's clothing and the other stuff that no one but a jury was ever supposed to see."

After a long pause, I admitted, "You're right. I signed it out."

Griffin grabbed his strands of blond hair and pulled them outward. "Oh, god. Did you look at it?"

"Yes, I did. Did you?"

"Yes. That's why it wasn't in your packet." After a very long exhale, he decided, "All right. What's done is done. Do you have any questions for me?"

I asked, "Why didn't they catch the guy? They knew what his tattoo looked like."

"They tried. They worked hard on it. The file is a thick one, believe me. But this isn't a TV episode, Roberta. Crimes don't get solved in an hour. Many times they don't get solved at all."

I asked him pointedly, "What's in this thick file?"

Griffin shook his head no. "There are regulations about this sort of thing. I can't talk about another detective's case." He glanced at the door. "I can tell you that he canvassed tattoo parlors along the Strip. He got no leads. Those tattoo guys are not a real cooperative bunch."

I tried, "Okay, can you tell me if he ever had a suspect?"

Griffin answered emphatically, "I can't tell you anything else."

I closed my eyes. I tried to remember the murder video — my mom's face, her look of fear, the moment when she took off around the counter. I felt tears welling up in my eyes. Then I felt them start to fall.

I waited Griffin out like that, sitting in the time-out office with tears rolling down my face. He gave in first. I heard him get up. Then I heard the sound of the door closing. I opened my watery eyes.

Griffin said, "You never heard a word of this from me." I nodded my agreement, and he sat back down. "There was a loan shark working the Strip back then. A big, bad guy named Sonny Santos. According to the detective, nothing happened on the Strip without Sonny knowing about it. The street punks were a lot more afraid of him than they were of the law. The detective figured that . . . Sonny knew about the bag of cash in the arcade, and that he sent someone in to grab it."

Griffin was looking at the floor as he continued. "All the evidence in the case was moving, slow but sure, in Sonny's direction."

I said, "Did he have a tattoo?"

"No. You're not following me, Roberta. He didn't do the crime himself. It was a street punk who grabbed the cash, who . . . committed the murder."

I started to shake, but I struggled to hide it.

"But I'm saying that no punk on the Strip would rob a store without Sonny's permission. Are you with me?"

I nodded. "So did they question this guy?"

Griffin exhaled loudly again. "No, because Sonny disappeared. One day he was cruising the Strip in his big El Dorado. The next day he was gone. Forever."

"What? He ran away?"

"Not likely. The detective's opinion was that Sonny had a disagreement with some business partners from Providence, Rhode Island, and that he and his El D were recycled somewhere in the Atlantic County Landfill."

I dried my cheeks with my hands. "Then . . . what? What happened next?"

Griffin admitted, "Not much. Everything was pointing one way, and suddenly everything was pointing nowhere. The case stalled out. It happens."

"There weren't any witnesses?"

"No."

Griffin squirmed a little after he said that, so I prodded him, "What? What aren't you telling me?"

There was a sharp knock on the door. Griffin opened it to Mrs. Biddulph. She asked him, "Why did you close the door, Detective?"

"We were discussing a sensitive matter, ma'am."

"We don't close doors around here. Not without an administrator present."

"Sorry, ma'am."

Mrs. Biddulph turned and walked to the counter. Griffin stood back to let me pass through the door. He told me, "If it's any consolation to you, the punk who did the crime is almost certainly dead. Long dead. Of AIDS, of a drug overdose. Who knows? Who cares?"

I told him, "I care. And I want to know."

He looked away, thinking. He said, "Roberta, I did a bad thing letting you see that tape."

"No, you didn't."

"Yes, I did. If I can make it up to you in any way, let me know."

Mrs. Biddulph cleared her throat in my direction, so I hurried out of the office and back to class.

After school, I stayed on the bus all the way back to Sawgrass Estates. I wanted to see if Dad had picked up Mrs. Biddulph's message about Griffin. He hadn't.

There were two lights blinking on the machine. I played Mrs. Biddulph's message right away and deleted it. Then I played the second message: "Roberta, this is Peter Herman calling from Channel Fifty-seven. I wanted to thank you. I had intended my farewell video only for my own classes, for the back row rabble, but I appreciate your initiative in providing me with a much wider audience."

My mouth fell open. I felt like a complete idiot. But Mr. Herman didn't seem to mind my blunder at all. He laughed lightly. "Anyway, I'm calling with a bit of news, which is not surprising since I am calling you from a newsroom. I have just heard that I will do my first commentary tonight, two entire minutes on the late news. That may not sound like much, but in a thirty-minute broadcast, two minutes is an eternity. If you are home from the family sweatshop by then, please tune in. Good-bye."

Work at the arcade droned on slowly today, until Nina's dramatic arrival.

Kristin, Karl, Will, and I were just hanging out at the counter. Suddenly Nina ran in, looked around to see who was listening, and told us in a tense whisper, "Listen, you guys. I gotta talk to you."

Kristin said, "There's no one around. Go ahead."

"The colonel's not around?"

"No. He's in the back. What's up?"

"Two things: I was talking to Betty. She told me that Devin is going to another after-hours party here. Tonight."

Kristin and I answered together, "Tonight?"

"Tonight. You didn't know?"

"No!"

"Then I'm glad I told you. But that's only half of it. I got a call from a guy on the football team. He said there's gonna be crack cocaine at the party."

Kristin practically shouted, "Here?"

"Yeah. This is where the party is. Right? About a dozen Xavier guys are putting in, like, a hundred bucks each — fifty bucks for the party and another fifty for the crack."

Kristin looked at me, bewildered. She started babbling, "What should we do? We have to do something. What should we do?"

I put my hand on hers. "I know."

"You do?"

"Yes. I know what to do. I need to get to a phone."

Nina whipped out her cell phone. "Here you go."

I stepped behind them, pulled out Griffin's card, and called his pager. The message started to come on, but suddenly it clicked off and I found myself speaking to him live. "This is Detective Griffin."

I said, "This is Roberta," and added, "from the West End Mall."

"You're the only Roberta I know."

"Remember you said you owed me a favor?"

He hesitated, then said, very slowly, "Yes."

"Would you like to make a drug bust tonight?"

"You have my complete attention."

"Uncle Frank is having another hardcore party after hours. Some Xavier boys are making it a drug party."

"What kind of drugs?"

"Crack cocaine."

"You're kidding. Those young gentlemen?"

"That's what we hear."

Griffin thought for a moment. "Do you want me to bust your uncle Frank?"

I hadn't thought about that. I answered, "No."

"But that's the likely scenario."

"Can you just bust the Xavier boys? And Devin? Is that possible?"

"Depends. If it goes down in the parking lot, yeah. We can do that."

"So . . . Will you come?"

Griffin paused, then replied, "Believe it or not, it's a slow night. We're looking for something to do. What time?"

"Nine o'clock. It will cost you fifty dollars to get in."

"Okay. How many partyers are we talking about?"

"I heard a dozen."

He whistled. "Whew. Six hundred bucks for Uncle Frank. That'll buy some vodka."

"Griffin!"

"Sorry. Cop humor. See you at nine."

I clicked the phone off and returned it to Nina. She said, "I gotta get back to my dad." Nina bounded down from the counter. "You guys are so lucky. You get to stay here."

Kristin and I just stared at her.

As soon as Nina left, I asked Kristin, Karl, and Will, "Did you hear all that with Griffin? Do you know what's going to happen?"

They nodded grimly.

At eight-thirty, Uncle Frank came out and told Karl, so that everyone could hear, "We're having another after-hours party tonight. It should be exactly the same as the last one. You know what to do." He handed over the hardcore CDs and legends and walked stiffly to the back.

We closed the doors at eight-forty-five and quickly changed out the discs and legends. Then we heard the back door open and the party guests come in.

Like last time, Uncle Frank collected their money in the back room. But tonight he stayed back there. Kristin, Karl, Will, and I were left out front to run the party.

Devin entered the arcade first. He was followed by Griffin, and then by a line of Xavier guys. Will stiffened when he saw two of them. He whispered to me, "Those are the guys who swirled me."

"Yeah? Do you want to leave?"

"No. I don't think they even see me. Anyway, I look different now."

I told him, "That's true. But let Kristin and me start the experiences for them. Why don't you go out back and see if they do any drugs?"

He agreed, "Okay."

Will slipped through the back door just as Greg Vandervelt and his two friends came in. I looked around to warn Kristin, but she had already spotted him. Greg headed for Kristin right away. He had a weird expression on his face, like Uncle Frank at the end of the night.

He stopped barely six inches from Kristin and said, "I heard you dropped out."

Kristin answered simply, "Do you want help with one of the experiences?"

"So what are you going to do now?"

"What do you mean?"

"You know what I mean. Now that you can't look down on everybody." Greg turned to include his two friends. "Not with a face like that." The friends laughed. Kristin braced herself, straightening her back. I was afraid she was going to lose it and cry.

But then the blond kid came in from the back, the one Kristin had kicked in the teeth. He was unsteady on his feet. Was he drugged? He pushed between Greg and Kristin, staring hard at Kristin's name tag.

The kid asked her, in too loud a voice, "What's that say?" He moved a hand toward her chest. "Can I see what this says?" He pulled Kristin's name tag up and out, stretching her shirt along with it. I couldn't tell if he touched her at the same time, but he came very close.

Anyway, it didn't matter to Kristin. Her eyes turned to flame. The heel of her right palm fired out like a rocket. It caught him under the chin so hard that he flew backward, releasing his grip on her name tag. His feet went up and his head went back, cracking on the platform of Serpent's Lair.

I looked over at Griffin. I watched him as he tried to decide what to do. Should he intervene? Should he blow his cover? Since the blond kid appeared to be conscious, and Greg was slowly backing away, he decided to do nothing.

The party never really got going. We were prepared to start the hardcore experiences, like we had last time, but no one ever asked us to. Maybe they were saving the virtual reality stuff for later.

But as it turned out, later never came.

One by one the Xavier boys went out through the back door. They went out, but they never came back.

Will hurried in and beckoned to Kristin and me. We huddled with him by the register. Will looked right at me. "I followed those two guys. They got into a car."

"Yeah? And are they doing drugs?"

"I think so."

"What did you see?"

"It looks like they have a soda can, like a Pepsi can, and they're using a lighter, and they're sniffing something up their noses."

Kristin broke in, "That's it! That's good enough for me. Come on." She led us over to Griffin. He was still pretending to be a partyer, but she told him outright, "Okay. Will just saw them. They're doing drugs in a car out back."

Griffin stopped pretending right away. He looked at Will. "You saw them smoking crack?"

"Yes, sir."

"In what kind of car?"

Kristin sputtered, "What does that matter?"

Griffin smiled at her. "It's just for identification purposes. What does it look like?"

Will reported, "I think it was a Mustang."

"Did you see a van parked out there?"

"Yeah. A gray van."

"Well, that van is full of cops."

Kristin's eyes grew wide with delight. "Really?"

"Really. Those party boys are being videotaped right now."

"That is great. That is so great."

Griffin laughed at her enthusiasm. Then he winked at us and strolled easily over to Greg's group. They were reading the legend for Crusader. He smiled and said in his best redneck voice, "Hey, boys, looks like we're the only ones left in this here shindig."

They didn't even look at him. Then Griffin whipped out a handset and spoke into it in his cop voice, "Vector One, this is Vector Two. The party's over. Let's move in."

Greg and his friends turned at the sound. This time

they looked at him. A loud voice answered over the handset, "Vector Two is moving."

Griffin reached behind him and pulled out his deputy's badge. He showed it and said, "Detective John Griffin, Atlantic County Sheriff's Department. I want you to turn around and place both your hands on this thing." He pointed to the black ring that encircled the Crusader experience.

Greg looked at the others. He let out a short laugh. He regretted that immediately.

Griffin grabbed him by the neck and pulled his head slowly downward and forward until it was an inch from his own. "Is there some part of that directive that you do not understand?"

Greg's face turned bright red. He squeaked a reply, "No."

Griffin let him go, and Greg put his hands on the ring. Griffin patted him down, but he found nothing. He looked at us, disappointed. Then he turned to the other two and snapped at them, "Get over here." They moved quickly.

"Empty out your pockets, and I mean empty them." They all thrust their hands into their pockets and pulled out an assortment of items — wallets, keys, Tic Tacs. Griffin didn't see what he was looking for.

He snapped again, "Single file, the three of you, out the back door to the parking lot. Move!"

Kristin, Karl, Will, and I fell in behind them. We all trooped through Uncle Frank's office, but Uncle Frank wasn't at his desk. The bathroom door was closed, so I figured he was in there.

Outside, in the muggy darkness, four cops in flak jackets had the Xavier boys lying on the asphalt with their hands cuffed behind them. One of the cops told Griffin, "These eight, from here to here, they all had at least one rock on them. And they were all in the car at least once."

The cop pointed to two at the end of the line. "Those two didn't have anything. They didn't go into the car, either."

Griffin nodded. "Okay." He pointed at Greg's group. "Check these fine young men out."

The cop took Greg by the elbow and forced him down onto the asphalt. His friends followed on their own.

Griffin bent over and picked up a clear little packet. He held it up to me so that I could see what was inside. It looked like little glass beads. He said, "Rock cocaine, a.k.a. crack. Cheaper than the powdered stuff, but just as bad."

The cops took eight of the Xavier boys to the police station. And they had the Mustang impounded. They had to let five boys, including Greg and his friends, go free because they had no drugs on them.

To everyone's surprise, neither did Devin. As Griffin removed his handcuffs, Devin told him, "I stopped taking drugs five years ago, man."

Griffin said, "Really? You'd never know it."

Devin rubbed his arms. "Can I go back to my store?"

"I suppose so."

Devin shambled away around the back of the trash trailer.

Griffin turned back to Greg and his friends. "Have any of you underage gentlemen had so much as one alcoholic beverage? Think before you answer that." The three of them nodded immediately, admitting that they had. Griffin handed Greg his cell phone and said, "Call Mommy and Daddy for a ride." Greg did what he was told.

I turned and saw Uncle Frank by the open door. I didn't know how long he had been standing there, but I'm sure it was long enough. He said, to no one in particular, "I had no idea they were taking drugs here."

Griffin looked at me. Then he answered him, "Technically, Colonel, they took no drugs on your property. They did them out here in the parking lot."

Uncle Frank muttered, "Thank you," quietly, and went back inside.

Kristin and Karl exchanged an embarrassed look, but then Kristin shook it off. She walked up to Griffin purposefully. She told him, "I think I'd like to do this."

"What?"

"What you're doing."

"Undercover work?"

"Yeah. Or regular work. Or whatever you call it. I'd like to be a police officer."

"Is that right?"

"What would I need to do?"

Griffin said, "Well, all those guys in the gray van,

and the women on our squad, too, are veterans. That helps."

"Really?"

"Yeah. I could put you in touch with a buddy of mine. He's an army recruiter."

Kristin looked at me and laughed. "The army?"

"Not everybody goes that route. I'm just saying it helps. Maybe you and I could go see him. We could talk about a plan."

Kristin was smiling wider than I had seen in a long time. "I don't know . . ."

Griffin assured her, "You could do it. You'd be great."

"Yeah? You really think so? Why?"

"You're super-straight. You're tough. Yeah, you could be the law." Griffin turned to include Karl, Will, and me. "Thanks for your help. You're all junior g-men now. We gotta go."

Kristin, Karl, Will, and I went back inside. Uncle Frank was now standing near the glass doors, right next to Crusader. I watched as he pulled on the black helmet and started it running. Then he just stood there, with his arms hanging at his sides, staring at the blood-thirsty infidels.

I was really exhausted when I finally left work, but my night wasn't over yet. As I made my left turn to go to Century Towers, I heard, "Hey! Roberta!"

I looked toward the wall and saw Nina and Dr. Navarro standing next to Nina's Corvette.

"My dad had to work late, so I stuck around. I wanted to see who got busted. Did they get Greg the Super-Anglo?"

"No. He didn't have anything on him."

"That's too bad."

Dr. Navarro shook his head sadly. He added a comment, "That's terrible. To think that boys from Xavier would do such a thing. To think that they would disgrace their school like that."

I thought, *That's a really odd way to describe what happened, Doctor,* but I didn't say anything.

Nina explained, "Papi, Roberta is the one who wrote the article about me being a supermodel."

Dr. Navarro smiled at me with those white teeth. "Ah yes. We have it on the coffee table at home. I make everybody read it. I'm so proud of my princesa."

Nina added sincerely, "You're a really great writer, Roberta. I mean that. Nobody ever wrote about me before. Maybe nobody's ever gonna do it again. So I'm glad I have that, you know, to remind me of what I was like. You know, when I was young."

I thought, *You're still young, Nina,* but all I said was, "Thanks."

The three of us stood there for a few uncomfortable seconds. I was wondering why she had called me over when Nina finally said, "My father's like a computer, Roberta. In fact, he's better than a computer. He has a better memory, like a million gig or something."

"Oh yeah?"

"Yeah."

I waited; then I asked her, as politely as I could, "So . . . what?"

"So, maybe the word *serpent* wasn't in the IBM, but it was in my father's brain. Go on, Papi. Tell her."

Dr. Navarro spoke to me matter-of-factly, but it made my heart race. "I remember a serpent guy. He was a real bad one."

Nina interjected, "Seven years ago."

Her father continued, "He used to hang out on the Strip — every day, every night. I remember that he gave me a weird phony name and a pair of hundred-dollar bills."

I shook my head up and down, letting him know that I was following his every word. I asked, "What was he like?"

Dr. Navarro stopped smiling. "Evil. He was evil. '*Libera nos a malo.*' That's from the Lord's Prayer in Latin. It means 'Deliver us from evil.'"

Nina asked him proudly, "How do you know things like that?"

"A doctor has to learn Latin, Princesa. It's the language of medicine. And science. And the law. It's the secret language you have to learn before they let you make any money."

I brought them back to the topic. "Doctor, is there any way this evil man might still be alive?"

"Oh, he is definitely alive."

"He is? How do you know?"

Nina told me, "Just listen to this part, Roberta."

Dr. Navarro explained, "He's that preacher guy. The

one on TV. Of course, he looks different after seven years. Now he looks like Jesus himself. But he can't fool me."

I looked at Nina and then back to him. I blurted out, "Not Stephen Cross!"

The doctor nodded. "Yes, that's the one, Stephen Cross. That was not the name he gave to me, though."

"Stephen Cross?"

"That's right."

I must have looked extremely upset. He put his hand on my arm and asked, "Are you all right? Can we give you a ride home?"

"No, thanks. I live right here."

Nina said, "Where?"

"In Century Towers."

"You're kidding."

"No. That's where I live now."

"I thought you had to be, like, ninety-nine to live there."

Dr. Navarro got into the car and started it up. All I could say was, "Thanks, Nina, for finding that out for me."

"Sure. Isn't that amazing?"

I started to back away. "Yeah. Good night."

"Good night."

They drove off, and I stood alone in the dark lot, repeating the name to myself, "Stephen Cross. Stephen Cross."

I wandered slowly toward Century Towers. I stopped and leaned with my back against the trash trailer for many minutes, trying to comprehend. *Was Stephen*

Cross really looking at me through that camera lens? Was he really speaking to me? Was he real at all?

I walked right past a sleeping guard to the elevators and to Mrs. Weiss's condo. She was asleep in her room, so I sat on the floor in front of the TV with the volume down low. I watched nearly all of the late news. The second story of the night was about "continuing unrest at Memorial High School." The Channel 57 news team really ran with the story, which isn't surprising, since they had helped to create it. They ran interviews with three other high school principals, who all insisted that they didn't agree with a word that Mr. Archer had said. Most of them must have been Mr. Archer's friends, since he has worked in the Atlantic County school system for thirty years, but not one stuck up for him.

The rest of the broadcast droned on, through the sports and weather, before they got to what I was waiting for. The anchor said, "And now here is Peter Herman with tonight's Channel Fifty-seven editorial." A graphic came up. It looked like the front page of a newspaper with a headline reading, CHANNEL 57 EDITORIAL: "THE GOOD OLD BOY NETWORK."

Then the camera cut to a desk. I recognized it as the same desk Mr. Herman had used for his Memorial High video. I recognized the desk quicker than I recognized Mr. Herman.

Mr. Herman was wearing a blue blazer and some nice designer glasses. On top of his shiny head, he was wearing a jet black toupee. He looked younger, of course, and not as thin, but he sounded exactly the same.

He looked slightly to the right of the camera and read these words off the TelePrompTer: "The good old boys began their teaching careers when Florida was a simpler place. The schools back then were local, each belonging to one particular community.

"The good old boys were men in a profession dominated by women, so they took on the manlier jobs. They became the coaches; they became the driving instructors. They taught gym; they taught history. When they got together in the teachers' lounge, they were more likely to talk about fishing than about education. The pay wasn't so great, but it was a steady job, and you got your summers off. Summer was prime fishing time, so they stuck with it.

"They were in the perfect position when the latest Florida boom began. About twenty years ago, young people with families started moving to Florida at a lemminglike rate. New school construction became the number-one priority for county governments everywhere.

"These new schools needed principals, and the good old boys were ready and waiting. They traded in their coaches' whistles for suits, and their driver's ed cars for Cadillac Coupe de Villes.

"They became the leaders of an educational system that for twenty years grew in quantity, but never in quality. How could it, with a leadership educated only to the level necessary to get by in a backwater Southern state?

"Now they find themselves and their appalling inadequacies in the spotlight. They find themselves adjudged by a population of students and parents from all over the United States, a population that is sophisticated, and demanding, and attuned to the philosophy that all races can live together in harmony.

"The principal of Memorial High School, in his comments to the media, may have inadvertently done public education in Florida a great service. By drawing a public spotlight to himself and to his peer group, he may have ensured that the good old boys will get their just reward for their twenty years of service to Florida's schools — an immediate and permanent fishing trip."

The camera cut back to the anchor girl. She thanked "Peter" and the other people on the broadcast, then it was over.

I switched off the set. I thought about Mr. Herman. I thought about his two video performances today. Was this his higher standard of journalism? I didn't think much of him for the way he left Memorial High School. I thought even less of him after this.

WEDNESDAY, THE 25TH ⋞ We're still on alert at school, although nothing bad seems to be happening. If anything, the kids are actually being nicer to each other.

Archie was our sub in Journalism II. Since Mr. Herman had left no sub plans, Archie told everybody to look at the *Atlantic News* while he graded his history papers.

I got up and waited in line behind two football players for a chance to speak to him. When my turn came, I said, "Mr. Herman offered to get me into AP classes and into the National Merit Scholarship Test. I've decided that I would like to do that."

Archie answered, "Okay," but I don't think he really understood what I said. I walked to the back and picked up a section of the newspaper. The football guys only read sports, so most of the other sections were available. I chose the letters to the editor.

People had written a lot of letters about Mr. Archer. They were all bad, but some were worse than others. Here are two samples:

> The remarks broadcast, and rebroadcast ad nauseum, by the local news stations about race relations at Memorial High School would have been offensive coming from a groundskeeper or from a student. What is mind-boggling is that they came from the school's principal. What do you have to do to get certified to teach in Florida these days? Flunk your real estate exam?

> For all those who were saddened or discouraged by the remarks made by the principal of Memorial High School, I want to share my own experience. My son has attended Xavier High School for four years now. He is part of a group of friends who are inseparable, whether they're in school, or at the mall, or at the beach. One of these friends is black, one is Hispanic, and one is white.

Maybe that principal should find out what they teach at Xavier and try it at Memorial High School. It might do his students a lot of good.

I looked up at Archie after I read the letters. Had he read them, too? He must have. What did he think? He had to be hurting for his father. He sure wasn't the happy-go-lucky guy he had been before.

As soon as I walked into the mall office, Suzie practically shouted at me, "I had to call your dad. I had to track him down on the beeper. Your uncle Frank never opened the store today."

"What?"

"He wasn't here at ten, like he should have been. Then he wasn't here at eleven. That's when I got worried."

"So what happened?"

"Your dad finally got here and opened up at noon."

I said, "I better help him," and hurried up to the arcade.

Dad looked up at me from behind the register and said, "Well, you've missed a wild day."

"What happened?"

"Your uncle is AWOL. Your cousins didn't show up, either."

I reached around and got my name tag. "You just ran the place by yourself? All day?"

"Sure. No biggie. It was just like the old days. I'm glad you're here, though. Now I can go get some food."

I covered the front while Dad took a long break. Shortly after he came back I had two visitors — Sam and Griffin.

Griffin no longer looked like a mall rat. He was dressed in black pants and an Atlantic County Sheriff's Department T-shirt.

I asked him, "Aren't you undercover anymore?"

"No. Not anymore. I've had too much exposure here."

Sam surveyed the arcade. He asked me, "Can your dad cover? I want to show you something."

I said, "Sure. What is it?"

Sam checked around him. "Griffin hasn't seen it yet, either. It's the latest turn in our case."

The three of us walked through the rotunda toward Crescent. Griffin asked Sam, "So what's the mystery? Did you catch somebody new?"

"No. There is nobody new."

We hurried through the Crescent showroom and into the back. Sam had a TV setup ready to go. He announced, "This was recorded at approximately eleven P.M. Colonel Frank Ritter has come back, and he has something to say."

Sam turned on the TV. "You have to listen close. He's on the other side of the glass."

I saw that the VCR was already on and cued. Uncle Frank was frozen on Pause. He was flickering and quivering like a bug on the sticky mallway flooring. Sam pressed Pause and the image of Uncle Frank was released. He walked straight up to the window of Crescent Electronics. He stood erect, nearly at attention, and talked into the camera in a slurred yet dignified voice. "Sam, I just want to say that I am sorry about all of this. All of it. I never wanted anything like this to happen.

"This was never about your race. Hell, I don't even know what your race is, and I certainly have nothing against it, or any other race. This was about money. About the recap. You wanted the recap to succeed to save the businesses in the mall; I wanted the recap to fail to save myself."

Here Uncle Frank started moving his arms in an effort to explain. "I can't get out of my franchise deal unless some force majeure thing happens — like the whole mall goes bankrupt. If the mall goes bankrupt, see, I can transfer the franchise, or sell it. I don't lose my savings. But if you save the mall, if you get the recap, I'm stuck with my deal. And I'm dead. Dead in the water."

He started to lose his composure. "I risked my life for twenty-five years to save that money. I was separated from my family more than I was with them. I fought in Desert Storm. I did it for this country. And that means I did it for you, too."

Now he was in tears. "I'm not waiting on tables in some restaurant at fifty years of age just to pay my mortgage. I'm not going to do that. I deserve better than to wind up like that. To wind up with nothing!"

Uncle Frank stared into the lens one last time. Then he turned and lurched off across the mallway.

Sam turned off the machines. He looked at me, and he saw that I was in tears. He looked at Griffin, but Griffin wasn't reacting at all. Sam finally asked him, "Well?"

"Well? Do you want the truth?"

"That's all I want."

"Okay. Here it is: That tape would never be admissible as evidence. He's obviously drunk. He's distraught. It's an amateur surveillance tape — no date and time on it, et cetera. Any lawyer with a functioning brain would get that thrown out."

Sam came back at him angrily. "He's confessing to the crime! What do you have to do to get arrested around here?"

"I'm not talking about getting arrested. I'm talking about getting convicted. It's great TV, Sam. It's just bad evidence. My advice would be to sell it to Angela del Fuego."

Sam looked with contempt at Griffin. He snapped at him, "Spare me any more of your advice. Okay? I'm pressing charges against this guy."

Griffin defended himself with, "Hey, you can press charges. I'm just saying, don't count on this confession holding up. It has, uh, legal problems." He paused and enunciated every syllable: "Prosecutorial problems."

Sam was turning red. "I have your records and your evidence, though. Right? You didn't lose those, did you?"

"No. I have it all. It's good to go."

Sam turned his attention to me. "And I have your

eyewitness account." He dropped his voice down. "Or do I?"

I assured him, "Yes."

"You did see him that night. Didn't you?"

"Yes, of course. We both saw him." But I remembered Griffin's words about Sam and me in that empty store. I thought about the dirty version a lawyer might make out of that.

Sam left us, obviously upset. I followed Griffin out through the store and into the mallway.

Once we were clear of Sam, I said, "Can I ask you something about my mom's case?"

Griffin eyed me sideways. "Okay."

"Have they stopped looking for the killer?"

"Actively, yes. If some new witness or other new evidence arises, we will reopen it. Why?"

"What if I found the killer?"

This time he smiled. A sideways smile. He said, "Roberta, I wouldn't be at all surprised."

I walked home after work. I passed the guard at the gate, took the elevator upstairs, and started down the walkway toward #303. That's where I stopped.

I thought I had seen some horrible sights lately — Mom on that videotape, Hawg spread out on that highway, Ironman blue and frozen against that trailer wall. But none of those hit me as hard as what I saw on that walkway, and it was a simple sight: a door.

The door to Mrs. Weiss's condo was open. Wide

open. The sight of it made me almost physically sick. Her door was open, with the light and the air-conditioning pouring out into the night. That would never, never happen. Never. Not if she could possibly prevent it.

I ran down the hall and turned inside. The kitchen and the living room were empty and quiet.

I hurried into the bedroom. There was Mrs. Roman, folding up the dark blue quilt from Mrs. Weiss's bed. She turned to me with tears in her eyes and said, "Oh, Roberta, sweetie, she's gone."

I said the stupidest thing. "Gone where?"

"She has passed away. Oh, Roberta, I blame myself. I should have been here."

Mrs. Roman started to talk, but her words sounded far away to me, as if I were underwater. "I drove her to the doctor this morning. He said it was pneumonia. He wrote out a prescription for her. We got back here, I got her settled in, and then I went out to Eckerds to get it filled. I should never have left. I came back, and I found her dead, in her bed. Dead of a heart attack."

I clutched at my heart, like it was going to stop, too.

But Mrs. Roman just kept on talking. "Her daughter is taking care of the funeral arrangements. You know, she didn't really have anybody down here."

I felt a surge of pain and cried out, "She had me!"

Mrs. Roman took in my words with such force that she dropped the quilt. She held out her arms for me to come to her, so I did. I ran and buried my face into her chest while she talked on and on. "I know she did, sweetie. Yes, she had you. You were the one. You were the one, Roberta. You were the apple of her eye."

THURSDAY, THE 26TH ✣ I didn't know what to do with myself today. At breakfast time I sat in Mrs. Weiss's kitchen, dwelling on all my problems, asking my mother over and over, *What should I do? What should I do?*

I didn't receive an answer, but that was okay. I didn't really expect to. It still felt comforting to talk to her.

I walked out of the apartment into the blinding heat and headed south. I rounded the anchor store, crossing the parking lot diagonally. I could have kept going down Everglades Boulevard to the school bus stop, but I didn't.

Instead I stopped at the spot where Will had placed his cross. It was long gone, but in my mind it still stood there, and it probably always would. I bowed my head at the spot, picturing Will's memorial cross as it was that first day. I listened to the traffic rushing by, thinking about life and death. Then, suddenly, I knew what to do about my mother's death. This was it: I had to make somebody else watch that videotape.

I crossed the northbound lanes and walked rapidly all the way to Sawgrass Estates. I entered the kitchen, headed straight into the bedroom, and dug the tape out of the back of my closet. I peeled off the ATLANTIC COUNTY EVIDENCE label and replaced it with a piece of white paper, taped down on four sides. Then I took a pen and wrote on the paper, *Stephen Cross as a teenager.* I stuck the tape into my backpack and hurried back outside, to the bus stop.

When I got off the bus, I walked up to the Channel 57 Studios like always. But this time I kept walking, past the modern white building to the sand-colored renovated church behind it, the Eternal Word Studios.

I went in and found myself facing a wall made of Sheetrock, covered with a thin coat of gray paint. The wall was about twelve feet high. The old church ceiling, however, was about forty feet high, so the wall stretched across the wide church entrance like a baby gate. An agile person could hop up on a desk and vault right over it.

I saw no one, and I heard no one, but I knew this was the place. Behind the desk was a poster of Stephen Cross under a banner that read, JOIN OUR CRUSADE.

I waited for a moment and listened. I heard water running somewhere, so I projected my voice over the wall of Sheetrock as best I could. "Hello? Is anybody in there?"

Footsteps started behind the wall. Then a lady in a blue dress, with heavy makeup, came around one end of the wall. She smiled at me. "Can I help you?"

"Yes, ma'am. I want to deliver this video to Stephen Cross." I reached into my backpack, pulled out the tape, and handed it to her.

She said, "Well, bless your heart," and took it from me. "Now, what is this exactly?"

"Do you see what it says on the label?"

The lady turned it around and read aloud, "*Stephen*

Cross as a teenager. Well, I bet that will be fun for the Reverend Cross to see. I'll show this to him when he arrives today." She stopped smiling, thought for a moment, and asked, "Now, how did you get it?"

"It belongs to me. It has belonged to my family for seven years."

"I see." She walked over to the desk and picked up a pack of big yellow Post-it notes. "Can I get your name and address?"

"Yes, ma'am. I am Roberta Ritter. My mother's name was Mary Ann Ritter. I can be reached at Arcane at the West End Mall."

She looked confused. "A mall?"

"Yes, ma'am. Out on Route Twenty-seven."

She wrote all of that down. "Okay. I will see that he gets it."

"Thank you." I walked back outside and stood at a hot-as-hell bus stop on Everglades Boulevard. I watched every car that drove by, hoping Stephen Cross might arrive before the bus. But that didn't happen.

As the bus pulled up to the mall entrance, I caught sight of Betty making her way through the parking lot. I waited for her and asked, "Are you out of school already?"

She squinted in the glare, then recognized me. "Yeah. We had Archie again for Journalism, so I split."

"You got past the cops?"

"Oh, they're all gone. The alert is over."

"That's good."

"Yeah. It was stupid."

I slowed down, and Betty did, too. I asked her, "Did you get a new job yet?"

"No, I'm still at Devin's."

"Are you still looking?"

"No." She added, "I'll be sixteen in another month. Then I can work wherever I want. Legally, even."

"I'm sixteen now."

"Yeah? It's weird. My mom was sixteen when she had me." Betty squinted at me and explained. "My mom's parents used to drive to Florida every year. They'd come here from Quebec for three months — January, February, and March. They'd drive down in a big Buick Roadmaster. I have a picture of my mom standing in front of it. Humongous car. They'd stay at one of the French-speaking hotels on the Strip, then they'd drive back up on April first."

"To Canada?"

"Yeah. Quebec City. That's where I was born."

"Really?"

"Uh-huh. She had me up there, like, nine months after she met my dad down here. My grandparents didn't even know she was pregnant until they got home to Canada. The next year they drove me down, in the big Roadmaster, and they gave me to my dad. I've been with him ever since."

I hadn't expected to hear that. I asked her, "Then . . . then, did your mom start to visit you?"

"Nope. I never saw her again. They stopped coming to Florida."

"So . . . do you hate her for that?"

Betty looked disappointed in me. "No. No way. I understand her. I have for a long time now. And now here I am, sixteen years old, just like she was. I'm glad I don't have two nasty parents, in a big Roadmaster, taking my baby away from me. I feel for her. I really do." Betty started toward the mall entrance. "I'd better get to Candlewycke."

When I got to Arcane, things appeared to be more depressing than usual. I went behind the counter and joined Kristin and Karl. Karl had obviously been crying. I looked at Kristin as if to say, *What's going on?*

She told me, "Karl's very upset about what's happening to our dad."

Kristin put an arm around Karl's shoulder. "Dad's always been so straight. You know? So responsible. And now this."

"And now what?"

"Bankruptcy. He filed for bankruptcy. We'll get to keep the house. But we'll lose our savings. All of it."

We stood for a while. Then I realized that they might not know my news. I said, "Has anyone told you about Mrs. Weiss?"

Kristin nodded sympathetically. "Yeah. The lady who talks all the time stopped over."

"Mrs. Roman?"

"Yeah. She told us about it. I'm really sorry, Roberta. I know she was your friend."

I nodded. "She was a lot more than that."

We all stood glumly in the dead mall. Finally Kristin

lightened the mood a little. "Hey, guess who called last night? Our mom."

"Oh? That's great."

"Yeah. She just got a new job. She was working for a small car company. Now she got a job with Daimler-Chrysler. They make the Mercedes-Benz."

"Great."

"That's not even the great part. She took the job because they have a big sales office in Miami, and they need German-speaking people over here."

I said, "That sounds good, right, Karl?" But Karl couldn't even look at me. I tried, "That sounds good for all of us."

At my break I walked over to Isabel's Hallmark. Mrs. Roman had written CLOSED on an envelope and taped it to the door. I leaned my face against the glass and thought about Mrs. Weiss.

I haven't been able to focus on the fact that she's gone. Even this morning, when I woke up in her empty condo, I couldn't understand the concept of her death. I guess it will hit me soon. I hope so.

FRIDAY, THE 27TH ❧ I decided to go back to school today.

In the guidance office Mrs. Biddulph pulled me aside and said, "I have a little job for you to do, Roberta. I'd like you to wheel the video camera into the principal's office."

"Yes, ma'am."

Mrs. Biddulph waited while I got the equipment and squeaked my way to the closed door. Then she opened it and pointed me inside.

Mr. Archer was in there, seated at his old desk. He looked pretty good, considering all the stuff that he was going through. He looked calm.

He said, "Good morning, Roberta. How are you today?"

"Fine, sir."

"Thank you for taking care of this for me."

"Sir?"

He smiled. "I'm sorry. Didn't Mrs. Biddulph explain?"

"No, sir."

"I see. Well, you're to tape a brief statement by me to the students. You can show it before the Pledge and Banner video, provided it's approved by Mrs. Biddulph."

I just stared at him.

He asked, "You ready?"

"Yes, sir." I removed the lens cap, aimed the camera at him, and said, "Rolling."

Mr. Archer looked into the camera. "Good morning, students. First I want to thank the county, and Mrs. Biddulph, the acting principal, for giving me a few minutes to say my piece. Thank you.

"I just want to say how sorry I am if I offended anyone on Monday. Let me tell you what happened. I got so busy that day that I forgot to take my blood-pressure medicine. I'm afraid I blew my stack at those reporters.

But make no mistake about it, the things I said that day were wrong. They were not true.

"I have spent thirty years teaching young people, and in that time I have seen great progress between all the races. I hope my . . . unfortunate remarks did not set back that progress to any degree. Now I am retiring from my duties as of immediately. I wish you all the very best, and I thank you again for giving me a final moment with you. God bless you all."

Mr. Archer smiled into the lens. Then he nodded at me, indicating that he was through.

I turned off the camera and pressed the Rewind button as Mr. Archer got to his feet. I felt really bad for him. I wanted to thank him for standing up for Hawg. And for going to the police station with him. And for calling him a fine young man. But I couldn't think of the right words, so I didn't.

I wheeled the camera back out, ejected the tape, and put it in the console. I was going to ask Mrs. Biddulph to preview it, but she wasn't around. So I played Mr. Archer's farewell, just as he had said it, before the Pledge and Banner tape.

I still felt really bad when I got to the mall today, bad about many things. I felt weighted down. I walked up to the card store, expecting to read the CLOSED envelope again. But instead I saw Mrs. Roman at the front, dusting a display.

I searched the store for customers. There weren't any. Mrs. Roman knocked off dusting to talk to me, but

I started talking first. I told her what had been on my mind for the past two days. "I caused Mrs. Weiss to die. She went out into that storm to save me."

I expected Mrs. Roman to be shocked. Instead she practically laughed. "You know what Isabel would say to that? Baloney!"

"You don't know what happened."

"She told me the whole thing. She had to. Her car looked like it was in the demolition derby. What am I going to do, ignore that?"

I shook my head in agreement. "No."

"No. Isabel accepted responsibility for everything that she did. I've been thinking about it too, sweetie. I think Isabel sent me to that drugstore so she could die in peace. I was talking too much, you know, trying to keep her spirits up? When all she really wanted to do was let go. Old people get that way, Roberta. They've had enough, and they want to go. They want to see their husbands, or wives, or parents."

I had a hard time with that concept. I said, "Do you really think she's with her husband?"

"Yes. I do. Her spirit is with his now. We have to get the rest of her there."

"What do you mean?"

Mrs. Roman suddenly got upset with herself. "Oh, Roberta. I'm so sorry. You, of all people, you should be the first to know these things." She stopped to collect her thoughts. "I'm sorry. I've never been in charge of so much important stuff. Okay. First of all, she's being buried in New York."

"Not next to her husband?"

"Yes, next to her husband. He's up in New York."

I corrected her. "No. He's not. He's in the Jewish section at Eternal Rest."

Mrs. Roman waved my words away. "Harry isn't buried at Eternal Rest. He hated Florida. He's up in Long Island, at Forest Lawn."

I insisted, "No. He was buried here. In the Jewish section. Mrs. Weiss would visit his grave when I visited my mom's."

"Did you ever see his grave? Did you ever read his headstone?"

I thought about those questions. I admitted, "No."

"She drove you out there so you could visit with your mother. I guess she figured you needed a reason to be alone, so she pretended she had something to do. That was a little silly, but Isabel could be silly."

I shook my head in disbelief. Mrs. Roman continued, "Do you know, that daughter of hers is not even having a ceremony down here? Listen to this, Roberta, and tell me what you think. She's having the undertaker drive Isabel to the airport tomorrow, and she's meeting 'the coffin,' as she puts it, up in Islip, Long Island.

"I said, 'I'll tell you what, miss. I'll go with Isabel to the airport, so she won't be alone. So they don't treat my friend like some package that's getting shipped Federal Express. She means too much to me to let anybody do that.' And do you know what she said?"

"What?"

"'You can do that if you like, but it won't be necessary.'" Mrs. Roman clenched her jaw in anger, reliving the conversation.

I asked her, "Can I go with you tomorrow, Mrs. Roman? I need to say good-bye, too."

"Of course you can. I expected that you would want to. I've already told the undertaker about you. He's a very nice man. He wears a nice suit.

"The flight is early, at nine A.M. I'll be here at the card shop at seven-thirty. The undertaker is going to pick me up here. He'll have Isabel's body with him." Mrs. Roman raised up her eyebrows. "At first I thought that sounded disrespectful, but then I thought, *Isabel wouldn't mind*. What do you think, Roberta?"

"No, I don't think she would mind. This was her home."

"Can you be here that early?"

"Most definitely. I'll meet you right here."

Uncle Frank returned today, but Karl drove him home at seven, "to sleep." And Will left after the late run to the trash trailer. By 9:01 Arcane was closed and locked up for the night. Only Kristin and I remained, which was the way I had planned it. I said, "I want to talk to you about something."

"What?"

"Surviving. Do you want to survive?"

She looked at me curiously. "Of course I do."

"Are you willing to fight to survive?"

Kristin gave me her most serious look. "I'm listening."

"Notice it's just you and me tonight. All the men are gone. Do you know why?"

"Why?"

"They've given up. Hawg, Will, Uncle Frank, Dad, even Sam — the men have all given up. They all think that Ray Lyons has won, and we have lost."

"Well, hasn't he won? Isn't the mall bankrupt?"

I pointed toward the rotunda. "He doesn't care about the mall! He never has. There's only one thing Ray Lyons cares about, and there's only one thing he wants to win. That's the election. He'll say or do anything to win the election."

Kristin shook her head back and forth quickly. "Help me out here, cuz."

"I have this crazy idea. I don't even know how it can work, and I can only tell you your part of it. That goes for anybody else who helps us. You only know your parts. The responsibility part, the blame part, is mine alone."

I knew Kristin was in. Definitely in. Her eyes lit up like they had the night she brought Will back from the dead. She said simply, "Where do we start?"

I took out Mrs. Knight's business card and held it up so that she could read it. I picked up the phone and said, "We start by using the power of the media."

Kristin dropped me off at Century Towers at ten o'clock. I grabbed a banana and some iced tea and flopped on the couch — Mrs. Weiss's couch. I called Karl at home, and then Will, and then Betty.

Then I turned on Mrs. Weiss's TV. There was no *Last Judgment* show tonight. Instead the Eternal Word Channel showed a rerun of a gospel choir performance. Stephen Cross did not appear at all. I wondered if he was watching his video.

SATURDAY, THE 28TH ❧ I arrived at the mall this morning at seven-thirty, in step with the early morning power-walkers. Mrs. Roman was already inside the card shop. She let me in, too, and we each selected a card from a Hallmark rack.

I found a white card embossed with a white dove; it was blank inside. Mrs. Roman found one with praying hands; it had a message about God inside. I don't know what she wrote in hers. But in mine I wrote, *I love you, Mrs. Weiss. I will not give up. Roberta.*

When that was taken care of, she said to me, "We should pay for these cards, Roberta, but I don't want to put a cash drawer in the register and then leave. What if somebody breaks in and robs the place? They do that, you know. People are such devils. They look in the paper to see who died, and to see when the funeral is going to be. Then they go and rob them during the funeral."

I said, "That's terrible."

"Of course. People are so rotten and dishonest. I feel dishonest just for taking this card without paying for it. Isabel wouldn't have liked that. She was always very strict about the rules in the store. You should be the same way."

"What do you mean?"

"Don't relax the rules. The rules are the rules, right? You should keep them that way."

I said, "What are you talking about, Mrs. Roman?"

Mrs. Roman stared at me. "I'm talking about your store policies. I'm saying you shouldn't change the rules, because they work."

I stared back at her blankly. Suddenly her expression changed. Her eyes grew wide. She pulled back and said, "Oh, my god. Roberta, you don't know."

"Know what?"

Mrs. Roman spoke very rapidly. "I asked her if you knew. I asked her a month ago. She said, 'I'm going to tell her. She'll know.'"

"What?"

"Oh, my god. She didn't tell you. She must have thought she still had time."

I was getting alarmed now. And a little fed up. "Mrs. Roman! What's going on?"

She held out her hands in an all-encompassing gesture. "Isabel left it to you. She left everything to you."

"To me? What to me?"

"Everything."

It took a long, eerie moment for those words to sink in. But they finally did. I understood. I understood that my life had just changed entirely. I repeated, "To me?"

"She never said anything?"

"No."

"It's all been going to you for a long time. For the last couple of years, at least. Isabel showed me the papers."

I bowed my head. I couldn't speak.

"And she asked me to handle executing the will. Can you believe that? Me? I never even balanced a checkbook before. Not until this year. My Joe always did all of that stuff. He paid all the bills for forty years. The first bill I ever paid was his hospital bill."

I interrupted her, "Please, Mrs. Roman, I need to understand this."

"What's to understand, Roberta? It's all yours. The business, the condo, the other properties."

I decided that I had to deal with this later. I couldn't fit one more complicated thing into my brain. It would have to wait.

Mrs. Roman assured me, "Listen, Roberta, we'll have plenty of time to talk about this . . . estate business. For now, I think we should stand outside and wait. I don't want a big spectacle outside, you know? People standing around staring at the hearse, wondering who's in there. Isabel wouldn't like that. Come on. You bring the cards."

We locked up and walked back through the rotunda toward the entrance. As soon as we made the turn, I could see that we were too late. A long black hearse was already parked in front of the glass doors, and a group of old people were looking at it. Mrs. Roman muttered to me, "Busybodies."

But when we pushed the doors open, she called out

to them in a friendly voice, "That's Isabel. Isabel Weiss. She lived in Number Three-oh-three at Century Towers. She owned the Hallmark store here in the mall."

The old people turned and looked at her; a couple of them nodded. Mrs. Roman added, "She was a nice lady."

The old people parted to let us through. The driver of the hearse jumped out and hurried around to open the back door. He was a small man with white hair and a blue suit.

He bowed slightly as he opened the door. "How are you, Mrs. Roman?"

"I'm fine, John. This is Roberta, the girl I was telling you about."

"Hello, Roberta. I'm very sorry about your loss."

I answered, "Thank you." And followed Mrs. Roman into the wide backseat.

I sat back and Mrs. Roman took my hand. I looked over at her and saw that she had begun to cry. She held my hand like that, and didn't speak, all the way to the airport.

We drove through a gate that said SPECIAL CARGO and stopped on the tarmac. Three workmen appeared and stood at the back of the hearse. As soon as John got out and unlocked the back, I started to get a panicky feeling. I turned to watch out of the dark-tinted window as John slid out a stretcher on wheels and the three guys arranged themselves around it.

I shouted, "Oh, Mrs. Roman! This is it! This is really it. This is good-bye." I threw open the door and scrambled out onto the tarmac. I ran back to the casket, shouting, "Wait!"

John held up one hand to the other men. They stopped and took a step backward. I reached my hand out and touched the dark metal of the casket. Then I tried to encircle the entire top section, where Mrs. Weiss's head was, with my arms. My arms would only go about halfway around, but I hugged her as best I could.

After a few seconds I stepped back. John put his hand down, and the men moved back to their positions. I stood there and watched them wheel her away. I didn't need to put any fingers up to my face this time. I knew I was crying. I could feel hot tears running down my cheeks.

Neither Mrs. Roman nor I spoke again all the way back to the mall. Then it was like a spell had been broken. The funeral duties were over, and the work duties had begun.

Mrs. Roman looked at me nervously and said the strangest thing. "Well, Roberta, I don't know what to do now. You're the owner of the store. You tell me."

"Please, Mrs. Roman, don't do this."

She held up one finger. "Okay. Let me make a suggestion. You let me run the store like I've been doing, at least for the next few weeks. That'll give you time to mourn, sweetie. People need time to mourn. Me, I've been through this. I know mourning. It's easier for me to handle than for you."

"All right. Thank you." I sat down numbly on the stool behind the register.

Mrs. Roman didn't let me mourn for long, though. She started right in, "Now, let me tell you some financial things that you may or may not know about. Your father signed a paper to open a trust fund that contains all of your money and property."

"He did?"

"He certainly did. Isabel showed me the paper. She showed me all the papers. One had his signature and, of course, a notarized seal."

I realized that I had probably tricked him into signing it, like everything else. I tried to focus on what she was saying. I asked her, "What is in this trust fund?"

"Everything that Isabel owned. Who else was she going to give it to? That daughter who didn't need her for anything? No. It's all yours, Roberta. And it's a lot — minus some money to the lawyer and whatever the funeral arrangements wind up costing. I have to pay those bills out of the estate. That's part of my job."

I pressed my fingers against my eyelids. "Because you're the executor?"

"Yes. I'm the executor of the will. That job only lasts for a week or two, until those bills get paid. But I'm also the guardian of the trust, because you're a minor. That job lasts until you turn eighteen. Get it?"

"Yes. I understand."

"You need a guardian of the trust to keep your father from getting his hands on the money. Isabel, of course, was very worried about that. Guess who the guardian was before I came along? Mr. Lombardo! Can you believe that?"

"I can't believe any of it."

"It's like you had a guardian angel."

"I guess."

"I don't guess. I know you did." Mrs. Roman turned on the register. I looked up at the clock. It was already ten-thirty. I gasped, "Oh no! Mrs. Roman! I have something I have to take care of today. I have to go."

"Then you should go. You should do whatever you have to do. I'll keep things running here." She unlocked the glass door enough to let me out.

I said, "Thank you. Thank you for everything." and hurried into the mallway. I walked quickly through the glass doors. Then I ran across the parking lot and down Everglades Boulevard until my side started to ache. I was walking fast along 111th Street when Kristin pulled up across from me in her Volkswagen. Karl was sitting next to her. I climbed into the back next to Will.

Karl turned toward me. His eyes were in focus. "So, cuz, I hear you got a secret plan."

"Yeah, I'll explain more when we pick up Betty."

Kristin asked, "So, where does our 'witch' live?"

We turned into the Golden Glades Mobile Home Community. A young guy with dark hair and a mustache was washing a pickup truck at the third trailer in. Kristin pulled into the driveway and rolled down the window. "Is this where Betty lives?"

The man turned off the hose. "Who?"

Kristin turned to me. "Oh no. Is that the wrong name?"

"I don't think so."

Kristin repeated, "Betty. The girl who works at the West End Mall."

The man said, "Yeah. She lives here." Betty came out of the mobile home. He turned to her and said, "Must be a mistake. This bunch looks normal."

Betty ignored him. She squeezed into the back with Will and me, and the man went back to washing his truck.

As soon as Kristin pulled out, Karl turned around again and said, "All right. We're all here. So what's this plan?"

I explained it this way: "I know the lady who books the guests for *Angela Live*. If we can pass an audition today, we'll be on the show on Monday."

Betty asked, "How is that supposed to save our jobs? Isn't *Angela Live* always a freak show? What are we supposed to be? Freaks?"

I told her simply, "Yeah. They want a freak show about kids who can't tell virtual reality from reality. We need to go in and give them that."

Karl asked, "So . . . what if we pass this audition?"

"They will do *Angela Live* from Arcane."

"Cool."

"Let me go over your parts, okay? It's very important that you understand your parts. Each of you is playing a different kind of freaky teenager."

I turned to Will. I noticed that he was wearing an

Ironman T-shirt. That had to be the first time he'd worn it since the trash trailer incident. I told Kristin, "Good idea, Kristin. Will has on the perfect shirt."

She said, "Yeah. And check out Karl's feet."

Karl struggled to show me. Instead of his usual sneakers, he had on shiny black combat boots.

I said, "Great. Great."

I turned back to Will. "Listen, Will, you need to talk about how you listened to too much heavy metal rock music, and now you hear voices telling you what to do."

Will looked very nervous. "What kinda voices?"

"I don't know. Like, deep, loud voices. Try to say something really scary and demonic."

"Like what?"

Kristin broke in, in a fake baritone, "Like, 'I am the voice of Satan. Do as I bid you.'"

But Will just repeated it back in his normal, high-pitched voice. "I am the voice of Satan. Do as I bid you."

Kristin laughed. She told him, "On second thought, maybe you should say that you can't remember what the voices tell you. Yeah, like, you have blackouts afterward."

I said, "Good. That's good. Now, Karl, you're going to have to say stuff about Nazis. Like, you think Hitler is good. Like, 'Hitler had the right idea.'"

Karl was still in a clearheaded time. He answered, "But I don't know anything about Hitler."

I said, "Come on, Karl. You grew up in Germany."

"Hey, I never even heard about him in Germany. It's like he never existed there."

"Well, then, you can say that you read about him over here. And you listen to him on television."

Kristin objected, "Hitler's not on television. He was too long ago."

"He certainly is on television. I've seen him. I've heard him make speeches in German on the History Channel. And you actually speak German, right, Karl?"

"*Ja, ich spreche.*"

"So you could listen to his speeches and actually understand what he's saying?"

"*Ja.*"

"Then you say that you spend all your time listening to Hitler. Okay, Karl?"

"*Jawohl.*"

I turned to Betty. "Now Betty, what you need to do is —"

She cut me off. "Never mind what I need to do. I know what I need to do."

"Okay. But we all need to —"

"I said I know. I understand. I don't even care about the stupid mall."

"All right. Sorry."

Betty looked out the window angrily. I thought it best to leave her alone.

Karl asked me, "What about you?"

"Me? I'm running the board. I hope."

We pulled into the studio lot. I directed Kristin to

park in back, between Channel 57 and the Eternal Word. I led the group around to the front door, past the equipment area, and into Angela's studio. Mrs. Knight, Bill, and Mr. McKay were already in there.

Mrs. Knight walked up and looked over the group carefully. She definitely liked what she saw. I quickly introduced everyone, but I didn't think she was listening. I guessed she was calculating how the show would work best, and that was fine with me.

Mrs. Knight told them, "Okay. Everybody follow me."

They all walked out onto the soundstage. Mrs. Knight seated them on three high stools — Betty to the left, Will in the center, and Karl on the right. Kristin stood off to the side, by Camera 1, where Will could see and hear her.

I joined Bill and Mr. McKay in the booth. It was my first time in there. The booth was a rectangular room with big soundproof windows. Most of its space was taken up by an awesome control board with hundreds of buttons and dials. While Bill stared at the dials, Mr. McKay opened up the studio mike and announced, "We're going to get some sound levels now. Girl on the left, go ahead and say something."

Kristin pointed up to the booth, indicating to Betty that she ought to answer. Betty finally said, "What?"

"This is your sound check. Please say something."

"Like what?"

"Like your name."

"My name is Elizabeth Lopez."

"Thank you. Next." That would have been Will, but

he didn't say anything, either. I could hear Kristin whispering to him and Will answering, "What?"

Mr. McKay said, "This isn't rocket science, people. When it's your turn to speak, you say your name, or something else, so we can get a sound level on you."

"My name is William Royce."

"Thank you. Next."

Karl looked up at the boom mike above him. He snapped his head back and shouted "*Achtung!*" as loud as he could.

Bill nearly jumped a foot. He yelled into the studio mike, "Don't do that again!"

I leaned over to the mike and said, "Mrs. Knight?"

She turned and looked up at the booth. "Yes?"

"Mrs. Knight, it's Roberta."

"Yes? What?"

"Remember, I said I wanted to learn how to run the board for this show?"

Mrs. Knight thought for a moment. "Right. Yes. Mr. McKay, is it all right if Roberta learns some of the cues?"

Mr. McKay leaned over in front of me. "Of course. That would be fine. Is everybody ready?"

Mrs. Knight said, "Yes, we're ready down here."

Mr. McKay told Bill, "Show Roberta what to do on the voice cues."

Bill looked at me with anger, but he did what he was told.

As the audition unfolded, Mr. McKay would say things like, "Camera One," "Camera Two," and "Open

Angela's mike," and Bill would push the necessary button or turn the necessary dial. Everything was clearly labeled, so it was no big deal. Of course, it *was* a big deal for Bill.

Mrs. Knight stood between Camera 1 and Camera 2, where Angela usually stands, but she made no attempt to do an Angela imitation. She pointed to Betty and asked her in a flat voice, "What would you reply if Angela asked you, 'Why are you a witch?'"

Betty thought for a moment, then answered like a Miss America contestant, "I am a witch because I believe in the ancient powers and the ancient wisdom. I believe they are better than anything we have today."

Mrs. Knight asked another question. "Do you believe in God?"

"I believe in many gods — including Jesus, Vishnu, and Zeus."

"Exactly how do you, yourself, practice witchcraft?"

"I practice witchcraft by calling on the arcane arts — such as herbology, astrology, tarot, and numerology."

"I see. And do you have a big black cat?"

I could almost feel Betty tense up at that one. She took a deep breath before answering. "Witches are just as likely to have little white dogs as big black cats. Myself, I have goldfish."

Mrs. Knight laughed. "All right. Thank you." Then she turned to Will. "Ironman? Why do they call you that?"

Will looked at Kristin, who pointed to his T-shirt. He

pulled his shirt out and answered, "Because of my shirt."

"I see. That's what it says on your shirt. And you also have what on your shirt — a death's-head?"

Will answered, "Yes, ma'am." Then he added, "Satan stuff."

Mrs. Knight seemed confused. "What do you mean?"

"I listen to so much heavy metal that I hear voices. Like Satan's."

"I see. And do you ever play the virtual reality games?"

Will looked at Kristin, who nodded. "Yeah. I play them every night. It's like I can't stop."

Mrs. Knight nodded and waited for more, but there wasn't any more. Will just stared at her.

Betty saw that and broke in, "I play them, too. They're so real that I can't tell where reality ends and fantasy begins."

Mrs. Knight turned back to her. "Ah! Tell me more about that."

"Sometimes when I'm in a virtual reality game, or 'experience' as we call it, I think it's real. When I get out of it and walk around the mall, I think the mall is the fantasy."

"Uh-huh."

Will said, "Me, too."

Mrs. Knight turned to Karl. "Now, Karl, are you a skinhead?"

"*Jawohl.*"

"Do you speak German?"

"*Ja, ich spreche Deutsch. Und Sie?*"

"Do you speak English?"

"I do. Although reluctantly, because it is the language of the weak and the inferior."

"Tell me more about that."

I noticed Angela over on the left side of the theater. I didn't know how long she had been in the studio, but she had obviously heard enough to pique her interest. I could hear her, through Mrs. Knight's mike, ask, "Is this the virtual reality show?"

Mrs. Knight answered proudly, "Yes, it is."

"They look great. Do they have a lot to say?"

"Oh yes. They sure do!"

Angela studied Betty, Will, and Karl, one by one. Then she said, "They're perfect. Go ahead and book it."

Mrs. Knight spun back to the auditioners and announced, "You heard the lady. You're in. We have some paperwork for you on the way out. Otherwise we'll see you at three o'clock Monday at Arcane."

I saw my opportunity, and I took it. I stepped out of the booth and said, "Angela?"

Angela smiled at me, thought about my name for a moment, then said, "Yes, Roberta?"

"I think Ray Lyons might like to appear on this show, too."

"Oh? Why?"

"Because the hate crimes at the West End Mall could be a direct result of these virtual reality games."

Angela focused on me more closely. "Keep talking."

"Mr. Lyons owns the mall. He's already trying to solve these hate crimes himself."

"Who are these crimes against? A black guy?"

"No. An Arab. And there's a virtual reality game there called Crusader that makes people want to attack Arabs."

Angela smiled at Mrs. Knight. "This is getting better and better." She asked me, "Can we get this Arab guy to come on?"

"Maybe. I'll ask him."

"Yeah. You do that. You get him, and I'll get Ray Lyons." She turned to Mrs. Knight. "Get Philip Knowlton on the phone."

Mrs. Knight left right away to do that. Angela turned to me again. "Do you have any more ideas for this show?"

I pulled a CD out of my backpack. "This is the virtual reality CD-ROM for Crusader. I thought we could use it as an intro to the show. The people could see the Arabs torturing the Christians and everything."

"Great. Mr. McKay will have to preview that, though."

"All right. I'll transfer part of it to videotape. I can put some of this hardcore CD on tape, too." I pulled out Krystallnacht and showed it to Angela. She seemed impressed.

"This is great stuff, Roberta. Maybe I'll make *you* my producer."

Suddenly I heard Betty call out, "Hey, Roberta! Can we go? I gotta get to work."

"Yeah. Thanks, Betty. Thanks, everybody. I guess you heard that the show is on for Monday. I still have to do some editing here, so I'll see you back at the mall."

Kristin, Karl, Will, and Betty gathered themselves up and trooped out the studio door.

I left the studio, too, and walked over to an editing machine in a small room off the lobby. I emptied out the items from my backpack and worked for about ninety minutes. When I was finished, I had made two highlight videos for Angela, one based on Crusader and one based on Krystallnacht. Then I made a different video for myself based on Ray Lyons's man-in-the-street interviews.

I left Angela's videos on Mr. McKay's chair in the booth, with a note on top, *Tapes for virtual reality show.*

As I finished the note, I heard Angela's voice from behind me, "What? You're still here?"

I turned and said, "Yeah, I was just finishing those tapes. Crusader and Krystallnacht."

"Oh yeah. I want to see those."

"Do you want me to play them for you?"

"No, not now. I gotta get to the spa. I just want to thank you again for being such a hardworking intern. They're not all like you."

"Well, I like learning this stuff."

"Is this what you want to do?"

"I think so. I think I'd like to be a news reporter."

Angela twisted up her mouth. "Well, I don't want to discourage you, but that's a tough job to break into. You might want to think about producing instead." She started off. "Thanks again for all that you're doing for the show."

"Sure."

I said, "Angela? Do you really think you can get Ray Lyons for the West End Mall show?"

"I already got him, kid. I talked to Knowlton ten minutes ago."

"Great."

"Yeah. I always get my man. See you."

SUNDAY, THE 29TH ❧ This morning, I woke up in Condo #303, showered, and ate breakfast. Then I called our answering machine at Sawgrass Estates. There was only one message: "This is Mr. Lewis from Arcane Industries in Antioch, Illinois. You have missed your third straight payment. Your franchise is officially in default. I believe you understand the consequences of that. If you do not, you are welcome to call me. You should probably call me anyway, so that I can make arrangements to reclaim our equipment."

I jotted down the number that he gave and then left for the mall. I pushed open the entrance doors exactly at noon. As soon as I reached the rotunda, I noticed something odd. Karl, Kristin, and Will were huddled together outside the glass doors. The arcade was not open.

Karl looked very upset. He was pumping his arms and rocking on his legs. He sputtered at Kristin, "No way! I'm not going in there."

She told him, "Karl, I can't pick him up by myself."

"No! Get somebody else. Get your boyfriend, here."

Will said, very maturely, "I'm not her boyfriend. I'm her friend."

Kristin clapped her hand on Karl's shoulder and held him still. She told him emphatically, "Karl, this isn't for friends or for anybody else to do. This is for us to do."

"I'm not going in there."

The three of them became aware of me all at once. They stopped talking and looked away, like they were embarrassed.

I said, "What's up?" No one replied, so I looked past them, through the sliding-glass doors. At first I didn't see anything unusual. But then I did.

It was Uncle Frank. He was curled up within the ring of Crusader, just lying there on the raised platform. A black helmet was half on and half off of his head. He appeared to be a total wreck, a broken man. I decided, "I'll go talk to him." I unlocked the door and slid it open a foot.

Kristin tried to stop me. "There's no talking to him, Roberta. Not when he's like this."

I said, "Let's find out."

"No. He's not himself. This is not my dad."

I looked her in the eye and answered, "Oh yes, it is."

I walked over to the Crusader platform. Uncle Frank was making a hollow sound, something in between snoring and gasping. I leaned over him. "Uncle Frank?"

His upper body jerked slightly, enough to make the helmet slide the rest of the way off his head. He managed to say, "What?" in a lost and confused voice.

"Uncle Frank, I just heard from Mr. Lewis, the guy from Arcane Industries, up in Antioch, Illinois. I know you haven't paid them in three months. I know it's all over."

Uncle Frank rolled onto all fours, like he was going to do push-ups. He shook his head furiously, trying to clear it.

I told him, "I just wanted to say this: At least you're here, Uncle Frank. At least you're upset, and angry, and broken up about it. That's because it matters to you. My dad, I'm sure, is at the beach now, or out test-driving a boat."

Uncle Frank looked up at me through bloodshot eyes. He spoke clearly. "You don't know what I did."

"Yes, I do. And I think it was a bad thing to do. A terrible thing. But I don't think it was an evil thing."

He wasn't buying that. He demanded to know, "Then what was it?"

"It was natural law. You fought to save what was yours. You fought with spray paint, and hate, and lies. You fought in a cowardly way" — he bristled at those words — "but I don't think you are really a coward. And I don't think you are really evil. You're just drunk, Uncle Frank. You're drunk, and you've given up. You gave up months ago."

Uncle Frank twisted his body left and right. Then he

managed to sit up. He even managed to regain a bit of his dignity. He reminded me quietly, "I was in Desert Storm."

"I know you were."

"I was sitting in a tank, in the middle of a desert, when your Mr. Samir Samad was sitting in a carseat, in the back of his daddy's BMW."

"Yes, sir. I know that."

Uncle Frank struggled all the way up to his feet. "That's all I have to say." He stepped down off the platform and walked, pretty steadily, into the back.

I watched him go. Then I squeezed back out though the door. I told Kristin, Karl, and Will, "It's over. We're out of business."

Kristin flopped back against the glass. She let herself slide down until she was on the floor. Will did the same, so Karl and I sat down, too. We remained there together for a few minutes, returning the curious stares of the early shoppers.

Then I felt the glass doors sliding against my back. I looked up and saw Uncle Frank. He stepped out, closed the door behind him, then turned and locked it with his key. He made no eye contact with anyone. He just said, "Let's go."

Kristin and Karl hopped up. They each put an arm around Uncle Frank. Then the three of them walked away, through the rotunda and out of sight.

Will and I stood up, too. He said, "I better go help my mom. Is your plan still on for tomorrow?"

"As far as I know. Mrs. Knight was supposed to set it all up."

"All right. I'll see you then." He wandered off to SpecialTees.

I thought about going in to help Mrs. Roman, but I just wasn't ready for that. I took off on a slow walk through the rotunda, into the south section of the mall.

Crescent Electronics had a table full of discounted software set up in the mallway to attract customers. I was surprised to see Sam himself manning the table. There weren't any customers around, so I walked up and said, "Mind if I hang out here with you for a few minutes?"

He shook his head. "No. Please do."

Sam seemed different. Almost lighthearted. I waited for a minute, then I took the opportunity to ask him, "What would you do if a lawyer asked you this: 'Why were you and a girl alone in an abandoned store late at night?'"

Sam looked at me curiously. "I'd tell the truth: 'We were looking to catch the guy who was vandalizing my property.' Why? What made you ask me that?"

"Griffin. He said Uncle Frank's lawyer would go after us for being together in that window."

"That wouldn't bother me. I have nothing to hide." Sam thought for a minute, then asked, "How old are you?"

"Sixteen."

"Oh, great. You're underage. Then I could be arrested. That would be a nice, ironic end to all of this, wouldn't it? Somebody finally gets arrested, but it turns out to be me." Sam looked at me closely. "What are you saying? That you're afraid to testify now?"

"No. Not at all. I just wanted to tell you what Griffin told me."

"Okay. You told me."

"I'm not afraid of anything. I just thought it was funny. Or, like you said, ironic. You know? Like anybody would think I was anybody's girlfriend."

Sam turned toward the store to get the attention of a clerk, a guy with black glasses and a white-blond crew cut. The clerk came out, and Sam said, "Could you watch the table, please? I'm going to take a little walk with Roberta."

The blond guy said, "Sure."

Sam started toward the rotunda, so I followed. After a few yards he said, "Let me tell you something. For the last two months, or more, I have felt like the biggest loser on earth. Think about it: I spent every night sitting in an empty store window. I kept saying, over and over, 'Why me? Why do they hate me? What's wrong with me?'

"That changed when you showed up. Suddenly I wasn't the only one sitting in that window." We entered the food court and turned left. "You know, Roberta, a lot of people saw the paint on my windows; they saw the scratches on my car. They knew what was happening. But you're the only one who actually did something about it, on your own time, just because it was the right thing to do. I'm not going to forget that."

We stopped at Soft Swirl Ice Cream. Sam asked, "Do you like chocolate?" I nodded. He told Geri, the owner, "Two chocolate cones."

When he handed me my cone, I suddenly felt elated. My heart started to pound. Then he said, "Let me tell you something else I've been feeling."

I stopped in midbite of my cone and waited. I guess I was waiting for something like words of love. I have no idea what they might have sounded like, or what I might have said back. As it turned out, that was a stupid thing for me to think.

Sam said, "I've been feeling sorry for your uncle Frank."

I went ahead and took the bite. I hoped my face didn't give away my ridiculous thoughts. I managed to say convincingly, "Why? After what he did to you?"

"Why? Because he had further to fall than most people. Everybody looked up to the colonel. Even strangers. You could see, when they met him, that they looked up to him. That's gone now. What can I do to him that's worse?" He paused and explained, "I've been thinking about forgiving him. About not pressing charges."

We finished our cones and started back toward Crescent. Sam said, "Those nights in the windows were bad, but they weren't wasted. I was forced to think, you know? To think through a lot of things. Anyway, the last two nights weren't bad at all."

That stupid feeling came back. I said, "They weren't?"

"No. They were exciting." He looked at me and smiled. "Hey, we cracked the case, didn't we?"

I smiled back. "Yeah."

We reached the Crescent sale table. Sam gave the clerk a little wave, indicating that he could go back into the store. Sam resumed his place behind the table. He said, "So what's this I hear? You're a store owner now?"

"Yeah. I guess so."

"Isabel's Hallmark?"

"Yes. Mrs. Weiss died. She left it to me."

"I heard that."

"Did you know her?"

"No. Not really. I knew her to say hi to. She used to yell at old Lombardo. I liked that."

I laughed. "Yeah. Inside, though, she was really nice."

"I'm sure she was."

"All the people here are nice."

Sam thought about that and nodded. "You're right. Everybody here is pretty decent, with some minor exceptions." He jerked his head toward Candlewycke. "These people deserve better than what they're getting. They work hard, they play by the rules, they deserve better."

I looked up and down the empty mallway. "So have you given up on the recap?"

"No. Not a hundred percent. Maybe ninety-nine percent."

"Why not a hundred percent?"

"Because" — he paused for emphasis — "ironically, the money is there. There is interest in this mall, Roberta. The problem is, the interest doesn't come from Ray Lyons, and Ray Lyons now holds a commanding lead in the election polls. As soon as he wins that election, you and I are out of business."

"I see. Well, now that I'm an owner, do I get to vote?"

"Sure."

"Then I vote that we don't give up."

Sam looked at me and smiled. "Okay. I'll register that vote."

"I'm not kidding, Sam. Promise me that you will not give up, either. We've all put too much of ourselves into this place to just . . . hold hands and jump into the grave."

Sam stopped smiling. He nodded seriously. He said, "Yeah, okay, Roberta. Okay."

I clapped Sam on the side of his right arm. It felt muscular, not soft at all. I took off walking quickly toward the rotunda. I knew he was watching me.

I turned right and went to the mall office. I sat down in front of Suzie and asked her point-blank, "Is the mall going bankrupt?"

She glared at me, but she finally answered, "That seems pretty obvious, doesn't it?"

"So what are we going to do about that?"

"Sometimes you have to cut your losses, Roberta." Suzie shook her blond bangs in the direction of Arcane. "Your dad finally talked Frank into not sending any more money to that franchisor. That's like flushing it down the toilet. At this point you have to protect what's important to you."

"What if your business is what's important to you?"

She shrugged. "Businesses come and go. So do jobs. I've probably had twenty different jobs. It's no big deal."

"So, has Uncle Frank told you it's over? Has he made it official?"

Suzie reached into her file drawer and pulled out a letter. "Yes, he has. Slot Number Thirty-two is officially vacant as of November first. Arcane is closed, permanently, to the public. However, it will be open tomorrow to tape the Angela del Fuego show live from the mall."

I asked her as innocently as I could, "Why?"

"Because Philip Knowlton wants it to be."

She placed a pink fingernail on a pink phone message on her desk. She paraphrased it for me. "The whole 'Ray Lyons for State Senate' team, including his wife, his son, and his daughters, is coming. Mr. Lyons will get another chance to speak out against hate crimes, and against witches, heavy metal rock music, skinheads, and other issues." Suzie slid the memo into the trash can. Then she returned Uncle Frank's letter to its file.

I left without saying good-bye.

I called Mrs. Roman at six o'clock and told her to close up.

She whispered, like she was frightened, "But what about the mall office?"

"The mall office doesn't care. The mall office has given up."

"Okay, Roberta. You're the owner."

I met Mrs. Roman outside of the card store at six-fifteen. We stopped at SunBelt Savings and deposited a cash bag. Then we stepped outside into the muggy evening. I could sense, all the way to the bus stop, that Mrs. Roman was having a difficult time walking. We crossed the parking lot, and then Route 27, but she kept going without complaint.

Once we were inside the bus stop, waiting, Mrs. Roman told me, "Isabel's beautiful white car was just sitting there getting wet."

"Wet? What do you mean?"

"That car is a foot longer than the carport. And it's had that broken window for a week. Every time it rains, the water seeps in through the back. So I had it towed in to the dealer to be repaired. My husband always said, 'Take it back to the dealer. They cost a little more, but they know what they're doing.' I hope you don't mind, Roberta."

"Why would I mind?"

"It's your car!"

I shook my head at the craziness of that. "I don't even have a license yet."

"No, but you will. Then you'll want to trade it in. You should get a good price for it. You could probably trade it in for a little sports car and not have to pay any extra at all."

The bus arrived. The regular driver was at the wheel. Mrs. Roman dumped six quarters into the box. She told the driver, "That's for two of us."

We got off the bus at Seventy-second Street and walked north. When we reached the cemetery, we started to go our separate ways, as usual. But I stopped and called after her, "Mrs. Roman?"

"What?"

"Your husband, Joe . . . Is he really buried here?"

"Are you kidding?"

"No."

"Where else would he be?"

"You're not just saying that so I'll have someone to go with to the cemetery?"

"No. Not me. I really come out here. Once a week."

"Good. That's what I want to do, too. We'll get somebody to cover on Sundays."

Mrs. Roman nodded in agreement. Then she pointed off to the side. "Look. It's Saint Francis of Assisi."

I looked. The Guardian Angel statue had been replaced with the statue of a small bald man with birds on his shoulders.

Mrs. Roman added, "That's nice."

I wasn't so sure. I walked on to the mausoleum. I stared at all the walls, studying them carefully, with new purpose. I made mental notes of the features I wanted and actually jotted down the numbers of the best ones: 107B, 103D, 101A.

Mrs. Roman came back fifteen minutes later, looking upset. She held up a golf ball. "Look at this! I found it next to Joe's grave."

I held out my hand. "That's terrible. Let me have it."

She handed it over, and I wedged it into my pocket. Then Mrs. Roman and I walked along the one-lane asphalt road. We followed it in a long curve until we got to the door of the mortuary office.

Inside, in the coolness, we were greeted by a pale man in a black suit. He wore thick, wavy glasses, which made his eyes seem teary with sympathy. He asked Mrs. Roman, "May I help you, madam?"

I answered, "No. You can help me, though."

The man turned his watery eyes to me. "Yes, miss. How may I be of service?"

"I want to talk about a burial."

"Certainly. Let's sit down over here." The man led us into a small room off the lobby. He sat behind a desk, and I sat in a chair in front of him. Although there was a second chair, Mrs. Roman chose to stand.

The man took out a self-carbon form and a pencil. "Who is the deceased, miss?"

"My mother."

"I am sorry. When did she pass away?"

"Seven years ago."

"Miss?"

"Seven years ago on October thirty-first. She is already buried here. She is in the Heaven Level, Number 109E. I would like to move her to a lower level. Can you do that?"

"Yes. Certainly. We can do that. We call that a reinterment."

"I want her to have a better spot, and I want her to have a better sign, a bronze one. And a bronze flower vase, and some other features."

The man started to write numbers on the form. He asked me many questions. Then he added everything up, punched some numbers on his desk calculator, and handed me the second page of the form. I never even looked at it. I folded it up, said, "Thank you," and put it in my backpack.

The man walked us toward the door. I said, "Oh, and one more thing. One of your employees, a groundskeeper I guess, has been playing golf on the graves."

The man's teary eyes came into focus. He looked genuinely concerned. "Oh no, miss, I assure you, they would not do that. We provide perpetual care for our graves. We treat them with utmost respect."

I reached into my pocket, held out the golf ball, and let it drop onto the tile floor. We all watched it bounce up and down until its momentum died. I told him, "I assure you, they do. This was on Mr. Joe Roman's grave, in the Catholic section."

The man gulped. He held the door for us. "Yes, miss. I'm very sorry. I will look into this immediately."

Mrs. Roman finally spoke up. "My Joe didn't even like golf."

"Yes, madam."

We walked back out into the sun. She added, "Except for that Arnold Palmer."

MONDAY, THE 30TH ～ I spent the morning by myself at Century Towers, making a list of the things I needed to do and then checking off things as I did them. Attending school was not on the list.

First I called Sam at Crescent Electronics. I explained the *Angela Live* show as best I could. He said, "Yeah. I heard all about it. From Suzie. I heard Lyons is coming, too."

"That's right. That's the most important part of the plan."

"What plan? What are you talking about?"

"I have a plan. I can't tell you any more than that."

Sam exhaled with a long whistling sound. "I don't understand any of this. Angela del Fuego is doing a show about how bad Arcane is?"

"Yeah."

"How can that be good?"

"It's publicity. All publicity is good, Sam. She has millions of viewers around here, millions of people who will hear about the West End Mall. And anyway, what do we have to lose?"

"I see. So is this part of not giving up?"

"Yeah. That's right."

"And I'm supposed to go on the show and be some offended Arab or something?"

That made me feel bad. I said, "Yeah. Look, Sam, I'm sorry. I know you're an American. I hate to keep bringing up this Arab stuff, but everybody is playing a character today. I was hoping you could play one, too."

He agreed, "Okay." Then he asked me, "Hey, did Suzie get a hold of you?"

"No. Why?"

"She just called me. Frantic, of course. She lost those man-in-the-street interviews that we did, or Knowlton never got them, or some such nonsense. Sounds like a typical Suzie screwup. Anyway, she's trying to get you, me, and Lombardo to come in and ask our questions again."

"When?"

"Right before the taping. Lyons and his family are going to be in the mall office during the show. She's got me setting up that wall of TVs again. We're supposed to stop by and pose with 'the candidate' and ask those stupid questions."

"Oh no. I don't have time for that."

"You sound like old Lombardo."

"I guess I'll have to, though."

"She told me three-thirty. On the dot."

I repeated, "Three-thirty. Okay. And then you'll go to Arcane and be on the *Angela* show?"

"Yeah, of course. I wouldn't miss it. Do you want me to wear a towel on my head?"

"Are you kidding?"

"Yes."

This time I exhaled. "Good. Thanks a million, Sam.

And I swear, for the rest of my life, I will never use the word *Arab* around you again."

"Hey, it's cool. I am an Arab. I'm other stuff, too."

"Gotcha. Bye."

Sam hung up. I went back to worrying. The sound check for the *Angela Live* broadcast was scheduled for 3:00 P.M. Now I had to be at the office at 3:30. Still, still, the plan could work. It could work.

I finally left the condo at two-forty-five and walked around the south anchor store. I walked slowly through the parking lot, looking up at the Toby the Turtle banners. Today they were flapping in the hot wind. I felt very, very nervous. I repeated to myself aloud, "You can do this. You can do this."

Then I stopped in my tracks. The glass entrance doors were propped open! The Channel 57 Studios RV was already there!

I ran in past the wall of TVs and into the rotunda. I stopped when I saw the RV. It was parked up against Slot #61, La Boutique de Paris. It was so large that it nearly blocked the entrance to Isabel's Hallmark, too. Thick black wires ran from it across the mallway. They passed under a ragged line of DANGER horses, snaked past the Sony monitor and the Crusader, and spread out inside Arcane.

I climbed up the RV's three steps and opened the door. Bill looked up and started to snarl, like he was going to kick me out, but then he recognized who I was. "Oh, so you're finally here."

I swallowed hard. "Mr. McKay said three o'clock."

"Mr. McKay doesn't work the remotes. I do. Mr. McKay has no idea what it takes to do one. I had to set the whole place up by myself."

"Sorry. That's what he said."

"I need you to guard this place while I set up the soundboard."

"Don't you need me to help set it up?"

Bill adjusted his glasses. He spoke angrily, tensely. "I need you to do exactly as I say. Understand?"

I swallowed hard again and tried to regain my composure. I took off my backpack and slid it behind a seat, where Bill could not see it. Then I took a deep breath and looked out the wide windows.

I had a great view of Arcane, similar to the mannequins' view from their window. Kristin, Karl, and Will were already in there. They were standing behind the register as always. Karl had the words HEIL HITLER written across his shirt in big, black letters.

The floor of the arcade had been completely rearranged. Dragon Slayer and Galactic Defender had been dragged all the way into the back. The rest of the experiences had been pushed against the walls, leaving an empty center area. A row of four high stools, illuminated by two tall light stands, now occupied that space. The Sony monitor was over by the counter. It was hooked up to one of the snaking black cables. Only the Crusader circle was in its original position. Bill was now sitting on its platform and struggling to set up the soundboard. I picked up his headset from the console and listened, but there was no sound.

When I looked back up, Bill was draping a black covering over the soundboard. He had positioned it directly behind the Crusader experience, making it harder to notice. Then, reluctantly I'm sure, he left it and walked back through the DANGER horses to the truck. He opened the door and asked, "Did McKay call?"

"No." I added, "I have to run down to the office for a few minutes. I have to ask a question of Mr. Lyons."

Bill looked at me and demanded to know, "Are you asking questions? Or are you interning?"

"Interning."

"You are?"

"Right. I'm running the board."

"Don't bet on it."

"What?"

"You're not running anything. Except errands."

"I'm running the board!"

"You're not to touch this console, or anything else, unless I tell you to."

"But I ran it at the studio, at the audition."

"You played on it for ten minutes. Do you really think we're going to let a kid intern run a live broadcast? And a remote one at that? No way."

"But —"

"But nothing. Put it out of your head. You're here to listen to me and to do what I tell you. Fast. This is live television."

Bill put on his headset, signaling that the discussion was over. The shock of his words had my head spinning.

I walked down to the mall office, fighting back a feeling of panic. I cut through the arrangement of chairs in front of the TVs. The office was already packed with people.

Ray Lyons and his group had arrived. Philip Knowlton wasn't taking any chances on unforeseen mall disasters today. He had that security guy, Joe Daley, two other sheriff's deputies, and an ambulance with a team of paramedics.

Joe the security guy was standing at the office door. I tried to push it open, but he blocked me. He asked, "What's your business here, miss?"

"I work here."

He turned and looked for Philip Knowlton. He held one finger over my head, pointing me out. Philip Knowlton looked at me and shook his head no. Daley said, "I'm sorry. This is a private party. You can't come in."

"But I work here. And I'm supposed to ask a question. I'm part of the man-in-the-street thing."

Knowlton had drifted closer to us. The guard called over to him. "She says she's in a man-in-the-street thing."

Knowlton thought for a moment. "Yes, that's right. She's the young person. Let her in, but have her stand over there." He pointed to the corner behind my computer.

The guard said, "Go stand over there."

I walked in, but I turned and told him, "This is my office. I'll stand where I like."

"I told him the same thing. Almost word for word." I turned to find Sam at my elbow. He looked at the bodyguard, but he spoke to me. "A little power is a dangerous thing."

Daley turned back to Philip Knowlton, I guess to see if he should kick us out, but Knowlton was talking to the candidate. He gave us one more dirty look, then went back to the door.

Sam said, "Do you remember your man-in-the-street question?"

"Not really. Do you?"

"Yeah. But I'm not gonna ask it. I'm gonna ask some new ones."

"They'll kick you out of the office."

Sam got very dramatic. "Then I'll scream, 'Hate crime! I'm the victim of a hate crime!'"

I laughed at his performance. "That's good."

Suzie came up behind me. She whispered angrily, "Is your father here?"

"I don't know."

Suzie suddenly smiled brightly over my shoulder. I turned to see Philip Knowlton approaching us. He told her, "Let's get started with the questions. The candidate only has about five minutes for this. Are the questioners here?"

Suzie said, "Two of them are. These two."

Knowlton looked us over. "Where's the old guy?"

Suzie said, "He's not here yet."

Knowlton called over to Angela, "Let's do the kid and the minority. We'll get an old guy afterward. Have each one ask a question, then Ray will answer it. Ray!"

Mr. Lyons left the people he was talking to and joined us. He looked the same as the last time. He even had on the same blue suit. I thought that a good omen for my plan.

Philip Knowlton explained to him, "This is that man-in-the-street thing. The one they lost the tape of? We have to do it again."

Mr. Lyons said, "Right. Let's be sure not to lose it this time."

"Do you remember the questions and answers?"

Mr. Lyons looked annoyed, like he had been over this too many times with Knowlton. He barely controlled his anger when he replied, "Phil, I can handle the questions. You can go do something else."

"I'm respecting your wishes, Ray. All the way. I'm going down to check out this arcade place before the show." He turned to Angela. "I don't want Ray to look like he's sitting in some loony bin. You can imagine what his opponent would do with that."

Angela smiled. They set up an area against the south wall of the office. Sam and I stood with Mr. Lyons and prepared to start. But then, at the last moment, Mr. Lombardo appeared. He was dressed in one of Sam's SAVE THE MALL T-shirts. He looked around defiantly, ready to take on whoever might ask him about it, but nobody did.

Angela looked at the cameraman. She said, "Okay, everybody. Whenever you're ready."

The red camera light came on. Angela said, "We're at the West End Mall office, October thirtieth. These questions are to replace the lost questions from September twenty-fifth."

Angela stopped speaking and stepped back. She pointed to Mr. Lombardo. He looked at Ray Lyons and demanded, "What about the recap? Are you going to do it or not? Yes or no?"

Mr. Lyons's eyes darted aside for a moment, like he was looking for Philip Knowlton. Then he remembered he had just kicked him out. He said, "I will answer questions about the fountain or about hate crimes. That's it."

Mr. Lombardo's voice lashed out at him again, filled with scorn. "Do you mean you have to be spoonfed the answers ahead of time or you won't talk?"

Mr. Lyons snapped, "No."

"Then what about the recap?"

"We haven't been able to convince a bank to recapitalize the mall. We're still working on it."

"All you're working on is your tan, you bum."

Joe the guard moved in. Mr. Lyons held up one hand to stop him. Mr. Lombardo put up both arms in front of himself, like a boxer, and shouted angrily, "You want to fight with me? Come on, put up your hands."

Angela stepped back in to try to calm things down. "Boys, boys, come on. It's almost showtime. Let's move on here."

Mr. Lyons agreed. "Yeah, that's enough of this. Let's get up to the show."

Sam said, "Hey! What about my question?"

Mr. Lyons looked suspicious, but he asked, "What is it?"

"I was the victim of hate crimes here at the mall. You made a statement about the guy they accused. Do you remember?"

Mr. Lyons nodded warily. "Yes, that's right. I did."

"Did you hear that he was proved innocent?"

"No. I did not hear that."

"Well, you're hearing it now. His name was Hugh Mason, and he was innocent."

"All right. Thank you for telling me. I hope they catch the real culprit."

Mr. Lyons walked out of the camera area, but Angela called after him, "Hold on, Ray. We only have one more. Roberta, what's your question?"

Mr. Lyons looked at me. He seemed less suspicious. He said, "Oh yes, the young-people question."

I looked at the red light, then at Mr. Lyons. I asked him, "A lot of young people work here at the mall. What will they do if you bulldoze it?"

He narrowed his eyes. "I'm not bulldozing anything, miss."

"But what will those young people do, Mr. Lyons, if they can't work here?"

"I would hope they would find work someplace else."

"Like at a golf course?"

"I don't know anything about that."

Sam jumped back in. "You don't know that your son has filed for a zoning variance to turn this site into a golf course and spa?"

A young man who must have been Richard Lyons stepped out of the family group and leveled a finger at Sam. "That's a lie. That's a lie, and you're a liar."

Sam said, "Excuse me. It wasn't you. It was your company that filed for it."

Ray Lyons held his hands up again. "That's enough! We're going up to the show now. This whole thing was a mistake."

Joe the bodyguard led the candidate out. Then Suzie herded the family and guests into the mallway and sat them in front of the TVs. As soon as Sam and I stepped through the door, Richard Lyons got back in Sam's face. "You're going to regret saying that."

Sam looked up at him. "You better watch who you're threatening, sonny boy. I'm a minority."

A lady who must have been Mrs. Lyons pulled Richard by the elbow. He took a step back. His teeth were clenched tight, but he didn't say anything else.

Sam and I followed Angela and the cameraman up to Arcane. I saw Mrs. Knight pushing the crowd back to let us through. I turned as I heard a frantic cry: "Roberta! Roberta!" Nina and her father were standing in the first row behind the DANGER horses. Nina had a pleading look in her eyes. She yelled, "Can Angela come over?"

Angela heard her. She asked me, "Who's that?"

I muttered, "A big fan. You met her on a studio tour last week."

Nina yelled, "I want my father to meet Angela!"

I was embarrassed. I said to Angela, "Sorry."

"What for? I love my fans. Let's go meet them."

Angela and I walked over to the barricade. The people started to push forward. Nina announced to Angela, as if she was an old friend, "Angela, this is my father, Dr. Jorge Navarro."

Angela smiled and shook hands with him. Nina added, "And this is my fiancé, Carlos." I hadn't noticed Carlos before, but there he was. He, too, shook hands with Angela.

Mrs. Knight called over to us, "Two minutes till the teaser, Angela."

Angela told them all, "I have to get to work. I hope you enjoy the show."

I followed Angela back inside. Two stationary cameras were set up, on the north and south ends, to catch all the action. I saw Kristin. She had staked out a place behind the north camera so Will could see her.

Karl, Will, and Betty were already sitting on stools in the middle of the floor. They looked extremely pale under the harsh lights, like a row of lab specimens. Karl appeared to be zoned out. Will seemed paralyzed. Betty looked distracted and unhappy. Studying their faces, I felt a surge of nausea, and of absolute terror; I was nearly overcome by it. But Karl's eyes suddenly snapped into focus, and he called to me, "What's wrong, cuz?"

I walked over to his stool and whispered to him, "This isn't working. There's no way this is going to work. I'm an idiot."

"No. You're not an idiot. I'm an idiot. You're a brain."

"I'm not, Karl. Not today."

"Let me ask you this: Do you still have the plan?"

"No. It's ruined now."

"How's it ruined?"

Bill uncovered the soundboard behind me. He tossed the black plastic cover aside. I rolled my eyes in that direction. "By him."

Karl nodded thoughtfully. "What do you need to happen to him?"

"I need to get him out of the RV."

"When?"

"After Angela brings in Ray Lyons."

Karl said simply, "You got it."

"What?"

"I'll take care of that part. You take care of your part."

Mrs. Knight walked Sam up to the remaining stool. She called over to Angela, "This is Sam the Arab."

Angela stepped up and shook hands with him. She asked him, "Do you understand what we're doing today?"

"Yes, I do. To a point."

"You sit on the stool. I ask you a question or two about these virtual reality games and these racist attacks against you. You answer nice and clear, and we'll have a great show. Okay?"

"Okay."

"Feel free to get excited, to get angry at people — but don't use any profanity."

"Gotcha."

Angela looked around carefully, getting her bearings. She asked Mrs. Knight, "Where'd you put Ray Lyons?"

"He's in an office in the back of the store. He's with that Mr. Knowlton."

"Okay."

Mrs. Knight called out in a loud voice, "One minute! Places, everybody!"

Everyone hushed. The tension was unbearable, but Angela was totally cool. I supposed she had done this a thousand times. She strolled over to check out the Crusader dummy. She whispered to Mrs. Knight, "Hey, real fast! Can we use this guy on the set?"

Mrs. Knight nodded. "If you want."

"Yeah. Drag him over there. Let's see."

Mrs. Knight grabbed Crusader and dragged him into camera range.

Angela laughed. "Oh yeah. Look at that. He is fine! Put him in my car after the show."

I figured I had better get to my place, too. I squeezed through the crowd and joined Bill at the console. He barely even looked up. He was totally focused on the broadcast now.

I didn't know what to do. I just stood there next to him and looked out at the strange sight. Arcane had been transformed into a soundstage by the powerful white lights. I finally dared to say, "What do you want me to do?"

"Stand there and wait. And don't touch anything."

Bill spoke through his headset to Mr. McKay. "I don't like this. Look at these lowlifes. Any one of them could utter a profanity." He turned to me and pointed to the *Angela* promo tape in the console. "You need to be ready with that."

I looked at the big console. The *Angela* promo tape was on top, ready to go. My Krystallnacht and Crusader tapes were stacked beneath it. Beside the console was an array of other tapes, marked with titles like *Heavy Metal/Satan*, *Nazi Teens in America*, *Witchcraft Covens*, and *Hate Crimes/Lynchings*. They had a backup tape ready for everything.

Angela put a tiny receiver in her ear, then covered it with her long red hair.

Bill said, "Ready for intro, Angela. On five, four, three, two, one."

Angela spoke into the camera: "By day, it's a typical kids' arcade in a typical South Florida mall. But what happens here when the mall is closed and the doors are locked will shock you — on today's *Angela Live!*"

The camera light went off. The opening montage came up on the Sony monitor next to Angela. She remained in place, reading notes on a small card. Then Bill said into her earpiece, "We're back in five, four, three, two, one."

Angela continued, "You have seen them in the

mall — without direction, without education, with no apparent sense of pride or self-respect — America's lost tribes of teenagers. In Africa, warlords would put machine guns in their hands, creating private armies of violent, unthinking children, ready to do their bidding, no matter what it is. Could that happen here?"

Angela spun around, and the cameraman got a wider view. "This is Arcane—The Virtual Reality Arcade. Teenagers come here to spend their last dollars on ultraviolent 'experiences' that seem frighteningly real. In many a tortured teenage mind, they *are* real."

Angela stood beside the Crusader. "Meet the future. Meet three teenagers who spend their lives in a state of virtual reality. They live only to pump money into mindblowing arcade games. Let me introduce you first to a youngster known only as Ironman."

As she stepped toward him, Will spoke up immediately, before Angela could even ask him a question. He said, "Satanic stuff. Heavy metal Satan worshiping."

Angela answered, "Uh-huh. I see. And do you think these virtual reality experiences fuel that?" Will looked at her dumbly. She tried, "Do they make you want to worship Satan?"

Will looked at Kristin, who nodded. He repeated, "Yeah. Satan-worship stuff."

"Satan? The prince of darkness? The source of all evil?" Will didn't answer. Angela looked into the camera. "Ironman is in his own twisted world, where reality itself is just another arcade game. We'll be back in a moment."

Bill yelled to Mr. McKay, "Watch out. She's going to a commercial."

The studio quickly took over the feed.

Angela spun around and looked for her producer. "Mrs. Knight? Did we prep these people?"

Mrs. Knight turned red. She answered, "I think Roberta prepped them."

"Yeah, well, Roberta is not my producer. You are."

Mrs. Knight turned red with shame. "I'm sorry, Angela."

Angela turned back to Will. She pointed a long red nail at his nose. "Do you have any other words that you could possibly work into your story? Or is this it?"

Will looked her in the eye. "Why? Isn't this what you want?"

Angela thought that over. She answered, "Okay. I guess I can work with this. You're possessed, right? It's a case of demonic possession?"

Will nodded. "Sure."

Bill warned her, "We're back in five, four, three . . ."

Angela looked into the camera. "Welcome back to the twisted reality of these American teenagers. Do any of them look familiar to you?" She moved toward Betty. "Betty the Witch, why do you call yourself that?"

"For you."

"Pardon me?"

"I call myself that because you want me to."

"I want you to? But I don't even know you."

Betty pointed to Will and Karl. "All of us, we're doing exactly what you want us to do. You want us to be scuzzbags so that you'll have somebody to look down on. So that you can feel better about yourself. So that you can say, 'At least I'm not a Nazi, Satan-worshiping witch hanging out in a scuzzbag mall.' So here we are. Look down on us and feel better. We're your four o'clock freak show for the day."

Angela said, "That's interesting. That's very interesting. Do the rest of you feel that way?"

She turned the mike to Will, who looked around for Kristin. Not seeing her in the lights, he mumbled, "Satan stuff."

Angela closed in on him, looking to change the topic. "What's that on your shirt? A death's-head? Does that signify allegiance to Satan?"

Will shot a quick look at Betty. Then he answered, very articulately, "No. It signifies a shirt. That's all. My mom makes them next door. She'll put whatever you want on there. You have to be very specific, though, or she might mess it up."

Angela stared at him hopelessly, then she snapped out of it. She turned to the camera. "Let's take a look at some of these heavy-metal groups in action, and at some of the Satanic symbols and imagery they employ."

The Sony monitor filled with a dark montage of rock videos while Angela rounded on Mrs. Knight. "What the hell is going on here?"

Mrs. Knight hung her head.

When the videos ended, Angela moved the mike over to Karl. "Skinhead Karl, tell me something: Why do you have HEIL HITLER written on your shirt?"

Karl looked into the camera. I could see that his eyes were out of focus. But he answered clearly enough, "Why don't you have HEIL HITLER written on yours?"

"For a number of very good reasons, Karl. Hitler was a monster responsible for the deaths of millions. Why would you walk around with the name of someone like that written on your shirt?"

Karl seemed at a loss to answer that one. He tried, "Why wouldn't I?"

Angela looked at the camera. "One of Arcane's most popular virtual reality experiences is called Krystall-nacht. In that experience, for five dollars, you can join Nazi stormtroopers beating and killing German Jews. We've come a long way since Pacman. Let's take a look."

My Arcane video came on, without sound, so that Angela could talk over it. "Watch with me, Karl, and tell me: When you play these virtual reality games, like this Krystallnacht, do you actually think you're in Nazi Germany?"

Karl replied, "No. To tell you the truth, I'm not really a skinhead. I just have bad skin. I bought these boots, and I wrote on the shirt with a Magic Marker."

The video soon ended. Angela must have felt punch-drunk by now, but she maintained control. She pretended Karl had never spoken. She took a step toward the right, toward Sam. "All right. Let me talk to Samir Samad for a moment. Sam, you are an Arab. You were the victim of a hate crime that directly followed an illegal after-hours party with hardcore, racist virtual reality experiences. Watch with me now as we show the audience part of a tape from an Arcane experience called Crusader."

Bill popped in the tape, and the screen filled with the image of a turbaned Arab's head being cut off and spewing out blood. The tape ended quickly. Angela picked up, "We can't show you much more on TV. Tell me, Sam, do you feel like one of those people?"

"No. Not really. I grew up in California."

"You were attacked following a late-night party during which people played virtual reality games like this. Were you not?"

"Yes."

"What did the mob do to you?"

"Well, it wasn't a mob. It was one guy. He didn't actually do anything to me. He did things to my store. And to my car."

"Didn't this hate crime happen because you're an Arab?"

"No. It turns out it was all about money. About recapitalizing the mall. By the way, I'd like to encourage your viewers to come shop at the West End Mall."

Angela looked into the camera. She spoke flatly. "We'll be right back with someone who has been fighting against hate crimes and racism in the West End Mall, state senate candidate Ray Lyons."

Another commercial came on. Angela looked at Mrs. Knight and told her bluntly, "This show is a loser."

Betty suddenly spoke up. "You're the loser, lady. You should look at yourself in a mirror sometime."

Angela turned to Betty and told her, in a voice loud

enough to carry into the mallway, "You're entitled to your opinion, Broomhilda, but not on my show. Now get the hell out of here."

Betty said, "No problem. I'm bored, anyway. This is stupid. You're stupid."

Angela was struggling now to keep cool. She rounded on her other guests. "I'll tell you what — I'd like to replace all four of you."

Betty slid off the stool, walked out into the mallway, and kept on going. Karl, Will, and Sam stayed put.

Suddenly a voice shouted out of the audience. It was Nina. She cried, "Angela! Yo, Angela! Maybe I could take her place."

Angela stepped over the cables and regarded Nina closely. I guess she was actually considering it, but then she said, "No. You don't look like a witch."

Nina was frantic. "Okay. I — I could be something else."

"What?"

"I could be Nina the Nympho."

Dr. Navarro's eyes snapped wide open. He shouted, "Princesa!"

Nina turned to him. "No. It wouldn't be true, Papi. I'd just be pretending. They're all just pretending. That's what you have to do to get on the show. You have to act like you're really messed up."

"You will pretend no such thing. Think of your family. Think of your mother."

She made one last plea to Angela, "What about Nina the Klepto?"

Dr. Navarro looked at his daughter closely — like he was examining her with his laser glasses, like he was seeing her for the first time.

Angela walked away and posed to start the next segment.

Bill counted it off, "Five, four, three . . ."

"Let me bring my last guest into the mix. He is the developer and owner of the West End Mall, which is the scene of our show today. He is also a candidate for the state senate, Ray Lyons."

Ray Lyons entered Arcane from the back office. He sat on Betty's stool and started to drone on about hate crimes. He was opposed to hate crimes against hard-working people like Sam. He was opposed to Satan-worshiping Nazis like Karl and Ironman.

Karl appeared to be completely zoned, and Angela knew it. She didn't direct any questions to him. She didn't direct any questions to anyone else, either. She didn't seem to care anymore. She let Mr. Lyons hijack the show.

I stood in the booth next to Bill with my hands motionless at my sides. I was devastated. I was humiliated. I felt like crawling into a ditch and dying. My plan was ridiculous, and I was ridiculous, and we were all going to lose everything because of me.

I lowered my head to cry, but no tears would come. I was still standing with my head down on my chest when I heard Bill mutter to Mr. McKay. "Oh no, check out Camera Two. The skinhead is moving."

I looked out through the glass. Karl had stepped

down from his stool. He was staring all around, like he might not know where he was.

Bill said, "Camera Two, get on Skinhead Karl." Then he spoke into the ear mike. "Angela, watch out. The skinhead is moving."

Angela spun toward Karl. She held up five long fingernails to Ray Lyons and told him, "Just a minute, Ray."

She moved slowly toward Karl, as you might approach a wild animal. "Skinhead Karl? Are you all right?" She asked Will and Sam, "What's happening? Is he dangerous?"

Will answered, "Oh yes, I'd say so."

Karl extended both arms and lurched forward, stiff legged, across the carpet, like Frankenstein in platform shoes. He went straight for the Crusader and clamped his big hands around the handle of that jeweled sword.

Angela said, "What's he doing now?" But no one answered her.

With a manic shriek, Karl yanked the Crusader's sword free, ripping it right out of the chain-mail gloves, exposing the wound-wire body to the air for the first time since we put him together. Karl then brandished the sword high over his head, continuing to shriek.

Angela started shrieking, too, "Skinhead Karl! Stop it! Put that down!"

But there was no stopping Karl now. He was a teenage psycho zombie from hell. He lurched toward Bill's one-hundred-thousand-dollar soundboard. He brought the sword down on it with a mighty whack, and the board gave up a shower of red sparks. Then he reared back and did it again. And again.

Bill turned to me and yelled, "What's he doing to my board?"

I watched Karl give it several more whacks. "Whompin' on it," I explained to him calmly. "He's whompin' on it."

Bill ripped off his headset and ran out to try to save the soundboard. I pulled the headset on in time to hear, "Bill! Where the hell are you?"

I said, "*I'm* here, Mr. McKay. This is Roberta, the intern."

"Oh, good, Roberta. Do you know what to do with the promo tape? Did Bill show you?"

"Yes, sir."

"All right, then. Go ahead and push it in. We've seen enough of this."

I pulled the *Angela* promo tape out of the slot and laid it on the console. I reached into my backpack, pulled out my own tape, and slid it in. The Sony monitor filled up with the tanned face of Ray Lyons. He was sitting in a chair, in the mall office, back on September 25.

I glanced quickly out the window. Bill and Karl had squared off against each other, face-to-face, over the shattered soundboard. Joe the bodyguard and two sheriff's deputies were circling behind Karl. Karl still held the Crusader sword high.

But Angela del Fuego was no longer looking at

them. She was looking up at the monitor with great curiosity. She, above all, knew that this was not her promo tape. She watched Ray Lyons from September 25. And she listened, along with two million viewers across Florida and the Southeast, as old Mr. Lombardo's voice asked him, "Mr. Lyons, what are you going to do about Century Towers? That's my home."

She heard him answer, "I'm going to let it sink back into the swamp. I'm Ray Lyons. I can do whatever the hell I like!"

Mr. Lombardo's voice protested, "That's the home to a lot of elderly people."

Ray Lyons replied, "Every time I go there I see nothing but old people. If you want to make money at that mall, open up a Depends undergarment outlet."

I heard Mr. McKay's voice over the headset. He was yelling to me, "That's it! Go to black! Go to black!"

I didn't respond, so he yelled to someone back at the station, "Take over the feed," and that was the last I heard. The screen went black.

I looked out. Angela was still gazing up at the Sony monitor with a puzzled expression. Bill was draped over the broken board. The two deputies were holding up Karl, who was now limp. One paramedic fit him into a Velcro straitjacket while another set up a stretcher.

A few seconds later the monitor came back to life with the real *Angela Live* promo. Angela threw up her hands in confusion. Philip Knowlton appeared from the back room. He was actually spinning in a circle, like he didn't know which way to go. I pulled my tape out of the slot. Then I walked over to Arcane, where chaos reigned.

Kristin reached me first. "My god, Roberta. What did you do?"

I told her, "I used the power of the media. I used it to help us survive."

She repeated "My god, Roberta."

Sam and Will came up to me. Sam said, "What was that? What did you do?"

"It's better if you don't know." Sam started to say something else, but I had to cut him off. "I'm sorry, you guys. I can't talk. I have to go."

"Go where?"

"This is the blame part. This is the responsibility part."

Sam insisted, "I'm going with you."

"No, you're not. It has to be me. Me alone."

I spun around and nearly crashed into the stretcher. The paramedics were wheeling Karl away. Kristin stepped in front of them. She demanded to know, "Where are you taking my brother?"

The straitjacket guy told her, "We're taking him to Atlantic Regional."

"Can we see him there?"

"I don't know." The guy pointed at the deputies. "The sheriff's department will have to decide from there."

Kristin's hand shot up to her mouth. "Oh, my god, Roberta! They'll take him right to the Positive Place."

I took Karl's bony hand in mine. I whispered in his ear, "Thanks, cuz. Thanks for the chance."

But Karl's eyes were staring vacantly at the ceiling. The window was now closed.

I told Kristin, "You go with Karl. Call your dad from the hospital."

She looked down toward the office. "You should come with us, too. You should get out of here."

"No. No, the plan's not finished yet. I have something to say to Mr. Ray Lyons."

We set off in our different directions. I hurried down to the mall office. The whole Ray Lyons family was still seated in front of the wall of TV sets, like they were hypnotized.

I ducked inside, followed immediately by Suzie. She screamed at me, "I watched that crazy show from in here. What happened?"

"I don't know. It was my first time in the booth. I guess I got the tapes messed up."

"Messed up? Roberta, I was at that interview. It was right here in this office. Mr. Lyons never said those things."

The door flew open and Richard Lyons stormed in. His tan face was tinged with red. Suzie looked at him. She continued to scream at me, but now it was in behalf of Ray Lyons. "How — how dare you treat Mr. Lyons and his family this way, after all he has done for the mall!"

But Richard Lyons had come in to do his own

screaming, first at Suzie. "What are you talking about? What did she do?"

"She switched the videotapes."

Richard Lyons stepped toward me menacingly. "My father owns this mall. He is one of the most important men in this state, you little . . . nobody! I promise you — you are going to pay for this stunt for the rest of your life."

The door banged open again and a horde of angry people flooded in — Knowlton, Daley, Ray Lyons, Angela, Mrs. Knight.

It was Bill who got to me first. "You did this! You put that tape in, didn't you!"

But Angela cut him off. "Oh, shut up, Bill. What were you doing out of the booth? It was your responsibility, not the intern's."

Bill sputtered, "I'm not going to take the fall for this."

Angela told him, "Yes, you are." And she told Mrs. Knight. "You are, too. You brought this kid to the show. You're responsible for her." Then she turned to me with cold, hard eyes. "As long as I am working in television, in any capacity, you will not be. You got that?"

Everybody seemed to be yelling and threatening me at the same time. Philip Knowlton turned out to be the voice of reason. He raised his arms straight up to get order. "Quiet! Be quiet! Listen to me: Every news station in South Florida has a crew on the way. This is the lead on the nightly news unless we kill it dead. Now."

But Ray Lyons didn't want to hear that. He was too

angry. He went after Angela. "This is too low even for the likes of you! This violates every standard of journalism. I'm going to sue you for your entire worth!"

Angela reacted very calmly. She pointed to me and said, "Hey, Ray. It was a mistake. The kid put the wrong tape in."

"The hell she did. First you tricked me with that old-people question —"

Knowlton interrupted, "I did not authorize any question about the elderly."

Mr. Lyons poked a finger at her. "You manufactured that tape! You're trying to destroy me!"

"Why would I do that?"

In the middle of all this yelling back and forth, I announced, "I did it." Then I said it again. And again.

Angela heard me first. She turned away from her eyelock with Lyons, so he looked at me, too. I waited until I had everybody's attention before I repeated, "I did it. I manufactured the tape."

Mr. Lyons himself said, "You? How?" as if he didn't believe I could be capable of doing such a thing.

"I used Suzie's videotape, and my intern skills, and a Channel Fifty-seven editing board."

He stared at me for several long seconds. Then he asked me, "Why?"

I stared back at him. I looked at the whole line of them: Philip Knowlton, Richard Lyons, Joe Daley, Suzie, Bill. I heard myself answer in a voice that began low but continued to rise: "Because you killed all those turtles, Mr. Lyons. Because your son wants to turn my world into his golf course. Because you're lying to us about the recap. And because of Hawg."

Ray Lyons looked at Knowlton, bewildered. "Who is Hawg?"

I continued. "Hugh Mason. From west Georgia. He's dead. So is Mrs. Weiss. Will tried to die, too, in the trash trailer, but we wouldn't let him. I guess we're all going to be dead someday, Mr. Lyons. But I'm alive right now. I'm standing here at the edge of your ditch, and I'm looking at you, with all your money, and all your people, and I'm saying, I will not jump in the ditch like all the others. You will have to shoot me. I will not give up! Do you understand? I will not give up — no matter what you do, I will never, ever give up!"

The whole wall of them stared at me as if I were insane. Time seemed to stand still.

Ray Lyons finally looked at Suzie and sputtered, "Who *is* this?"

I answered, "I am Roberta Ritter. My mother was Mary Ann Ritter."

Suzie stammered, "She's — she's just a girl. She's just an employee here at the mall."

I said, "I'm more than that, Suzie. I'm your step-daughter."

A look of horror came over Suzie's face. She stammered, "That's not true!"

Ray Lyons glared at her. But before he could say anything else, Philip Knowlton cut in, "Ray. It's crunch time. It's time to circle the wagons. There are network crews setting up out there right now. Here's what you're going to say to them to try to salvage this election."

Ray Lyons looked completely lost. Knowlton instructed him, "You are going to announce that the recap has come through. You are going to announce that the new phase of Century Towers is starting."

Richard Lyons shouted, "What?"

Knowlton cut him off dead. "Butt out, Richard! It's off. The golf course deal is off."

Richard glared at him, seething with rage.

Joe Daley and the candidate made their way outside to meet with the reporters. Before he followed, Philip Knowlton turned to me. He said, coldly and quietly, "And when I'm through with you, miss, you'll be —"

But I cut Knowlton off dead. "I'll be what? A poor kid with no job?"

Knowlton stood there for many seconds, many seconds longer than he had time for. He finally said, as if thinking out loud, "Huh! I underestimated you. Didn't I?" Then he went outside.

I had no intention of staying in that office, either. I pushed my way through Ray Lyons's family and hurried into the parking lot. I found a good spot to watch the on-air newspeople in action.

Tonight there was a new face among them.

Mr. Herman, in his black toupee, was jostling for position among the mob of younger reporters. He was sticking his microphone into Ray Lyons's face and shouting at him, just like all the others.

I heard Ray Lyons tell them, "I never said what you

heard on that tape. Like a lot of my elderly constituents, I have been the victim of a fraud. I was set up. That tape you saw was doctored."

One of them shouted, "Who set you up, Ray?"

"I don't know. Not yet. For now, let me set the record straight. Ten years ago I committed my company to building a mall and a condo community for the elderly on this site. I am still committed to that. I am committed to getting this project recapitalized immediately. I am committed to proceeding with the next phase of Century Towers. And I am committed to an investment in the mall infrastructure, so no more kids have to get rescued. The last time I was here I had to carry a dozen children to safety."

The reporters all started shouting at once. Mr. Herman shouted right along with them. I couldn't believe what I was seeing. I wanted to walk up to him, shove a microphone in his face, and ask, "Mr. Herman? What high standard is guiding you now? What ideal are you pursuing?" But I didn't.

Mr. Lyons finally turned away from them all and disappeared into his limo. Philip Knowlton shouted, "No further questions! You have your story. The candidate was set up. He's the victim of a political dirty trick. We'll have an official press conference in an hour."

The reporters all packed up quickly and hurried back to their trucks. Mr. Herman was running right along with them. I realized that I had never seen him run before.

He looked ridiculous.

After being in crowds for so long, it felt odd to walk alone back to the condo. I felt light. I felt giddy. I told myself out loud, "Way to go, Roberta. You lost your job yesterday. You lost your internship today. If you can get expelled tomorrow, you'll have all the time in the world."

After I got into the condo, I walked straight out to the balcony. I picked up the portable phone, checked a number, and dialed.

A gruff voice answered, "Yes?"

"Mr. Lewis?"

"Yes."

"This is Roberta Ritter from the West End Mall in South Florida. Do you know who I am?"

"Yes, I do, Roberta. What can I do for you?"

"Nothing. I had a message to call you back, so I'm calling."

"Oh? Oh yeah. Well, you know we got stuck with the shipping charges for your franchise materials."

"Were we supposed to pay them?"

"Technically, yes. It's part of the contract. You always pay your own shipping."

"We have to pay even after we've lost everything?"

"Technically, yes. Or it comes out of your collateral. Colonel Frank Ritter's collateral, I should say."

"I think I speak for my uncle, Colonel Frank Ritter, when I say that he doesn't care anymore."

"Oh. Okay. I just wanted to let you know."

"Is that it?"

"Yeah. I guess so."

I wondered, "Is this how it ends for your franchisees?"

"Some of them."

"How many of them?"

"I'd say maybe half."

"And we were in the wrong half?"

"I guess so. Oh well. *Deus vult,* right?"

I held the phone out for a moment. "What did you say?"

"*Deus vult.* It was the motto of the crusaders."

"It was?"

"Yeah. Didn't you ever see it written on his collar?"

"Isn't it *volt?*"

"No. It's not supposed to be, anyway."

"What does it mean?"

"It means 'God wills it.'"

"It doesn't mean 'Two volts'?"

"No. It's Latin."

"Of course." I stopped for a moment to collect my thoughts. Mr. Lewis hung on the line, so I asked him, "Mr. Lewis?"

"Yes?"

"What did God will?"

"What?"

"*Deus vult.* 'God wills it.' So what did God will?"

"I don't know. I guess God willed that the crusaders should take back the Holy Land from the infidel. That's what the legend says, right?"

"Right. So you don't mean that God willed Hawg's death, do you?"

"Hawg?"

"Because I was there, and Hawg did that to himself. I didn't see God do anything."

"Uh-huh."

"Or did God will Ironman's death? Because if He did, He didn't get His way. We saved him."

"Ironman?"

"Or do you just mean, no matter what happens, either way, whether it's good or bad, God wills it?"

"You lost me, kid. Are you okay?"

"Yeah. I'm okay. I just don't know what God wills."

"Neither do I. But I think we'd better wrap this up."

"Okay." I hung up. Then I went into my bedroom, got undressed, and crawled into bed. I knew it was the wrong night, but I switched on the TV and lay there with the remote control anyway, searching the airwaves in vain for Stephen Cross.

TUESDAY, THE 31ST ⁓ I woke up early today. I poured a glass of orange juice and stood on the balcony, taking in the swamp view.

I noticed a peculiar smell. Peculiar, but familiar. Then I recognized it. It was the swamp gas smell that had filled the mall during the Santa seat disaster. I had never noticed it out here before. I stood in that damp, sulfurous air and thought about the day that stretched before me.

I thought about this: Today was Halloween. Seven years ago, this day became my mom's last on earth. What would today become for me?

When I passed through the entrance, I spotted a clumsily printed CLOSED sign on the door of the mall office. I walked through the rotunda and stopped before the door of Arcane, Slot #32. It was dark inside.

I turned around and leaned with my back against the door, waiting for someone to show up. A pair of power-walkers huffed by, then I saw a flash of motion across the way. Someone was in the window of Slot #61. I crossed over there and peered in.

It was Leo. I watched him drag the three mannequins to the back and stack them up, like cords of firewood. I rapped on the window. Leo looked up, annoyed, but then he saw who it was. He hurried over and let me in.

Right away he started explaining something to me, like I knew what he was talking about. "Mrs. Weiss had this planned for a long time, but she had to get it approved. I guess it came through too late for her."

"What did?"

"The expansion." He explained further, "The thing I've been talking to Millie — uh, Mrs. Roman — about. Don't you know?"

"No."

"The card store's gonna expand into Slot #61 here. It's gonna be a double slot, like Eyes and Ears, and Sports Authority. It's gonna be one of those Hallmark Gold Crown Stores. You know what those are?"

"No."

"They're the big ones. They don't just sell cards. They sell those collectible things, bears and stuff. They sell boxes of candy, stationery, wedding napkins. All kinds of stuff. Expensive stuff."

I looked around at the empty, dusty space. "Do you think this is a good idea, Leo? What if the mall goes under?"

One of the mannequins started to slip off the pile. Leo gave it a kick back into place. "Ah, there's no use thinking like that, Roberta. You gotta move forward in life. Who knows what's gonna happen? Mrs. Weiss always made money here. You just have to make up your mind to do it, too."

"Yeah. Hey, Leo, did Suzie know about this? Did she know the card shop was expanding?"

Leo gave a delighted snort. "Suzie? What did she ever know?"

"She must have. I'm going to ask her."

"I don't think so. Suzie don't work here no more."

"What?"

Leo beamed with pleasure. "It was a beautiful thing to behold. Lyons sent that rent-a-cop of his back last night. I was right outside the door, helpin' Sam move those TVs. I watched the whole thing. He came in and told her she was canned. Then he stood there while she packed up her stuff. He did everything but take his gun out and shoot her. She walked out with a cardboard box full of things, then he took her key away and locked up the office."

I couldn't help myself — I smiled along with him. Then I turned and looked across the way. I saw Dad opening the glass doors of our slot. By the time I said good-bye to Leo, left La Boutique de Paris, and crossed the mallway, Kristin and Will had arrived, too. Once we all got inside, Dad slid the doors closed again.

He said, "Good morning, everybody," but no one answered. We were a sullen group today, there for one purpose only: to dismantle the hardware of Arcane — The Virtual Reality Arcade, and to pack it into boxes.

Dad started to say something else, but he thought better of it. He led the way back to the office and opened the outside door, revealing a big pile of cardboard boxes. We started to haul them in; still, no one spoke.

I broke the silence when I asked Kristin, "What do you hear about Karl?"

She shook her head grimly. "Nothing yet. Dad was at the Atlantic County Medical Center all night. He's trying to get Karl released, but it's just not happening. That judge's order has him bound for the Positive Place for at least ten days."

"Oh, god. What's he going to do?"

Kristin's eyes filled with tears. "I don't know. Karl is really very fragile. Last time he was there, he shut down completely."

"How bad a place is it?"

"They put, like, criminally insane kids there. Kids who kill their parents in their sleep. Kids who stuff their pets into microwaves. Stuff like that." Kristin's tears poured out. "And what did Karl ever do? He never killed anybody. He tried to get out of here with Hawg. Who can blame him for that?"

"I'm really sorry, Kristin."

"I just wish I knew why he did that."

I knew I had to tell her. "He did it to help me."

Kristin pressed her T-shirt against her wet eyes. "What do you mean?"

"I told him I needed a distraction. I needed to get Bill out of the RV. He figured the rest out himself."

Kristin nodded, slowly and thoughtfully. "He did?"

"Yeah."

She wiped her eyes some more. Then she smiled as best she could. She said aloud, "Not bad, Karl."

I tried to smile, too. "No. Not bad at all. He did his part. Now we have to wait and see if I did mine."

"What do you think is going to happen?"

"Did you hear what Lyons told the reporters?"

"No."

"He said the recap would come through for the mall. He even said he would start building at Century Towers again."

"Those could all be lies."

"They could. But Philip Knowlton is a smart man. And a politician. I'm betting we see a new Ray Lyons from here on out."

We heard a rap on the glass. It was Suzie. Her eyes looked puffy, like she had been crying. Or drinking. Dad walked over and let her in. He asked her, "Where were you last night?"

Kristin went back to work, but I stayed by the door. Suzie looked over at me and then mumbled, "At home."

"At your old place?"

"Yeah. It's mine until November first."

"I thought you were coming out to the beach place."

Suzie looked at me again, as if to say it would be nice if I left them alone, but I didn't. She turned back to Dad. "I got fired last night."

"No!"

"Yes. After that . . . zoo left, I stayed to try to sort some things out. Mr. Lyons sent that Joe Daley guy back with orders to fire me. He wasn't very nice about it, either."

"Why? What for?"

"He didn't even know. Or care. All he would say was, 'Orders from Mr. Lyons.'" Suzie blew her nose into a Kleenex. "I get blamed for everything that goes wrong in this damn place. And I get credit for nothing."

Dad said, "Come here." He put his arm around her and walked her toward an empty wall.

I wanted to get to work, but I heard another rap on the glass. I turned to see two little girls. They were dressed in Halloween costumes with pointy black witches' hats. I slid the door open a crack, and the taller of the two said, "Trick or treat."

"Uh, sorry. We're closed."

The taller girl turned to go, but the other one persisted, "The stores in the mall are supposed to give us candy."

"But we're not open anymore. We're out of business."

"The stores are supposed to give us candy."

The taller one added, "We're not allowed to trick-or-treat in our neighborhood. There are too many crazy people. They put razor blades in the candy."

I said, "Yeah. I know."

"So we're supposed to go around the mall instead."

I reached into my pocket and pulled out a ten-dollar bill. "Here. Take this to Lombardo's Drugs and get some bags of candy. Then bring the bags back here. I'll leave them outside, and kids can help themselves."

"Can we help ourselves?"

"Sure. You can be the first ones."

"Okay." The taller witch took the money, and the two of them ran off toward Lombardo's.

I joined Kristin and Will in the center of the arcade. We quickly disassembled King Kong, Vampire's Feast, Viking Raid, Serpent's Lair, Mekong Massacre, Genghis Khan Rides!, Galactic Defender, and Dragon Slayer.

Soon only Crusader remained. Will and I set to work to dismantle what was left of him. I knew we were both thinking about that day with Hawg when we put him together. Will wasn't grinning. Far from it. He started to sniffle and then to cry.

By eleven-thirty all of the Arcane experiences, legends, CDs, helmets, wands, and promotional displays were packed away. Dad was saying a long good-bye to Suzie somewhere near the front of the store, so Kristin, Will, and I hung out in the back waiting for the UPS guy.

He arrived right on time. As soon as I opened the door, he told me, "I got a notice this morning that your account is closed. No more deliveries."

"That's right. No more deliveries. Just one more pickup."

"If I pick anything up, you're going to have to pay cash."

"No. These are cash on delivery."

"No way. I'm not taking anything from here COD."

Kristin stepped between us. She leveled a stare right in the UPS guy's face. "Fine. Leave them, then. But these cartons aren't our property anymore. They belong to Arcane Industries, in Antioch, Illinois."

The guy leaned backward. "Listen, you gotta work it out with them. I'll pick the boxes up tomorrow."

"No, you listen. There is no tomorrow. This is it. This arcade is out of business."

The guy looked around like he was trying to see a way out.

Kristin opened the office door and indicated that we should all leave. She called back to him, "Tell you what, chump. I'll go get my father, the colonel. He'll explain it to you so that you'll understand."

The UPS guy smiled nervously, like Will used to do. Then he said, "Okay. Since you're not going to be here tomorrow, I guess I'll have to take them today."

Kristin, Will, and I continued through the door, leaving him to cart them away. Kristin and Will kept walking to the front of the store, but I stopped and turned back. For some reason I wanted to see the boxes go, especially Crusader's.

When I joined them at the front, Dad was seated cross-legged on the carpet. He was rolling up the h n-dreds of yards of wires that had electrified the Arcane experiences.

As Will slid the door open, Dad called out, "Thanks for your help, guys."

Kristin didn't look at him, so Will didn't, either. But Will did look at me. He said, "Hey, Roberta. Thanks for doing that."

"What?"

"For standing up to that guy. That politician guy. We didn't just take it from him, you know? We didn't just stand there with our mouths shut and take it from him."

Kristin added, "He's right, Roberta. No matter what happens, at least we put up a fight. And that's because of you." She hugged me and whispered so that only I could hear, "You are your mother's daughter." Then she and Will slipped through the opening and left.

Just as I lost sight of them, the two little witches returned. They set down three big bags of candy — Smartees, Junior Mints, and Bit-o-Honeys. The taller one held out her fist. "Here's your change." She dropped some coins into my hand.

I said, "Thanks. Did you help yourselves?"

"No. Not yet."

"Well, go ahead. Take as much as you want." They giggled and started ripping the bags open. I left them to it.

I took a deep breath and got my mind focused. Then I sat down on the floor next to Dad. I said to him, "We've been here before, Dad. Do you remember?"

He looked at me and smiled. "What do you mean, honey?"

"The Family Arcade. You and I packed that up, too."

"Oh yeah. That's right. You were there for that one, too, weren't you?"

I asked him, "What are you going to do now?"

"I think I'm gonna take it easy for a while. Maybe manage somebody else's store. Maybe something on the beach. You know? I'll let somebody else have all the headaches."

"It sounds like Suzie's going to need a new job, too."

"Yeah. Poor kid. She's really upset." When I didn't respond, he continued, "She's going to come over to the house and help me clear out my stuff."

I said, "I have stuff there, too."

"You'd better come with us, then. This is a day for clearing things out. Right?" Dad finished rolling up the cables. He got up, tossed them into the debris pile, and announced, "That's it. I'm finished, and I'm hungry. I'm going to get something for the road. How about you?"

I started to answer, but I suddenly became distracted by a flash of white in the mallway. I looked and saw a small, thin man out there. He was wearing black pants and a white, white shirt. He had long hair and sandals, like Jesus.

Dad said, "What do you say? A calzone from Brothers? A fajita from the Taco Stop?"

"No. No, Dad. I'm not hungry."

"No? Did you have breakfast?"

"Oh yeah. I had a big breakfast. Tell you what, I'll meet you back at the house."

The man in the mallway was holding a bag, a plastic supermarket bag. Dad must have followed my gaze to the guy, because he asked, "Who is that?"

"Who?"

"That hippie outside. Do you know him?"

"No. Do you?"

"No. He looks like he might be one of Devin's friends."

Neither of us said anything for a moment. The hippie wasn't going away, though, so Dad decided, "I'll get rid of him." He opened the glass door and called out, "We're closed. We're out of business."

The guy looked at Dad with piercing eyes, then he turned and walked away. Dad said, "Okay. He's gone. Last call, honey. Can I get you something to drink, at least?"

"No. Not a thing."

"Then I'll see you at home." Dad let himself out.

I kept watching the mallway closely. Just as I expected, the man returned. He walked up to the door and slid it open. I wasn't afraid, because I knew who he was.

When he entered I spoke his name. "Stephen Cross."

He nodded in a quick, jerky way. As he got close I could see that he did not look well. He was sweating; his leathered skin looked yellow; his lips were cracked. But when he spoke, it was with Stephen Cross's voice. "Are you Roberta Ritter?"

"Yes, I am."

"This tape is yours?" He reached into the plastic bag and pulled it out.

"That's right."

He looked at me with those fiery eyes, but his voice trembled. "I swear to you, before Christ my savior, that I did not remember that horrible scene. Not for all these years. Not until last night. And then . . . I did remember."

I leaned back until I was resting against my elbows. I asked him coldly, "What did you remember?"

"Everything. I remembered putting on that Halloween mask, that demon mask. I could barely see out of it. I remembered running in there. I grabbed a bag and started to run out. I swear, I . . ." His voice trailed off. I could see the sweat ooze up on his forehead. I watched it, wondering if it would turn to blood.

He found his voice and continued, "A few seconds after that videotape came on, I was struck down. I fell to the floor, like I had been struck by a bolt of lightning. No one was there to help me. I lay there, paralyzed, while the tape rolled on, all the way to the end."

He parted his cracked lips and looked at me. I did not move. I scarcely breathed. He asked me hoarsely, "Do you know of my ministry?"

I nodded.

"I have made it my mission to find the truth. To find the truth —"

I completed the phrase for him, "To ask forgiveness. To seek redemption."

He closed his eyes, like he was praying. Then he said, "I have spoken to the police. They weren't interested in me, or my tape, or my story."

"They let you go?"

"Let me go? They made me go! They wouldn't listen. They treated me like a . . . a nuisance. They told me that I was 'raving,' that it was only a dream."

Stephen Cross closed his eyes again. "That was what I had thought, too. I have had this horrible dream in the past. This recurring nightmare where I walk into a store in a demon mask, and then I —" He broke off, pale and shaking. "But now I know it was not a dream. Now I know that it was real. I remember it now. I remember everything."

I looked closely at his right arm. It bore no tattoo, but it was discolored, like with a blue bruise. So was his left. I said, "That was your arm in the tape?"

"God knows that was my arm. God knows that was my crime. The police don't want to hear it, so I've come to you. Tell me, Roberta, what can I possibly do?"

I told him. "You can answer my questions."

His head bobbed quickly, eagerly. "Yes. Yes. Of course."

I began, "Why did you murder my mother?"

He answered simply, "For money."

"Why did you need the money?"

"For drugs. All my money went for drugs."

"Why that night? And why the Family Arcade?"

He thought for a moment, then said, "I remember that I had to meet a man in a parking lot."

"What parking lot?"

"The 7-Eleven's. I met a man there who told me what to do."

"And what was that?"

"Walk into the arcade, reach behind the counter, grab the money bag, and run."

"Did you know this man in the parking lot?"

"Kind of. I knew him to see. I'd dealt him some coke."

"What's that mean? You used to sell him cocaine?"

"Yes."

I swallowed hard. I tried to speak evenly. "So why did you murder her? Why didn't you just push her away? She was a small woman. You already had the bag."

Stephen Cross's head dropped forward, like his neck could no longer bear the weight. He told me, "I reacted. I reacted like the animal that I was. I remember she came up behind me. I remember — lashing out with my knife. I remember running."

"Where was the man? The man who sent you in there? Was he waiting outside?"

Stephen Cross's eyes shifted to the mallway and then back. "I don't know. I don't think so. He was probably waiting for me in that parking lot, but I never went back there. I just kept on running, all the way up to Daytona."

"You never gave him the money?"

"No, I never gave it to him. I never gave him anything."

I stopped asking my questions. I had to think. I put my head down, too, to think about his answers.

But Stephen Cross interrupted my thoughts. He said, "I've been praying all night. This morning I received an answer from God. I was to come here and tell you the truth. I was to ask you for your forgiveness. Can I ask you, Roberta, to kneel and pray with me?"

I answered, "No."

"Will you forgive me?"

"No. I don't think so."

He looked away. "I understand." Stephen Cross placed the video on the floor in front of me. His eyes were red and runny. "All I can say is, 'I'm sorry.' I know that is pitifully, immeasurably short of what you need. I want you to know — I will do anything to help you through this pain. Anything you ask, including surrendering my own life."

I just shook my head.

He continued, "Anything. Anytime. For the rest of my life."

I told him, "You had better go now." I added, though only to myself, *Go find your redemption someplace else.*

Stephen Cross got up and walked to the glass, but he couldn't pass through the door. Not yet. He wasn't finished. He had one more thing to say. I knew that, and my heart started to pound. "Roberta, the man who hired me —"

I started to cover my ears, but I fought back the impulse. I put my arms down at my side and looked him in the eye.

"You know what I'm going to say, don't you? The man who hired me to steal the money . . . He just left here. He's the one who told me, 'We're closed. We're out of business.'"

All I could do was nod my head.

His eyes looked at me with infinite pity. "Your father?"

I met his gaze. I told him, "No."

Stephen Cross knew a lie when he heard one, but he didn't speak again. He turned and left.

I sat alone on the stained mall carpeting. My mind started filling up with agony and terror. The void started to open beneath me, but I fought against it with everything that I had.

I grabbed the tape, struggled to my feet, and ran through the empty arcade, pushing my way through two doors to the back parking lot. I ran to the trash trailer and punched at it savagely. Then I ran past George the guard, shouting, "Shut up!" at him, just in case he was thinking about opening his stupid mouth. I didn't stop running until I threw open the door of #303. I yanked the phone out of its wall cradle and called Griffin's pager. I left my number and stood there, panting wildly, until he called back.

I shouted at him, "Griffin! I need to talk to you right now!"

"Roberta? I'm working an undercover. This'll have to be fast."

"It will be fast if you tell me the truth."

He started with his usual, "Hey, Roberta —"

But I cut him off. "I don't want to hear about your department regulations. I want to hear the truth. Do you understand me?"

Griffin tried to calm me down. "Okay. Okay. What do you want to hear?"

"What *aren't* you telling me? What did you start to tell me in the guidance office? You'd better tell me now, Griffin. If you don't, here's what I do: I call nine-one-one. I tell them it's not an emergency, but I need to speak to the platoon sergeant. Then I tell him how you 'back-door' evidence out of the sheriff's department."

Griffin broke in. "Whoa! Whoa! Whoa!" He let out a grunt, like a trapped bear. Then he asked me, "Okay — do you remember the blue smocks?"

"Yes."

"Well, guess what? They confiscated three blue smocks from the Family Arcade that night — a small, a medium, and an extra-large. You didn't get the extra-large one back, did you?"

"No."

"That's because the extra-large one had a problem. It tested positive for cocaine."

"Cocaine? For drugs?"

"Powder cocaine. A very popular drug back then."

I stammered, "You're telling me my dad used drugs?"

"Yes, ma'am. An expensive drug. A drug for people with cash to spend."

I covered the receiver, fighting back a wave of nausea. I finally managed to say, "So . . . so what is the whole truth, Griffin? What really happened that night?"

"I only know the detective's theory of the truth. Here it is: The detective figured the Family Arcade robbery was bogus. It was an inside job. He figured your father owed big Sonny some big money. Your father went to his savings account to get the big money out and discovered that it wasn't there. Why? Your mother had other plans for it, and she had already withdrawn it."

I knew what those other plans were. I answered dully, "The Florida Prepaid College Program. It cost her five thousand dollars."

"That's right. So your father panicked. He didn't make a bank deposit for two days. Instead he put a large amount of cash in a deposit bag; then he got some street kid to go in and grab it. He planned to give that cash to Sonny, to avoid personal injury, and then collect it all back from the insurance company. It's a common scam. We see it all the time. But usually nobody gets hurt."

My ear was still next to the phone, listening. But my mouth was hanging open in horror, thinking about my dead mother. Griffin finally said, "You okay, Roberta?"

I wasn't, but I muttered, "Yeah, thanks," and hung up. I stood frozen like that for a long time. Frozen in horror. Then I remembered something. I thought very hard about my mother. I formed a picture of her, alive and strong, and I asked her what I should do.

I don't remember much about my walk to Sawgrass Estates. I traversed the mall parking lot, the highway, and the side road with an intense, singleminded purpose, never pausing until I had reached the carport. My father's Malibu was parked there. I listened carefully through the wall and heard the noise of the TV.

I eased open the door and walked quickly through to the bathroom, unnoticed. I reached under the sink and pulled up Kristin's makeup bag. I dumped the contents — bottles and tubes — into the sink basin. Then I set to work on myself with toilet paper and a brush.

At last, when I had finished, I cracked open the bathroom door. I could see my father now. He was seated in the living room, watching something very noisy and loud. I slipped quietly across the hall into my bedroom. I reached into the back of my closet and pulled out the medium-size blue smock. I put it on, zippering it up just as we all used to do.

I listened to the sound coming from the living room — a chaotic sound. Then I picked up the videotape and went in there, treading as lightly as a ghost.

I passed by my father on his right. He was seated on the couch watching a car race. I kept my back to him as I reached the VCR.

He remarked, "Oh, Roberta, you're here."

I didn't answer. I pushed the tape in and changed the car race channel to Channel 3. He must have been curious by now, but his voice barely showed it. He asked me, "Honey? Did you want to watch something?"

I said, "Yes. Can I?"

"Sure. I'm not really watching this. I've got the car packed. I'm just waiting for Suzie."

I pressed Play, stepped to the side, and said, "Then I'd like you to watch this with me."

I could hear the blip as the tape interrupted the show on Channel 3.

He asked, "What is it?"

But still I would not turn around.

He asked, "Did you just comb your hair or something?"

Then he stopped talking. The evil taped played out its evil story just for him — the lightning; the fearful look; the man, the mask, the tattoo. He muttered to himself, troubled and confused, "What? What is this thing?"

I answered, "You know what it is."

"No, I don't. Is this — is this another prank, Roberta? Suzie told me what you did to Mr. Lyons."

"No. No one has altered this tape. This is real."

I finally turned around. I showed him my hair, pulled back and clipped, like my mother's hair in the video. I showed him my blue vinyl smock, my mother's own smock. And I showed him my face, the face that I had worked on so long in the bathroom.

It was my modeling face.

It was my mother's face.

He stared at me in horror for ten seconds, like he had just looked into hell. Then he started to melt down. Like a candle. Like a Candlewycke candle in the shape of a man, he began to melt down. He babbled two words, "Mary Ann."

I answered him, ghostlike, "Seven years ago tonight."

"My god. Mary Ann."

"Seven years of life ago."

"Please, god! Stop this. Please!" He slid completely off the couch. He curled into a ball on the floor and cried uncontrollably. I sat down on the edge of the couch and waited him out.

It took several minutes, but he finally stopped. He regained enough composure to uncurl himself, and then to crawl a few feet away from me. He reached the wall, turned, and sat up with his back against it. He managed to say to me, like a dying man, with his last breath, "Roberta, what are you doing to me?"

The tape was still running. Now it was into the long section, the section where nothing was happening on-screen, the section where my mother was bleeding to death outside. I asked him, "Do you want to see it again from the beginning?" I pointed at the TV screen.

He begged, "Please! Please, no!"

"Then tell me the truth. Do not dishonor my mother's memory with one more lie."

I leaned toward him to hear the truth. To finally hear the truth.

He started to blabber, with stuff coming out his nose and eyes, like it had so long ago: "Okay, Roberta. This guy . . . This awful, this big guy, he was gonna kill me. And not just me. He said he would go after Mommy and you, too. He said the next thing that would happen to me would be I would go to drive my family to the beach one day and my car would explode. I swear that's what he told me. And he meant it. He meant it! I had to do it. I don't know why Mommy fought with that punk. That wasn't like her."

"I'll tell you why. She fought with him for me. So that I could go to college. She wanted to use her money for me, for college — not for you, for drugs."

He struggled up to his knees, breathing hard, trying to regain control. He protested, "Listen to me, Roberta! I did what I had to do. Your mother did not. Your mother *had* to give up that bag of money to that punk. That's what she had to do. The insurance would have covered it. Instead she grabbed him, and . . . I swear to god, Roberta, I never in a million years thought your mother would do that. She wouldn't even raise a hand to spank you. I never in a million years thought she would go after a robber."

I asked him coldly, "So it was all Mom's fault?"

He screamed, "Of course not! It was all my fault. I'm just saying it should have turned out different. Honey, the night before Mommy's funeral, this man, he caught me outside our apartment. He took a baseball bat. He took a bat and he cracked open my kneecap. Just broke my leg! Just like that! Like I was some kind of cockroach. I told him we had insurance money coming, but he didn't care. Do you see the kind of man I was dealing with?"

"So it was this bad man's fault?"

"Yes!"

"This bad man, did he come up to you one day and say, 'Take my money and buy drugs with it'?"

"What?"

"Or did you go to him?"

He understood the question. And he understood that he was beaten. He admitted, "Ahh . . . I went to him. You know the answer to that. I went to him." He buried his face in his hands. Then he wiped his eyes and said, "Roberta, don't you think this has been killing me? Honey, I haven't even been able to look at you lately. You've gotten so big — I can't stand to see her face in you. Don't you think this has been killing me? All these years?"

I told him, "No. I don't think so. I don't think you're like that. I think it's all about you. You and only you."

He started to answer that, but I held up my hand and stopped him. I was going to do the rest of the talking: "First of all, you're not to call me honey or anything like that ever again."

I reached into my right pocket and pulled out the cemetery form. I threw it at him. "Second, you're going to give my mother a decent burial. I know the manager at Eternal Rest. I'm going to call him on Friday. If you haven't placed this order by noon on Friday, then I will call Detective Griffin and tell him that I've solved Mary Ann Ritter's murder.

"Third, we're not going to be part of each other's lives. Don't you ever show up asking me for money. I don't care if somebody is about to chop your head off. Don't you ever contact me again. Anywhere. Ever.

"I will mail you whatever papers you need to sign,

and you will sign them, like always. You will mail them back to me immediately. If at any time I feel you are not cooperating, I will go to the police and have you arrested for murder. Do you understand?"

I think he did, although he looked too stunned to show it. He eventually whispered, "Roberta, what about the videotape? What will happen to that?"

I answered, "It'll stay with me, for as long as I need it."

We heard the kitchen door open. Suzie came in. She stopped still and beheld the eerie scene. The video was running without sound. My father was on the floor, in a helpless state. And I was sitting on the couch, made up like a model.

She spoke to me. "What's going on, Roberta? Why are you dressed like that? Is that your Halloween costume?"

I didn't bother to look at her, but I answered, "Here is all you need to know: You're not part of my life anymore. Not in any way. My father is leaving with you now. For good. You're getting him, but I doubt very much that you're getting a boat. So I guess that means you're only getting half of everything you always wanted."

Suzie looked at her broken fiancé. "Bob, what's going on here?"

He struggled to his feet. He moved stiffly toward the door, like an old man. "Let's just go. I'll tell you in the car. Let's go."

They left immediately. I wondered, for a moment,

what he would tell her in the car. Then I forgot all about them.

I laid my head back on top of the couch. The video played on, its lightning flashes illuminating the room as they had the Family Arcade seven Halloweens ago.

I snapped forward, though, when the phone rang. I picked it up, but I wasn't able to speak. I heard, "Roberta? It's Griffin. Are you all right?"

I managed to whisper, "Yes."

"You don't sound all right."

"Give me a minute." I set the phone down, stretched my arms straight out, and shook my head. I got back on and told him, "I'm all right. Really. What do you want?"

"I have some news for you. Stephen Cross, the TV preacher guy, wandered into the station today and confessed to your mother's murder."

"I know. I talked to him."

Griffin got upset. "You know? How could you know before —" But then he stopped himself. He changed his tone. "Damn. I told you, Roberta, I wouldn't be surprised by you. And I'm not going to be."

I cut in, "So what do we do now?"

"I want to reopen the case, but I need that video. Tonight."

"I'm sorry. I threw it away."

He shouted, "You what? Where?"

"In a garbage can at the food court. A week ago. It's somewhere in the county landfill now. Like Sonny Santos."

"Roberta —"

"Why is the tape important if the killer came in and confessed?"

"Why? Because we're talking about the recollection of a junkie from seven years ago. A recollection he never had until he saw a certain videotape. By the way, Roberta, he saw the videotape on Monday. That was not a week ago. It was a day ago."

"Yeah. That's what I meant."

Griffin stopped talking. I could hear what he was thinking: *She's lying. But what can I do about it? Pursue the lies, like a good detective? Or let them go?*

He let them go.

He told me, calmly, "I called you because the case suddenly had potential. But if the tape is gone, the potential is gone, too. If evidence has been lost, then the case is a dog. The state's attorney doesn't like dogs."

He cleared his throat before asking me, "So . . . Did Cross tell you who sent him in there?"

"Yes."

"Bob Ritter?"

"Yes, sir."

Griffin let me sweat about that for a minute. Then he said, "Is there any chance of Bob Ritter coming down here and confessing, too?"

"No, sir. He doesn't have it in him to do that. He'll deny it all the way."

"Then all we have is Cross saying he saw a video that you're saying no longer exists."

"Correct."

"You see? There's no way we're gonna prosecute that. It's a dog with fleas." Griffin changed tones once more. "Roberta? Why don't you want to get Cross? You know what he did. Hell, you saw him do it."

"I asked myself, *What would my mother want me to do?* And this is it."

"What? Let a killer walk free?"

"He's not a killer anymore. He has changed. I truly believe that. Stephen Cross is not who he used to be."

"And what about Bob Ritter?"

Now it was Griffin's turn to wait. I finally said, "I talked to my mother about him, and she told me what to do. Let's just say I'm taking care of his punishment."

Griffin whistled like he thought I was crazy.

I changed the subject. "So what'll happen to you when they find out about the videotape? Will you get fired?"

He answered quickly, "No. They might catch some flak down at the County Services building. It makes the department look bad, losing evidence. The state's attorney does not like his department to look bad."

I heard some commotion in the background. He told me, "Listen, Roberta, I gotta go. You have my number if I can ever help you or any member of your family."

I said, "Okay," and he hung up.

At around nine o'clock, some trick-or-treaters came to the door. That's never happened in Sawgrass Estates, not since I've lived here. Too many psychos. I listened to them knock, waiting for them to give up and go away. And that's what they finally did.

No one else followed.

That's how Halloween night ended. It ended with me losing my father. It ended with me sitting alone, thinking about my lost mother. I fell asleep right there — wearing my mother's makeup and hair, wearing my mother's smock, frozen in the video snow.

NOVEMBER

THURSDAY, THE 16TH ❧ The *Angela Live* broadcast from the West End Mall was more than two weeks ago. It has taken all this time for me to sort out its effects. They seemed to change every day. I have felt like both a hero and a fool, sometimes in the same day.

Philip Knowlton managed to contain the local damage very well. Mr. Lyons was treated by the local media as a victim of a dirty political trick. The TV news shows even ran companion pieces demonstrating how easy it was to alter a videotape, to make anybody look like he or she had said anything, anywhere, at any time.

But beyond the local outlets, the damage was not so easily contained. The video quickly surfaced on news broadcasts all over the state, and then all over the country. Mr. Lyons, his comments, and how I had stitched them together became a topic for magazine writers, TV commentators, and stand-up comics. No matter where it was discussed, or who was discussing it, one line was always picked up, verbatim — the one about the Depends undergarments. Ray Lyons became a national figure, but not in the way he had hoped.

The Philip Knowlton damage-control team made a

great show of presenting a check to Mr. Lombardo and Sam. It was a gigantic prop check from SunBelt Savings, measuring six feet long and four feet tall. It said, on the lower left, FOR THE RECAPITALIZATION OF THE WEST END MALL.

Mr. Lombardo and Sam insisted on posing for the check photo beneath a Toby the Turtle banner. Philip Knowlton was furious, but he had to keep his big mouth shut. Knowlton did succeed in dragging some of the elderly power-walkers into the photo. Then Mr. Lyons posed over a shovel and broke ground for the next phase of Century Towers. All the while, Ray Lyons hammered home the message: That he has always been for the poor and the elderly, that he was the victim of a dirty trick.

Philip Knowlton even went so far as to post a "fact sheet" about me on the Ray Lyons for State Senate web site. He called me "a disturbed teen, with gender confusion, who had recently been tested for drug abuse." He forgot to add that I kicked my dog.

But none of it did them any good. People had caught a glimpse of the real Ray Lyons, uncontrolled and unmanaged, for a few pirated seconds. They did not forget what they saw, or what they heard. The election was two days ago, and Mr. Lyons lost. He lost big. "The old people got him," as Mrs. Weiss would have said.

There is other news, too, but there is no more mall newsletter to report it in. People still tell me things as I walk through the mall, and I still observe things on my own, so here are some items. I'll call them my People Pieces for November. It's already been a busy month:

PEOPLE PIECES

My mom's reinterment took place last week. The ceremony was very nice. Family and friends from the mall gathered before the mausoleum wall. They were all astonished when the minister arrived. I know that teary-eyed undertaker, for one, was very impressed to meet Stephen Cross. The Reverend Cross said some beautiful and heartfelt prayers and then delivered a stirring eulogy. Afterward, he kept thanking me, over and over again, for "having mercy." My father didn't show up, but I didn't expect him to. He had followed his instructions. That was all he needed to do. That is all he ever needs to do from now on.

Karl was released from the Positive Place this morning. I wanted to visit him there, but they only let immediate family in. My aunt Ingrid, uncle Frank, and Kristin saw him for every minute of every visiting period. They said he was doing much better this time around. I hope to see him tonight, or as soon as he is ready.

Kristin has stopped working altogether. She wants to spend as much time as she can with her mother. She is also thinking seriously about joining the army.

Uncle Frank pulled himself together and went to talk to Sam. Sam shook hands with him. According to

Kristin, Sam even offered him a job at Crescent, but Uncle Frank turned him down. He hopes to use his knowledge of German, and Germany, to get a job with DaimlerChrysler.

Will Royce now works part-time for SpecialTees and part-time at the card shop. He still talks to Kristin a lot, but he seems to be standing more on his own.

All the merchants, including Mr. Lombardo, voted to let Sam control the recap money. He's making many physical improvements. The empty slots are starting to fill up, and pushcarts with names like Seashell Art and the Curry Pot now line the middle of the mallway.

The renovation of Isabel's Hallmark into a Hallmark Gold Crown Store is complete. We now occupy two prime slots, #60 and #61, just off the rotunda. In addition to the store, it turns out that Mrs. Weiss left me a small fortune. I haven't even had time to sort it all out. People seem to look at me differently, but I don't feel any different.

And Archie, believe it or not, came through. He got me into the Latin AP class at school. Latin just seems to come up a lot. I intend to take as many AP classes as I can and to win a National Merit scholarship. Furthermore, I intend to change the world as a journalist. And I'm not kidding. I have seen myself doing just that.

All of these changes, and these opportunities, have left me with much more to do at school and at work. I have a lot less time to stare out the window at the mallway. When I do now, it is from Isabel's Gold Crown Hallmark. Occasionally I pause and lift my head up from my various duties. I stare, absently, at the windows of Slot #32, the former home of Arcane — The Virtual Reality Arcade.

THURSDAY, THE 23RD ✻ Mrs. Roman and I left extra-early on Thanksgiving to visit the cemetery. She thought it was to try to catch that guy playing golf again, but I had my own secret plan. I drove the restored Lincoln Town Car down Everglades Boulevard in the first light of dawn.

Mrs. Roman said, "I'm glad there's no traffic. With a car this big, you might hit something."

"It's okay, Mrs. Roman. I've driven it before. I practiced with Mrs. Weiss."

"You could have a little car."

"No, I like this car."

"Did you remember your license?"

"Yes, ma'am."

We turned into the gate just as the sun was coming up. First I accompanied Mrs. Roman to her husband's grave. It doesn't have a headstone, but it has a nice bronze plaque in the ground. The plaque notes that he served in the U.S. Army in World War II. I knelt with Mrs. Roman on the wet grass as she said a prayer. I laid one red rose on the grave.

Then we trekked over to my mom's new crypt, #103A, on the Eye Level. Mrs. Roman commented on the delicate swirls of flowers carved in the marble facade, and on the thick bronze nameplate. I placed another red rose in the vase that projects from the wall like a Statue of Liberty arm.

As we walked back to the car, Mrs. Roman said, "The roses were a lovely idea, dear. And it was lovely of you to remember my Joe. You didn't even know him."

"I feel like I do."

"It was a very thoughtful thing to do."

When we reached the Lincoln, she asked me, "Now, what is that other bouquet you made? The one in the backseat? Who is that for?"

I said, "That one's for my mom. It's to give thanks to her."

"What? Did you forget to bring it out?"

"No. It's not for here. It's going someplace else."

"We're driving someplace else?"

"Yes. Do you mind?"

"No. As long as I'm back before ten — I have cooking to do."

"Oh, we'll be back before then."

"Leo's coming at noon. He wants to watch some football game. I'm going to ask him to look at the toilet, too. It's making noise. Me, I enjoy the Macy's parade. I like to see Santa come every year."

"We'll be back in plenty of time, Mrs. Roman."

I started up the Lincoln and circled slowly around the rectangle of crypts. Mrs. Roman said, "I like your hair back like that."

"Thanks."

"And is that a little rouge you have on?"

"I think it's blush."

"Same thing. You look very nice today. Very nice for a special day. When is your family coming over?"

"At noon."

"That's nice."

Mrs. Roman actually made our Thanksgiving plans for us. I had told her that no one in my family, including my aunt Ingrid, had ever cooked a turkey. She came into the store the next day with a newspaper ad for the Hollywood Cafeteria. They're having a Thanksgiving Day special — turkey and all the trimmings for $9.95. I called Aunt Ingrid and mentioned the ad, so now the five of us are going to go eat there. She's picking me up at twelve in her new Mercedes, with *"meiner Kristi, meinen Karly, und meinen Franz."*

I pulled carefully out of Eternal Rest and drove the big Lincoln all the way down Seventy-second Street to its eastern end, at A1A. Then I turned north. I'm sure Mrs. Roman had no idea where we were going. I doubt she has even heard of the Strip. I parked on the beach side, directly across from the Third Eye Tattoo Parlor.

Mrs. Roman said, "It's here? You wanted to go to the beach? What? Did you want to see your father?"

I answered, "No," and thought, *I intend to never see my father again. And today, I intend to not even think about him. Today is for someone else.* I reached over and brought my memorial wreath into the front seat.

Mrs. Roman commented, "That's lovely. Isabel would approve."

"I know she would."

"She told me that story, too. About the concentration camp. And her mother."

"She did?"

"Yes. That was a sad story." Mrs. Roman looked at the ocean. "There are a lot of sad stories. It seems like everybody has one to tell." She touched the items in my wreath. "So what's the story with this?"

I pointed out different parts of the arrangement. "These are the books my mom and I used to read together. Especially *The Sneetches and Other Stories* and *The Cat in the Hat*."

A disapproving look crossed her face. "Don't you want to save them? For your children?"

"No."

Mrs. Roman stared at me momentarily, then said, "Go ahead. I won't interrupt."

"This is a letter I wrote to my mom, telling her that I love her."

"That's nice."

"This blue material is from the smocks she and I wore when we worked together. I worked with her right here, across the street."

Mrs. Roman looked at the other side of the street for the first time. Worry lines appeared around her eyes. I finished up, "And I included some photos of the two of us."

Mrs. Roman couldn't help herself. "Roberta, dear, aren't you afraid you're going to lose all of these things? These precious things?"

I told her as simply as I could. "It's time to lose all these things."

She nodded uncertainly. I opened the car door and grabbed the wreath. "You stay in here, okay?" As I crossed A1A, I could hear the car locks clicking down behind me.

Early as it was, the street kids were already out there. I crossed over diagonally to the 7-Eleven parking lot, clutching my wreath. I saw the chubby girl and her boyfriend take off from their spot by the phone and hurry to cut me off.

The girl said to me, "Are you looking to cop?"

I stopped. "Cop? I'm not a cop."

"No, *cop*. Buy. Buy drugs."

I heard myself say, "No. No, not at all. That stuff destroys lives. Don't you know that by now? Doesn't everyone know that by now? Nothing but evil comes from it."

The two of them nodded warily and started to back away. I said, "Wait a minute. Can I ask you something?"

"Yeah?"

"You know that tall guy who hangs out by the phone? He has a short partner, with a dog collar on? They both deal drugs?"

The boy spoke for the first time. "The dude who only wore cutoffs?"

"Yeah. Yeah. Are they still around?"

"No. Those dudes disappeared, man. They were here every day, and then they just disappeared."

"No one knows what happened?"

"No, man. But I bet it wasn't good. Those dudes were down."

I nodded uncertainly.

The girl looked at the boy, trying to get his attention. When she did, the two of them took off toward the beach without saying another word.

I found myself alone in front of the Third Eye Tattoo Parlor. I closed my eyes and pictured my mother. Then I opened them and carried the wreath forward slowly, stepping like the soldiers on Memorial Day. I focused on the spot, ten feet in front of the entrance. I remembered the video vault, and the hideous stain that became the second story on the nightly news. I remembered the lightning, like flash cameras popping, illuminating a woman's last moments on earth. I remembered a mask, an arm, a serpent.

I knelt at the spot and laid the wreath down. The tears welled up and then rolled out of my eyes. I lowered my face, letting the tears fall on the cement. I stayed like that until they stopped falling. I have no idea how long that was. But then I leaned back onto my heels.

I slid the note out of the wreath, ceremonially, and read it aloud.

Dear Mom,

Thank you for reading to me. And for buying me Slurpees. And for fighting for me when you had to. I'll do the best I can. I'll make you proud of me.

Love,
Roberta

Then I slid it back into its place.

I reached up with both hands and wiped my face. I felt good. I felt lighter and younger than I had in a long time. And I felt loved, still loved, by someone who just happened to be far away.

I must have seemed a bizarre sight when the two street kids came back my way. I heard them first, calling out and running across A1A. I looked sideways at them as they approached. They were both soaking wet from jumping in the ocean.

The girl shook her long, curly hair and greeted me with a vivacious, "Hey!"

I said, "Hey."

She studied my face closely; then she turned and looked over at what I had done. She said, "Hey, can I ask you something?"

"Yeah."

"Why do you keep coming back here?"

I pointed at the place where the memorial wreath now lay. "Something happened here. My mother died here. She left the world right here, on this spot."

"Wow. So what's all that stuff?"

"It's our stuff. Hers and mine. It's a wreath to give thanks for my mother. Today is Thanksgiving, so I'm giving thanks. And then I'm moving on."

"Wow. Today is Thanksgiving?"

The boy spoke again. "I liked Thanksgiving. I was in a Thanksgiving play."

The girl said, "No way."

"Yeah. At school. I was an Indian."

"You were an Indian?"

"Yeah. I was Squanto. You know, he helped the Pilgrims?"

"Yeah."

We all stared at the memorial wreath for another moment. I got up on my feet, turned back, and waved at Millie. She was looking at me wide-eyed through the car windows, scared to death.

But I wasn't ready to leave these two yet. I wanted very badly to talk to them. Or at least, I wanted them to listen to me. I said, "My mother is gone, but I have a picture of her in my heart, so she is always with me."

The boy started saying, "Yeah, yeah. That's all you need is friends, man. Someone to watch your back, you know."

I disagreed. "No. That's not it. That's not it at all. You need more than that."

The girl sided with him. She explained to me, "The kids who get wasted out here are the kids with no friends. They say this one chick, she was from, like, Alabama. She went with a guy, and now she's a slave on a plantation, like, down in South America. White slavery. I saw a show about it on TV. They pick up white girls and they drug them, and they wake up in South America and they're slaves."

The boy asked her, "Was that that chick with the Tweetie Bird tattoo?"

"No, that chick OD'd. They found her out behind the Dumpster."

"No, man. That wasn't her."

"Yeah, it was. I saw the tattoo. Don't tell me it wasn't her. I was there when they loaded her on the stretcher."

I interrupted to say, "I'll bet the Greek Isles Family Restaurant is having turkey dinners today." I reached into my pocket and pulled out my wallet. I took out the folded hundred-dollar bill Mrs. Weiss had given me and said, "Here. I want you guys to have some turkey today."

The boy just looked at it.

The girl took it. "Thanks a lot. We'll keep an eye on your wreath. You know? We'll protect your mom's wreath. We'll, like, Mace anybody who messes with it."

"No. No, don't do that. Just let it happen. Whatever's going to happen, just let it. The important thing is that I did this. And now I am going to go live my life. And I hope you will live your lives, too."

The girl started to get that wary look again. So I just told her, "Good luck to you."

She smiled. I added, "And good luck to you, Squanto."

He laughed out loud.

I retraced my steps across A1A. Mrs. Roman unlocked the doors to let me in. Then she locked them again. She said, "Those children look so sickly. Like they have ringworm. I saw you give them a dollar. What? Did they ask you for a dollar?"

"No, they didn't ask me for anything. They were asking me about my mom and her memorial."

"You shouldn't give money away. It encourages beggars."

I put on my seat belt. I told her, "We all need encouragement sometimes, don't we?"

Mrs. Roman laughed. And she made a dismissive gesture with her hand, like she thought I was kidding. "Ah, you . . ." She added, "That memorial was a nice thing to do, Roberta. A very nice thing."

I told her, "I'm going to do one for Mrs. Weiss someday, too, with my diplomas and some of my first big stories. I'll leave it outside the card store someday, some Thanksgiving Day."

"That'd be nice, dear."

I looked over, but the street kids were gone. They had disappeared that quickly. I was taken aback for a moment. Suddenly I no longer knew what to do. I said, "Pardon me, Mrs. Roman. I need to think for a minute or two. Okay?"

"You go ahead. You think. I'm not here to stop you."

I stared in rising confusion at that spot, the spot where the three of us had just stood.

It's funny. Ever since Stephen Cross asked me to pray with him, and I refused, I have had the urge to do just that. But I don't know how. The best I can do is think about things, really hard. That's what I call praying. So that's what I did.

I looked out the window onto the Strip, and I prayed like this: I thought hard about all the kids who were gone — about the ones who didn't make it, and about the ones who weren't going to make it. I thought about the Brazilian street kids who left their *favelas*. I thought about the American street kids who left their broken homes. I thought about Hawg and his Arkansas T-shirt. I thought about the girl sold into white slavery, and about the one behind the Dumpster, with the Tweetie Bird tattoo. I wished them all well. I wished they could find their way, somehow, out of the void.

When I was finished praying, I checked up and down the Strip again for my two street kids. They were still nowhere to be seen. I thought for a moment, really hard, about them. I envisioned them sitting down to a big Thanksgiving dinner. I envisioned them trying, and then finding, something in their lives to be thankful for.

Then I looked back at the site of the old Family Arcade. I stared at the Dr. Seuss memorial for a long, long moment. It looked cheerful sitting there, a cheerful package on a gray sidewalk. Once I was certain that I would never, ever forget what it looked like, I turned my head away. I would not be turning back. I put on the left signal, checked the mirror, and pulled out onto the empty morning highway.